Charlotte Mary Yonge

**Magnum bonum : or, Mother Carey's brood**

Charlotte Mary Yonge

**Magnum bonum : or, Mother Carey's brood**

ISBN/EAN: 9783337057282

Printed in Europe, USA, Canada, Australia, Japan

Cover: Foto ©Andreas Hilbeck / pixelio.de

More available books at **www.hansebooks.com**

# MAGNUM BONUM

OR

## MOTHER CAREY'S BROOD

BY

### CHARLOTTE M. YONGE

AUTHOR OF 'THE HEIR OF REDCLYFFE,' ETC.

London

MACMILLAN AND CO., LIMITED

NEW YORK: THE MACMILLAN COMPANY

1899

# CONTENTS

# LIST OF ILLUSTRATIONS

# MAGNUM BONUM;

## OR

## MOTHER CAREY'S BROOD

## CHAPTER I

### JOE BROWNLOW'S FANCY

'The lady said, " An orphan's fate
Is sad and hard to bear."'

SCOTT.

'MOTHER, you could do a great kindness.'

'Well, Joe?'

'If you would have the little teacher at the Miss Heaths' here for the holidays. After all the rest, she has had the measles last and worst, and they don't know what to do with her, for she came from the asylum for officers' daughters, and has no home at all, and they must go away to have the house purified. They can't take her with them, for their sister has children, and she will have to roam from room to room before the white-washers, which is not what I should wish in the critical state of chest left by measles.'

'What is her name?'

'Allen. The cry was always for Miss Allen when the sick girls wanted to be amused.'

'Allen! I wonder if it can be the same child as the one Robert was interested about. You don't remember, my dear. It was the year you were at Vienna, when one of Robert's brother-officers died on the voyage out to China, and he sent home urgent letters for me to canvass right and left for the orphan's election. You know Robert writes much better than he speaks, and I copied over and over again his account of the poor young man to go with the cards. "Caroline Otway Allen, aged seven years, whole orphan, daughter of Captain Allen, 107th Regiment;" yes, that's the way it ran.'

'The year I was at Vienna, and Robert went out to China.

B

That was eleven years ago.  She must be the very child, for she
is only eighteen.  They sent her to Miss Heath's to grow a little
older, for though she was at the head of everything at the asylum,
she looks so childish that they can't send her out as a governess.
Did you see her, mother ?'

'Oh no !  I never had anything to do with her ; but if she
is daughter to a friend of Robert's——'

Mother and son looked at each other in congratulation.
Robert was the stepson, older by several years, and was
viewed as the representative of sober common sense in
the family.  Joe and his mother *did* like to feel a plan quite
free from Robert's condemnation for enthusiasm or unpractic-
ability, and it was not the worse for his influence, that he had
been generally with his regiment, and when visiting them was
a good deal at the United Service Club.  He had lately married
an heiress in a small way, retired from the army, and settled in
a house of hers in a country town, and thus he could give his
dicta with added weight.

Only a parent or elder brother would, however, have looked
on 'Joe' as a youth, for he was some years over thirty, with a
mingled air of keenness, refinement, and alacrity about his
slight but active form, altogether with the air of some imple-
ment, not meant for ornament but for use, and yet absolutely
beautiful, through perfection of polish, finish, applicability, and
a sharpness never meant to wound, but deserving to be cherished
in a velvet case.

This case might be the pretty drawing-room, full of the choice
artistic curiosities of a man of cultivation, and presided over by
his mother, a woman of much the same bright, keen, alert
sweetness of air and countenance : still under sixty, and in
perfect health and spirits—as well she might be, having preserved, as well as deserved, the exclusive devotion of her only
child during all the years in which her early widowhood had
made them all in all to each other.  Ten years ago, on his election to a lectureship at one of the London hospitals, the son had
set up his name on the brass plate of the door of a comfortable
house in a once fashionable quarter of London , she had joined
him there, and they had been as happy as affection and fair
success could make them.  He became lecturer at a hospital,
did much for the poor, both within and without its walls, and
had besides a fair practice, both among the tradespeople, and
also among the literary, scientific, and artistic world, where
their society was valued as much as his skill.

Mrs. Brownlow was well used to being called on to do the
many services suggested by a kind heart in the course of a
medical man's practice, and there was very little within, or
beyond, reason that she would not have done at her Joe's bidding.  So she made the arrangement, exciting much gratitude
in the heads of the Pomfret House Establishment for Young
Ladies ; though without seeing little Miss Allen, till, from the

Doctor's own brougham, but escorted only by an elderly maid-servant, there came climbing up the stairs a little heap of shawls and cloaks, surmounted by a big brown mushroom hat.

'Very proper of Joe. He can't be too particular—but such a child!' thought Mrs. Brownlow, as the mufflings disclosed a tiny creature, angular in girlish sort, with an odd little narrow wedge of a face, sallow and wan, rather too much of teeth and mouth, large greenish-hazel eyes, and a forehead with a look of expansion, partly due to the crisp waves of dark hair being as short as a boy's. The nose was well cut, and each delicate nostril was quivering involuntarily with emotion—or fright, or both.

Mrs. Brownlow kissed her, made her rest on the sofa, and talked to her, the shy monosyllabic replies lengthening every time as the motherliness drew forth a response, until, when conducted to the cheerful little room which Mrs. Brownlow had carefully decked with little comforts for the convalescent, and with the ornaments likely to please a girl's eye, she suddenly broke into a little irrepressible cry of joy and delight. 'Oh! oh how lovely! Am I to sleep here? Oh! it is just like the girls' rooms I always *did* long to see! Now I shall always be able to think about it.'

'My poor child, did you never even see such a room?'

'No; I slept in the attic with the maid at old Aunt Mary's, and always in a cubicle after I went to the asylum. Some of the girls who went home in the holidays used to describe such rooms to us, but they could never have been so nice as this! Oh! oh! Mrs. Brownlow, real lilies of the valley! Put there for me! Oh! you dear, delicious, pearly things! I never saw one so close before!'

'Never before.' That was the burthen of the song of the little bird with wounded wing who had been received into this nest. She had the dimmest remembrance of home or mother, something a little clearer of her sojourn at her aunt's, though there the aunt had been an invalid who kept her in restraint in her presence, and her pleasures had been in the kitchen and in a few books, probably *Don Quixote* and *Evelina*, so far as could be gathered from her recollection of them. The week her father had spent with her, before his last voyage, had been the one vivid memory of her life, and had taught her at least how to love. Poor child, that happy week had had to serve her ever since, through eleven years of unbroken school! Not that she pitied herself. Everybody had been kind to her—governesses, masters, girls, and all. She had been happy and successful, and had made numerous friends, about whom, as she grew more at home, she freely chatted to Mrs. Brownlow, who was always ready to hear of Mary Ogilvie and Clara Cartwright, and liked to draw out the stories of the girl-world, in which it was plain that Caroline Allen had been a bright, good, clever girl, getting on well, trusted and liked. She had been half sorry to leave her dear old school, half glad to go on to something new. She was evidently not so comfortable, while Miss Heath's lowest teacher, as she had been while she was the asylum's senior pupil. Yet when on Sunday evening the Doctor was summoned and the ladies were left *tête-à-tête*, she laughed rather than complained. But still she owned, with her black head on Mrs. Brownlow's lap, that she had always craved for something—something, and she had found it now !

Everything was a fresh joy to her ; every print on the walls, every ornament on the brackets, seemed to speak to her eye and to her soul both at once, and the sense of comfort and beauty and home, after the bareness of school, seemed to charm her above all. 'I always did want to know what was inside people's windows,' she said.

And in the same way it was a feast to her to get hold of a 'real book,' as she called it, not only the beginnings of every-thing, and selections that always broke off just as she began to care about them. She had been thoroughly well grounded, and had a thirst for knowledge too real to have been stifled by the routine she had gone through—though, said she, 'I do want time to get on further, and to learn what won't be of any use !'

'Of no use ! said Mr. Brownlow, laughing—having just found her trying to make out the old English of King Alfred's *Boëthius* —'such as this?'

'Just so ! They always are turning me off with " This won't be of any use to you." I hate use——

'Like Ridley, who says he reads a book with double pleasure if he is not going to review it.'

'That Mr. Ridley who came in last evening?'

'Even so. Why that opening of eyes?'

'I thought a critic was a most formidable person.'

'You expected to see a mess of salt and vinegar prepared for his diet ?'

'I should prepare something quite different—milk and sweet-breads, I think.'

'To soften him? Do you hear, mother? Take advice.'

Caroline—or Carey, as she had begged to be called—blushed, and drew back half alarmed, as she always was when the Doctor caught up any of the little bits of fun that fell so shyly and demurely from her, as they were evoked by the more congenial atmosphere.

It was a great pleasure to him and to his mother to show her some of the many things she had never seen, watch her enjoy-ment, and elicit whether the reality agreed with her previous imaginations. Mr. Brownlow used to make time to take the two ladies out, or to drop in on them at some exhibition, check-ing the flow of half-droll, half-intelligent remarks for a moment, and then encouraging it again, while both enjoyed that most amusing thing, the fresh simplicity of a grown-up clever child.

'How will you ever bear to go back again ?' said Carey's

school-friend, Clara Cartwright, now a governess, whom Mrs. Brownlow had, with some suppressed growls from her son, invited to share their one day's country outing under the horse-chestnut trees of Richmond.

'Oh! I shall have it all to take back with me,' was the answer, as Carey toyed with the burnished celandine stars in her lap.

'I should never dare to think of it! I should dread the contrast!'

'Oh no!' said Carey. 'It is like a blind person who has once seen, you know. It will be always warm about my heart to know there are such people.'

Mrs. Brownlow happened to overhear this little colloquy while her son was gone to look for the carriage, and there was something in the bright unrepining tone that filled her eyes with tears, more especially as the little creature still looked very fragile—even at the end of a month. She was so tired out with her day of almost rapturous enjoyment that Mrs. Brownlow would not let her come downstairs again, but made her go at once to bed, in spite of a feeble protest against losing one evening.

'And I am afraid that is a recall,' said Mrs. Brownlow, seeing a letter directed to Miss Allen on the side-table. 'I will not give it to her to-night, poor little dear; I really don't know how to send her back.'

'Exactly what I was thinking,' said the Doctor, leaning over the fire, which he was vigorously stirring.

'You don't think her strong enough? If so, I am very glad,' said the mother, in a delighted voice. 'Eh, Joe?' as there was a pause; and as he replaced the poker, he looked up to her with a colour scarcely to be accounted for by the fire, and she ended in an odd, startled, yet not displeased tone, 'It is *that*—is it?'

'Yes, mother, it is *that*,' said Joe, laughing a little, in his relief that the plunge was made. 'I don't see that we could do better for your happiness or mine.'

'Don't put mine first' (half-crying).

'I didn't know I did. It all comes to the same thing.'

'My dear Joe, I only wish you could do it to-morrow, and have no fuss about it! What will Robert do?'

'Accept the provision for his friend's daughter,' said Joe gravely; and then they both burst out laughing. In the midst came the announcement of dinner, during which meal they refrained themselves, and tried to discuss other things, though not so successfully but that it was reported in the kitchen that something was up.

Joseph was just old enough for his mother, who had always dreaded his marriage, to have begun to wish for it, though she had never yet seen her ideal daughter-in-law, and the enforced silence during the meal only made her more eager, so that she began at once as soon as they were alone.

'When did you begin to think of this, Joe?'

'Not when I asked you to invite her—that would have been treacherous. No, but when I began to realise what it would be to send her back to her treadmill; though the beauty of it is that she never seems to realise that it is a treadmill.'

'She might now, though I tried so hard not to spoil her. It is that content with such a life which makes me think that in her you may have something more worth than the portion, which—which I suppose I ought to regret and say you will miss.'

'I shall get all that plentifully from Robert, mother.'

'I am afraid it does entail harder work on you, and later on in life, than if you had chosen a person with something of her own.'

'Something of her own? Her own, indeed! Mother, she has that of her own which is the very thing to help and inspire me to make a name, and work out an idea, worth far more than any pounds, shillings, and pence, or even houses or lands I might get with a serene and solemn dame, even with clear notions as to those same *l. s. d.!*'

'For shame, Joe! You may be as much in love as you please, but don't be wicked.'

For this description was applicable to the bride whom Robert had presented to them about a year ago, on retiring with a colonel's rank.

'So I may be as much in love as I please? Thank you. I always knew you were the very best mother in the world:' and he came and kissed her.

'I wonder what she will say, the dear child!'

'May be that she has no taste for such an old fellow. Hush, mother. Seriously, my chief scruple is whether it be fair to ask a girl to marry a man twice her age, when she has absolutely seen nothing of his kind but the German master!'

'Trust her,' said Mrs. Brownlow. 'Nay, she never could have a freer choice than now, when she is too young and simple to be weighted with a sense of being looked down on. It is possible that she may be startled at first, but I think it will be only at life opening on her; so don't be daunted, and imagine it is your old age and infirmity,' said the mother, smoothing back the locks which certainly were not the clustering curls of youth.

How the mother watched all the next morning, while the unconscious Carey first marvelled at her nervousness and silence, and then grew almost infected by it. It was very strange, she thought, that Mrs. Brownlow, always so kind, should say nothing but 'humph' on being told that Miss Heath's workmen had finished, and that she must return next Monday morning. It was the Doctor's day to be early at the hospital, and he had had a summons to see some one on the way, so that he was gone before breakfast, when Carey's attempts to discuss her happy day in the country met with such odd, fitful answers;

for, in fact, Mrs. Brownlow could not trust herself to talk, and had no sooner done breakfast than she went off to her house-keeping affairs and others, which she managed unusually to prolong.

Carey was trying to draw some flowers in a glass before her —a little purple, green-winged orchis, a cowslip, and a quivering dark-brown tuft of quaking grass. He came and stood behind her, saying—

'You've got the character of those.'

'They are very difficult,' sighed Carey; 'I never tried flowers before, but I wanted to take them with me.'

'To take them with you?' he repeated, rather dreamily.

'Yes, back to another sort of Heath,' she said, with a little laugh; 'don't you know I go next Monday?'

'If you go, I hope it will only be to come back.'

'Oh! if Mrs. Brownlow is so good as to let me come again in the holidays!' and she was all one flush of joy, looking round, and up in his face, to see whether it could be true.

'Not only for holidays—for work days,' he said, and his voice shook.

'But Mrs. Brownlow can't want a companion?'

'But I do. Caroline, will you come back to us to make home doubly sweet to a busy man, who will do his best to make you happy?'

The little creature looked up in his face bewildered, and then said shyly, the colour surging into her face—

'Please, what did you say?'

'I asked if you would stay with us, and make this place bright for us, as my wife,' he said, taking both the little brown hands into his own, and looking into the widely-opened wondering eyes; while she answered, 'If I may'—the very words, almost the very tone, in which she had replied to his invitation to come to recover at his house.

'Ah, my poor child, you have no one's leave to ask!' he said; 'you belong to us, only to us'—and he drew her into his arms, and kissed her.

Then he felt and heard a great sob, and there were two tears on her cheek when he could see her face, but she smiled with happy, quivering lip, and said—

'It was like when papa kissed me before he went away; he would be so glad.'

In the midst of the caress that answered this, a bell sounded, and in the certainty that the announcement of luncheon would instantly follow, they started apart.

Two seconds later they met Mrs. Brownlow on the landing—

'There, mother,' said the Doctor.

'My child!' and Carey was in her arms.

'Oh, may I?—Is it real?' said the girl in a stifled voice.

After that, they took it very quietly. Carey was so young and ignorant of the world that she was not nearly so much over-

powered as if she had had the slightest external knowledge
either of married life or of the exceptional thing the Doctor was
doing. Her mother had died when she was three years old, and
she had never since that time lived with wedded folk, while
even her companions at school being all fatherless, she had
gathered nothing of even second-hand experience from them.
All she knew was from books, which had given glimpses into
happy homes; and though she had feasted on a few novels
during this happy month, they had been very select, and chiefly
historical romance. She was at the age when nothing is impossible to youthful dreams, and if Tancredi had come out of the
*Gerusalemme* and thrown himself at her feet, she would hardly
have felt it more strangely dream-like than the transformation
of her kind doctor into her own Joe: and on the other hand,
she had from the first moment nestled so entirely into the home
that it would have seemed more unnatural to be torn away
from it than to become a part of it. As to her being an extraordinary and very disadvantageous choice for him, she simply
knew nothing of the matter; she was used to passiveness as to
her own destiny, and now that she did indeed 'belong to somebody' she let those somebodies think and decide for her, with
the one certainty that what Mr. Brownlow and his mother
liked was sure to be the truly right and happy thing.

So, instead of being alarmed and scrupulous, she was sweetly,
shyly, and yet confidingly gay and affectionate, enchanting both
her companions, but revealing by her naïve questions and
remarks such utter ignorance of all matters of common life that
Mrs. Brownlow had no scruples in not stirring the question,
that had never occurred to her son or his little betrothed,
namely, her own retirement. Caroline needed a mother far too
much for her to be spared.

What was to be done about Miss Heath? It was due to her
for Miss Allen to offer to return till her place could be supplied,
Mrs. Brownlow said—but that was only to tease the lovers—for
a quarter, at which Joe made a snarling howl, whereat Carey
ventured to laugh at him, and say she should come home for
every Sunday, as Miss Pinniwinks, the senior governess, did.
'Come *home*—it is enough to say that,' she added.

Mrs. Brownlow undertook to negotiate the matter, her son
saying privately—

'Get her off, if you have to advance a quarter. I'd rather do
anything than send her back for even a week, to have all manner
of nonsense put into her head. I'd sooner go and teach there
myself.'

'Or send me?' asked his mother.

'Anything short of that,' he said.

Miss Heath, as Mrs. Brownlow had guessed, thought an engaged girl as bad as a barrel of gunpowder, and was quite as
much afraid of Miss Allen putting nonsense into her pupils'
heads as the Doctor could be of the reverse process; so, young

teachers not being scarce, Carey's brief connection with Miss Heath was brought to an end in a morning call, whence she returned endowed with thirteen book-markers, five mats, and a sachet.

Carey had of her own, as it appeared, twenty-five pounds a year, which had hitherto clothed her, and of which she only knew that it was paid to her quarterly by a lawyer at Bath, whose address she gave. Mr. Brownlow followed up the clue, but could not learn much about her belongings. The twenty-five pounds was the interest of the small sum which had remained to poor Captain Allen when he wound up his affairs, after paying the debts in which his early and imprudent marriage had involved him. He did not seem to have had any relations, and of his wife nothing was known but that she was a Miss Otway, and that he had met her in some colonial quarters. The old lady with whom the little girl had been left was her mother's maternal aunt, and had lived on an annuity so small that on her death there had not been funds sufficient to pay expenses without a sale of all her effects, so that nothing had been saved for the child except a few books with her parents' names in them—John Allen and Caroline Otway—which she still kept as her chief treasures. The lawyer, who had acted as her guardian, would hand over to her £500 on her coming of age.

That was all that could be discovered, nor was Colonel Robert Brownlow as much flattered as had been hoped by the provision for his friend's daughter. Nay, he was inclined to disavow the friendship. He was sorry for poor Allen, he said, but as to making a friend of such a fellow, pah! No! there was no harm in him, he was a good officer enough, but he never had a grain of common sense; and whereas he never could keep out of debt, he must needs go and marry a young girl, just because he thought her uncle was not kind to her. It was the worst thing he could have done, for it made her uncle cast her off on the spot, and then she was killed with harass and poverty. He never held up his head again after losing her, and just died of fever because he was too broken down to have energy to live. There was enough in this to weave out a tender little romance, probably really another aspect of the truth, which made Caroline's bright eyes overflow with tears, when she heard it couched in tenderer language from Joseph; and the few books and treasures that had been rescued agreed with it—a Bible with her father's name, a few devotional books of her mother's, and Mrs. Heman's poems, with 'To Lina, from her devoted J. A.'

Caroline would fain have been called Lina, but the name did not fit her, and would not *take*.

Colonel Brownlow was altogether very friendly, if rather grave and dry towards her, as soon as he was convinced that 'it was only Joe,' and that pity, not artfulness, was to blame

for the undesirable match.   He was too honourable a man not
to see that it could not be given up, and he held that the best
must now be made of it, and that it would be more proper,
since it was to be, for him to assume the part of father, and let
the marriage take place from his house at Kenminster.   This
was a proposal for which it was hard to be as grateful as it
deserved, since it had been planned to walk quietly into the
parish church, be married 'without any fuss,' and then to take
the fortnight's holiday, which was all that the doctor allowed
himself.

But as Robert was allowed to be judge of the proprieties,
and as the kindness on his part was great, it was accepted;
and Caroline was carried off for three weeks to keep her
residence, and make the house feel what a blank her little
figure had left.

Certainly, when the pair met again on the eve of the
wedding, there never was a more willing bride.

She said she had been very happy.   The Colonel and Ellen,
as she had been told to call her future sister, had been very
kind indeed; they had taken her for long drives, shown her
everything, introduced her to quantities of people; but, oh
dear! was it absolutely only three weeks since she had been
away?   It seemed just like three years, and she understood
now why the girls who had homes made calendars, and checked
off the days.   No school term had ever seemed so long; but at
Kenminster she had had nothing to do, and besides, now she
knew what home was!

So it was the most cheerful and joyous of weddings, though
the bride was a far less brilliant spectacle than the bride of last
year, Mrs. Robert Brownlow, who with her handsome oval face,
fine figure, and her tasteful dress, perfectly befitting a young
matron, could not help infinitely outshining the little girlish
angular creature, looking the browner for her bridal white, so
that even a deep glow and a strange misty beaminess of
expression could not make her passable in Kenminster eyes.

How would Joe Brownlow's fancy turn out?


## CHAPTER II          .

### THE CHICKENS

'John Gilpin's spouse said to her dear,
    "Though wedded we have been
    These twice ten tedious years, yet we
    No holiday have seen."'

                                        COWPER.

No one could have much doubt how it had turned out, who
looked, after fifteen years, into that room where Joe Brownlow
and his mother had once sat *tête-à-tête*.

They occupied the two ends of the table still, neither looking much older, in expression at least, for the fifteen years that had passed over their heads, though the mother had—after the wont of active old ladies—grown smaller and lighter, and the son somewhat more bald and gray, but not a whit more careworn, and, if possible, even brighter.

On one side of him sat a little figure, not quite so thin, some angles smoothed away, the black hair coiled, but still in resolute little mutinous tendrils on the brow, not ill set off by a tuft of carnation ribbon on one side, agreeing with the colour that touched up her gauzy black dress ; the face, not beautiful indeed — but developed, softened, brightened with more of sweetness and tenderness—as well as more of thought—added to the fresh responsive intelligence it had always possessed.

On the opposite side of the dinner-table were a girl of fourteen and a boy of twelve ; the former, of a much larger frame than her mother, and in its most awkward and uncouth stage, hardly redeemed by the keen ardour and inquiry that glowed in the dark eyes, set like two hot coals beneath the black overhanging brows of the massive forehead, on which the dark smooth hair was parted. The features were large, the complexion dark but not clear, and the look of resolution in the square-cut chin and closely-shutting mouth was more boy-like than girl-like. Janet Brownlow was assuredly a very plain girl, but the family habit was to regard their want of beauty as rather a mark of distinction, capable of being joked about, if not triumphed in.

Nor was Allen, the boy, wanting in good looks. He was fairer, clearer, better framed in every way than his sister, and had a pleasant, lively countenance, prepossessing to all. He had a well-grown, upright figure, his father's ready suppleness of movement, and his mother's hazel eyes and flashing smile, and there was a look of success about him, as well there might be, since he had come out triumphantly from the examination for Eton College, and had been informed that morning that there were vacancies enough for his immediate admission.

There was a pensiveness mixed with the satisfaction in his mother's eyes as she looked at him, for it was the first break into the home. She had been the only teacher of her children till two years ago, when Allen had begun to attend a day school a few streets off, and the first boy's first flight from under her wing, for ever so short a space, is generally a sharp wound to the mother's heart.

Not that Allen would leave an empty house behind him. Lying at full length on the carpet, absorbed in a book, was Robert, a boy on whom the same capacious brow as Janet's sat better than on the feminine creature. He was reading on, undisturbed by the pranks of three younger children, John Lucas, a lithe, wiry, restless elf of nine, with a brown face and black curly head, and Armine and Barbara, young persons of seven and six, on whom nature had been more beneficent in the matter of looks, for though brown was their prevailing complexion, both had well-moulded, childish features, and really fine eyes.  The hubbub of voices, as they tumbled and rushed about the window and balcony, was the regular accompaniment of dinner, though on the first plaintive tone from the little girl, the mother interrupted a 'Well, but, papa,' from Janet, with 'Babie, Babie.'

'It's Jock, Mother Carey!  He *will* come into Fairyland too soon.'

'What's the last news from Fairyland, Babie?' asked the father as the little one ran up to him.

'I want to be Queen Mab, papa, but Armine wants to be Perseus with the Gorgon's head, and Jock is the dragon ; but the dragon *will* come before we've put Polly upon the rock.'

'What! is Polly Andromeda——?' as a gray parrot's stand was being transferred from the balcony.

'Yes, papa,' called out Armine.  'You see she's chained, and Bobús won't play, and Babie will be Queen Mab——'

'I suppose,' said the mother, 'that it is not harder to bring Queen Mab in with Perseus than Oberon with Theseus and Hippolyta——'

'You would have us infer,' said the Doctor with grave humour, 'that your children are at their present growth in the Elizabethan age of culture——'

But again began a 'Well, but, papa!' but he exclaimed, 'Do look at that boy— Well wallopped, dragon !' as Jock with preternatural contortions, rolled, kicked, and tumbled himself with extended jaws to the rock, *alias* stand, to which Polly was chained, she remarking in a hoarse, low whisper, 'Naughty boy——'

'Well moaned, Andromeda !'

'But papa,' persisted Janet, 'when Oliver Cromwell——

'Oh ! look at the Gorgon !' cried the mother, as the battered head of an ancient doll was displayed over his shoulder by Perseus, decorated with two enormous snakes, one made of stamps, and the other a spiral of whalebone shavings out of a box.

The monster immediately tumbled over, twisted, kicked, and wriggled so that the scandalised Perseus exclaimed : 'But Jock —monster, I mean—you're turned into stone——'

'It's convulsions,' replied the monster, gasping frightfully, while redoubling his contortions, though Queen Mab observed in the most admonitory tone, touching him at the same time with her wand, 'Don't you know, Skipjack, that's the reason you don't grow——'

'Eh !  What's the new theory !  Who says so, Babie?' came from the bottom of the table.

'Nurse says so, papa,' answered Allen ; 'I heard her telling Jock yesterday that he would never be any taller till he stood still and gave himself time.'

'Get out, will you!' was then heard from the prostrate Robert, the monster having taken care to become petrified right across his legs.

'But, papa,' Janet's voice was heard, 'if Oliver Cromwell had not helped the Waldenses——'

It was lost, for Bobus and Jock were rolling over together with too much noise to be bearable; grandmamma turned round with an expostulatory 'My dears,' mamma with 'Boys, please don't when papa is tired——'

'Jock is such a little ape,' said Bobus, picking himself up. 'Father, can you tell me why the moon draws up the tides on the wrong side?'

'You may study the subject,' says the Doctor; 'I shall pack you all off to the seaside in a day or two.'

There was one outcry from mother, wife, and boys, 'Not without you?'

'I can't go till Drew comes back from his outing——'

'But why should we? It would be so much nicer all together.'

'It will be horribly dull without: indeed I never can see the sense of going at all,' said Janet.

There was a confused outcry of indignation, in which waves —crabs—boats and shrimps, were all mingled together.

'I'm sure that's not half so entertaining as hearing people talk in the evening,' said Janet.

'You precocious little piece of dissipation,' said her mother, laughing.

'I didn't mean fine lady nonsense,' said Janet, rather hotly; 'I meant talk like——'

'Like big guns. Oh, yes, we know,' interrupted Allen; 'Janet does not think any one worth listening to that hasn't got a whole alphabet tacked behind his name.'

'Janet had better take care, and Bobus too,' said the Doctor, 'or we shall have to send them to vegetate on some farm, and see the cows milked and the pigs fed.'

'I'm afraid Bobus would apply himself to finding how much caseine matter was in the cow's milk,' said Janet in her womanly tone.

'Or by what rule the pigs curled their tails,' said her father, with a mischievous pull at the black plaited tail that hung down behind her.

And then they all rose from the table, little Barbara starting up as soon as grace was said. 'Father, please, you *are* the giant Queen Mab always rides!'

'Queen Mab, or Queen Bab, always rides me, which comes to the same thing. Though as to the size of the giant——'

There was a pause to let grandmamma go up in peace, upon Mother Carey's arm, and then a general romp and scurry all the way up the stairs, ending by Jock's standing on one leg on the top post of the baluster, like an acrobat, an achievement which

made even his father so giddy that he peremptorily desired it
never to be attempted again, to the great relief of both the
ladies. Then, coming into the drawing-room, Babie perched
herself on his knee, and began, without the slightest preparation, the recitation of Cowper's 'Colubriad'—

> 'Fast by the threshold of a door nailed fast
> Three kittens sat, each kitten looked aghast.'

And just as she had with great excitement—

> 'Taught him never to come there no more,'

Armine broke in with 'Nine times one are nine.'

It was an institution dating from the days when Janet made
her first acquaintance with the 'Little Busy Bee,' that there should
be something, of some sort, said or shown to papa whenever he
was at home or free between dinner and bedtime, and it was
considered something between a disgrace and a misfortune to
produce nothing.

So when the two little ones had been kissed and sent off to
bed, with mamma going with them to hear their prayers, Jock,
on being called for, repeated a Greek declension with two
mistakes in it, Bobus showed a long sum in decimals, Janet
brought a neat parallelism of the present tense of the verb 'to
be' in five languages—Greek, Latin, French, German, and
English.

'And Allen—reposing on your honours ?  Eh, my boy ?'

Allen looked rather foolish, and said, 'I spoilt it, papa, and
hadn't time to begin another.'

'It—I suppose I am not to hear what till it has come to
perfection.  Is it the same that was in hand last time ?'

'No, papa, *much* better,' said Janet emphatically.

'What I want to see,' said Dr. Brownlow, 'is something
finished.  I'd rather have that than ever so many magnificent
beginnings.'

Here he was seized upon by Robert, with his knitted brow
and a book in his hands, demanding aid in making out why, as
he said, the tide swelled out on the wrong side of the earth.

His father did his best to disentangle the question, but Bobus
was not satisfied till the clock chimed his doom, when he went
off with Jock, who was walking on his hands.

'That's too tough a subject for such a little fellow,' said the
grandmother ; 'so late in the day too !'

'He would have worried his brain with it all night if he had
not worked it out,' said his father.

'I'm afraid he will, any way,' said the mother  'Fancy
being troubled with dreams of surging oceans rising up the
wrong way !'

'Yes, he ought to be running after the tides instead of
theorising about them.  Carry him off, Mother Carey, and the
whole brood, without loss of time.'

'But, Joe, why should we not wait for you? You never did send us away all forlorn before!' she said pleadingly. 'We are all quite well, and I can't bear going without you.'

'I had much rather all the chickens were safe away, Carey,' he said, sitting down by her. 'There's a tendency to epidemic fever in two or three streets, which I don't like in this hot weather, and I had rather have my mind easy about the young ones.'

'And what do you think of my mind, leaving you in the midst of it?'

'Your mind, being that of a mother bird and a doctor's wife, ought to have no objection.'

'How soon does Dr. Drew come home?'

'In a fortnight, I believe. He wanted rest terribly, poor old fellow. Don't grudge him every day.'

'A fortnight!' (as if it was a century). 'You can't come for a fortnight. Well, perhaps it will take a week to fix on a place.'

'Hardly, for see here, I found a letter from Acton when I came in. They have found an unsophisticated elysium at Kyve Clements, and are in raptures which they want us to share—rocks and waves and all.'

'And rooms?'

'Yes, very good rooms, enough for us all,' was the answer, flinging into her lap a letter from his friend, a somewhat noted artist in water-colours, whom, after long patience, Carey's school-friend, Miss Cartwright, had married two years ago.

There was nothing to say against it, only grandmamma observed, 'I am too old to catch things; Joe will let me stay and keep house for him.'

'Please, please let me stay with granny,' insisted Janet; 'then I shall finish my German classes.'

Janet was granny's child. She had slept in her room ever since Allen was born, and trotted after her in her 'housewife-skep,' and the sense of being protected was passing into the sense of protection. Before she could be answered, however, there was an announcement. Friends were apt to drop in to coffee and talk in the evening, on the understanding that certain days alone were free—people chiefly belonging to a literary, scientific, and artist set, not Bohemian, but with a good deal of quiet ease and absence of formality.

This friend had just returned from Asia Minor, and had brought an exquisite bit of a Greek frieze, of which he had become the happy possessor, knowing that Mrs. Joseph Brownlow would delight to see it, and mayhap to copy it.

For Carey's powers had been allowed to develop themselves; Mrs. Brownlow having been always housekeeper, she had been fain to go on with the studies that even her preparation for governess-ship had not rendered wearisome, and thus had become a very graceful modeller in clay—her favourite pursuit —when her children's lessons and other occupations left her free to indulge in it. The history of the travels, and the account of the discovery, were given and heard with all zest, and in the midst others came in—a barrister and his wife to say good-bye before the circuit, a professor with a ticket for the gallery at a scientific dinner, two medical students, who had been made free of the house because they were nice lads with no available friends in town.

It was all over by half-past ten, and the trio were alone together. 'How amusing Mr. Leslie is!' said the young Mrs. Brownlow. 'He knows how to describe as few people do.'

'Did you see Janet listening to him,' said her grandmother, 'with her brows pulled down and her eyes sparkling out under them, wanting to devour every word?'

'Yes,' returned the Doctor, 'I saw it, and I longed to souse that black head of hers with salt water. I don't like brains to grow to the contempt of healthful play.'

'People never know when they are well off! I wonder what you would have said if you had had a lot of stupid dolts, boys always being plucked, etc.'

'Don't plume yourself too soon, Mother Carey; only one chick has gone through the first ordeal.'

'And if Allen did, Bobus will.'

'Allen is quite as clever as Bobus, granny, if——' eagerly said the mother.

'If——' said the father; 'there's the point. If Allen has the stimulus, he will do well. I own I am particularly pleased with his success, because perseverance is his weak point.'

'Carey kept him up to it,' said granny. 'I believe his success is quite as much her work as his own.'

'And the question is, how will he get on without his mother to coach him?'

'Now you know you are not one bit uneasy, papa!' cried his wife indignantly. 'But don't you think we might let Janet have her will for just these ten days? There can't be any real danger for her with grandmamma, and I should be happier about granny.'

'You don't trust Joe to take care of me?'

'Not if Joe is to be out all day. There will be nobody to trot up and down stairs for you. Come, it is only what she begs for herself, and she really is perfectly well.'

'As if I could have a child victimised to me,' said granny.

'The little Cockney thinks the victimising would be in going to the deserts with only the boys and me,' laughed Carey; 'but I think a week later will be quite time enough to sweep the cobwebs out of her brain.'

'And you can do without her?' inquired Mrs. Brownlow. 'You don't want her to help to keep the boys in order?'

'Thank you, I can do that better without her,' said Carey. 'She exasperates them sometimes.'

'I believe granny is thinking whether she is not wanted to keep Mother Carey in order as well as her chickens. Hasn't mother been taken for your governess, Carey?'

'No, no, Joe, that's too bad. They asked Janet at the dancing-school whether her sister was not going to join.'

'Her younger sister?'

'No, I tell you, her half-sister. But Clara Acton will do discretion for us, granny; and I promise you we won't do anything her husband says is very desperate! Don't be afraid.'

'No,' said grandmamma, smiling as she kissed her daughter-in-law, and rose to take her candle; 'I am never afraid of anything a mother can share with her boys.'

'Even if she is nearly a tomboy herself,' laughed the husband, with rather a teasing air, towards his little wife. 'Good-night, mother. Shall not we be snug with nobody left but Janet, who might be great-grandmother to us both?'

'I really am glad that Janet should stay with granny,' said Carey, when he had shut the door behind the old lady; 'she would be left alone so many hours while you are out, and she does need more waiting on than she used to do.'

'You think so? I never see her grow older.'

'Not in the least older in mind or spirits; but she is not so strong, nor so willing to exert herself, and she falls asleep more in the afternoon. One reason for which I am less sorry to go on before, is that I shall be able to judge whether the rooms are comfortable enough for her, and I suppose we may change if they are not.'

'To another place, if you think best.'

'Only you will not let her stay at home altogether. That's what I'm afraid of.'

'She will only do so on the penalty of keeping me, and you may trust her not to do that,' said Joe, laughing with the confidence of an only son.

'I shall come back and fetch you if you don't appear under a fortnight. Did you do any more this morning to the great experiment, Magnum Bonum?'

She spoke the words in a proud, shy, exulting semi-whisper, somewhat as Gutenberg's wife might have asked after his printing-press.

'No. I haven't had half an hour to myself to-day; at least when I could have attended to it. Don't be afraid, Carey, I'm not daunted by the doubts of our good friends. I see your eyes reproaching me with that.'

'Oh no, as you said, Sir Matthew Fleet mistrusts anything entirely new, and the professor is never sanguine. I am almost glad they are so stupid, it will make our pleasure all the sweeter.'

'You silly little bird, if you sit on that egg it will be sure to be addled. If it should come to any good, probably it will take longer than our life-time to work into people's brains.'

'No,' said Carey, 'I know the real object is the relieving pain and saving life, and that is what you care for more than the honour and glory. But do you remember the fly on the coach wheel ?'

'Well, the coach wheel means to stand still for a little while. I don't mean to try another experiment till my brains have been turned out to grass, and I can come to it fresh.'

'Ah! 'tis you that really need the holiday,' said Carey wistfully; 'much more than any of us. Look at this great crow's foot,' tracing it with her finger.

'Laughing, my dear. That's the outline of the risible muscle. A Mother Carey and her six ridiculous chickens can't but wear out furrows with laughing at them.'

'I only know I wish it were you that were going, and I that were staying at home.'

> ' " You shall do my work to-day,
> And I'll go follow the plough," '

said her husband, laughing. 'There are the notes of my lecture, if you'll go and give it.'

'Ah! we should not be like that celebrated couple. You would manage the boys much better than I could doctor your patients.'

'I don't know that. The boys are never so comfortable when I've got them alone. But, considering the hour, I should think the best preliminary would be to put out the lamp and go to bed.'

'I suppose it is time; but I always think this last talk before going upstairs the best thing in the whole day !' said the happy wife as she took the candle.

## CHAPTER III

### THE WHITE SLATE

> 'Dark house, by which once more I stand
>     Here in the long unlovely street,
>     Doors, where my heart was used to beat
> So quickly, waiting for a hand,
>
> A hand that can be clasp'd no more—
>     Behold me, for I cannot sleep.'
>
> TENNYSON.

'MOTHER CAREY,' to call her by the family name that her husband had given the first day she held a baby in her arms, had a capacity of enjoyment that what she called her exile could not destroy. Even Bobus left theory behind him and became a holiday boy, and the whole six climbed rocks, paddled, boated,

hunted seaweeds and sea animals, lived on the beach from
morning to night ; and were exceedingly amused by the people,
who insisted on addressing the senior of the party as 'Miss,'
and thought them a young girl and her brothers under the
charge of Mrs. Acton. She, though really not a year older than
her friend, looked like a worn and staid matron by her side, and
was by no means disposed to scramble barefoot over slippery
seaweed, or to take impromptu a part in the grand defence of
the sand and shingle edition of Raglan Castle.

Even to Mrs. Acton it was a continual wonder to see how
entirely under control of that little merry mother were those
great, lively, spirited boys, who never seemed to think of dis-
obeying her first word, and, while all made fun together, and
she was hardly less active and enterprising than they, always
considered her comforts and likings.

So went things for a fortnight, during which the coming of
the others had been put off by Dr. Drew's absence. One morning Mr. Acton sought Mrs. Brownlow on the beach, where she
was sitting with her brood round her, partly reading from a
translation, partly telling them the story of Ulysses.

He called her aside, and told her that her husband had telegraphed to him to bid him to carry her the tidings that good
old Mrs. Brownlow had been taken from them suddenly in the
night, evidently in her sleep.

Carey turned very white, but said only, 'Oh ! why did I go
without them ?'

It was such an overwhelming shock as left no room for tears.
Her first thought, the only one she seemed to have room for,
was to get back to her husband by the next train. She would
have taken all the children, but that Mrs. Acton insisted, almost
commanded, that they should be left under her charge, and
reminded her that their father wished them to be out of London ;
nor did Allen and Robert show any wish to return to a house of
mourning, being just of the age to be so much scared at sorrow
as to ignore it. And indeed their mother was equally new to
any real grief ; her parents had been little more than a name to
her, and the only loss she had actually felt was that of a favourite
schoolfellow.

She had no time to think or feel till she had reached the train
and taken her seat, and even then the first thing she was conscious of was a sense of numbness within, and frivolous observation without, as she found herself trying to read upside down
the direction of her opposite neighbour's parcels, counting the
flounces on her dress, and speculating on the meetings and
partings at the stations ; yet with a terrible weight and soreness on her all the time, though she could not think of the dear
granny, of whom it was no figure of speech to say that she had
been indeed a mother. The idea of her absence from home for
ever was too strange, too heartrending to be at once embraced ;
and as she neared the end of her journey on that long day,

Carey's mind was chiefly fixed on the yearning to be with her husband and Janet, who had suffered such a shock without her. She seemed more able to feel through her husband—who was so devoted to his mother—than for herself, and she was every moment more uneasy about her little daughter, who must have been in the room with her grandmother. Comfort them? How, she did not know! The others had always petted and comforted her, and now—— No one to go to when the children were ailing or naughty—no one to share little anxieties when Joe was out late—no one to be the backbone she leant on—no dear welcome from the easy-chair. That thought nearly set her crying; the tears burnt in her strained eyes, but the sight of the people opposite braced her, and she tried to fix her thoughts on the unseen world, but they only wandered wide as if beyond her own control, and her head was aching enough to confuse her.

At last, late on the long summer day, she was at the terminus, and with a heart beating so fast that she could hardly breathe, found herself in a cab, driving up to her own door, just as the twilight was darkening.

How dark it looked within, with all the blinds down! The servant who opened the door thought Miss Janet was in the drawing-room, but the master was out. It sounded desolate, and Carey ran upstairs, craving and eager for the kiss of her child—the child who must have borne the brunt of the shock.

The room was silent, all dusky and shadowed; the window-frames were traced on the blinds by the gas freshly lighted out-side, and moving in the breeze with a monotonous dreariness. Carey stood a moment, and then her eyes getting accustomed to the darkness, she discerned a little heap lying curled up before the ottoman, her head on a great open book, asleep—poor child! quite worn out. Carey moved quietly across and sat down by her, longing but not daring to touch her. The lamp was brought up in a minute or two, and that roused Janet, who sprang up with a sudden start and dazzled eyes, exclaiming, 'Father! Oh, it's Mother Carey! Oh, mother, mother, please don't let him go!'

'And you have been all alone in the house, my poor child,' said Carey, as she felt the girl shuddering in her close embrace.

'Mrs. Lucas came to stay with me, but I didn't want her,' said Janet, 'so I told her she might go home to dinner. It's father——'

'Where is father?'

'Those horrid people in Tottenham Court Road sent for him just as he had come home,' said Janet.

'He went out as usual?'

'Yes, though he had such a bad cold. He said he could not be spared; and he was out all yesterday till bedtime, or I should have told him grandmamma was not well.'

'You thought so!'

'Yes, she panted and breathed so oddly; but she would not let me say a word to him. She made me promise not, but being anxious about him helped to do it. Dr. Lucas said so.'

There was a strange hardness and yet a trembling in Janet's voice; nor did she look as if she had shed tears, though her face was pale and her eyes black-ringed; and when old nurse, now very old indeed, tottered in sobbing, she flung herself to the other end of the room. It was more from nurse than from Janet that Carey learnt the particulars, such as they were, namely, that the girl had been half-dressed when she had taken alarm from her grandmother's unresponsive stillness, and had rushed down to her father's room. He had found that all had long been over. His friend, old Dr. Lucas, had come immediately, and had pronounced the cause to have been heart complaint.

Nurse said her master had been 'very still,' and had merely given the needful orders and written a few letters before going to his patients, for the illness was at its height, and there were cases for which he was very anxious.

The good old woman, who had lived nearly all her life with her mistress, was broken-hearted; but she did not forget to persuade Caroline to take food, telling her she must be ready to cheer up the master when he should come in, and assuring her that the throbbing headache which disgusted her with all thoughts of eating would be better for the effort. Perhaps it was, but it would not allow her to bring her thoughts into any connection, or to fix them on what she deemed befitting; and when she saw that the book over which Janet had been asleep in the twilight was *The Last of the Mohicans*, she was more scandalised than surprised.

It was past Janet's bedtime, but though too proud to say so, she manifestly shrank from her first night of loneliness, and her mother, herself unwilling to be alone, came with her to her room, undressed her, and sat with her in the darkness, hoping for some break in the dull reticence, but disappointed, for Janet hid her head in the clothes, and slept, or seemed to sleep.

Perhaps Carey herself had been half dozing, when she heard the well-known sounds of arrival, and darted downstairs, meeting indeed the welcoming eye and smile; but 'Ah, here she is!' was said so hoarsely and feebly that she exclaimed, 'O Joe, you have knocked yourself up!'

'Yes,' said Dr. Lucas, whom she only then perceived. 'He must go to bed directly, and then we will see to him. Not another word, Brownlow, till you are there, nor then if you are wise.'

He strove to disobey, but cough and choking forbade; and as he began to ascend the stairs, Caroline turned in dismay to the kind, fatherly old man, who had always been one of the chief intimates of the house, and was now retired from practice, except for very old friends.

He told her that her husband was suffering from a kind of

sore throat that sometimes attacked those attending on this
fever, though generally not unless there was some predisposition,
or unless the system had been unduly lowered. Joe had indeed
been overworked in the absence of several of the regular practitioners and of all those who could give extra help; but this
would probably have done little harm, but for a cold caught in
a draughty room, and the sudden stroke with which the day had
begun. Dr. Lucas had urged him to remain at home, and had
undertaken his regular work for the day, but summonses from
his patients had been irresistible; he had attended to every one
except himself, and finally, after hours spent over the critical
case of the wife of a small tradesman, he had found himself so
ill that he had gone to his friend for treatment, and Dr. Lucas
had brought him home, intending to stay all night with him.

Since the wife had arrived, the good old man, knowing how
much rather they would be alone, consented to sleep in another
room, after having done all that was possible for the night, and
cautioned against talking.

Indeed Joe, heavy, stupefied, and struggling for breath,
knew too well what it all meant not to give himself all possible
chance by silent endurance, lying with his wife's hand in his, or
sometimes smoothing her cheek, but not speaking without
necessity. Once he told her that her head was aching, and
made her lie down on the bed, but he was too ill for this rest to
last long, and the fits of struggling with suffocation prevented
all respite save for a few minutes.

With the early light of the long summer morning Dr. Lucas
looked in, and would have sent her to bed, but she begged off,
and a sign from her husband seemed to settle the matter, for
the old physician went away again, perhaps because his eyes
were full of tears.

The first words Joe said when they were again alone were
'My tablets.' She went in search of them to his dressing-room,
and not finding them there, was about to run down to the consulting-room, when Janet came out already dressed, and fetched
them for her, as well as a white slate, on which he was accustomed to write memorandums of engagements.

Her father thanked her by a sign, but there was possibility
enough of infection to make him wave her back from kissing
him, and she took refuge at the foot of the bed, on a sofa shut
off by the curtains which had been drawn to exclude the light.

Joe meantime wrote on the slate the words '*Magnum bonum.*'

'*Magnum bonum?*' read his wife, in amazement.

'Papers in bureau,' he wrote; 'lock all in my desk. Mention
to no one.'

'Am I to put them in your desk?' asked Caroline, bewildered as to his intentions, and finding it hard to read the
writing, as he went on—

'No word to *any one,*' scoring it under, 'not till one of the
boys is ready.'

'One of the boys!' in utter amazement.

'Not as a chance for *himself*,' he wrote, 'but as a great trust.'

'I know,' she said, 'it is a great trust to make a discovery which will save life. It is my pride to know you are doing it, my own dear Joe.'

'It seems I am not worthy to do it,' was traced by his fingers. 'It is not developed enough to be listened to by any one. Keep it for the fit one of the boys. Religion, morals, brains, balance.'

She read each word aloud, bending her head in assent; and, after a pause, he wrote, 'Not till his degree. He could not work it out sooner. There is peril to self and others in experimenting—temptation to rashness. It were better unknown than trifled with. Be an honest judge—promise. Say what I want.'

Spellbound, almost mesmerised by his will, Caroline pronounced—'I promise to keep the *magnum bonum* a secret till the boys are grown up, and then only to confide it to the one that seems fittest, when he has taken his degree, and is a good, religious, wise, able man, with brains and balance, fit to be trusted to work out and apply such an invention, and not make it serve his own advancement, but be a real good and blessing to all.'

He gave her one of his bright, sweet smiles, and as she sealed her promise by a kiss, he took up the slate again and wrote, 'My dear comfort, you have always understood. You are to be trusted. It must be done worthily or not at all.'

That was the burthen of everything; and his approval and affection gave a certain sustaining glow to the wife, who was besides so absorbed in attending to him as not to look beyond the moment. He wrote presently, after a little more, 'You know all my mind for the children. With God's help you can fill both places to them. I should like you to live at Kenminster, under Robert's wing.'

After that he only used the tablets for temporary needs, and to show what he wanted Dr. Lucas to undertake for his patients. The husband and wife had little more time for intimate communings, for the strangulation grew worse, more remedies were tried, and one of the greatest physicians of the day was called in, but only to make unavailing efforts.

Colonel Brownlow arrived in the middle of the day, and was thunderstruck at the new and terrible disaster. He was a large, tall man, with a good-humoured, weather-beaten face and an unwieldy, gouty figure; and he stood, with his eyes brimming over with tears, looking at his brother, and at first unable to read the word Joe traced for him—for writing had become a great effort—'Carey.'

'We will do our best for her, Ellen and I, my dear fellow. But you'll soon be better. Horrid things, these quinsies; but they pass off.'

Poor Joe half smiled at this confident opinion, but he merely

wrung his brother's hand, and only twice more took up the
pencil—once to write the name of the clergyman he wished to
see, and lastly to put down the initials of all his children:
'Love to you all. Let God and your mother be first with
you.—J. B.'

The daylight of the second morning had come in before that
deadly suffocation had finished its work and the strong man's
struggles were ended.

When Colonel Brownlow tried to raise his sister-in-law, he
found her fainting, and, with Dr. Lucas's help, carried her to
another room, where she lay, utterly exhausted, in a kind of
faint stupor, apparently unconscious of anything but violent
headache, which made her moan from time to time if anything
stirred her. Dr. Lucas thought this the effect of exhaustion,
for she had not slept, and hardly taken any food since her breakfast at Kyve three days ago; and finding poor old nurse too
entirely broken down to be of any use, he put his own kind
wife in charge of her, and was unwilling to admit any one else
—even Mrs. Robert Brownlow, who arrived in the course of the
day. She was a tall, fine-looking person, with an oval face—
soft, pleasant brown skin, mild brown eyes, and much tenderness of heart and manner, but not very well known to Caroline;
for her periodical visits had been wholly devoted to shopping
and sight-seeing. She was exceedingly shocked at the tidings
that met her, and gathered Janet into her arms with many
tears over the poor orphan girl! It was an effusiveness that
overwhelmed Janet, who had a miserable, hard, dried-up feeling of wretchedness, and injury too; for the more other people
cried, the less she could cry, and she heard them saying to one
another that she was unfeeling.

Still Aunt Ellen's presence was a sort of relief, for it made
the house less empty and dreary, and she took upon her the
cares that were greatly needed in the bereaved household,
where old nurse had lost her head and could do nothing, and
the most effective maid was away with the children. So Janet
wandered about after her aunt, with an adverse feeling at
having her home meddled with, but answering questions and
giving opinions, called or uncalled for. Her longing was for her
brothers, and it was a great blow to find that her uncle had
written to both Allen and Mr. Acton that they had better not
come home at present. She thought it cruel and unjust both
towards them and herself; and in her sickening sense of solitude and injury she had a vague expectation that they were all
going to be left wholly orphans, like the children of fiction,
dependent on their uncle and aunt, who would be unjust, and
prefer their own children; and she had a prevision of the battles
she was to fight, and the defensive influence she was to exert.

That brought to her mind the white slate on which her father
had been writing, and she hurried to secure it, though she
hardly knew where to go or to look; but straying into her

father's dressing-room, she found both it and the tablets among a heap of other small matters that had been cleared away when the other chamber had been arranged into the solemnity of the death-room. Hastily securing them, she carried them to her own desk in the deserted schoolroom, feeling as if they were her charge, and thus having no scruple in reading them.

She had heard what passed aloud , and, as the eldest girl, had been so constantly among the seniors, and so often supposed to be intent on her own occupations when they were conversing, that she had already the knowledge that *magnum bonum* was the pet home term for some great discovery in medical science that her father had been pursuing, with many disappointments and much incredulity from the few friends to whom it had been mentioned, but with absolute confidence on his own part. What it was she did not know, but she had fully taken in the injunction of secrecy and the charge to hand on the task to one of her brothers ; only, while her father had spoken of it as a grave trust, she viewed it as an inheritance of glory ; and felt a strange longing and repining that it could not be given to her to win and wear the crown of success.

Janet did not, however, keep the treasure long, for that very evening Mrs. Lucas sought her out to tell her that her mother had been saying something about a slate, and Dr. Lucas thought it was one on which her father had been writing. If she could find it, they hoped her mother would rest better.

Janet produced it, and being evidently most unwilling to let it go out of her hands, was allowed to carry it in, and to tell her mother that she had it. There was no need for injunctions to do so softly and cautiously, for she was frightened by her mother's dull, half-closed eye and pale, leaden look ; but there was a little air of relief as she faltered, 'Here's the slate, dear mother': and the answer, so faint that she could hardly hear it, was, 'Lock it up, my dear, till I can look.'

Mrs. Lucas told Janet she might kiss her, and then sent the girl away. There was need of anxious watch lest fever should set in, and therefore all that was exciting was kept at a distance as the poor young widow verged towards recovery.

Once, when she heard voices on the stairs, she started nervously, and asked Mrs. Lucas, 'Is Ellen there?'

'Yes, my dear ; she shall not come to you unless you wish it,' seeing her alarm ; and she laid her head down again.

The double funeral was accomplished while she was still too ill to hear anything about it, though Mrs. Lucas had no doubt that she knew ; and when he came home, Colonel Brownlow called for Janet, and asked her whether she could find her grandmother's keys and her father's for him.

'Mother would not like any one to rummage their things,' said Janet, like a watch-dog.

'My dear,' said her uncle, in a surprised but kind tone, as one who respected yet resented her feeling ; 'you may trust me not to rummage, as you call it, unnecessarily; but I know that I am executor, if you understand what that means, my dear.'

'Of course,' said Janet, affronted as she always was by being treated as a child.

'To both wills,' continued her uncle; 'and it will save your mother much trouble and distress if I can take steps towards acting on them at once; and if you cannot tell where the keys are, I shall have to look for them.'

'Janet ought to obey at once,' said her aunt, not adding to the serenity of Janet's mind; but she turned on her heel, ungraciously saying, 'I'll get them'; and presently returned with her grandmother's key-box, full of the housekeeping keys, and a little key, which she gave to her uncle with great dignity, adding, 'The key of her desk is the Bramah one; I'll see for the others.'

'A strange girl, that!' said her uncle, as she marched out of the room.

'I am glad our Jessie has not her temper!' responded his wife; and then they both repaired to old Mrs. Brownlow's special apartment, the back drawing-room, while Janet quietly dropped downstairs with the key she had taken from her father's table on her way to the consulting-room. She intended to prevent any search, by herself producing the will from among his papers, for she was in an agony lest her uncle should discover the clue to the *magnum bonum*, of which she regarded herself the guardian.

Till she had actually unlocked the sloping lid of the old-fashioned bureau, it did not occur to her that she did not know either what the will was like, nor yet the *magnum bonum*, which was scarcely likely to be so ticketed. She only saw piles of letters and papers, marked; some with people's names, some with a Greek or Latin word, or one of the curious old Arabic signs, for which her father had always a turn, having, as his mother used to tell him, something of the alchemist in his composition. One of these parcels, fastened with elastic rings, must be *magnum bonum*, and Janet, though without much chance of distinguishing it, was reading the labels with a strange, sad fascination, when, long before she had expected him, her uncle stood before her, with greatly astonished and displeased looks, and the word 'Janet.'

She coloured scarlet, but answered boldly, 'There was something that I know father did not want any one but mother to see.'

'Of course there is much,' said her uncle gravely—'much that I am fitter to judge of than any little girl.'

Words cannot express the offence thus given to Janet. Something swelled in her throat as if to suffocate her, but there could be no reply, and to burst out crying would only make him think her younger still; so as he turned to his mournful task, she ensconced herself in a high-backed chair and watched him from under her dark brows.

She might comfort herself by the perception that he was less likely than even herself to recognise the *magnum bonum*. He would scarcely have thought it honourable to cast a glance upon the medical papers, and pushing them aside from where she had pulled them forward, searched till he had found a long cartridge-paper envelope, which he laid on the table behind him while he shut up the bureau, and Janet, by cautiously craning up her neck, managed to read that on it was written, 'Will of Joseph Brownlow. Executors: Mrs. Caroline Otway Brownlow, Lieutenant-Colonel Robert Brownlow.'

Her uncle then put both that and the keys in his pocket, either not seeing her, or not choosing to notice her.


## CHAPTER IV

### THE STRAY CHICKENS

'But when our father came not here,
I thought if we could find the sea
We should be sure to meet him there,
And once again might happy be.'

*Ballad.*

'WHAT was Dr. Lucas saying to you?' asked Carey, sitting up in bed after her breakfast.

'He said, my dear, that you were really well now,' said Mrs. Lucas tenderly, 'and that you only wanted rousing.'

She clasped her hands together.

'Yes, I know it. I have been knowing it all yesterday and last night. It hasn't been right of me, keeping you all this time, and not facing it.'

'I don't think you could, my dear.'

'Not at first. It seems to me like having been in a whirlpool, and those two went down in it.' She put her hands to her temples. 'But I must do it all now, and I will. I'll get up now. Oh! dear, if they only would let me come down and go about quietly.' Then smiling a piteous smile. 'It is very naughty, but of all things I dread the being cried over and fondled by Ellen!'

Mrs. Lucas shook her head, though the tears were in her eyes, and bethought her whether she could caution Mrs. Robert Brownlow not to be too demonstrative; but it was a delicate matter in which to interfere, and after all, whatever she might think beforehand, Caroline might miss these tokens of feeling.

She had sat up for some hours the evening before, so that there was no fear of her not being strong enough to get up as she proposed; but how would it be when she left her room, and beheld all that she could not have realised?

However, matters turned out contrary to all expectation.
Mrs. Lucas was in the drawing-room, talking to the Colonel's
wife, and Janet upstairs helping her mother to dress, when there
was a sound of feet on the stairs, the door hastily opened for a
moment, and two rough-headed, dusty little figures were seen
for one moment, startling Mrs. Brownlow with the notion of
little beggars; but they vanished in a moment, and were heard
chattering upstairs with calls of 'Mother! Mother Carey!'
And looking out, they beheld at the top of the stairs the two
little fellows hanging one on each side of Carey, who was just
outside her door, with her hair down, in her white dressing-
gown, kneeling between them, all the three almost devouring
one another.

'Jockie! Armie! my dears! How did you come? Where
are the rest?'

'Still at Kyve,' said Jock. 'Mother, we have done such a
thing—we came to tell you of it.'

'We've lost the man's boat,' added Armine, 'and we must
give him the money for another.'

'What is it? What is it, Caroline?' began her sister-in-law;
but Mrs. Lucas touched her arm, and as a mother herself, she
saw that mother and sons had best be left to one another, and
let them retreat into the bedroom, Carey eagerly scanning her
two little boys, who had a battered, worn, unwashed look that
puzzled her as much as their sudden appearance, which indeed
chimed in with the strange dreamy state in which she had lived
ever since that telegram. But their voices did more to restore
her to ordinary life than anything else could have done; and
their hearts were so full of their own adventure that they
poured it out before remarking anything—

'How did you come, my dear boys?'

'We walked, after the omnibus set us down at Charing Cross,
because we hadn't any more money,' said Armine. 'I'm so
tired.' And he nestled into her lap, seeming to quell the beating of her aching heart by his pressure.

'This is it, mother,' said Jock, pulling her other arm round
him. 'We two went down to the beach yesterday, and we saw
a little boat—Peter Lary's pretty little boat, you know, that is
so light—and we got in to rock in her, and then I thought I
would pull about in her a little.'

'Oh! Jock, Jock, how could you?'

'I'd often done it with Allen and young Pete,' said Jock
defensively.

'But by yourselves!' she said in horror.

'Nobody told us not,' said Jock rather defiantly; and Armine,
who, with his little sister Barbara, always seemed to live where
dreamland and reality bordered on each other, looked up in her
face and innocently said—

'Mrs. Acton read us about the Rocky Island, and she said
father and granny had brought their boats to the beautiful

country, and that we ought to go after them, and there was the bright path along the sea, and I thought we would go too, and that it would be nicer if Jock went with me.'

'I knew it did not mean that,' said Jock, hanging his mischievous black head a little, as he felt her shudder; 'but I thought it would be such fun to be Columbus.'

'And then? Oh! my boys, what a fearful thing! Thank God I have you here.'

'I wasn't frightened,' said Jock, with uplifted head; 'we could both row, couldn't we, Armie? and the tide was going out, and it was so jolly; it seemed to take us just where we wanted to go, out to that great rock, you know, mother, that Bobus called the Asses' Bridge.'

Carey knew that the current at the mouth of the river did, at high tide, carry much drift to the base of this island, and she could understand how her two boys had been floated thither. Jock went on—

'We had a boathook, and I pulled up to the island; I did, mother, and I made fast the boat to a little stick, and we went out to explore the island.'

'It has a crater in the top, mother, and we think it must be an *instinct* volcano,' said Armine, looking up sleepily.

'And there were such lots of jolly little birds,' went on Jock.

'Never mind that now. What happened?'

'Why, the brute of a boat got away,' said Jock, much injured, 'when I'd made her ever so fast. She pulled up the stick, I'm sure she did, for I can tie a knot as well as Pete.'

'So you could not get away?'

'No, and we'd got nothing to eat but chocolate creams and periwinkles, and Armie wouldn't look at them, and I don't think I could while they were alive. So I hoisted a signal of distress, made of my tie, for we'd lost our pocket-handkerchiefs. I was afraid they would think we were pirates, and not venture to come near us, for we'd only got black flags, and it was a very, very long time, but at last, just as it got a little darkish, and Armie was crying—poor little chap—that steamer came by that always goes between Porthole and Kyvemouth on Tuesdays and Thursdays. I hailed and I hailed, and they saw or heard, and sent a boat and took us on board. The people all came and looked at us, and one of them said I was a plucky little chap; he did, mother, and that I'd the making of an admiral in me; and a lady gave us such a jolly paper of sandwiches. But you see the steamer was going to Porthole, and the captain said he could not anyhow put back to Kyve, but he must take us on, and we must get back by train.'

Mother Carey understood this, for the direct line ran to Porthole, and there was a small junction station whence a branch ran to Kyvemouth, from which Kyve St. Clements was some three miles distant.

'Were you carried on?' she asked.

'Well, yes, but we meant it,' said Jock. 'I remembered the boat. I knew father would say we must buy another, so I asked the captain what was the price of one, for Armine and I had each got half a sovereign.'

'How was that?'

'An old gentleman the day before was talking to Mr. Acton. I think he is some great swell, for he has got a yacht, and servants, and a carriage, and lots of things; and he said, "What! are those poor Brownlow's boys? bless me!" and he tipped us each. Allen and Bobus were to go with Mr. Acton and have a sail in his yacht, but they said we should be too many, so we thought we'd get a new boat, but the captain——'

'Said your money would go but a little way,' put in Caroline.

'He laughed!' said Jock, as a great offence; 'and said that was a matter for our governor, and we had better go home and tell as fast as we could. There was a train just starting when we got in to Porthole, and somebody got our tickets for us, and Armine went fast off to sleep, and I, when I came to think about it, thought we would not get out at the junction, but come on home at once, Mother Carey, and tell you all about it. When Armie 'woke—why, he's asleep now—he said he would rather come home than to Kyve.'

'Then you travelled all night?'

'Yes, there was a jolly old woman who made us a bed with her shawl, only I tumbled off three times and bumped myself, and she gave us gooseberries, and cake, and once when we stopped a long time a porter got us a cup of tea. Then when we came to where they take the tickets, I think the man was going to make a row, but the guard came up and told him all about it, and I gave him my two half-sovereigns, and he gave me back fourteen shillings change, for he said we were only half price and second class. Then when once I was in London,' said Jock, as if his foot was on his native heath, 'of course I knew what to be at.'

'Have you had nothing to eat?'

'We had each a bun when we got out at Charing Cross, but I'm awfully hungry, mother!'

'I should think so. Janet, my dear, go and order some breakfast for them.'

'And,' said Janet, 'must not the others be dreadfully frightened about them at Kyve?'

That question startled her mother into instant action.

'Of course they must! Poor Clara! Poor Allen! They must be in a dreadful state. I must telegraph to them at once.'

She lifted Armine off gently to her bed, scarcely disturbing him, twisted up her hair in summary fashion, and the dress, which her friends had dreaded her seeing, was on, she hardly knew how, as she bade old nurse see to Jock's washing, dressing, and making himself tidy, and then amazed the other ladies by running into the drawing-room, crying breathlessly—

'I must telegraph to the Actons,' and plunging to the depths of a drawer in the davenport.

'Caroline, your cap!'

For it was on the back of the head that had never worn a cap before. And not only then, but for the most part whenever they met, those tears and caresses, that poor Mother Carey so much feared, were checked midway by the instinct that made Aunt Ellen run at her with a great pin and cry—

'Caroline, your cap.'

She was still, after having had it fixed, kneeling down, searching for a form for telegraphing, when the door was opened, and in came Colonel Brownlow, looking very pale and fearfully shocked.

'Ellen!' he began, 'how shall I ever tell that poor child? Here is Mr. Acton.'

But at that moment up sprang Mother Carey, and as Mr. Acton entered the room she leapt forward—

'Oh! I was just going to telegraph! They are safe! they are here! Jock, Jock!'

And downstairs came tumbling and rushing that same little imp, while the astonishment of his uncle and aunt only allowed them to utter the one word 'John!'

Mr. Acton drew a long breath, and said, 'You have given us a pretty fright, boy.'

'Here's the paper,' added Carey; 'telegraph to Clara at once. Ring the bell, Jock; I'll send to the office.'

All questions were suspended while Mr. Acton wrote the telegram, and then it appeared that the boat had been picked up empty, with Armine's pocket-handkerchief full of shells in it, and the boys had been given up for lost, it having been concluded that, if they had been seen, the boat also would have been taken in tow, and not cast loose to tell the tale. The two elder boys were almost broken-hearted, and would have been wild to come back to their mother, had it not been impossible to leave poor little Barbara, who clung fast to them, as the only shreds left to her of home and protection. They would at least be comforted in the space of a quarter of an hour!

Carey was completely herself and full of vigour while Mr. Acton was there, consoling him when he lamented not having taken better care, and refusing when he tried to persuade her to accompany him back to Kyve. Neither would Janet return with him, feeling it impossible to relax such watch as she could keep over the *magnum bonum* papers, even though she much longed for her brothers.

'I should insist on her going,' said Aunt Ellen, 'after all she has gone through.'

'I don't think I can,' said Carey. 'You would not send away your Jessie?'

Ellen did not quite say that her pretty, sweet, caressing Jessie was different, but she thought it all the same.

Carey did not fulfil her intentions of going into matters of business with her brother-in-law that day, for little Armine, always delicate, had been so much knocked up by his course of adventures that he needed her care all the rest of the day. Nor would she have been fit for anything else, for when his aunt recommended a totally different treatment for his ailments, she had no spirit to argue, but only looked pale and determined, being too weary and dejected to produce her arguments.

Jock was sufficiently tired to be quiescent in the nursery, where she kept him with her, feeling, in his wistful eyes, and even in poor little Armine's childish questions, something less like blank desolation than her recent apathy had been, as if she were waking to thrills of pain after the numbness of a blow.

Urged by a restless night and an instinctive longing for fresh air, she took a long walk in the park before any one came down the next morning, with only Jock for her companion, and she came to the breakfast table with a freshened look, though with a tremulous faintness in her voice, and she let Janet continue tea-maker, scarcely seeming to hear or understand the casual remarks around her; but afterwards she said in a resolute tone, 'Robert, I am ready whenever you wish to speak to me.'

So in the drawing-room the Colonel, with the two wills in his hand, found himself face to face with her. He was the more nervous of the two, being much afraid of upsetting that composure which scandalised his wife, but which he preferred to tears; and as he believed her to be a mere child in perception, he explained down to her supposed level, while she listened in a strange inert way, feeling it hard to fix her attention, yet half-amused by the simplicity of his elucidations. 'Would Ellen need to be told what an executor meant?' thought she.

She was left sole guardian of the children, 'the greatest proof of confidence a parent can give,' impressively observed the Colonel, wondering at the languor of her acquiescence, and not detecting the thought, 'Dear Joe! of course! as if he would have done anything else!'

'Of course,' continued the Colonel, 'he never expected that it would have proved more than a nominal matter, a mere precaution. For my own part, I can only say that I shall be always ready to assist you with advice or authority if ever you should find the charge too onerous for you.'

'Thank you,' was all she could bring herself to say at that moment, feeling that her boys were her own, though the next she was recollecting that this was no doubt the reason Joe had bidden her live at Kenminster, and, in a pang of self-reproach, was hardly attending to the technicalities of the matters of property which were being explained to her.

Her husband had not been able to save much, but his life

insurance was for a considerable sum, and there was also the amount inherited from his parents. A portion of the means which his mother had enjoyed passed to the elder brother, and Mrs. Brownlow had sunk most of her individual property in the purchase of the house in which they lived. By the terms of Joseph's will, everything was left to Caroline unreservedly, save for a stipulation that all, on her death, should be divided among the children, as she should appoint. The house was not even secured to Allen, so that she could let or sell it as she thought advisable.

'I could not sell it,' said Carey quickly, feeling it her first and only home. 'I hope to see Allen practising there some day.'

'It is not in a situation where you could sell it to so much advantage as you would have by letting it to whoever takes the practice.'

She winced, but it was needful to listen, as he told her of the offers that had been made for the house and the good-will of the practice. What he had thought the best offer was, however, rejected by her with vehemence. She was sure that Joe would never stand that man coming in upon his patients, and when asked for her reasons, would only reply that 'None of us could bear him.'

''That is no reason why he should not be a good practitioner and respectable man. He may not be what you like in society, and yet——'

'Ask Dr. Lucas,' hastily interrupted Carey.

'Perhaps that will be the best way,' said the Colonel gravely. 'Will you promise to abide by his decision?'

'I don't know! I mean, if every one decided against me, *nothing* should induce me to let *that* Vaughan into Joe's house to meddle with his patients.'

Colonel Brownlow made a sign of displeased acquiescence, so like his brother when Carey was a little impetuous or naughty, that she instantly felt shocked at herself, and faltered, 'I beg your pardon.'

He seemed not to notice this, but went on, 'As you say, it may be wise to consult Dr. Lucas. Perhaps, putting it up to competition would be the best way.'

'Oh no,' said Caroline. 'Have you a letter from Dr. Drake?'

'No.'

'Then depend upon it he must have too much delicacy to begin about it so soon. I had rather he had it than any one else.'

'Can he make a fair offer for it? You cannot afford to throw away a substantial benefit for preferences,' said the Colonel. 'At the outside, you will not have more than £500 a year, and I fear you will feel much straitened after what you are used to, with four boys, and such ideas as to their education,' he added, smiling.

'I don't know, but I am sure it is what Joe would wish. He had rather trust his patients to Harry—to Dr. Drake—than to any one, and he is just going to be married, and wants a practice ; I shall write to him. It is so nice of him not to have pressed forward.'

'You will not commit yourself?' said Colonel Brownlow. 'Remember that your children's interests are at stake, and must not be sacrificed to a predilection.'

Again Caroline felt fiery and furious, and less inclined than ever to submit her judgment as she said, 'You can inquire, but I know what Joe thought of him.'

'His worthiness is not the point, but whether he can indemnify you.'

'His worthiness not the point !' cried Caroline indignantly. 'I think it all the point.'

'You misunderstand me ; you totally misunderstand me,' exclaimed the Colonel, trying hard to be gentle. 'I never meant to recommend an unworthy man.'

'You wanted Vaughan,' murmured Mother Carey, but he did not regard the words, perhaps did not hear them, for he went on : 'My brother in such a case would have taken a reasonable view, and placed the good of his children before any amiable desire to benefit a—a—one unconnected with him. However,' he added, 'there is no reason against writing to him, provided you do not commit yourself.'

Caroline hated the word, but endured it, and the rest of the interview was spent upon some needful signatures, and on the question of her residence at Kenminster, an outlook which she contemplated as part of the darkness into which her life seemed to have suddenly dashed forward. One place would be much the same as another to her, and she could only hear with indifference about the three houses possible, and the rent, garden, and number of rooms.

She was very glad when it was over, and the Colonel, saying he should go and consult Dr. Lucas, gave her back the keys he had taken from Janet, and said that perhaps she would prefer looking over the papers before he himself did so, with a view to accounts ; but he should much advise all professional records to be destroyed.

It may be feared that the two executors did not respect or like each other much the better for the interview, which had made the widow feel herself even more desolate and sore-hearted.

She ran downstairs, locked the door of the consulting-room, opened the lid of the bureau, and kneeling down with her head among all the papers, she sobbed with long-drawn, tearless sobs, 'O father ! O Joe ! how could you bid me live there ? He makes me worse ! They *will* make me worse and worse, and now you are gone, and granny is gone, there's nobody to make me good ; and what will become of the children ?'

Then she looked drearily on the papers that lay before her, as if his handwriting at least gave a sort of nearness. There was a memorandum book which had been her birthday present to him, and she felt drawn to open it. The first she saw after her own writing of his name was—

'Magnum Bonum. So my sweet wife insists on calling this possibility, of which I will keep the notes in her book.

'Magnum Bonum! Whether it so prove, and whether I may be the means of making it known, must be as God may will. May He give me the power of persevering, to win, or to fail, or to lay the foundation for other men, whichever may be the best, with a true heart, heeding His glory, and acting as His servant to reveal His mysteries of science for the good of His children.

'And above all, may He give us all to know and feel the true and only Magnum Bonum, the great good, which alone makes success or failure, loss or gain, life or death, alike blessed in Him and through Him.'

Carey gazed on those words, as she sat in the large arm-chair, whither she had moved on opening the book. She had always known that religion was infinitely more to her husband than ever it had been to herself. She had done what he led her to do, and had a good deal of intellectual and poetical perception, and an uprightness, affection, and loyalty of nature that made her anxious to do right, but devotion was duty, and not pleasure to her; she was always glad when it was over, and she was feeling that the thoughts which were said to comfort others were quite unable to reach her grief. There was no disbelief nor rebellion about her, only a dull weariness, and an inclination which she could hardly restrain, even while it shocked her, to thrust aside those religious consolations that were powerless to soothe her. She knew it was not their fault, she did not doubt of their reality; it was she who was not good enough to use them.

These words of Joe were to her as if he were speaking to her again. She laid them on her knee, murmured them over fondly, looked at them, and finally, for she was weak still and had had a bad night, fell fast asleep over them, and only wakened as shouts of 'Mother' were heard over the house.

She locked the bureau in a hurry, and opened the door, calling back to the boys, and then she found that Aunt Ellen had taken all the three out walking, when Jock and Armine, with the remains of their money burning in their pockets, had insisted on buying two little ships, which must necessarily be launched in the Serpentine. Their aunt could by no means endure this, and Janet did not approve, so there seemed to have been a battle royal, in which Jock would have been the victor if his little brother had not been led off captive between his aunt and sister, when Jock went along on the opposite side of the road, asserting his independence by every sort of monkey trick most trying to his aunt's rural sense of London propriety.

It was very ridiculous to see the tall, grave, stately Mrs. Robert Brownlow standing there describing the intolerable naughtiness of that imp, who, not a bit abashed, sat astride on the balustrade in the comfortable conviction that he was not hers.

'I hope, at least,' concluded the lady, 'that you will make them feel how bad their behaviour has been.'

'Jock,' said Carey mechanically, 'I am afraid you have behaved very ill to your aunt.'

'Why, Mother Carey,' said that little wretch, 'it is just that she doesn't know anything about anything in London.'

'Yes,' chimed in little Armine, who was hanging to his mother's skirts; 'she thought she should get to the Park by Duke Street.'

'That did not make it right for you not to be obedient,' said Carey, trying for severity.

'But we couldn't, mother.'

'Couldn't?' both echoed.

'No,' said Jock, 'or we should be still in Piccadilly. Mother Carey, she told us not to cross till it was safe.'

'And she stood up like the Duke of Bedford in the square,' added Armine.

Janet caught her mother's eye, and both felt a spasm of uncontrollable diversion in their throats, making Janet turn her back, and Carey gasp and turn on the boys.

'All that is no reason at all. Go up to the nursery. I wish I could trust you to behave like a gentleman, when your aunt is so kind as to take you out.'

'I *did*, mother! I did hand her across the street, and dragged her out from under all the omnibus horses,' said Jock in an injured tone, while Janet could not refrain from a whispered comparison, 'Like a little steam-tug,' and this was quite too much for all of them, producing an explosion which made the tall and stately dame look from one to another in such bewildered amazement, that struck the mother and daughter as so comical that the one hid her face in her hands with a sort of hysterical heaving, and the other burst into that painful laughter by which strained spirits assert themselves in the young.

Mrs. Robert Brownlow, in utter astonishment and discomfiture, turned and walked off to her room. Somehow Carey and Janet felt more on their ordinary terms than they had done all these sad days, in their consternation and a certain sense of guilt.

Carey could adjudicate now, though trembling still. She made Jock own that his Serpentine plans had been unjustifiable, and then she added, 'My poor boy, I must punish you. You must remember it, for if you are not good and steady, what *will* become of us.'

Jock leapt at her neck. 'Mother, do anything to me. I don't mind, if you only won't look at me like that!'

She sat down on the stairs, all in a heap again with him, and sentenced him to the forfeit of the ship, which he endured with more tolerable grace, because Armine observed, 'Never mind, Skipjack, we'll go partners in mine. You shall have half my cargo of gold dust.'

Carey could not find it in her heart to check the voyages of the remaining ship over the uncarpeted dining-room; but as she was going, Armine looked at her with his great soft eyes, and said, 'Mother Carey, have you got to be the scoldy and punishy one now?'

'I must if you need it,' said she, going down on her knees again to gather the little fellow to her breast; 'but oh, don't —don't need it.'

'I'd rather it was Uncle Robert and Aunt Ellen,' said Jock, 'for then I shouldn't care.'

'Dear Jock, if you only care, I think we shan't want many punishments. But now I must go to your aunt, for we did behave horribly ill to her.'

Aunt Ellen was kind, and accepted Carey's apology when she found that Jock had really been punished. Only she said, 'You must be firm with that boy, Caroline, or you will be sorry for it. My boys know that what I have said is to be done, and they know it is of no use to disobey. I am happy to say they mind me at a word; but that John of yours needs a tight hand. The Colonel thinks that the sooner he is at school the better.'

Before Carey had time to get into a fresh scrape, the Colonel was ringing at the door. He had to confess that Dr. Lucas had said Mrs. Joe Brownlow was right about Vaughan, and had made it plain that his offer ought not to be accepted, either in policy, or in that duty which the Colonel began to perceive towards his brother's patients. Nor did he think ill of her plan respecting Dr. Drake; and said he would himself suggest the application which that gentleman was no doubt withholding from true feeling, for he had been a favourite pupil of Joe Brownlow, and had been devoted to him. He was sure that Mrs. Brownlow's good sense and instinct were to be trusted, a dictum which not a little surprised her brother-in-law, who had never ceased to think of 'poor Joe's fancy' as a mere child, and who forgot that she was fifteen years older than at her marriage.

He told his wife what Dr. Lucas had said, to which she replied, 'That's just the way. Men know nothing about it.'

However, Dr. Drake's offer was sufficiently eligible to be accepted. Moreover, it proved that the most available house at Kenminster could not be got ready for the family before the winter, so that the move could not take place till the spring. In the meantime, as Dr. Drake could not marry till Easter, the lower part of the house was to be given up to him, and Carey and Janet felt that they had a reprieve.

## CHAPTER V

### BRAINS AND NO BRAINS

'I do say, thou art quick in answers:
Thou heatest my blood.'

*Love's Labour's Lost.*

KEM'STER, as county tradition pronounced what was spelt Kenminster, a name meaning St. Kenelm's minster, had a grand collegiate church and a foundation-school which, in the hands of the Commissioners, had of late years passed into the rule of David Ogilvie, Esq., a spare, pale, nervous, sensitive-looking man of eight or nine and twenty, who sat one April evening under his lamp, with his sister at work a little way off, listening with some amusement to his sighs and groans at the holiday tasks that lay before him.

'Here's an answer, Mary. What was Magna Charta? The first map of the world.'

'Who's that ingenious person?'

'Brownlow Major, of course; and here's French, who says it was a new sort of cow invented by Henry VIII—a happy feminine, I suppose, to the Papal Bull. Here's a third! The French fleet defeated by Queen Elizabeth. Most have passed it over entirely.'

'Well, you know this is the first time you have tried such an examination, and boys never do learn history.'

'Nor anything else in this happy town,' was the answer, accompanied by a ruffling over of the papers.

'For shame, David! The first day of the term!'

'It is the dead weight of Brownlows, my dear. Only think! There's another lot coming! A set of duplicates. They haven't even the sense to vary the Christian names. Three more to be admitted to-morrow.'

'That accounts for a good deal!'

'You are laughing at me, Mary; but did you never know what it is to feel like Sisyphus? Whenever you think you have rolled it a little way, down it comes, a regular dead weight again, down the slope of utter indifference and dulness, till it seems to crush the very heart out of you!'

'Have you really nobody that is hopeful?'

'Nobody who does not regard me as his worst enemy, and treat all my approaches with distrust and hostility. Mary, how am I to live it down?'

'You speak as if it were a crime!'

'I feel as if it were one. Not of mine, but of the pedagogic race before me, who have spoilt the relations between man and boy; so that I cannot even get one to act as a medium.'

'That would be contrary to *esprit de corps*.'

'Exactly; and the worst of it is, I am not one of those genial fellows, half boys themselves, who can join in the sports *con amore;* I should only make a mountebank of myself if I tried, and the boys would distrust me the more.'

'Quite true. The only way is to be oneself, and one's best self, and the rest will come.'

'I'm not so sure of that. Some people mistake their vocation.'

'Well, when you have given it a fair trial, you can turn to something else. You are getting the school up again, which is at least one testimony.'

David Ogilvie made a sound as if this were very base kind of solace, and his sister did not wonder when she remembered the bright hopes and elaborate theories with which he had undertaken the mastership only nine months ago. He was then fresh from the university, and the loss of constant intercourse with congenial minds had perhaps contributed as much as the dulness of the Kenminster youth to bring him into a depressed state of health and spirits, which had made his elder sister contrive to spend her Easter at the seaside with him, and give him a few days at the beginning of the term. Indeed, she was anxious enough about him, when he went down to the old grammar-school, to revolve the possibility of acceding to his earnest wish, and coming to live with him, instead of continuing in her situation as governess.

He came back to luncheon next day with a brightened face, that made his sister say, 'Well, have you struck some sparks?'

'I've got some new material, and am come home saying, "What's in a name?"'

'Eh! Is it those very new Brownlows, that seemed yesterday to be the last straw on the camel's back?'

'I wish you could have seen the whole scene, Mary. There were half a dozen new boys to be admitted, four Brownlows! Think of that! Well, there stood manifestly one of the old stock, with the same oval face and sleepy brown eyes, and the very same drawl I know so well in the "No—a——" to the vain question, "Have you done any Latin?" And how shall I do justice to the long, dragging drawl of his reading? Aye, here's the sentence I set him on : "The—Gowls—had—con—sen—ted—to—accept—a—sum—of—gold—and—retire. They were en—gagged—in—wagging out the sum—required, and——" I had to tell him what to call Brennus, and he proceeded to cast the sword into the scale, exclaiming, just as to a cart-horse, "Woh! To the Worsted" (pronounced like yarn). After that you may suppose the feelings with which I called his ditto, another Joseph Armine Brownlow; and forth came the smallest sprite, with a white face and great black eyes, all eagerness, but much too wee for this place. "Begun Latin?" "Oh yes;" and he rattled off a declension and a tense with as much ease as if he had been born speaking Latin. I gave him Phædrus to see whether that would stump him, and I don't

think it would have done so if he had not made or a mouth
instead of a bone, in dealing with the "Wolf and the Lamb."
He was almost crying, so I put the Roman history into his
hand, and his reading was something refreshing to hear. I
asked him if he knew what the sentence meant, and he answered,
"Isn't it when the geese cackled?" trying to turn round the
page. "What do you know about the geese?" said I. To
which the answer was, "We played at it on the stairs! Jock
and I were the Romans, and Mother Carey and Babie were the
geese."'

'Poor little fellow! I hope no boys were there to listen, or
he will never hear the last of those geese.'

'I hope no one was within earshot but his brothers, who
certainly did look daggers at him. He did very well in sum-
ming and in writing, except that he went out of his way to
spell *fish*, p-h-y-c-h, and *shy*, s-c-h-y; and at last I could not
resist the impulse to ask him what Magna Charta is. Out came
the answer, "It is yellow, and all crumpled up, and you can't
read it, but it has a bit of a great red seal hanging to it."'

'What, he had seen it?'

'Yes, or a facsimile, and what was more, he knew who signed
it. Whoever taught that child knew how to teach, and it is a
pity he should be swamped among such a set as ours.'

'I thought you would be delighted.'

'I should be, if I had him alone, but he must be put with a
crew who will make it their object to bully him out of his
superiority, and the more I do for him, the worse it will be for
him, poor little fellow; and he looks too delicate to stand the
ordeal. It is sheer cruelty to send him.'

'Hasn't he brothers?'

'Oh yes! I was going to tell you, two bigger boys, another
Robert and John Brownlow—about eleven and nine years old.
The younger one is a sort of black spider monkey, wanting the
tail. We shall have some trouble with that gentleman, I
expect.'

'But not the old trouble?'

'No, indeed; unless the atmosphere affects him. He answered as no boy of twelve can do here; and as to the elder
one, I must take him at once into the fifth form, such as
it is.'

'Where have they been at school?'

'At a day school in London. They are Colonel Brownlow's
nephews. Their father was a medical man in London, who died
last summer, leaving a young widow and these boys, and they
have just come down to live in Kenminster. But it can't be
owing to the school. No school would give all three that kind
of—what shall I call it?—culture, and intelligence, that they
all have; besides, the little one has been entirely taught at
home.'

'I wonder whether it is their mother's doing?'

'I am afraid it is their father's. The Colonel spoke of her as a poor helpless little thing, who was thrown on his hands with all her family.'

After the morning's examination and placing of the boys, there was a half-holiday ; and the brother and sister set forth to enjoy it together, for Kenminster was a place with special facilities for enjoyment. It was built, as it were, within a crescent, formed by low hills sloping down to the river; the church, school, and other remnants of the old collegiate buildings lying in the flat at the bottom, and the rest of the town, one of the small decayed wool staples of Somerset, being in terraces on the hillside, with steep streets dividing the rows. These were of very mixed quality and architecture, but, as a general rule, improved the higher they rose, and were all interspersed with gardens running up or down, and with a fair sprinkling of trees, whose budding green looked well amid the yellow stone.

On the summit were some more ornamental villa-like houses, and gray stone buildings with dark tiled roofs, but the expansion on that side had been checked by extensive private grounds. There were very beautiful woods coming almost close to the town, and in the absence of the owner, a great moneyed man, they were open to all those who did not make themselves obnoxious to the keepers ; and these, under an absentee proprietor, gave a free interpretation to rights of way. Thither were the Ogilvies bound, in search of primrose banks, but their way led them past two or three houses on the hill-top, one of which, being constructed on supposed Chinese principles of architecture, was known to its friends as 'the Pagoda,' to its foes as 'the Folly.' It had been long untenanted, but this winter it had been put into complete repair, and two rooms, showing a sublime indifference to consistency of architecture, had been lately built out with sash windows and a slated roof, contrasting oddly with the frilled and fluted tiles of the tower from which it jutted.

Suddenly there sounded close to their ears the words— 'School time, my dear !'

Starting and looking round for some impertinent street boy, Mr. Ogilvie exclaimed, 'What's that?'

'Mother Carey ! We are all Mother Carey's chickens.'

'See, there,' exclaimed Mary, and a great parrot was visible on the branch of a sumach, which stretched over the railings of the low wall of the Pagoda garden. 'O you appropriate bird, you surely ought not to be here !'

To which the parrot replied, '*Hic, hæc, hoc !*' and burst out in a wild scream of laughing, spreading her gray wings, and showing intentions of flying away ; but Mr. Ogilvie caught hold of the chain that hung from her leg.

Just then voices broke out—

'That's Polly ! Where is she ? That's you, Jock, you horrid

boy.' 'Well, I didn't see why she shouldn't enjoy herself.' 'Now you've been and lost her.  Poll, Poll!'

'I have her!' called back Mr. Ogilvie.  'I'll bring her to the gate.'

Thanks came through the hedge, and the brother and sister walked on.

'It's old Ogre.  Cut!' growled in what was meant to be an aside, a voice the master knew full well, and there was a rushing off of feet, like ponies in a field.

When the sheep gate was reached, a great furniture van was seen standing at the door of the 'Folly,' and there appeared a troop of boys and girls in black, eager to welcome their pet.

'Thank you, sir; thank you very much.  Come, Polly,' said the eldest boy, taking possession of the bird.

'I think we have met before,' said the schoolmaster to the younger ones, glad to see that two—*i.e.* the new Robert and Armine Brownlow—had not joined in the *sauve qui peut.*

Nay, Robert turned and said, 'Mother, it is Mr. Ogilvie.'

Then that gentleman was aware that one of the black figures had a widow's cap, with streamers flying behind her in the breeze, but while he was taking off his hat and beginning, 'Mrs. Brownlow,' she held out her hands to his sister, crying, 'Mary, Mary Ogilvie,' and there was an equally fervent response.  'Is it?  Is it really Caroline Allen?' and the two friends linked eager hands in glad pressure, turning, after the first moment, towards the house, while Mary said, 'David, it is my dear old schoolfellow; Carey, this is my brother.'

'You were very kind to these boys,' said Carey, warmly shaking hands with him.  'The name sounded friendly, but I little thought you were Mary's brother.  Are you living here, Mary?  How delightful!'

'Alas, no; I am only keeping holiday with David.  I go back to-morrow.'

'Then stay now; stay and let me get all I can of you, in this frightful muddle,' entreated Caroline.  'Chaos is come again, but you won't mind.'

'I'll come and help you,' said Mary.  'David, you must go on alone and come back for me.'

'Can't I be of use?' offered David, feeling rather shut out in the cold; 'I see a bookcase.  Isn't that in my line?'

'And here's the box with its books,' said Janet.  'Oh! mother, do let that be finished off at least!  Bobus, there are the shelves, and I have all their pegs in my basket.'

The case was happily in its place against the wall, and Janet had seized on her recruit to hold the shelves while she pegged them, while the two friends were still exchanging their first inquiries, Carey exclaiming, 'Now, you naughty Mary, where have you been, and why didn't you write?'

'I have been in Russia, and I didn't write, because nobody answered, and I didn't know where anybody was.'

'In Russia! I thought you were with a Scottish family, and wrote to you to the care of some laird with an unearthly name.'

'But you knew that they took me abroad.'

'And Alice Brown told me that letters sent to the place in Scotland would find you. I wrote three times, and when you did not answer my last——' and Caroline broke off with things unutterable in her face.

'I never had any but the first when you were going to London. I answered that. Yes, I did! Don't look incredulous. I wrote from Sorrento.'

'That must have miscarried. Where did you address it?'

'To the old place, inside a letter to Mrs. Mercer.'

'I see! Poor Mrs. Mercer went away ill, and did not live long after, and I suppose her people never troubled themselves about her letters. But why did not you get ours?'

'Mrs. M'Ian died at Venice, and the aunts came out, and considering me too young to go on with the laird and his girls, they fairly made me over to a Russian family whom we had met. Unluckily, as I see now, I wrote to Mrs. Mercer, and as I never heard more I gave up writing. Then the Crimean war cut me off entirely, even from David. I had only one letter all that time.'

'How is it that you are a governess? I thought one was sure of a pension from a Russian grandee!'

'These were not very grand grandees, only counts, and though they paid liberally, they could not pension one. So when I had done with the youngest daughter, I came to England and found a situation in London. I tried to look up our old set, but could not get on the track of any one except Emily Collins, who told me you had married very soon, but was not even sure of your name. Very soon! Why, Caroline, your daughter looks as old as yourself.'

'I sometimes think she is older! And have you seen my Eton boy?'

'Was it he who received the delightful popinjay, who "Up and spak" so much to the purpose?' asked Mr. Ogilvie.

'Yes, it was Allen. He is the only one you did not see in the morning. Did they do tolerably?'

'I only wish I had any boys who did half as well,' said Mr. Ogilvie, the lads being gone for more books.

'I was afraid for John and Armine, for we have been unsettled, and I could not go on so steadily with them as before,' she said eagerly, but faltering a little. 'Armine told me he blundered in Phædrus, but I hope he did fairly on the whole.'

'So well that if you ask my advice, I should say keep him to yourself two years more.'

'Oh! I am so glad,' with a little start of joy. 'You'll tell his uncle? He insisted—he had some impression that they were very naughty boys, whom I could not cope with, poor little fellows.'

'I can decidedly say he is learning more from you than he would in school among those with whom, at his age, I must place him.'

'Thank you, thank you. Then Babie won't lose her companion. She wanted to go to school with Armie, having always gone on with him. And the other two—what of them? Bobus is sure to work for the mere pleasure of it; but Jock?'

'I don't promise that he may not let himself down to the standard of his age and develop a capacity for idleness, but even he has time to spare, and he is at that time of life when boys do for one another what no one else can do for them.'

'The Colonel said the boys were a good set and gentlemanly,' said Carey wistfully.

'I think I may say that for them,' returned their master. 'They are not bad boys as boys go. There is as much honour and kindliness among them as you would find anywhere. Besides, to boys like yours this would be only a preparatory school. They are sure to fly off to scholarships.'

'I don't know,' said Carey. 'I want them to be where physical science is an object. Or do you think that thorough classical training is a better preparation than taking up any individual line?'

'I believe it is easier to learn *how* to learn through languages than through anything else.'

'And to be taught *how* to learn is a much greater thing than to be crammed,' said Carey. 'Of course when one begins to teach oneself, the world has become "mine oyster," and one has the dagger. The point becomes how to sharpen the dagger.'

At that moment three or four young people rushed in with arms full of books, and announcing that the uncle and aunt were coming. The next moment they appeared, and stood amazed at the accession of volunteer auxiliaries. Mr. Ogilvie introduced his sister, while Caroline explained that she was an old friend,—meanwhile putting up a hand to feel for her cap, as she detected in Ellen's eyes those words, 'Caroline, your cap.'

'We came to see how you were getting on,' said the Colonel kindly.

'Thank you, we are getting on capitally. And oh, Robert, Mr. Ogilvie will tell you; he thinks Armine too—too—I mean he thinks he had better not go into school yet,' she added, thankful that she had not said 'too clever for the school.'

The Colonel turned aside with the master to discuss the matter, and the ladies went into the drawing-room, the new room opening on the lawn, under a verandah, with French windows. It was full of furniture, in the most dire confusion. Mrs. Robert Brownlow wanted to clear off at once the desks and other things that seemed school-room properties, saying that a little room downstairs had always served the purpose.

'That must be nurse's sitting-room,' said Carey

'Old nurse! She can be of no use, my dear!'

'Oh yes, she is; she has lived with us ever since dear grand-mamma married, and has no home, and no relations. We could not get on without dear old nursey!'

'Well, my dear, I hope you will find it answer to keep her on. But as to this room! It is such a pity not to keep it nice, when you have such handsome furniture too.'

'I want to keep it nice with habitation,' said Caroline. 'That's the only way to do it. I can't bear fusty, shut-up, smart rooms, and I think the family room ought to be the pleasantest and prettiest in the house for the children's sake.'

'Ah, well,' said Mrs. Brownlow, with a serene good-nature, contrasting with the heat with which Caroline spoke, 'it is your affair, my dear, but my boys would not thank me for shutting them in with my pretty things, and I should be sorry to have them there. Healthy country boys like to have their fun, and I would not coop them up.'

'Oh, but there's the studio to run riot in, Ellen,' said Carey. 'Didn't you see? The upper story of the tower. We have put the boys' tools there, and I can do my modelling there, and make messes and all that's nice,' she said, smiling to Mary, and to Allen, who had just come in.

'Do you model, Carey?' Mary asked, and Allen volunteered to show his mother's groups and bas-reliefs, thereby much increasing the litter on the floor, and delighting Mary a good deal more than his aunt, who asked, 'What will you do for a store-room then?'

'Put up a few cupboards and shelves anywhere.'

It is not easy to describe the sort of air with which Mrs. Robert Brownlow received this answer. She said nothing but 'Oh,' and was perfectly unruffled in a sort of sublime contempt, as to the hopelessness of doing anything with such a being on her own ground.

There did not seem overt provocation, but poor Caroline, used to petting and approval, chafed and reasoned: 'I don't think anything so important as a happy home for the boys, where they can have their pursuits and enjoy themselves.'

Mrs. Brownlow seemed to think this totally irrelevant, and observed, 'When I have nice things, I like to keep them nice.'

'I like nice boys better than nice things,' cried Carey.

Ellen smiled as though to say she hoped she was not an unnatural mother, and again said 'Oh!'

Mary Ogilvie was very glad to see the two gentlemen come in from the hall, the Colonel saying, 'Mr Ogilvie tells me he thinks Armine too small at present for school, Caroline.'

'You know I am very glad of it, Robert,' she said, smiling gratefully, and Ellen compassionately observed, 'Poor little fellow, he is very small; but country air and food will soon make a man of him if he is not overdone with books. I make it a point never to force my children.'

'No, *that* you don't,' said Caroline, with a dangerous smile about the corners of her mouth.

'And my boys do quite as well as if they had their heads stuffed and their growth stunted,' said Ellen. 'Joe is only two months older than Armine, and you are quite satisfied with him, are you not, Mr. Ogilvie?'

'He is more on a level with the others,' said Mr. Ogilvie politely; 'but I wish they were all as forward as this little fellow.'

'Schoolmasters and mammas don't always agree on those points,' said the Colonel good-humouredly.

'Very true,' responded his wife. 'I never was one for teasing the poor boys with study and all that. I had rather see them strong and well grown. They'll have quite worry enough when they go to school.'

'I'm sorry you look at me in that aspect,' said Mr. Ogilvie.

'Oh, I know you can't help it,' said the lady.

'Any more than Trois Echelles and Petit André,' said Carey in a low voice, giving the two Ogilvies the strongest desire to laugh.

Just then out burst a cry of wrath and consternation, making every one hurry out into the hall, where, through a perfect cloud of white powder, loomed certain figures, and a scandalised voice cried, 'Aunt Caroline, Jock and Armine have been and let all the arrowroot fly about.'

'You told me to be useful and open parcels,' cried Jock.

'Oh, jolly, jolly! first-rate!' shouted Armine in ecstasy. 'It's just like Paris in the cloud! More, more, Babie. You are Venus, you know.'

'Master Armine, Miss Barbara! For shame,' exclaimed the nurse's voice. 'All getting into the carpet, and in your clothes, I do declare! A whole case of best arrowroot wasted, and worse.'

''Twas Jessie's doing,' replied Jock. 'She told me.'

Jessie, decidedly the most like Venus of the party, being a very pretty girl, with an oval face and brown eyes, had retreated, and was with infinite disgust brushing the white powder out of her dress, only in answer ejaculating, 'Those boys!'

Jock had not only opened the case, but had opened it upside down, and the classical performances of Armine and Barbara had powdered themselves and everything around, while the draught that was rushing through all the wide open doors and windows dispersed the mischief far and wide.

'Can you do nothing but laugh, Caroline?' gravely said Mrs. Brownlow. 'Janet, shut that window. Children, out of the way! If you were mine, I should send you to bed.'

'There's no bed to be sent to,' muttered Jock, running round to give a sly puff to the white heap, diffusing a sprinkling of white powder over his aunt's dress.

'Jock,' said his mother, with real firmness and indignation in her voice, 'that is not the way to behave. Beg your aunt's pardon this instant.'

And to every one's surprise the imp obeyed the hand she had laid on him, and muttered something like 'Beg pardon,' though it made his face crimson.

His uncle exclaimed, 'That's right, my boy,' and his aunt said, with dignity, 'Very well, we'll say no more about it.'

Mary Ogilvie was in the meantime getting some of the powder back into the tin, and Janet running in from the kitchen with a maid, a soup tureen, and sundry spoons, every one became busy in rescuing the remains—in the midst of which there was a smash of glass.

'Jock again !' quoth Janet.

'Oh, mother !' called out Jock. 'It's so long ! I thought I'd get the feather-brush to sweep it up with, and the other end of it has been and gone through this stupid lamp.'

'Things are not unapt to be and go through, where you are concerned, Mr. Jock, I suspect,' said Mr. Ogilvie. 'Suppose you were to come with me, and your brothers too, and be introduced to the swans on the lake at Belforest.'

The boys brightened up ; the mother said, 'Thank you most heartily, if they will not be a trouble ,' and Babie put her hand entreatingly into the schoolmaster's, and said, 'Me too ?'

'What, Venus herself ! I thought she had disappeared in the cloud ! Let her come, pray, Mrs. Brownlow.'

'I thought the children would have been with their cousins,' observed the aunt.

'So we were,' returned Armine ; 'but Johnnie and Joe ran away when they saw Mr. Ogilvie coming.'

Babie having by this time had a little black hat tied on, and as much arrowroot as possible brushed out of her frock, Carey warned the schoolmaster not to let himself be chattered to death, and he walked off with the three younger ones.

Caroline would have kept her friend, but Mary, seeing that little good could be gained by staying with her at present, replied that she would take the walk now, and return to her friend in a couple of hours' time ; and Carey was fain to consent, though with a very wistful look in her eyes.

At the end of that time, or more, Janet met the party at the garden gate. 'You are to go down to my uncle's, children,' she said ; 'mother has one of her very bad headaches.'

There was an outcry that they must take her the flowers, of which their hands and arms were full ; but Janet was resolute, though Babie was very near tears.

'To-morrow—to-morrow,' she said. 'She must lie still now, or she won't be able to do anything. Run away, Babie, they'll be waiting tea for you. Allen's there. He'll take care of you.'

'I want to give Mother Carey those dear white flowers,' still entreated Babie.

'I'll give them, my dear. They want you down there—Ellie and Esther.'

'I don't want to play with Ellie and Essie,' sturdily declared Barbara. 'They say it is telling falsehoods when one wants to play at anything.'

'They don't understand pretending,' said Armine. '*Do* let us stay, Janet, we'll not make one smallest little atom of noise, if Jock doesn't stay.'

'You can't,' said Janet, 'for there's nothing for you to eat, and nurse and Susan are as savage as Carribee islanders.'

This last argument was convincing. The children threw their flowers into Janet's arms, gave their hands to Miss Ogilvie, and Babie between her two brothers scampered off, while Miss Ogilvie uttered her griefs and regrets.

'My mother would like to see *you*,' said Janet; 'indeed, I think it will do her good. She told me to bring you in.'

'Such a day of fatigue,' began Mary.

'That and all the rest of it,' said Janet moodily.

'Is she subject to headaches?'

'No, she never had one till——' Janet broke off, for they had reached her mother's door.

'Bring her in,' said a weary voice, and Mary found herself beside a low iron bed, where Carey, shaking off the handkerchief steeped in vinegar and water on her brow, and showing a tear-stained, swollen-eyed face, threw herself into her friend's arms.

But she did not cry now, her tears all came when she was alone, and when Mary said something of being so sorry for her headache, she said, 'Oh! it's only with knocking one's head against a mattress, like mad people,' in such a matter-of-fact voice, that Mary for a moment wondered whether she had really knocked her head.

Mary doubted what to say, and wetted the kerchief afresh with the vinegar and water.

'Oh, Mary, I wish you were going to stay here.'

'I wish! I wish I could, my dear!'

'I think I could be good if you were here!' she sighed. 'Oh, Mary, why do they say that troubles make one good?'

'They ought,' said Mary.

'They don't,' said Carey. 'They make me wicked!' and she hid her face in the pillow with a great gasp.

'My poor Carey!' said the gentle voice.

'Oh! I want to tell you all about it. Oh, Mary, we have been so happy!' and what a wail there was in the tone. 'But I can't talk,' she added faintly, 'it makes me sick, and that's all *her* doing too.'

'Don't try,' said Mary tenderly. 'We know where to find each other now, and you can write to me.'

'I will,' said Caroline; 'I can write much better than tell. And you will come back, Mary?'

'As soon as I can get a holiday, my dear, indeed I will.'

Carey was too much worn out not to repose on the promise, and though she was unwilling to let her friend go, she said very little more.

Mary longed to give her a cup of strong coffee, and suggested it to Janet; but headaches were so new in the family, that domestic remedies had not become well known. Janet instantly rushed down to order it, but in the state of the house at that moment it was nearly as easy to get a draught of pearls.

'But she shall have it, Miss Ogilvie,' said Janet, putting on her hat. 'Where's the nearest grocer?'

'Oh, never mind, my dear,' sighed the patient. 'It will go off of itself, when I can get to sleep.'

'You *shall* have it,' returned Janet.

And Mary having taken as tender a farewell as Caroline was able to bear, they walked off together; but the girl did not respond to the kindness of Miss Ogilvie.

She was too miserable not to be glum, too reserved to be open to a stranger. Mary guessed a little of the feeling, though she feared that an uncomfortable daughter might be one of poor Carey's troubles, and she could not guess the girl's sense of banishment from all that she had enjoyed, society, classes, everything, or her feeling that the *Magnum Bonum* itself was imperilled by exile into the land of dulness, which of course the poor child exaggerated in her imagination. Her only consolation was to feel herself the Masterman Ready of the shipwreck.

## CHAPTER VI

### ENCHANTED GROUND

'And sometimes a merry train
Comes upon us from the lane
All through April, May, or June,
Every gleaming afternoon;
All through April, May, and June,
Boys and maidens, birds and bees,
Airy whisperings from all trees.'

KEBLE, *Petition of the Flowers.*

THE headache had been carried off by a good night's rest; a droll, scrambling breakfast had been eaten, German fashion, with its headquarters on the kitchen table; and everybody running about communicating their discoveries. Bobus and Jock had set off to school, and poor little Armine, who firmly believed that his rejection was in consequence of his confusion between *os, ossis,* and *os, oris,* and was very sore about it, had gone with Allen and Barbara to see them on their way, and Mother Carey

E

and Janet had agreed to get some real work done, and were actually getting through business, when in rushed, rosy and eager, Allen, Armine, and Babie, with arms stretched and in breathless haste.

'Mother Carey!  Oh, mother! mammie, dear! come and see!'

'Come—where?'

'To fairyland.  Get her bonnet, Babie.'

'Out of doors, you boy? just look there!'

'Oh! bother all that!  It can wait.'

'Do pray come, mother,' entreated Armine; 'you never saw anything like it!'

'What is it?  Will it take long?' said she, beginning to yield, as Babie danced about with her bonnet, Armine tugged at her, and Allen looked half-commanding, half-coaxing.

'She is not to know till she sees!  No, don't tell her,' said Armine.  'Bandage her eyes, Allen.  Here's my silk handkerchief.'

'And Janet.  She mustn't see,' cried Babie in ecstasy.

'I'm not coming,' said Janet, rather crossly.  'I'm much too busy, and it is only some nonsense of yours.'

'Thank you,' said Allen, laughing; 'mother shall judge of that.'

'It does seem a shame to desert you, my dear,' said Carey, 'but you see——'

What Janet was to see was stifled in the flap of the handkerchief with which Allen was binding her eyes, while Armine and Babie sang rapturously—

> 'Come along, Mother Carey,
> Come along to land of fairy;'

an invocation to which, sooth to say, she had become so much accustomed that it prevented her from expecting a fairyland where it was not necessary to 'make believe very much.'

Janet so entirely disapproved of the puerile interruption that she never looked to see how Allen and Babie managed the bonnet.  She only indignantly picked up the cap, which had fallen from the sofa to the floor, and disposed of it for security's sake on the bronze head of Apollo, which was waiting till his bracket could be put up.

Guided most carefully by her eldest son, and with the two little ones dancing and singing round her, and alternately stopping each other's mouths when any premature disclosure was apprehended, pausing in wonder when the cuckoo note, never heard before, came on them, making them laugh with glee.

Thus she was conducted much farther than she expected. She heard the swing of the garden gate and felt her feet on the road and remonstrated, but she was coaxed on and through another gate, and a path where Allen had to walk in front of her and the little ones fell behind.

Then came an eager 'Now.'

Her eyes were unbound, and she beheld what they might well call enchanted ground.

She was in the midst of a curved bank where the copsewood had no doubt been recently cut away, and which was a perfect marvel of primroses, their profuse bunches standing out of their wrinkled leaves at every hazel root or hollow among the exquisite moss, varied by the pearly stars of the wind-flower, purple orchis spikes springing from black-spotted leaves, and deep-gray crested dog-violets. On one side was a perfect grove of the broad-leaved, waxen-belled Solomon's seal, sloping down to moister ground where was a golden river of king-cups, and above was a long glade between young birch-trees, their trunks gleaming silvery white, the boughs overhead breaking out into foliage that looked yellow rather than green against the blue sky, and the ground below one sheet of that unspeakably intense purple blue which is only produced by masses of the wild hyacinth.

'There!' said Allen.

'There!' re-echoed the children. 'Oh, mammy, mammy dear! Is it not delicious?'

Carey held up her hand in silence, for a nightingale was pouring out his song close by; she listened breathlessly, and as it ceased she burst into tears.

'O mother!' cried Allen, 'it is too much for you.'

'No, dear boy, it is—it is—only too beautiful. It is what papa always talked of and would have so enjoyed.'

'Do you think he has better flowers up there?' asked Babie. 'I don't think they can be much better.' And without waiting for more she plunged down among the primroses and spread her little self out with a scream of ecstasy.

And verily the strange sense of rapture and enchantment was no less in the mother herself. There is no charm perhaps equal to that of a primrose bank on a sunny day in spring, sight, sound, scent all alike exquisite. It comes with a new and fresh delight even to those to whom this is an annual experience, and to those who never saw the like before it gives, like the first sight of the sea or of a snowy mountain, a sensation never to be forgotten. Fret, fatigue, anxiety, sorrow, all passed away like dreams in that sweet atmosphere. Carey, like one of her children, absolutely forgot everything in the charm and wonder of the scene, in the pure, delicate, unimaginable odour of the primroses, in debating with Allen whether (cockneys that they were) it could be a nightingale 'singing by day when every goose is cackling,' in listening to the marvellous note, only pausing to be answered from further depths, in the beauty of the whole, and in the individual charm of every flower, each heavily-laden arch of dark blue-bells with their curling tips, so infinitely more graceful than their pampered sister, the hyacinth of the window-glass, of each pure delicate anemone she gathered, with its winged stem, of the smiling primrose of that inimitable tint it only wears in its own woodland nest; and when Allen lighted on a bed of wood-sorrel, with its scarlet stems, lovely trefoil leaves, and purple striped blossoms like insect's wings, she absolutely held her breath in an enthusiasm of reverent admiration. No one can tell the happiness of those four, only slightly diminished by Armine's getting bogged on his way to the golden river of king-cups, and his mother in going after him, till Allen from an adjacent stump pulled them out, their feet deeply laden with mud.

They had only just emerged when the strokes of a great bell came pealing up from the town below, Allen and his mother looked at each other in amused dismay, then at their watches. It was twelve o'clock! Two hours had passed like as many minutes, and the boys would be coming home to dinner.

'Ah! well, we must go,' said Carey, as they gathered up their armloads of flowers. 'You naughty children, to make me forget everything.'

'You are not sorry you came, though, mother. It has done you good,' said Allen solicitously. He was the most affectionate of them all.

'Sorry! I feel as if I cared for nothing while I have a place like that to drink up delight in.'

With which they tried to make their way back to the path again, but it was not immediately to be found; and their progress was further impeded by a wood-pigeon dwelling impressively on the notes 'Take *two* cows, Taffy: Taffy take TWO!' and then dashing out, flapping and gray, in their faces, rather to Barbara's alarm, and then by Armine's stumbling on his first bird's nest, a wren's in the moss of an old stump, where the tiny bird unadvisedly flew out of her leafy hole full before their eyes. That was a marvel of marvels, a delight equal to that felt by any explorer the world has seen. Armine and Barbara, who lived in one perpetual fairy tale, were saying to one another that

'One needn't make believe here, it was every bit real.'

'And more,' added the other little happy voice.

Barbara did, however, begin to think of the numerous children in the wood, and to take comfort that it was unprecedented that their mother and big brother should be with them, but they found the park palings at last, and then a little wicket gate, where they were very near home.

'Mother, where *have* you been?' exclaimed Janet, somewhat suddenly emerging from the door.

'In Tom Tiddler's ground, picking up gold and silver,' said Carey, pointing to the armsful of king-cups, cuckoo-flowers, and anemones, besides blue-bells, orchises, primroses, etc. 'My poor child, it was a great shame to leave you, but they got me into the enchanted land and I forgot all about everything.'

'I think so,' said a gravely kind voice, and Caroline was aware of Ellen's eye looking at her as the Court Queen might have looked at Ophelia if she had developed her taste for 'long purples' as Hamlet's widow.  At least so it struck Mother Carey, who immediately became conscious that her bonnet was awry, having been half pulled off by a bramble, that her ankles were marked by the bog, and that bits of green were sticking all over her.

'Have you been helping Janet?  Oh, how kind!' she said, refreshed by her delightsome morning into putting a bright face on it.

'We have done all we could in your absence,' said her sister-in-law in a reproachful voice.

'Thank you: I'm sure it is very good of you.  Janet—Janet, where's the great Dutch bowl—and the little Salviati?  Nothing else is worthy of this dear little fairy thing.'

'What is it?  Just common wood-sorrel,' said the other lady, in utter amaze.

'Ah, Ellen, you think me demented.  You little know what it is to see spring for the first time.  Ah! that's right, Janet. Now, Babie, we'll make a little bit of fairyland——'

'Don't put all those littering flowers on that nice clean chintz, children,' exclaimed the aunt, as though all her work were about to be undone.

And then a trampling of boys' boots being heard and shouts of 'Mother,' Carey darted out into the hall to hear fragments of school intelligence as to work and play, tumbling over one another, from Bobus and Jock both at once, in the midst of which Mrs. Robert Brownlow came out with her hat on, and stood, with her air of patient serenity, waiting for an interval.

Caroline looked up, and said, 'I beg your pardon, Ellen—what is it?'

'If you can attend a moment,' said she gravely; 'I must be going to my boys' dinner.  But Robert wishes to know whether he shall order this paper for the drawing-room.  It cannot be put up yet, of course; but Smith has only a certain quantity of it, and it is so stylish that he said the Colonel had better secure it at once.'

She spread the roll of paper on the hall table.  It was a white paper, slightly tinted, and seemed intended to represent coral branches, with starry-looking things at the ends.

'The aquarium at the Zoo,' muttered Bobus; and Caroline herself, meeting Allen's eye, could not refrain from adding—

> 'The worms they crawled in,
>   And the worms they crawled out.'

'Mother!' cried Jock, 'I thought you were going to paint it all over with jolly things.'

'Frescoes,' said Allen; 'shan't you, mother?'

'If your uncle does not object,' said his mother, choking down a giggle. 'Those plaster panels are so tempting for frescoes. Ellen.'

'Frescoes! Why, those are those horrid improper-looking gods and goddesses in clouds and chariots on the ceilings at Belforest,' observed that lady in a half-puzzled, half-offended tone of voice, that most perilously tickled the fancy of Mother Carey and her brood! and she could hardly command her voice to make answer, 'Never fear, Ellen; we are not going to attempt allegorical monstrosities, only to make a bower of green leaves and flowers such as we see round us; though after what we have seen to-day that seems presumptuous enough. Fancy, Janet! golden green trees and porcelain blue ground, all in one bath of sunshine. Such things must be seen to be believed in.'

Poor Mrs. Robert Brownlow! She went home and sighed, as she said to her husband, 'Well, what is to become of those poor things I do not know. One would sometimes think poor Caroline was just a little touched in the head.'

'I hope not,' said the Colonel, rather alarmed.

'It may be only affectation,' said his lady in a consolatory tone. 'I am afraid poor Joe did live with a very odd set of people—artists, and all that kind of thing. I am sure I don't blame her, poor thing! But she is worse to manage than any child, because you can't bid her mind what she is about, and not talk nonsense. When she leaves her house in such a state, and no one but that poor girl to see to anything, and comes home all over mud, raving about fairyland, and gold trees and blue ground; when she has just got into a bog in Belforest coppice—littering the whole place, too, with common wild flowers. If it had been Essie and Ellie, I should just have put them in the corner for making such a mess!'

The Colonel laughed a little to himself, and said consolingly, 'Well, well, you know all these country things are new to her. You must be patient with her.'

Patient! That had to be the burthen of the song on both sides. Carey was pushing back her hair with a fierce, wild sense of impatience with that calm assumption that fretted her beyond all bearing, and made her feel desolate beyond all else. She would have, she thought, done well enough alone with her children, and scrambled into her new home; but the directions, however needful, seemed to be continually insulting her understanding. When she was advised as to the best butcher and baker, there was a ring in her ears as if Ellen meant that these were safe men for a senseless creature like her, and she could not encounter them with her orders without wondering whether they had been told to treat her well.

Indeed, one of the chief drawbacks to Carey's comfort was her difficulty in attending to what her brother and sister-in-law said to her. Something in the measured tones of the Colonel always made her thoughts wander as from a dull sermon ; and this was more unlucky in his case than in his wife's—for Ellen used such reiterations that there was a fair chance of catching her drift the second or third time, if not the first, whereas all he said was well weighed and arranged, and was only too heavy and sententious.

Kencroft, the home of the Colonel and his family, Mrs. Robert Brownlow's inheritance, was certainly 'a picture of a place.' It had probably been an appendage of the old minster, though the house was only of the seventeenth century ; but that was substantial and venerable of its kind, and exceedingly comfortable and roomy, with everything kept in perfect order. Caroline could not quite think the furniture worthy of it, but that was not for want of the desire to do everything handsomely and fashionably. Moreover, in spite of the schoolroom and nursery-ful of children, marvels of needlework and knitting adorned every table, chair, and sofa, while even in the midst of the town Kencroft had its own charming garden ; a lawn, once devoted to bowls and now to croquet, an old-fashioned walled kitchen garden, sloping up the hill, and a paddock sufficient to make cows and pigs part of the establishment.

The Colonel had devoted himself to gardening and poultry with the mingled ardour and precision of a man who needed something to supply the place of his soldierly duties ; and though his fervour had relaxed under the influence of ease, gout, and substantial flesh, enough remained to keep up apple-pie order without-doors, and render Kencroft almost a show place. The meadow lay behind the house, and a gravel walk leading along its shaded border opened into the lane about ten yards from the gate of the Pagoda, as Colonel and Mrs. Brown-low and the post-office laboured to call it ; the Folly, as came so much more naturally to every one's lips. It had been the work of the one eccentric man in Mrs. Robert Brownlow's family, and was thus her property. It had hung long on hand, being difficult to let, and after making sufficient additions, it had been decided that, at a nominal rent, it would house the family thrown upon the hands of the good Colonel.

## CHAPTER VII

### THE COLONEL'S CHICKENS

'They censured the bantam for strutting and crowing,
In those vile pantaloons that he fancied looked knowing ;
And a want of decorum caused many demurs
Against the game chicken for coming in spurs.'
                                        *The Peacock at Home.*

LEFT to themselves, Mother Carey, with Janet and old nurse, completed their arrangements so well that when Jessie looked

in at five o'clock, with a few choice flowers covering a fine
cucumber in her basket, she exclaimed in surprise, 'How nice
you have made it all look ! I shall be so glad to tell mamma.'

'Tell her what ?' asked Janet.

'That you have really made the room look nice,' said Jessie.

'Thank you,' said her cousin ironically. 'You see we have
as many hands as other people. Didn't Aunt Ellen think we
had ?'

'Of course she did,' said Jessie, a pretty, kindly creature, but
slow of apprehension ; 'only she said she was very sorry for
you.'

'And why ?' cried Janet, leaping up in indignation.

'Why ?' interposed Allen, 'because we are raw cockneys, who
go into raptures over primroses and wild hyacinths ; eh, Jessie ?'

'Well, you have set them up very nicely,' said Jessie ; 'but
fancy taking so much trouble about common flowers.'

'What would you think worth setting up ?' asked Janet. 'A
big dahlia, I suppose, or a great red cactus ?'

'We have a beautiful garden,' said Jessie : 'papa is very particular about it, and we always get the prize for our flowers.
We had the first prizes for hyacinths and forced roses last week,
and we should have had the first for forced cucumbers if the
gardener at Belforest had not had a spite against Spencer because he left him for us. Everybody said there was no comparison between the cucumbers, and Mr. Ellis said——'

Janet had found the day before how Jessie could prattle on
in an endless quiet stream without heeding whether any one
entered into it or replied to it ; but she was surprised at Allen's
toleration of it, though he changed the current by saying, ' Belforest seems a jolly place.'

'But you've only seen the wood, not the gardens,' said Jessie.

'I went down to the lake with Mr. Ogilvie,' said Allen, 'and
saw something splendiferous looking on the other side.'

'Oh ! they are beautiful !' cried Jessie, 'all laid out in ribbon
gardens and with the most beautiful terrace, and a fountain—
only that doesn't play except when you give the gardener half
a crown, and mamma says that is exorbitant — and statues
standing all round—real marble statues.'

'Like the groves of Blarney,' muttered Janet :

> ' Heathen goddesses most rare,
> Homer, Venus, and Nebuchadnezzar,
> All standing naked in the open air.'

Allen, seeing Jessie scandalised, diverted her attention by
asking, 'Whom does it belong to ?'

'Mr. Barnes,' said Jessie ; 'but he is hardly ever there. He
is an old miser, you know—what they call a millionaire, or mill-
owner ; which is it ?'

'One is generally the French for the other,' put in Janet.

'Never mind her, Jessie,' said Allen, with a look of infinite displeasure at his sister. 'What does he do which keeps him away?'

'I believe he is a great merchant, and is always in Liverpool,' said Jessie. 'Any way, he is a very cross old man, and won't let anybody go into his park and gardens when he comes down here; and he is very cruel too, for he disinherited his own nephew and niece for marrying. Only think, Mrs. Watson at the grocer's told our Susan that there's a little girl, who is his own great-niece, living down at River Hollow Farm with Mr. and Mrs. Gould, just brought up by common farmers, you know, and he won't take any notice of her, nor give one farthing for bringing her up. Isn't it shocking? And even when he is at home, he only has two chops or two steaks, or just a bit of kidney, and that when he is literally rolling in gold.'

Jessie opened her large brown eyes to mark her horror, and Allen made a gesture of exaggerated sympathy, which his sister took for more earnest than it was, and she said scornfully, 'I should like to see him literally rolling in gold. It must be like Midas. Do you mean that he sleeps on it, Jessie? How hard and cold!'

'Nonsense,' said Jessie; 'you know what I mean.'

'I know what literally rolling in gold means, but I don't know what you mean.'

'Don't bully her, Janet,' said Allen; 'we are not so stupid, are we, Jessie? Come and show me the walnut tree you were telling me about.'

'What's the matter, Janet?' said her mother, coming in a moment or two after, and finding her staring blankly out of the window, where the two had made their exit.

'O mother, Jessie has been talking such gossip, and Allen likes it, and won't have it stopped! I can't think what makes Allen and Bobus both so foolish whenever she is here.'

'She is a very pretty creature,' said Carey, smiling a little.

'Pretty!' repeated Janet. 'What has that to do with it?'

'A great deal, as you will have to find out in the course of your life, my dear.'

'I thought only foolish people cared about beauty.'

'It is very convenient for us to think so,' said Carey, smiling.

'But, mother—surely everybody cares for you just as much or more than if you were a great handsome, stupid creature! How I hate that word "handsome"!'

'Except for a cab,' said Carey.

'Ah! when shall I see a hansom again?' said Janet in a slightly sentimental tone. But she returned to the charge, 'Don't go, mother, I want you to answer.'

'Beauty *versus* brains! My dear, you had better open your eyes to the truth. You must make up your mind to it. It is only very exceptional people who, even in the long run, care most for feminine brains.'

'But, mother, every one did.'

'Every one in our world, Janet; but your father made our home set of those exceptional people, and we are cast out of it now!' she added, with a gasp and a gesture of irrepressible desolateness.

'Yes, that comes of this horrid move,' said the girl in quite another tone. 'Well, some day——' and she stopped.

'Some day?' said her mother.

'Some day we'll go back again, and show what we are,' she said proudly.

'Ah, Janet! and that's nothing now without *him*.'

'Mother, how can you say so, when——?' Jane just checked herself, as she was coming to the great secret.

'When we have his four boys,' said her mother. 'Ah! yes, Janet—if—and when—But that's a long way off, and, to come back to our former subject,' she added, recalling herself with a sigh, 'it will be wise in us owlets to make up our minds that owlets we are, and to give the place to the eaglets.'

'But eaglets are very ugly, and owlets very pretty,' quoth Janet.

Carey laughed. 'That does not seem to have been the opinion of the Beast Epic,' said she, and the entrance of Babie prevented them from going further.

Janet turned away with one of her grim sighs at the unappreciative world to which she was banished. She had once or twice been on the point of mentioning the *Magnum Bonum* to her mother, but the reserve at first made it seem as if an avowal would be a confession, and to this she could not bend her pride, while the secrecy made a strange barrier between her and her mother. In truth, Janet had never been so devoted to Mother Carey as to either granny or her father, and now she missed them sorely, and felt it almost an injury to have no one but her mother to turn to.

Her character was not set in the same mould, and though both could meet on the common ground of intellect, she could neither enter into the recesses of her mother's grief, nor understand those flashes of brightness and playfulness which nothing could destroy. If Carey had chosen to unveil the truth to herself, she would have owned that Allen, who was always ready, tender, and sympathetic to her, was a much greater comfort than his sister; nay, that even little Babie gave her more rest and peace than did Janet, who always rubbed against her whenever they found themselves *tête-à-tête* or in consultation.

Meantime Babie had been out with her two little cousins, and came home immensely impressed with the Belforest gardens. The house was shut up, but the gardens were really kept up to perfection, and the little one could not declare her full delight in the wonderful blaze she had seen of banks of red, and flame coloured, and white, flowering trees. 'They said they would show me the Americans,' she said. 'Why was it, mother? I thought Americans were like the gentleman who dined with you one day, and told me about the snow birds. But there were only these flower-trees, and a pond, and statues standing round it, and I don't think they were Americans, for I know one was Diana, because she had a bow and quiver. I wanted to look at the rest, but Miss James said they were horrid heathen gods, not fit for little girls to look at; and, mother, Ellie is so silly, she thought the people at Belforest worshipped them. Do come and see them, mother. It is like the Crystal Palace out-of-doors.'

'Omitting the Crystal,' laughed some one; but Babie had more to say, exclaiming, 'O mother, Essie says Aunt Ellen says Janet and I are to do lessons with Miss James; but you won't let us, will you?'

'Miss James!' broke out Janet indignantly; 'we might as well learn of old nurse! Why, mother, she can't pronounce French, and she never heard of terminology, and she thinks Edward I. killed the bards!' For the girls had spent a day or two with their cousins in the course of the move.

'Yes,' broke in Barbara, 'and she won't let Essie and Ellie teach their dolls their lessons! She was quite cross when I was showing them how, and said it was all nonsense when I told her I heard you say that I half taught myself by teaching Juliet. And so the poor dolls have no advantages, mother, and are quite stupid for want of education,' pursued the little girl indignantly. 'They aren't people, but only dolls, and Essie and Ellie can't do anything with them but just dress them and take them out walking.'

'That's what they would wish to make Babie like!' said her elder sister.

'But you'll not let anybody teach me but you, dear, dear Mother Carey,' entreated the child.

'No, indeed, my little one.' And just then the boys came rushing in to their evening meal, full of the bird's nest that they had been visiting in their uncle's field, and quite of opinion that Kenminster was 'a jolly place.'

'And then,' added Jock, 'we got the garden engine, and had such fun, you don't know.'

'Yes,' said Bobus, 'till you sent a whole cataract against the house, and that brought out her Serene Highness!'

The applicability of the epithet set the whole family off into a laugh, and Jock further made up a solemn face, and repeated—

> ' Buff says Buff to all his men,
> And I say Buff to you again.
> Buff neither laughs nor smiles,
> But carries his face
> With a very good grace.'

It convulsed them all, and the mother, recovering a little, said, 'I wonder whether she ever can laugh.'

'Poor Aunt Ellen!' said Babie, in all her gravity; 'she is like King Henry I. and never smiled again.'

And with more wit than prudence, Mrs. Buff, her Serene Highness, Sua Serenità, as Janet made it, became the *sobriquets* for Aunt Ellen, and were in continual danger of oozing out publicly  Indeed the younger population at Kencroft probably soon became aware of them, for on the next half-holiday Jock crept in with unmistakable tokens of combat about him, and on interrogation confessed, 'It was Johnnie, mother. Because we wanted you to come out walking with us, and he said 'twas no good walking with one's mother, and I told him he didn't know what a really jolly mother was, and that his mother couldn't laugh, and that you said so, and he said my mother was no better than a tomboy, and that she said so, and so——'

And so, the effects were apparent on Jock's torn and stained collar and swelled nose.

But the namesake champions remained unconvinced, except that Johnnie may have come over to the opinion that a mother no better than a tomboy was not a bad possession, for the three haunted the 'Folly' a good deal, and made no objection to their aunt's company after the first experiment.

Unfortunately, however, their assurances that their mother could laugh as well as other people were not so conclusive but that Jock made it his business to do his utmost to produce a laugh, in which he was apt to be signally unsuccessful, to his own great surprise, though to that of no one else. For instance, two or three days later, when his mother and Allen were eating solemnly a dinner at Kencroft, by way of farewell ere Allen's return to Eton, an extraordinarily frightful noise was heard in the poultry yard, where dwelt various breeds of Uncle Robert's prize fowls.

Thieves—foxes—dogs—what could it be? Even the cheese and celery were deserted, and out rushed servants, master, mistress, and guests, being joined by the two girls from the school-room; but even then Carey was struck by the ominous absence of boys. The poultry-house door was shut—locked—but the noises within were more and more frightful—of convulsive cocks and hysterical hens, mingled with human scufflings and hushes and snortings and snigglings that made the elders call out in various tones of remonstrance and reprobation, 'Boys, have done! Come out! Open the door.'

A small hatch door was opened, a flourish on a tin trumpet was heard, and out darted, in an Elizabethan ruff and cap, a respectable Dorking mother of the yard, cackling her displeasure, and instantly dashing to the top of the wall, followed at once by a stately black Spaniard, decorated with a lace mantilla of cut paper off a French plum box, squawking and curtseying. Then came a dapper pullet, with a doll's hat on her unwilling head, etc. etc.

The outsiders were choking with breathless surprise at first, then the one lady began indignantly to exclaim, 'Now, boys! Have done—let the poor things alone. Come out this minute.'

The other fairly reeled against the wall with laughter, and Janet and Jessie screamed at each fresh appearance, till they made as much noise as the outraged chickens, though one shrieked with dismay, the other with diversion. At last the Colonel, slower of foot than the rest, arrived on the scene, just as the pride of his heart, the old King Chanticleer of the yard, made his exit, draped in a royal red paper robe and a species of tinsel crown, out of which his red face looked most ludicrous as he came, halting and stupefied, having evidently been driven up in a corner and pinched rather hard ; but close behind him, chuckling forth his terror and flapping his wings, came the pert little white bantam, belted and accoutred as a page.

Colonel Brownlow's severe command to open the door was not resisted for one moment, and forth rushed a cloud of dust and feathers, a quacking, waggling substratum of ducks, and a screaming, flapping rabble of chickens, behind whom, when the mist cleared, were seen, looking as if they had been tarred and feathered, various black and gray figures, which developed into Jock, Armine, Robin, Johnnie, and Joe. Jock, the foremost, stared straight up in his aunt's face, Armine ran to his mother with—'Did you see the old king, mother, and his little page? Wasn't it funny——' But he was stopped by the sight of his uncle, who laid hold of his eldest son with a fierce 'How dare you, sir?' and gave him a shake and blow. Robin stood with a sullen look on his face, and hands in his pockets, and his brothers followed suit. Armine hid his face in his mother's dress, and burst out crying ; but Jock stepped forth, and, with that impish look of fearlessness, said, 'I did it, Uncle Robert ! I wanted to make Aunt Ellen laugh. Did she laugh, mother?' he asked in so comical and innocent a manner that, in spite of her full consciousness of the heinousness of the offence, and its general unluckiness, Mother Carey was almost choked. This probably added to the gravity with which the other lady decreed with Juno-like severity, 'Robin and John must be flogged. Joe is too young.'

'Certainly,' responded the Colonel ; but Caroline, instead of, as they evidently expected of her, at once offering up her victim, sprang forward with eager, tearful pleadings, declaring it was all Jock's fault, and he did not know how naughty it was —but all in vain. 'Robert knew. He ought to have stopped it,' said the Colonel. 'Go to the study, you two.'

Jock did not act as the generous hero of romance would have done, and volunteer to share the flogging. He cowered back on his mother, and put his arm round her waist, while she said, 'Jock told the truth, so I shall not ask you to flog him, Uncle Robert. He shall not do such mischief again.'

'If he does,' said his uncle, with a look as if her consent would not be asked to what would follow.

## CHAPTER VIII

### THE FOLLY

> ' There will we sit upon the rocks,
> And see the shepherds feed their flocks
> By summer rivers, by whose falls
> Melodious birds sing madrigals.'
>
> MARLOWE.

'How does my little schoolfellow get on?' asked Mary Ogilvie, when she had sat down for her first meal with her brother in her summer holidays.

'Much as Ariel did in the split pine, I fancy.'

'For shame, David! I'm afraid you are teaching her to see Sycorax and Caliban in her neighbours.'

'Not I! How should I ever see her? Do you hear from her?'

'Sometimes; and I heard of her from the Actons, who had an immense regard for her husband, who, they say, was a very superior man.'

'It is hardly necessary to be told so.'

'They mean to take lodgings somewhere near here this next month, and see what they can do to cheer her in her present life, which must be the greatest possible contrast to her former one. Do you wish to set out on our expedition before August, Davie? I should like you to see them.'

'By all means let us wait for them. Indeed I should not be at liberty till the last week in July.'

'And how go the brains of Kenminster? You look enlivened since last time I saw you.'

'It is the infusion the brains have received. That one woman has made more difference to the school than I could have done in ten years.'

'You find her boys, at any rate, pupils worth teaching.'

'More than that. Of course it is something to have a fellow capable of ideas before one; but besides that, lads who had gone on contentedly at their own level have had to bestir themselves not to be taken down by him. When he refused to have it forced upon him that study was not the thing at Kenminster, they found the only way to make him know his place was to keep theirs, and some of them have really found the use of their wits, and rejoice in them. Even in the lower form, the Colonel's second boy has developed an intellect. Then the way those boys bring their work prepared has raised the standard!'

'I heard something of that on my way.'

'You did?'

'Yes; two ladies were in full career of talk when the train stopped at the Junction, and I heard—"I am always obliged to

spend one hour every evening seeing that Arthur knows his
lessons. So troublesome, you know ; but since that Mrs. Joseph
Brownlow has come, she helps her boys so with their home-work
that the others have not a chance if one does not look to it
oneself." Then it appeared that she told Mr. Ogilvie it wasn't
fair, and that he would give her no redress.'

'Absurd woman ! It is not a matter of unfairness, as I told
her. They don't get help in sums or exercises ; they only have
grammar to learn and construing to prepare, and all my concern is that it should be got up thoroughly. If their mothers
help them, so much the better.'

'The mothers don't seem to think so. However, she branched
off into incredulity that Mrs. Joe Brownlow could ever really
teach her children anything, for she was always tramping all
over the country with them at all hours of the day and night.
She has met her herself, with all those boys after her, three
miles from home, in a great straw hat, when her husband hadn't
been dead a year.'

'I'm sure she is always in regulation veils, and all the rest of
it, at church, if that's what you ladies want.'

'But the crown of the misdoings seemed to be that she had been
met at some old castle, sacred to picnics, alone with her children
—no party nor anything. I could not make out whether the
offence consisted in making the ruin too cheap, or in caring for
it for its own sake, and not as a lion for guests.'

'The latter probably. She has the reputation of being very
affected ! ! !'

'Poor dear ! I heard that she was a great trial to dear Mrs.
Brownlow,' said Mary in an imitative voice. 'Why, do you
know, she sometimes is up and out with her children before six
o'clock in the morning ; and then Colonel Brownlow went in
one day at twelve o'clock, and found the whole family fast
asleep on different sofas.'

'The sensible way, too, to spend such days as these. To go
out in the cool of the morning, and take a *siesta*, is the only
rational plan !'

'I'm afraid one must conform to one's neighbours' ways.'

'Trust a woman for being conventional.'

'I confess I did not like the tone in which my poor Carey
was spoken of. I am afraid she can hardly have taken care
enough not to be thought flighty.'

'Mary ! you are as absurd as the rest of them !'

'Why ? what have you seen of her ?'

'Nothing, I tell you, except once meeting her in the street,
and once calling on her to ask whether her boy should learn
German.' And David Ogilvie spoke with a vehemence that
somewhat startled his sister.

It was a July evening, and though the walls of the schoolmaster's house were thick, it was sultry enough within to lead
the brother and sister out immediately after dinner, looking

first into the play-fields, where cricket was of course going on among the bigger boys, but where Mary looked in vain for her friend's sons.

'No, they are not much of cricketers,' said her brother; 'they are small for it yet, and only take their turn in watching-out by compulsion. I wish the senior had more play in him. Shall we walk on by the river?'

So they did, along a paved causeway which presently got clear of the cottages and gables of old factories, and led along, with the bright glassy sheet of water on one side, and the steep wooded slope on the other, loose-strife and meadow-sweet growing thickly on the bank, amid long weeds with feathery tops, rich brown fingers of sedge, and bur-reeds like German morgensterns; while above the long wreaths of dog-roses projected, the sweet honeysuckle twined about, and the white blossoms of traveller's-joy hung in festoons from the hedge of the bordering plantation. After a time they came on a kind of glade, opening upwards through the wood, with one large oak-tree standing alone in the centre, and behold! on the grass below sat or lay a company—Mrs. Joseph Brownlow in the midst, under the obnoxious mushroom-hat, reading aloud. Radiating from her were five boys, the biggest of all on his back, with his hat over his eyes, fast asleep; another cross-legged, with a basket between his knees, dividing his attention between it and the book; two more lying frog-like, with elbows on the ground, feet erected behind them, chin in hand, devouring the narrative with their eyes; the fifth wriggling restlessly about, evidently in search of opportunities of mischief or of tormenting tricks. Just within earshot, but sketching the picturesque wooden bridge below, sat one girl. The little one, with her youngest brother, was close at their mother's feet, threading flowers to make a garland. It was a pretty sight, and so intent were most of the party on their occupations that they never saw the pair on the bank till Joe, the idler, started and rolled round with 'Hollo!' when all turned, it may be feared with muttered growls from some of the boys; but Carey herself gave a cry of joy, ran down the bank like a girl, and greeted Mary Ogilvie with an eager embrace.

'You are holding a court here,' said the schoolmaster.

'We have had tea out here. It is too hot for indoors, and I am reading them the *Water Babies*.'

'To a large audience, I see.'

'Yes, and some of which are not quite sure whether it is fact or fiction. Come and sit down.'

'The boys will hate us for breaking up their reading,' said Mary.

'Why should not we listen?' said her brother. 'Don't disturb yourselves, boys; we've met before to-day.'

Bobus and Jock were, however, on their feet, and Johnnie had half risen; Robin lay still snoring, and Joe had retreated into the wood from the alarming spectacle of the 'schoolmaster abroad.'

After a greeting to the two girls, who comported themselves, according to their ages, as young ladies might be expected to do, the Ogilvies found accommodation on the roots of the tree, and listened. The *Water Babies* were then new, and Mr. Ogilvie had never heard them. Luckily the reading had just come to the history of the 'Do as You Likes,' and the interview between the last of the race and M. Du Chaillu diverted him beyond measure. He laughed so much over the poor fellow's abortive attempt to say 'Am I not a man and a brother?' that his three scholars burst out into a second edition of shouts of laughter at the sight of him, and thus succeeded in waking Robin, who, after a great contortion, sat up on the grass, and, rubbing his eyes, demanded in an injured tone what was the row?

' "The Last of the Do as You Likes," ' said Armine.

'Oh I say—isn't it jolly,' cried Jock, beating his breast gorilla-fashion and uttering a wild murmur of 'Am I not a man and a brother?' then tumbling head over heels, half in ecstasy, half in imitation of the fate of the Do as You Like, setting everybody off into fits again.

'It's just what Robin is coming to,' observed Bobus, as his namesake stretched his arms and delivered himself of a waking howl; then suddenly becoming conscious of Mr. Ogilvie, he remained petrified, with one arm fully outstretched, the other still lifted to his head.

'Never mind, Brownlow maximus,' said his master; 'it was hardly fair to surprise you in private life, was it?'

The boy made no answer, but scrambled up, sheepish and disconcerted; and indeed the sun was entirely down and the dew almost falling, so that the mother called to the young ones to gather up their things and come home.

Such a collection! Bobus picked up a tin case and basket full of flowers, interspersed with bottles of swimming insects. The trio and Armine shouldered their butterfly-nets, and had a distribution of pill-boxes and bottles, in some of which were caterpillars intended to live, in others butterflies dead (or dying, it may be feared) of laurel leaves. Babie had a mighty nosegay; Janet put up the sketch, which showed a good deal of power; and the whole troop moved up the slope to go home by the lanes.

'What collectors you are!' said Mr. Ogilvie.

'For the museum,' answered Armine eagerly.

'Haven't you seen our museum?' cried Barbara, who had taken his hand. 'Oh, it is such a beauty! We have got an *Orobanche major*, only it is not dry yet.'

'I'm afraid Babie likes fine words,' said her mother; 'but our museum is a great amusement to us Londoners.'

They all walked home together, talking merrily, and Mr. and Miss Ogilvie came in with them, on special entreaty, to share

the supper—milk, fruit, bread and butter and cheese, and sandwiches, which was laid out on the round table in the octagon
vestibule, which formed the lowest story of the tower.  It was
partaken of standing, or sitting at ease on the window-seats, a
form or two, an old carved chair, or on the stairs, the children
ascending them after their meal, and after securing in their own
fashion their treasures for the morrow.  The two cousins had
already bidden good-night at the gate and gone home, and the
Ogilvies followed their example in ten minutes, Caroline begging
Mary to come up to her as soon as Mr. Ogilvie was disposed of
by school hours.

'But you will be busy?' said Mary.

'Never mind, I am afraid we are not very regular,' said
Carey.

It was by this time ten o'clock, and the two younger children
were still to be heard shouting to one another upstairs about
the leaves for their chrysalids.  So when Mary came up the hill
at half-past ten the next morning, she was the less surprised to
find these two only just beginning breakfast, while their mother
was sitting at the end of the table knitting, and hearing Janet
repeat German poetry.  The boys had long been in school.

Caroline jumped up and threw her arms round Mary's neck,
declaring that now they would enjoy themselves.  'We are very
late,' she added, 'but these late walks make the little people
sleep, and I think it is better for them than tossing about, hot
and cross.'

Mary was rather entertained at this new code, but said
nothing, as Carey pointed out to the children how they were to
occupy themselves under Janet's charge, and the work they had
to do showed that for their age they had lost no time.

The drawing-room showed indeed a contrast to the chaotic
state in which it had been left.  It was wonderfully pleasant-
looking.  The windows of the deep bay were all open to the
lawn, shaded with blinds projecting out into the garden, where
the parrot sat perched on her pole ; pleasant nooks were arranged
in the two sides of the bay window, with light chairs and small
writing-tables, each with its glass of flowers ; the piano stood
across the arc, shutting off these windows into almost a separate
room ; low book-cases, with chiffonier cupboards and marble
tops, ran round the walls, surmounted with many artistic ornaments.  The central table was crowned with a tall glass of ex-
quisitely-arranged grasses and wild flowers, and the choice and
graceful nicknacks round it were such as might be traced to a
London life in the artist world, and among grateful patients.

Brackets with vases and casts here and there projected from
the walls, and some charming crayons and water-colours hung
round them.  The plastered walls had already been marked out
in panels, and a growth of frescoes of bulrushes, ivy, and leaves
of all kinds was beginning to overspread them, while on a
nearer inspection the leaves proved to be fast becoming peopled

with living portraits of butterflies and other insects; indeed
Mary started at finding herself in, as she thought, unpleasant
proximity to a pair of cockchafers.

'Ah! I tell the children that we shall be suspected of putting
those creatures there as a trial to the old ladies' nerves,' said
Caroline, laughing.

'I confess they are startling to those who don't like creeping
things. Have you many old ladies, Carey?'

'Not very many. I fancy they don't take to me more than I
take to them, so we are mutually satisfied.'

'But is that a good thing?' said Mary anxiously.

'I don't know,' said Carey indifferently. 'At least I do
know,' she added, 'that I always used to be told I didn't try
to make small talk, and I can do it less than ever now that
it is the smallest of small, and my heart faints from it. O
Mary!'

'My poor dear Caroline! But you say that you were told
you ought to do it?'

'Well, yes. Dear granny wished it; but I think that was
rather with a view to Joe's popularity, and we haven't any
patients to think of now. I should think the less arrant gossip
the children heard, the better.'

'But is it well to let them despise everybody?'

'Then the less they see of them, the better.'

'For shame, Carey!'

'Well, Mary, I dare say I am naughty. I do feel naughtier
now than ever I did in my life; but I can't help it! It just
makes me mad to be worried or tied down,' and she pushed back
her hair so that her unfortunate cap was only withheld from
tumbling entirely off by the pin that held it.

'Oh, that wretched cap!' she cried, jumping up petulantly,
and going to the glass to set it to rights, but with so hasty a
hand that the pin became entangled in her hair, and it needed
Mary's quiet hand to set it to rights; 'it's just an emblem of all
the rest of it; I wouldn't wear it another day, but that I'm
afraid of Ellen and Robert, and it perfectly drives me wild.
And I know Joe couldn't have borne to see me in it.' At the
Irishism of which she burst out laughing, and laughed herself
into the tears that had never come when they were expected of
her.

Mary caressed and soothed her, and told her she could well
guess it was sadder to her now than even at first.

'Well, it is,' said Carey, looking up. 'If one was sent out to
sea in a boat, it wouldn't be near so bad as long as one could see
the dear old shore still, as when one had got out—out into the
wide open—with nothing at all.'

And she stretched out her hands with a dreary, yearning
gesture into the vacant space, such as it went to her friend's
heart to see.

'Ah! but there's a haven at the end.'

'I suppose there is,' said Carey; 'but it's a long way off, and there's dying first, and when people want to begin about it, they get so conventional, and if there's one thing above another that I can't stand, it is being bored.'

'My poor child!'

'There, don't be angry with me, because I'm telling you just what I am!'

Before any more could be said Janet opened the door, saying, 'Mother, Emma wants to see you.'

'Oh! I forgot,' cried Carey, hurrying off, while Janet came forward to the guest in her grown-up way, and asked—

'Have you been to the Water-Colour Exhibition, Miss Ogilvie?'

'Yes; Mr. Acton took me one Saturday afternoon.'

'Oh! then he would be sure to show you Nita Ray's picture. I want so much to know how it strikes people.'

And Janet had plunged into a regular conversation about exhibitions, pictures, artists, concerts, lectures, etc., before her mother came back, talking with all the eagerness of an exile about her native country. As a governess in her schoolroom, Miss Ogilvie had had little more than a keyhole view of all these things; but then what she had seen and heard had been chiefly through the Actons, and thus coincided with Janet's own side of the world, and they were in full discussion when Caroline came back.

'There, I've disposed of the butcher and baker!' she said. 'Now we can be comfortable again.'

Mary expected Janet to repair to her own lessons, or to listen to those scales which Babie might be heard from a distance playing; but she only appealed to her mother about some picture of last year, and sat down to her drawing, while the conversation on pictures and books continued in animated style. So far from sending her away, Mary fancied that Carey was rather glad to keep to surface matters, and to be prevented from another outbreak of feeling.

The next interruption was from the children, each armed with a pile of open books on the top of a slate. Carey begged Mary to wait, and went outside the window with them, sitting down under a tree whence the murmured sounds of repetition could be heard, lasting about twenty minutes between the two, and then she returned, the little ones jumping on each side of her, Armine begging that Miss Ogilvie would come and see the museum, and Barbara saying that Jock wanted to help to show it off.

'Well, run now and put your own corners tidy,' suggested their mother. 'If Jock does not stay in the playground, he will come back in a quarter of an hour.'

'And Mr. Ogilvie will come then. I invited him,' said Babie.

At which Carey laughed incredulously; but Janet, observing

that she must go and see that the children did not do more
harm than good, walked off, and Mary said—

'I should not wonder if he did act on the invitation.'

'I hope he will. It would have only been civil in me to have
asked him, considering that I have taken possession of you,'
said Caroline.

'I fully expect to see him on Miss Barbara's invitation. Do
you know, Carey, he says you have transformed his school.'

'Translated it, like Bottom the Weaver.'

'In the reverse direction. He says you have made the
mothers see to their boys' preparation, and wakened up the
intellects.'

'Have I? I thought I had only kept my own boys up to the
mark. Yes, and there's Johnnie. Do you know, Mary, it is very
funny, but that boy Johnnie has adopted me. He comes after
me everywhere like a shadow, and there's nothing he won't do
for me, even learning his lessons. You see the poor boy has a
good deal of native sense, Brownlow sense, and mind had been
more stifled than wanting in him. Nobody had ever put things
to him by the right end, and when he once let me do it for him,
it was quite a revelation, and he has been so happy and
prosperous that he hardly knows himself. Poor boy, there is
something very honest and true about him, and so affectionate!
He is a little like his uncle, and I can't help being fond of him.
Then Robin is just as devoted to Jock, though I can't say the
results are so very desirable, for Jock is a monkey, I must
confess, and it is irresistible to a monkey to have a bear that
he can lead to do anything. I hear that Robin used to be the
good boy of the establishment, and I am afraid he is not that
now.'

'But can't you stop that?'

'My dear, nobody could think of Jock's devices so as to stop
them, who had not his own monkey brain. Who would have
thought of his getting the whole set to dress up as nigger
singers, with black faces and banjoes, and coming to dance and
sing in front of the windows?'

'There wasn't much harm in that.'

'There wouldn't have been if it had been only here. And,
oh dear, the irresistible fun of Jock's capering antics, and Rob
moving by mechanism, as stiff and obedient as the giant porter
to Flibbertigibbet.' Carey stopped to laugh. 'But then I
never thought of their going on to present themselves to Ellen
in the middle of a mighty and solemn dinner party! All the
grandees, the county people' (this in a deep and awful voice),
'sitting up in their chignons of state, in the awful pause during
the dishing-up, when these five little wretches, in finery filched
from the rag-bag, appear on the smooth lawn, mown and
trimmed to the last extent for the occasion, and begin to strike
up at their shrillest, close to the open window. Ellen rises with
great dignity. I fancy I can see her, sending out to order them

off. And then, oh dear, Jock only hopping more frantically than ever round the poor man the hired waiter, who, you must know, is the undertaker's chief mute, and singing—

> " Leedle, leedle, leedle
> Our cat's dead.
> What did she die wi' ?
> Wi' a sair head.
> A' you that kenned her
> While she was alive,
> Come to her burying
> At half-past five."

And then the Colonel, bestirring himself to the rescue, with "Go away, boys, or I'll send for the police." And then the discovery, when in the height of his wrath, Jock perked up, and said, "I thought you would like to have the ladies amused, Uncle Robert." He did box his ears then—small blame to him, I must say. I could stand that better than the jaw Ellen gave us afterwards. I beg your pardon, Mary, but it really was one. She thinks us far gone in the ways of depravity, and doesn't willingly let her little girls come near us.'

'Isn't that a pity?'

'I don't know ; Essie and Ellie have feelings in their clothes, and don't like our scrambling walks, and if Ellie does get allured by our wicked ways, she is sure to be torn, or splashed, or something, and we have shrieks and lamentations, and accusations of Jock and Joe, amid floods of tears ; and Jessie comes to the rescue, primly shaking her head and coaxing her little sister, while she brings out a needle and thread. I can't help it, Mary. It does aggravate me to look at her !'

Mary could only shake her head with a mixture of pity, reproof, and amusement, and as a safer subject could not help asking—

'By the by, why do you confuse your friends by having all the two families named in pairs?'

'We didn't know we were going to live close together,' said Carey. 'But the fact is that the Janets were named after their fathers' only sister, who seems to have been an equal darling to both. We would have avoided Robert, but we found that it would have been thought disrespectful not to call the boy after his grandfather and uncle.'

'And Bobus is a thoroughly individual name.'

'Then Jock's name is John Lucas, and we did mean to call him by the second, but it wouldn't stick. Names won't sometimes, and there's a formality in Lucas that would never fit that skipjack of a boy. He got called Jock as a nickname, and now he will abide by it. But Joseph Armine's second name does fit him, and so we have kept to it ; and Barbara was dear grandmamma's own name, and quite our own.'

Therewith Babie rushed downstairs with 'He's coming,

Mother Carey,' and darted out at the house door to welcome Mr. Ogilvie at the gate, and lead him in in triumph, attended by her two brothers. The two ladies laughed, and Carey said, with a species of proud apology—

'Poor children, you see they have been used to be noticed by clever men.'

'Mr. Ogilvie is come to see our museum,' cried Babie in her patronising tone, jumping and dancing round during his greetings and remarks that he hoped he might take advantage of her invitation; he had been thinking whether to begin a school museum would not be a very good thing for the boys, and serve to open their minds to common things. On which, before any one else could answer, the parrot, in a low and sententious tone, observed, 'Excellent.'

'There, you have the consent of your first acquaintance,' said Carey, while the bird, excited by one of those mysterious likings that her kind are apt to take, held her gray head to Mr. Ogilvie to be scratched, chuckling out, 'All Mother Carey's chickens;' and Janet exclaimed—

'That's an adoption.'

The troop were climbing the stairs to the third story, where Armine and Bobus were already within an octagon room, corresponding to the little hall below, and fitted with presses and shelves, belonging to the store-room of the former thrifty inhabitant; but now divided between the six children, Mother Carey, as Babie explained, being 'Mine own, and helping me more specially.'

The table was likewise common to all; but one of the laws of the place was that everything left there after twelve o'clock on Saturday was, as Babie's little mouth rolled out the long words, 'confiscated by the inexorable Eumenides.'

'And who are they?' asked Mr. Ogilvie, who was always much entertained by the simplicity with which the little maid uttered the syllables as if they were her native speech.

'Janet, and Nurse, and Emma,' she said; 'and they really are inex-ō-rable. They threw away my snail shell that a thrush had been eating, though I begged and prayed them.'

'Yes, and my femur of a rabbit,' said Armine, 'and said it was a nasty old bone, and the baker's Pincher ate it up; but I did find my turtle-dove's egg in the ash-heap, and discovered it over again, and you don't see it is broken now; it is stuck down on a card.'

'Yes,' said his mother, 'it is wonderful how valuable things become precisely at twelve on Saturday.'

Each had some department: Janet's, which was geology, was the fullest, as she had inherited some youthful hoards of her father's; Bobus's, which was botany, was the neatest and most systematic. Mary thought at first that it did not suit him; but she soon saw that with him it was not love of flowers, but the

study of botany. He pronounced Jock's butterflies to be perfectly disgraceful.

'You said you'd see to them,' returned Jock.

'Yes, I shall take up insects when I have done with plants,'
said Bobus coolly.

'And say, "Solomon, I have surpassed thee?"' asked Mr.
Ogilvie.

Bobus looked as if he did not like it; but his mother shook
her head at him as one who well deserved the little rebuke for
self-sufficiency. There was certainly a wonderful winning way
about her—there was a simplicity of manner almost like that of
Babie herself, and yet the cleverness of a highly-educated
woman. Mary Ogilvie did not wonder at what Mr. and Mrs.
Acton had said of the charm of that unpretending household,
now broken up.

There was, too, the perception that, beneath the surface on
which, like the children, she played so lightly, there were depths
of sorrow that might not be stirred, which added a sweetness
and pathos to all she said and did.

Of many a choice curiosity the children said, in lowered tones
of reverence, that '*he* found it'; and these she would not allow
to be passed over, but showed fondly off in all their best points,
telling their story as if she loved to dwell upon it.

Barbara, who had specially fastened herself on Mr. Ogilvie,
according to the modern privileges of small girls, after having
much amused him by doing the honours of her own miscellaneous treasury, insisted on exhibiting 'Mother Carey's studio.'

Caroline tried to declare that this meant nothing deserving
of so grand a name; it was only the family resort for making
messes in. She never touched clay now, and there was nothing
worth seeing; but it was in vain; Babie had her way; and
they mounted to the highest stage of the Pagoda, where the
eaves and the twisted monsters that supported them were in
close juxtaposition with the four windows.

The view was a grand one. Belforest Park on the one side,
the town almost as if in a pit below, with a bird's-eye prospect
of the roofs, the gardens and the schoolyard, the leaden-covered
church, lying like a great gray beetle with outspread wings.
Beyond were the ups-and-downs of a wooded, hilly country, with
glimpses of blue river here and there, and village and town
gleaming out white; a large house, 'bosomed high in tufted
trees'; a church-tower and spire, nestled on the hillside, up to
the steep gray hill with the tall land-mark tower, closing in the
horizon—altogether, as Carey said, a thorough 'allegro' landscape, even to 'the tanned haycock in the mead.' But the
summer sun made the place dazzling and almost uninhabitable,
and the visitors, turning from the glare, could hardly see the
casts and models that filled the shelves; nor was there anything
in hand; so that they let themselves be hurried away to share
the mid-day meal, after which Mr. Ogilvie and the boys betook

themselves to the school, and Carey and her little ones to the shade of the garden-wall, to finish their French reading, while Mary wondered the less at the Kenminster ladies.

## CHAPTER IX

### FLIGHTS

'Have you no wit, manners, nor honesty, but to gabble like tinkers at this time of night? Is there no respect of place, persons, nor time in you?'—*Twelfth-Night.*

THE summer holidays not only brought home Allen Brownlow from Eton, but renewed his mother's intercourse with several of her friends, who so contrived their summer outing as to 'see how poor little Mrs. Brownlow was getting on,' and she hailed them as fragments of her dear old former life.

Mr. and Mrs. Acton came to a farmhouse at Redford, about a mile and a half off, where Mr. Acton was to lay up a store of woodland and home sketches, and there were daily meetings for walks, and often out-of-door meals. Mr. Ogilvie declared that he was thus much more rested than by a long expedition in foreign scenery, and he and his sister stayed on, and usually joined in the excursion, whether it were premeditated or improvised, on foot into copse or glade, or by train or waggonette to ruined abbey or cathedral town.

Then came two sisters, whom old Mrs. Brownlow had befriended when the elder was struggling, as a daily governess, to provide home and education for the younger. Now, the one was a worthy, hard-working law-copier, the other an artist in a small way, who had transmogrified her name of Jane into Juanita or Nita, wore a crop, short petticoats, and was odd. She treated Janet on terms of equal friendship, and was thus a much more charming companion than Jessie. They always came into cheap seaside lodgings in the vacation, but this year had settled themselves within ten minutes' walk of the Folly, a title which became more and more applicable, in Kenminster eyes, to the Pagoda, and above all in those of its proper owner. Mrs. Robert Brownlow, in the calm dignity of the heiress, in a small way, of a good family, had a bare toleration for professional people, had regretted the vocation of her brother-in-law, and classed governesses and artists as 'that kind of people,' so that Caroline's association with them seemed to her absolute love of low company. She would have stirred up her husband to remonstrate, but he had seen more of the world than she had, and declared that there was no harm in Caroline's friends. 'He had met Mr. Acton in the reading-room, smoked pipes with him in the garden, and thought him a very nice fellow; his wife was the daughter of poor Cartwright of the Artillery, and a sensible ladylike woman as ever he saw.'

With a resigned sigh at the folly of mankind, his wife asked, 'How about the others? That woman with the hair? and that man with the velvet coat? Jessie says Jock told her that he was a mere play-actor!'

'Jock told Jessie! Nonsense, my dear! The man is going out to China in the tea trade, and is come to take leave. I believe he did sing in public at one time; but Joe attended him in an illness which damaged his voice, and then he put him in the way of other work. You need not be afraid. Joe was one of the most particular men in the world in his own way.'

Mrs. Brownlow could do no more. She had found that her little sister-in-law could be saucy, and personal squabbles, as she justly thought, had better be avoided. She could only keep Jessie from the contamination by taking her out in the carriage and to garden parties, which the young lady infinitely preferred to long walks that tired her and spoilt her dress; to talk and laughter that she could not understand, and games that seemed to her stupid, though everybody else seemed to find them full of fun. True, Allen and Bobus were always ready to push and pull her through, and to snub Janet for quizzing her; but Jessie was pretty enough to have plenty of such homage at her command, and not specially to prefer that of her cousins, so that it cost her little to turn a deaf ear to all their invitations.

Her brothers were not of the same mind, for Rob was never happy out of sight of Jock. Johnnie worshipped his aunt, and Joe was gregarious, so there was generally an accompanying rabble of six or seven boys, undistinguishable by outsiders, though very individual indeed in themselves, and adding a considerable element of noise, high spirits, and mischievous enterprise. The man in the velvet coat, whose proper name was Orlando Hughes, was as much of a boy as any of them, and so could Mr. Acton be on occasion, thus giving a certain Bohemian air to their doings.

Things came to a crisis on one of the dog-days. Young Dr. Drake had brought his bride to show to his old friend, and they were staying at the Folly, while a college friend of Mr. Ogilvie's, a London curate, had come to see him in the course of a cathedral tour, and had stayed on, under the attraction of the place, taking the duty for a few Sundays.

The weather was very sultry, forbidding exertion on the part of all save cricketers; but there was a match at Redford, and Kenminster was eager about it, so that all the boys, grown up or otherwise, walked over to see it, accompanied by Nita Ray with her inseparable Janet, meaning to study village groups and rustic sports. The other ladies walked in the cool to meet them at the Actons' farmhouse, chiefly, it was alleged, in deference to the feelings of the bride, who could not brave the heat, but had never yet been so long separated from her bridegroom.

The little boys, however, were alone to be found at the farm, reporting that their elders had joined the cricket supper. So Mrs. Acton made them welcome, and spread her cloth in the greensward, whence could be seen the evening glow on the harvest fields. Then there was a feast of cherries, and delicious farmhouse bread and butter, and inexhaustible tea, which was renewed when the cricketers joined them, and called for their share.

Thus they did not set out on their homeward walk, over fragrant heath and dewy lanes, till just as the stars were coming out, and a magnificent red moon, scarcely past the full, was rising in the east, and the long rest, and fresh dewiness after the day's heat, gave a delightful feeling of exhilaration.

Babie went skipping about in the silvery flood of light, quite wild with delight as they came out on the heath, and, darting up to Mr. Ogilvie, asked if now he did not think they might really see a fairy.

'Perhaps I do,' he said.

'Oh where, where, show me?'

'Ah! you're the one that can't see her.'

'What, not if I did my eyes with that Euphrasia and Verbena officinalis?' catching tight hold of his hand, as a bright red light went rapidly moving in a straight line in the valley beneath their feet.

'Robin Goodfellow,' said Mr. Hughes, overhearing her, and immediately began to sing—

'I know a bank——'

Then the curate, as he finished, began to sing some other appropriate song, and Nita Ray and others joined in. It was very pretty, very charming in the moonlight, very like *Midsummer Night's Dream;* but Mary Ogilvie, who was a good way behind, felt a start of dismay as the clear notes pealed back to her. She longed to suggest a little expediency; but she was impeded; for poor Miss Ray, entirely unused to long country walks and nocturnal expeditions, and further tormented by tight boots, was panting up the hill far in the rear, half-frightened, and a good deal distressed, and could not, for very humanity's sake, be left behind.

'And after all,' thought Mary, as peals of the boys' merry laughter came to her, and then again echoes of 'spotted snakes with double tongue' awoke the night echoes, 'this is such a solitary place that it cannot signify, if they will only have the sense to stop when we get into the roads.'

But they hadn't. Mary heard a chorus from *Der Freischütz* beginning just as she was dragging her companion over a stile, which had been formidable enough by day, but was ten times worse in the confusing shadows. That brought them into a lane darkened by its high hedges, where there was nothing for it but to let Miss Ray tightly grapple her arm, while the songs

came farther and farther on the wind, and Mary felt the conviction that middle-aged spinsters must reckon on being forgotten, and left behind alike by brothers, sisters, and friends.

Nor did they come up with the party till they found them
waiting in the road, close to the Rays' lodgings, having evidently
just missed them, for Mr. Ogilvie and the clergyman were turning back to look for them when they were gladly hailed, half
apologised to, half laughed at by a babel of voices, among which
Nita's was the loudest, informing her sister that she had lost the
best bit of all, for just at the turn of the lane there had come
on them Babie's fiery-eyed monster, which had 'burst on the
path,' when they were in mid song, flashing over them, and
revealing, first a horse, and then a brougham, wherein there sat
the august forms of Colonel and Mrs. Brownlow, going home
from a state dinner, the lady's very marabouts quivering with
horror.

Mary stepped up to Nita, and gave her a sharp, severe
grasp.

'Hush! remember their boys are here,' she whispered; and,
with an exaggerated gesture, Nita looked about her in affected
alarm, and, seeing that none were near, added—

'Thank you; I was just going to say it would be a study for
*Punch.*'

'O do send it up, they'll never know it,' cried Janet; but
there Caroline interfered—

'Hush, Janet, we ought to be at home. Don't stand here,
Armine is tired to death! 11.5 at the station to-morrow.
Good-night.'

They parted, and Mary and her brother turned away to their
own home. If it had not been for the presence of the curate, Mary
would have said a good deal on the way home. As it was, she
was so silent as to inspire her brother with enough compunction
for having deserted her, to make him follow her, when she went
to her own room. 'Mary, I am sorry we missed you,' he said;
'I ought to have looked about for you more, but I thought——'

'Nonsense, David; of course I do not mind that, if only I
could have stopped all that singing.'

'That singing; why it was very pretty, wasn't it?'

'Pretty indeed! Did it never occur to you what a scrape
you may be getting that poor little thing into with her relations,
and yourself too?'

David looked more than half-amused, and she proceeded more
resolutely—

'Well! what do you think must be Mrs. Brownlow's opinion
of what she saw and heard to-night? I blame myself exceedingly for not having urged the setting off sooner; but you must
remember that what is all very well for holiday people, only
here for a time, may do infinite mischief to residents.'

David only observed, 'I didn't want all those men, if that's
what you mean. They made the noise, not I.'

'No, nor I ; but we swelled the party, and I am much disposed to believe that the best thing we can do is to take ourselves off, or do anything to break up this set.'

He looked for a moment much disconcerted ; but then with a little masculine superiority, answered—

'Well, well, we'll think over it, Mary. See how it appears to you to-morrow when you aren't tired,' and then, with a smile and a kiss, bade her good-night.

'So that's what we get,' said Mary to herself, half amused, half annoyed ; 'those men think it is all because one is left behind in the dark ! David is the best boy in the world, but there's not a man of them all who has a notion of what gets a woman into trouble ! I believe he was rather gratified than otherwise to be found out on a lark. Well, I'll talk to Clara ; she will have some sense !'

They were all to meet at the station the next morning, to go to an old castle, about an hour from Kenminster by railway ; and they filled the platform, armed with sketching tools, sandwich baskets, botanical tins, and all other appliances ; but when Mr. Ogilvie accosted Mrs. Joseph Brownlow, saying, 'You have only half your boys,' she looked up, with a drolly guilty air, saying, 'No, there's an embargo on the other poor fellows.'

They had just taken their seats, and the train was in motion, when a heated headlong boy came dashing over the platform, and clung to the door of the carriage, standing on the step. It was Johnnie. Orlando Hughes, who was next the window, grasped his hands, and, in answer to the cries of dismay and blame that greeted him, he called out, 'Yes, here I am ; Rob and Joe couldn't run so fast.'

'Then you've got leave ?' asked his aunt.

Johnnie's grin said 'No.'

She looked up at Mr. Ogilvie in much vexation and anxiety.

'Don't say any more to him now. It might put him in great danger. Wait till the next station,' he said.

It was a stopping train, and ten minutes brought a halt, when the guard came up in a fury, and Johnnie found no sympathy for his bold attempt. Carey had no notion of fostering flat disobedience, and she told Johnnie that unless he would promise to go home by himself and beg his father's pardon, she should stay behind and go back with him, for she could have no pleasure in an expedition with him when he was behaving so outrageously.

The boy looked both surprised and abashed. His affection for his aunt was very great, as for one who had opened to him the gates of a new world, both within himself and beyond himself. He would not hear of her giving up the expedition, and promised her with all his heart to walk home, and confess, 'Though 'twasn't papa, but mamma !' were his last words, as they left him on the platform, crestfallen, but with a twinkle in his eye, and with the stationmaster keeping watch over him as a dangerous subject.

Mr. Ogilvie said it would do the boy good for life ; Caroline mourned over him a little, and wondered how his mother would treat him ; and Mary sat and thought till the arrival at their destination, when they had to walk to the castle, dragging their appurtenances, and then to rouse their energies to spread out the luncheon.

Then, when there had been the usual amount of mirth, mischief, and mishap, and the party had dispersed, some to sketch, some to scramble, some to botanise, the 'Duck and Drake to spoon'—as said the boys, Mary Ogilvie found a turfy nook where she could hold counsel with Mrs. Acton about their poor little friend, for whose welfare she was seriously uneasy.

But Clara did not sympathise as much as she expected, having been much galled by Mrs. Robert Brownlow's supercilious manner, and thinking the attempt to conciliate her both unworthy and useless.

'Of course I do not mean that poor Carey should truckle to her,' said Mary, rather nettled at the implication ; 'but I don't think these irregular hours, and all this roaming about the country at all times, can be well in themselves for her or the children.'

'My dear Mary, did you never take a party of children into the country in the spring for the first time ? If not, you never saw the prettiest and most innocent of intoxications. I had once to take the little Pyrtons to their place in the country one April and May, months that they had always spent in London ; and I assure you they were perfectly mad, only with the air, the sight of the hawthorns, and all the smells. I was obliged to be content with what they *could* do, not what ought to be done, of lessons. There was no sitting still on a fine morning. I was as bad myself; the blood seemed to dance in one's veins, and a room to be a prison.'

'This is not spring,' said Mary.

'No, but she began in spring, and habits were formed.'

'No doubt, but they cannot be good. They keep up flightiness and excitability.'

'Oh, that's grief, poor dear !'

'We bain't carousing, we be dissembling grief, as the farmer told the clergyman who objected to merry-making after a funeral,' said Mary, rather severely. Then she added, seeing Clara looked annoyed, 'You think me hard on poor dear Carey, but indeed I am not doubting her affection or her grief.'

'Remember, a woman with children cannot give herself entirely up to sorrow without doing them harm.'

'Poor Carey, I am sure I do not want to see her given up to sorrow, only to have her a little more moderate, and perhaps select—so as not to do herself harm with her relations—who, after all, must be more important to her than any outsiders.'

The **artist's wife** could not but see things a little differently from the schoolmaster's sister, who **moreover** knew nothing of Carey's former life ; and Clara made answer—

'Sending her down to these **people** was the greatest error of dear good Dr. Brownlow's life.'

'I am not sure of that. **Blood is thicker than water.'**

'But between sisters-in-law it is apt to be only ill-blood, and very turbid.'

'For shame, Clara.'

'Well, Mary, you **must allow** something for human **nature's** reluctance to be **treated as** something not quite **worthy of a** handshake from **a little** country town Serene Highness ! I may be allowed to **doubt** whether Dr. Brownlow would **not have** done better **to leave her** unbound to those who **can never be** congenial.'

'Granting that (not that I do grant it, for the Colonel is worthy), should not she be persuaded to conform herself?'

'To purr and lay eggs ? My dear, that did not succeed with the ugly duckling, even in early life.'

'Not after it had been among the swans ? You vain Clara !'

'I only lay claim to having seen the swans—not to having brought many specimens down here.'

'Such as *that* Nita, or Mr. Hughes?'

'More like the other bird, certainly,' said Clara, smiling ; 'but Mary, if you had but seen what that house was. Joe Brownlow was one of those men who make themselves esteemed and noted above their actual position. He was much thought of as a lecturer, and would have had a much larger practice but for his appointment at the hospital. It was in the course of the work he had taken for a friend gone out of town that he caught the illness that killed him. His lectures brought men of science about him, and his practice had made him acquainted with us poor Bohemians, as you seem to think us. Old Mrs. Brownlow had means of her own, and theirs was quite a wealthy house among our set. Any of us were welcome to drop into five o'clock tea, or at nine at night, and the pleasantness and good influence were wonderful. The motherliness and yet the enthusiasm of Mrs. Brownlow made her the most delightful old lady I ever saw. I can't describe how good she was about my marriage, and many more would say they owed all that was brightest and best in them to that house. And there was Carey, like a little sunshiny fairy, the darling of every one. No, not spoilt—I see what you are going to say.'

'Only as we all spoilt her at school. Nobody but her Serene Highness ever could help making a pet of her.'

'That's more reasonable, Mary,' said Mrs. Acton, in a more placable voice ; 'she did plenty of hard work, and did not spare herself, or have what would seem indulgences to most women ; but nobody could see the light of her eyes and smile without trying to make it sparkle up ; and she was just the first thought

in life to her husband and his mother. I am sure in my governess days I used to think that house paradise, and her the undoubted queen of it. And now, that *you* should turn against
her, Mary, when she is uncrowned, and unappreciated, and
browbeaten.'

She had worked herself up, and had tears in her eyes.

Mary laughed a little.

'It is hard, when I only want to keep her from making herself be unappreciated.'

'And I say it is in vain!' cried Clara; 'for it is not in the
nature of the people to appreciate her, and nothing will make
them get on together'

Poor Mary! she had expected her friend to be more reasonable and less defensive; but she remembered that even at school
Clara had always protected Caroline whenever she had attempted
to lecture her. All she further tried to say was—

'Then you won't help me to advise her to be more guarded,
and not shock them?'

'I will not tease the poor little thing, when she has enough
to torment her already. If you had known her husband, and
watched her last winter, you would be only too thankful to see
her a little more like herself.'

Mary was silent, finding that she should only argue round and
round if they went on, and feeling that Clara thought her old-
maidish, and could not enter into her sense that, the balance-
weight being gone, gusts of wind ought to be avoided. She sat
wondering whether she herself was prim and old-maidish, or
whether she was right in feeling it a duty to expostulate and
deliver her testimony.

There was no doing it on this day. Carey was always surrounded by children and guests, and in an eager state of
activity; but though again they all went home in the cool of
the evening, an attempt to sing in the second-class carriage,
which they filled entirely, was quashed immediately—no one
knew how, and nothing worse happened than that a very dusty
set, carrying odd botanical, entomological, and artistic wares,
trailed through the streets of Kenminster, just as Mrs. Coffinkey, escorted by her maid, was walking primly home from
drinking tea at the vicarage.

Still Mary's reflections only strengthened her resolution. On
the next day, which was Sunday, she ascended to the Folly at
about four o'clock in the afternoon, and found the family,
including the parrot, spread out upon the lawn under the shade
of the acacia, the mother reading to them.

'Oh, please don't stop, mother,' cried Babie; while the more
courteous Armine exclaimed—

'Miss Ogilvie, don't you like to hear about Bevis and Jocelin
Joliffe?'

'You don't mind waiting while we finish the chapter,' added
their mother; 'then we break up our sitting.'

'Pray go on with the chapter,' said Mary, rather coolly, for she was a good deal taken aback at finding them reading *Woodstock* on a Sunday ; 'but afterwards, I do want to speak to you.'

'Oh ! don't want to speak to me. The Colonel has been speaking to me,' she said, with a cowering, shuddering sort of action, irresistibly comic.

'And he ate up half our day,' bemoaned more than one of the boys.

Miss Ogilvie sat down a little way off, not wishing to listen to *Woodstock* on a Sunday, and trying to work out the difficult Sabbatarian question in her mind.

'There !' said Caroline, closing the book, amid exclamations of 'I know who Lewis Kerneguy was.' 'Wasn't Roger Wildrake jolly ?' 'O mother, didn't he cut off Trusty Tomkins' head ?' 'Do let us have a wee bit more, mother ; Miss Ogilvie won't mind.'

But Carey saw that she did mind, and answered—

'Not now ; there won't be time to feed all the creatures, or to get nurse's Sunday nosegays, if you don't begin.' Then, coming up to her guest, she said, 'Now is your time, Mary ; we shall have the Rays and Mr. Hughes in presently ; but you see we are too worldly and profane for the Kencroft boys on Sunday ; and so they make experiments in smoking, with company less desirable, I must say, than Sir Harry Lee's. Am I very bad to read what keeps mine round me ?'

'Is it an old fashion with you ?'

'Well, no ; but then we had what was better than a thousand stories ! And this is only a feeble attempt to keep up a little watery reflection of the old sunshine.'

It was a watery reflection indeed !

'And could it not be with something that would be——'

'Dull and goody ?' put in Carey. 'No, no, my dear, that would be utterly futile. You can't catch my birds without salt. Can we, Polly ?'

To which the popinjay responded, 'We are all Mother Carey's chickens.'

'I did mean salt—very real salt,' said Mary, rather sadly.

'I have not got the recipe,' said Carey. 'Indeed I do try to do what must be done. My boys can hold their own in Bible and Catechism questions ! Ask your brother if they can't. And Armie is a dear little fellow, with a bit of the angel, or of his father, in him ; but when we've done our church, I see no good in decorous boredom ; and if I did, what would become of the boys ?'

'I don't agree to the necessity of boredom,' said Mary ; 'but let that pass. There are things I wanted to say.'

'I knew it was coming. The Colonel has been at me already, levelling his thunders at my devoted head. Won't that do ?'

'Not if you heed him so little.'

'My dear, if I heeded, I should be annihilated. When he

G

says "My good little sister," I know he means "You little idiot;"
so if I did not think of something else, what might not be the
consequence? Why, he said I was not behaving decently!'

'No more you are.'

'And that I had no proper feeling,' continued she, laughing
almost hysterically.

'No one can wonder at his being pained. It ought never to
have happened.'

'Are you gone over to Mrs. Grundy? However, there's this
comfort, you'll not mention Mrs. Coffinkey's sister-in-law.'

'I'm sure the Colonel didn't!'

'Ellen does though, with tragic effect.'

'You are not like yourself, Carey.'

'No, indeed I'm not! I was a happy creature a little while
ago; or was it a very long, long time ago? Then I had everybody to help me and make much of me! And now I've got into
a great dull mist, and am always knocking my head against
something or somebody; and when I try to keep up the old
friendships and kindnesses—poor little fragments as they are—
everybody falls upon me, even you, Mary.'

'Pardon me, dearest. Some friendships and kindnesses that
were once admirable, may be less suitable to your present circumstances.'

'As if I didn't know that!' said Carey, with an angry, hurt
little laugh; 'and so I waited to be chaperoned up to the eyes
between Clara Acton and the Duck in the very house with me.
Now, Mary, I put it to you. Has one word passed that could
do harm? Isn't it much more innocent than all the Coffinkey
gossip? I have no doubt Mrs. Coffinkey's sister-in-law looks up
from her black-bordered pocket-handkerchief to hear how Mrs.
Brownlow's sister-in-law went to the cricket-match. Do you
know, Robert really thought I had been there? I only wonder
how many I scored. I dare say Mrs. Coffinkey's sister-in-law
knows.'

'It just shows how careful you should be.'

'And I wonder what would become of the children if I shut
myself up with a pile of pocket-handkerchiefs bordered an inch
deep. What right have they to meddle with my ways, and my
friends, and my boys?'

'Not the Coffinkeys, certainly,' said Mary; 'but indeed,
Carey, I myself was uncomfortable at that singing in the lanes
at eleven at night.'

'It wasn't eleven,' said Carey perversely.

'Only 10.50—eh?'

'But what was the possible harm in it?'

'None at all in itself, only remember the harm it may do to
the children for you to be heedless of people's opinion, and to
get a reputation for flightiness and doing odd things.'

'I couldn't be like the Coffinkey pattern any more than I
could be tied down to a rope walk.'

'But you need not do things that your better sense must tell you may be misconstrued. Surely there was a wish that you should live near the Colonel and be guided by him.'

'Little knowing that his guidance would consist in being set at me by Ellen and the Coffinkeys!'

'Nonsense,' said Mary, vexed enough to resume their old schoolgirl manners. 'You *know* I am not set on by anybody, and I tell you that if you do not pull up in time, and give no foundation for ill-natured comments, your children will never get over it in people's estimation. And as for themselves, a little steadiness and regularity would be much better for their whole dispositions.'

'It is holiday time,' said Carey in a tone of apology.

'If it is only in holiday time——'

'The country has always seemed like holiday. You see we used to go—all of us—to some seaside place, and be quite free there, keeping no particular hours, and being so intensely happy. I haven't yet got over the feeling that it is only for a time, and we shall go back into the dear old home and its regular ways.' Then clasping her hands over her side as though to squeeze something back, she broke out, 'O Mary, Mary, you mustn't scold me! You mustn't bid me tie myself to regular hours till this summer is over. If you knew the intolerable stab when I recollect that he is gone—gone—gone for ever, you would understand that there's nothing for it but jumping up and doing the first thing that comes to hand. Walking it down is best. Oh! what will become of me when the mornings get dark, and I can't get up and rush into those woods? Yes'—as Mary made some affectionate gesture—'I know I have gone on in a wild way, but who would not be wild who had lost *him?* And then they goad me, and think me incapable of proper feeling,' and she laughed that horrid little laugh. 'So I am, I suppose; but feeling won't go as other people think *proper*. Let me alone, Mary, I won't damage the children. They are Joe's children, and I know what he wanted and wished for them better than Robert or anybody else. But I must go my own way, and do what I can bear, and as I can, or—or I think my heart would break quite, and that would be worse for them than anything.'

Mary had tears in her eyes, drawn forth by the vehement passion of grief apparent in the whole tone of her poor little friend. She had no doubts of Carey's love, sorrow, or ability, but she did seriously doubt of her wisdom and judgment, and thought her undisciplined. However, she could say no more, for Nita Ray and Janet were advancing on them.

The next day Caroline was in bed with one of her worst headaches. Mary felt that she had been a cruel and prim old duenna, and meekly bore Clara's reproachful glances.

# CHAPTER X

### ELLEN'S MAGNUM BONUMS

'He put in his thumb
And he pulled out a plum,
And cried, " What a good boy am I ! " '

*Jack Horner.*

WHETHER it were from the effects of the warnings, or from that of native good sense, from that time forward Mrs. Joseph Brownlow sobered down, and became less distressing to her sister-in-law. Mary carried off her brother to Wales, and the Acton and Ray party dispersed, while Dr. and Mrs. Lucas came for a week, giving much relief to Mrs. Brownlow, who could discuss the family affairs with them in a manner she deemed unbecoming with Mrs. Acton or Miss Ogilvie. Had Caroline heard the consultation, she would have acquitted Ellen of malice ; and indeed her Serene Highness was much too good to gossip about so near a connection, and had only confided her wonder and perplexity at the strange phenomenon to her favourite first cousin, who unfortunately was not equally discreet.

With the end of the holidays finished also the trying series of first anniversaries, and their first excitements of sorrow, so that it became possible to be more calm and quiet.

Moreover, two correctives came of themselves to Caroline. The first was Janet's inordinate correspondence with Nita Ray, and the discovery that the girl held herself engaged to stay with the sisters in November.

'Without asking me !' she exclaimed, aghast.

'I thought you heard us talking,' said Janet, so carelessly that her mother put on her dignity.

'I certainly had no conception of an invitation being given and accepted without reference to me.'

'Come now, Mother Carey,' said this modern daughter, 'don't be cross ! We really didn't know you weren't attending.'

'If I had I should have said it was impossible, as I say now. You can never have thought over the matter !'

'Haven't I? When I am doing no good here, only wasting time ?'

'That is my fault. We will set to work at once steadily.'

'But my classes and my lectures !'

'You are not so far on but that our reading together will teach you quite as much as lectures.'

Janet looked both sulky and scornful, and her mother continued—

'It is not as if we had not modern books, and I think I know how to read them so as to be useful to you.'

'I don't like getting behindhand with the world.'

'You can't keep up even with the world without a sound foundation. Besides, even if it were more desirable, the Rays cannot afford to keep you, nor I to board you there.'

'I am to pay them by helping Miss Ray in her copying.'

'Poor Miss Ray!' exclaimed Carey, laughing. 'Does she know your handwriting?'

'You do not know what I can do,' said Janet, with dignity.

'Yes, I hope to see it for myself, for you must put this notion of going to London out of your head. I am sure Miss Ray did not give the invitation—no, nor second it. Did she, Janet?'

Janet blushed a little, and muttered something about Miss Ray being afraid of stuck-up people.

'I thought so! She is a good, sensible person, whom grand-mamma esteemed very much; but she has never been able to keep her sister in order; and as to trusting you to their care, or letting you live in their set, neither papa nor grandmamma would ever have thought of it.'

'You only say so because her Serene Highness turns up her nose at everything artistic and original.'

'Janet, you forget yourself,' Caroline exclaimed, in a tone which quelled the girl, who went muttering away; and no more was ever heard of the Ray proposal, which no doubt the elder sister at least had never regarded as anything but an airy castle.

However, Caroline was convinced that the warnings against the intimacy had not been so uncalled for as she had believed; for she found, when she tried to tighten the reins, that her daughter was restive, and had come to think herself a free agent, as good as grown up. Spirit was not, however, lacking to Caroline, and when she had roused herself, she made Janet understand that she was not to be disregarded or disobeyed. Regular hours were instituted, and the difficulty of getting broken into them again was sufficient proof to her that she had done wrong in neglecting them. Armine yawned portentously, and declared that he could not learn except at his own times; and Babie was absolutely naughty more than once, when her mother suffered doubly in punishing her from the knowledge of whose fault it was. However, they were good little things, and it was not hard to re-establish discipline with them. After a little breaking in, Babie gave it to her dolls as her deliberate opinion that 'Wegulawity settles one's mind. One knows when to do what.'

Janet could not well complain of the regularity in itself, though she did cavil at the actual arrangements, and they were altered all round to please her, and she showed a certain con-tempt for her teacher in the studies she resumed with her mother; but after the dictionary, encyclopædia, and other authorities, including Mr. Ogilvie, proved almost uniformly to be against her whenever there was a difference of opinion, she had sense enough to perceive that she could still learn something at home.

Moreover, after one or two of these references, Mr. Ogilvie offered to look over her Latin and Greek exercises, and hear her construe on his Saturday half-holidays, declaring that it would be quite a refreshment. Caroline was shocked at the sacrifice, but she could not bear to affront her daughter, so she consented; but as she thought Janet was not old enough to need a *chaperon*, and as her boys did want her, she was hardly ever present at the lessons.

Moreover, Mr. Ogilvie had a lecturer from London to give weekly lectures on physical science to his boys, and opened the doors to ladies. This was a great satisfaction, chiefly for the sake of Bobus and Jock, but also for Janet's and her mother's. The difficulty was to beat up for ladies enough to keep one another in countenance; but happily two families in the country, and one bright little bride in the town, were found glad to open their ears, so that Ellen had no just cause of disapproval of the attendance of her sister and niece.

Ellen had more cause to sigh when Michaelmas came, and for the first time taught poor Carey what money matters really meant. Throughout her married life, her only stewardship had concerned her own dress and the children's; Mrs. Brownlow's occasional plans of teaching her housekeeping had always fallen through, Janet being always her grandmamma's deputy.

Thus Janet and nurse had succeeded to the management when poor Carey was too ill and wretched to attend to it; and it had gone on in their hands at the Pagoda. Janet was pleased to be respected accordingly by her aunt, who always liked her the best, in spite of her much worse behaviour, for were not her virtues her own, and her vices her mother's?

Caroline had paid the weekly books, and asked no questions, until the winding up of the executor's business; and the quarterly settlement of accounts made startling revelations that the balance at her bankers was just eleven shillings and fourpence halfpenny, and what was nearly as bad, the discovery was made in the presence of her fellow-executor, who could not help giving a low whistle. She turned pale, and gasped for breath, in absolute amazement, for she was quite sure they were living at much less expense than in London, and there had been no outgoings worth mentioning for dress or journeys. What were they to do? Surely they could not live upon less! Was it her fault?

She was so much distressed, that the good-natured Colonel pitied her, and answered kindly—

'My good little sister, you were inexperienced. You will do better another year.'

'But there's nothing to go on upon!'

He reminded her of the rent for the London house, and the dividends that must soon come in.

'Then it will be as bad as ever! How can we live more cheaply than we do?'

'Ellen is an excellent manager, and you had better consult her on the scale of your expenditure.'

Caroline's spirit writhed, but before she had time to say anything, or talk to Janet, the Colonel had heard his excellent housewife's voice, and called her into the council. She was as good as possible, too serenely kind to manifest surprise or elation at the fulfilment of her forebodings. To be convicted of want of economy would have been so dreadful and disgraceful that she deeply felt for poor Caroline, and dealt with her tenderly and delicately, even when the weekly household books were opened, and disclosed how much had been spent every week in items, the head and front of which were oft repeated in old nurse's self-taught writing—

| | | | | | | | | |
|---|---|---|---|---|---|---|---|---|
| 'Man | . | . | . | . | . | Glas of beare. | | 1d. |
| Creme | . | . | . | . | . | . | . | 3d.' |

For had not the Colonel's wife warned against the endless hospitality of glasses of beer to all messengers ; and had not unlimited cream with strawberries and apple tarts been treated as a kind of spontaneous luxury produced at the Belforest farm agent's? To these, and many other small matters, Caroline was quite relieved to plead guilty, and to promise to do her best by personal supervision ; and Ellen set herself to devise further ways of reduction, not realising how hopeless it is to prescribe for another person's household difficulties. It is not in the nature of things that such advice should be palatable, and the proverb about the pinching of the shoe is sure to be realised.

'Too many servants,' said prudence. 'If old nurse must be provided for—and she ought to have saved enough to do without—it would be much better to pension her off, or get her into an almshouse.'

Caroline tried to endure, as she made known that she viewed nurse as a sacred charge, about whom there must be no question.

Ellen quietly said—

'Then it is no use to argue, but she must be allowed no more discretion in the housekeeping.'

'No, I shall do that myself,' said Caroline.

'An extravagant cook.'

'That may be my fault. I will try to judge of that.'

'Irregular hours.'

'They shall end with the holidays.'

There was still another maid, whom Ellen said was only kept to wait on nurse, but who, Caroline said, did all their needlework, both making and mending.

'That,' said Ellen, 'I should have thought you and Janet could do. I do nearly all our work with the girls' help ; I am happy to say that Jessie is an excellent needlewoman, and Essie and Ellie can do something. I only direct the nurserymaid; I never trust anything to servants.'

'I could never bear not to trust people,' said Caroline.

Ellen sighed, believing that she would soon be cured of that; and Carey added—

'On true principles of economy, surely it is better that Emma, who knows how, should mend the clothes, than that I should botch them up in any way, when I can earn more than she costs me!'

'Earn!'

'Yes; I can model, and I can teach. Was I not brought up to it?'

'Yes, but *now* it is impossible! It is not a larger income that you want, but proper attention to details in the spending of it, as I will show you.'

Whereupon Mrs. Brownlow, in her neat figures, built up a pretty little economical scheme, based on a thorough knowledge of the subject. Caroline tried to follow her calculations, but a dreaminess came over her; she found herself saying 'Yes,' without knowing what she was assenting to; and while Ellen was discoursing on coals and coke, she was trying to decide which of her casts she could bear to offer for sale, and going off into the dear old associations connected with each, so that she was obliged at the end, instead of giving an unqualified assent, to say she would think it over; and Ellen, who had marked her wandering eye, left off with a conviction that she had wasted her breath.

Certainly she was not prepared for the proposal with which Mother Carey almost rushed into the room the next day, just as she was locking up her wine, and the Colonel lingering over his first glance at the day's *Times*.

'I know what to do! Miss James is not coming back? And you have not heard of any one? Then, if you would only let me teach your girls with mine! You know that is what I really can do. Yes, indeed, I would be regular. I always was. You know I was, Robert, till I came here, and didn't quite know what I was about; and I have been regular ever since the end of the holidays, and I really can teach.'

'My dear sister,' edged in the Colonel, as she paused for breath, 'no one questions your ability, only the fitness of——'

'I had thought over two things,' broke in Caroline again. 'If you don't like me to have Jessie, and Essie, and Ellie, I would offer to prepare little boys. I've been more used to them than to girls, and I know Mr. Ogilvie would be glad. I could have the little Wrights, and Walter Leslie, and three or four more directly, but I thought you might like the other way better.'

'I can see no occasion for either,' said Ellen. 'You need no increase in income, only to attend to details.'

'And I had rather do what I can—than what I can't,' said Caroline.

'Every lady should understand how to superintend her own household,' said her Serene Highness.

'Granted ; oh, granted, Ellen ! I'm going to superintend with all my might and main, but I don't want to be my own upper servant, and I know I should make no hand of it, and I had much rather earn something by my wits. I can do it best in the way I was trained ; and you know it is what I have been used to ever since my own children were born.'

Ellen heaved a sigh at this obtuseness towards what she viewed as the dignified and ladylike mission of the well-born woman, not to be the bread-winner, but the preserver and steward, of the household. Here was poor little Caroline so ignorant as actually to glory in having been educated for a governess !

The colonel, wanting to finish his *Times* in peace, looked up and said, with the gracious tone he always used to his brother's wife—

'My good little sister, it is very praiseworthy in you to wish to exert yourself, and very kind and proper to desire to begin at home, but you must allow us a little time to consider.'

She took this as a hint to retreat ; and her Serene Highness likewise feeling it a dismissal, tried at once to obviate all ungraciousness by saying, 'We are preserving our *magnum bonums*, Caroline dear ; I will send you some.'

'*Magnum bonum !*' gasped Caroline, hearing nothing but the name. 'Do you know——?'

'I know the recipe of course, and can give you an excellent one. I will come over by and by and explain it to you.'

Caroline stood confounded. Had Joe revealed all to his brother ? Was it to be treated as a domestic nostrum ? 'Then you know what the *magnum bonum* is ?' she faltered.

'Are you asking as a philosopher ?' said the Colonel, amused by her tone.

'I don't know what you mean Colonel,' said his wife. 'I offered Caroline a basket of *magnum bonums* for preserving, and one would think I had said something very extraordinary.'

'Perhaps it is my cockney ignorance,' said Caroline, beginning to breathe freely, and thinking it would have been less oppressive if Sua Serenità would have either laughed or scolded, instead of gravely leading her past the red-baize door which shut out the lower regions to the room where white armies of jam-pots stood marshalled, and in the midst two or three baskets of big yellow plums, which awoke in her a remembrance of their name, and set her laughing, thanking, and preparing to carry home the basket.

This, however, as she was instantly reminded, was not country-town manners. The gardener was to be sent with them, and Ellen herself would copy out the recipe, and by and by bring it, with full directions.

Each lady felt herself magnanimously forbearing, as Caroline went home to the lessons, and Ellen repaired to her husband on his morning inspection of his hens and chickens.

'Poor thing,' she said, 'there are great allowances to be made for her. I believe she wishes to do right.'

'She knows how to teach,' rejoined the Colonel. 'Bobus is nearly at the head of the school, and Johnnie has improved greatly since he has been so much with her.'

'Johnnie was always clever,' said his mother. 'For my part, I had rather see them playing at good honest games than messing about with that museum nonsense. The boys did not do half so much mischief, nor destroy so many clothes, before they were always running down to the Pagoda. And as to this setting up a school, you would never consent to have Joe's wife doing that !'

'There is no real need.'

'None at all, if she only would—if she only knew how to attend to her proper duties.'

'At the same time, I should be very glad of an excuse for making her an advance, enough to meet the weekly bills, till her rent comes in, so that she may not begin a debt. Could you not send the girls to her for a few hours every day ?'

'That's not so bad as her taking pupils, for nobody need know that she was paid for it,' said his wife, considering. 'I don't believe it will answer, or that she will ever keep to it steadily ; but it can hardly hurt the children to try, if Jessie has an eye on Essie and Ellie. I will *not* have them brought on too fast, nor taught Latin, and all that poor little Babie is learning. I am sure it is dreadful to hear that child talk. I am always expecting that she will have water on the brain.'

The decision, which really involved a sacrifice and a certain sense of risk on the part of these good people, was conveyed in a note, together with a recipe for the preservation of *magnum bonums*, and a very liberal cheque in advance for the first quarter of her three pupils, stipulating that no others should be admitted, that the terms should be kept secret, that the hours should be regular, and above all, that the pupils should not be forced.

Caroline was touched and grateful, but could hardly keep a little satire out of her promise that Essie and Ellie should not be too precocious. She wrote her note of thanks, despatched it, and then, in the interest of some arithmetical problems which she was working with Janet, forgot everything else, till a sort of gigantic buzz was heard near at hand. A sudden thought struck her, and out she darted into the hall. There stood the basket in the middle of the table, just where the boys were wont to look for refections of fruit or cake when they tumbled in from school. Six boys and Babie hovered round, each in the act of devouring a golden-green, egg-like plum, and only two or three remained in the leaves at the bottom!

'Oh, the *magnum bonums!*' she cried; and Janet came rushing out in dismay at the sound, standing aghast, but not exclaiming.

'Weren't they for us?' asked Bobus, the first to get the stone out of his mouth.

'No; oh no!' answered his mother, as well as laughter would permit; 'they are your aunt's precious plums, which she gave us as a great favour, and I was going to be so good and learn to preserve and pickle them! Oh dear!'

'Never mind, Mother Carey,' mumbled her nephew Johnnie, with his stone swelling out his cheek, where it was tucked for convenience of speech; 'I'll go and get you another jolly lot more.'

'You can't,' grunted Robin; 'they are all gathered.'

'Then we'll get them off the old tree at the bottom of the orchard, where they are just as big and yellow, and mamma will never know the difference.'

'But they taste like soap!'

'That doesn't matter. She'd no more taste a *magnum bonum* before it is all titivated up with sugar than—than—than—'

'Babie's head with brain sauce,' gravely put in Bobus, as his cousin paused for a comparison. 'It's a wasting of good gifts to make jam of these, for jam is nothing but a vehicle for sugar.'

'Then the grocer's cart is jam,' promptly retorted Armine, 'for I saw a sugarloaf come in one yesterday.'

'Come on, then,' cried Jock, ripe for the mischief; 'I know the tree! They are just like long apricots. Aunt Ellen will think her plums have been all a-growing!'

'No, no, boys!' cried his mother, 'I can't have it done. To steal your aunt's own plums to deceive her with!'

'We always may do as we like with that tree,' said Johnnie, 'because they are so nasty, and won't keep.'

'How nice for the preserves!' observed Bobus.

'They would do just as well to hinder Mother Carey from catching it.'

'No, no, boys; I ought to "catch it!" It was all my fault for not putting the plums away.'

'You won't tell of us,' growled Robin, between lips that he opened wide enough the next moment to admit one of three surviving plums.

'If I tell her I left them about in the boys' way, she will arrive at the natural conclusion.'

'Do they call those things *magnum bonum?*' asked Janet, as the boys drifted away.

'Yes,' said her mother, looking at her rather wonderingly;

and adding, as Janet coloured up to the eyes, 'My dear, have you any other association with the name?'

Many a time Janet had longed to tell all she knew; now, when so good an opportunity had come, all was choked back by the strange leaden weight of reserve, and shame in that long reserve.

She opened her eyes and stared as stupidly at her mother as Robin could have done, feeling an utter incapacity of making any reply; and Caroline, who had for a moment thought she understood, was baffled, and durst not pursue the subject for fear of betraying her own secret, deciding within herself that Janet might have caught up the word without understanding.

They were interrupted the next minute, and Janet ran away, feeling that she had had an escape, yet wishing she had not.

Caroline did effectually shelter her nephews under her general term 'the boys,' and if their mother was not conciliated, their fellow-feeling with her was strengthened, as well as their sense of honour. Nay, Johnnie actually spent the next half-holiday in walking three miles and back to his old nurse, whom he beguiled out of a basket of plums—hard, little blue things, as unlike *magnum bonums* as could well be, but which his aunt received as they were meant, as full compensation; nay, she took the pains to hunt up a recipe, and have them well preserved, in hopes of amazing his mother.

It was indeed one difficulty that the two sisters-in-law had such different notions of the aim and end of economy. The income at Kencroft had not increased with the family, which numbered eight, for there were two little boys in the nursery, and it was only by diligent housewifery that Mrs. Brownlow kept up the somewhat handsome establishment she had started with at her marriage. Caroline felt that she neither could nor would have made herself such a slave to domestic details; yet this was life and duty and interest to Ellen. Where one sister would be unheeding of shabby externals, so that all her children might be free and on an equality, if they did not go beyond her, in all enjoyments, physical, artistic, or intellectual; the other toiled to keep up appearances, kept her children under restraint and in the background, and made all sorts of unseen sacrifices to the supposed duty of always having a handsome dinner for whomsoever the Colonel might bring in, and keeping the horses, carriages, and servants that she thought his due.

But then Ellen had a husband, and, as Caroline sighed to herself, that made all the difference! and she was no Serene Highness, and had no dignity.

The three girls from Kencroft did actually become pupils at the Folly, but the beginnings were not propitious, for, in her new teacher's eyes, Jessie knew nothing accurately, but needed to have her foundations looked to—to practise scales, draw square boxes, and work the four first rules of arithmetic.

'Simple things,' complained Jessie to her mother, 'that I used to do when I was no bigger than Essie, and yet she is always teasing one about how and why! She wanted me to tell why I carried one.'

'Have a little patience for the present, my dear; your papa wants to help her just at present, and after this autumn we will manage for you to have some real good music lessons.'

'But I don't like wasting time over old easy things made difficult,' sighed Jessie.

'It is very tiresome, my dear; but your papa wishes it, and you see, poor thing, she can't teach you more than she knows herself; and while you are there, I am sure it is all right with Essie and Ellie.'

'She does not teach them a bit like Miss James,' said Jessie. 'She makes their sums into a story, and their spelling lessons too. It is like a game.'

Indeed, Essie and Ellie were so willing to go off to their lessons every morning, that their mother often thought it could not be all right, and that the progress, which they undoubtedly made, must be by some superficial trick; but as their father had so willed it, she submitted to the present arrangement, deciding that 'poor Caroline was just able to teach little children.'

The presence of Essie and Ellie much assisted in bringing Babie back to methodical habits; nor was she, in spite of her precocious intelligence, too forward in the actual drill of education to be able to work with her little cousins.

The incongruous elements were the two elder girls, who could by no means study together, since they were at the two opposite ends of the scale; but as Jessie was by no means aggressive, being in fact as sweet and docile a shallow girl as ever lived, things went on peaceably, except when Janet could not conceal her displeasure that Bobus would not share her contempt for Jessie's intellect.

If she told him that Jessie thought that the *Odyssey* was about a voyage to Odessa, and was written by Alfred Tennyson, he only declared that anything was better than being a spiteful cat; and when he came in from school, and found his cousin in wild despair over the conversion of 2861 florins into half-crowns, he stood by, telling her every operation, and leaving her nothing to do but to write down the figures. He was reckless of Janet, who tried to wither them both by her scorn; but Jessie looked up with her honest eyes, saying—

'I wish you hadn't put it into my head, Janet, for now I must rub it out and do it again, and it won't be so hard now Bobus has shown me how.'

'No, no, Jessie,' said Bobus; 'I wouldn't be bullied.'

'For shame, Bobus,' said his sister; 'how is she to learn anything in that way?'

'And if she doesn't?' said Bobus.

'That's a disgrace.'

'A grace,' said provoking Bobus. 'She is much nicer as she is, than you will ever be.'

'Don't talk such nonsense,' said Janet, with an elder sisterly air. 'It is not kind to encourage Jessie to think any one can care for an empty-headed doll.'

'Empty-headed dolls are all the go,' said Bobus. 'Never mind, Jessie, a girl's business is to be pretty and good-humoured, not to stuff herself with Latin and Greek. You should leave that to us poor beggars!'

'Yes, I know, that's all your envy and jealousy,' retorted Janet.

All the time Jessie stood by, plump, gentle, and pretty, though with a certain cloud of perplexity on her white open brow, and as her aunt returned into the room she said—

'I think my sum is right now, Aunt Caroline; but Bobus helped me. Must I do it over again?'

'You shall begin with it to-morrow, my dear,' said her aunt; 'then I dare say it will go off easily.'

Jessie thanked with an effusion of gratitude which made her prettier than ever, and then was claimed by Bobus to help him in the making of some paper bags that he needed for some of his curiosities.

Janet liked to fancy that it was beauty *versus* genius that made Jessie the greater favourite. She had not taken into account that she was always too much engrossed with her own concerns to be helpful, while Jessie's pretty dexterous hands were always at every one's service, and without in the least entering into the cause of science, she was invaluable in the museum, whenever her ideas of neatness and symmetry were not in too absolute opposition to the requirements of system.

The two little ones, Essie and Ellie, were equally graceful, or indeed still more so, as being still in their kittenhood, and their attitudes were so charming as to revive their aunt's artistic instincts.

All the earlier part of the year, when her time was her own, it had been mere wretchedness and heart-sickness to think of the art which had given her husband so much pleasure, and, but for Allen, the studio would never have been arranged. But no sooner was her time engrossed, than the artist fever awoke in her, and all the time she could steal by early rising, or on wet afternoons and birthday holidays, was devoted to her clay.

Before the end of the autumn she had sent up to Mr. Acton some lovely little groups of children, illustrating Wordsworth's poems. She had been taught anatomy enough to make her work superior to that of most women, and Mr. Acton found no difficulty in disposing of them to a porcelain manufactory, to be copied in Parian, bringing in a sum that made her feel rich.

Vistas opened before her sanguine eyes of that clay educating her son for the Magnum Bonum, her great thought. Her boys must be brought up to be worthy of the quest, high-minded, disinterested, and devoted, as well as intellectual and religious. So said their father ; and thus the Magnum Bonum had become very nearly a religion to her, giving her a definite aim and principle.

Unfortunately there was not much in her present surroundings to lead her higher. The vicar, Mr. Rigby, was a dull, weak man, of a worn-out type, a careful visitor of the sick and poor, but taking little heed to the educated, except as subscribers and Sunday-school teachers. Carey had done little in the first capacity, Janet had refused to act in the latter.

His sermons were very sleepy performances, except for a tendency to jumble up metaphors, that kept the audience from the Folly just awake enough to watch for them. The hearer was proud who could repeat by heart such phrases as 'Let us not, beloved brethren, as gaudy insects, flutter out life's little day, bound to the chariot wheels of vanity, whirling in the vortex of dissipation, until at length we lie moaning over the bitter dregs of the intoxicating draught.' Some of these became household proverbs at the Folly, under the title of 'Rigdum Funnidoses,' and might well be an extreme distress to the good, reverent, and dutiful Jessie.

Mrs. Rigby was an inferior woman, a sworn member of the Coffinkey clique, admiring and looking up to her Serene Highness as the great lady of the place, and wearing an almost abject manner when receiving good counsels from her. Neither of them commanded respect, nor were they likely to change the belief, which prevailed at the Folly, that all ability resided among the London clergy.

## CHAPTER XI

### UNDINE

'Lithest, gaudiest harlequin,
Prettiest tumbler ever seen,
Light of heart and light of limb.'
WORDSWORTH.

LONG walks continued to be almost a necessity to Mrs. Joseph Brownlow, even when comparatively sobered down, and there were few days on which she was not to be met a mile or two from Kenminster, attended by a train of boys larger or smaller, according to the demands of the school for work or play.

The winter was of the description least favourable to collective boyish sports, as there was no snow and very little frost. The Christmas holidays led to more walking than ever. The gravelled roads of Belforest were never impassable, even in moist weather ; and even the penetralia of the place had been laid open to the Brownlows, in consequence of a friendship which the two Johns had established with Alfred Richards, the agent's son. They had brought him in to see the museum, and he had proved so nice and intelligent a lad, that Mother Carey, to the great scandal of her Serene Highness, allowed Jock to ask him to partake of a birthday feast.

When Allen came home at Christmas, he introduced stilt walking, and the Coffinkey world had the pleasure of communicating to one another that 'Mrs. Folly Brownlow' had been seen with all her boys walking on stilts ; and of course in the next stage, Mrs. 'Folly' Brownlow herself was said to have been walking on stilts with all her boys, a libel which caused Mrs. Robert Brownlow much pain and trouble in the contradiction.

'Poor Caroline ! walking seemed to be necessary to her health, and she was out a great deal, but always walking along in the lanes on foot with her little girls—yes, I assure you, always on foot !'

It was thus that Caroline, with Babie and Armine, was descending a hill on the other side of Belforest Park, fully employed in picking the way through the mud from stone to stone, when a cry of dismay came to them from a distance, and whilst they were still struggling towards a gate, which broke the line of the high hedge, the two Johns came back at speed, crying, 'Mother, Mother Carey ! come quick, here's Allen had a spill— came down on his shoulder—his stilt went into a hole, and he went right over ; they think he must have broken something, he howls so when they touch him.'

Feeling her limbs and breath inadequate to bear her on as fast as her spirit flew forward, Caroline dashed through the slippery mud far too swiftly for poor little Babie to keep up with her, leaving one boy to take care of the little ones, while the other acted as her guide down the long steep lane. She was unable to see over the hedges till she came through a gate into a meadow, where Jock looked about, rubbed his eyes, and exclaimed, 'Hallo, where are they ?' pointing to the place where Allen had fallen, but whence he seemed to have been spirited away like Sir Piercie Shafton. However, Rob and Joe came running out of a farmyard at a little distance, with tidings that Allen had been taken in there, and replying to her breathless question, that they could not tell how much he was hurt.

A fine-looking white-haired farmer met her next, saying, 'Your young gentleman is not very seriously hurt, ma'am. I think a dislocation of the shoulder is the extent of the injury. He is feeling rather faint, but you must not be alarmed.'

It was spoken with a kind courtesy that gave her confidence, and the old man led her to the parlour, where his daughter-in-law, a gentle-looking person, was most kindly attending on Allen, who lay on the sofa, exceedingly white, and in much pain, but able to smile at his mother, and assure her that he should soon be all right.

'Had they sent for a surgeon ?'

'No, but they had sent for a bone-setter, who would be there in a minute.'

The old farmer explained that it would be two hours at the least before a surgeon could be fetched from Kenminster, while Higg, the blacksmith, who lived close at hand, was better for man and beast than any surgeon he had known, and his son had instantly set out to fetch him. As the mother doubtfully asked of his fitness, instances were quoted of his success. The family had a 'gift,' inherited and kept up from time immemorial, and the farmer's wife declared that he was as tender as possible; she had seen him operate on a neighbour's child, and should not be afraid to trust him with one of her own.

The man's voice was heard; they went out to speak to him, and Caroline was left with her boy.

'What do you think, Ali, my dear,' she said, kneeling by him, 'I have often heard dear papa speak of the wonderful instinct of those bone-setting families.'

'I'd have nothing to do with a humbugging quack,' put in Bobus.

'He may humbug as much as he likes, if he'll only get me out of this pain,' said poor Allen.

'He will only make it ever so much worse, and then you'll have to have it done over again,' croaked Bobus.

'That is not the way to talk of it, Bobus,' said his mother. 'I know a dislocated shoulder does not require any great skill, and that promptness is of greater use than knowledge in such a case.'

'Well, if you like to encourage abominable humbug and have Allen lamed for life, I don't,' said Bobus. 'I shan't stay in the house with the blackguard.'

He stalked out of the room with great loftiness of demeanour, just as the operator was being introduced—a tall, sinewy man, with one of those strong yet meek faces often to be found among the peasantry. He came in after the old farmer, pulling his forelock to the lady, and waiting for orders as if he had been sent for to mend the gate; but Caroline saw in a moment that he was a man to trust in, and that his hands were not only clean, but were well-formed and powerful, with a great air of dexterity.

'I am afraid my boy's arm is put out,' she said, trembling a good deal.

'Yes, ma'am.'

'And—and,' said she, feeling sick, and more desolate and left to her own judgment than ever before, 'can you undertake to push it in again?'

'Please God, ma'am,' Higg said gravely, coming nearer for examination.

Allen shrank and shuddered.

'Won't it hurt awfully?' he asked.

'Well, sir, it won't just be a bed of roses, but it won't last, not long, if you sets your will to it.'

He asked for various needments, and while he was inspecting them, Allen's courage began to fail, and he breathed out whispers that the man was rougher and more ignorant than he expected, and they had better wait and send to Kenminster for a doctor ; but those who thought Caroline helpless and childish would have been amazed at the gentle resolution with which she refused to listen to his falterings, and braced him to endure, knowing well that her husband had said that skill was hardly needed in such a case, only resolution. She would not let herself be taken out of the room, and indeed never thought of herself, only of Allen, whose other hand she held, and to whom she seemed to give patience and courage. When all was well over, there was a hospitable invitation to the patient to remain till he was fit to return, and an extension of the invitation to his mother, but with promises of every care if she must leave him, and this she was forced to decide on doing, as such a household as hers could not well spare her, especially on a Saturday evening ; and she also saw that the inconvenience to her hosts would have been great.

Allen was so much relieved that she had no fear of leaving him to these kind people, to whom she had taken a great fancy.

'I shall learn the habits of the genuine species, British farmer,' said he, as his mother kissed him, and declared him the best and most conformable of boys.

Old Mr. Gould would not be denied driving her home in his gig, and when she thought about it, she found she had a strange relaxed aching of the knees, which made her glad of kindness for herself and the little ones. In the fine old kitchen she found that Armine had had an overpowering fit of crying, which had been kindly soothed by motherly Mrs. Gould, and the whole party were partaking of a luxurious tea, enlivened by mince pies and rosy-cheeked apples, which had diverted his attention to the problem why the next year's prosperity should depend on the number of mince pies consumed before Christmas.

Bobus was not among them, having marched off in his contempt of the bone-setter, and his mother was not without fears that he might bring a real surgeon down on her at any moment, so she quickly drank off her cup of tea, and took her seat in Farmer Gould's gig with Babie as bodkin in front, and Joe and Armine in the little seat behind. Robin and the two Johns were to stilt themselves home, while she was taken so long and rugged a way, that at every jolt she was ready to renew her thanks for sparing it to her son's shoulder ; and they were at home before her.

The whole family came pouring out to meet her, and the Colonel made warm acknowledgments of the farmer's kindness, speaking of him when he was gone as one of the most estimable men in the neighbourhood, staunch in his politics, and very ill-used by old Barnes of Belforest.

Caroline looked anxiously for Bobus; and Janet, who had stayed at home to finish some papers for her essay society, said that he had only hurried in to tell her and take off his stilts, and had then gone down to Dr. Leslie's.

'Then has Dr. Leslie gone? We did not meet him, but he may have gone through Belforest,' exclaimed Caroline.

'Oh no, he has not gone; he would not when he heard about that Higg,' said Janet, with uneasy and much disgusted face. 'He couldn't do any good after his meddling.'

'Do you mean that he said so?' asked Carey, much alarmed.

'Never mind,' said the Colonel, 'you did quite right, Caroline, whatever the doctor says. Any man of sense, with good strong hands, can manage a shoulder like that, and I should have thought Leslie had sense to see it; but those professional men can't stand outsiders.'

'Where is Bobus?' asked Caroline; 'I should like to distinguish between what Dr. Leslie said to him and what he told Janet. He might be more zealous for Dr. Leslie than Dr. Leslie for himself.'

Bobus was unearthed, and by much pumping was made to allow that Dr. Leslie had told him that there was nothing more to be done, and that his brother was quite safe in Higg's hands; but Bobus evidently did not believe it. He kept silence while his uncle remained, but he had hunted up his father's surgical books, and went on about humeral clavicles and ligatures all the evening, till his mother felt sick in the nervous contemplation of possibilities, though her better sense was secure that she had done right, while Janet was moodily silent and angered with her, in the belief that she had weakly let Allen be injured for life; and Bobus seemed as if he had rather it should be so than that he should be wrong, and Higg's native endowments turn out a reality.

Caroline abstained from looking at the book herself, partly because she thought she might only alarm herself the more without confuting Bobus, and partly because she knew that the old law which forbade Janet to meddle with the medical books would be considered as abrogated if she touched them herself.

Both she and Janet were much more anxious than they confessed, except by the looks which betrayed their broken rest the next morning. Each was bent on walking to River Hollow, and they would fain have done so immediately after breakfast, but to take the whole tribe was impossible; and to let them go to church without her would infallibly lead to Jock's getting into a scrape with his relatives, if not with the whole congregation. Was it not all her eyes could do to hinder palpable smiles in the sermon, and her monkey from playing tricks on his bear, who, by some fatality, always sat in front, with his irresistible broad back, down which, in spite of all her vigilance, Jock had once thrust a large bluebottle fly? She also knew that both her

husband and his mother would have thought she ought to go to
church, and that if matters went amiss with her boy, she should
reproach herself with the omission. Her children, too, in-
fluenced her, though very oppositely, for Janet was found preparing to start for River Hollow, and on being told that she
must wait, to go with her mother, till after church, declared
defiantly that 'she saw no sense in staying at home to hear
Rigdum when she did not know how ill Allen might be.'

'You would not have said that to grandmamma,' said Carey.

'Well, if you like to go to church, you can. I can go alone.'

'No, I will not have you take that long walk alone.'

'Then I will take one of the boys.'

'No, Janet, I mean to be obeyed. Go and put on your other
hat, and do not make us late for church.'

Janet was forced to submit, for she never came to the point
of actual disobedience to her mother. Caroline's ruffled feelings were soothed by little Armine, who ran in from feeding
his rabbits to ask to have the place in his prayer-book shown
to him where he should pray for poor Allen. She marked the
Litany sentence for him, and meant to have thrown her own
heart into it, but when the moment came, her mind was far
astray, building vague castles about her boys.

Still she felt as if her church-going had its reward, for Dr.
Leslie met her a little way outside the porch, and, after asking
after her boy, said—

'I hope his brother explained to you that Higg is quite to be
trusted. He always knows what he can do, and when a case is
beyond him. If I had come, there would have been nothing for
me to do.'

'There!' said Jock triumphantly to his brother and sister.

'Much you know about it,' grunted Bobus.

'Mother Carey was right. She always is,' persisted Jock.

'It would have been just the same if the man had known
nothing about it,' said Janet. 'I hate your irregular practitioners, and it was very weak in mother to encourage them.'
Then, as Bobus snarled at the censure of his mother—'You
said so yourself yesterday.'

'I didn't say any such beastly thing of mother. She could
tell whether it was just a simple dislocation, and she was right,
having ever so much more sense than you, Janet.'

'You didn't say so yesterday,' repeated Janet.

'I don't like irregular practitioners a bit better than you do,
Janet,' said Bobus with dignity; 'and I thought it right to call
in a qualified surgeon, but I never said mother couldn't judge.'

However, Bobus would not countenance the irregular
practitioner by escorting his mother to River Hollow; and as
he was in one of the surly moods in which he was dangerous to
any one who meddled with him, especially Janet, his mother
was glad not to have to keep the peace between them.

Janet, though not in the most amiable mood, chose to go with

her, and they set forth by the shorter way, across Belforest
Park, skirting the gardens where the statues stood up, looking
shivery and forlorn, as if they were not suited to English
winters, and the huge house looked down on them like a
London terrace that had lost its way, with a dreary uninhabited
air about it. Even by this private way they had two miles and
a half of park to traverse, before they reached a heavy miry
lane, where the beds of mud, alternated with rugged masses of
stone, intended to choke them. It led up between high hedges
to the brow of one of the many hills of the county, whence
they could look down into the hollow, a perfect cup, scooped
out as it were between the hills that closed it in, except at the
outlet of the river that intersected it, making the meadow on
either side emerald green, even in the winter. Corn lands of
rich red soil, pasture fields dotted with cattle, and broad belts
of copse-wood between clothed the slopes; and a picturesque
wooden bridge, with a double handrail, crossed the river. The
farmhouse, built of creamy stone, stood on the opposite side of
the river, some way above the bank, and the mother and
daughter agreed that it deserved to be sketched next summer.

They had to pick their way down a lane that was almost a
torrent, and emerging at the foot of the bridge, they stood still
in amazement, for in the very centre was something vibrating
rapidly, surrounded by a perfect halo of gold and scarlet. It
was like a gigantic humming-bird moth at first, but it presently
resolved itself into a little girl, clad in something dark purple
below, and above with a bright scarlet cloaklet, which flew out
and streamed back, beneath the floating locks of glistening
gold that glinted in the sun, as with a hand on each rail of the
bridge she swung herself backwards and forwards with the most
bewildering rapidity. Suddenly becoming aware of the approach
of strangers, she stood for one moment gazing in astonishment,
then fled so swiftly that she almost seemed to fly, and vanished
in the farm buildings!

They stood laughing and declaring that Babie would be convinced that fairies came out on Sunday, then crossed the river
and were beginning to ascend the path when a volley of sounds
broke on them, a shrill yap giving the alarm, louder notes
joining in, and the bass being supplied by a formidable deep-
mouthed bark, as out of the farmyard gate dashed little terrier,
curly spaniel, slim greyhounds, surly sheep-dog of the old
tailless sort, and big and mighty Newfoundland, and there they
stood in a row, shouting forth defiance in all gradations of
note, so that, though frightened, Carey and Janet could not
help laughing, as the former said—

'This comes of gadding about on Sunday.'

'If we went on boldly they would see we are not tramps,'
said Janet.

'Depend on it, they will let no one pass in church time.'

So it proved, for Janet's attempt to move forward elicited a growl from the sheep-dog, and a leap forward of the 'little dogs and all,' which daunted even her stout heart.

However, calls were heard, and the bright vision of the bridge came darting among the dogs, scolding and driving them in, and Allen himself came out to the gate, all bandaged up on one side, but waving his arm as a signal to his mother and sister to advance. They did so nervously but safely, while the growls of the sheep-dog sounded like distant thunder, and the terrier uttered his protest from the door. Allen declared himself much better, and said he should be quite able to go home to-morrow, only this was such a jolly place; and then he brought them into the beautiful old kitchen with a magnificent open hearth, enclosed by two fine dark walnut-wood settles, making a little carpeted chamber between them. Here Allen had the farmer's arm-chair and a footstool, and with *Foxe's Martyrs* open at a flaming illustration on the little round table before him, appeared to be spending his Sunday as luxuriously as the big tabby cat who shared the hearth with him.

'They have only one service at Woodbridge, morning and afternoon by turns,' he explained, 'and so they are all gone to it.'

'Who is that girl?' asked Janet.

'Undine,' he coolly replied.

'She certainly appeared on the bridge,' said his mother, 'but I should think Undine's colouring had been less radiant—more of the blue and white.'

'She had not a whiter skin nor bluer eyes,' said Allen, 'nor made herself more ridiculous either. Did you ever see such hair, mother? Hullo, Elfie. There she is, peeping in at the window, just as Undine did. Come in!' he cried at the door. 'No, not she,' as he returned baffled; 'she is off again!'

'But, Allen, who is she? Not Farmer Gould's daughter.'

'Of course not. Don't you know she was fished up in a net, and belonged to a palace under the ocean full of pearls and diamonds? She took such a fancy to me that no power on earth would make her go to church with the rest. She ran away, and hid, and when they were all gone she came out and curled herself up at my feet and chattered, till I happened to offend her majesty, and off she went like a shot. I'm only thankful that she did not make her pearly teeth meet in my finger in true Undine fashion.'

'But who is she, really?'

'I can't quite make out. They call her Elfie, and she calls them grandpapa, and uncle and aunt, but she has been sitting here complaining of everything being cold and dull, and talking about seas and islands, palm-trees, and coral caves, and humming birds, yes, and black slaves, and strings of pearls, so that if she is romancing, like Armine and Babie, she does it uncommonly naturally.'

They saw no more of this mysterious little being, and the family soon returned from church. The father was a fine, old-fashioned yeoman, the son had the style of a modern farmer, and the wife was so quiet, sensible, and matronly as to be almost ladylike. Her two little girls were dressed as well as Essie and Ellie, but all were essentially commonplace. They were very kind and friendly, anxious that Allen should stay as long as was good for him, as well as pressing in their hospitality to the two ladies. Mr. Gould was very anxious to drive them home in his gig, though he allowed that the road was very rough unless you went through Belforest Park, and that he never did.

This was surprising, for Belforest had always seemed as free as the turnpike-road, and River Hollow was apparently part of the estate, but there was an air of discouraging questions, so Carey suspected quarrels and asked none.

She was enlightened the next day when Colonel Brownlow brought his phaeton to fetch Allen home over the smooth park road. He told her that the Goulds were freeholders who had owned River Hollow from time immemorial, though each successive lord of Belforest tried to buy them out. The alienation between them and Mr. Barnes, the present master, had, however, much stronger grounds than these. His nephew and intended heir had stolen a match with the old man's pretty daughter, and this had never been forgiven. The young couple had gone out to the West Indian isles, where the early home of her husband had been, and where he held some government office, and there fell a victim to the climate. Old Mr. Gould had gone home to fetch his daughter and her child, but the former had died before he reached her, and he had only brought back the little girl about two years ago.

Mr. Barnes ignored her entirely, and the Goulds, who had a good deal of pride, did not choose to apply to him. It was very unfortunate, for unless he had any other relations the child must be heiress to his immense wealth, though it was as likely as not that he would leave it all to hospitals out of pure vindictiveness.

They found Allen out of doors attended by the three little girls, all eagerly watching the removal of a sheepfold. He was a pleasant-mannered boy, ready to adapt himself to all circumstances and to throw ready intelligent interest into everything, and he had won the hearts of the whole River Hollow establishment, from old Mr. Gould down to the smallest puppy

Elfie, as he called her, stood her ground, and as she looked up under her brown mushroom hat, Caroline was struck with her beauty, fair, but with a southern richness of bloom and glow—the carnation cheek of a depth of tint more often found in brunette complexions. The eyes were not merely blue by courtesy, but of a wonderful deep azure, shaded by very long lashes, dark except when the sun glinted them with gold, and round her shoulders hung masses of hair of that exquisite light auburn which cannot be accused of being red.

She let herself be greeted by the strangers with much more ease and grace than the other two children, but the slow walk of her grandfather and Colonel Brownlow seemed more than she could brook, and she went off, flying and spinning round like a little dog.

While all the acknowledgments and farewells were being made, and Colonel Brownlow was taking directions for finding Higg's house and forge so as to remunerate him for his services, Elfie came hurrying up to Allen, holding out a great, gorgeous, pink-lined shell, and laid within it two heads of scarlet geranium on a green leaf.

'O Elfie, Elfie! how could you?' exclaimed he, knowing them to be the only flowers in bloom.

'You must have them. There's nothing else pretty to give you, and I love you,' said the child, holding up her face to kiss him.

'Elvira!' said her aunt in warning, 'how can you! What will this lady think of you?'

Elvira's gesture would in any other child have seemed a sulky thrust of the elbow, but in her it was more like the flutter of the wing of a brilliant bird.

'You must,' she repeated; and when he hesitated with 'If Mrs. Gould,' she broke away, dashed the flowers, shell and all, into the middle of a clump of rosemary, and rushed out of sight like a little fury.

'You will excuse her, Mrs. Brownlow,' said Mrs. Gould, much annoyed. 'She has been sadly spoilt, living among negro servants and having her own way, so that she is sometimes quite ungovernable.'

'Nay, nay, she is a warm-hearted little thing if you don't cross her,' said the old farmer; 'and the young gentleman has been very kind to her.'

Mrs. Gould looked as if she thought she knew her niece better than grandpapa did, but she was too wise to speak; and the little girls having assisted Allen in the recovery of the shell and the flowers, he tendered them again to her.

'You had better keep them, Mr. Brownlow,' she said. 'The shell is her own, and if you did not take it, she is so *tenacious* that she would be sure to smash it to atoms.'

Allen accepted perforce and proceeded with his farewells, but as he was stooping down to kiss little five-year-old Kate Gould, something wet, cold, and sloppy came with great force on them both, almost knocking them down and bespattering them both with black drops. The missile proved to be a dripping sod pulled up from the duck-pond in the next field, and a glimpse might be caught of Elvira's scarlet legs disappearing over the low wall between.

Over poor Mrs. Gould's apologies a veil had best be drawn.

Mother Carey pitied her heartily, but it was impossible not to make fun at home over the black tokens on Allen's shirt-collar. His brothers and sisters laughed excessively, and Janet twitted him with his Undine, till he, contrary to his wont, grew so cross as to make his mother recollect that he was still a suffering patient, and insist on his lying quiet on the sofa, while she banished every one, and read Tennyson to him. Poetry, read aloud by her, was Allen's greatest delight, but not often enjoyed, as Bobus and Jock scouted it, and Janet was getting too strong-minded and used to break in with inopportune criticisms.

So to have Mother Carey to read 'Elaine' undisturbed was as great an indulgence as Allen could well have, but she had not gone far before he broke out—

'Mother, please, I wish you could do something for that girl. She really is a lady.'

'So it appears,' said Carey, much disposed to laugh.

'Now, mother, don't be tiresome. You have more sense than Janet. Her father was Vice-consul at San Ildefonso, one of the Antilles.'

'But, my dear, I am afraid that is not quite so grand as it sounds——'

'Hush, mother. He was nephew to Mr. Barnes, and they lived out of the town in a perfect paradise of a place, looking out into the bay. Mr. Gould says he can hardly believe he ever saw anything so gorgeously beautiful, and there this poor little Elvira de Menella lived like a princess with a court of black slaves. Just fancy what it must be to her to come to that farm, an orphan too, with an aunt who can't understand a creature like that.'

'Poor child.'

'Then she can't get any education. Old Gould is a sensible man, who says any school he could afford would only turn her out a sham, and he means, when Mary and Kate are a little older, to get some sort of governess for the three. But, mother, couldn't you just let him bring her in on market days and teach her a little ?'

'My dear boy, what would your aunt do? We can't have sods of mud flying about the house.'

'Now, mother, you know better ! You could make anything of her, you know you could ! And what a model she would make ! Think what a poor little desolate thing she is. You always have a fellow-feeling for orphans, and we do owe those people a great deal of gratitude.'

'Allen, you special pleader, it really will not do ! If I had not undertaken Essie and Ellie, I might think about it, but I promised your aunt not to have any other pupils.'

Allen bothered Essie and Ellie, but was forced to acquiesce, which was fortunate, for when on the last day of the holidays it was found that he had walked to River Hollow to take leave of the Goulds, his aunt administered to his mother a serious warning on the dangers of allowing him to become intimate there.

Caroline tingled all over during the discourse, and at last jumped up, exclaiming—

'My dear Ellen, half the harm in the world is done by making a fuss. Things don't die half so hard when they die a natural death.'

Ellen knew Carey thought she had said something very clever, but was all the more unconvinced.


## CHAPTER XII

### KING MIDAS.

'When I did him at this advantage take,
An ass's nowl I fixed upon his head.'
*Midsummer Night's Dream.*

IN the early spring an unlooked-for obstacle arose to all wanderings in the Belforest woods. The owner returned and closed the gates. From time that seemed immemorial, the inhabitants of Kenminster had disported themselves there as if the grounds had been kept up for their sole behoof, and their indignation at the monopoly knew no bounds.

Nobody saw Mr. Barnes save his doctor, whose carriage was the only one admitted within the lodge gates, intending visitors being there informed that Mr. Barnes was too unwell to be disturbed.

Mrs. 'Folly' Brownlow's aberrations lost their interest in the Coffinkey world beside the mystery of Belforest. Opinions varied as to his being a miser, or a lunatic, a prey to conscience, disease, or deformity ; and reports were so diverse, that at the Folly a journal was kept of them, with their dates, as a matter of curiosity—their authorities marked :—

March 4th.—Mr. Barnes eats nothing but fresh turtle. Brings them down in tubs alive and flapping. Mrs. Coffinkey's Jane heard them cooing at the station. Gives his cook £300 per annum.

5th.—Mr. Barnes so miserly that he turned away the housemaid for burning candles eight to the pound. (H. S. H.)

6th.—Mr. B. keeps a bloodhound trained to hunt Indians, and has six pounds of prime beef steaks for it every day. (Emma.)

8th.—Mr. B.'s library is decorated with a string of human ears, the clippings of his slaves in 'the Indies.' (Nurse.)

12th.—Mr. B. whipped a black boy to death, and is so haunted by remorse that he can't sleep without wax candles burning all round him. (Mrs. Coffinkey's sister-in-law.)

14th.—Mr. Barnes's income is £500,000, and he does not live at the rate of £200. (Col. Brownlow.)

15th.—He has turned off all his gardeners, and the place will be desolation.  (H. S. H.)

16th.—He did turn off one gardener's boy for staring at him when he was being wheeled about in his bath-chair.  (Alfred Richards.)

17th.—He threw a stone, which cut the boy's head open, and he lies at the hospital in a dangerous state.  (Emma.)

18th.—Mr. Barnes was crossed in love when he was a young man by one Miss Anne Thorpe, and has never been the same man since, but has hated all society.  (Query : Is this a version of being a misanthrope ?)

19th.—He is a most unhappy man, who has sacrificed all family affections and all humanity to gold, and whose conscience will not let him rest.  He is worn to a shadow, and is at war with mankind.  In fine, he is a lesson to weak human nature.  (Mrs. Rigby.)

22d.—All his toilet apparatus is of 'virgin gold': he lets nothing else touch him.  (Jessie.)

'Exactly like King Midas.'  (Babie.)

The exclusion from the grounds was a serious grievance, entailing much loss of time and hindrance to the many who had profited by the private roads.  The Sunday promenade was a great deprivation ; nurses and children were cut off from grass and shade, and Mother Carey and her brood from all the delights of the enchanted ground.

She could bear the loss better than in that first wild restlessness, which only free nature could allay.  She had made her occupations, and knew of other haunts, though many a longing eye was cast at the sweet green wilderness, and many regrets spent on the rambles, the sketches, the plants, and the creatures that had seemed the certain entertainment of the summer.

To one class of the population the prohibition only gave greater zest—namely, the boys.  Should there be birds' nests in Belforest unscathed by the youth of St. Kenelm's ?  What were notice-boards, palings, or walls to boys with arms and legs ready to defy even the celebrated man-traps of Ellangowan, 'which, if a man goes in, they will break a horse's leg'?  The terrific bloodhound alarmed a few till his existence was denied by Alfred Richards, the agent's son ; and dodging the keepers was a new and exciting sport.  At first, these men were not solicitous for captures, but their negligence was so often detected, that they began to believe that their master kept telescopes that could penetrate through trees, and their vigilance increased.

Bobus, in quest of green hellebore, got off with a warning ; but a week later, Robin and Jock were inspecting the heronry, when they caught sight of a keeper, and dashed off to find themselves running into the jaws of another.  Swift as lightning, Jock sprung up into an ivied ash ; but the less ready Rob was caught by the leg as he mounted, and pulled down again,

while his captor shouted, 'If there's any more of you young
varmint up yonder, you'd best come down before I fires up into
the hoivy.'

He made a click and pointed his gun, and Robin shrieked,
'Oh, don't! We are Colonel Brownlow's sons; at least, I mean
nephews. Don't! I say. Skipjack, come down.'

'You ass!' muttered Jock, as he crackled down, and was
collared by the keeper. 'Hollo! what's that for?'

'Now, young gents, why will you come larking here to get a
poor chap out of his situation? It's as much as my place is
worth not to summons you, and yet I don't half like to do it to
young gents like you.'

'What could they do to us?' asked Jock.

'Well, sir, may be they'd keep you in the lock-up all night;
and what would your papa and mamma say to that?'

'My father is Colonel Brownlow,' growled Robin.

'More shame for you, sir, to want to get a poor man out of
his place.'

'Look here, my man,' said Jock with London sharpness and
impudence, 'if you want to bully us into tipping you, it's no go.
We've only got one copper between us, and nothing else but
our knives; and if we had, we wouldn't do such a sneaking
thing!'

'I never meant no such thing, sir,' said the keeper; 'only in
case Mr. Barnes should hear of our good nature.'

'Come along, Robin,' said Jock; 'if we are had up, we'll let
'em know how Leggings wanted us to buy off!'

Wherewith Jock made a rush, Rob plunged after him into
the brambles, and they never halted till they had tumbled over
the park wall, and lay in a breathless heap on the other side.
The adventure was the fruitful cause of mirth at the Folly, but
not a word was breathed of it at Kencroft.

A few other lads did actually pay toll to the keepers, and
some penniless ones were brought before the magistrates and
fined for trespass, 'because they could not afford it,' as Caroline
said, and to the Colonel's great disgust she sent two sovereigns
by Allen to pay their fines and set them free.

'It was my own money,' she said, in self-defence, 'earned by
my models of fungi.'

The Colonel thought it an unsatisfactory justification, and
told her that she would lay up trouble for herself by thus
encouraging insubordination. He little thought that the laugh
in her eyes was at his complacent ignorance of his own son's
narrow escape.

Allen was at home for Easter, when Eton gave longer
holidays than did St. Kenelm, so that his brothers were at
work again long before he was. One afternoon, which had
ended in a soaking mist, the two pairs of Roberts and Johns
encountered him at the Folly gate so disguised in mud that they
hardly recognised the dainty Etonian.

'That brute Barnes,' he ejaculated; 'I had to come miles round through a disgusting lane. I wish I had gone on. I'd have proved the right of way if he chose to prosecute me!'

'Father says that's no go,' said Robin.

'I say, Allen, what a guy you are,' added Johnnie.

'And he's got his swell trousers on,' cried Jock, capering with glee.

'I see,' gravely observed Bobus, 'he had got himself up regardless of expense for his Undine, and she has treated him to another dose of her native element.'

'She had nothing to do with it,' asseverated Allen, 'she was as good as gold——'

'Ah! I knew he wasn't figged out for nothing,' put in Jock.

'Don't be ashamed, Ali, my boy,' added Bobus. 'We all understand her little tokens.'

'Stop that!' cried Allen, catching hold of Jock's ear so as to end his war-dance in a howl, bringing the ponderous Rob to the rescue, and there was a general *mêlée*, ending by all the five rolling promiscuously on the gravel drive. They scrambled up with recovered tempers, and at the sight of an indignant house-maid rushed in a general stampede to the two large attics opening into one another, which served as the lair of the Folly lads. There, while struggling, with Jock's assistance, to pull off his boots, Allen explained how he had been waylaid 'by a beast in velveteens' and walked off to the nearest gate.

'Will he summons you, Ali? We'll all go and see the Grand Turk in the dock,' cried Jock.

'Don't flatter yourself; he wouldn't think of it.'

'How much did you fork out?' asked Bobus.

Allen declaimed in the last refinement of Eton slang (care-fully treasured up by the others for reproduction) against the spite of the keeper, who he declared had grinned with malice as he turned him out at a little back gate into a lane with a high stone wall on each side, and two ruts running like torrents with water, leading in the opposite direction to Kenminster, and ending in a bottom where he was up to the ankles in red clay.

'The Eton boots, oh my!' cried Jock, falling backwards with one of them, which he had just pulled off.

'And then,' added Allen, 'as I tried to get along under the wall by the bank, what should a miserable stone do but turn round with me and send me squash into the mud and mire, floundering like a hippopotamus. I should like to get damages from that villain! I should!'

Allen was much more angry than was usual with him, and the others, though laughing at his Etonian airs, fully sym-pathised with his wrath.

'He ought to be served out.'

'We *will* serve him out!'

'How?'

'Get all our fellows and make a jolly good row under his windows,' said Robin.

'Decidedly low,' said Allen.

'And impracticable besides,' said Bobus. 'They'd kick you out before you could say Jack Robinson.'

'There was an old book of father's,' suggested Jock, 'with an old scamp who starved and licked his apprentices, till one of them dressed himself up in a bullock's hide, horns and hoofs, and tail and all, and stood over his bed at night and shouted—

> ' " Old man, old man, for thy cruelty,
>    Body and soul thou art given to me ;
>    Let me but hear those apprentices' cries,
>    And I'll toss thee, and gore thee, and bore out thine eyes."

And he was quite mild to the apprentices ever after.'

Jock acted and roared with such effect as to be encored, but Rob objected. 'He ain't got any apprentices.'

'It might be altered,' said Allen.

> ' Old man, old man, thy gates thou must ope,'

Bobus chimed in.

> ' Nor force Eton swells in quagmire to grope.'

'Bother you, don't humbug and put me out.

> 'Old man, old man, if for aught thou wouldst hope,
>    Thy heart, purse, and gates thou must instantly ope.
>    Let me but——'

'Get Mother Carey to write it,' suggested his cousin John.

'No ; she must know nothing about it,' said Bobus.

'She'd think it a jolly lark,' said Jock.

'When it's over,' said Allen. 'But it's one of the things that the old ones are sure to stick at beforehand, if they are ever so rational and jolly.'

''Tis a horrid pity she is not a fellow,' sighed Johnnie.

'And who'll do the verses ?' said Rob.

'Oh, any fool can do them,' returned Bobus. 'The point is to bell the cat.'

'There'd be no getting in to act the midnight ghost,' said Allen.

'No,' said Jock ; 'but one could hide in the big rhododendron in the wolf-skin rug, and jump out on him in his chair.'

In Allen's railway rug Jock rehearsed the scene, and was imitated if not surpassed by both cousins ; but Allen and Bobus declared that it could not be carried out in the daylight.

'I could do it still better,' said Jock, 'if I blacked myself all over, not only my face, but all the rest, and put on nothing but my red flannel drawers and a turban. They'd take me for the ghost of the little nigger he flogged to death, and Allen could write something pathetic and stunning.'

'You might cut human ears out of rabbit-skins and hang them round your neck,' added Bobus.

'You'd be awfully cold,' said Allen.

'You could mix in a little iodine,' suggested Bobus. 'That stings like fun, and a coppery tinge would be more natural.'

There was great acclamation, but the difficulty was that the only time for effecting an entrance into the garden was between four and five in the morning, and it would be needful to lurk there in this light costume till Mr. Barnes went out. No one would be at liberty from school but Allen, and he declined the oil and lamp-black, even though warmed up with iodine.

'Could it not be done by deputy?' said Bobus; 'we might blacken the little fat boy riding on a swan—the statue, I mean.'

'What, and gild the swan, to show how far his golden goose can carry him?' said Jock.

'Or,' said Allen, 'there's the statue they say is himself, though that's all nonsense. We could make a pair of donkey's ears in Mother Carey's clay, and clap them on him, and gild the thing in his hand.'

'What would be the good of that?' asked Robert.

However, the fun was irresistible, and the only wonder was that the secret was kept for the whole day, while Allen moulded in the studio two things that might pass for ass's ears, and secreted cement enough to fasten them on. The performance elicited such a rapture of applause that the door had to be fast locked against the incursion of the little ones to learn the cause of the mirth. When Mother Carey asked at tea what they were having so much fun about, they only blushed, sniggled, and wriggled in their chairs in a way that would have alarmed a more suspicious mother, but only made her conclude that some delightful surprise was preparing, for which she must keep her curiosity in abeyance.

Nor was she dismayed by the creaking of boots on the attic stairs before dawn, and when the boys appeared at breakfast with hellebore, blue periwinkle, and daffodils, clear indications of where they had been, she only exclaimed—

'Forbidden sweets! O you naughty boys!' when ecstatic laughter alone replied.

She heard no more till the afternoon, when the return from school was notified by shouts from Allen, and the boys rushed up to the verandah where he was reading.

'I say! here's a go. He thinks Richards has done it, and has written to Ogilvie to have him expelled.'

'How do you know?'

'He told me himself.'

'But Ogilvie has too much sense to expel him!'

'Of course, but there's worse, for old Barnes means to turn

off his father.   Nothing will persuade the old fellow that it
wasn't his work, for he says that it must be a grammar-school
boy.'

'Does Dicky Bird guess ?'

'Yes, but he's all right, as close as wax.   He says he was
sure no one but ourselves could have done it, for nobody else
could have thought of such things or made them either.'

'Then he has seen it ?'

'Yes, and he was fit to kill himself with laughing, though
his father and old Barnes were mad with rage and fury.   His
father believes him, but old Barnes believes neither of them,
and swears his father shall go.'

'We shall have to split on ourselves,' elegantly observed
Johnnie.

'We had better tell Mother Carey.   Hullo ! here she is, inside
the window.'

'Didn't you know that ?' said Allen.

Therefore the boys, leaning and sprawling round her, half in
and half out of the window, told the story, the triumph over-
coming all compunction, as they described the morning raid,
the successful scaling of the park-wall, the rush across the
sward, the silence of the garden, the hoisting up of Allen to
fasten on the ears, and the wonderful charms of the figure when
it wore them and held a golden apple in its hand.   'Right of
Way' and 'Let us in' had been written in black on all the
pedestals.

'It is a peculiar way of recommending your admission,' said
Caroline.

'That's Rob's doing,' said Allen.   'I couldn't look after him
while I was gilding the apple or I would have stopped him.
He half blacked the little boy on the swan too——'

'And broke the swan's bill off, worse luck,' added Johnnie.

'Yes,' said Allen, 'that was altogether low and unlucky !   I
meant the old fellow simply to have thought that his statue had
grown a pair of ears in the night.'

'And what would have been the use of that ?' said Robin.

'What was the use of all your scrawling,' said Allen,
'except just to show it was not the natural development of
statues.'

'Yes,' added Bobus, 'it all came of you that poor Dickey
Bird is suspected and it is all blown up.'

'As if he would have thought it was done by nobody,' said
Rob.

'Why not ?' said Jock.   'I'm sure I'd never wonder to see
ass's ears growing on you.   I think they are coming.'

There was a shout of laughter as Rob hastily put up his
hands to feel for them, adding in his slow, gruff voice—

'A statue ain't alive.'

'It made a fool of the whole matter,' proceeded Bobus.   'I
wish we'd kept a lout like you out of it.'

'Hush, hush, Bobus,' put in his mother, 'no matter about that. The question is what is to be done about poor Mr. Richards and Alfred.'

'Write a poetical letter,' said Allen, beginning to extemporise in Hiawatha measure.

> ' O thou mighty man of money,
>   Barnes, of Belforèst, Esquire,
>   Innocent is Alfred Richards ;
>   Innocent his honest father ;
>   Innocent as unborn baby
>   Of development of Midas,
>   Of the smearing of the Cupid,
>   Of the fracture of the goose-bill,
>   Of the writing of the mottoes.
>   All the Brownlows of St. Kenelm's,
>   From the Folly and from Kencroft,
>   Robert, the aspiring soldier,
>   Robert, too, the sucking chemist,
>   John, the Skipjack full of mischief,
>   John, the great originator,
>   Allen, the ——'

'Allen, the uncommon gaby,' broke in Bobus. 'Come, don't waste time, something must be done.'

'Yes, a rational letter must be written and signed by you all,' said his mother. 'The question is whether it would be better to do it through your uncle or Mr Ogilvie.'

'I don't see why my father should hear of it, or Mr. Ogilvie either,' growled Rob. 'I didn't do those donkeyfied ears.'

'You did the writing, which was five hundred times more donkeyfied,' said Jock.

'It is quite impossible to keep either of them in ignorance,' said Caroline.

'Yes,' repeated all her own three ; Jock adding, 'Father would have known it as soon as you, and I don't see that my uncle is much worse.'

'He ain't so soft,' exclaimed Johnnie, roused to loyal defence of his parent.

'Soft !' cried Jock indignantly ; 'I can tell you father did pitch into me when I caught the old lady's bonnet out at the window with a fishing-rod.'

'He never flogged you,' said Johnnie contemptuously.

'He did !' cried Jock triumphantly. 'At least he flogged Bobus, when——'

'Shut up, you little ape,' thundered Bobus, not choosing to be offered up to the manes of his father's discipline.

'You think you must explain it to my uncle, mother,' said Allen, rather ruefully.

'Certainly. He ought to be told first, and Mr. Ogilvie next. Depend upon it, he will be far less angry if it is freely confessed and put into his hands, and what is more important, Mr. Barnes must attend to him, and acquit the Richardses.'

The general voice agreed, but Rob writhed and muttered, 'Can't you be the one to tell him, Mother Carey?'

'That's cool,' said Allen, 'to ask her to do what you're afraid of.'

'He couldn't do anything to her,' said Rob.

However, public opinion went against Rob, and the party of boys dragged him off in their train, the less reluctantly that Allen would be spokesman, and he always got on well with his uncle. No one could tell how it was, but the boy had a frank manner, with a sort of address in the manner of narration, that always went far to disarm displeasure, and protected his comrades as well as himself. So it was that, instead of meeting with unmitigated wrath, the boys found that they were allowed the honours and graces of voluntary confession. Allen even thought that his uncle showed a little veiled appreciation of the joke, but this was not deemed possible by the rest.

To exonerate young Richards was the first requisite, and Allen, under his uncle's eye, drew up a brief note to this effect :—

SIR—We beg to apologise for the mischief done in your grounds, and to assure you on our word and honour that it was suggested by no one, that no one admitted us, and no one had any share in it except ourselves.

ALLEN BROWNLOW.
ROBERT FRIAR BROWNLOW.
ROBERT OTWAY BROWNLOW.
JOHN FRIAR BROWNLOW.
JOHN LUCAS BROWNLOW.

This letter was taken up the next morning to Belforest by Colonel Brownlow, and the two eldest delinquents, one curious, amused, and with only compunction enough to flavour an apology, the other cross, dogged, and sheepish, dragged along like a cur in a sling, 'just as though he were going to be hanged,' said Janet.

The report of the expedition as given by Allen was thus :— 'The servant showed us into a sort of ante-room, and said he would see whether his master would see us. Uncle Robert sent in his card and my letter, and we waited with the door open, and a great screen in front, so that we couldn't help hearing every word. First there was a great snarl, and then a deferential voice, "This alters the case, sir." But the old man swore down in his throat that he didn't care for Colonel Brownlow or Colonel anybody. "A gentleman, sir ; one of the most respected." "Then he should bring up his family better." "Indeed, sir, it might be better to accept the apology. This might not be considered actionable damage." "We'll see that!" "Indeed, don't you agree with me, Mr. Richards, the magistrates would hardly entertain the case." "Then I'll appeal; I'll send a representation to the Home Office." "Is it not to be considered, sir, whether some of these low papers might not put it in a ludicrous light?" Then,' continued Allen, who had been most dramatically mimicking the two voices, 'we heard a crackling as if he were opening my letter, and after an odd noise or two, he sent to call us in to where he was sitting with Richards and the attorney he had got to prosecute us. He is a regular old wizened stick, the perfect image of an old miser; almost hump-backed, and as yellow as a mummy. He looked just ready to bite off our heads, but he was amazingly set on finding out which was which among us, and seemed uncommonly struck with my name and Bobus's. My uncle told him I was called after your father, and he made a snarl just like a dog over a bone. He ended with, "So you are Allen Brownlow! You'll remember this day's work, youngster." I humbly said I should, and so the matter ended.'

'He did not mean any prosecution?'

'Oh no, that was all quashed, even if it was begun. He must have been under an hallucination that he was a stern parent, cutting me off with a shilling.'

The words had also struck the Colonel, who sought the first opportunity of asking his sister-in-law whether she knew the names of any of her mother's relations.

'Only that her name was Otway,' said Caroline. 'You know I lived with my father's aunt, who knew nothing about her, and I have never been able to find anything out. Do you know of any connection? Not this old man! Then you would have known.'

'That does not follow, for I was scarcely in Jamaica at all. I had a long illness immediately after going there, was sent home on leave, and then to the depôt, and only joined again after the regiment had gone to Canada, when the marriage had taken place. I may have heard the name of Mrs. Allen's uncle, but I never bore it in my mind.'

'Is there any way of finding out?'

'I will write to Norton. If he does not remember all about it, his wife will.'

'He is the present lieutenant-colonel, I think.'

'Yes, and he was your father's chief friend. Now that they are at home again, we must have him here one of these days.'

'It would be a wonderful thing if this freak were an introduction to a relation,' said Caroline.

'There was no doubt of his being struck by the combination of Allen and Otway. He chose to understand which were my sons and which my nephews, and when I said that Allen bore your maiden name he assented as if he knew it before, and spoke of your boy having cause to remember this; I am afraid it will not be pleasantly.'

'No,' said Caroline, 'it sounded much like a threat. But one would like to know, only I thought Farmer Gould's little grand-daughter was his niece.'

'That might be without preventing your relationship ; I will do my best to ascertain it.'

Colonel Norton's letter gave decisive information that Barnes was the name of the uncle with whom Caroline Otway had been living at the time of her marriage. She had been treated as a poor relation, and seemed to be half-slave, half-governess to the children of the favoured sister, little semi-Spanish tyrants. This had roused Captain Allen's chivalry, and his friend remembered his saying that, though he had little or nothing of his own, he could at least make her happier than she was in such a family. The uncle was reported to have grown rich in the mahogany trade, and likewise by steamboat speculations, coupled with judicious stock-jobbing among the distressed West Indians after the emancipation.

'He was a sinister-looking old fellow,' ended Colonel Norton, 'and I should think not very particular ; but I should be glad to hear that he had done justice to poor Allen's daughter. He was written to when she was left an orphan, but vouchsafed no answer.'

'Still he may have kept an eye upon you,' added Uncle Robert. 'I do not think it was new to him that you had married into our family.'

'If only those unfortunate boys have not ruined everything,' sighed Ellen.

'Little Elvira's father must have been one of those cousins,' said Caroline. 'I wonder what became of the others ? She must be—let me see—my second cousin.'

'Not very near,' said Ellen.

'I never had a blood relation before since my old aunt died. I am so glad that brilliant child belongs to me !'

'I daresay old Gould could tell you more,' said the Colonel.

'Is it wise to revive the connection ?' asked his wife.

'The Goulds are not likely to presume,' said the Colonel ; 'and I think that if Caroline takes up the one connection, she is bound to take up the other.'

'How am I to make up to this cross old man ?' said Carey. 'I can't go and fawn on him.'

'Certainly not,' said her brother-in-law ; 'but I think you ought to make some advance, merely as a relation.'

On the family vote, Caroline rather unwillingly wrote a note, explaining that she had only just discovered her kinship with Mr. Barnes, and offering to come and see him ; but not the smallest notice was taken of her letter, rather to her relief, though she did not like to hear Ellen augur ill for the future.

Another letter, to old Mr. Gould, begging him to call upon her next market day, met with a far more ready response. When at his entrance she greeted him with outstretched hands, and 'I never thought you were a connection,' the fine old weather-beaten face was strangely moved, as the rugged hand took hers, and the voice was husky that said—

'I thought there was a likeness in the voice, but I never imagined you were grandchild to poor Carey Barnes; I beg your pardon, to Mrs. Otway.'

'You knew her? You must let me see something of my little cousin! I know nothing of my relations, and my brother-in-law said he thought you could tell me.'

'I ought to be able, for the family lived at Woodbridge all my young days,' said the farmer.

The history was then given. The present lord of the manor had been the son of a land surveyor. He was a stunted, sickly, slightly-deformed lad, noted chiefly for skill in ciphering, and therefore had been placed in a clerkship. Here a successful lottery ticket had been the foundation of his fortunes; he had invested it in the mahogany trade, and had been one of those men with whom everything turned up a prize. When a little over thirty, he had returned to his own neighbourhood, looking any imaginable age. He had then purchased Belforest, furnished it sumptuously, and laid out magnificent gardens in preparation for his bride, a charming young lady of quality. But she had had a young Lochinvar, and even in her wedding-dress, favoured by sympathising servants, had escaped down the back stairs of a London hotel, and been married at the nearest church, leaving poor Mr. Barnes in the case of the poor craven bridegroom, into whose feelings no one ever inquired.

Mr. Barnes had gone back to the West Indies at once, and never appeared in England again till he came home, a broken and soured old man, to die. There had been two sisters, and Caroline fancied that the old farmer had had some tenderness for the elder one, but she had married, before her brother's prosperity, a poor struggling builder, and both had died young, leaving their child dependent on her uncle. His younger sister had been the favourite; he had taken her back with him to America, and married her to a man of Spanish blood, connected with him in business. The only one of her children who survived childhood was educated in England, treated as his uncle's heir, and came to Belforest for shooting. Thus it was that he had fallen in love with Farmer Gould's pretty daughter, and as it seemed, by her mother's contrivance, though without her father's consent, had made her his wife.

The wrath of Mr. Barnes was implacable. He cast off the favourite nephew as entirely as he had cast off the despised niece, and deprived him of all the means he had been led to look on as his right. The young man had nothing of his own but an estate in the small island of San Ildefonso, of very little value, and some of his former friends made interest to obtain a vice-consulship for him at the Spanish town. Then, after a few years, both husband and wife died, leaving this little orphan to the care of her grandfather, who had written to Mr. Barnes on her father's death, but had heard nothing from him, and had too much honest pride to make any further application.

'My little cousin,' said Caroline, 'the first I ever knew. Pray bring her to see me, and let her stay with me long enough for me to know her.'

The old man began to prepare her for the child's being shy and wild, though perhaps her aunt was too particular with her, and expected too much. Perhaps she would be homesick, he said, so wistfully that it was plain that he did not know how to exist without his darling; but he was charmed with the invitation, and Caroline was pleased to see that he did not regard her as his grandchild's rival, but as representing the cherished playmate of his youth.

## CHAPTER XIII

### THE RIVAL HEIRESSES

'	You smile, their eager ways to see,
	But mark their choice when they
	To choose their sportive garb are free,
	The moral of their play.'

			KEBLE.

ONE curious part of the reticence of youth is that which relates to its comprehension of grown-up affairs. There is a smile with which the elders greet any question on the subject, half of wonder, half of amusement, which is perfectly intolerable to the young, who remain thinking that they are regarded as presumptuous and absurd, and thus will do anything rather than expose themselves to it again.

Thus it was that Mrs. Brownlow flattered herself that her children never put two and two together when she let them know of the discovery of their relationship. Partly she judged by herself. She was never in the habit of forecasting, and for so clever and spirited a woman, she thought wonderfully little. She had plenty of intuitive sense, decided rapidly and clearly, and could easily throw herself in other people's thoughts, but she seldom reflected, analysed, or moralised, save on the spur of the moment. She lived chiefly in the present, and the chief events of her life had all come so suddenly and unexpectedly upon her, that she was all the less inclined to guess at the future, having always hitherto been taken by surprise.

So when Jock observed in public, 'Mother, they say at Kencroft that the old miser ought to leave you half his money. Do you think he will?' it was with perfect truth that she answered, 'I don't think at all about it.'

It was taken in the family as an intimation that she would not talk about it, and while she supposed that the children drew no conclusions, they thought the more.

Allen was gone to Eton, but Janet and Bobus had many

discussions over their chemical experiments, about possibilities
and probabilities, odd compounds of cleverness and ignorance.

'Mother must be heir-at-law, for her grandmother was
eldest,' said Janet.

'A woman can't be heir-at-law,' said Bobus.

'The Salique law doesn't come into England.'

'Yes it does, for Sir John Gray got Graysnest only last year,
instead of the old man's daughter.'

'Then how comes the Queen to be Queen?'

'Besides'—Bobus shifted his ground to another possibility—
'when there's nobody but a lot of women, the thing goes into
abeyance among them.'

'Who gets it, then?'

'Chancery, I suppose, or some of the lawyers.   They are all
blood-suckers.'

'I'm sure,' said Janet, superior by three years of wisdom,
'that abeyance only happens about Scotch peerages ; and if he
has not made a will, mother will be heiress.'

'Only halves with that black Undine of Allen's,' sturdily
persisted Bobus.   'Is she coming here, Janet?'

'Yes, to-morrow.   I did not think we wanted another child
about the house ; Essie and Ellie are quite enough.'

'If mother gets rich she won't have all that teaching to
bother her,' said Bobus.

'And I can go on with my education,' said Janet.

'Girl's education does not signify,' said Bobus.   'Now I shall
be able to get the very best instruction in physical science, and
make some great discovery.   If I could only go and study at
Halle, instead of going on droning here.'

'Oh! boys can always get educated if they choose.   You are
going to Eton or Winchester after this term.'

'Not if I can get any sense into mother.   I don't want to
waste my time on those stupid classics and athletics.   I say,
Janet, it's time to see whether the precipitation has taken
place.'

The two used to try experiments together, in Bobus's end of
the attic, to an extent that might make the presence of a strange
child in the house dangerous to herself as well as to every one
else.

Mrs. Gould herself brought the little girl, trying to impress
on Mrs. Brownlow that if she was indocile it was not her fault,
but her grandfather could not bear to have her crossed.

The elders did not wonder at his weakness, for the creature
was wonderfully lovely and winning, with a fearless imperious-
ness that subdued every one to her service.   So brilliant was
she, that Essie and Ellie, though very pretty little girls, looked
faded and effaced beside this small empress, whose air seemed
to give her a right to bestow her favours.

'I'm glad to be here !' she observed graciously to her hostess,
for you are my cousin and a lady.'

'And pray what are you?' asked Janet.

'I am La Señora Doña Elvira Maria de Guadalupe de Menella," replied the damsel, with a liquid sonorousness so annihilating, that Janet made a mocking courtesy; and her mother said it was like asking the head of the house of Hapsburg if she were a lady!

With some disappointment at Allen's absence, the little Donna motioned Bobus to sit by her side at dinner-time, and when her grandfather looked in somewhat later to wish her good-bye, in mingled hope and fear of her insisting on going home with him, she cared for nothing but his admiration of her playing at kings and queens with Armine and Barbara, in *the* cotton velvet train of the dressing-up wardrobe.

'No, she did not want to go home. She never wanted to go back to River Hollow.'

Nor would she even kiss him till she had extorted the assurance that he had been shaved that morning.

The old man went away blessing Mrs. Brownlow's kindness to his child, and Janet was universally scouted for muttering that it was a heartless little being. She alone remained unenthralled by Elvira's chains. The first time she went to Kencroft, she made Colonel Brownlow hold her up in his arms to gather a bough off his own favourite double cherry; and when Mother Carey demurred, she beguiled Aunt Ellen into taking her on her own responsibility to the dancing lessons at the assembly rooms.

There she electrified the dancing-master and all beholders, seeming to catch inspiration from the music, and floating along with a wondrous swimming grace, as her dainty feet twinkled, her arms wreathed themselves, and her eyes shone with enjoyment.

If she could only have always danced, or acted in the garden! Armine's and Babie's perpetual romantic dramas were all turned by her into homage to one and the same princess. She never knew or cared whether she were goddess or fairy, Greek or Briton, provided she had the crown and train; but as Babie much preferred action to magnificence, they got on wonderfully well without disputes. There was a continual performance, endless as a Chinese tragedy, of Spenser's *Faery Queene*, in which Elfie was always Gloriana, and Armine and Babie were everybody else in turn, except the wicked characters, who were represented by the cabbages and a dummy.

'Reading was horrid,' Elvira said, and certainly hers deserved the epithet. Her attainments fell far behind those of Essie and Ellie, and she did not mean to improve them. Her hostess let her alone till she had twice shaken her rich mane at her grandfather, and refused to return with him; and he had shown himself deeply grateful to Mrs. Brownlow for keeping her there, and had said he hoped she was good at her lessons.

The first trial resulted in Elvira's going to sleep over her book, the next in her playing all sorts of ridiculous tricks, and sulking when stopped, and when she was forbidden to speak or go out till she had repeated three answers in the multiplication table, she was the next moment singing and dancing in defiance in the garden. Caroline did not choose to endure this, and went to fetch her in, thus producing such a screaming, kicking, rolling fury that Mrs. Coffinkey might have some colour for the statement that Mrs. Folly Brownlow was murdering all her children. The cook, as the strongest person in the house, was called, carried her in, and put her to bed, where she fell sound asleep, and woke hungry, in high spirits, and without an atom of compunction.

When called to lessons she replied, 'No, I'm going back to grandpapa.'

'Very well,' was all Caroline answered, thinking wholesome neglect the best treatment.

In an hour's time Mr. Gould made his appearance with his grandchild. She had sought him out among the pigs in the market-place, pulled him by the coat, and insisted on being taken home.

His politeness was great, but he was plainly delighted, and determined to believe that her demand sprang from affection, and not naughtiness. Elvira stood caressing him, barely vouchsafing to look at her hostess, and declaring that she never meant to come back.

Not a fortnight had passed, however, before she burst upon them again, kissing them all round, and reiterating that she hated her aunt, and would live with Mother Carey. Mr. Gould had waited to be properly ushered in. He was distressed and apologetic, but he had been forced to do his tyrant's behest. There had been more disturbances than ever between her and her aunt, and Mrs. Gould had declared that she would not manage the child any longer, while Elvira was still more vehement to return to Mother Carey. Would Mrs. Brownlow recommend some school or family where the child would be well cared for? Mrs. Brownlow did more, offering herself to undertake the charge.

Spite of all the naughtiness, she loved the beautiful wild creature, and could not bear to think of entrusting her to strangers; she knew, too, that her brother and sister-in-law had no objection, and it was the obvious plan. Mr. Gould would make some small payment, and the child was to be made to understand that she must be obedient, learn her lessons, and cease to expect to find a refuge with her grandfather when she was offended.

She drew herself up with childish pride and grace, saying, 'I will attend to Mrs. Brownlow, for she is my cousin and my equal.'

To a certain degree the little maiden kept her word. She was the favourite plaything of the boys, and got on well with

Babie, who was too bright and yielding to quarrel with any one.

But Janet's elder-sisterly authority was never accepted by the newcomer. 'I couldn't mind her, she looked so ugly,' said she in excuse ; and probably the heavy, brown, dull complexion and large features were repulsive in themselves to the sensitive fancy of the creature of life and beauty. At any rate, they were jarring elephants, as said Eleanor, who was growing ambitious, and sometimes electrified the public with curious versions of the long words more successfully used by Armine and Babie.

Caroline succeeded in modelling a very lovely profile in bas-relief of the exquisite little head, and then had it photographed. Mary Ogilvie, coming to Kenminster as usual when her holidays began in June, found the photograph in the place of honour on her brother's chimney-piece, and a little one beside it of the artist herself.

So far as Carey herself was concerned, Mary was much better satisfied. She did not look so worn or so flighty, and had a quieter and more really cheerful tone and manner, as of one who had settled into her home and occupations. She had made friends, too—few, but worth having ; and there were those who pronounced the Folly the pleasantest house in Kenminster, and regarded the five o'clock tea, after the weekly physical science lecture at the school, as a delightful institution.

Of course, the schoolmaster was one of these ; and when Mary found how all his paths tended to the Pagoda, she hated herself for being a suspicious old duenna. Nevertheless, she could not but be alarmed by finding that her project of a walking tour through Brittany was not, indeed, refused, but deferred, with excuses about having work to finish, being in no hurry, and the like.

'I think you ought to go,' said Mary at last.

'I see no ought in the case. Last year the work dragged, and was oppressive ; but you see how different it has become.'

'That is the very reason,' said Mary, the colour flying to her cheeks. 'It will not do to stay lingering here as we did last summer, and not only on your own account.'

'You need not be afraid,' was the muttered answer, as David bent down his head over the exercise he was correcting. She made no answer, and ere long he began again, 'I don't mean that her equal exists, but I am not such a fool as to delude myself with a spark of hope.'

'She is too nice for that,' said Mary.

'Just so,' he said, glad to relieve himself when the ice had been broken. 'There's something about her that makes one feel her to be altogether that doctor's, as much as if he were present in the flesh.'

'Are you hoping to wear that out? For I don't think you will.'

'I told you I had no hope,' he answered, rather petulantly.

'Even were it otherwise, there is another thing that must withhold me. It has got abroad that she may turn out heiress to the old man at Belforest.'

'In such a hopeless case, would it not be wiser to leave this place altogether?'

'I cannot,' he exclaimed; then remembering that vehemence told against him, he added, 'Don't be uneasy; I am a reasonable man, and she is a woman to keep one so; but I think I am useful to her, and I am sure she is useful to me.'

'That I allow she has been,' said Mary, looking at her brother's much improved appearance; 'but——'

'Moths and candles to wit,' he returned; 'but don't be afraid, I attract no notice, and I think she trusts me about her boys.'

'But what is it to come to?'

'I have thought of that. Understand that it is enough for me to live near her, and be now and then of some little service to her.'

'You troubadour!'

They were interrupted by a note, which Mr. Ogilvie read, and handed to his sister with a smile—

DEAR MR. OGILVIE—Could you and Mary make it convenient to look in this evening? Bobus has horrified his uncle by declining to go up for a scholarship at Eton or Winchester, and I should be very glad to talk it over with you. Also, I shall have to ask you to take little Armine into school after the holidays.—Yours sincerely,     C. O. BROWNLOW.

'What does the boy mean?' asked Mary. 'I thought he was the pride of your heart.'

'So he is; but he is ahead of his fellows, and ought to be elsewhere. All measures have been taken for sending him up to stand at one of the public schools, but I thought him very passive about it. He is an odd boy—reserved and self-concentrated—quite beyond his uncle's comprehension, and likely to become headstrong at a blind exercise of authority.'

'I used to like Allen best,' said Mary.

'He is the pleasantest, but there's more solid stuff in Bobus. That boy's school character is perfect, except for a certain cool opinionativeness, which seldom comes out with me, but greatly annoys the undermasters.'

'Is he a prig?'

'Well, yes, I'm afraid he is. He's unpopular, for he does not care for games; but his brother is popular enough for both.'

'Jock?—the monkey!'

'His brains run to mischief. I've had to set him more impositions than any boy in the school, and actually to take his form myself, for simply the undermasters can't keep up discipline or their own tempers. As to poor M. le Blanc, I find him dancing and shrieking with fury in the midst of a circle of snorting, giggling boys; and when he points out *ce petit monstre*, Jock coolly owns to having translated "*Croquons les*," let us croquet them; or "*Je suis blessé*," I am blest.'

'So the infusion of brains produces too much effervescence.'

'Yes, but the whole school has profited, and none more so than No. 2 of the other family, who has quite passed his elder brother, and is above his namesake whenever it is a case of plodding ability *versus* idle genius. But, after all, how little one can know of one's boys.'

'Or one's girls,' said Mary, thinking of governess experiences.

It was a showery summer evening when the brother and sister walked up to the Folly in a partial clearing, when the evening sun made every bush twinkle all over with diamond drops. Childish voices were heard near the gate, and behind a dripping laurel were seen Elvira, Armine, and Barbara engaged in childhood's unceasing attempt to explore the centre of the earth.

'What do you expect to find there?' they were asked.

'Little kobolds, with pointed caps, playing at ball with rubies and emeralds, and digging with golden spades,' answered Babie.

'And they shall give me an opal ring,' said Elfie. 'But Armine does not want the kobolds.'

'He says they are bad,' said Babie. 'Now are they, Mr. Ogilvie? I know elder women are, and erl kings and mist widows, but poor Neck, that sat on the water and played his harp, wasn't bad, and the dear little kobolds were so kind and funny. Now are they bad elves?'

Her voice was full of earnest pleading, and Mr. Ogilvie, not being versed in the spiritual condition of elves, could best reply by asking why Armine thought ill of their kind.

'I think they are nasty little things that want to distract and bewilder one in the real great search.'

'What search, my boy?'

'For the source of everything,' said Armine, lowering his voice and looking into his muddy hole.

'But that is above, not below,' said Mary.

'Yes,' said Armine reverently; 'but I think God put life and the beginning of growing into the earth, and I want to find it.'

'Isn't it Truth?' said Babie. 'Mr. Acton said Truth was at the bottom of a well. I won't look at the kobolds if they keep one from seeing Truth.'

'But I must get my ring and all my jewels from them,' put in Elfie.

'Should you know Truth?' asked Mr. Ogilvie. 'What do you think she is like?'

'So beautiful!' said Babie, clasping her fingers with earnestness. 'All white and clear like crystal, with such blue, sweet, open eyes. And she has an anchor.'

'That's Hope?' said Armine.

'Oh! Hope and Truth go hand in hand,' said Babie; 'and

Hope will be all robed in green like the young corn-fields in the spring.'

'Ah, Babie, that emerald Hope and crystal Truth are not down in the earth, earthy,' said Mary again.

'Nay, perhaps Armine has got hold of a reality,' said Mr. Ogilvie. 'They are to be found above by working below.'

'Talking paradox to Armine?' said the cheerful voice of the young mother. 'My dear sprites, do you know that it is past eight? How wet you are! Good-night, and mind you don't go upstairs in those boots.'

'It is quite comfortable to hear anything so commonplace,' said Mary, when the children had run away, to the sound of its reiteration after full interchange of good-nights. 'Those imps make one feel quite eerie.'

'Has Armine been talking in that curious fashion of his?' said Carey, as they began to pace the walks. 'I am afraid his thinker is too big — as the child says in Miss Tytler's book. This morning over his parsing he asked me—"Mother, which is *reallest*, what we touch or what we feel?" knitting his brows fearfully when I did not catch his meaning, and going on—"I mean is that fly as real as King David?" and then as I was more puzzled he went on—"You see we only need just see that fly now with our outermost senses, and he will only live a little while, and nobody cares or will think of him any more, but everybody always does think, and feel, and care a great deal about King David." I told him, as the best answer I could make on the spur of the moment, that David was alive in heaven, but he pondered in and broke out—"No, that's not it! David was a real man, but it is just the same about Perseus and Siegfried, and lots of people that never were men, only just thoughts. Ain't thoughts *realler* than things, mother?"'

'But much worse for him, I should say,' exclaimed Mary.

'I thought of Pisistratus Caxton, and wrote to Mr. Ogilvie. It is a great pity, but I am afraid he ought not to dwell on such things till his body is grown up to his mind.'

'Yes, school is the approved remedy for being too clever,' said Mr. Ogilvie. 'You are wise. It is a pity, but it will be all the better for him by and by.'

'And the elder ones will take care the seasoning is not too severe,' said Caroline, with a resolution she could hardly have shown if this had been her first launch of a son. 'But it was about Bobus that I wanted to consult you. His uncle thinks him headstrong and conceited, if not lazy.'

'Lazy he is certainly not.'

'I knew you would say so, but the Colonel cannot enter into his wish to have more physical science and less classics, and will not hear of his going to Germany, which is what he wishes, though I am sure he is too young.'

'He ought not to go there till his character is much more formed.'

'What do you think of his going on here?'

'That's a temptation I ought to resist. He will soon have outstripped the other boys, so that I could not give him the attention he needs, and besides, the being with other boys, more his equals, would be invaluable to him.'

'Well, he is rather bumptious.'

'Nothing is worse for a lad of that sort than being cock of the walk. It spoils him often for life.'

'I know exactly the sort of man you mean, always liking to lay down the law and talking to women instead of men, because they don't argue with him. No, Bobus must not come to that, and he is too young to begin special training. Will you talk to him, Mr. Ogilvie? You know if my horse is not convinced, I may bring him to the water, but it will be all in vain.'.

They had reached the outside of the window of the dining-room, where the schoolboys were learning their lessons for the morrow. Bobus was sitting at the table with a small lamp so shaded as to concentrate the light on him and to afford it to no one else. On the floor was a servant's flat candlestick, mounted on a pile of books, between one John sprawling at full length preparing his Virgil, the other cross-legged, working a sum with ink from a doll's tea-cup placed in the candlestick, and all the time there was a wonderful mumbling accompaniment, as there always was between those two.

'I say, what does *pulsum* come from?'

'What a brute this is of a fraction! Skipjack, what will go in 639 and 852?'

'*Pulsum*, a pulse—*volat*, flies. Eh! Three'll do it. Or common measure it at once.'

'Bother common measure. The threes in——'

'*Fama*, fame; *volat*, flies; *pulsum*, the pulse; *cecisse*, to have ceased; *paternis regnis*, in the paternal kingdom. I say, wouldn't that rile Perkins like fun?'

'The threes in seven—two—in eighteen——'

'I say, Johnnie, is *pulsum* from *pulco*?'

'Never heard of it.'

'Bobus, is it *pulco, pulxi, pulsum*?'

'*Pulco*—I make an ass of myself,' muttered Bobus.

'Oh murder,' groaned Johnnie, 'it has come out 213.'

'Not half so much murder as this *pulsum*. Why, it will go in them both. I can see with half an eye.'

'Isn't it *pello—pulsum*?'

'*Pello*, to drive out. Hurrah! That fits it.'

'Look out, Skipjack, there's a moth.'

'Anything worth having?' demanded Bobus.

'Only a grass eggar *Fama*, fame; *volat*, flies; *Idomaea ducem*, that Idomaeus the leader; *pulsum*, expelled. Get out, I say, you foolish beggar' (to the moth).

'Never mind catching him,' said Bobus, 'we've got dozens.'

'Yes, but I don't want him frizzling alive in my candle.'

'Don't kick up such a shindy,' broke out Johnnie, as a much-stained handkerchief came flapping about.

'You've blotted my sum. Thunder and ages!' as the candle-stick toppled over, ink and all. 'That is a go!'

'I say, Bobus, lend us your Guy Fawkes to pick up the pieces.'

'Not if I know it,' said Bobus. 'You always smash things.'

'There's a specimen of the way we learn our lessons,' said Caroline in a low voice, still unseen, as Bobus wiped, sheathed, and pocketed his favourite pen, then proceeded to turn down the lamp, but allowed the others to relight their candle at the expiring wick.

'The results are fair,' said Mr. Ogilvie.

'I think of your carpet,' said Mary quaintly.

'We always lay down an ancient floorcloth in the bay window before the boys come home,' said Carey, laughing. 'Here, Bobus.'

And as he came out headforemost at the window, the two ladies discreetly drew off to leave the conversation free.

'So, Brownlow,' said Mr. Ogilvie, 'I hear you don't want to try your luck elsewhere.'

'No, sir.'

'Do you object to telling me why?'

'I see no use in it,' said Bobus, never shy, and further aided by the twilight; 'I do quite well enough here.'

'Should you not do better in a larger field among a higher stamp of boys?'

'Public schoolboys are such fools!'

'And what are the Kenites?'

'Well, not much,' said Bobus, with a twitch in the corner of his mouth; 'but I can keep out of their way.'

'You mean that you have gained your footing, and don't want to have to do it again.'

'Not only that, sir,' said the boy, 'but at a public school you're fagged, and forced to go in for cricket and football.'

'You would soon get above that.'

'Yes, but even then you get no peace, and are nobody unless you go in for all that stuff of athletics and sports. I hate it all, and don't want to waste my time.'

'I don't think you are quite right as to there being no distinction without athletics.'

'Allen says it is so now.'

'Allen may be a better judge of the present state of things, but I should think there was always a studious set who were respectable.'

'Besides,' proceeded Bobus, warming with his subject, 'I see no good in nothing but classics. I don't care what ridiculous lies some old man who never existed, or else was a dozen people at once, told about a lot of ruffians who never lived, killing each other at some place that never was. I like what you can lay your finger on, and say it's here, it's true, and I can prove it, and explain it, and improve on it.'

'If you can,' said Mr. Ogilvie, struck by the contrast with the little brother.

'That's what I want to do,' said Bobus ; 'to deal with real things, not words and empty fancies. I know languages are necessary ; but if one can read a Latin book, and understand a Greek technical term, that's all that is of use. If my uncle won't let me study physical science in Germany, I had rather go on here, where I can be let alone to study it for myself.'

'I do not think you understand what you would throw away. What is the difference between Higg, the bone-setter, and Dr. Leslie ?'

'Higg can do that one thing just by instinct. He is un-educated.'

'And in a measure it is so with all who throw themselves into some special pursuit without waiting for the mind and character to have full training and expansion. If you mean to be a great surgeon——'

'I don't mean to be a surgeon.'

'A physician, then.'

'No, sir. Please don't let my mother fancy I mean to be in practice, at every one's beck and call. I've seen too much of that. I mean to get a professorship, and have time and apparatus for researches, so as to get to the bottom of everything,' said the boy, with the vast purposes of his age.

'Your chances will be much better if you go up from a public school, trained in accuracy by the thorough work of language, and made more powerful by the very fact of not having followed merely your own bent. Your contempt for the classics shows how one-sided you are growing. Besides, I thought you knew that the days are over of unmitigated classics. You would have many more opportunities, and much better ones, of studying physical science than I can provide for you here.'

This was a new light to Bobus, and when Mr. Ogilvie proved its truth to him, and described the facilities he would have for the study, he allowed that it made all the difference.

Meantime the two ladies had gone in, Mary asking where Janet was.

'Gone with Jessie and her mother to a birthday party at Polesworth Lawn.'

'Not a good day for it.'

'It is the perplexing sort of day that no one knows whether to call it fine or wet ; but Ellen decided on going, as they were to dance in the hall if it rained. I'm sure her kindness is great, for she takes infinite trouble to make Janet producible ! Poor Janet, you know dressing her is like hanging clothes on a wooden peg, and a peg that won't stand still, and has curious theories of the beautiful, carried out in a still more curious

way. So when, in terror of our aunt, the whole female household have done their best to turn out Miss Janet respectable,
between this house and Kencroft, she contrives to give herself
some twitch, or else is seized with an idea of the picturesque,
which sets every one wondering that I let her go about such a
figure. Then Ellen and Jessie put a tie here, and a pin there,
and reduce the chaotic mass to order.'

It was not long before Janet appeared, and Jessie with her,
the latter having been set down to give a message. The two
girls were dressed in the same light black-and-white checked
silk of early youth, one with pink ribbons and the other with
blue ; but the contrast was the more apparent, for one was fresh
and crisp, while the other was flattened and tumbled ; one said
everything had been delightful, the other that it had all been
very stupid, and the expression made even more difference than
the complexion, in one so fair, fresh, and rosy, in the other so
sallow and muddled. Jessie looked so sweet and bright, that
when she had gone Miss Ogilvie could not help exclaiming,
'How pretty she is !'

'Yes, and so good-tempered and pleasant. There is something always restful to me in having her in the room,' said
Caroline.

'Restful?' said Janet, with one of her unamiable sneers.
'Yes, she and H. S. H. sent me off to sleep with their gossip on
the way home ! O mother, there's another item for the Belforest
record. Mr. Barnes has sent off all his servants again, even the
confidential man is shipped off to America.'

'You seem to have slept with one ear open,' said her mother.
'And oh !' as Janet took off her gloves, 'I hope you did not show
those hands !'

'I could not eat cake without doing so, and Mr. Glover
supposed I had been photographing.'

'And what had you been doing?' inquired Mary, at sight of
the brown stains.

'Trying chemical experiments with Bobus,' said her mother.

'Yes !' cried Janet, 'and I've found out why we did not
succeed. I thought it out during the dancing.'

'Instead of cultivating the "light fantastic toe," as the *Courier*
calls it.'

'I danced twice, and a great plague it was. Only with Mr.
Glover and with a stupid little middy. I was thinking all the
time how senseless it was.'

'How agreeable you must have been !'

'One can't be agreeable to people like that. O Bobus !' as
he came into the room with Mr. Ogilvie, 'I've found out——'

'I thought Jessie was here,' he interrupted.

'She's gone home. I know what was wrong yesterday. We
ought to have isolated the hypo——'

'Isolated the grandmother,' said Bobus. 'That has nothing to
do with it.'

K

'I'm sure of it.  I'll show you how it acts.'

'I'll show you just the contrary.'

'Not to-night,' cried their mother, as Bobus began to relight the lamp.  'You two explosives are quite perilous enough by day without lamps and candles.'

'You endure a great deal,' said Mr. Ogilvie.

'I'm not afraid of either of these two doing anything dangerous singly, for they are both careful, but when they are of different minds, I never know what the collision may produce.'

'Yes,' said Bobus, 'I'd much sooner have Jessie to help me, for she does what she is bid, and never thinks.'

'That's all you think women good for,' said Janet.

'Quite true,' said Bobus coolly

And Mr. Ogilvie was acknowledged by his sister to have done a good deed that night, since the Folly might be far more secure when Janet tried her experiments alone.


## CHAPTER XIV

### PUMPING AWAY

'The rude will scuffle through with ease enough ;
Great schools best suit the sturdy and the rough.
Soon see your wish fulfilled in either child,
The pert made perter, and the tame made wild.'

COWPER.

ROBERT OTWAY BROWNLOW came out fourth on the roll of newly-elected scholars of S. Mary, Winton, and his master was, as his sister declared, unwholesomely proud of it, even while he gave all credit to the Folly, and none to himself.

Still Mary had her way and took him to Brittany, and though her present pupils were to leave the schoolroom at Christmas, she would bind herself to no fresh engagement, thinking that she had better be free to make a home for him, whether at Kenminster or elsewhere.

When the half-year began again, Bobus was a good deal missed, Jock was in a severe idle fit, and Armine did not come up to the expectations formed of him, and was found, when 'up to Mr. Perkins,' to be as bewildered and unready as other people.

All the work in the school seemed flat and poor, except perhaps Johnnie's, which steadily improved.  Robert, whose father wished him to be pushed on so as to be fit for examination for Sandhurst, opposed to all pressure the passive resistance of stolidity.  He was nearly sixteen, but seemed incapable of understanding that compulsory studies were for his good and not a cruel exercise of tyranny.  He disdainfully rejected an offer from his aunt to help him in the French and arithmetic

which had become imminent, while of the first he knew much
less than Babie, and of the latter only as much as would serve
to prevent his being daily 'kept in.'

One chilly autumn afternoon, Armine was seen, even by the
unobservant under-master, to be shivering violently, and his
teeth chattering so that he could not speak plainly.

'You ought to be at home,' said Mr. Perkins. 'Here you,
Brownlow maximus, just see him home, and tell his mother that
he should be seen to.'

'I can go alone,' Armine tried to say; but Mr. Perkins
thought the head-master could not say he neglected one who
was felt to be a favoured scholar if he sent his cousin with him.

So presently Armine was pushed in at the back door, with
these words from Rob to the cook—'Look here, he's been and
got cold or something.'

Rob then disappeared, and Armine struggled in to the kitchen
fire, white, sobbing and panting, and, as the compassionate
maids discovered, drenched from head to foot, his hair soaked,
his boots squishing with water. His mother and sisters were
out, and as cook administered the hottest draught she could
compound, and Emma tugged at his jacket, they indignantly
demanded what he had been doing to himself.

'Nothing,' he said. 'I'll go and take my things off; only
please don't tell mother.'

'Yes,' said old nurse, who had tottered in, but who was past
fully comprehending emergencies;' 'go and get into bed, my
dear, and Emma shall come and warm it for him.'

'No,' stoutly said the little boy; 'there's nothing the matter,
and mother must not know.'

'Take my word for it,' said cook, 'that child have a been
treated shameful by those great nasty brutes of big boys.'

And when Armine, too cold to sit anywhere but by the only
fire in the house, returned with a book and begged humbly for
leave to warm himself, he was installed on nurse's footstool, in
front of a huge fire, and hot tea and 'lardy-cake' tendered for
his refreshment, while the maids by turns pitied and questioned
him.

'Have you had a haccident, sir?' asked cook.

'No,' he wearily said.

'Have any one been doing anything to you, then?' And as
he did not answer, she continued: 'You need not think to blind
me, sir; I sees it as if it was in print. Them big boys have been
a-misusing of you.'

'Now, cook, you ain't to say a word to my mother,' cried
Armine vehemently. 'Promise me.'

'If you'll tell me all about it, sir,' said cook coaxingly.

'No,' he answered, 'I promised!' and he buried his head in
nurse's lap.

'I calls that a shame,' put in Emma; 'but you could tell we,
Master Armine. It ain't like telling your ma nor your master.'

'I said no one,' said Armine.

The maids left off tormenting him after a time, letting him fall asleep with his head on the lap of old nurse, who went on dreamily stroking his damp hair, not half understanding the matter, or she would have sent him to bed.

Being bound by no promise of secrecy, Emma met her mistress with a statement of the surmises of the kitchen, and Caroline hurried thither to find him waking to headache, fiery cheeks, and aching limbs, which were not simply the consequence of the position in which he had been sleeping before the fire. She saw him safe in bed before she asked any questions, but then she began her interrogations, as little successfully as the maids.

'I can't, mother,' he said, hiding his face on the pillow.

'My little boy used to have no secrets from me.'

'Men must have secrets sometimes, though they rack their hearts and—their backs,' sighed poor Armine, rolling over. 'O mother, my back is so bad! Please don't bother besides.'

'My poor darling! Let me rub it. There, you might trust Mother Carey! She would not tell Mr. Ogilvie, nor get any one into trouble.'

'I promised, mother. Don't!' And no persuasions could draw anything from him but tears. Indeed he was so feverish and in so much pain that she called in Dr. Leslie before the evening was over, and rheumatic fever was barely staved off by the most anxious vigilance for the next day or two. It was further decreed that he must be carefully tended all the winter, and must not go to school again till he had quite got over the shock, since he was of a delicate frame that would not bear to be trifled with.

The boy gave a long sigh of content when he heard that he was not to return to school at present; but it did not induce him to utter a word on the cause of the wetting, either to his mother or to Mr. Ogilvie, who came up in much distress, and examined him as soon as he was well enough to bear it. Nor would any of his schoolfellows tell. Jock said he had had an imposition, and was kept in school when 'it' happened; John said 'he had nothing to do with it'; and Rob and Joe opposed surly negatives to all questions on the subject, Rob adding that Armine was a disgusting little idiot, an expression for which his father took him severely to task.

However, there were those in Kenminster who never failed to know all about everything, and the first afternoon after Armine's disaster that Caroline came to Kencroft she was received with such sympathetic kindness that her prophetic soul misgave her, and she dreaded hearing either that she was letting herself be cheated by some tradesman, or that she was to lose her pupils.

No. After inquiries for Armine, his aunt said she was very

sorry, but now he was better she thought his mother ought to know the truth.

'What——?' asked Caroline, startled; and Jessie, the only other person in the room, put down her work, and listened with a strange air of determination.

'My dear, I am afraid it is very painful.'

'Tell me at once, Ellen.'

'I can't think how he learnt it. But they have been about with all sorts of odd people.'

'Who? What, Ellen? Are you accusing my boy?' said Caroline, her limbs beginning to tremble and her eyes to flash, though she spoke as quietly as she could.

'Now do compose yourself, my dear. I dare say the poor little fellow knew no better, and he has had a severe lesson.'

'If you would only tell me, Ellen.'

'It seems,' said Ellen, with much regret and commiseration, 'that all this was from poor little Armine using such shocking language that Rob, as a senior boy, you know, put him under the pump at last to put a stop to it.'

Before Caroline's fierce, incredulous indignation had found a word, Jessie had exclaimed 'Mamma!' in a tone of strong remonstrance; then, 'Never mind, Aunt Carey, I know it is only Mrs. Coffinkey, and Johnnie promised he would tell the whole story if any one brought that horrid nonsense to you about poor little Armine.'

Kind, gentle Jessie seemed quite transported out of herself, as she flew to the door and called Johnnie, leaving the two mothers looking at each other, and Ellen, somewhat startled, saying, 'I'm sure, if it is not true, I'm very sorry, Caroline, but it came from——'

She broke off, for Johnnie was scuffling across the hall, calling out 'Holloa, Jessie, what's up?'

'Johnnie, she's done it!' said Jessie. 'You said if the wrong one was accused you would tell the whole story!'

'And what do they say?' asked John, who was by this time in the room.

'Mamma has been telling Aunt Carey that Rob put poor little Armine under the pump for using bad language.'

'I say!' exclaimed John; 'if that is not a cram!'

'You said you knew nothing of it,' said his mother.

'I said I didn't do it. No more I did,' said John.

'No more did Rob, I am sure,' said his mother.

But Johnnie, though using no word of denial, made it evident that she was mistaken, as he answered in an odd tone of excuse, 'Armie was cheeky.'

'But he didn't use bad words!' said Caroline, and she met a look of comfortable response.

'Let us hear, John,' said his mother, now the most agitated. 'I can't believe that Rob would so ill-treat a little fellow like

Armie, even if he did lose his temper for a moment. Was Armine impertinent?'

'Well, rather,' said John. 'He wouldn't do Rob's French exercise.' And then, as the ladies cried out, he added, 'Oh yes, he knows ever so much more French than Rob, and now Bobus is gone Rob could not get any one else.'

'Bobus?'

'Oh yes, Bobus would do anybody's exercises at a penny for Latin, two for French, and three for Greek,' said John, not aware of the shock he gave.

'And Armine would not?' said his mother. 'Was that it?'

'Not only that,' said John; 'but the little beggar must needs up and say he would not help to act a falsehood, and you know nobody could stand that.'

Caroline understood the gravity of such an offence better than Ellen did, for that good lady had never had much in common with her boys after they outgrew the nursery. She answered, 'Armine was quite right.'

'So much the worse for him, I fear,' said Caroline.

'Yes,' said John, 'it would have been all very well to give him a cuff and tell him to mind his own business.'

'All very well!' ejaculated his mother.

'But, you know,' continued Johnnie to his aunt, 'the seniors are always mad at a junior being like that; and there was another fellow who dragged him to the great school pump, and put him in the trough, and they said they would duck him till he swore to do whatever Rob ordered.'

'Swore!' exclaimed his mother. 'You don't mean that, Johnnie?'

'Yes, I do, mamma,' said John. 'I would tell you the words, only you wouldn't like them. And Armine said it would be breaking the Third Commandment, which was the very way to aggravate them most. So they pumped on his head, and tried if he would say it. "No," he said. "You may kill me like the forty martyrs, but I won't," and of course that set them on to pump the more.'

'But, Johnnie, did you see it all?' cried Caroline. 'How could you?'

'I couldn't help it, Aunt Carey.'

'Yes, Aunt Carey,' again broke in Jessie, 'he was held down. That horrid—well, I won't say whom, Johnnie—held him, and his arm was so twisted and grazed that he was obliged to come to me to put some lily-leaves on it, and if he would but show it, it is all black and yellow still.'

Carey, much moved, went over and kissed both her boy's champions, while Ellen said, with tears in her eyes, 'O Johnnie, I'm glad you were at least not so bad. What ended it?'

'The school-bell,' said Johnnie. 'I say, please don't let Rob know I told, or I shall catch it.'

'Your father——'

'Mamma! You aren't going to tell him!' cried Jessie and Johnnie, both in horror, interrupting her.

'Yes, children, I certainly shall. Do you think such wickedness as that ought to be kept from him? Nearly killing a fatherless child like that, because he was not as bad as they were, and telling falsehoods about it too! I never could have believed it of Rob. Oh! what school does to one's boys!' She was agitated and overcome to a degree that startled Carey, who began to try to comfort her.

'Perhaps Rob did not understand what he was about, and you see he was led on. Armine will soon be all right again, and though he is a dear, good little fellow, maybe the lesson may have been good for him.'

'How can you treat it so lightly?' cried poor Ellen, in her agitated indignation. 'It was a mercy that the child did not catch his death; and as to Rob——! And when Mr. Ogilvie always said the boys were so improved, and that there was no bullying! It just shows how much he knows about it! To think what they have made of my poor Rob! His father will be so grieved! I should not wonder if he had a fit of the gout!'

The shock was far greater to her than to one who had never kept her boys at a distance, and who understood their ways, characters, and code of honour; and besides Rob was her eldest, and she had credited him with every sterling virtue. Jessie and Johnnie stood aghast. They had only meant to defend their little cousin, and had never expected either that she would be so much overcome, or that she would insist on their father knowing all, as she did with increasing anger and grief at each of their attempts at persuading her to the contrary. Caroline thought he ought to know. Her children's father would have known long ago, but then his wrath would have been a different thing from what seemed to be apprehended from his brother; and she understood the distress of Jessie and John, though her pity for Rob was but small. Whatever she tried to say in the way of generous mediation or soothing only made it worse; and poor Ellen, far from being her Serene Highness, was, between scolding and crying, in an almost hysterical state, so that Caroline durst not leave her or the frightened Jessie, and was relieved at last to hear the Colonel coming into the house, when, thinking her presence would do more harm than good, and longing to return to her little son, she slipped away, and was joined at the door by her own John, who asked—

'What's up, mother?'

'Did you know all about this dreadful business, Jock?'

'Afterwards, of course; but I was shut up in school, writing three hundred disgusting lines of Virgil, or I'd have got the brutes off some way.'

'And so little Armie is the brave one of all!'

'Well, so he is,' said Jock; 'but I say, mother, don't go

making him cockier. You know he's only fit to be stitched up
in one of Jessie's little red Sunday books, and he must learn to
keep a civil tongue in his head, and not be an insufferable little
donkey.'

'You would not have had him give in and do it! Never,
Jock!'

'Why, no ; but he could have got off with a little chaff instead
of coming out with his testimony like that, and so I've been telling him. So don't you set him up again to think himself forty
martyrs all in one, or there will be no living with him.'

'If all boys were like him.'

Jock made a sound of horror and disgust that made her
laugh.

'He's all very well,' added he in excuse ; 'but to think of all
being like *that*. The world would be only one big muff.'

'But, Jock, what's this about Bobus being paid for doing
people's exercises?'

'Bobus is a cute one,' said Jock.

'I thought he had more uprightness,' she sighed. 'And you,
Jock?'

'I should think not!' he laughed. 'Nobody would trust me.'

'Is that the only reason?' she said sadly, and he looked up in
her face, squeezed her hand, and muttered—

'One mayn't like dirt without making such a row.'

'That's like father's boy,' she said, and he wrung her hand
again.

They found Armine coiled up before the fire with a book, and
Jock greeted him with—

'Well, you little donkey, there's such a shindy at the Croft
as you never heard.'

'Mother, you know!' cried Armine, running into her outstretched arms and being covered with her kisses. 'But who
told?' he asked.

'John and Jessie,' said Jock. 'They always said they would
if any one said anything against you to mother or Uncle
Robert.'

'Against me?' said Armine.

'Yes,' said Jock. 'Didn't you know it got about through
some of the juniors or their sisters that it was Brownlow
maximus gently chastising you for bad language?—and of course
Mrs. Coffinkey told Aunt Ellen.'

'Oh! but, Jock,' cried Armine, turning round in consternation,
'I hope Rob does not know.'

And on further pressing it was extracted that Rob, when sent
home with him, had threatened him with the great black
vaulted cellars of Kencroft if he divulged the truth. When
Jock left them, the relief of pouring out the whole history to
the mother was evidently great.

'You know, mother, I couldn't,' he cried, as if there had been
a physical impossibility.

'Why, dear child? How did you bear their horrid cruelty?'

'I thought it could not be so bad as it was for the forty soldiers on the lake. Dear grandmamma read us the story out of a little red book one Sunday evening when you were gone to church. They froze, you know, and it was only cold and nasty for me.'

'So the thought of them carried you through?'

'God carried me through,' said the child reverently. 'I asked Him not to let me break His commandment.'

Just then the Colonel's heavy tread was heard, and with him came Mr Ogilvie, whom he had met on the road and informed. The good man was indeed terribly grieved, and his first words were, 'Caroline, I cannot tell you how much shocked and concerned I am', and then he laid his hand on Armine's shoulder, saying, 'My little boy, I am exceedingly sorry for what you have suffered. One day Robert will be so too. You have been a noble little fellow, and if anything could console me for the part Robert has played it would be the seeing one of my dear brother's sons so like his father.'

He gave the downcast brow a fatherly kiss, so really like those of days gone by that the boy's overstrained spirits gushed forth in sobs and tears, of which he was so much ashamed that he rushed out of the room, leaving his mother greatly overcome, his uncle distressed and annoyed, and his master not much less so, at the revelation of so much evil, so hard either to reach or to understand.

'I would have brought Robert to apologise,' said the Colonel, 'if he had been as yet in a mood to do so properly.'

'Oh! that would have been dreadful for us all,' ejaculated Caroline, under her breath.

'But I can make nothing of him,' continued he. 'He is perfectly stolid, and seems incapable of feeling anything, though I have talked to him as I never thought to have to speak to any son of mine; but he is deaf to all.'

The Colonel, in his wrath, even while addressing only Caroline and Mr. Ogilvie, had raised his voice as if he were shouting words of command, so that both shrank a little, and Carey said—

'I don't think he knew it was so bad.'

'What? Cheating his masters and torturing a helpless child for not yielding to his tyranny?'

'People don't always give things their right names even to themselves,' said Mr. Ogilvie. 'I should try to see it from the boy's point of view.'

'I have no notion of extenuating ill-conduct or making excuses! That's the modern way! So principles get lowered! I tell you, sir, there are excuses for everything. What makes the difference is only the listening to them or not.'

'Yes,' ventured Caroline; 'but is there not a difference between finding excuses for oneself and for other people?'

'All alike, lowering the principle,' said the Colonel, with

something of the same slowness of comprehension as his son.
'If excuses are to be made for everything, I don't wonder that
there is no teaching one's boys truth or common honesty and
humanity.'

'But, Robert,' said Caroline, roused to defence, 'do you
really mean that in your time nobody bullied or cribbed?'

'There was some shame about it if they did,' said the Colonel.
'Now, I suppose, I am to be told that it is an ordinary custom
to be connived at.'

'Certainly not by me,' said Mr. Ogilvie. 'I had hoped that
the standard of honour had been raised, but it is very hard to
mete the exact level of the schoolboy code from the outside.'

'And your John and mine have never given in to it,' added
Caroline.

'What do you propose to do, Mr. Ogilvie?' said the Colonel.
'I shall do my part with my boy as a father. What will you do
with him and the other bully, who I find was Cripps?'

'I shall see Cripps's father first. I think it might be well if
we both saw him before deciding on the form of discipline.
We have to think not only of justice but of the effect on their
characters.'

'That's the modern system,' said the Colonel indignantly.
'Fine work it would make in the army. I know when punishment is deserved. I don't set up to be Providence, to know
exactly what work it is to do. I leave that to my Maker and
do my duty.'

He was cut short by his son Joe rushing in headlong, exclaiming—

'Papa, papa, please come! Rob has knocked Johnnie
down and he doesn't come round.'

Colonel Brownlow hurried off, Caroline trying to make him
hear her offer to follow if she could be useful, and sending Jock
to see whether there was any opening for her. Unless the
emergency were very great indeed she knew her absence would
be preferred, and so she and Mr. Ogilvie remained, talking the
matter over, with more pity for the delinquent than his own
family would have thought natural.

'It really is a terrible thing to be stupid,' she said. 'I don't
imagine that unlucky boy ever entered into his father's idea of
truth and honour, which really is fine in its way.'

'Very fine, and proved to have made many fine fellows in
its time. I dare say the lad will grow up to it, but just now he
simply feels cruelly injured by interference with a senior's
claim to absolute submission.'

'Which he sees as singly as his father sees the simple duty
of justice.'

'It would be comfortable if we poor moderns could deal out
our measures with that straightforward military simplicity. I
cannot help seeing in that unfortunate boy the victim of examinations for commissions. Boys must be subjected to high

pressure before they can thoroughly enter into the importance of the issues that depend upon it; and when a sluggish, dull intellect is forced beyond endurance, there is an absolute instinct of escape, impelling to shifts and underhand ways of eluding work. Of course the wrong is great, but the responsibility rests with the taskmaster in the same manner as the thefts of a starved slave might on his owner.'

'The taskmaster being the country?'

'Exactly so. Happy those boys who have available brains, like yours.'

'Ah! I am very sorry about Bobus; what ought I to do?'

'Hardly more than write a few words of warning, since the change may probably have put an end to the practice.'

Jock presently brought back tidings that his namesake was all right, except for a black eye, and was growling like ten bears at having been sent to bed.

'Uncle Robert was more angry than ever, in a white heat, quiet and terrible,' said Jock in an awe-struck voice. 'He has locked Rob up in his study, and here's Joe, for Aunt Ellen is quite knocked up, and they want the house to be very quiet.'

No tragical consequences, however, ensued. Mother and sons both appeared the next morning, and were reported as 'all right' by the first inquirer from the Folly; but Jessie came to her lessons with swollen eyelids, as if she had cried half the night; and when her aunt thanked her for defending Armine, she began to cry again, and Essie imparted to Barbara that Rob was 'just like a downright savage with her.'

'No; hush, Essie, it is not that,' said Jessie; 'but papa is so dreadfully angry with him, and he is to be sent away, and it is all my fault.'

'But Jessie, dear, surely it is better for Rob to be stopped from those deceitful ways.'

'Oh yes, I know. But that I should have turned against him!' And Jessie was so thoroughly unhappy that none of her lessons prospered and her German exercise had three great tear-blots on it.

Rob's second misdemeanour had simplified matters by deciding his father on sending him from home at once into the hands of a professed coach, who would not let him elude study, and whose pupils were too big to be bullied. To the last he maintained his sullen, dogged air of indifference, though there might be more truth than the Folly was disposed to allow in his sister's allegations that it was because he did feel it so very much, especially mamma's looking so ill and worried.

Ellen did in truth look thoroughly unhinged, though no one saw her give way. She felt her boy's conduct sorely, and grieved at the first parting in her family. Besides, there was anxiety for the future. Rob's manner of conducting his studies was no hopeful augury of his success, and the expenses of sending him to a tutor fell the more heavily because unexpectedly. A horse and man were given up, and Jessie had to resign the hope of her music lessons. These were the first retrenchments, and the diminution of dignity was felt.

The Colonel showed his trouble and anxiety by speaking and tramping louder than ever, ruling his gardener with severe precision, and thundering at his boys whenever he saw them idle. Both he and his wife were so elaborately kind and polite that Caroline believed that it was an act of magnanimous forgiveness for the ill luck that she and her boys had brought them. At last the Colonel had the threatened fit of the gout, which restored his equilibrium, and brought him back to his usual condition of kindly, if somewhat ponderous, good sense.

He had not long recovered before Number Nine made his appearance at Kencroft, and thus his mother had unusual facilities for inquiries of Dr. Leslie respecting the master of Belforest.

The old man really seemed to be in a dying state. A hospital nurse had taken charge of him, but there was not a dependent about the place, from Mr. Richards downwards, who was not under notice to quit, and most were staying on without his knowledge on the advice of the London solicitor, to whom the agent had written. There was even more excitement on the intelligence that Mr. Barnes had sent for Farmer Gould.

On this there was no doubt, for Mr. Gould, always delicately honourable towards Mrs. Brownlow, came himself to tell her about the interview. It seemed to have been the outcome of a yearning of the dying man towards the sole survivor of the companions of his early days. He had talked in a feeble wandering way of old times, but had said nothing about the child, and was plainly incapable of sustained attention. He had asked Mr. Gould to come again, but on this second visit he was too far gone for recognition, and had returned to his moody instinctive aversion to visitors, and in three days more he was dead.

## CHAPTER XV

### THE BELFOREST MAGNUM BONUM

' Where is his golden heap?'
              *Divine Breathings.*

MRS. ROBERT BROWNLOW was churched with all the expedition possible, in order that she might not lose the sight of the funeral procession, which would be fully visible from the studio in the top of the tower.

The excitement was increased by invitations to attend the funeral being sent to the Colonel and to his two eldest nephews, who were just come home for the holidays, also to their mother to be present at the subsequent reading of the will.

A carriage was sent for her, and she entered it, not knowing or caring to find out what she wished, and haunted by the line, 'Die and endow a college or a cat.'

Allen met her at the front door, whispering, 'Did you see, mother, he has still got his ears?' And the thought crossed her —'Will those ears cost us dear?'

She was the only woman present in the library—a large room, but with an atmosphere as if the open air had not been admitted for thirty years, and with an enormous fire, close to which was the arm-chair whither she was marshalled, being introduced to the two solicitors, Mr. Rowse and Mr. Wakefield, who, with Farmer Gould, the agent, Richards, the Colonel, and the two boys, made up the audience.

The lawyers explained that the will had been sent home ten years ago from Yucatan, and had ever since been in their hands. Search had been made for a later one, but none had been found, nor did they believe that one could exist.

It was very short. The executors were Charles Rowse and Peter Ball, and the whole property was devised to them, and to Lieutenant-Colonel Robert Brownlow, as trustees for the testator's great-niece, Mrs. Caroline Otway Brownlow, daughter of John and Caroline Allen, and wife of Joseph Brownlow, Esq., M.D., F.R.C.S., the income and use thereof to be enjoyed by her during her lifetime; and the property, after her death, to be divided among her children in such proportions as she should direct.

That was all; there was no legacy, no further directions.

'Allow me to congratulate——' began the elder lawyer.

'No—no—oh, stay a bit,' cried she, in breathless dismay and bewilderment. 'It can't be! It can't mean only me. There must be something about Elvira de Menella.'

'I fear there is not,' said Mr. Rowse; 'I could wish my late client had attended more to the claims of justice, and had divided the property, which could well have borne it; but unfortunately it is not so.'

'It is exactly as he led us to expect,' said Mr. Gould. 'We have no right to complain, and very likely the child will be much happier without it. You have a fine family growing up to enjoy it, Mrs. Brownlow, and I am sure no one congratulates you more heartily than I.'

'Don't; it can't be,' cried the heiress, nearly crying, and wringing the old farmer's hand. 'He must have meant Elvira. You know he sent for you. Has everything been hunted over? There must be a later will.'

'Indeed, Mrs. Brownlow,' said the solicitor, 'you may rest assured that full search has been made. Mr. Richards had the same impression, and we have been searching every imaginable receptacle.'

'Besides,' added Colonel Brownlow, 'if he had made another will there would have been witnesses.'

'Yes,' said Mr. Richards; 'but to make matters certain, I wrote to several of the servants to ask whether they remembered any attestation, but no one did; and indeed I doubt whether, after his arrival here, poor Mr. Barnes ever had sustained power enough to have drawn up and executed a will without my assistance, or that of any legal gentleman.'

'It is too hard and unjust,' cried Caroline; 'it cannot be. I must halve it with the child, as if there had been no will at all. Robert! you know that is what your brother would have done.'

'That would be just as well as generous, indeed, if it were practicable,' said Mr. Rowse; 'but unfortunately Colonel Brownlow and myself (for Mr. Ball is dead) are in trust to prevent any such proceeding. All that is in your power is to divide the property among your own family by will, in such proportion as you may think fit.'

'Quite true, my dear sister,' said the Colonel, meeting her despairing, appealing look, 'as regards the principal, but the ready money at the bank and the income are entirely at your own disposal, and you can, without difficulty, secure a very sufficient compensation to the little girl out of them.'

'No doubt,' said Mr. Rowse.

'You'll let me—you'll let me, Mr. Gould,' implored Caroline; 'you'll let me keep her, and do all I can to make up to her. You see the Colonel thinks it is only justice; don't you, Robert?'

'Mrs. Brownlow is quite right,' said the Colonel, seeing that her vehemence was a little distrusted; 'it will be only an act of justice to make provision for your granddaughter.'

'I am sure, Colonel Brownlow, nothing can be handsomer than your conduct and Mrs. Brownlow's,' said the old man; 'but I should not like to take advantage of what she is good enough to say on the spur of the moment, till she has had more time to think it over.'

Therewith he took leave, while Caroline exclaimed—

'I always say there is no truer gentleman in the county than old Mr. Gould. I shall not be satisfied about that will till I have turned everything over and the partners have been written to.'

Again she was assured that she might set her mind at rest, and then the lawyers began to read a statement of the property, which made Allen utter, under his breath, an emphatic 'I say!' but his mother hardly took it in. The heated room had affected her from the first, and the bewilderment of the tidings seemed almost to crush her; her heart and temples throbbed, her head ached violently, and while the final words respecting arrangements were passing between the Colonel and the lawyers, she was conscious only of a sickening sense of oppression, and a fear of committing the absurdity of fainting.

However, at last her brother-in-law put her into the

brougham, desiring the boys to walk home, which they did very willingly, and with a wonderful air of lordship and possession.

'Well, Caroline,' said the Colonel, 'I congratulate you on being the richest proprietor in the county.'

'O Robert, don't! If—if,' said a suffocated voice, so miserable that he turned and took her hand kindly, saying—

'My dear sister, this feeling is very—it becomes you well. This is a fearful responsibility.'

She could not answer. She only leant back in the carriage, with closed eyes, and moaned—

'O Joe! Joe!'

'Indeed,' said his brother, greatly touched, 'we want him more than ever.'

He did not try to talk any more to her, and when they reached the Pagoda, all she could do was to hurry upstairs, and, throwing off her bonnet, bury her face in the pillow.

Janet and her aunt both followed, the latter with kind and tender solicitude; but Caroline could bear nothing, and begged only to be left alone.

'Dear Ellen, it is very kind, but nothing does any good to these headaches. Please don't—please leave me alone.'

They saw it was the only true kindness, and left her, after all attempts at bathing her forehead, or giving her sal volatile, proved only to molest her. She lay on her bed, not able to think, and feeling nothing but the pain of her headache and a general weight and loneliness.

The first break was from Allen, who came in tenderly with a cup of coffee, saying that they thought her time was come for being ready for it. His manner always did her good, and she sat up, pushed back her hair, smiled, took the cup, and thanked him lovingly.

'Uncle Robert is waiting to hear if you are better,' he said.

'Oh yes,' she said; 'thank him; I am sorry I was so silly.'

'He wants me to dine there to-night, mother, to meet Mr. Rowse and Mr. Wakefield,' said Allen, with a certain importance suited to a lad of fifteen, who had just become 'somebody.'

'Very well,' she said, in weary acquiescence, as she lay down again, just enough refreshed by the coffee to become sleepy.

'And, mother,' said Allen, lingering in the dark, 'don't trouble about Elfie. I shall marry her as soon as I am of age, and that will make all straight.'

Her stunned sleepiness was scarcely alive to this magnanimous announcement, and she dreamily said—

'Time enough to think of such things.'

'I know,' said Allen; 'but I thought you ought to know this.'

He looked wistfully for another word on this great avowal, but she was really too much stupefied to enter into the purport of the boy's words, and soon after he left her she fell sound

asleep. She had a curious dream, which she remembered long
after. She seemed to have identified herself with King Midas,
and to be touching all her children, who turned into hard, cold,
solid golden statues fixed on pedestals in the Belforest gardens,
where she wandered about, vainly calling them. Then her
husband's voice, sad and reproachful, seemed to say, 'Magnum
Bonum! Magnum Bonum!' and she fancied it the elixir which
alone could restore them, and would have climbed a mountain
in search of it, as in the Arabian tale ; but her feet were cold,
heavy, and immovable, and she found that they too had become gold, and that the chill was creeping upwards. With a
scream of 'Save the children, Joe,' she awoke.

No wonder she had dreamt of cold golden limbs, for her feet
were really chilly as ice, and the room as dark as at midnight.
However, it was not yet seven o'clock ; and presently Janet
brought a light, and persuaded her to come downstairs and
warm herself. She was not yet capable of going into the dining-
room to the family tea, but crept down to lie on the sofa in the
drawing-room ; and there, after taking the small refreshment
which was all she could yet endure, she lay with closed eyes,
while the children came in from the meal. Armine and Babie
were the first. She knew they were looking at her, but was too
weary to exert herself to speak to them.

'Asleep,' they whispered. 'Poor Mother Carey.'

'Armie,' said Babie, 'is mother unhappy because she has got
rich ?'

Armine hesitated. His brief experience of school had made
him less unsophisticated, and he seldom talked in his own
peculiar fashion even to his little sister, and she added--

'Must people get wicked when they are rich ?'

'Mother is always good,' said faithful little Armine.

'The rich people in the Bible were all bad,' pondered Babie.
'There was Dives, and the man with the barns.'

'Yes,' said Armine ; 'but there were good ones too—Abraham
and Solomon.'

'Solomon was not always good,' said Babie ; 'and Uncle
Robert told Allen it was a fearful responsibility. What is a
responsibility, Armie ? I am sure Ali didn't like it.'

'Something to answer for !' said Armine.

'To who ?' asked the little girl.

'To God,' said the boy reverently. 'It's like the talent in
the parable. One has got to do something for God with it,
and then it won't turn to harm.'

'Like the man's treasure that changed into slate stones when
he made a bad use of it,' said Babie. 'Oh ! Armie, what shall
we do ? Shall we give plum-puddings to the little thin girls
down the lane ?'

'And I should like to give something good to the little gray
workhouse boys,' said Armine. 'I should so hate always walking
out along a straight road as they do.'

'And oh! Armie, then don't you think we may get a nice book to write out Jotapata in?'

'Yes, a real jolly one. For you know, Babie, it will take lots of room, even if I write my very smallest.'

'Please let it be ruled, Armie. And where shall we begin?'

'Oh! at the beginning, I think, just when Sir Engelbert first heard about the Crusade.'

'It will take lots of books then.'

'Never mind, we can buy them all now. And do you know, Bab, I think Adelmar and Ermelind might find a nice lot of natural petroleum and frighten Mustafa ever so much with it!'

For be it known that Armine and Barbara's most cherished delight was in one continued running invention of a defence of Jotapata by a crusading family, which went on from generation to generation with unabated energy, though they were very apt to be reduced to two young children who held out their fortress against frightful odds of Saracens, and sometimes conquered, sometimes converted their enemies. Nobody but themselves was fully kept *au courant* with this wonderful siege, which had hitherto been recorded in interlined copy-books, or little paper books pasted together, and very remarkably illustrated.

The door began to creak with an elaborate noisiness intended for perfect silence, and Jock's voice was heard.

'Bother the door! Did it wake mother? No? That's right;' and he squatted down between the little ones while Bobus seated himself at the table with a book.

'Well! what colour shall our ponies be?' began Jock, in an attempt at a whisper.

'Oh! shall we have ponies?' cried the little ones.

'Zebras if we like,' said Jock. 'We'll have a team.'

'Can't,' growled Bobus.

'Why not? They can be bought!'

'Not tamed. They've tried it at the *Jardin d'Acclimatisa-tion.*'

'Oh, that was only Frenchmen. A zebra is too jolly to let himself be tamed by a Frenchman. I'll break one in myself and go out with the hounds upon him.'

'Jack-ass on striped-ass—or off him,' muttered Bobus.

'Oh! don't, Jock,' implored Babie, 'you'll get thrown.'

'No such thing. You'll come to the meet yourself, Babie, on your Arab.'

'Not she,' said Bobus in his teasing voice. 'She'll be governessed up and kept to lessons all day.'

'Mother always teaches us,' said Babie.

'She'll have no time, she'll be a great lady, and you'll have three governesses—one for French, and one for German, and one for deportment, to make you turn out your toes, and hold up your head, and never sit on the rug.'

'Never mind, Babie,' said Jock. 'We'll bother them out of their lives if they do.'

'You'll be at school,' said Bobus, 'and they'll all three go out walking with Babie, and if she goes out of a straight line one will say, "Fi donc, Mademoiselle Barbe," and the other will say, "Schämen sie sich, Fräulein Barbara," and the third will call for the stocks.'

'For shame, Robert,' cried his mother, hearing something like a sob ; 'how can you tease her so !'

'Mother, must I have three governesses?' asked poor little Barbara.

'Not one cross one, my sweet, if I can help it !'

'Oh ! mother, if it might be Miss Ogilvie?' said Babie.

'Yes, mother, do let it be Miss Ogilvie,' chimed in Armine. 'She tells such jolly stories !'

'She ain't a very nasty one,' quoted Jock from Newman Noggs, and as Janet appeared he received her with—'Moved by Barbara, seconded by Armine, that Miss Ogilvie become bear-leader to lick you all into shape.'

'What do you think of it, Janet?' said her mother.

'It will not make much difference to me,' said Janet. 'I shall depend on classes and lectures when we go back to London. I should have thought a German better for the children, but I suppose the chief point is to find some one who can manage Elfie if we are still to keep her.'

'By the by, where is she, poor little thing?' asked Caroline.

'Aunt Ellen took her home,' said Janet. 'She said she would send her back at bedtime, but she thought we should be more comfortable alone to-night.'

'Real kindness,' said Caroline ; 'but remember, children, all of you, that Elfie is altogether one of us, on perfectly equal terms, so don't let any difference be made now or ever.'

'Shall I have a great many more lessons, mother?' asked Babie.

'Don't be as silly as Essie, Babie,' said Janet. 'She expects us all to have velvet frocks and gold-fringed sashes, and Jessie's first thought was "Now, Janet, you'll have a ladies' maid."'

'No wonder she rejoiced to be relieved of trying to make you presentable,' said Bobus.

'Shall we live at Belforest?' asked Armine.

'Part of the year,' said Janet, who was in a wonderfully expansive and genial state ; 'but we shall get back to London for the season, and know what it is to enjoy life and rationality again, and then we must all go abroad. Mother, how soon can we go abroad?'

'It won't make a bit of difference for a year. We shan't get it for ever so long,' said Bobus.

'Oh !'

'Fact. I know a man whose uncle left him a hundred pounds last year, and the lawyers haven't let him touch a penny of it.'

'Perhaps he is not of age,' said Janet.

'At any rate,' said Jock, 'we can have our fun at Belforest.'

'Oh yes, Jock, only think,' cried Babie, 'all the dear tadpoles belong to mother!'

'And all the dragon-flies,' said Armine.

'And all the herons,' said Jock.

'We can open the gates again,' said Armine.

'Oh! the flowers!' cried Babie in an ecstasy.

'Yes,' said Janet. 'I suppose we shall spend the early spring in the country, but we must have the best part of the season in London now that we can get out of banishment, and enjoy rational conversation once more.'

'Rational fiddlestick,' muttered Bobus.

'That's what any girl who wasn't such a prig as Janet would look for,' said Jock.

'Well, of course,' said Janet. 'I mean to have my balls like other people; I shall see life thoroughly. That's just what I value this for.'

Bobus made a scoffing noise.

'What's up, Bobus?' asked Jock.

'Nothing, only you keep up such a row, one can't read.'

'I'm sure this is better and more wonderful than any book!' said Jock.

'It makes no odds to me,' returned Bobus, over his book.

'Oh! now!' cried Janet, 'if it were only the pleasure of being free from patronage it would be something.'

'Gratitude!' said Bobus.

'*I'll* show my gratitude,' said Janet; 'we'll give all of them at Kencroft all the fine clothes and jewels and amusements that ever they care for, more than ever they gave us; only it is we that shall give and they that will take, don't you see?'

'Sweet charity,' quoth Bobus.

Those two were a great contrast; Janet had never been so radiant, feeling her sentence of banishment revoked, and realising more vividly than any one else was doing, the pleasures of wealth. The cloud under which she had been ever since the coming to the Pagoda seemed to have rolled away, in the sense of triumph and anticipation; while Bobus seemed to have fallen into a mood of sarcastic ill-temper. His mother saw, and it added to her sense of worry, though her bright sweet nature would scarcely have fathomed the cause, even had she been in a state to think actively rather than to feel passively. Bobus, only a year younger than Allen, and endowed with more force and application, if not with more quickness, had always been on a level with his brother, and felt superior, despising Allen's Eton airs and graces, and other characteristics which most people thought amiable. And now Allen had become son and heir, and was treated by every one as the only person of importance. Bobus did not know what his own claims might be, but at any rate his brother's would transcend them, and his temper was thoroughly upset.

Poor Caroline! She did not wholly omit to pray, 'In all time of our tribulation, in all time of our wealth, deliver us!' but if she had known all that was in her children's hearts, her own would have trembled more.

And as to Ellen, the utmost she allowed herself to say was, 'Well, I hope she will make a good use of it!'

While the Colonel, as trustee and adviser, had really a very considerable amount of direct importance and enjoyment before him, which might indeed be—to use his own useful phrase—'a fearful responsibility,' but was no small boon to a man with too much time on his hands.


## CHAPTER XVI

### POSSESSION

' Vainglorious Elf, said he, dost thou not weete
  That money can thy wants at will supply ;
  Shields, steeds and armes, and all things for thee meet,
  It can purvey in twinkling of an eye.'

SPENSER.

BOBUS'S opinion that it would be long before anything came of this accession of wealth was for a few days verified in the eyes of the impatient family, for Christmas interfered with some of the necessary formalities ; and their mother, still thinking that another will might be discovered, declared that they were not to go within the gates of Belforest till they were summoned.

At last, after Colonel Brownlow had spent a day in London, he made his appearance with a cheque-book in his hand, and the information that he and his fellow-trustee had so arranged that the heiress could open an account, and begin to enter on the fruition of the property. There were other arrangements to be made, those about the out-door servants and keepers could be settled with Richards, but she ought to remove her two sons from the foundation of the two colleges, though of course they would continue there as pupils.

'And, Robert,' she said, colouring exceedingly, 'if you will let me, there is a thing I wish very much—to send your John to Eton with mine. He is my godson, you know, and it would be such a pleasure to me.'

'Thank you, Caroline,' said the Colonel, after a moment's hesitation ; 'Johnnie is to stand at the Eton election, and I should prefer his owing his education to his own exertions rather than to any kindness.'

'Yes, yes ; I understand that,' said Caroline ; 'but I do want you to let me do anything for any of them. I should be so grateful,' she added imploringly, with a good deal of agitation ; 'please—please think of it, as if your brother were still here. You would never mind how much he did for them.'

'Yes, I should,' said the Colonel decidedly, but pausing to collect his next sentence. 'I should not accept from him what might teach my sons dependence. You see that, Caroline.'

'Yes,' she humbly said. 'He would be wise about it! I don't want to be disagreeable and oppressive, Robert; I will never try to force things on you; but please let me do all that is possible to you to allow.'

There was something touching in her incoherent earnestness which made the Colonel smile, yet wink away some moisture from his eyes, as he again thanked her without either acceptance or refusal. Then he said he was going to Belforest, and asked whether she would not like to come and look over the place. He would go back and call for her with the pony carriage.

'But would not Ellen like to go?' she said. 'I will walk with the boys.'

The Colonel demurred a little, but knowing that his wife really longed to go, and could not well be squeezed into the back seat, he gave a sort of half-assent; and as he left the house, Mother Carey gave a summoning cry to gather her brood, rushed upstairs, put on what Babie called her 'most everydayest old black hat;' and when Colonel and Mrs. Brownlow, with Jessie behind, drove into the park, it was to see her careering along by the short cut over the hoar-frosty grass, in the midst of seven boys, three girls, and two dogs, all in a most frisky mood of exhilaration.

Distressed at appearing to drive up like the lady of the house, her Serene Highness insisted on stopping at the iron gates of the stately approach. There she alighted, and waited to make the best setting to rights she could of the heiress's wind-tossed hat and cloak, and would have put her into the carriage, but that no power could persuade her to mount that triumphal car, and all that could be obtained was that she should walk in the forefront of the procession with the Colonel.

There was nobody to receive them but Richards, for the servants had been paid off, and only a keeper and his wife were living in the kitchen in charge. There was a fire in the library, where the Colonel had business to transact with Richards, while the ladies and children proceeded with their explorations. It was rather awful at first in the twilight gloom of the great hall, with a painted mythological ceiling, and cold white pavement, varied by long perspective lines of black lozenges, on which every footfall echoed. The first door that they opened led into a vast and dreary dining-room, with a carpet, forming a crimson roll at one end, and long ranks of faded leathern chairs sitting in each other's laps. At one end hung a huge picture by Snyders, of a bear hugging one dog in his fore paws and tearing open the ribs of another with his hind ones. Opposite was a wild boar impaling a hound with his tusk, and the other walls were occupied by Herodias smiling at the contents of her

charger, Judith dropping the gory head into her bag, a brown
St. Sebastian writhing among the arrows; and Juno extracting
the painfully flesh and blood eyes of Argus to set them in her
peacock's tail.

'I object to eating my dinner in a butcher's shop,' observed
Allen.

'Yes, we must get them out of this place,' said his mother.

'They are very valuable paintings,' interposed Ellen.  'I
know they are in the county history.  They were collected by
Sir Francis Bradford, from whom the place was bought, and he
was a great connoisseur.'

'Yes, they are just the horrid things great connoisseurs of
the last century liked, by way of giving themselves an appetite,'
said Caroline.

'Are not fine pictures always horrid?' asked Jessie, in all
simplicity.

The drawing-rooms, a whole suite—antechamber, saloon,
music-room, and card-room, were all swathed up in brown
holland, hanging even from the picture-rods along the wall.
Even in the days of the most liberal housekeeper, Ellen had
never done more than peep beneath.  So she revelled in investi-
gations of gilding and yellow satin, ormolu and marble, big
mirrors and Sèvres clocks, a three-piled carpet, and a dazzling
prismatic chandelier, though all was pervaded with such a chill
of unused dampness and odour of fustiness, that Caroline's first
impression was that it was a perilous place for one so lately recovered.  However, Ellen believed in no danger till she came on
two monstrous stains of damp on the walls, with a whole crop
of curious fungi in one corner, and discovered that all the
holland was flabby, and all the damask clammy !  Then she enforced the instant lighting of fires, and shivered so decidedly
that Caroline and Jessie begged her to return to the fire in the
library, while Jessie went in search of Rob to drive her home.

All the rest of the younger population had deserted the state
apartments, and were to be heard in the distance, clattering
along the passages, banging doors, bawling and shouting to
each other, with freaks of such laughter as had never awakened
those echoes during the Barnes's tenure, but Jessie returned
not ; and her aunt, going in quest of her up a broad flight of
shallow stairs, found herself in a grand gallery, with doors leading to various corridors and stairs.  She called, and the tramp
of the boots of youth began to descend on her, with shouts of
'All right!' and downstairs flowed the troop, beginning with
Jock, and ending with Armine and Babie, each with some
breathless exclamation, all jumbled together—

*Jock.* 'Oh, mother !  Stunning !  Lots of bats fast asleep.'

*Johnnie.* 'Rats ! rats !'

*Rob.* 'A billiard-table.'

*Joe.* 'Mother Carey, may Pincher kill your rats?'

*Armine.* 'One wants a clue of thread to find one's way.'

*Janet.* 'I've counted five-and-thirty bedrooms already, and that's not all.'

*Babie.* 'And there's a little copper tea-kettle in each. May my dolls have one?'

*Bobus.* 'There's nothing else in most of them ; and, my eyes! how musty they smell.'

*Elvira.* 'I will have the room with the big red bed, with a gold crown at the top.'

*Allen.* 'Mother, it will be a magnificent place, but it must have a vast deal done to it.'

But Mother Carey was only looking for Jessie. No one had seen her. Janet suggested that she had taken a rat for a ghost, and they began to look and call in all quarters, till at last she appeared, looking rather white and scared at having lost herself, being bewildered by the voices and steps echoing here, there, and everywhere. The barrenness and uniformity did make it very easy to get lost, for even while they were talking, Joe was heard roaring to know where they were, nor would he stand still till they came up with him, but confused them and himself by running to meet them by some deluding stair.

'We've not got a house, but a Cretan labyrinth,' said Babie.

'Or the bewitched castle mother told us of,' said Allen, 'where everybody was always running round after everybody.'

'You've only to have a grain of sense,' said Bobus, who had at last recovered Joe, and proceeded to give them a lecture on the two main arteries, and the passages communicating with them, so that they might always be able to recover their bearings.

They were more sober after that. Rob drove his mother home, and the Colonel made the round to inspect the dilapidations, and estimate what was wanting. The great house had never been thoroughly furnished since the Bradfords had sold it, and it was, besides, in manifest need of repair. Damp corners and piles of crumbled plaster told their own tale. A builder must be sent to survey it, and on the most sanguine computation it could hardly be made habitable till the end of the autumn.

Meantime, Caroline must remain a tenant of the Pagoda, though, as she told the eager Janet, this did not prevent a stay in London for the sake of the classes and the society, of whom she was always talking, only there must be time to see their way.

The next proposition gave universal satisfaction. Mother Carey would take her whole brood to London for a day, to make purchases, the three elder children each with £5, the younger with £2 apiece. She actually wanted to take two-thirds of those from Kencroft also, with the same bounty in their pockets, but to this their parents absolutely refused consent. To go about London with a train of seven was bad enough ; but that was her own affair, and they could not prevent it ; and they absolutely would not swell the number to thirteen. It would

be ridiculous; she would want an omnibus to go about
in.

'I did not mean all to go about together. The elder boys
will go their own way.'

But, as the Colonel observed, that was all very well for boys
whose home had always been in London, but she would find
his country lads much in her way. She then reduced her demand by a third, for she really wished for Johnnie; but the
Colonel's principles would not allow him to accept so great an
indulgence for Rob.

That unlucky fellow had, of course, failed in his examination,
and this had renewed the Colonel's resentment at his laziness
and shuffling. He was, however, improved by contact with
strangers, looked and behaved less bearishly, and had acquired
a will to do better. Still, it was not possible to regret his
absence, except because it involved that of his brother; and,
with a great effort, and many assurances of her being really
needed, Jessie's company was secured.

Never was the taste of wealth sweeter than in that over-filled
railway carriage, before it was light on the winter morning,
with a vista of endless possibilities contained in those crackling
notes and round gold pieces, Jessie being, of course, as well off
as the rest, and feeling the novelty and wonder even
more.

Mrs. Acton's house was to be the place of rendezvous, and
she would take charge of the girls for part of the day; the boys
wished to shift for themselves; and Allen and Bobus had
friends of their own with whom they meant to lunch.

Clara met her friend with an agitated manner, half-laughing,
half-crying, as she said—

'Well, Mother Carey dear, you haven't quite soared above us
yet?'

'Petrels never take high flights,' said Carey; 'I hope and
trust that it may prove impossible to make a fine lady of me. I
am caught late, you see.'

'Your daughters are not. You won't like to have them
making excuses for mamma's friends.'

'Janet's exclusiveness will not be of that sort, and for warm-
hearted little Babie, trust her. Do you know where the Ogilvies
can be written to, Clara? Are they at Rome, or Florence?'

'They were to be at Florence by the 14th. Mary has learnt
to be such a traveller that she always drags her brother abroad
for however short a time St. Kenelm may give her.'

'I hope I shall catch her in time. We want her for our
governess.'

'Now, really, Carey, you are a woman for old friends! But
do you think you will get on? You know she won't spare you.'

'That's the very reason I want her.'

'It is very generous of you! You always were the best little
thing in the world, with a strong turn for being under the lash;

so you're going to keep the slave in the back of your triumphal
chariot, like the Roman general.'

'I see, you're afraid she will teach me to be too proper
behaved for you.'

'Precisely so, after her experience of Russian countesses.
I don't know whether she will let you be mistress of your own
house.'

'She will make me mistress all the more,' said Caroline; 'for
she will make me all the more "queen o'er myself."'

Then began the shopping, such shopping extraordinary as
none of the family had ever enjoyed except in dreams; and
when it was the object of everybody to conceal their purchases
from everybody else. Caroline contrived to make time for a
quiet luncheon with Dr. and Mrs. Lucas, to which she took her
two youngest boys, since Jock was the godson of the house, and
had moreover been shaken off by his two elder brothers.
Happily he was too good-tempered to grumble at being thrown
over, and his mind was in a beatific state of contemplation of
his newly-purchased treasures, a small pistol, a fifteen-bladed
knife, and a box of miscellaneous sweets, although his mother
had so far succumbed to the weakness of her sex as to prevent
the weapon from being accompanied by any ammunition.

As to Armine, she wanted to consult Dr. Lucas about the
fragile looks and liability to cold that had alarmed her ever
since Rob's exploit. Besides, he was so unlike the others!
Had she not seen him quietly make his way into the drawing-
room, where Mrs. Lucas kept a box for the Children's Hospital,
and drop into it two bright florins, one of which she had seen
Babie hand over to him?

'I do think it is not canny,' she said, as if it had been one of
his symptoms.

'Do you want me to prescribe for it?'

'I did try one prescription for having too big a soul; I
turned my poor little boy loose into school, and there they half
killed him for me, and made the original complaint worse.'

'Happily no prescription, "neither life, nor death, nor any
other creature," can cure that complaint,' said the good old
doctor, 'though, alas! it is only too apt to dry up from
within.'

'Still I can't help feeling it rather awful to have to do with
a being so spiritual as that, and it appears to me to increase on
him, so that he never seems quite to belong to me. And pre-
cocity is a dangerous sign, is it not?'

'I see,' said the doctor, smiling; 'you are going to be a
treasure to the faculty, and indulge in anxieties and consultations.'

'Now, Dr. Lucas, you know that we were always anxious
about Armine. You remember his father said he needed more
care than the rest.'

Dr. Lucas allowed that this was true; but he only recommended flannel, pale ale, moderation in study, and time to recover the effects of the pump.

Both the good old friends were very kind and full of tender congratulation, mingled with a little anxiety, though they were pleased with her good taste and simplicity and absence of all elation. But then she had hardly realised the new position, and seemed to look neither behind nor before. Her only scheme seemed to be to take a house in London for a few months, and then perhaps to go abroad, but of this she could not talk in those old scenes which vividly brought back that castle in the air, never fulfilled, of a holiday in Switzerland with Joe.

On leaving the Lucases, she sent her boys on before her to the nearest bazaar, and was soon at her old home. Kind Mrs. Drake effaced herself as much as possible, and let her roam about the house alone; but furniture had altered every room, so that no responsive chord was touched till she came to the study, which was little changed. There she shut herself in and strove to recall the touch of the hand that was gone, the sound of the voice that was still. She stood, where she had been wont to stand over her husband when he had been busy at his table and she had run down with some inquiry, and with a yearning ache of heart she clasped her hands, and almost breathed out the words, 'O Joe, Joe, dear father ! Oh ! for one moment of you to tell me what to do, and how to keep true to the charge you gave me—your Magnum Bonum !'

So absolutely had she asked the question, that she waited, almost expecting a reply, but there was no voice and none to answer her ; and she was turning away with a sickening sense of mockery at her own folly in seeking the empty shrine whence the oracle of her life had departed, when her eye fell on the engraving over the mantelpiece. It was the one thing for which Mr. Drake had begged as a memorial of Joe Brownlow, and it still hung in its old place. It was of the Great Physician, consoling and healing all around—the sick, the captive, the self-tormenting genius, the fatherless, the widow.

Was this the answer ? Something darted through her mind like a pang followed by a strange throb—'Give yourself up to Him. Seek the true good first. The other may lie on its way.'

But it was only a pang. The only too-natural recoil came the next minute. Was not she as religious as there was any need to be, or at least as she could be without alienating her children or affecting more than she felt ? Give herself to Him ? How ? Did that mean a great deal of church-going, sermon-reading, cottage-visiting, prayers, meditations, and avoidance of pleasure ? That would never do ; the boys would not bear it, and Janet would be alienated ; besides, it would be hypocrisy in one who could not sit still and think, or attend to anything lengthy and wearisome.

So, as a kind of compromise, she looked at the photograph which hung below, and to it she almost spoke out her answer.

'Yes, I'll be very good, and give away lots of things. Mary Ogilvie shall come and keep me in order, and she won't let me be naughty, if I ever want to be naughty when I get away from Ellen. Then Magnum Bonum shall have its turn too. Don't be afraid, dearest. If Allen does not take to it now, I am sure Bobus will be a great chemical discoverer, able to give all his time and spare no expense, and then we will fit up this dear old house for a hospital for very poor people. That's what you would have done if you had been here! Oh, if this money had only come in time! But here are these horrid tears! If I once begin crying, I shall be good for nothing. If I don't go at once, there's no saying what Jock mayn't have bought.'

She was just in time to find Jock asking the price of all the animals in the Pantheon Bazaar, and expecting her to supply the cost of a vicious-looking monkey. The whole flock collected in due time at the station, and so did their parcels. Allen brought with him his chief purchase, the most lovely toy-terrier in the world, whom he presented on the spot to Elvira, and who divided the journey between licking himself and devouring the fragments of biscuit with which Jock supplied him. Allen had also bought a beautiful statuette for himself, and a set of studs. Janet had set herself up with a case of mathematical instruments and various books; Bobus's purchases were divers chemical appliances and a pocket microscope, also what he thrust into Jessie's lap and she presently proclaimed to be a lovely little work-case; Jessie herself was hugging a parcel, which turned out to contain warm pelisses for the two nursery boys just above the baby. For the adaptation of their seniors' last year's garments had not proved so successful as not to have much grieved the good girl and her mother.

Elvira's money had all gone into an accordion and a necklace of large blue beads.

'Didn't you get anything for your grandfather or your cousins?' said Caroline.

'I wanted it all,' said Elfie; 'and you only gave me two sovereigns, or I would have had the bracelets too.'

'Never mind, Elfie,' cried Babie, 'I've got something for Mr. Gould and for Kate and Mary.'

'Have you, Babie? So have I,' returned Armine; and the two, who had been wedged into one seat, began a whispering conversation, by which the listeners might have learnt that there was a friendly rivalry as to which had made the two pounds provide the largest possible number of presents. Neither had bought anything for self, for the chest of drawers, bath, and broom were for Babie's precious dolls, not for herself. Mother Carey, uncle and aunt, brothers, sisters, cousins, servants, Mr. Gould, the gardener's grandson, the old apple-woman, 'the little thin girls,' had all been provided for at that wonderful German Bazaar, and the only regret was that gifts for Mr. Ogilvie and Alfred Richards could not be brought within the powers of even

two pounds. What had Mother Carey bought? Ah! Nobody
was to know till Twelfth-day, and then the first tree cut at
Belforest would be a Christmas-tree. Then came a few regrets
that everybody had proclaimed their purchases, and therewith
people began to grow weary and drop asleep. It was by gaslight that they arrived at home and bundled into the flies that
awaited them, and then in the hall at home came Elvira's
cry—

'Where's my doggie, my Chico?'

'Here; I took him out,' said Jock.

'That's not Chico; that's a nasty, horrid, yellow cur. Chico
was black. You naughty boy, Jock, you've been and changed
my dog.'

'Has Midas changed him to gold?' cried Babie.

'Ah!' said Bobus meaningly.

'You've done it then, Bobus! You've put something to
him.'

'I haven't,' said Bobus, 'but he's been licking himself all the
way home. Well, we all know green is the sacred colour of the
Grand Turk.'

'No! You don't mean it!' said Allen, catching up the dog
and holding him to the lamp, while Janet observed that he was
a sort of chameleon, for his body, which had been black, was
now yellow, and his chops, which had been tan, had become
black.

Elvira began to cry angrily, still uncomprehending, and
fancying Bobus and Jock had played her a trick and changed
her dog; Allen abused the horrid little brute, and the more
horrid man who had deceived him; and Armine began pitying
and caressing him, seriously distressed lest the poor little beast
should have poisoned himself. Caroline herself expected to have
heard that he was dead the next morning, and would have felt
more compassion than regret; but, to her surprise and Allen's
chagrin, Chico made his appearance, very rhubarb-coloured and
perfectly well.

'I think,' said Elvira, 'I will give Chico to grandpapa for a
nice London present.'

Everybody burst out laughing at this piece of generosity, and
though the young lady never quite understood what amused
them, and Allen heartily wished Chico among the army of dogs
at River Hollow, he did somehow or other remain at the Folly,
and, after the fashion of dogs, adopted Jock as the special object
of his devotion.

Ellen came in, expecting to regale her eyes with the newest
fashions. Or were they all coming down from the dressmaker?

'I had no time to be worried with dressmakers,' said Caroline.

'I thought you went there while the girls were going about
with Mrs. Acton.'

'Indeed no. I had just got my new bonnet for the winter.'

'But!'

'And *indeed*, I have not inherited any more heads.'

Ellen sighed at the impracticability of her sister-in-law and the blindness of fortune. But nobody could sigh long in the face of that Twelfth-day Christmas-tree. What need be said of it but that each member of the house of Brownlow, and each of its dependents, obtained the very thing that the bright-eyed fairy of the family had guessed would be most acceptable.

## CHAPTER XVII

### POPINJAY PARLOUR

'Happiest of all, in that her gentle spirit
Commits itself to yours to be directed.'

*Merchant of Venice.*

'It is our melancholy duty to record the demise of James Barnes, Esq., which took place at his residence at Belforest Park, near Kenminster, on the 20th of December. The lamented gentleman had long been in failing health, and an attack of paralysis, which took place on the 19th, terminated fatally. The vast property which the deceased had accumulated, chiefly by steamboat and railway speculations in the West Indies, rendered him one of the richest proprietors in the county. We understand that the entire fortune is bequeathed solely to his grand-niece, Mrs. Caroline Otway Brownlow, widow of the late Joseph Brownlow, Esq., and at present resident in the Pagoda, Kenminster Hill. Her eldest son, Allen Brownlow, Esq., is being educated at Eton.'

That was the paragraph which David Ogilvie placed before the eyes of his sister in a newspaper lent to him in the train by a courteous fellow-traveller.

'Poor Caroline!' said Mary.

They said no more till the next day, when, after the English service at Florence, they were strolling together towards San Miniato, and feeling themselves entirely alone.

'I wonder whether this is true,' began Mary at last.

'Why not true?'

'I thought Mr. Barnes had threatened the boys that they should remember the Midas escapade.'

'It must have been only a threat. It could only lie between her and the Spanish child; and, if report be true, even the half would be an enormous fortune.'

'Will it be fortune or misfortune, I wonder?'

'At any rate, it puts an end to my chances of being of any service to her. Be it the half or the whole, she is equally beyond my reach.'

'As she was before.'

'Don't misinterpret me, Mary. I mean out of reach of helping her in any way. I was of little use to her before. I could

not save little Armine from those brutal bullies, and never suspected the abuse that engulphed Bobus. I am not fit for a
schoolmaster.'

'To tell the truth, I doubt whether you have enough high
spirits or geniality.'

'That's the very thing! I can't get into the boys, or prevent
their thinking me a don. I had hoped there was improvement,
but the revelations of the half-year have convinced me that I
knew just nothing at all about it.'

'Have you thought what you will do?'

'As soon as I get home, I shall send in my notice of resignation at midsummer. That will see out her last boy, if he stays
even so long.'

'And then?'

'I shall go for a year to a theological college, and test my
fitness to offer myself for holy orders.'

A look of satisfaction on his sister's part made him add,
'Perhaps you were disappointed that I was not ordained on my
fellowship seven years ago.'

'Certainly I was; but I was in Russia, and I thought you
knew best, so I said nothing.'

'You were right. You would only have heard what would
have made you anxious. Not that there was much to alarm
you, but it is not good for any one to be left so entirely without
home influences as I was all the time you spent abroad. I fell
among a set of daring talkers, who thought themselves daring
thinkers; and though the foundations were never disturbed
with me, I was not disposed to bind myself more closely to what
might not bear investigation, and I did not like the aspect of
clerical squabbles on minutiæ. There was a tide against the
life that carried me along with it, half from sound, half from
unsound motives, and I shrank from the restraint, outward and
inward.'

'Very likely it was wise, and the best thing in the end. But
what has brought you to it?'

'I hope not as the resource of a shelved schoolmaster.'

'Oh no; you are not shelved. See how you have improved
the school. Look at the numbers.'

'That is no test of my real influence over the boys. I teach
them, I keep them in external order, but I do not get into them.
The religious life is at a low ebb.'

'No wonder, with that vicar; but you have done your best.'

'Even if my attempts are a layman's best, they always get
quenched by the cold water of the Rigby element. It is hard
for boys to feel the reality of what is treated with such business-
like indifference, and set forth so feebly, not to say absurdly.'

'I know. It is a terrible disadvantage.'

'Listening to Rigby has, I must say, done a good deal to
bring about my present intention.'

'By force of contradiction.'

'If that means of longing to be in his place and put the thing as it ought to be put.'

'It is a contradiction in which I most sincerely rejoice, David,' she said ; 'one of the wishes of my heart fulfilled when I had given it up.'

'You do not know that it will be fulfilled.'

'I think it will, though you are right to take time, in case the decision should be partly due to disappointment.'

'If there can be disappointment where hope has never existed. But if a man finds he can't have his great good, it may make him look for the greater.'

Mary sighed a mute and thankful acquiescence.

'The worst of it is about you, Mary. It is throwing you over just as you were coming to make me a home.'

'Never mind, Davie. It is only deferred, and at any rate we can keep together till midsummer. Then I can go out again for a year or two, and perhaps you will settle somewhere where the curate's sister could get a daily engagement.'

The next day they found the following letter at the post-office :—

THE FOLLY, 3d Jan.

MY DEAR MARY — I suppose you may have attained the blessed realms that lie beyond the borders of gossip, and may not have heard the nine days' wonder that Belforest had descended on the Folly, and that poor old Mr. Barnes has left his whole property to me. My dear, it would be something awful even if he had done his duty and halved it between Elvira and me, and he has ingeniously tied it up with trustees so as to make restitution impossible. As it is, my income will be not less than £40,000 a year, and when divided among the children they will all be richer than perhaps is good for them.

And now, my dear old dragon, will you come and keep me in order under the title of governess to Barbara and Elvira? For, of course, the child will go on living with us, and will have it made up to her as far as possible. You know that I shall do all manner of foolish things, but I think they will be rather fewer if you will only come and take me in hand. My trustees are the Colonel and an old solicitor, and will both look after the estate ; but as for the rest, all that the Colonel can say is, that it is a frightful responsibility, and her Serene Highness is awestruck. I could not have conceived that such a thing could have made so much difference in so really good a woman. Now I don't think you will be subject to gold dust in the eyes, and I believe you will still see the same little wild goose, or stormy petrel, that you used to bully at Bath, and will be even more willing to perform the process. As I should have begun by saying, on the very first evening Babie showed her sense by proposing you as governess, and you were unanimously elected in full and free parliament. It really was the child's own thought and proposal, and what I want is to have those two children made wiser and better than I can make them, as well as that you should be the dear comrade and friend I need more than ever. You will see more of your brother than you could otherwise, for Belforest will be our chief home, and I need not say how welcome he will always be there. It is not habitable at present, so I mean to stay on in the Folly till Easter, and then give Janet the London lectures and

classes she has been raving for these two years, and take Jessie also for
music lessons, if she can be spared.

I'm afraid it is a come-down for a finisher like you to condescend to my
little Babie, but she is really worth teaching, and I would say, make your
own terms, but that I am afraid you would not ask enough.    Please let it
be £150, there's a good Mary!   I think you would come if you knew what
a relief it would be.   Ever since that terrible August, two years and a half
ago, I have felt as if I were drifting in an endless mist, with all the children depending on me, and nobody to take my hand and lead me.   You
are one of the straws I grasp at.   Not very complimentary after all, but
when I thought of the strong, warm, guiding hands that are gone, I could
not put it otherwise.   Do, Mary, come, I do need you so.—Your affectionate                                               C. O. Brownlow.

'May I see it?' asked David.

'If you will; but I don't think it will do you any good.   My
poor Carey!'

'Few women would have written such a letter in all the first
flush of wealth.'

'No; there's great sweetness and humility and generosity in
it, dear child.'

'It changes the face of affairs.'

'I'm engaged to you.'

'Nonsense!   As if that would stand in the way.   Besides,
she will be at Kenminster till Easter.   You are not hesitating,
Mary?'

'I don't think I am, and yet I believe I ought to do so.'

'You are not imagining that I——'

'I was not thinking of you; but I am not certain that it
would not be better for our old friendship if I did not accept
the part poor Carey proposes to me.   I might make myself more
disagreeable than could be endured by forty thousand a year.'

'You do yourself and her equal injustice.'

'I shall settle nothing till I have seen her.'

'Then you will be fixed,' he said, in a tone of conviction.

So she expected, though believing that it would be the ruin
of her pleasant old friendship.   Her nineteen years of governess-
ship had shown her more of the shady side of high life than was
known to her brother or her friend.   She knew that, whatever
the owner may be at the outset, it is the tendency of wealth
and power to lead to arbitrariness and impatience of contradiction and censure, and to exact approval and adulation.
Even if Caroline Brownlow's own nature should, at five-and-
thirty, be too much confirmed in sweetness and generosity to
succumb to such temptation, her children would only too probably resent any counter-influence, and set themselves against
their mother's friend, and guide, under the title of governess.
Moreover, Mary was too clear-sighted not to feel that there
was a lack in the Brownlow household of what alone could give
her confidence in the charming qualities of its mistress.   Yet
she knew that her brother would never forgive her for refusing,

and that she should hardly forgive herself for following—not so much her better, as her more prudent, judgment. For she was infinitely touched and attracted by that warm-hearted letter, and could not bear to meet it with a refusal. She hoped, for a time at least, to be a comfort, and to make suggestions, with some chance of being attended to. Such aid seemed due from the old friendship at whatever peril thereto, and she would leave her final answer till she should see whether her friend's letter had been written only on the impulse of the moment, and half retracted immediately after.

The brother and sister crossed the Channel at night, and arrived at Kenminster at noon, on a miserably wet day. At the station they were met by Jock and a little yellow dog. His salutation, as he capped his master, was—

'Please, mother sent me up to see if you were come by this train, because if you'd come to early dinner, she would be glad, because there's a builder or somebody coming with Uncle Robert about the repairs afterwards. Mother sent the carriage because of the rain. I say, isn't it jolly cats and dogs ?'

Mary was an old traveller, who could sleep anywhere, and had made her toilet on landing, so as to be fresh and ready ; but David was yellow and languid enough to add force to his virtuous resolution to take no advantage of the invitation, but leave his sister to settle her affairs her own way, thinking perhaps she might trust his future discretion the more for his present abstinence, so he went off in the omnibus. Jock, with the unfailing courtesy of the Brood, handed Miss Ogilvie into a large closed waggonette, explaining, 'We have this for the present, and a couple of job horses ; but Uncle Robert is looking out for some real good ones, and ponies for all of us. I am going over with him to Woolmarston to-morrow to try some.'

It was said rather magnificently, and Mary answered, 'You must be glad to get back into the Belforest grounds.'

'Ain't we? It was just in time for the skating,' said Jock. 'Only the worst of it is, everybody will come to the lake, and so mother won't learn to skate. We thought we had found a jolly little place in the wood, where we could have had some fun with her, but they found it out, though we halloed as loud as ever we could to keep them off.'

'Can your mother skate ?'

'No, you see she never had a chance at home. Father was so busy, and we were so little ; but she'd learn. Mother Carey can learn anything, if one could hinder her Serene Highness from pitching into her. I say, Miss Ogilvie, you'll give her leave to skate, won't you ?' he asked in an insinuating tone.

'I give her leave !'

'She always says she'll ask you when we want her to be jolly and not mind her Serene Highness.'

Mary avoided pledging herself, and Jock's attention was

diverted to the dog, who was rising on his hind legs, vainly
trying to look out of the window ; and his history, told with
great gusto by Jock, lasted till they reached home.

The drawing-room was full of girls about their lessons as
usual—sums, exercises, music, and grammar all going on at
once ! but Caroline put an end to them, and sent the Kencroft
party home at once in the carriage.

'So you have not dropped the old trade ? ' said Mary.

'I couldn't. Ellen is not strong enough yet to have the
children on her hands all day. I said I'd be responsible for
them till Easter, and I dare say you won't mind helping me
through it as the beginning of everything. Will you condescend ? You know I want to be your pupil too.'

'You can be no one's pupil but your own, my dear ! no one's
on earth, I mean.'

'Oh, don't ! I know that, Mary. I'm trying and trying to
be *their* pupil still. Indeed I am ! It makes me patient of
Robert, and his fearful responsibility, and his good little sister,
to know that my husband always thought him right, and meant
him to look after me. But as one lives on, those dear voices
seem to get farther and farther away, as if one was drifting
more out of reach in the fog. I do hate myself for it, but I
can't help it.'

'Is there not a voice that can never go out of reach, and that
brings you nearer to them ? '

'You dear old Piety, Prudence, and Charity all in one ! That
is if you have the charity to come and infuse a little of your
piety and prudence into me. You know you could always make
me mind you, and you'll make me—what is it that Mrs. Coffinkey says ?—a credit to my position before you've done. I've
had your room got ready ; won't you come and take off your
things ? '

'I think, if you don't object, I had better sleep at the schoolhouse, and come up here after David's breakfast.'

'Very well ; I won't try to rob him of you more than can be
helped. Though you know he would be welcome here every
evening if he liked.'

'Thank you very much, I can help him more at home ; but
I'll come for the whole day, for I am sure you must have a great
deal on your hands.'

'Well ! I've almost as many classes as pupils, and then there
are so many interruptions. The Colonel is always bringing
something to be signed, and then people will come and offer
themselves, though I'm sure I never asked them. Yesterday
there was a stupendous butler and house-steward who could
also act as courier, and would do himself the honour of
arranging my household in a truly ducal style. Just as I got
rid of him, came a man with a future history of the landed
gentry in quest of my coat of arms and genealogy, also three
wine merchants, a landscape gardener, and a woman with a

pitcher of gold fish. Emma is so soft she thinks everybody is a gentleman. I am trying to get the good old man-servant we had in our old home to come and defend me ; not that he is old, for he was a boy whom Joe trained. O Mary, the bewilderment of it !' and she pushed back the little stray curly rings of hair on her forehead, while a peal at the bell was heard and a card was brought in. 'Oh ! Emma ! don't bring me any more ! Is it a gentleman ?'

'Y—es, ma'am. Leastways it is a clergyman.'

The clergyman turned out to be a Dissenting minister seeking subscriptions, and he was sent off with a sovereign.

'I know it was very weak,' she said ; 'but it was the only way to stop his mouth, and I must have time to talk to you, so don't begin your mission by scolding me.'

Terms were settled ; Mary would remain at the schoolhouse, but daily come to the Pagoda till the removal to London, when her residence was to begin in earnest.

She took up her line from the first as governess, dropping her friend's Christian name, and causing her pupils to address herself as Miss Ogilvie, a formality which was evidently approved by Mrs. Robert Brownlow, and likewise by Janet.

That young lady was wonderfully improved by prosperity. She had lost her caustic manner and air of defiance, so that her cleverness and originality made her amusing instead of disagreeable. She piqued herself on taking her good fortune sensibly, and, though fully seventeen, professed not to know or care whether she was out or not, but threw herself into hard study, with a view to her classes, and gladly availed herself of Miss Ogilvie's knowledge of foreign languages.

Mrs. Coffinkey supposed that she would be presented at court with her dear mamma ; but she laughed at courts and ceremonies, and her mother said that the first presentation in the family would be of Allen's wife when he was a member of parliament. But Janet was no longer at war with Kenminster. She laughed good-humouredly, and was not always struggling for self-assertion, since the humiliations of going about as the poor, plain cousin of the pretty Miss Brownlow were over. Now that she was the rich Miss Brownlow, she was not likely to feel that she was the plain one.

The sense of exile was over when the house in London was taken, and so Janet could afford to be kind to Kenminster ; and she was like the Janet of old times, without her slough of captious disdain. Even then there was a sense that the girl was not fathomed ; she never seemed to pour out her inner self, but only to talk from the surface, and certainly not to have any full confidence with her mother—nay, rather to hold her cheap.

Mary Ogilvie detected this disloyal spirit, and was at a loss whether to ascribe it to modern hatred of control, to the fact that Caroline had been in her old home more like the favourite child than the mother, or to her own eager naturalness of

demeanour and total lack of assumption. She was anything
but weak, yet she could not be dignified, and was quite ready
to laugh at herself with her children. Janet could hardly be
overawed by a mother who had been challenged by her own
gamekeeper creeping down a ditch, with the two Johns, to see
a wild duck on her nest, and with her hat half off, and her hair
disordered by the bushes.

The 'Folly' laughed till its sides ached at the adventure, and
Caroline asked Mary if she were not longing to scold her.

'No, I think you will soon grow more cautious about getting
into ridiculous positions.'

'Isn't laughing a wholesome pastime?'

'Not when it is at those who ought to be looked up to.'

'Oh! I'm not made to be looked up to. I'm not going to be
a hero to my *valet de chambre*, or to anybody else, my dear, if
that's what you want of me!'

Mary secretly hoped that a little more dignity would come in
the London life, and was relieved when the time came for the
move. The new abode was a charming house, with the park
behind it, and the space between nearly all glass. Great ferns,
tall citrons, fragrant shrubs, brilliant flowers, grew there; a
stone-lined pool, with water-lilies above, gold-fish below, and a
cool, sparkling, babbling fountain in the middle. There was an
open space round it, with low chairs and tables, and the parrot
on her perch. Indeed, Popinjay Parlour was the family title of
this delightful abode; but it might almost as well have been
called Mother Carey's bower. Here, after an audience with the
housekeeper, who was even more overpowering than her Serene
Highness, would Caroline retreat to write notes, keep accounts,
and hear Armine's lessons, secure before luncheon from all unnecessary interruption; and here was her special afternoon and
evening court.

This first summer she was free to take her own course as to
society, for Janet cared for the Cambridge examination far
more than for gaiety, and thus she had no call, and no heart for
'going out,' even if she had as yet been more known. Some
morning calls were exchanged, but she sent refusals on mourning cards to invitations to evening parties, though she took her
young people to plays, concerts, and operas, and all that was
pleasant. Her young people included Jessie. Colonel and Mrs.
Brownlow made her a visit as soon as she was settled, and were
so much edified by the absence of display and extravagance
that they did not scruple to trust their daughter to her for the
long-desired music-lessons.

Caroline had indeed made no attempt to win her way into
the great world; but she had brought together as much as possible of the old society of her former home. On two evenings
in the week the *habitués* of Joe Brownlow's house were secure
of finding her either in the drawing-room or conservatory;
beautiful things, and new books and papers on the tables, good

HEARING ARMINE'S LESSONS IN POPINJAY PARLOUR.

music on the piano, sometimes acted charades, or paper games, according to the humour or taste of the party. If she had been a beautiful duchess, Popinjay Parlour would have been a sort of *salon bleu ;* but it was really a kind of paradise to a good many clever, hardworked men and women. Those of the upper world, such as Kenminster county folks, old acquaintances of her husband, or natural adherents of Midas, who found their way to these receptions, either thought them odd but charming, or else regretted that Mrs. Brownlow should get such queer people together, and turn Hyde Corner House into another Folly.

Mary Ogilvie enjoyed, but not without misgivings. It was delightful, and yet, what with Joe Brownlow and his mother had been guarded, might become less safe with no leader older or of more weight than Carey, who could easily be carried along by what they would have checked. The older and more intimate friends always acted as a wholesome restraint ; but when they were not present there was sometimes a tone that jarred on the reverent ear, or dealt with life and its mysteries in a sneering, mocking style. This was chiefly among newcomers, introduced by former acquaintances, and it never went far ; but Mary was distressed by seeing Janet's relish for such conversation. Nita Ray was the chief female offender in this way, and this was the more unfortunate, as Sunday was her only free day.

Those Sundays vexed Mary's secret soul. No one interfered with her way of spending them ; but that was the very cause of misgiving. Everybody went to church in the morning, but just where and as they pleased, meeting at luncheon with odd anecdotes of their adventures, and criticisms of music or of sermons. It was an easy-going meal, lasting long, and haunted by many acquaintances, for whose sake the table was always at its full length, and spread with varieties of delicacies that would endure waiting.

People dropped in, helped themselves, ate and drank, and then adjourned to Popinjay Parlour, where the afternoon was spent in an easy-going, loitering way, more like a foreign than an English Sunday. Miss Ogilvie used to go to the Litany at one of the churches near ; Armine always came with her, and often brought Babie, and Jessie came too, as soon as that good girl had swallowed the fact that the Litany could stand alone.

Janet was apt to be walking with Nita, or else in some eager and amusing conversation in the conservatory ; and as to Elvira, she was the prettiest, most amusing plaything that Mrs. Brownlow's house afforded, a great favourite, and a continual study to the artist friends. Mary used to find her chattering, coquetting, and romping on coming in to the afternoon tea, which she would fain have herself missed ; but that her absence gave pain, and as much offence as one so kind as Mrs. Brownlow could take.

Carey argued that most of her guests were people who seldom

had leisure to enjoy rest, conversation, and variety of pretty things, and that it would be mere Puritan crabbedness to deny them the pleasures of Popinjay Parlour on the only day they could be happy there. It was not easy to answer the argument, though the strong feeling remained that it was not keeping Sunday as the true Lord's Day. While abstinence from such enjoyments created mere negative dulness, there must be something wrong.

Otherwise, Mary was on the happiest terms, made her own laws and duties, and was treated like a sister by Caroline, while the children were heartily fond of her, all except Elvira, who made a fierce struggle against her authority, and then, finding that it was all in vain, conformed as far as her innate idleness and excitability permitted.

She behaved better to Miss Ogilvie than to Janet, with whom she kept up a perpetual petty warfare, sometimes, Mary thought, with the pertinacity of a spiteful elf, making a noise when Janet wanted quiet, losing no opportunity of upsetting her books or papers, and laughing boisterously at any little mishap that befell her. The only reason she ever gave when pushed hard was that 'Janet was so ugly, she could not help it,' a reason so utterly ridiculous that there was no going any further.

Janet, on the whole, behaved much better under the annoyance than could have been expected. She entered enough into the state of affairs to see that the troublesome child could hardly be expelled, and she was too happy and too much amused to care much about the annoyance. There was magnanimity enough about her not to mind midge bites, and certainly this summer was exceptionally delightful with all the pleasures of wealth, and very few of its drawbacks.

By the time the holidays were coming round, Belforest was not half habitable, and they had to return to the Pagoda. A tenant had been found for it, and such of the old furniture as was too precious to be parted with was to be removed to Belforest. Things were sufficiently advanced there for the rooms to be chosen, and orders given as to the decoration and furniture, and then, gathering up her sons, Caroline meant to start for the Rhine, Switzerland, and Italy. Old nurse was settled in a small pair of rooms, with Emma to wait on her, and promises from Jessie to attend to her comforts; but the old woman had failed so much in their absence, and had fretted so much after 'Mrs. Joseph' and the children, that it was hard to leave her again.

Everything that good taste and wealth could do to make a place delightful was at work. The 'butcher's shop' was relegated to a dim corner of the gallery, and its place supplied from the brushes of the artists whom Caroline viewed with loving respect; the drawing-room was renovated, a forlorn old library resuscitated into vigorous life, a museum fitted with shelves,

drawers, and glass cases, which Caroline said would be as
dangerous to the vigorous spirit of natural history as new
clothes to a Brownie, and a billiard and gun room were ceded to
the representations of Allen, who comported himself as befitted
the son and heir.

Caroline would not part with her room-mate, little Barbara,
and was to have for herself a charming bedroom and dressing-
room, with a balcony and parapet overlooking the garden
and park, and a tiny room besides, for Babie to call her
own.

Janet chose the apartments which had been Mr. Barnes', and
which, being in the oldest part of the house and wainscoted
with dark oak, she could take possession of at once. There was
one room downstairs with very ugly caryatides supporting the
wooden mantelpiece and dividing the panels, one of which had
a secret door leading by an odd little stair to the bedroom
above—that in which Mr. Barnes had died.

It had of course another door opening into the corridor, and
it was on these rooms that Janet set her affections. To the
general surprise, Elvira declared that this was the very room
she had chosen, with the red velvet curtains and gold crown,
the day they went over the house, and that Mother Carey had
promised it to her, and she *would* have it.

No one could remember any such promise, and the curtains
of crimson moreen did not answer Elfie's description ; but she
would not be denied, and actually put all her possessions into
the room.

Janet, without a word, quietly turned them out into the
passage, and Elfie flew into one of those furious kicking and
screaming passions which always ended in her being sent to
bed. Caroline felt quite shaken by it, but stood firm, though,
as she said, it went to her heart to deny the child who ought to
have had equal shares with herself, and she would have been
thankful if Janet would have given way.

Of this, however, Janet had no thoughts, strong in the conviction that the child could not make the same reasonable use
of the fittings of the room as she could herself, and by no means
disposed not 'to seek her own.'

She had numerous papers, notes of lectures, returned essays
from her society, and the like to dispose of, and she rejoiced in
placing them in the compartments of the great bureau in the
lower room. The lawyers had cleared all before her, and the
space was delightful. All personals must have been carried off
by the servants as perquisites, for she found no traces of the
former occupant till she came to a little bedside table. The
drawer was not locked, but did not open without difficulty,
being choked with notes and letters in envelopes, directed to J.
Barnes, Esquire. This perhaps accounted for the drawer not
having been observed and emptied. Janet shook the contents
out into a basket, and was going to take them to her uncle, but

thought it could do no harm first to see whether there were
anything curious or interesting in them.

Several were receipted bills : but then she came to her
mother's handwriting, and read her conciliatory note, which
whetted her curiosity ; and looking further she got some amusement out of the polite notes and offers of service, claims to old
family friendship, and congratulations which had greeted Mr.
Barnes, and he had treated with grim disregard.

Presently, thrust into an envelope with another letter, and
written on a piece of note-paper, was something that made her
start as if at the sting of a viper.  No! it could not be a will!
She knew what wills were like.  They were sheets of foolscap,
written by lawyers, while this was only an old man's cramped
and crooked writing.  Perhaps, when he was in a rage, he had
so far carried out his threat that Allen should remember King
Midas as to make a rough draft of a will, leaving everything
to Elvira de Menella, for there at the top was the date, plainly
visible, the very April when the confession had been made.
But no doubt he had never carried out his purpose so far as to
get it legally drawn out and attested.  As Mr. Richards had
said, he had never been in health to take any active measures,
and probably he had rested satisfied with this relief to his
feelings.

Should she show it to her mother and uncle, and let them
know their narrow escape?  No.  Mother Carey and Allen
made quite fuss enough already about that little vixen, and if
they discovered how nearly she had been the sole heiress, they
would be far worse.  Besides, her mother might have misgivings as to this unhappy document being morally, though not
legally, binding.  Suppose she were seized with a fit of generosity,
and gave all up! or even half.  Elfie, the little shrew, to have
equal rights!  The sweets of wealth only just tasted to be
resigned, and the child, overweening enough already, to be set
in their newly gained place!

The sagacity of seventeen decided that mother had better not
be worried about it for her own sake and that of every one else.
So what was to be done.  No means of burning it were at hand,
and to ask for them might excite suspicion.  The safest way
was to place it in one of the drawers of the bureau, lock it up,
and keep the key.

# CHAPTER XVIII

## AN OFFER FOR MAGNUM BONUM

'They had gold and gold and gold without end,
  Gold to lay by and gold to spend,
  Gold to give and gold to lend,
 . And reversions of gold in futuro.
  In gold his family revelled and rolled,
  Himself and his wife and his sons so bold,
  And his daughters who sang to their harps of gold
                    O bella età dell' oro.'

FOUR years of wealth had not made much external alteration in Mrs. Joseph Brownlow. As she descended the staircase of her beautiful London house, one Monday morning late in April, between flower-stands filled with lovely ferns and graceful statues, she had still the same eager girlish look. It was true that her little cap was of the most costly lace, her hair manipulated by skilful hands, and her thin black summer dress was of material and make such as a scientific eye alone could have valued in their simplicity. But dignity still was wanting. Silks and brocades that would stand alone, and velvets richly piled only crushed and suffocated the little light swift figure, and the crisp curly hair was so much too wilful for the maid that she had been even told that madame's style would be to cut it short, and wear it à l'ingénue, which she viewed as insulting ; and altogether her general air was precisely what it had been when her dress cost a twentieth part of what it did at present.

Her face looked no older. It was thin, eager, bright, and sunny, yet with an indescribable wistfulness in the sparkling eyes, and something worn in the expression, and, as usual, she moved with a quiet nimbleness peculiar to herself.

The breakfast-table, sparkling with silver and glass, around a magnificent orchid in the centre, and a rose by every plate, was spread in the dining-room, sweet sounds and scents coming in through the widely-opened glass doors of the conservatory, while a bright wood fire, still pleasant to look at, shone in the grate.

As she rang the bell, Bobus came in from the conservatory, book in hand, to receive the morning kiss, for which he had to bend to his little mother. He was not tall, but he had attained his full height, and had a well-knit sturdy figure which, together with his heavy brow and deep-set eyes, made him appear older than his real age—nineteen. His hair and upper lip were dark, and his eyes keen with a sense of ready power and strong will.

'Good morning, Bobus ; I didn't see you all day yesterday,' said his mother.

'No, I couldn't find you before you went out on Saturday
night, to tell you I was going to run down to Belforest
with Bauerson. I wanted to enlighten his mind as to wild
hyacinths. They are in splendid bloom all over the copses, and
I thought he would have gone down on his knees to them, like
Linnæus to the gorse.'

'I'm afraid he didn't go on his knees to anything else.'

'Well, it is not much in his line.'

'Then can he be a nice Sunday companion?'

'Now, mother, I expected credit for not scandalising the
natives. We got out at Woodgate and walked over, quite "un-
knownst," to Kenminster.'

'I was not thinking of the natives, but of yourself.'

'As you are a sensible woman, Mother Carey, wasn't it a more
goodly and edifying thing to put a man like Bauerson in a
trance over the bluebells, than to sit cramped up in foul air
listening to the glorification of a wholesale massacre.'

'For shame, Bobus; you know I never allow you to say such
things.'

'Then you should not drag me to church. Was it last Sunday that I was comparing the Prussians at Bazeille with——'

'Hush, my dear boy, you frighten me; you know it is all explained. Fancy, if we had to deal with a nation of Thugs, and
no means of guarding them—a different dispensation and all.
But here come the children, so hush.'

Bobus gave a nod and smile, which his mother understood
only too well as intimating acquiescence with wishes which he
deemed feminine and conventional.

'My poor boy,' she said to herself, with vague alarm and
terror, 'what has he not picked up? I must read up these
things, and be able to talk it over with him by the time he
comes back from Norway.'

There, however, came the morning greeting of Elvira and
Barbara, girls of fourteen and eleven, with floating hair and
short dresses, the one growing up into all the splendid beauty
of her early promise, the other thin and brown, but with a
speaking face and lovely eyes. They were followed by Miss
Ogilvie, as trim and self-possessed as ever, but with more ease
and expansiveness of manner.

'So, Babie,' said her brother, 'you've earned your breakfast;
I heard you hammering away.'

'Like a nut-hatch,' was the merry answer.

'And Elfie?' asked Mrs. Brownlow.

'I'm not so late as Janet,' she answered; and the others
laughed at the self-defence before the attack.

'It is a lazy little Elf in town,' said Miss Ogilvie; 'in the
country she is up and out at impossible hours.'

'Good morning, Janet,' said Bobus, at that moment, 'or
rather, "Marry come up, mistress mine, good lack, nothing is
lacking to thee save a pointed hood graceless."'

For Janet was arrayed in a close-fitting pale blue dress, cut in semblance of an ancient kirtle, and with a huge chatelaine, from which massive chains dangled, not to say clattered—not merely the ordinary appendages of a young lady, but a pair of compasses, a safety inkstand, and a microscope. Her dark hair was strained back from a face not calculated to bear exposure, and was wound round a silver arrow.

Elfie shook with laughter, murmuring—

'Oh dear! what a fright!' in accents which Miss Ogilvie tried to hush; while Babie observed as a sort of excuse, 'Janet always is a figure of fun when she is picturesque.'

'My dear, I hope you are not going to show yourself to any one in that dress,' added her mother.

'It is perfectly correct,' said Janet, 'studied from an old Italian costume.'

'The Marchioness of Carabbas, in my old fairy-tale book. Oh yes, I see!' and Babie went off again in an ecstatic fit of laughter.

'I hope you've got boots and a tail ready for George,' added Bobus. 'Being a tiger already, he may serve as cat.'

Therewith the post came in, and broke up the discourse; for Babie had a letter from Eton, from Armine, who was shut up with a sore throat.

Her mother was less happy. She had asked a holiday for the next day for her two Eton boys and their cousin John, and the reply had been that though for two of the party there could be no objection, her elder boy was under punishment for one of the wild escapades to which he was too apt to pervert his excellent abilities.

'Are not they coming, mother?' asked Babie. 'Armie does not say.'

'Unfortunately Jock has got kept in again.'

'Poor Jock!' said Bobus; 'sixpence a day and no expectations would have been better pasture for his brains.'

'Yes,' said his mother, with a sigh, 'I doubt if we are any of us much the better or the wiser for Belforest.'

'The wiser, I'm sure, because we've got Miss Ogilvie,' cried Babie.

'Do I hear babes uttering the words of wisdom?' asked Allen, coming into the room, and pretending to pull her hair, as the schoolroom party rose from the breakfast-table, and he met them with outstretched hands.

'Ay, to despise Lag-last,' said Elvira, darting out of his reach, and tossing her dark locks at him as she hid behind a fern plant in the window; and there was a laughing scuffle, ended by Miss Ogilvie, who swept the children away to the schoolroom, while Allen came to the table, where his mother had poured out his coffee, and still waited to preside over his breakfast, though she had long finished her own.

Allen Brownlow, at twenty, was emphatically the Eton and

Christchurch production, just well made and good-looking
enough to do full justice to his training and general getting up,
without too much individual personality of his own.  He looked
only so much of a man as was needful for looking a perfect
gentleman, and his dress and equipments were in the most perfect quietly exquisite style, as costly as possible, yet with no
display, and nothing to catch the eye.

'Well, Bobus,' he said, 'you made out your expedition.  How
did the place look?'

'Wasting its sweetness,' said his mother; 'it is tantalising to
think of it.'

'It could hardly be said to be wasted,' said Bobus; 'the
natives were disporting themselves all over it.'

'Where?' asked Allen, with displeased animation.

'Oh, Essie and Ellie were promenading a select party about
the gardens.  I could almost hear Mackintyre gnashing his teeth
at their inroads on the forced strawberries, and the park and
Elmwood Spinney were dotted so thick with people that we
had to look sharp not to fall in with any one.'

'Elmwood Spinney!' exclaimed Allen; 'you don't mean that
they were running riot over the preserves?'

'I don't think there were more than half a dozen there.
Bauerson was quite edified.  He said "So! they had on your
English Sunday quite falsely me informed."  There were a
couple of lovers spooning and some children gathering flowers,
and it had just the Arcadian look dear to the German eye.'

'Children,' cried Allen, as if they were vipers.  'That's just
what I told you, mother.  If you will persist in throwing open
the park, we shall not have a pheasant on the place.'

'My dear boy, I have seen them running about like chickens
in a farmyard.'

'Yes, but what's the use, if all the little beggars in Kenminster are to be let in to make them wild!  And when you
knew I particularly wished to have something worth asking
Prince Siegfried down to.'

'Never mind, Allen,' put in Janet; 'you can ask him to shoot
into the poultry yard.  The poor things are just as thick there,
and rather tamer, so the sport will be the more noble.'

'You know nothing about it, Janet,' said Allen in displeasure.

'But, Allen,' said his mother apologetically, though she felt
with Janet, 'the woods are locked up.'

'Locked!  As if that was any use when you let a lot of boys
come marauding all over the place!'

'Really, Allen,' said his mother, 'when I remember what we
used to say about old Mr. Barnes, I cannot find it in my heart to
play the same game!'

'It is quite a different thing.'

'How?'

'He did it out of mere surliness.'

'I don't suppose it makes much difference to the excluded whether it is done out of mere surliness, or for the sake of the preserves.'

'Mother!' Allen spoke as if the absurdity of the argument were quite too much for him; but his brother and sister both laughed, which nettled him into adding—

'Well! All I have to say is, that if Belforest is to be nothing but a people's park for all the ragamuffins in Kenminster, there will soon not be a head of game in the place, and I shall be obliged to shoot elsewhere!'

Poor Caroline! If there was a thing she specially hated, it was a *battue*, both for the thing itself, and all the previous preparation of preserving, and of prosecuting poachers; and yet sons have their mothers so much in their power by that threat of staying away from home, that she could not help faltering, 'Oh, Allen, I'll do my best, and tell the keepers to be very careful, and lock the gates of all the preserves.'

Allen saw she was vexed, and spoke more kindly, 'There, never mind, mother. It is more than can be expected that ladies should see things in a reasonable light.'

'What is the reasonable light?' asked Bobus.

Allen did not choose to hear, regarding Bobus not indeed as a woman, but as something as little capable of appreciating his reason. It was Janet who took up the word. 'The reasonable light is that the enjoyment of the many should be sacrificed to the vanity of the few, viz. that all Kenminster should be confined to dusty roads all the year round in order that Allen may bring down the youngest son of the youngest son of a German prince for one day to fire amongst some hundreds of tame pheasants who come up expecting to be fed.'

'Oh yes,' said Allen, 'we all know that you are a regular out-and-out democrat, Janet.'

'I confess, without being a democrat,' said his mother, 'that I do wonder that you gentlemen, who wish the game laws to continue, should so work them as to be more aggravating than ever.'

'It is a simple question of the rights of property,' said Allen. 'If I do a thing, I like it to be well done, and not half-and-half.'

Caroline rose from the table, dreading, like many a mother, a regular skirmish about game-preserving, between those who cared to shoot and those who did not. Like other ladies, she could never understand exaggerated preserving, nor why men who loved sport should care to have game multiplied and tamed so as apparently to spoil all the zest of the chase; but she had let Allen and his uncle do whatever they told her was right by the preserves, except shutting up the park and all the footpaths. Colonel Brownlow, whose sporting instincts were those of a former generation, was quite satisfied; Allen never would be so; and it was one of the few bones of contention in the family.

For Allen was walking through Oxford in a quiet, amiable way, not troubling himself more about study than to secure himself from an ignominious pluck, and doing whatever was supposed to be 'good form.'

His brother accused him of carrying his idolatry of 'good form' to a snobbish extent, but Allen could carry it out so naturally that no one could have suspected that he had not been to the manner born. If he did appreciate the society of people with handles to their names, he comported himself among them as their easy equal; and he was so lavish as to be a very popular man. He had no vicious tastes or tendencies, and was too gentlemanly and quiet ever to come into collision with the authorities. At home, except when his notions of 'good form' were at variance with strong opinions of his mother's, nothing could be more chivalrously deferential than his whole demeanour to her; and the worst that could be said of him was that he managed to waste a large amount of time and money with very little to show for it. His profession was to be son and heir to a large fortune, and he took to the show part of the affair very kindly.

But was this being the man his father had expected him to be? The thought would come across Caroline at times, but not very often, as she floated along easily in the stream of life. Most of the business troubles of her property were spared her by her trustees, and her income was so large that even Allen's expenditure had not yet been felt as an inconvenience. As to the responsibilities, she contributed largely to county subscriptions, gave her clergyman whatever he asked, provided Christmas treats and summer teas for their school-children, and permitted Miss Ogilvie and Babie to do whatever they pleased among the poor when they were at home. But she was not very much at Belforest. She generally came there at Midsummer and at Christmas, and filled the house with friends. All kinds of amusements astonished the neighbourhood, and parties of the newest kinds, private theatricals, *tableaux*, charades, all that taste or ingenuity could devise, were in vogue.

But before the spring east winds the party were generally gone to some more genial climate, and the early autumn was often spent in Switzerland. Pictures, art, and scenery were growing to be necessaries of life, and to stay at home with no special diversion in view seemed unthought of. The season was spent in London, not dropping the artist society on the one hand, but adding to it the amount of intercourse into which she was drawn by the fact of her being a rich and charming woman, having a delightful house, and a son and daughter who might be '*grands partis*.' Allen liked high life for her, so she did not refuse it; but probably her social success was all the greater from her entire indifference, and that of her daughter, to all the questions of exclusiveness and fashion. If they had been born duchesses they could not have been less concerned about obtaining invitations to what their maid called 'the first circles,' and they would sometimes reduce Allen to despair by giving the preference to a lively literary *soirée*, when he wanted them to show themselves among the aristocracy at a drum.

Engagements of all kinds grew on them with every season, and in this one especially, Caroline had grown somewhat weary of the endeavour to satisfy both him and Janet, and was not sorry that her two eldest sons were starting on a yacht voyage to Norway, where Allen meant to fish, and Bobus to study natural history. She had her interview with the housekeeper, and proceeded to her own place in Popinjay Parlour, a quiet place at this time of day, save for the tinkling of the fountain and the twitterings of the many little songsters in the aviary, whom the original parrot used patronisingly to address as 'Pretty little birds.'

Janet was wandering about among the flowers, evidently waiting for her, and began, as she came in—

'I wanted to speak to you, mother.'

'Well, Janet,' said Caroline, reviewing in one moment every unmarried man, likely or unlikely, who had approached the girl, and with a despairing conviction that it would be some one very unlikely indeed !

'You know I am of age, mother.'

'Certainly. We drank your health last Monday.'

'I made up my mind that till I was of age I would go on studying, and at the same time see something of the world and of society.'

'Certainly,' said Caroline, wondering what her inscrutable daughter was coming to.

'And having done this, I wish to devote myself to the study of medicine.'

'Be a lady doctor, Janet !'

'Mother, you are surely above all the commonplace, old-world nonsense !'

'I don't think I am, Janet. I don't think your father would have wished it.'

'He would have gone on with the spirit of the times, mother ; men do, while women stand still.'

'I don't think he would in this.'

'I think he would, if he knew me, and the issues and stake, and how his other children are failing him.'

'Janet !'—and the colour flushed into her mother's face—' I don't quite know what you mean ; but it is time we came to an understanding.'

'I think so,' returned Janet.

'Then you know——'

'I heard what papa said to you. I kept the white slate till you thought of it,' said Janet, in a tone that sounded soft from her

'And why did you never say so, my dear?'

'I can hardly tell. I was shy at first; and then reserve grows on a person; but I never ceased from thinking about it through all these years. Mother, you do not think there is any chance of the boys taking it up as my father wished?'

'Certainly not Allen,' said Caroline, with a sigh. 'And as to Bobus, he would have full capacity; but a great change must come over him, poor fellow, before he would fulfil your father's conditions.'

'He has no notion of the drudgery of the medical profession,' said Janet; 'he means to read law, get up social and sanitary questions, and go into parliament.'

'I know,' said her mother, 'I have always lived in hopes that sanitary theories would give him his father's heart for the sufferers, and that search into the secrets of nature would lead him higher; but as long as he does not turn that way of himself, it would be contrary to your father's charge to hold this discovery out to him as an inducement.'

'And Jock?' said Janet, smiling. 'You don't expect it of the born soldier—nor of Armine?'

'I am not sure about Armine, though he may not be strong enough to bear the application.'

'Armine will walk through life like Allen,' scornfully said Janet: 'besides he is but fourteen. Now, mother, why should not I be worthy?'

'My dear Janet, it is not a question of worthiness; it is not a thing a woman could work out.'

'I do not ask you to give it to me now, nor even to promise it to me,' said Janet, with a light in those dark wells, her eyes; 'but only to let me have the hope, that when in three years' time I am qualified, and have passed the examinations, if Bobus does not take it up, you will let me claim that best inheritance my father left, but which his sons do not heed.'

'My child, you do not know what you ask. Remember, I know more about it than only what you picked up on that morning. It is a matter he could not have made sure of without a succession of experiments very hard even for him, and certainly quite impossible for any woman. The exceeding difficulty and danger of the proof was one reason of his guarding it so much, and desiring it should only be told to one good as well as clever—clever as well as good.'

'Can you give me no hint of the kind of thing?' said Janet wistfully.

'That would be a betrayal of his trust.'

Janet looked terribly disappointed.

'Mother,' said she, 'let me put it to you. Is it fair to shut up a discovery that might benefit so many people?'

'It is not his fault, Janet, that it is shut up. He talked of it to several of the most able men he was connected with, and they thought it a chimera. He could not carry it on far enough to

convince them. I do not know what he would have done if his
illness had been longer, or he could have talked it out with any
one, but I know the proof could only be made out by a course
of experiments which he could not commit to any one not
highly qualified, or whom he could not entirely trust. It is not
a thing to be set forth broadcast, while it might yet prove a
fallacy.'

'Is it to be lost for ever, then?'

'I shall try to find light as to the right thing to be done
about it.'

'Well,' said Janet, drawing a long breath, 'three years of
study must come, any way, and by that time I may be able to
triumph over prejudice.'

There was no time to reply, for at that moment the letters
of the second delivery were brought in ; and the first that
Caroline opened told her that the cold which Armine had mentioned on Saturday seemed to be developing into an attack of a
rather severe hybrid kind of illness, between measles and scarla-
tina, from which many persons had lately been suffering.

Armine was never strong, and his illnesses were always a
greater anxiety than those of other people, so that his mother
came to the immediate decision of going to Eton that same
afternoon and remaining there, unless she found that it had
been a false alarm.

She did not find it so ; and as she remained with her boy,
Janet's conversation with her could not be resumed. There
was so much chance of infection that she could not see any of
the family again. Both the Johns sickened as soon as Armine
began to improve, and Miss Ogilvie took the three girls down
to Belforest.

After the first few days it was rather a pleasant nursing.
There was never any real alarm ; indeed, Armine was the least
ill of the three, and Johnnie the most, and each boy was perfectly delighted to have her to attend to him, her nephew
almost touchingly grateful. The only other victim was Jock's
most intimate friend, Cecil Evelyn, whose fag Armine was.
He became a sharer of her attentions and the amusements she
provided. She received letters of grateful thanks from his
mother, who was, like herself, a widow, but was prevented from
coming to him by close attendance on her mother-in-law, who
was in a lingering state of decay when every day might be the
last.

The eldest son, Lord Fordham, was so delicate that he was
on no account to be exposed to the infection, and the boys were
exceedingly anxious that Cecil should join them in the expedition that their mother projected making with them, to air them
in Switzerland before returning to the rest of the family. But
Mrs. Evelyn (her husband had not lived to come to the title)
declined this. Fordham was in the country with his tutor, and
she wished Cecil to come and spend his quarantine with her in

N

London before joining him. The boys grumbled very much, but Caroline could hardly wonder when she talked with their tutor.

He, like every one else, liked, and even loved personally, that perplexing subject, John Lucas Brownlow, *alias* Jock. The boy was too generous, honourable, truthful, and kindly to be exposed to the stigma of removal; but he was the perplexity of everybody. He could not be convinced of any necessity for application, and considered a flogging as a slight risk quite worth encountering for the sake of diversion. He would execute the most audacious pranks, and if he was caught, would take it as a trial of skill between the masters and himself, and accept punishment as amends, with the most good-humoured grace in the world. Fun seemed to be his only moving spring, and he led everybody along with him, so as to be a much more mischievous person than many a worse lad.

The only exceptions in the house to his influence seemed to be his brother and cousin. Both were far above the average boy—Armine for talent, John Friar Brownlow at once for industry and steadiness. They had stood out resolutely against more than one of his pranks, and had been the only boys in the house not present on the occasion of his last freak—a champagne supper, when parodies had been sung, caricaturing all the authorities; and when the company had become uproarious enough to rouse the whole family, the boys were discovered in the midst of the most audacious but droll mimicry of the masters.

As to work, Jock was developing the utmost faculties for leaving it undone, trusting to his native facility for putting on the steam at any crisis; and not believing in the warnings that he would fail in passing for the army.

What was to be done with him? Was he to be taken away and sent to a tutor? His mother consulted himself as he sat in his arm-chair.

'Like Rob!' he said, and made up a face.

'Rob is doing very well in the militia.'

'No; don't do that, mother! Never fear, I'll put on a spurt when the time comes!'

'I don't believe a spurt will do. Now, seriously, Jock——'

'Don't say "seriously," mother; it's like H.S.H.'

'Perhaps, if I had been like her, you would not be vexing me so much now.'

'Come, come, mother, it's nothing to be vexed about. My tutor needn't have bothered you. I've done nothing sneaking nor ungentlemanly.'

'There is plenty of wrong without that, Jock. While you never heed anything but fun and amusement I do not see how you are to come to anything worth having; and you will soon get betrayed into something unworthy. Don't let me have to

take you away in disgrace, my boy; it would break my
heart.'

'You shan't have to do that, mother.'

'But don't you think it would be wiser to be somewhere with
fewer inducements to idleness?'

'Leave Eton? Oh no, mother! I can't do that till the last
day possible. I shall be in the eight another year.'

'You will not be here another year unless you go on very
differently. Your tutor will not allow it, if I would.'

'Has he said so?'

'Yes; and the next half is to be the trial.'

Jock applied himself to extracting a horsehair from the
stuffing of the elbow of his chair; and there was a look over
his face as near sullenness as ever came to his gay, careless
nature.

Would he attend? or even could he?

When his bills came in Caroline feared, as before, that he
was the one of all her children whom Belforest was most
damaging. Allen was expensive, but in an elegant, exquisite
kind of way; but Jock was simply reckless; and his pleasures
were questionable enough to be on the borders of vices, which
might change the frank, sweet, merry face that now looked
up to her into a countenance stained by dissipation and
licence!

A flash of horror and dismay followed the thought! But
what could she do for him, or for any of her children? Censure
only alienated them and made them worse, and their love for
her was at least one blessing. Why had this gold come to take
away the wholesome necessity for industry?

## CHAPTER XIX

### THE SNOWY WINDING-SHEET

' Cold, cold, 'tis a chilly clime
That the youth in his journey hath reached;
And he is aweary now,
And faint for lack of food.
Cold! cold! there is no sun in heaven.'

SOUTHEY.

VERY merry was the party which arrived at the roughly-built
hotel of Schwarenbach, which serves as a half-way house to the
Altels.

Never had expedition been more enjoyed than that of Mrs.
Brownlow and her three boys. They had taken a week by the
sea to recruit their forces, and then began their journey in
earnest, since it was too late for a return to Eton, although so
early in the season that to the Swiss they were like the first
swallows of the spring; and they came in for some of the

wondrous glory of the spring flowers, so often missed by tourists.

In her mountain dress, all state and ceremony cast aside, Caroline rode, walked, and climbed like the jolly Mother Carey she was, to use her son's favourite expression ; and the boys, full of health and recovery, gambolled about her, feeling her companionship the very crown of their enjoyment.

Johnnie, to whom all was more absolutely new than to the others, was the quietest of the three. He was a year older than Lucas, as Jock was now called to formal outsiders, while Friar John, a reversal of his cousin's two Christian names, was a school title that sometimes passed into home use. Friar John then had reached an age open to the influences of beautiful and sublime scenery, and when the younger ones only felt the exhilaration of mountain air, and longings to get as high as possible, his soul began to expand, and fresh revelations of glory and majesty to take possession of him. He was a very different person from the rough, awkward lad of eight years back. He still had the somewhat loutish figure which, in his mother's family, was the shell of fine-looking men, and he was shy and bashful, but Eton polish had taken away the rude gruffness, and made his manners and bearing gentlemanly. His face was honest and intelligent, and he had a thoroughly good, conscientious disposition ; his character stood high, and he was the only Brownlow of them all who knew the sweets of being 'sent up for good.' His aunt could almost watch expression deepening on his open face, and he was enjoying with soul and mind even more than with body. Having had the illness later and more severely than the other two, his strength had not so fully returned, and he was often glad to rest, admire, and study the subject with his aunt, to whose service he was specially devoted, while the other two climbed and explored. For even Armine had been invigorated with a sudden overflow of animal health and energy, which made him far more enterprising and less contemplative than he had ever been before.

They four had walked up the mountain after breakfast from Kandersteg, bringing their bags for a couple of nights, the boys being anxious to go up the Altels the next day, as their time was nearly over and they were to be in school in ten days' time again. After luncheon and a good rest on the wooden bench outside the door, they began to stroll towards the Daubensee, along a path between desolate boulders, without vegetation, except a small kind of monkshood.

'I call this dreary,' said the mother. 'We don't seem to get a bit nearer the lake. I shall go home and write to Babie.'

'I'll come back with you,' said Johnnie. 'My mother will be looking for a letter.'

'Not giving in already, Johnnie,' said Armine. 'I can tell you I mean to get to the lake.'

'The Friar is the slave of his note-book,' said Jock. 'When

are we to have it—"Crags and Cousins," or "From Measles to Mountains"?'

'I don't want to forget everything,' said Johnnie, with true Kencroft doggedness.

'Do you expect ever to look at that precious diurnal again?'

'He will leave it as an heirloom to his grandchildren!'

'And they will say how slow people were in the nineteenth century.'

'There will have been a reaction by that time, and they will only wonder how anybody cared to go up into such dreary places.'

'Or perhaps they will have stripped them all, and eaten the glaciers up as ices and ice-creams!'

'I think I'll set up that as my pet anxiety,' said their mother, laughing; 'just as some people suffer from perplexity as to what is to become of the world when all the coal is used up! You are not turning on my account, are you, Johnnie? I am quite happy to go back alone.'

'No, indeed. I want to write my letter, and I have had enough,' said John.

'Tired!' said Armine. 'Poor old Monk! Swiss air always makes me feel like a balloon full of gas. I could go on, up and up, for ever!'

'Well, keep to the path, and don't do anything imprudent,' she said, turning back, the boys saying, 'We'll only have a look down the pass! Here, Chico! Chico! Chick! Chick!'

Chico, the little dog so disdainfully rejected by Elvira, had attached himself from the first to Jock. He had been in the London house when they spent a day there, and in rapture at the meeting had smuggled himself, not without his master's connivance, among the rugs and wrappers, and had already been the cause of numerous scrapes with officials and travellers, whence sometimes money, sometimes politeness, sometimes audacity, bought off his friends as best they could.

There was a sort of grave fascination in the exceeding sternness of the scene—the gray heaps of stone, the mountains raising their shining white summits against the blue, the dark, fathomless, lifeless lake, and the utter absence of all forms of life. Armine's spirit fell under the spell, and he moved dreamily on, hardly attending to Jock, who was running on with Chico, and alarming him by feints of catching him and throwing him into the water.

They came to the gap where they expected to look over the pass, but it was blotted out by a mist, not in itself visible though hiding everything, and they were turning to go home when, in the ravine near at hand, the white ruggedness of the Wildstrube glacier gleamed on their eyes.

'I didn't know it was so near,' said Jock. 'Come and have a look at it.'

'Not on it,' said Armine, who had somewhat more Swiss

experience than his brother. 'There's no going there without a guide.'

'There's no reason we should not get on the moraine,' said Jock; and they presently began to scramble about among the rocks and boulders, trying to mount some larger one whence they might get a more general view of the form of the glacier. Chico ran on before them, stimulated by some reminiscence of the rabbit-holes of Belforest, and they were looking after him and whistling him back; Armine heard a sudden cry and fall— Jock had disappeared. 'Never mind!' he called up the next instant. 'I'm all right. Only come down here! I've twisted my foot somehow.'

Armine scrambled round the rock over which he had fallen, a loose stone having turned with him. He had pulled himself up, but even with an arm round Armine's neck he could not have walked a step on even ground, far less on these rough *débris*, which were painful walking even for the lightest, most springy tread.

'You must get to the inn and bring help,' he said, sinking down with a sigh.

'I suppose there's nothing else to be done,' said Armine unwillingly. 'You'll have a terrible time to wait, unless I meet some one first. I'll be as quick as I can.'

'Not too quick till you get off this place,' said Jock, 'or you'll be down too, and here, help me off with this boot first.'

This was not done quickly or easily. Jock was almost sick with the pain of the effort, and the bruise looked serious. Armine tried to make him comfortable, and set out, as he thought, in the right direction, but he had hardly gone twenty steps before he came to a sudden standstill with an emphatic 'I say!' then came back repeating, 'I say, Jock, we are close upon the glacier; I was as near as possible going down into an awful blue crack!'

'That's why it's getting so cold,' said Jock. 'Here, Chick, come and warm me. Well, Armie, why ain't you off?'

'Yes,' said Armine, with a quiver in his voice, 'if I keep down by the side of the glacier, I suppose I must come to the Daubensee in time.'

'What! Have we lost the way?' said Jock, beginning to look alarmed.

'There's no doubt of that,' said Armine, 'and what's worse, that fog is coming up; but I've got my little compass here, and if I keep to the south-west, and down, I must strike the lake somewhere. Good-bye, Jock.'

He looked white and braced up for the effort. Jock caught hold of him. 'Don't leave me, Armie,' he said; 'you can't— you'll fall into one of those crevasses.'

'You'd better let me go before the fog gets worse,' said Armine.

'I say you can't; it's not fit for a little chap like you. If you fell, it would be ever so much worse for us both.'

'I know! But it is the less risk,' said Armine gravely.

'I tell you, Armie, I can't have you go. Mother will send out for us, and we can make no end of a row together. There's a much better chance that way than alone. Don't go, I say——'

'I was only looking out beyond the rock. I don't think it would be possible to get on now. I can't see even the ridge of stones we climbed over.'

'I wish it was I,' said Jock, 'I'll be bound I could manage it!' Then impatiently—'Something must be done, you know, Armie. We can't stay here all night.'

Yet when Armine went a step or two to see whether there was any practicability of moving, he instantly called out against his attempting to go away. He was in a good deal of pain, and, high-spirited boy as he was, was thoroughly unnerved and appalled, and much less able to consider than the usually quieter and more timid Armine. Suddenly there was a frightful thunderous roar and crash, and with a cry of 'An avalanche,' the brothers clasped one another fast and shut their eyes, but ere the words 'Have mercy' were uttered all was still again, and they found themselves alive!

'I don't think it was an avalanche,' said Armine, recovering first. 'It was most likely to be a great mass of ice tumbling off the arch at the bottom of the glacier. They do make a most awful row. I've heard one before, only not so near. Any way, we can't be far from the bottom of the glacier, if I only could crawl there.'

'No, no,' cried Jock, holding him tight; 'I tell you, you can't do it.'

Jock could not have defined whether he was most actuated by fears for his brother's safety or by actual terror at being left alone and helpless. At any rate, Armine much preferred remaining, in all the certain misery and danger, to losing sight of his brother, with the great probability of only being further lost himself.

'I wonder whether Chico would find mother,' he said.

Jock brightened; Armine found an envelope in his pocket, and scribbled—

'On the moraine　Jock's ankle sprained—Come.'

Then Jock produced a bit of string, wherewith it was fastened to the dog's collar, and then authoritatively bade Chico go to mother.

Alas! cleverness had never been Chico's strong point, and the present extremity did not inspire him with sagacity. He knew the way as little as his masters did, and would only dance about in an unmeaning way, and when ordered home crouch in abject entreaty. Jock grew impatient and threatened him, but this only made him creep behind Armine, put his tail between his legs, hold up his little paw, and look piteously imploring.

'There's no use in the little brute,' sighed Jock at last, but the attempt had done him good and recalled his nerve and good sense.

'We are in for a night of it,' he said, 'unless they find us : and how are they ever to do that in this beastly fog?'

'We must halloo,' said Armine, attempting it.

'Yes, and we don't know when to begin ! We can't go on all night, you know,' said Jock ; 'and if we begin too soon, we may have no voice left just at the right time.'

'It is half-past seven now,' said Armine, looking at his watch. 'The food was to be at seven, so they must have missed us by this time.'

'They won't think anything of it till it gets dark.'

'No. Give them till half-past eight. Somewhere about nine or half-past it may be worth while to jodel.'

'And how awfully cold it will be by that time. And my foot is aching like fun !'

Armine offered to rub it, and there was some occupation in this and in watching the darkening of the evening, which was very gradual in the dense white fog that shut them in with a damp, cold, moist curtain of undeveloped snow.

The poor lads were thinly clad for a summer walk, Jock had left his plaid behind him, and they were beginning to feel only too vividly that it was past supper-time, when they could dimly see that it was past nine, and began to shout, but they soon found this severe and exhausting.

Armine suggested counting ten between each cry, which would husband their powers and give them time to listen for an answer. Yet even thus there was an empty, feeble sound about their cries, so that Jock observed—

'It's very odd that when there's no good in making a row, one can make it fast enough, and now, when it would be of some use, one seems to have no more voice than a little sick mouse.'

'Not so much, I think,' said Armine. 'It is hunger partly.'

'Hark ! That sounded like something.'

Invigorated by hope they shouted again, but though several times they did hear a distant jodel, the hope that it was in answer to themselves soon faded, as the sound became more distant, and their own exertions ended soon in an utter break-down—into a hoarse squeak on Jock's part, and a weak, hungry cry on Armine's. Jock's face was covered with tears, as much from the strain as from despair.

'There !' he sighed, 'there's our last chance gone ! We are in for a night of it.'

'It can't be a very long night,' Armine said, through chattering teeth. 'It's only a week to the longest day.'

'Much that will matter to us,' said Jock impatiently. 'We shall be frozen long before morning.'

'We must keep ourselves awake.'

'You little ass,' said poor Jock, in the petulant inconsistency
of his distress, 'it is not come to that yet.'

Armine did not answer at once. He was kneeling against
the rock, and a strange thrill came over Jock, forbidding him
again to say—'It was not come to *that ;*' but a shoot of aching
pain in his ankle presently drew forth an exclamation.

Armine again offered to rub it for him, and the two arranged
themselves for this purpose, the curtain of damp woolliness
seeming to thicken on them. There was a moon somewhere, and
the darkness was not total, but the dreariness and isolation
were the more felt from the absence of all outlines being manifest. They even lost sight of their own hands if they stretched
out their arms, and their light summer garments were already
saturated with damp and would soon freeze. No part of their
bodies was free from that deadly chill save where they could
press against one another.

They were brave boys. Jock had collected himself again, and
for some time they kept up a show of mirth in the shakings and
buffetings they bestowed on one another, but they began to
grow too stiff and spent to pursue this discipline. Armine
thought that the night must be nearly over, and Jock tried to
see his watch, but decided that he could not, because he could
not bear to believe how far it was from day.

Armine was drowsily rubbing the ankle, mechanically murmuring something to himself. Jock shook him, saying—

'Take care, don't doze off. What are you mumbling about
leisure ?'

'O tarry thou the Lord's leisure. Be strong and—— Was I
saying it aloud ?' he broke off with a start.

'Yes ; go on.'

Armine finished the verse, and Jock commented—

'Comfort thine heart. Does the little chap mean it in a fix
like this ?'

'Jock,' said Armine, now fully awake, 'I *do* want to say
something.'

'Cut on.'

'If you get out of this and I don't——'

'Stop that ! We've got heat enough to last till morning.'

'Will they find us then ? These fogs last for days and turn
to snow.'

'Don't croak, I say. I can't face mother without you.'

'She'll be glad enough to get you. Please listen, Jock, while
I'm awake. I want you to give her and all of them my love,
and say I'm sorry for all the times I've vexed them.'

'As if you had ever——'

'And please, Jock—if I was nasty and conceited about the
champagne——'

'Shut up, I can't stand this,' cried Jock, chiefly from force of
habit, for it was a tacit agreement among the elder brothers
that Armine must not be suffered to 'be cocky and humbug,' by

which they meant no implication on his sincerity, but that they did not choose to hear remonstrances or appeals to higher motives, and this had made him very reticent with all except his sister Barbara and Miss Ogilvie, but he now persisted.

'Indeed I want you to forgive me, Jock. You don't know how often I've thought all sorts of horridness about you.'

Jock laughed, 'Not more than I deserved, I'll be bound. How can you be so absurd? If any one wants forgiveness, it is I. I say, Armie, this is all nonsense. You don't really think you are done for, or you would not take it so coolly.'

'Of course I know who can bring us through if He will,' said Armine. 'There's the Rock. I've been asking Him all this time—every moment—only I get so sleepy.'

'If He will; but if He won't?'

'Then there's Paradise. And Himself and father,' said Armine, still in a dreamy tone.

'Oh yes; that's for you! But how about a mad fellow like me? It's so sneaking just to take to one's prayers because one's in a bad case.'

'O Jock! He is always ready to hear! More ready than we to pray!'

'Now don't begin to improve the occasion,' broke out Jock. 'By all the stories that ever were written, I'm the one to come to a bad end, not you.'

'Don't,' said Armine, with an accent of pain that made Jock cry, hugging him tighter. 'There, never mind, Armie; I'll let you say all you like. I don't know what made me stop you, except that I'm a beast, and always have been one. I'd give anything not to have gone on playing the fool all my life, so as to be able to mind this as little as you do.'

'I don't seem awake enough to mind anything much,' said the little boy, 'or I should trouble more about mother and Babie; but somehow I can't.'

'Oh!' wailed Jock, 'you must! You must get out of it, Armie. Come closer. Shove in between me and the rock. Here, Chico, lie down on the top of us! Mother must have you back any way, Armie.'

The little fellow was half dozing, but words of prayer and faith kept dropping from his tongue. Pain and a stronger vitality alike kept Jock free from the torpor, and he used his utmost efforts to rouse his brother; but every now and then a horrible conviction of the hopelessness of their condition came over him.

'Oh!' he groaned out, 'how is it to be if this is the end of it? What is to become of a fellow that has been like me?'

Armine only spoke one word—the Name that is above every name.

'Yes, you always cared! But I never cared for anything but fun! Never went to Communion at Easter. It is too late.'

'Oh no, no!' cried Armine, rousing up, 'not too late! Never! You are His! You belong to Him! He cares for you!'

'If He does, it makes it all the worse. I never heeded; I thought it all a bore. I never let myself think what it all meant. I've thrown it all away.'

'Oh, I wish I wasn't so stupid,' cried Armine, with a violent effort against his exhaustion. 'Mother loves us, however horrid we are! He is like that; only let us tell Him all the bad we've done, and ask Him to blot it out. I've been trying—trying—only I'm so dull; and let us give ourselves more and more out and out to Him, whether it is here or there.'

'That I must,' said Jock; 'it would be shabby and sneaking not.'

'Oh, Jock,' cried Armine joyfully, 'then it will all be right any way;' and he raised his face and kissed his brother. 'You promise, Jock. Please promise.'

'Promise what? That if He will save us out of this, I'll take a new line, and be as good as I know how, and——'

Armine took the word, whether consciously or not: 'And manfully to fight under His banner, and continue Christ's faithful soldiers and servants unto our lives' end. Amen!'

'Amen,' Jock said after him.

After that, Jock found that the child was repeating the Creed, and said it after him, the meanings thrilling through him as they had never done before. Next followed lines of 'Rock of Ages,' and for some time longer there was a drowsy murmur of sacred words, but there was no eliciting a direct reply any more; and with dull consternation, Jock knew that the fatal torpor could no longer be broken, and was almost irritated that all the words he caught were such happy, peaceful ones. The very last were, 'Inside angels' wings, all white down.'

The child seemed almost comfortable—certainly not suffering like himself, bruised and strained, with sharp twinges rending his damaged foot; his limbs cramped, and sensible of the acute misery of the cold, and the full horror of their position; but as long as he could shake even an unconscious murmur from his brother, it seemed like happiness compared with the utter desolation after the last whisper had died away, and he was left intolerably alone under the solid impenetrable shroud that enveloped him, and the senseless form he held on his breast. And if he tried to follow on by that clue which Armine had left him, whirlwinds of dismay seemed to sweep away all hope and trust, while he thought of wilfulness, recklessness, defiance, irreverence, and all the yet darker shades of a self-indulgent and audacious schoolboy life!

It was a little lighter, as if dawn might be coming, but the cold was bitterer, and benumbing more than paining him. His clothes were stiff, his eyelashes white with frost, he did not feel equal to looking at his watch, he *would* not see Armine's face, he found the fog depositing itself in snow, but he heeded it no longer. Fear and hope had alike faded out of his mind, his ankle seemed to belong to some one else far away, he had left off wishing to see his mother, he wanted nothing but to be let alone !

He did not hear when Chico, finding no comfort, no sign of life in his masters, stood upon them as they lay clasped together in the drift of fine small snow, and in the climax of misery he lifted up the long and wretched wailing howlings of utter dog-wretchedness.

## CHAPTER XX

### A RACE

' Speed, Malise, speed ! such cause of haste
Thine active sinews never braced ;
Bend 'gainst the steepy hill thy breast,
Burst down like torrent from its crest.'

SCOTT.

'HARK !'

The guides and the one other traveller, a Mr. Graham, who had been at the inn, were gathered at the border of the Daubensee, entreating, almost ready to use force, to get the poor mother home before the snow should efface the tracks, and render the return to Schwarenbach dangerous.

Ever since the alarm had been given there had been a going about with lights, a shouting and seeking, all along the road where she had parted with her sons. It was impossible in the fog to leave the beaten track, and the traveller told her that rewards would be but temptations to suicide.

Johnnie had fortunately been so tired out that he had gone to bed soon after coming in, and had not been wakened by the alarm till eleven o'clock. Then, startled by the noises and lights, he had risen and made his way to his aunt. Substantial help he could not give—even his German was halting ; but he was her stay and help, and she would—as she knew afterwards—have been infinitely more desolate without him. And now, when all were persuading her to wait, as they said, till more aid could be sent for to Kandersteg, he knew as well as she did that it was but a kindly ruse to cover their despair, and was striving to insist that another effort in daylight should be made.

He it was who uttered the 'Hark,' and added, 'That is Chico !'

At first the tired, despairing guides did not hear, but going along the road by the lake in the direction from which the sound came, the prolonged wail became more audible.

'It is on the moraine,' the men said, with awestruck looks at one another.

They would fain not even have taken John with them, but with a resolute look he uttered ' Ich komm.'

Mr. Graham, an elderly man, not equal to a moraine in the snow, stayed with the mother. He wanted to take her back to prepare for them, as he said—in reality to lessen any horrors there might be to see.

But she stood like a statue, with clasped hands and white face, the small feathery snow climbing round her feet and on her shoulders.

'O God, spare my boys! Though I don't deserve it—spare them!' had been her one inarticulate prayer all night.

And now—shouts and jodels reach her ears. They are found! But how found? The cries are soon hushed. There is long waiting—then, through the snow, John flashes forward and takes her hand. He does not speak; only, as their eyes meet, his pale lips tremble, and he says, 'Don't fear; they will revive at the inn. Jock is safe, they are sure.'

Safe? What? that stiff, white-faced form, carried between two men, with the arm hanging lifelessly down? One man held the smaller figure of Armine, and kept his face pressed inwards. Kind words of 'Liebe Frau,' and assurances that were meant to be cheering, passed around her, but she heard them not. Some brandy had, it seemed, been poured into their mouths. They thought Jock had swallowed; Armine had not.

At intervals on the way back a little more was administered, and the experienced guides had no doubt that life was yet in him. When they reached the hotel the guides would not take them near the stove, but carried them up at once by the rough stair to the little wood-partitioned bedrooms. There were two beds in each room, and their mother would have had them both together; but the traveller, and the kindly, helpful young land-lady, Fräulein Rosalie, quietly managed otherwise, and when Johnnie tried to enforce his aunt's orders, Mr. Graham, by a sign, made him comprehend why they had thus arranged, filling him with blank dismay.

A doctor? The guides shook their heads. They could hardly make their way to Leukerbad while it was snowing as at present, and if they had done so, no doctor could come back with them. Moreover, the restoratives were known to the moun-taineers as well as to the doctors themselves, and these were vigorously applied. All the resources of the little wayside house were put in requisition. Mr. Graham and Johnnie did their best for Jock; his mother seemed to see and think of nothing but Armine, who lay senseless and cold in spite of all their efforts.

It was soon that Jock began to moan and turn and struggle painfully back to life. When he opened his eyes with a dazed half-consciousness, and something like a word came from between his lips, Mr. Graham sent John to call the mother, saying very low, 'Get her away. She will bear it better when she sees this one coming round.'

John had deep and reverent memories connected with

Armine. He knew—as few did know—how steadfastly that
little gentle fellow could hold the right, and more than once the
two had been almost alone against their world. Besides, he was
Mother Carey's darling! Johnnie felt as if his heart would
break, as with trembling lips he tried to speak as if in glad
hope, as he told his aunt that Jock was speaking and wanted
her, while he looked all the time at the still, white, inanimate
face.

She looked at him half in distrust.

'Yes! Indeed, indeed,' he said, 'Jock wants you.'

She went; Johnnie took her place. The efforts at restoration
were slackening. The attendants were shaking their heads and
saying, '*der Arme*.'

Mr. Graham came up to him, saying in his ear, 'She is engrossed with the other. He will not let her go. Let them do
what is to be done for this poor little fellow. So it will be
best for her.'

There was a frantic longing to do something for Armine, a
wild wonder that the prayers of a whole night had not been
more fully answered in John's mind, as he threw himself once
more over the senseless form, propped with pillows, and kissed
either cheek and the lips. Then suddenly he uttered a low cry,
'He breathed. I'm sure he did; I felt it! The spoon! Oh,
quick!'

Mr. Graham and the Fräulein looked pitifully at one another
at the delusion; but they let the lad have the spoon with the
drops of brandy. He had already gained experience in giving
it, and when they looked for disappointment, his eyes were
raised in joy.

'It's gone down,' he said.

Mr. Graham put his hand on the pulse and nodded.

Another drop or two, and renewed rubbing of hands and
feet. The icy cold, the deadly white, were certainly giving
way, the lips began to quiver, contract, and gasp.

Was it for death or life? They would not call his mother for
that terrible, doubtful minute; but she could not long stay
away. When Jock's fingers first relaxed on hers, she crept to
the door of the other room, to see Armine upheld on Johnnie's
breast, with heaving chest and working features, but with eyes
opening: yes, and meeting hers.

Johnnie always held that he never had so glad a moment in
all his life as that when he saw her countenance light up.

The first word was 'Jock!'

Armine's full perceptions were come back, unlike those of
Jock, who was moaning and wandering in his talk, fancying
himself still in the desolation of the moraine, with Armine dead
in his arms, and all the miseries, bodily, mental, and spiritual,
from which he had suffered were evidently still working in his
brain, though the words that revealed them were weak and dis-
jointed. Besides, he screamed and moaned with absolute and

acute pain, which alarmed them much, though Armine was sufficiently himself to be able to assure them that there had been no hurt beyond the strain.

It was well that Armine was both rational and unselfish, for nothing seemed to soothe Jock for a moment but his mother's hand and his mother's voice. It was plain that fever and rheumatism had a hold upon him, and what or who was there to contend with them in this wayside inn? The rooms, though clean, were bare of all but the merest necessaries, and though the young hostess was kind and anxious, her maids were the roughest and most ignorant of girls, and there were no appliances for comfort—nothing even to drink but milk, bottled lemonade, and a tisane made of yellow flowers, horrible to the English taste.

And Jock, ill as he was, did not fill his mother with such dread for the future as did Armine, when she found him, quiet indeed, but unable to lie down, except when supported on John's breast and in his arms—with a fearful oppression and pain in his chest, and every token that the lungs were suffering. He had not let them call her. Jock's murmurs and cries were to be heard plainly through the wooden partition, and the little fellow knew she could not be spared, and only tried to prevent John and Mr. Graham from alarming her. 'She—can't—do—any--good,' he gasped out in John's ear.

No, nobody could, without medical skill and appliances. The utmost that the house could do was to produce enough mustard to make two plasters, and to fill bottles with hot water, to warm stones, and to wrap them in blankets. And what was this, in such cold as penetrated the wooden building, too high up in the mountains for the June sun as yet to have full power? The snow kept blinding and drifting on, and though every one said it could not last long at that time in the summer, it might easily last too long for Armine's fragile life. Here was evening drawing on and no change outside, so that no offer of reward could make it possible for any messenger to attempt the Gemmi to fetch advice from Leukerbad.

Caroline could not think. She was in a dull, dreary state of consternation, and all she could dwell on was the immediate need of the moment, soothing Jock's terrors, and, what was almost worse, his irritable rejection of the beverages she could offer him, and trying to relieve him by rubbing and hot applications. If ever she could look into Armine's room, she was filled with still greater dismay, even though a sweet, patient smile always met her, and a resolute endeavour to make the best of it.

'It—does—not—make—much—difference,' gasped Armine. 'One would not like anything.'

John came out in a character no one could have expected. He showed himself a much better nurse, and far more full of resource than the traveller. It was he who bethought him of

keeping a kettle in the room over the inevitable charcoal, so as
slightly to mitigate the chill of the air, or the fumes of the charcoal, which were equally perilous and distressing to the labouring lungs.  He was tender and handy in lifting, tall and strong,
so as to be efficient in supporting, and then Armine and he
understood one another.  They had never been special companions ; John had too much of the Kencroft muscularity about
him to accord with a delicate, imaginative being like Armine,
but they respected one another, and made common cause, and
John had more than once been his little cousin's protector.  So
when they were so much alone that all reserves were overcome,
Armine had comfort in his cousin that no one else in the place
could have afforded him.  The little boy perfectly knew how ill
he was, and as he lay in John's arms, breathed out his messages
to Babie as well as he could utter them.

'And please, you'll be always mother's other son,' said
Armine.

'Won't I?  She's been the making of me every way,' said
John.

'If ever—she does want anybody——' said Armine, feeling,
but not uttering, a vague sense of want of trust in others
around her.

'I will, I will.  Why, Armie, I shall never care for any one
so much.'

'That's right.'

And again, after an interval, Armine spoke of Jock, saying,
'You'll help him, Johnnie.  You know sometimes he can be put
in mind——'

John promised again, perhaps less hopefully, but he saw that
Armine hoped.

'Would you mind reading me a Psalm?' came, after a great
struggle for breath.  'It was so nice to know Babie was saying
her Psalms at night, and thinking of us.'

So the evening wore away and night came on, and John,
after full six-and-twenty hours' wakeful exertion and anxiety,
began to grow sleepy, and dozed even as he held his cousin,
whenever the cough did not shake the poor little fellow.  At
last, with Armine's consent, or rather at his entreaty, Mr.
Graham, though knowing himself a bad substitute, took him
from the arms of the outwearied lad, who, in five minutes more,
was lying, dressed as he was, in the soundest of dreamless
slumbers.

When he awoke, the sun was up, an almost midsummer sun,
streaming on the fast-melting snow with a dazzling brilliancy.
Armine was panting under the same deadly oppression on his
pillows, and Mother Carey was standing by him, talking to Mr.
Graham about despatching a message to Leukerbad in search of
one of the doctors, who were sure to be found at the baths.  How
haggard her face looked, and Armine gasped out—

'Mother, your hair.'

The snow had been there; the crisp black waves on her brow were quite white. Jock had fallen into a sort of doze from exhaustion, but moaning all the time. She could call him no better, and Armine's sunken face told that he was worse.

John went in search of more hot water, and on the way heard voices which made him call Mr. Graham, who knew more of the vernacular German *patois* than himself, to understand it. He thought he had caught something about English, and a doctor at Kandersteg.

It was true. A guide belonging to the other side of the pass, who had been weather-bound at Kandersteg, had just come up with tidings that an English party were there, who had meant to cross the Gemmi but had given it up, finding it too early in the season for the *kränklicher* Milord, who was accompanied by his doctor.

'An English doctor! Oh!' cried John, 'there's some good in that. Some one must take a note down to him at once.'

But after some guttural conversation, of which he understood only a word or two, Mr. Graham said—

'They declare it is of no use. The carriage was ordered at nine. It is past seven now.'

'But it need not take two hours to go that distance downhill, the lazy blackguards!' exclaimed John.

'In the present state of the path, they say that it will,' said Mr. Graham. 'In fact, I suspect a little unwillingness to deprive their countrymen of the job.'

'I'll go,' said John, 'then there will be no loss of time about writing. You'll look after Armine, sir, and tell my aunt.'

'Certainly, my boy; but you'll find it a stiffish pull.'

'I came in second for the mile race last summer at Eton,' said Johnnie. 'I'm not in training now; but if a will can do it——'

'I believe you are right. If you don't catch him, we shall hardly have lost time, for they say we must wait an hour or two for the Gemmi road to get clear of snow. Stay; don't go without eating. You won't keep it up on an empty stomach. Remember the proverb.'

Prayer had been with him all night, and he listened to the remonstrance as to provender enough to devour a bit of bread, put another into his pocket, and swallow a long draught of new milk. Mr. Graham further insisted on his taking a lad to show him the right path through the fir woods; and though Johnnie looked more formed for strength than speed, and was pale-cheeked and purple-eyed with broken rest, the manner in which he set forth had a purpose-like air that was satisfactory—not over-swift at the outset over the difficult ground, but with a steadfast resolution, and with a balance and knowledge of the management of his limbs due to Eton athletics.

Mr. Graham went up to encourage Mrs. Brownlow. She clasped her hands together with joy and gratitude.

'That dear, dear boy,' she said, 'I shall owe him everything.'

Jock had wakened rational, though only to be conscious of severe suffering. He would hardly believe that Armine was really alive till Mr. Graham actually carried in the boy, and let them hold each other's hands for a moment before placing Armine on the other bed.

Indeed it seemed that this might be the poor boys' last meeting. Armine could only look at his brother, since the least attempt to speak increased the agonised struggle for breath, which, doctor or no doctor, gave Mr. Graham small expectation that he could survive another of these cold mountain nights.

Their mother was so far relieved to have them together that it was easier to attend to them; and Armine's patient eyes certainly acted as a gentle restraint upon Jock's moans, lamentations, and requisitions for her services. It was one of those times that she only passed through by her faculty of attending only to present needs, and the physical strength and activity that seemed inexhaustible as long as she had anything to do, and which alone alleviated the despair within her heart.

Meantime John found the rock slippery, the path heavy, and his young guide a drag on him. The path through the fir woods, which had been so delightful two days (could it be only two days?) ago, was now a baffling, wearisome zigzag; yet when he tried to cut across, regardless of the voice of his guide, he found he lost time, for he had to clamber, once fell and rolled some distance, happily with no damage, as he found when he picked himself up, and plodded on again, without even stopping to shake himself.

At last came an opening where he could see down into the Kandersteg valley. There was the hotel in clear sunshine, looking only too like a house in a German box of toys, and alas! there was also a toy carriage coming round to the front!

Like the little foot-page of old ballads, John 'let down his feet and ran,' ran determinately on, down the now less precipitous slope—ran till he was beyond the trees, with the summer sun beating down on him, and in sight of figures coming out from the hotel to the carriage.

Johnnie scarce ventured to give one sigh. He waved his hat in a desperate hope of being seen. No, they were in the carriage. The horses were moving!

But he remembered a slight steep on the further road where they must go slower. Moreover, there were a few curves in the horse-road. He set his teeth with the desperate resolution of a moment, clenched his hands, intensified his mental cry to Heaven, and with the dogged determination of Kencroft dashed on, not daring to look at the carriage, intent only on the way.

He was past the inn, but his breath was short and quick; his

knees were failing, an invisible hand seemed to be on his chest
making him go slower and slower ; yet still he struggled on, till
the mountain-tops danced before his eyes, cascades rushed into
his ears, the earth seemed to rise up and stop him ; but through
it all he heard a voice say, 'Hullo, it's the Monk ! What is the
matter ?'

Then he knew he was on the ground on his face, with kind
but tormenting hands busy about him, and his heart going so
like a sledge-hammer that the word he would have given his
life to utter would not come out of his lips, and all he could do
was to grasp convulsively at something that he believed to be a
garment of the departing travellers.

'Here, the flask ! Don't speak yet,' said a man's voice, and
a choking stimulant was poured into his mouth. When the
choking spasm it cost him was over, his eyes cleared, and he
could at least gasp. Then he saw that it was his housemate,
Evelyn, at whom he was clutching, and who asked again in
amaze—

'What is up, old fellow ?'

'Hush, not yet,' said the other voice ; 'let him alone till he
gets his breath. Don't hurry, my boy,' he added, 'we will
wait.'

Johnnie, however, felt altogether absorbed in getting out one
panting whisper, 'A doctor.'

'Yes, yes, he is,' cried Evelyn. 'What's the matter ? Not
Brownlow !'

'Both—oh,' sobbed John in the agony of contending with the
bumping, fluttering heart which *would* not let him fetch breath
enough to speak.

'You will tell us presently. Don't be afraid. We will wait,'
said the voice of the man who, as John now felt, was supporting
him. 'Hush, Cecil, another minute, and he will be able to
tell us.'

Indeed the rushing of every pulse was again making it vain
for Johnnie to try to utter anything, and he shut his eyes in the
realisation that he had succeeded and found help. If his heart
would have not bumped and fluttered so fearfully, it would
have been almost rest, as he was helped up by those kind, strong
arms. It was really for little more than five seconds before
he gathered his powers to say, still between gasps—

'Out all night—the moraine—fog—snow—Jock—very bad—
Armine—worse—up there.'

'At Schwarenbach ?'

'Yes. Oh, come ! They are so ill.'

'I am sure Dr. Medlicott will do all he can for them,' said
another voice, which John saw proceeded from a very tall,
slight youth, with a fair, delicate, girlish face. 'Had he not
better get into the carriage and return to the hotel ?'

'By all means.'

And John found himself without much volition lifted and

helped into the carriage, where Cecil Evelyn scrambled up beside him, and put an arm round him.

'Poor old Monk, you are dead beat,' he said, as the carriage turned, the other two walking beside it. 'Did you come that pace all the way down?'

'Only after the wood.'

'Well, 'twas as plucky a thing as I ever saw. But is Skipjack so bad?'

'Dreadful! Light-headed all yesterday—horrid pain! But not so bad as Armine. If something ain't done soon—he'll die.'

'Poor little Brownlow! You've come to the right shop. Medlicott is first-rate. Did you know it was we?'

'No—only—an English doctor,' said John.

'Mother sent us abroad with him, because they said Fordham must have Swiss air; and poor old Granny still goes on in the same state,' said Cecil. 'We got here on Tuesday evening, and saw your names; but then the fog came, and it snowed all yesterday, and the doctor said it would not do for Fordham to go so high. And the more I wanted them to come up with you, the more they would not. Were they out in that snow?'

Here came an order from the doctor not to make his friend talk, and Johnnie was glad to obey, and reserve his breath for the explanation. He did not hear what passed between the other two, as they walked behind the carriage.

'A fine fellow that! Is he Cecil's friend?'

'No, I wish he were. However, it can't be helped now, in common humanity; and my mother will understand.'

'You mean that it was her wish that we should avoid them.'

'She thinks the influence has not been good for Cecil.'

'That was the reason you gave up the Gemmi so easily.'

'It was. But, as I say, it can't be helped now, and no harm can be done by going to see whether they are really so ill.'

'Brownlow is the name. I wonder if they are any relation to a man I once knew— a lecturer at one of the hospitals?'

'Not likely. These are very rich people, with a great house in Hyde Park regions, and a place in the country. They are always asking Cecil there; only my mother does not fancy it. It is not a matter of charity after the first stress. They can easily have advice from England, or anywhere they like.'

By this time they reached the hotel, and John alighted briskly enough, and explained the state of affairs in a few words.

'My dear boy,' said Dr. Medlicott, 'I'll go up at once, as soon as I can get at our travelling medicine-chest. Luckily we have what is most likely to be useful.'

'Thank you,' said Johnnie, and therewith he turned dizzy, and reeled against the wall.

'It is nothing—nothing,' he said, as the doctor, having helped him into a sitting-room, laid his hand on his pulse. 'Don't delay about me! I shall be all right in a minute.'

'They are getting down the boxes. No time is lost,' said the doctor quietly. 'See whether they can let us have some soup, Cecil.'

'I couldn't swallow anything,' said Johnnie imploringly.

'Have you had any breakfast this morning?'

'Yes, a bit of bread and a drink of milk. There was not time for more.'

'And you had been searching all one night, and nursing the next?'

'Most of it,' was the confession. 'But I shall be all right— if there is any pony I could ride upon.'

'You shall by and by; but first, Reeves,' as a servant with grizzled hair and moustache brought in a neatly-fitted medicine-chest, 'I give this young gentleman into your care. He is to lie down on my bed for half an hour, and Mr. Evelyn is not to go near him. Then, if he is awake——'

'If——' ejaculated John.

'Give him a basin of soup—Liebig, if you can't get anything here.'

'Liebig,' broke out John. 'Oh, please take some. There's nothing up there but old goat, and nothing to drink but milk and lemonade, like beastly hair-oil; and Jock hates milk.'

'Never fear,' said Dr. Medlicott; 'Liebig is going, and a packet of tea. Mrs. Evelyn does not send us out unprovided. If you eat your soup like a good boy, you may then ride up —not walk—unless you wish to be on your mother's hands too.'

'She's my aunt; but it is all the same. Tell her I'm coming.'

'I shall go with you, doctor,' said Cecil. 'I must know about Brownlow.'

'Much good you'll do him! But I'd rather leave this fellow in Fordham's charge than yours.'

So Johnnie had no choice but to obey, growling a little that it was all nonsense, and he should be all right in five minutes, but that expectation continued, without being realised, for longer than Johnnie knew. He awoke with a start to find the Liebig awaiting him; and Lord Fordham's eyes fixed on him, with (though neither understood it) the generous, though melancholy, envy of an invalid youth for a young athlete.

'Have I been asleep?' he asked, looking at his watch. 'Only ten minutes since I looked last? Well, now I am all right.'

'You will be when you have eaten this,' said Lord Fordham. Johnnie obeyed, and ate with relish.

'There!' said he; 'now I am ready for anything.'

'Don't get up yet. I'll go and order a horse for you.'

When Lord Fordham came back from doing so, he found his patient really fast asleep, and with a little colour coming into the pale cheeks. He stole back, bade that the pony should

wait, went on writing his letter, and waited till one hour, two,
three hours had passed, and at last the sleeper woke, greatly
disgusted, willing to accept the bath which Lord Fordham
advised him to take, and which made him quite himself
again.

'You'll let me go now,' he said. 'I can walk as well as
ever.'

'You'll be of more use now, if you ride,' said Lord Fordham.
'There, I hear our luncheon coming in. You must eat while the
pony is coming round.'

'If it won't lose time—thank you,' said Johnnie, recovered
enough now to know how hungry he was. 'But I ought not to
have stayed away. My aunt has no one but me.'

'And you can really help her?' said Lord Fordham, with
some experience of his brother's uselessness.

'Not well, of course,' said Johnnie; 'but it is better than
nobody; and Armine is so patient and so good, that I'm the
more afraid. Is not it a very bad sign?' he added confidentially;
for he was quite won by the youth's kind, considerate way, and
evident liking and sympathy.

'I don't know,' faltered Lord Fordham. 'My brother Walter
was like that! Is this the little fellow who is Cecil's fag?'

'Yes; Jock asked him to take him, because he was sure never
to bully him or lick him when he wouldn't do things.'

This not very lucid description rejoiced Lord Fordham.

'I am glad of that,' he said. 'But I hope the little boy will
get over this. My mother had a very excellent account of Dr.
Medlicott's skill; and you know an illness from a misadventure
is not like anything constitutional.'

'No; but Armine is always delicate, and my aunt has had
to take care of him.'

'Do you live with them?'

'Oh no; I have lots of people at home. I only came with
them because I had had these measles at Eton; and my aunt is
—well, the very jolliest woman that ever was.'

Lord Fordham smiled.

'Yes, indeed she is. I don't mean only kind and good-natured.
But if you just knew her! The whole world and everything else
have just been something new and glorious ever since I knew
her. I seem to myself to have lived in a dark hole till she made
it all light.'

'Ah! I understand that you would do anything for her.'

'*That* I would, if there was anything I could do,' said
Johnnie, hastily finishing his meal.

'Well, you've done something to-day.'

'That—oh, that was nothing. I shouldn't have made such a
fool of myself if I hadn't been seedy before. I hear the pony,'
he added. 'Excuse me.' And, with a murmured grace, he
rose. Then, recollecting himself, 'No end of thanks. I don't
know how to thank you enough.'

'Don't; I've done nothing,' said Lord Fordham, wringing his hand. 'I only hope——'

The words stuck in his throat, and with a sigh he watched the lad ride off.

## CHAPTER XXI

### AN ACT OF INDEPENDENCE

'Soldier now and servant true;
Earth behind and heaven in view.'

ISAAC WILLIAMS.

MARMADUKE ALWYN EVELYN, Viscount Fordham, was the fourth bearer of that title within ten years. His father had not lived to wear it, and his two elder brothers had both died in early youth. His precarious existence seemed to be only held on a tenure of constant precaution, and if his mother ventured to hope that it might be otherwise with the two youngest of the family, it was because they were of a shorter, sturdier, more compact form and less transparent complexion than their elders, and altogether seemed of a different constitution.

More delicate from the first than the two brothers who had gone before him, Lord Fordham had never been at school, had studied irregularly, and had never been from under his mother's wing till this summer, when she was detained by the slow decay of his grandmother. Languor and listlessness had beset the youth, and he had been ordered mountain air, and thus it was that Mrs. Evelyn had despatched both her sons to Switzerland, under the attendance of a highly-recommended physician, a young man, bright and attractive, who had overworked himself at an hospital and needed thorough relaxation. Rightly considering Lucas Brownlow as the cause of most of Cecil's Eton follies, she had given her elder son a private hint to elude joining forces with the family, and he was the most docile and obedient of sons. Yet was it the perversity of human nature that made him infinitely more animated and interested in John Brownlow's race and the distressed travellers on the Schwarenbach than he had been since—no one could tell when?

Perhaps it was the novelty of being left alone and comparatively unwatched. Certain it was that he ate enough to rejoice the heart of his devoted and tyrannical attendant Reeves; and that he walked about in much anxiety all the afternoon, continually using his telescope to look up the mountain wherever a bit of the track was visible through the pine woods.

In due time Cecil rode back the pony which John had taken up. The alacrity with which the long, lank, bending figure stepped to meet him was something unwonted, but the boy himself was downcast and depressed.

'I'm afraid you've nothing good to tell.'

Cecil shook his head, and after some more seconds broke out—

'It's awful!'

'What is?'

'Brownlow's pain. I never saw anything like it!'

'Rheumatism? If that is from the exposure, I hope it will not last long.'

'No. They've sent for some opiates to Leukerbad, and the doctor says that is sure to put him to sleep.'

'Medlicott stays there?'

'Yes. He says if little Armine is any way fit, he must move him away to-morrow at all risks from the night-cold up there, and he wants Reeves to see about men to carry him, that is, if —if to-night does not——'

Cecil could not finish.

'Then it is as bad as we heard?'

'Quite,' said Cecil, 'or worse. That dear little chap, just fancy!' and his eyes filled with tears. 'He tried to thank me for having been good to him—as if I had.'

'He was your fag?'

'Yes; Skipjack asked me to choose him because he's that sort of little fellow that won't give in to anything that goes against his conscience, and if one of those fellows had him that say lower boys have no business with consciences, he might be licked within an inch of his life and he'd never give in. He did let himself be put under a pump once at some beastly hole in the country, for not choosing to use bad language, and he has never been so strong since.'

'Mother would be glad that at least you allowed him the use of his conscience.'

'I'm glad I did now,' said Cecil, with a sigh, 'though it was a great nuisance sometimes.'

'Was the Monk, as you call him, one of that set?'

'Bless you, no, he's a regular sap, as steady as old time.'

'I wonder if he is the son of the doctor whom Medlicott talks of.'

'No; his father is alive. He is a colonel, living near their place. The other two are the doctor's sons; their mother came into the property after his death. Their Maximus was in college at first, and between ourselves, he was a bit of a snob, who couldn't bear to recollect it.'

'Not your friend?'

'No, indeed. The eldest one, who has left these two years, and is at Christchurch.'

'I am sure the one who came down here was a gentleman.'

'So they are, all three of them,' said Cecil, who had never found his brother so ready to hear anything about his Eton life, since in general accounts of the world, from which he was debarred, so jarred on his feelings that he silenced it with apparent indifference, contempt, or petulance. Now, however, Cecil, with his heart full of the Brownlows, could not say more of them than Fordham was willing to hear ; **nay,** he even found an amused listener to some of his good **stories of** courageous pranks.

Fordham was not yet up the next morning when there was a knock at his door, and the doctor came in, answering his eager question with—

'Yes, he has got through this night, but another up in that place would be fatal. We **must** get them **down to Leukerbad.**'

'Over that long precipitous path ?'

'It is the only chance. I came down to look up bearers, and rig up a couple of hammocks, as well as to see how you are getting on.'

'Oh ! I'm **very well,**' said Lord Fordham, in a tone that meant it, sitting up in bed. 'We might ride on to Leukerbad with Reeves, and get rooms **ready.**'

'The best thing **you could do,**' said Dr. Medlicott joyfully. 'When we are there we can consider what can be done next ; and if you wish to **go on,** I could look up some one there in whose charge **to leave them till they could get advice from home ;** but it is **touch and go with that little fellow.**'

'I'm in no particular hurry,' said Lord Fordham, answering the doctor's tone rather than his words. 'I would not do anything hasty or that might add **to** their **distress. Are there likely to be** good doctors at this place ?'

'It is a great watering-place, chiefly for rheumatic complaints, and that is all very well for the elder boy. As to the little one, he is in as critical a state as I ever saw, and—— His mother is an excellent linguist, that is one good **thing.**'

'Yes ; it would be very trying for **her to have** a foreigner to attend **the boy** in such a state, however skilled he might be,' said Lord Fordham. 'I think we might make up our minds to stay **with them till they can get some one** from England.'

Dr. Medlicott caught at the words.

'It rests **with you,**' he said. 'Of course I am your property and Mrs. Evelyn's, but I should like to tell you why this is more to me than a matter of common humanity. I went **up** to study in London, a simple, foolish lad, bred **up** by three good old aunts, more ignorant of **the world than their** own tabby cat. Of course I instantly fell in with the worst stamp of fellows, and was in a fair way of being done for, body and soul, if **one** of **the** lecturers, after taking **us to task** for some heartless, disgusting piece of levity, seeing perhaps that it was **more** than **half** bravado on my part and nearly made me sick, managed to get **me alone.** He talked it out with me, found out the innocenthearted **fool I** was, cured me of my false shame **at** what the good old **souls** at home had taught me, showed me **what** manhood was, found **a** good friend and a better lodging for me, in short, was the saving of **me.** He died three months after I first **knew** him, but whatever **is worth** having in me is owing to him.'

'Was he the father of these boys?'

'Yes; I saw a likeness in the nephew who came down yesterday, and I see it in both the others.'

'Of course you would wish to do all that is possible for them?'

'I should feel it the greatest honour. Still my first duty is to you, and you have told me that your mother wished you to keep your brother out of the way of his schoolfellow.'

'My mother would not wish to deprive her worst enemy of your care in such need as this,' said Lord Fordham, smiling. 'Besides, if this friend of Cecil's were ever so bad, he couldn't do him much harm while he is ill, poor boy. We will at any rate stay to get them through the next few days, and then we can judge. I will settle it with my mother.'

'I knew you would say so,' rejoined the doctor. 'Thank you. Then it seems to me that the right course will be to write to Mrs. Evelyn, inclosing a note to Dr. Lucas—who, it seems, is Mrs. Brownlow's chief reliance—asking him to find some one to send out. She can send it on to him if she disapproves of our remaining together longer than is absolutely necessary, or if Leukerbad disagrees with you. Meantime, I'll go and see whether Reeves has found any men to carry the poor boys.'

Unfortunately it was too early in the season for the hotels to have marshalled their full establishment, and such careful and surefooted bearers as the sufferers needed could not be had in sufficient numbers, so that Dr. Medlicott was forced to decide on leaving the elder patient for a night at Schwarenbach. The move might be matter of life or death to Armine; but Jock was better, the pain could be somewhat allayed by anodynes, the fever was abating, and he would rather gain than lose by another day of rest, provided he would only accept his fate patiently, and also if he could be properly attended to. If Mr. Graham would stay with him——

So breakfast was eaten, bills were paid, horses hired, and the whole cavalcade started from Kandersteg in time to secure the best part of a bright hot day for the transit.

They met Mr. Graham, who had been glad to escape as soon as Mrs. Brownlow had found other assistance, so that the doctor was disappointed in his hope of a guardian for Jock. Lord Fordham offered to lend Reeves, but that functionary absolutely refused to separate himself from his charge, observing—

'I am responsible for your lordship to your mamma, and it does not lie within my province to leave you on any account.'

Reeves always called Mrs. Evelyn 'your mamma' when he wished to be particularly authoritative with his young gentlemen. If they were especially troublesome he called her 'your ma.'

'And after all,' said the doctor, 'I don't know what sort of preparations the young gentlemen would make if we let them go by themselves. A bare room, perhaps—with no bedclothes, and nothing to eat till the *table d'hôte*.'

Reeves smiled. He had found the doctor much less of a rival than he had expected, and he was a kind-hearted man, so long as his young lord was made the first object ; so he declared his willingness to do anything that lay in his power for the assist- ance of the poor lady and her sons. He would gladly sit up with them, if it were in the same house with his lordship.

No one came out to meet the party. John was found with Armine, who had been taken back at night to his own room ; Mrs. Brownlow, as usual, with Jock, who would endure no presence but hers, and looked exceedingly injured when, sending Cecil in to sit with him, the doctor called her out of the room.

It was a sore stroke on her to hear that her charges must be separated ; and there was the harrowing question whether she should stay with one or go with the other.

'Please decide,' she said.

'I think you should be with the most serious case.'

'And that, I fear, means my little Armine. Yes, I will do as you tell me. But what can be done for Jock ?—poor Jock, who thinks he needs me most. And perhaps he does. You know best, though, Dr. Medlicott, and you shall settle it.'

'That is a wise nurse,' said he kindly ; 'I wish I could take your place myself, but I must be with the little fellow myself ; and I am afraid we can only leave his brother to your nephew for this one night. Should you be afraid to be sole nurse ?' he added, as Johnnie came to Armine's door.

'I think I know what to do, if Jock can stand having me,' said Johnnie stoutly, as soon as he understood the question.

'Mother !' just then shouted Jock, and as Johnnie obeyed the call, he began, 'I want my head higher—no—I say, not you— Mother Carey !'

'She is busy with the doctor.'

'Can't she come and do this ? No, I say,' and he threw the nearest thing at hand at him.

'Come,' said Cecil, 'I'm glad you can do such things as that.'

But Jock gave a cry of pain, and protested that it was all John's fault for making him hurt himself instead of fetching mother.

'You had better let me lift you,' said John ; 'you know she is tired, and I *really* am stronger.'

'No, you shan't touch me—a great clumsy lout.'

In the midst of these amenities, the doctor appeared, and Jock looked slightly ashamed, especially when the doctor, in- stead of doing what was wanted, directed John where to put an arm, and how to give support, while moving the pillow, adding that he was a handy fellow, more so than many a pupil after half a year's training at the hospital, and smiling down Jock's growls and groans, which were as much from displeasure as from pain. They were followed by some despairing sighs at the horrors of the prospect of being moved.

'Ah! what will you give me for letting you off?' said the doctor.

Jock uttered a sound of relief, then, rather distrustfully, asked, 'Why?'

'We can only get bearers enough for one; and as it is most important to move your brother, while you will gain by a night's rest, he must have the first turn.'

'And welcome,' said Jock; 'my mother will stay with me.'

'That's the very point,' said Dr. Medlicott. 'I want you not only to give her up, but to do so cheerfully.'

'I'm sure mother wants to stay with me. Armine does not need her half so much.'

'He does not require the same kind of attention; but he is in so critical a state that I do not think I ought to separate her from him.'

'Why, what is the matter with him?' asked Jock, startled.

'Congestion of the right lung,' said the doctor, seeing that he was strong enough to bear the information, and feeling the need of rousing him from his monopolising self-absorption.

'People get over that, don't they?' said Jock, with an awe-struck interrogation in his voice.

'They *do;* and I hope much from getting him into a warmer atmosphere, but the child is so much reduced that the risk is great, and I should not dare not to have his mother with him.' Then, as Jock was silent, 'I have told you because you can make a great difference to their comfort by not showing how much it costs you to let her go.'

Jock drew the bedclothes over his face, and an odd stifled sound was heard from under them. He remained thus *perdu* while directions were being given to John for the night, but as the doctor was leaving the room, emerged and said—

'Bring him in before he goes.'

In a short time, for it was most important not to lose the fine weather, the doctor carried Armine in, swathed in rugs and blankets, a pale, sunken, worn face, and great hollow eyes looking out at the top.

The mother said something cheerful about a live mummy, but the two poor boys gazed at one another with sad, earnest, wistful eyes, and wrung one another's hands.

'Don't forget,' gasped Armine, labouring for breath.

And Jock answered—

'All right, Armie; good-bye. I'm coming to-morrow,' with a choking, quivering attempt at bravery.

'Yes, to-morrow,' said poor Mother Carey, bending over him. 'My boy—my poor good boy, if I could but cut myself in two! I can't tell you how thankful I am to you for being so good about it. That dear good Johnnie will do all he can, and it is only till to-morrow. You'll sleep most of the time.'

'All right, mother,' was again all that Jock could manage to utter, and the kisses that followed seemed to him the most precious he had known. He hid his face again, bearing his trouble the better because of the lull of violent pain quelled by opiates, so that his senses were all as in a dream bound up. When he looked up again at the clink of glass, it was Cecil whom he saw measuring off his draught.

'You !' he exclaimed.

'Yes, Medlicott said I might stay till four, and give the Monk a chance of a sleep. That fellow can always snooze away off hand, and he is as sound as a top in the next room ; but I was to give you this at two.'

'You're sure it's the right stuff ?'

'I should think so. We've practice enough in the family to know how to measure off a dose by this time.'

'How is it you are out here still ? This is Thursday, isn't it ? We meant to have been half-way home, to be in time for the matches.'

'I'm not going back this half, worse luck. They were mortally afraid these measles would make me get tender in the chest, like all the rest of us, so I've got nothing to do but be dragged about with Fordham after churches and picture galleries and mountains,' said Cecil, in a tone of infinite disgust. 'I declare it made me half mad to look at the Lake of Lucerne, and recollect that we might have been in the eight.'

'Not this year.'

'No, but next.'

In this contemplation Cecil was silent, only fondling Chico, until Jock, instead of falling asleep again, said, 'Evelyn, what does your doctor really think of the little chap ?'

Cecil screwed up his face as if he had rather not be asked.

'Never you think about it,' he said. 'Doctors always croak. He'll be all right again soon.'

'If I was sure,' sighed Jock ; 'but you know he has always been such a religious little beggar. It's a horrid bad sign.'

'Like my brother Walter,' said Cecil gravely. 'Now, Duke can be ever so snappish and peevish ; I'm not half so much afraid for him.'

'You never heard anything like the little fellow that night,' said Jock, and therewith he gave his friend by far the most connected account of the adventure that had yet been arrived at. He even spoke of the resolution to which he had been brought, and in a tone of awe described how he had pledged himself for the future.

'So you see I'm in for it,' he concluded ; 'I must give up all our jolly larks.'

'Then I shan't get into so many rows with my mother and uncle,' said Cecil, by no means with the opposition his friend had anticipated.

'Then you'll stand by me ?' said Jock.

'Gladly. My mother was at me all last Easter, telling me my goings on were worse to her than losing George or Walter, and talking about my confirmation and all. She only let me be a communicant on Easter Day because I did mean to make a fresh start—and I did mean it with all my heart; only when that supper was talked of, I didn't like to stick out against you, Brownlow; I never could, you know, and I didn't know what it was coming to.'

'Nor I,' said Jock; 'that's the worst of it. When a lark begins, one doesn't know how far one will get carried on. But that night I thought about the confirmation, and how I had made the promise without really thinking about it, and never had been to Holy Communion.'

'I meant it all,' said Cecil, 'and broke it, so I'm worst.'

'Well!' said Jock, 'if I go back from the promise little Armie made me make about being Christ's faithful soldier and servant, I could never face him again—no, nor death either! You can't think what it was like, Evelyn, sitting in the dead stillness—except for an awful crack and rumbling in the ice, and the solid snow fog shutting one in. How ugly, and brutish, and horrid all those things did look; and how it made me long to have been like the little fellow in my arms, or even this poor little dog, who knew no better. Then somehow came now and then a wonderful sense that God was all round us, and that our Lord had done *all that* for my forgiveness, if I only meant to do right in earnest. Oh! how to go on meaning it!'

'That's the thing,' said Cecil. 'I mean it fast enough at home, and when my mother talks to me, and I look at my brothers' graves, but it all gets swept away at Eton. It won't now, though, if you are different, Brownlow. I never liked any fellow like you. I knew you were best, even when you were worst. So if you go in for doing right, I shan't care for any one else—not even Cressham and Bulford.'

'If they choose to make asses of themselves they must,' said Jock. 'It will be a bore, but one mustn't mind things. I say, Evelyn, suppose we make that promise of Armine's over again together now.'

'It is only the engagement we made when we were sworn into Christ's army at our baptism,' said the much more fully instructed Cecil. 'We always were bound by it.'

'Yes, but we knew nothing about it then, and we really mean it now,' said Jock. 'If we do it for ourselves together, it will put us on our honour to each other, and to Christ our Captain, and that's what we want. Lay hold of my hand.'

The two boys, with clasped hands, and grave, steadfast eyes, with one voice, repeated together——

'We, John Lucas Brownlow and Cecil Fitzroy Evelyn, promise with all our hearts manfully to fight under Christ's banner, and continue His faithful soldiers and servants to our lives' end. Amen.'

Then Cecil touched Lucas's brow with his lips, and said—
'Fellow-soldiers, Brownlow.'
'Brothers in arms,' responded Jock.

It was one of those accesses of deep enthusiasm, and even of sentiment, which modern cynicism and false shame have not entirely driven out of youth. Their hearts were full ; and Jock, the stronger, abler, and more enterprising, had always exercised a fascination over his friend, who was absolutely enchanted to find him become an ally instead of a tempter, and to be no longer pulled two opposite ways.

'Ought we not to say a prayer to make it really firm ? We can't stand alone, you know,' he said diffidently.

'If you like ; if you know one,' said Jock.

Cecil knelt down and said the Lord's Prayer and the collect for the Fourth Epiphany Sunday.

'That's nice,' was Jock's comment. 'How did you know it ?'

'Mother made us learn the collects every Sunday, and she wrote that in my little book. I always begin the half with it, but afterwards I can't go on.'

'Then it doesn't do you much good,' was the not unnatural remark.

'I don't know,' said Cecil, hesitating ; 'may be *all this*—your getting right, I mean, is the coming round of prayers—my mother's, I mean, for if you take this turn, it will be much easier for me ! Poor mother ! it's not for want of her caring and teaching.'

'My mother doesn't bother about it.'

'I wish she did,' said Cecil. 'If she had gone on like mine, you would have been ever so much better than I.'

'No, I should have been bored and bothered into being regularly good-for-nothing. You don't know what she's really like. She's nicer than any one—as jolly as any fellow, and yet a lady all over.'

'I know that,' said Cecil ; 'she was uncommonly jolly to me at Eton, and I know my mother and she will get on like a house on fire. We're too old to have a scrimmage about them like disgusting little lower boys,' he added, seeing Jock still bristling in defence of Mother Carey.

This produced a smile, and he went on—

'Look here, Skipjack, we *will* be fellow-soldiers every way. My Uncle James can do anything at the Horse Guards, and he shall have us set down for the same regiment. I'll tell him you are my good influence.'

'But I've been just the other way.'

'Oh, but you will be—a year or two will show it. Which shall it be ? Do you go in for cavalry or infantry ? I like cavalry, but he's all for the other.'

Jock was wearied enough not to have much contribution to make to the conversation, and he thus left Cecil such a fair field as he seldom enjoyed for Uncle James's Indian and Crimean campaigns, and for the comparative merits of the regiments his nephew had beheld at reviews.

He was interrupted by a message from the guide that there was a cloud in the distance, and the young Herr had better set off quickly unless he wished to be weather-bound.

Johnnie was on his feet as soon as there was a step on the stairs, and was congratulated on his ready powers of sleeping.

'It's in the family,' said Jock. 'His brother Rob went to sleep in the middle of the examination for his commission.'

'Then I should think he could sleep on the rack,' said Cecil.

'I'm sure I wish I could,' rejoined Jock.

'What a sell for the torturers, to get some chloroform !' said John. And so Cecil departed amid laughter, which gave John little idea how serious the talk had been in his absence.

The rain came on even more rapidly than the guide had foretold, and it was a drenched and dripping object that rode into the court of the tall hotel at Leukerbad, and immediately fell into the hands of Dr. Medlicott and Reeves, who deposited him ignominiously in bed, in spite of all his protestations and murmurs. However, he had the comfort of hearing that his little fag was recovering from the exhaustion of the journey. He had at first been so faint that the doctor had watched, fearing that he would never revive again, and he had not yet attempted to speak ; but his breathing was certainly already less laboured, and the choking, struggling cough less frequent. 'He really seems likely to have a little natural sleep,' was Lord Fordham's report somewhat later, on coming in to find Cecil sitting up in bed to discuss a very substantial supper. 'I hope that, with Reeves and the doctor to look to him, his mother may get a little rest to-night.'

'Have you seen her ?'

'Only for a moment or two, poor thing ; but I never did see such eyes or such a wonderful sad smile as she tried to thank us with. Medlicott is ready to do anything for her husband's sake ; I am sure any one would do the same for hers. To get such a look is something to remember !'

'Well done, Duke !' ejaculated Cecil under his breath, for he had never seen his senior so animated or so enthusiastic. 'Then you mean to stay, and let Medlicott look after them ?'

'Of course I do,' said Fordham, in a much more decided tone than he had used in the morning. 'I'm not going to do anything so barbarous as to leave them to some German practitioner ; and when we are here, I don't see why they should have advice out from home—not half so good probably.'

'You're a brick, Duke,' uttered Cecil ; and though Fordham hated slang, he smiled at the praise.

'And now, Duke, be a good fellow, and give me some clothes. That brute Reeves has not brought me in one rag.'

'Really it is hardly worth while. It is nearly eight o'clock, and I don't know where your portmanteau was put. Shall I get you a book?'

'No; but if you'd get me a pen and ink, I want to write to mother.'

Such a desire was not too frequent in Cecil, and Fordham was glad enough to promote it, bringing in his own neat apparatus, with only a mild entreaty that his favourite pen might be well treated, and the sheets respected. He had written his own letter of explanation of his first act of independence, and he looked with some wonder at his brother's rapid writing, not without fear that some sudden pressure for a foolish debt might have been the result of his *tête-à-tête* with his dangerous friend. Cecil's letters were too apt to be requests for money or confessions of debts, and if this were the case, what would be Mrs. Evelyn's view of the conduct of the whole party in disregarding her wishes?

Had he been with his mother, he would have probably been called into consultation over the letter, but he was forced to remain without the privilege here offered to the reader :—

BADEN HOTEL, LEUKERBAD, *14th June.*

DEAREST MOTHER—Duke has written about our falling in with the Brownlows, and how pluckily Friar caught us up. It was a regular mercy, for the little one couldn't have lived without Dr. Medlicott, and most likely Lucas is in for a rheumatic fever. He has been telling me all about it, and how frightful it was to be all night out on the edge of the glacier in a thick fog with his ankle strained, and how little Armine went on with his texts and hymns and wasn't a bit afraid, but quite happy. You never would believe what a fellow Brownlow is. We have had a great talk, and you will never have to say again that he does me harm.

Mammy, darling, I want to tell you that I was a horrible donkey last half, worse than you guessed, and I am sorrier than ever I was before, and this is a real true resolution not to do it again. Brownlow and I have promised to stand by one another about right and wrong to our lives' end. He means it, and what Brownlow means he does, and so do I. We said your collect, and somehow I do feel as if God would help us now.

Please, dearest mother, forgive me for all I have not told you.

Duke is very well and jolly. He is quite smitten with Mrs. Brownlow, and, what is more, so is Reeves, who says she is 'such a lady that it is a pleasure to do anything for her.'—Your loving son,        C. F. E.

Cecil's letter went off with his brother's in early morning; but it was such a day as only mails and postmen encounter. Mountains, pine-woods, nay, even the opposite houses, were blotted out by sheets of driving rain, and it was impossible to think of bringing Jock down! Dr. Medlicott heard and saw with dismay. What would the mother say to him—nay, what ought he to have done? He could hardly expect her not to reproach him, and he fairly dreaded meeting her eyes when they turned from the streaming window.

But all she said was, 'We did not reckon on this.'

'If I had——' began the doctor.

P

'Please don't vex yourself,' said she; 'you could not have done otherwise, and perhaps the move would have hurt him more than staying there. You have been so very kind. See what you have done here!'

For Armine, after some hours that had been very distressing, had sunk into a calm sleep, and there was a far less oppressed look on his wan little face.

The doctor would have had her take some rest, but she shook her head. The only means of allaying the gnawing anxiety for Jock, and the despairing fancies about his suffering and Johnnie's helplessness, was the attending constantly to Armine.

'Any way, I will see him to-day,' said Dr. Medlicott, impelled far more by the patient silence with which she sat, one hand against her beating heart, than he would have been by any entreaty. But how she thanked him when she found him really setting forth! She insisted on his taking a guide, as much for his own security as to carry some additional comforts to the prisoners, and she committed to him two little notes, one to each boy, written through a mist of tears. Yes; tears, unusual as they were with her, were called forth as much by the kindness she met with as by her sick yearning after the two lonely boys. And when she knew the doctor was on his way, she could yield to Armine's signs of entreaty, lie back in her chair and sleep, while Reeves watched over him.

When the doctor, by a strong man's determination, had made his way up the pass, he found matters better than he had dared to expect. The patient was certainly not worse, and the medicine had kept him in a sleepy, tranquil state, in which he hardly realised the situation. His young attendant was just considering how to husband the last draught, when the welcome, dripping visitor appeared. The patient was not in bad spirits considering, and could not but feel himself reprieved by the weather. He was too sleepy to feel the dulness of his present position, and even allowed that his impromptu nurse had done tolerably well. Johnnie had been ready at every call, had rubbed away an attack of pain, hurt wonderfully little in lifting him, and was 'not half a bad lot altogether'—an admission of which doctor and nurse knew the full worth.

Johnnie himself was pleased and grateful, and had that sort of satisfaction which belongs to the finding out of one's own available talent. He had done what was pronounced the right thing; and not only that, but he had liked the doing it, and he declared himself not afraid to encounter another night alone with his cousin. He had picked up enough vernacular German to make himself understood, and indeed was a decided favourite with Fräulein Rosalie, who would do anything for her dear young Herr. It was possible to get a fair amount of sleep, and Dr. Medlicott felt satisfied that the charge was not too much for him, and indeed there was no other alternative. The doctor stayed as long as he could, and did his best to enliven the dulness by producing a pocketful of Tauchnitzes, and sitting talking while the patient dozed. Johnnie showed such intelligent curiosity as to the how and why of the symptoms and their counteraction, that after some explanation the doctor said, 'You ought to be one of us, my friend.'

'I have sometimes thought about it,' said John.

'Indeed !' cried the doctor, like an enthusiast in his profession ; and John, though not a ready speaker, was drawn on by his notes of interest to say, 'I don't really like anything so much as making out about man and what one is made of.'

'Physiology ?'

'Yes,' said the boy, who had been shy of uttering the scientific term. 'There's nothing like it for interest, it seems to me. Besides, one is more sure of being of use that way than in any other.'

'Capital ! Then what withholds you ? Isn't it *swell* enough ?'

Johnnie laughed and coloured. 'I'm not such a fool, but I am not sure about my people.'

'I thought your uncle was Joseph Brownlow.'

'My aunt would be delighted, but it is my own people. They would say my education—Eton and *all that*—was not intended for it.'

'You may tell them that whatever tends to make you more thoroughly a man and gentleman, and less of a mere professional, is a benefit to your work. The more you are in yourself, the higher your work will be. I hope you will go to the university.'

'I mean to go up for a scholarship next year ; but I've lost a great deal of time now, and I don't know how far that will tell.'

'I think you will find that what you may have lost in time, you will have gained in power.'

'I *do* want to go in for physical science, but there's another difficulty. One of my cousins does so, but the effect on him has not made my father like it the better—and—and to tell the truth—' he half mumbled, 'it makes me doubt——'

'The effect on his faith ?'

'Yes.'

'If faith is unsettled by looking deeper into the mysteries of God's works it cannot have been substantial faith, but merely outward, thoughtless reception,' said the doctor, as he met two thoughtful dark eyes fixed on him in inquiry and consideration.

'Thank you, sir,' after a pause.

'Had this troubled you ?'

'Yes,' said John ; 'I couldn't stand doubt *there*. I would rather break stones on the road than set myself doubting !'

'Why should you think that there is danger ?'

'It seems to be so with others.'

'Depend upon it, Doubting Castle never lay on the straight road. If men run into it, it is not simple study of the works of creation that leads them there ; but either they have only acquiesced, and never made their faith a living reality, or else they are led away by fashion and pride of intellect. One who begins and goes on in active love of God and man, will find faith and reverence not diminished but increased.'

'But aren't there speculations and difficulties ?'

'None which real active religion and love cannot regard as the mere effects of half-knowledge—the distortions of a partial view. I speak with all my heart, as one who has seen how it has been with many of my own generation, as well as with myself.'

Johnnie bent his head, and the young physician, somewhat surprised at finding himself saying so much on such points, left that branch of the subject, and began to talk to him about his uncle.


## CHAPTER XXII

### SHUTTING THE STABLE DOOR

' Presumptuous maid, with looks intent,
Again she gazed, again she bent,
Nor knew the gulf between.'

GRAY.

'HURRAH ! It's Johnnie !'

'Georgie. Recollect yourself.'

'But, mamma, it was Johnnie.'

'Johnnie does not come till evening. Sit still, children, or I shall have to send you to dine in the nursery.'

'Somebody did pass the window, mamma, but I thought it was Rob,' said Jessie, now grown into a very fine-looking, tall, handsome maiden, with a grandly-formed head and shoulders, and pleasant soft brown eyes.

'It was Johnnie,' reiterated little George ; and at that moment the dining-room door opened, and the decorum of the luncheon dinner entirely giving way, the three little ones all precipitated themselves towards the entering figure, while Jessie and her mother rose at their two ends of the table, and the Colonel, no luncheon eater, came in from the study.

'What, Johnnie, already !'

'The tidal train was earlier than I expected, so I have another half-day. Well ! are you all well ?'

'Quite well. Why—how you are grown ! I thought it was Rob when you passed my window,' said his father.

'So did I at first,' added Jessie, 'but Rob is much broader.'

'Yes,' said his mother. 'I am glad you are come back, Johnnie ; you look thin and pale. Sit down. Some mutton or some rabbit-pie ? No, no, let Jessie help you ; you shan't have all the carving ; I'm sure you are tired ; you don't look at all well.'

'I was crossing all night, you know,' said Johnnie, laughing, 'and am as hungry as a hunter, that's all. What a blessing to see a nice clean English potato again without any flummery!'

'Ah! I thought so,' said his mother; 'they didn't know how to feed you. It was an unfortunate business altogether.'

'How did you leave those poor boys, Johnnie?' asked his father.

'Better,' said Johnnie. 'Jock is nearly well—will be quite so after the baths; and Armine is getting better. He sat up for an hour the day before I came away.'

'And your aunt?' said his father.

'Wonderful,' said John, with a quiver of feeling on his face. 'You never saw anything like her. She keeps up, but she looks awfully thin and worn. I couldn't have left her, if Dr. Medlicott and Lord Fordham and his man had not all been bent on saving her whatever they could.'

Her Serene Highness virtuously forbore a sigh. She never could believe those chains with which Caroline bound all men to her service to be either unconscious or strictly proper. However, she only said—

'It was high time that you came away; you were quite knocked up with being left a week alone with Lucas in that horrid place. I can't think how your aunt came to think of it.'

'She didn't think,' said John bluntly. 'It was only a week, and it couldn't be helped. Besides, it was rather jolly.'

'But it knocked you up.'

'Oh! that was only a notion of the doctor and my aunt. They said I was done up first because I caught cold, and I was glad to wait a day or two longer at Leukerbad, in hopes Allen and Bobus would have come out before I went.'

'They come out! Not they!' said the Colonel. '"Tis not the way of young men nowadays to give up anything for their fathers and mothers. No, no, Bobus can't spare a week from his reading-party, but must leave his mother to a set of chance acquaintance; and Allen—whom poor Caroline always thinks the affectionate one, if he is nothing else—can't give up going to gape at the sun at midnight; and Rob was wanting to make one of their freight of fools, but I told him it was quite enough to have one son wandering abroad at other people's expense, when it couldn't be helped, and that I wouldn't have another unless he was prepared to lay down his share in the yacht out of his pay and allowance. I'm glad you are come home, Johnnie: it was quite right to come as soon as your aunt could spare you, poor thing! She writes warmly about you; I am glad you were able to be of use to her, but you ought not to waste any more time.'

'No. I wrote to my tutor that I would be at Eton to-morrow night, in time to begin the week's work.'

'Papa!' cried out Mrs. Brownlow, 'you will never let him

start so soon ? He is so pulled down, I must have him at home
to get him right again ; and there are all his clothes to look
over !'

Colonel Brownlow gave the odd little chuckling noise that
meant to all the family that he did not see the force of mamma's
objections, and John asseverated that he was perfectly well,
and that his Eton garments were all at Hyde Corner, where he
should take them up. Meantime, he thought he ought to walk
to Belforest to report to his cousins, and carry a key which his
aunt had sent by him to Janet.

'They will be coming in this evening,' said his mother ; 'you
had better stay and rest.'

'I must go over, thank you,' said John. 'There is a book
Armine wants to have sent out to him. Jessie, will you walk
with me ?'

'And me !' cried George.

'And me !' cried Edmund.

'And me, Lina go !' cried the smallest voice.

But the Colonel disconcerted the petitioners by announcing
that he had business at Belforest, and would drive Johnnie over
in the dog-cart. So Jessie had to console herself by agreeing
with her mother that Johnnie looked much more manly, yes,
and had an air and style about him which both admired very
much, though, while Mrs. Brownlow deemed it the true outcome
of the admixture of Friar and Brownlow, Jessie gave more
credit to Eton and Belforest, for Jessie was really fond of her
aunt, to whom she had owed most of her extra gaieties. Moreover, Mrs. Brownlow, though often chafing secretly, had the
power of reticence, and would not set the minds of her children
against one who was always doing them kindnesses. True,
these favours were more than she could easily brook, since her
pride and independence were not, like her husband's, tempered
by warm affection. It was his doing that the expenses of
Johnnie's education had been accepted, and that Esther and
Ellen had been sent by their aunt to a good school ; thus
gratitude, unpalatable though it were, prevented unguarded
censure. She abstained from much ; and as there was no quick
intuition in the family, even Jessie, the most in her confidence,
only vaguely knew that mamma thought Aunt Caroline too
clever and fly-away ; but mamma was grave and wise, and it
was very nice to have an aunt who was young and lively, and
always had pleasant things going on in her house. Jessie
always had her full share, not indeed appreciating the intellect,
but possessing beauty and charm enough to be always appreciated there. 'Sweetly pretty,' as Mrs. Coffinkey called her,
was exactly what she was, for she was thoroughly good and
unselfish, and a happy, simple nature looked out through her
brown smiling eyes. She was very fond of her cousins, had
shared all the anxieties of the last fortnight to the utmost, and
was a good deal disappointed at being baulked of the walk with

her brother, in which she would have heard so much more about
Armine, Jock, and Aunt Caroline than would be communicated
in public.

Johnnie, however, was glad of the invitation, even though a
little shy of it. The *tête-à-tête* drive was an approach to the
serious business of life, since it was evidently designed to give
opportunity for answering a letter which he had thought out
and written while laid up at Leukerbad by a bad cold and the
reaction from his exertions at Schwarenbach.

Still his father did not speak till they had driven up the hill,
and were near the gates of Belforest. Then he said—

'That was not a bad letter that you wrote me, Johnnie.'

Johnnie flushed with pleasure. The letter had cost him
much thought and pains, and commendation from his father
was rare.

'But it will take a great deal of consideration.'

'Yes,' said Johnnie. 'You don't disapprove, do you, papa?'

'Well,' said the Colonel, in his ponderous way, 'you have
advantages, you know, and you might do better for yourself.'

There was a quivering impulse on Johnnie's lips to say that
it was not to himself that he wanted to do good ; but when his
father was speaking in that deliberate manner, he was not to be
interrupted, and there was nothing for it but to hear him out.

' Your aunt is providing you with the best of educations, you
have good abilities and industry, and you will be a well-looking
fellow besides,' added the Colonel, glancing over him with an
approving eye of fatherly satisfaction ; 'and it seems to me
that you could succeed in some superior line. Your mother
and I had always hoped to see you at the bar. Every opportunity for distinction is given you, and I do not understand this
sudden desire to throw them up for a profession of much greater
drudgery and fewer chances of rising, unless it were from some
influence of your aunt.'

'She never spoke of it. She does not know that I have
thought of it, nor of my letter to you.'

'Then it is simply from enthusiasm for this young doctor?'

'Not exactly,' said John, 'but I always wished I could be like
my uncle. I remember hearing mamma read a bit of one of the
letters of condolence which said, "His was one of the most
beautiful lives I have ever known," and I never forgot it. It
stayed in my mind like a riddle, till I gradually found out that
the beauty was in the good he was always doing——'

'Ah !' said the Colonel, in a tone betokening that he was
touched, and which encouraged John to continue—

'Besides, I really do like and enter into scientific subjects
better than any others ; I believe it is my turn.'

'Perhaps—you do sometimes put me in mind of your uncle.
But why have you only spoken of it now?'

'I don't think I really considered what I should be,' said
John. 'There was quite enough to think of with work, and

cricket, and all the rest, till this spring, when I have been off it all, and then when I talked it over with Dr Medlicott, he settled my mind about various things that I wanted to know.'

'Did he persuade you?'

'No more than saying that I managed well for Jock when I was left alone with him, and that he thought I had the makings of a doctor in me. He loves his profession, of course, and thinks it a grand one. Yes, papa, indeed I think it is. To be always learning the ways of God's working, for the sake of lessening all the pain and grief in the world——'

'Johnnie! That's almost what my brother said to me thirty years ago, and what did it come to? Being at the beck and call night and day of every beggar in London, and dying at last in his prime, of disease caught in their service.'

'Yes,' said John, with a low gruff sound in his voice, 'but is not that like being killed in battle?'

'The world doesn't think it so, my boy,' said the soldier. 'Well! what is it you propose to do?'

'I don't suppose it will make much difference yet,' said John, 'except that at Oxford I should go in more for physical science.'

'You don't want to give up the university?'

'Oh no! Dr. Medlicott said a degree there is a great help; besides that, all the general study one can get is the more advantage, lifting one above the mere practitioner.'

'That is well,' said the Colonel. 'If you are to go to the university, there is no need to dwell further on the matter at present. You will have had time to see more of the world, and you will know whether this wish only comes from enthusiasm for a pleasant young man who has been kind to you, or if it be your real deliberate choice, and if so, your mother will have had time to reconcile herself to the notion. At any rate, we will say no more about it for the present. Though I must say, Johnnie,' he added, as he turned his horse's head between the ribbon borders of the approach, 'you have thought and spoken like a sensible lad, and so like my dear brother that I could not deny you.'

If Johnnie could hardly believe in the unwonted commendation, which made his heart throb and sent a flood of colour into his cheeks, Colonel Brownlow was equally amazed at the boy's attainment of a manly and earnest thought and purpose, so utterly unlike anything he had hitherto seen in the stolid Rob, or the easy-going Allen, or even in Bobus, who—whatever there might be in him—never thought it worth while to show it to his uncle.

However, discussion was cut short by a little flying figure which came rushing across the garden, and Babie with streaming hair clung to her cousin, gasping—

'Oh, Johnnie, Johnnie, tell me about Armie and Jock!'

'They are ever so much better, Babie,' said Johnnie, lifting the slim little thing up in his arms, as he had lifted his own five-year-old brother ; 'I've got a thick parcel of acrostics for you ; Armine makes them in bed, and Lord Fordham writes them out.'

'Will you come to the rosary, Uncle Robert?' said Babie, recovering her manners, as Johnnie set her down. 'It is the coolest place, and they are sitting there.'

'Why, Babie, what a sprite you look,' said Johnnie. 'You look as if you were just off the sick-list too !'

'I'm all right,' said Babie, shaking her hair at him, and bounding on before with the tidings of their coming, while her uncle observed in a low voice—

'Poor little thing ! I believe she has been a good deal knocked up between the heat and the anxiety ; there was no making her eat or sleep. Ah ! Miss Elfie, are you acting queen of roses?' as Babie returned, together with Elvira, who with a rich dark red rose over one ear, and a large bouquet at her bosom, justified the epithet at which she bridled, and half curtsied in her graceful stately archness, as she gave her hand in greeting, and exclaimed—

'Ah, Johnnie ! are you come ? When is Mother Carey going to send for us?'

'When they leave Leukerbad, I fancy,' said John. 'That's a tiresome place for any one who does not need to lead the life of a hippopotamus.'

'It can't be more tiresome than this is,' said Elvira, with a yawn. 'Lessons all day, and nobody to come near us.'

'Isn't this a dreadful place?' said John merrily, as he looked into the rosary, a charming bowery circle of fragrance, inclosed by arches of trellis-work on which roses were trained, their wreaths now bearing a profusion of blossoms of every exquisite tint, from deep crimson or golden-yellow to purest white, while their more splendid standard sisters bloomed out in fragrant and gorgeous magnificence under their protection.

At the shady end there was a little grass plat round a tiny fountain, whose feather of spray rose and plashed coolness. Near it were seats, where Miss Ogilvie and Janet were discovered with books and work. They came forward with greetings and inquiries, which Johnnie answered in detail.

'Yes, they are both better. Armine sat by the window for an hour the day before I came away.'

'Will they be able to come back to Eton after the holidays?' asked his father.

'Certainly not Armine, but Jock seems to be getting all right. If he was to catch rheumatism he did it at the right place, for that's what Leukerbad is good for. Oh, Babie, you never saw such a lark ! Fancy a great room, and where the floor ought to be, nothing but muddy water or liquid mud, with steps going down, and a lot of heads looking out of it, some with curly heads, some in smoking-caps, some in fine caps of lace and ribbons.'

'Oh, Johnnie ; like women !'

'Like women ! They are women.

'Not both together.'

'Yes, I tell you, the whole boiling of them, male and female. There's a fat German Countess, who always calls Jock her *liebes Kind*, and comes floundering after him, to his very great disgust. The only things they have to show they are human still, and not frogs, are little boards floating before them with their pocket-handkerchiefs and coffee-cups and newspapers.'

'Oh ! like the little blacks in the dear bright bays at San Ildefonso,' cried Elvira.

'You don't mean that they have no clothes on ?' said Babie, with shocked downrightness of speech that made everybody laugh ; and Johnnie satisfied her on that score, adding that Dr. Medlicott had made a parody of Tennyson's 'Merman,' for Jock's benefit, on giving him up to a Leukerbad doctor, who was to conduct his month's *Kur*. It was to go into the *Traveller's Joy*, a manuscript magazine, the first number of which was being concocted and illustrated amongst the Leuker-bad party, for the benefit of Babie and Sydney Evelyn. As a foretaste, Johnnie produced from the bag he still carried strapped on his shoulder, a packet of acrostics addressed to Miss Barbara Brownlow, and a smaller envelope for Janet.

'Is it the key ?' asked Colonel Brownlow.

'Yes,' said Janet, 'the key of her davenport, and directions in which drawer to find the letters you want. Do you like to have them at once, Uncle Robert ?'

'Thank you—yes, for then I can go round and settle with that fellow Martin, which I can't do without knowing exactly what passed between him and your mother.'

Janet went off, observing—'I wonder whether that is a possibility ;' while Miss Ogilvie put in an anxious inquiry for Mrs. Brownlow's health and spirits, and a good many more details were elicited than Johnnie had given at home. She had never broken down, and now that she was hopeful, was, in spite of her fatigue, as bright and merry as ever, and was contributing comic pictures to the *Traveller's Joy*, while Lord Fordham did the sketches. Those kind people were as careful of her as any could be.

'And what are her further plans ?' asked Miss Ogilvie. 'Has she been able to form any ?'

'Hardly,' said Johnnie. 'They must stay at Leukerbad for a month for Jock to have the course of waters rightly, and indeed Armine could hardly be moved sooner. I think Dr. Medlicott wants them to keep in Switzerland till the heat of the weather is over, and then winter in the south.'

'And when may I go to Armine ?'

'When shall we get away from here ?' asked Babie and Elfie in a breath.

'I don't quite know,' said John. 'There is not much room to

spare in the hotel where they are at Leukerbad, and it is a
dreadfully slow place. Evelyn is growling like a dozen polar
bears at it.'

'Why isn't he gone back with you to Eton?'

'I believe it was settled that he was not to go back this half,
for fear of his lungs, and you see he is a swell who takes it
easily. He would have been glad enough to return with me
though, and would scarcely have endured staying, but that he
is so fond of Jock.'

'What is there to be done there?'

'Nothing, except to wade in tepid mud. Fordham has
routed out a German to read *Faust* with, and that puts Evelyn
into a sweet temper. They go on expeditions, and do sketching
and botany, which amuses Armine; but they get up some fun
over the queer people, and *do* them for the mag., but it is all
deadly lively; not that I saw much of it, for we only got down
from Schwarenbach on Monday, and they kept me in bed all
the two next days; but Jock and Evelyn hate it awfully. Indeed Jock is so down in the mouth altogether I don't know
what to make of him, and just when the German doctors say the
treatment makes people particularly brisk and lively.'

'Perhaps what makes a German lively makes an Englishman
grave,' sagely observed Babie.

'Jock grave must be a strange sight,' said the Colonel; 'I am
afraid he can't be recovering properly.'

'The doctor thinks he is,' said John; 'but then he doesn't
know the nature of the Skipjack. But,' he added in a low
voice, 'that night was enough to make any one grave, and it
was much the worst to Jock, because he kept his senses almost
all the time, and was a good deal hurt besides to begin with.
His sprain is still so bad that he has to be carried upstairs and
to go to the baths in a chair.'

'And do you think,' said the Colonel, 'that this young lord is
going to stay on all this time in this dull place for the sake of
an utter stranger?'

'Jock and Evelyn were always great friends at Eton,' said
John. 'Then my uncle did something, I don't know what, that
Medlicott is grateful for, and they have promised to see Armine
through this illness. The place agrees with Fordham; they say
he has never been so well or active since he came out.'

'What is he like?' inquired Babie.

'Like, Babie? Like anything long and limp you can think
of. He sits all in a coil and twist, and you don't think there's
much of him; but when he gets up and pulls himself upright,
you go looking and looking till you don't know where's the top
of him, till you see a thin white face in washed-out hair. He is
a good fellow, awfully kind, and I suppose he can't help being
such a tremendous——' John hesitated, in deference to his
father, for a word that was not slang, and finally chose
'don.'

'Oh,' sighed Babie, 'Armie said in his note he was jolly beyond description.'

'Well, so he is,' said John ; 'he plays chess with Armie, and brings him flowers and books, and waits on him as you used to do on a sick doll. And that's just what he is ; he ought to have been a woman, and he would have been much happier too, poor fellow. I'd rather be dead at once than drag about such a life of coddling as he does.'

'Poor lad !' said his father. 'Did Janet understand that I was waiting for those letters, I wonder ?'

'You had better go and see, Babie,' said Miss Ogilvie. 'Perhaps she cannot find them.'

Babie set off, and John proceeded to explain that Mrs. Evelyn was still detained in London by old Lady Fordham, who continued to be kept between life and death by her doctors. Meantime, the sons could dispose of themselves as they pleased, while under the care of Dr. Medlicott, and were not wanted at home, so that there was little doubt but that they would remain with Armine as long as he needed their physician's care.

All the while Elfie was flitting about, pelting Johnnie with handfuls snatched from over-blown roses, and though he returned the assault at every pause, his gray travelling suit was bestrewn with crimson, pink, cream, and white petals.

At last the *débris* of a huge Eugénie Grandet hit him full on the bridge of his nose, and caused him to exclaim—

'Nay, Elfie, you little wretch ; that was quite a good rose— not fair game,' and leaping up to give her chase in and out among the beds, they nearly ran against Janet returning with the letters, and saying 'she was sorry to have been so long, but mother's hoards were never easy places of research.'

Barbara came more slowly back, and looked somewhat as if she had had a sharper rebuke than she understood or relished.

Poor child ! she had suffered much in this her first real trouble, and a little thing was enough to overset her. She had not readily recovered from the petulant tone of anger with which Janet told her not to come peeping and worrying.

Janet had given a most violent start when she opened the door of her mother's bedroom where the davenport stood ; and Janet much resented being startled ; no doubt that was the reason she was so cross, thought Barbara, but still it was very disagreeable.

That room was the child's also. She had been her mother's bedfellow ever since her father's death, and she felt her present solitude. The nights were sultry, and her sleep had been broken of late.

That night she was in a slumber as cool as a widely-opened window would make it, but not so sound that she was not haunted all the time by dread for Armine.

Suddenly she was awakened to full consciousness by seeing a

light in the room. No, it was not the maid putting away her dresses. It was Janet, bending over her mother's davenport.

Babie started up.

'Janet! Is anything the matter?'

'Nothing! Nonsense! go to sleep, child.'

'What are you about?'

'Never mind. Only mother keeps her things in such a mess; I was setting them to rights after disturbing them to find the book.'

There was something in the tone like an apology. Babie did not like it, but she well knew that she should be contemptuously put down if she attempted an inquiry, far less a remonstrance, with Janet. Only, with a puzzled sort of watch-dog sense, she sat up in bed and stared.

'Why don't you lie down?' said Janet.

Babie did lie down, but on her back, her head high up on the pillow, and her eyes well open still.

Perhaps Janet did not like it, for she gave an impatient shuffle to the papers, shut the drawer with a jerk, locked it, took up her candle, and went away without vouchsafing a 'good-night.'

Babie lay wondering. She knew that the davenport contained all that was most sacred and precious to her mother, as relics of her old life, and that only dire necessity would have made her let any one touch it. What could Janet mean? To speak would be of no use. One-and-twenty was not likely to listen to thirteen, though Babie, in her dreamy wakefulness, found herself composing conversations in which she made eloquent appeals to Janet, which she was never likely to utter.

At last the morning twitterings began outside, doves cooed, peacocks miawed, light dawned, and Babie's perceptions cleared themselves. In the wainscoted room was a large closet, used for hanging up cloaks and dresses, and fortunately empty. No sooner did the light begin to reflect itself in its polished oak-panelled door, than an idea struck Babie, and bounding from her bed, she opened the door, wheeled in the davenport, shut it in, turned the big rusty key with both hands and a desperate effort, then repairing to her own little inner room, disturbed the honourable retirement of the last and best-beloved of her dolls in a pink-lined cradle in a disused doll's house, and laying the key beneath the mattress, felt heroically ready for the thumbscrew rather than yield it up. She knew Armine would say she was right, and be indignant that Janet should meddle with mother's private stores. So she turned over on the pillow, cooled by the morning breeze, and fell into a sound sleep, whence she was only roused by the third 'Miss Barbara' from her maid.

She heard no more of the matter, and but for the absence of the davenport could really have thought it all a dream.

She was driving her two little fairy ponies to Kenminster with

Elvira, to get the afternoon post, when a quiet, light step came into the bedroom, and Janet stood within it, looking for the davenport, as if she did not quite believe her senses. However, remembering Babie's eyes, she had her suspicions. She looked into the little girl's room and saw nothing, then tried the closet door, and finding it locked, came to a tolerably correct guess as to what had become of it, and felt hotly angry at 'that conceited child's meddling folly.'

For the awkward thing was that the clasped memorandum-book, containing 'Magnum Bonum,' was in her hand, locked out of, instead of into, its drawer.

When searching for the account-book for her uncle, it had, as it were, offered itself to her; and though so far from being green, with 'Garden' marked on it, it was Russia leather, and had J. B. upon it. She had peeped in and read 'Magnum Bonum' within the lid. All day the idea had haunted her, that there lay the secret, in the charge of her little thoughtless mother, who, ignorant of its true value, and deterred by uncomprehended words and weak scruples, was withholding it from the world, and depriving her own family, and what was worst of all, her daughter, of the chances of becoming illustrious.

'I am his daughter as much as hers,' thought she. 'Why should she deprive me of my inheritance?'

Certainly Janet had been told that the great arcanum could not be dealt with by a woman; but this she did not implicitly believe, and she was in consequence the more curious to discover what it really was, and whether it was reasonable to sacrifice the best years of her life to preparing for it. The supposed unfairness of her exclusion seemed to her to justify the act, and thus it was that she had stolen to the davenport when she supposed that her little sister would be asleep, and finding it impossible to attend or understand with Babie's great brown eyes lamping on her, she had carried off the book.

She had been reading it even till the morning light had surprised her, and had been able to perceive the general drift, though she had leaped over the intermediate steps. She had just sufficient comprehension of the subject for unlimited confidence that the achievement was practicable, without having knowledge enough to understand a tithe of the difficulties, though she did see that they could hardly be surmounted by a woman unassisted. However, she might see her way by the time her studies were completed, and in the meantime her mother might keep the shell while she had the essence.

However, to find the shell thus left on her hands was no slight perplexity. Should she, as eldest daughter left in charge, demand the desk, Barbara would produce her reasons for its abstraction, and for this Janet was not prepared. Unless something else was wanted from it, so as to put Babie in the wrong, Janet saw no alternative but to secure the book in her own bureau, and watch for a chance of smuggling it back.

Thus Babie escaped all interrogation, but she did not release the captive davenport, and indeed she soon forgot all about it in her absorption in Swiss letters.

## CHAPTER XXIII

### THE LOST TREASURE

'But solemn sound or sober thought
  The Fairies cannot bear ;
They sing, inspired with love and joy,
  Like skylarks in the air.
Of solid sense, or thought that's grave,
  You find no traces there.'

*Young Tamlane.*

WHEN old Lady Fordham's long decay ended in death, Mrs. Evelyn would not recall her sons to the funeral, but meant to go out herself to join them, and offered to escort Mrs. Brownlow's daughters to the meeting-place. This was to be Engelberg, for Dr. Medlicott had decided that after the month at Leukerbad all his patients would be much the better for a breath of the pine-woods on the Alpine height, and undertook to see them conveyed thither in time to meet the ladies.

This proposal set Miss Ogilvie free to join her brother, who had a curacy in a seaside place where the season began just when the London season ended. Her holiday was then to begin, and Janet was to write to Mrs. Evelyn and declare herself ready to meet her in London at the time appointed.

The arrangement was not to Janet's taste. She thought herself perfectly capable of escorting the younger ones, especially as they were to take their maid, a capable person named Delrio, daughter of an Englishwoman and a German waiter, and widow of an Italian courier, who was equal to all land emergencies, and could speak any language. She belonged to the young ladies. Their mother, not liking strangers about her, had, on old nurse's death, caused Emma to learn enough of the lady's maid's art for her own needs at home, and took care of herself abroad.

Babie was enraptured to be going to Mother Carey and Armine, and Elvira was enchanted to leave the schoolroom behind her, being fully aware that she always had more notice and indulgence from outsiders than at home, or indeed from any one who had been disappointed at her want of all real affection.

'You are just like a dragon fly,' said Babie to her, 'all brightness outside and nothing within.'

This unusually severe remark came from Babie's indignation at Elvira's rebellion against going to River Hollow to take leave. It would be a melancholy visit, for her grandfather had

become nearly imbecile, since he had had a paralytic stroke in
the course of the winter, and good sensible Mrs. Gould had died
of fever in the previous autumn.

Elvira, who had never liked the place, now loathed it, and
did not seem capable of understanding Babie's outburst.

'Not like to go and see them when they are ill and unhappy!
Elfie, how can you?'

'Of course I don't! Grandpapa kisses me and makes me
half sick.'

'But he is so fond of you.'

'I wish he wasn't, then. Why, Babie, are you going to cry?
What's the matter?'

'It is very silly,' said Babie, winking hard to get rid of her
tears; 'but it does hurt me so to think of the good old gentleman caring more for you than anybody, and you not liking to
go near him.'

'I can't see what it matters to you,' said Elvira; 'I wish
you would go instead of me, if you are so fond of him.'

'He wouldn't care for me,' said Babie; 'I'm not his ain
lassie.'

'*His* lassie! I'm a lady,' exclaimed the señorita, with the
haughty Spanish turn of the neck peculiar to herself.

'That's not what I mean by a lady,' said Babie.

'What do you mean by it?' said Elvira, with a superior
air.

'One who never looks down on anybody,' said Babie thoughtfully.

'What nonsense!' rejoined the Elf; 'as if any lady could
like to hear grandpapa maunder, and Mary scold and scream at
the farm people, just like the old peahen.'

'Miss Ogilvie said poor Mary was overstrained with having
more to attend to than she could properly manage, and that
made her shrill.'

'I know it makes her very disagreeable; and so they all are.
I hate the place, and I don't see why I should go,' grumbled
Elvira.

'You will when you are older, and know what proper feeling
is,' said Miss Ogilvie, who had come within earshot of the last
words. 'Go and put on your hat; I have ordered the pony
carriage.'

'Shall I go, Miss Ogilvie?' asked Babie, as Elfie marched off
sullenly, since her governess never allowed herself to be disobeyed.

'I think I had better go, my dear; Elfie may be under more
restraint with me.'

'Please give old Mr. Gould and Mary and Kate my love, and
I will run and ask for some fruit for you to take to them,' said
Babie, her tender heart longing to make compensation.

Miss Ogilvie and her pouting companion were received by
a fashionable — nay, extra fashionable-looking person, whom

Mary and Kate Gould called Cousin Lisette, and the old farmer, Eliza Gould. While the old man in his chair in the sun in the hot little parlour caressed and asked feeble repetitions of questions of his impatient granddaughter, the lady explained that she had thrown up an excellent situation as instructress in a very high family to act in the same capacity to her motherless little cousins. She professed to be enchanted to meet Miss Ogilvie, and almost patronised.

'I know what the life is, Miss Ogilvie, and how one needs companionship to keep up one's spirits. Whenever you are left alone, and would drop me a line, I should be quite delighted to come and enliven you; or whenever you would like to come over here, there's no interruption by uncle; and he, poor old gentleman, is quite—quite *passé*. The children I can always dismiss. Regularity is my motto, of course, but I consider that an exception in favour of my own friends does no harm, and indeed it is no more than I have a right to expect, considering the sacrifices that I have made for them. Mary, child, don't cross your ankles; you don't see your cousin do that. Kate, you go and see what makes Betsy so long in bringing the tea. I rang long ago.'

'I will go and fetch it,' said Mary, an honest, but harassed-looking girl.

'Always in haste,' said Miss Gould, with an effort at good humour, which Miss Ogilvie direfully mistrusted. 'No, Mary, you must remain to entertain your cousin. What are servants for but to wait on us? She thinks nothing can be done without her, Miss Ogilvie, and I am forced to act repression sometimes.'

'Indeed we do not wish for any tea,' said Miss Ogilvie, seeing Elvira look as black as thunder; 'we have only just dined.'

'But Elfie will have some sweet-cake; Elfie likes auntie's sweet-cake, eh?' said the old man.

'No, thank you,' said Elfie glumly, though in fact she did care considerably for sweets, and was always buying bonbons.

'No cake! Or some strawberries—strawberries and cream,' said her grandfather. 'Mr. Allen always liked them. And where is Mr. Allen now, my dear?'

'Gone to Norway. It's the fifth time I've told him so,' muttered Elvira.

'And where is Mr. Robert? And Mr. Lucas?' he went on. 'Fine young gentlemen all of them; but Mr. Allen is the pleasant-spoken one. Ain't he coming down soon? He always looks in and says, "I don't forget your good cider, Mr. Gould,"' and there was a feeble chuckling laugh and old man's cough.

'Do let me go into the garden; I'm quite faint,' cried Elvira, jumping up.

It was true that the room was very close, rather medicinal,

and not improved by Miss Gould's perfumes ; but there was an alacrity about Elfie's movements, and a vehemence in the manner of her rejection of the said essences, which made her governess not think her case alarming, and she left her to the care of the young cousins, while trying to make up for her incivility by courteously listening to and answering her grand-father, and consuming the tea and sweet-cake.

When she went out to fetch her pupil to say good-bye, Miss Gould detained her on the way to obtain condolence on the 'dreadful trial that old uncle was,' and speak of her own great devotion to him and the children, and the sacrifices she had made. She said she had been at school with Elvira's poor mamma, 'a sweetly pretty girl, poor dear, but so indulged.'

And then she tried to extract confidences as to Mrs. Brown-low's intentions towards the child, in which of course she was baffled.

Elvira was found ranging among the strawberries, with Mary and Kate looking on somewhat dissatisfied.

Both the poor girls looked constrained and unhappy, and Miss Ogilvie wondered whether 'Cousin Lisette's' evident in-tentions of becoming a fixture would be for their good or the reverse.

'Are you better, my dear?' asked she affectionately.

'Yes, it was only the room,' said Elvira.

'You are a good deal there, are not you?' said Miss Ogilvie to Mary, who had the white flabby look of being kept in an un-wholesome atmosphere.

'Yes,' said Mary wistfully, 'but grandpapa does not like having me half so much as Elvira. He is always talking about her.'

'You had better come back to him now, Elfie,' said Miss Ogilvie.

'It makes me ill,' said Elvira, with her crossest look.

Her governess laid her hand on her shoulder, and told her in a few decided words, in the lowest possible voice, that she was not going away till she had taken a properly respectful and affectionate leave of her grandfather. Whereupon she knew further resistance was of no use, and going hastily to the door of the room, called out—

'Good-bye, then, grandpapa.'

'Ah! my little beauty, are you there?' he asked, in a tone of bewildered pleasure, holding out the one hand he could use.

Elvira was forced to let herself be held by it. She hoped to kiss his brow, and escape ; but the poor knotted fingers which had once been so strong would not let her go, and she had to endure many more kisses and caresses and blessings than her proud thoughtless nature could endure before she made her escape. And then 'Cousin Lisette' insisted on a kiss for the sake of her dear mamma ; and Elfie could only exhale her exasperation by rushing to the pony-carriage, avoiding all kisses to her young cousins, taking the driving seat, and whipping up the ponies more than their tender-hearted mistress would by any means have approved.

Miss Ogilvie abstained from either blame or argument, knowing that it would only make her worse ; and recollecting the old Undine theory, wondered whether the Elf would ever find her soul, and think with tender regret of the affection she was spurning.

The next day the travellers started, sleeping a couple of nights in Hyde Corner, for convenience of purchases and preparations.

They were to meet Mrs. Evelyn at the station ; but Janet, who foretold that she would be another Serene Highness, soured by having missed the family title, retarded their start till so late that there could be no introduction on the platform ; but seats had to be rushed for, while a servant took the tickets.

However, a tall, elderly, military-looking gentleman, with a great white moustache, was standing by the open door of a carriage.

'Miss Brownlow,' said he, handing them in—Babie first, next Janet, and then Elvira.

He then bowed to Miss Ogilvie, took his seat, handed in the appurtenances, received, showed, and pocketed the tickets, negotiated Janet's purchase of newspapers, and constituted himself altogether cavalier to the party.

Sir James Evelyn ! Janet had no turn for soldiers, and was not gratified ; but Elvira saw that her blue eyes and golden hair were producing the effect she knew how to trace ; so she was graciously pleased to accept *Punch*, and to smile a bewitching acceptance of the seat assigned to her opposite to the old General.

Barbara was opposite to Mrs. Evelyn, and next to Sydney, a girl a few months older than herself, but considerably taller and larger. Mother and daughter were a good deal alike, save that the girl was fresh, plump, and rosy, and the mother worn, with the red colouring burnt as it were into her thin cheeks. Yet both looked as if smiles were no strangers to their lips, though there were lines of anxiety and sorrow traced round Mrs. Evelyn's temples. Their voices were sweet and full, and the elder lady spoke with a tender intonation that inspired Babie with trustful content and affection, but caused Janet to pass a mental verdict of 'Sugared milk and water.'

She immersed herself in her *Pall Mall*, and left Babie to exchange scraps of intelligence from the brothers' letters, and compare notes on the journey.

By and by Mrs. Evelyn retired into her book, and the two little girls put their heads together over a newly-arrived acrostic, calling on Elfie to assist them.

'Do *you* like acrostics?' she said, peeping up through her long eyelashes at the old General.

'Oh, don't tease Uncle James,' hastily interposed Sydney, as yet inexperienced in the difference between the importunities

of a merely nice-looking niece and the blandishments of a
brilliant stranger.   Sir James said kindly—

'What, my dear?'

And when Elvira replied—

'Do help us to guess this.   What does man love most below?'
he put on a droll face, and answered—

'His pipe.'

'Oh, Uncle James, that's too bad,' cried Sydney.

'If Jock had made this acrostic, it might be pipe,' said
Babie; 'but this is Armine's.'

It was thereupon handed to the elders, who read, in a boyish
handwriting—

> Twins, parted from their rocky nest,
>   We run our wondrous race,
> And now in tumult, now at rest,
>   Flash back heaven's radiant face.
>
> 1. While both alike *this* name we bear,
>     And both like life we flow,
> 2. And near us nestle sweet and fair
>     What man most loves below.
>
> Alike it is our boasted claim
>   To nurse the precious juice
> 3. That maddened erst the Theban dame,
>     With streaming tresses loose.
>
> 4. The evening land is sought by one,
>     One rushes towards mid-day,
>   One to a vigil song has run,
>     One heard Red Freedom's lay.
>
> Tall castles, glorious battlefields
>   Graced *this* in ages past,
> But now its mighty power *that* yields
> 5.    To work my busy last.

'Is that your brother Armine's own? asked Sir James,
surprised.

'Oh yes,' said Janet with impressive carelessness, 'all my
brothers have a facility in stringing rhymes.'

'Not Bobus,' said Elvira.

'He does not think it worth while,' said Janet, again absorb-
ing herself in her paper, while the public united in guessing the
acrostic; and the only objection was raised by the exact
General, who would not allow that the 'Marseillaise' was sung
at the mouth of the Rhone, and defended Ino's sobriety.

Barbara and Sydney lived upon those acrostics in their
travelling bags till they reached Folkestone, and had grown
intimate over them.   Sir James looked after the luggage,
putting gently aside Janet's strong-minded attempt to watch
over it, and she only retained her own leathern travelling case,
where she carried her personals, and which, heavy as it was, she
never let out of her immediate charge.

They all sat on deck, for there was a fine smooth summer sea, and no one was deranged except the two maids, whom every one knew to be always disabled on a voyage.

Janet had not long been seated, and was only just getting immersed in her *Contemporary*, when she received a greeting which gratified her. It was from somewhat of a lion, the author of some startling poems and more startling essays much admired by Bobus, who had brought him to some evening parties of his mother's, not much to her delectation, since there were ugly stories as to his private character. These were ascribed by Bobus to pious malevolence, and Janet had accepted the explanation, and cultivated a bowing acquaintance.

Hyde Corner was too agreeable a haunt to be despised, and Janet owed her social successes more to her mother's attractions than her own. Conversation began by an inquiry after her brothers, whose adventures had figured in the papers, and it went on to Janet's own journey and prospects. Her companion was able to tell her much that she wanted to know about the university of Zurich, and its facilities for female study. He was a well-known advocate of woman's rights, and she scrupled not to tell him that she was inquiring on her own account. Many men would have been bored, and have only sought to free themselves from this learned lady, but the present lion was of the species that prefer roaring to an intelligent female audience, without the rough male argumentative interruption, and Janet thus made the voyage with the utmost satisfaction to herself.

Mrs. Evelyn asked Babie who her sister's friend was. The answer was, 'Do you know, Elfie? You know so many more gentlemen than I do.'

'No,' replied Elvira, 'I don't. He looks like the stupid sort of man.'

'What is the stupid sort of man?' asked the General, as she intended.

'Oh! that talks to Janet.'

'Is every one that talks to Janet stupid?'

'Of course,' said Elvira. 'They only go on about stupid things no better than lessons.'

Sir James laughed at her arch look, and shook his head at her, but then made a tour among the other passengers, leaving her pouting a little at his desertion. On his return, he sat down by his sister-in-law and mentioned a name, which made her start and glance an inquiry whether she heard aright. Then as he bent his head in affirmation, she asked, 'Is there anything to be done?'

'It is only for the crossing, and she is quite old enough to take care of herself.'

'And it is evidently an established acquaintance, for which I am not responsible,' murmured Mrs. Evelyn to herself.

She was in perplexity about these friends of her son's. Ever since Cecil had been at Eton, his beloved Brownlow had seemed to be his evil genius, whose influence none of his resolutions or promises could for a moment withstand. If she had acted on her own judgment, Cecil would never have returned to Eton, but his uncle disapproved of his removal, especially with the disgrace of the champagne supper unretrieved; and his penitent letter had moved her greatly. Trusting much to her elder son and to Dr. Medlicott, she had permitted the party to continue together, feeling that it might be life or death to that other fatherless boy in whom Duke was so much interested; and now she was going to judge for herself, and Sir James had undertaken to escort her, that they might together come to a decision whether the two friends were likely to be doing one another good or harm.

Mrs. Evelyn had lived chiefly in the country since her husband's death, and knew nothing of Mrs. Joseph Brownlow. So she looked with anxiety for indications of the tone of the family who had captivated not only Cecil, but Fordham, and seemed in a fair way of doing the same by Sydney. The two hats, brown and black, were almost locked together all the voyage, and indeed the feather of one once became entangled with the crape of the other, so that they had to be extricated from above. There was perhaps a little maternal anxiety at this absorption; but as Sydney was sure to pour out everything at night, her mother could let things take their course, and watch her delight in expanding, after being long shut up in a melancholy house without young companions.

Elvira had a tone of arch simplicity which, in such a pretty creature, was most engaging, and she was in high spirits with the pleasure of being with new people, away from her school-room and from England, neither of which she loved, so she chattered amiably and amusingly, entertained Mrs. Evelyn, and fascinated Sir James.

Janet and her companion were less complacently regarded. Certainly the girl (though less ancient-looking at twenty-one than at fourteen) had the air of one well used to independence, so that she was no great subject for responsibility; but she gave no favourable impression, and was at no pains to do so. When she rejoined the party, Mrs. Evelyn asked whether she had known that gentleman long.

'He is a friend of my brother Robert,' she answered. Shall I introduce you?'

Mrs. Evelyn declined in a quiet civil tone, that provoked a mental denunciation of her as strait-laced and uncharitable, and as soon as the gentleman returned to the neighbourhood, Janet again sought his company, let him escort her ashore, and only came back to the others in the refreshment-room, whither she brought a copy of a German periodical which he had lent her. With much satisfaction Mrs. Evelyn filled the railway carriage with her own party, so that there was no room for any

addition to their number. Nor indeed did they see any more
of their unwelcome fellow-traveller, since he was bound for the
Hotel du Louvre, and, to Janet's undisguised chagrin, rooms
were already engaged at the Hotel Castiglione.

They came too late for the *table d'hôte*, and partook of an
extemporised meal in their sitting-room immediately on their
arrival, as the start was to be early. Then it was that Janet
missed her bag, her precious bag! Delrio was sent all over the
house to make inquiries whether it had been taken to any other
person's room, but in vain. Mrs. Evelyn said she had last seen
it when they took their seats on board the steamer.

'Yes,' added Elvira, 'you left it there when you went to walk
up and down with that gentleman.'

'Then why did not you take care of it? I don't mean Elfie
—nobody expects her to be of any use; but you, Babie?'

'You never told me!' gasped Babie, aghast.

'You ought to have seen; but you never think of anything
but your own chatter.'

'It is a very inconvenient loss,' said Mrs. Evelyn kindly.
'Have you sent to the station?'

'I shall, as soon as I am satisfied that it is not here. I can
send out for the things I want for use; but there are books and
papers of importance, and my keys.'

'The key of mother's davenport?' cried Babie. 'Was it
there? O Janet, Janet!'

'You should have attended to it, then,' said Janet sharply.

Delrio knocked at the door with an account of her unsuccessful mission, and Sir James, little as the young lady deserved it,
concerned himself about sending to the station, and if the bag
were not forthcoming there, telegraphing to Boulogne the first
thing in the morning.

While Janet was writing particulars and volubly instructing
the commissionaire, Mrs. Evelyn saw Babie's eyes full of tears,
and her throat swelling with suppressed sobs. She held out an
arm and drew the child to her, saying kindly, 'I am sure you
would have taken care of the bag if you had been asked, my
dear.'

'It's not that, thank you,' said Babie, laying her head on the
kind shoulder, 'for I don't think it was my fault; but mother
will be so sorry for her key. It is the key of her davenport,
and father's picture is there, and grandmamma's, and the card
with all our hairs, and she will be so sorry.'

And Babie cried the natural tears of a tired child, whom
anything would overcome after her long absence from her
mother. Mrs. Evelyn saw how it was, and, as Delrio was
entirely occupied with the hue and cry, she herself took the
little girl away, and helped her to bed, tenderly soothing and
comforting her, and finding her various needments. Among
them were her 'little books,' but they could not be found, and
her eyes looked much too tired to use them, especially as the

loss again brought the ready moisture. 'My head feels so funny, I can't think of anything,' she said.

'Shall I do as I used when Sydney was little?' and Mrs. Evelyn knelt down with her, and said one or two short prayers.

Babie murmured her thanks, nestled up to her and kissed her, but added imploringly, 'My Psalm. Armie and I always say our Psalm at bed-time and think of each other. He did it out on the moraine.'

'Will it do if you lie down and I say it to you?'

There was another fond, grateful, nestling kiss, and some of the Psalms were gone through in the soft, full cadences of a voice that had gained unconscious pathos by having many times used them as a trustful lullaby to a weary sufferer.

If Babie heard the end, it was in the sweetness of sleep, and when Mrs. Evelyn left her, it was with far less judicial desire to inquire into the subject of that endless conversation which had lasted, with slight intermission, from London to Paris. She was not long left in ignorance, for no sooner had Sydney been assured that nothing ailed Barbara but fatigue, than she burst out, 'Mamma, she is the nicest girl I ever saw.'

'Do you like her better than Elvira?'

'Of course I do,' most emphatically. 'Mamma, she loves Sir Kenneth of the Leopard as much as I do.'

Mrs. Evelyn was satisfied. While Sir Kenneth of the Leopard remained the object of the young ladies' passion, there was not much fear of any nonsense that was not innocent and happy.

No news of the bag. Janet was disposed to go back herself or send Delrio, but Sir James declared this impossible; nor would the Evelyns consent to disturb the plan of the journey, and disappoint those who expected them at Engelberg on Saturday by waiting at Paris for tidings. Janet in vain told herself that she was not under their control, and tried to remain behind by herself with her maid. They had a quiet, high-bred, decisive way of taking things for granted, and arranging for her, and she found herself unable to resist; but whenever, in after times, she was unpleasantly reminded of her loss, she always charged it upon them.

Otherwise the journey was prosperous. Elfie was on the terms of a saucy pet with the General, and Babie's bright, gentle courtesy and unselfishness won Mrs. Evelyn's heart, while she and Sydney were as inseparable as ever.

In fact Sydney had been made free of Jotapata. That celebrated romance had been going on all these years with the elision of several generations; because though few members of the family were allowed to see their twenty-fifth year, it was impossible to squeeze them all into the crusading times; and besides, the reigning favourites must be treated to an adventure with Cœur de Lion.

Even thus abridged, it bade fair to last throughout the

journey, both the little maidens being sufficiently experienced
travellers to care little for the sights from the French railway,
and being only stimulated to talk and listen the more eagerly
when interrupted by such trifles as meals, companions, and calls
to look at objects far less interesting.

'Look, my dears ; we are coming to the mountains. There is
the first snowy head.'

'Yes, mamma,' but the hats were together again in the
corner.

'Come, Sydney, don't lose this wonderful winding valley.'

'I see, Uncle James. Beautiful !' popping back instantly
with, 'Go on, Babie, dear. How did Sir Gilbert get them out
of that horrid defile full of Turks ? It is true, you said.'

'True that Louis VII and Queen Eleanor got into that
dreadful mess. Armine found it in Sismondi, but nobody knew
who Sir Gilbert was except ourselves ; and we are quite sure
he was Sir Gilbert of the Ermine, the son of the brother who
thought it his duty to stay at home.'

'Sir Philibert ? Oh yes ! I know.'

'There are some verses about the Iconium Pass, written out
in our spotted book, but I can say some of them.'

'Oh, do !'

> '"The rock is steep, the gorge is deep,
>     Mount Joye St. Denys ;
> But King Louis bold his way doth hold,
>     Mount Joye St. Denys.
>
> " Ho, ho, the ravine is narrow, I ween,
>     Lah billah el billah, hurrah.
> The hills near and far the Frank's way do bar,
>     Lah billah el billah, hurrah."

It ought to be "Allah el Allah," but you know that really does
mean a holy name, and Armine thought we ought not to have
it. It was delightful making the ballad, for all the Christian
verses have "Mount Joye St. Denys" in the different lines, and
all the Turkish ones "Lah billah," till Sir Gilbert comes in, and
then his war-cry does instead—

> ' "On, on, ye Franks, hew down their ranks,
>     Up, merry men, for the Ermine !
> For Christian right 'gainst Pagan might,
>     Up, merry men, for the Ermine ! "

but one day Jock got hold of it, and wrote a parody on it.'

'Oh, what a shame ! Weren't you very angry ?'

'It was so funny, one could not help laughing.

> ' "Come on, old Turk, you'll find hot work—
>     Pop goes the weasel !
> They cut and run ; my eyes, what fun !—
>     Pop goes the weasel ! " '

'How could you bear it ? I won't hear a bit more. It is
dreadful.'

'Miss Ogilvie says if one likes a thing very much, parodies don't hurt one's love,' said Babie.

'But what did Sir Gilbert do?'

'He rode up to where Louis was standing with his back against a rock, and dismounted, saying "My liege——"'

'I thought he was an Englishman?'

'Oh, but you always called a king "my liege," whoever you were. "My liege," he said——'

'Look at that charming little church tower.'

'I see, thank you.'

'I see, Uncle James. No, thank you, I don't want to look out any more. I saw it. Well, Babie, "My liege——"'

'Never mind, James,' said Mrs. Evelyn, 'one can't be *more* than in Elysium.'

There were fewer conveniences for the siege on the last day of the journey, when railroads were no more; but something could be done on board the steamer in spite of importunities from those who thought it a duty to look at the shores of the Lake of Lucerne, and when arrival became imminent, happy anticipation inclined Barbara to a blissful silence. Mrs. Evelyn saw her great hazel eyes shining like stars, and began to prefer the transparent mask of that ardent little soul to the external beauty which made Elvira a continual study for an artist.


## CHAPTER XXIV

### THE ANGEL MOUNTAIN

'To your eager prayer, the Voice
    Makes awful answer, " Come to Me."
Once for all now seal your choice
    With Christ to tread the boisterous sea.'

                                        KEBLE.

THE Leukerbad section of the party had only three days' start of the others, for Jock was not released till after a whole month's course of the baths, and Armine's state fluctuated so much that the journey would not have been sooner possible.

It had been a trying time. While Dr Medlicott thought he could not rouse Mrs. Brownlow to the sense of the little fellow's precarious condition, deadly alarm lay couched in the bottom of her heart, only kept at bay by defiantly cheerful plans and sanguine talk.

Then Jock was depressed, and at his age (and, alas! at many others) being depressed means being cross, and very cross he was to his mother and his friend, and occasionally to his brother, who, in some moods, seemed to him merely a rival invalid and candidate for attention, and whom he now and then threatened with becoming as frightful a muff as Fordham. He missed Johnnie, too, and perhaps longed after Eton. He was

more savage to Cecil than to any one else, treating his best
attentions with growls, railings, and occasionally showers of
slippers, books, and cushions, but, strange as it sounds, the
friendship only seemed cemented by this treatment, and this
devoted slave evidently preferred being abused by Jock to
being made much of by any one else.

The regimen was very disagreeable to his English habits,
and the tedium of the place was great. His mother thought it
quite enough to account for his captiousness, and the doctor
said it was recovery, but no one guessed how much was due to the
good resolutions he had made on the moraine and ratified with
Cecil. To no one else had he spoken, but all the more for his
reserve did he feel himself bound by the sense of the shame and
dishonour of falling back from vows made in the time of
danger. No one else was aware of it, but John Lucas Brownlow was not of a character to treat a promise or a resolution
lightly. If he could have got out of his head the continual
echo of the two lines about the monastic intentions of a certain personage when sick, he would have been infinitely better
tempered.

For to poor Jock steadiness appeared renunciation of all
'jest and youthful jollity,' and religion seemed tedious endurance of what might be important, but, like everything important, was to him very wearisome and uninteresting. To him all
zest and pleasure in life seemed extinguished, and he would
have preferred leaving Eton, where he must change his habits
and amaze his associates. Indeed, he was between hoping and
fearing that all this would there seem folly. But then he would
break his word, the one thing that poor half-heathen Jock truly
cared about.

Meantime he was keeping it as best he knew how under the
circumstances, by minding his prayers more than he had ever
done before, trying to attend when part of the service was read
on Sundays, and endeavouring to follow the Evelyn sabbatical
code, but only succeeding in making himself more dreary and
savage on Sunday than on any other day.

By easy journeys they arrived at Engelberg early on a Friday
afternoon, and found pleasant rooms in the large hotel, looking
out in front on the grand old monastery, once the lord of half
the Canton, and in the rear upon pine-woods, leading up to a
snow-crowned summit. The delicious scent seemed to bring
invigoration in at the windows.

However, Jock and Armine were both tired enough to be
sent to bed, if not to sleep, immediately after the—as yet,
scantily-filled *table d'hôte*. The former was lying dreamily
listening to the evening bells of the monastery, when Cecil
came in, looking diffident and hesitating.

'I say, Jock,' he began, 'did you see that old clergyman at
the *table d'hôte*?'

'Was there one?'

'Yes ; and there is to be a Celebration on Sunday.'

'Oh ! Then Armine can have his wish.'

'Fordham has been getting the old cleric to talk to your mother about it.'

Armine was unconfirmed. The other two had been confirmed just before Easter, but on the great Sunday Jock had followed his brother Robert's example and turned away. He had recollected the omission on that terrible night, and when after a pause Cecil said, 'Do you mean to stay?' he answered rather snappishly, 'I suppose so.'

'I fancied,' said Cecil, with wistful hesitation, 'that if we were together it would be a kind of seal to——'

Jock actually forced back the words, 'Don't humbug,' which were not his own, but his ill-temper's, and managed to reply—

'Well, what?'

'Being brothers in arms,' replied Cecil, with shy earnestness that touched the better part of Jock, and he made a sound of full assent, letting Cecil, who had a turn for sentiment, squeeze his hand.

He lay with a thoughtful eye, trying to recall some of the good seed his tutor had tried to sow on a much-trodden wayside, very ready for the birds of the air. The outcome was—

'I say, Evelyn, have you any book of preparation? Mine is —I don't know where.'

Neither his mother, nor Reeves, nor, to do him justice, Cecil himself, would have made such an omission in his packing, and he was heartily glad to fetch his manual, feeling Jock's reformation his own security in the ways which he really preferred.

Poor Jock, who, whatever he was, was real in all his ways, and could not lead a double life, as his friend too often did, read and tried to fulfil the injunctions of the book, but only became more confused and unhappy than ever. Yet still he held on, in a blind sort of way, to his resolution. He had undertaken to be good, he meant therefore to communicate, and he believed he repented, and would lead a new life—if—if he could bear it.

His next confidence was—

'I say, Cecil, can you get me some writing things? We—at least I—ought to write and tell my tutor that I am sorry about that supper.'

'Well, he was rather a beast.'

'I think,' said Jock, who had the most capacity for seeing things from other people's point of view, 'we did enough to put him in a wax. It was more through me than any one else, and I shall write at once, and get it off my mind before to-morrow.'

'Very well. If you'll write, I'll sign,' said Cecil. 'Mother said I ought when I saw her in London, but she didn't order me. She said she left it to my proper feeling.'

'And you hadn't any?'

'I was going to stick by you,' said Cecil, rather sulkily, on which Jock rewarded him with something sounding like—

'What a donkey you can be!'

However, with many writhings and gruntings the letter was indited, and Jock was as much wearied out as if he had taken a long walk, so that his mother feared that Engelberg was going to disagree with him. He had not energy enough to go out in the evening of Saturday to meet the new arrivals, but stayed with Armine, who was in a state of restless joy and excitement, marvelling at him, and provoking him by this surprise as if it were censure.

With his forehead against the window, Armine watched and did his utmost to repress the eagerness that seemed to irritate his brother, and at last gave vent to an irrepressible hurrah.

'There they are! Cecil has got his sister! Oh! and there she is! Babie—holding on to mother, and that must be Mrs. Evelyn with Fordham—and there's Elf making up already to the doctor! Aren't you coming down, Jock?'

'Not I! I don't want to see you make a fool of yourself before everybody!—I say—you'll have to come upstairs again, you know! Shut the door, I say!' shouted Jock, as he found Armine deaf to all his expostulations, and then getting up, he banged it himself, and then shuffling back to the sofa, put his hands over his face and exclaimed, 'There! What an eternal brute I am!'

A few moments more and the door was open again, and Cecil, with his arm round his sister, thrust her forwards, exclaiming—

'Here he is, Syd.'

Jock had recovered his gentlemanly manners enough to shake hands courteously, as well as to receive and return Babie's kiss, when she and Armine staggered in together, reeling under their weight of delight. Janet kissed him too, and then, scanning both brothers, observed to her mother—

'I think Lucas is the more altered of the two.' In which sentiment Elvira seemed to agree, for she put her hands behind her and exclaimed—

'O Jock, you do look such a fright; I never knew how like Janet you were!'

'You are letting every one know what a spiteful little Elf *you* can be,' returned Janet indignantly. 'Can't you give poor Jock a kinder greeting?'

Whereupon the Elf put on a cunning look of innocence and said—

'I didn't know it was unkind to say he was like you, Janet.'

The Evelyn pair had gone—after this introduction of Jock and Sydney—to their own sitting-room, which opened out of that of the Brownlows, and the door was soon unclosed, for the two families meant to make up only one party. The two mothers seemed as if they had been friends of old standing, and Mrs. Evelyn was looking with delighted wonder at her elder son, who had gained much in flesh and in vigour ever since Dr.

Medlicott's last and most successful prescription of a more pressing subject of interest than his own cough.

She had an influence about her that repressed all discords in her presence, and the evening was a cheerful and happy one, leaving a soothing sense upon all.

Then came the awakening to the sounds of the monastery bells, and in due time the small English congregation assembled, and one at least was trying to force an attention that had freely wandered over before.

The preacher was the chance visitor, an elderly clergyman with silvery hair.  He spoke extempore from Job xxviii.

> ' Where shall wisdom be found ?
> And where is the place of understanding ?
> Man knoweth not the price thereof ;
> Neither is it found in the land of the living.
> The depth saith, It is not in me :
> And the sea saith, It is not with me.
> It cannot be gotten for gold,
> Neither shall silver be weighed for the price thereof.'

What he said was unlike any sermon the young people had heard before.  It began with a description of the alchemist's labours, seeking for ever for the one great arcanum, falling by the way upon numerous precious discoveries, yet never finding the one secret which would have rendered all common things capable of being made of priceless value.  He drew this quest into a parable of man's search for the One Great Good, the wisdom that is the one thing necessary to give weight, worth, and value to the life which, without it, is vanity of vanities. Many a choice gift of thought, of science, of philosophy, of beauty, of poetry, has been brought to light in its time by the seekers, but in vain.  All rang empty, hollow, and heartless, like sounding brass or tinkling cymbal, till the secret should be won.  And it is no unattainable secret.  It is the love of Christ that truly turneth all things into fine gold.  One who has attained that love has the true transmuting and transforming power of making life golden—golden in brightness, in purity, in value, so as to be 'a present for a mighty King.'

Then followed a description of the glory and worth of the true, noble, faithful manhood of a 'happy warrior,' ever going forward and carrying through achievements for the love of the Great Captain.  Each in turn—the protector of the weak, the redresser of wrong, the patriot, the warrior, the scholar, the philosopher, the parent, the wife, the sister, or the child, the healthful or the sick, whoever has that one constraining secret, the love of Christ—has his service even here, whether active or passive, veritably golden, the fruit unto holiness, the end everlasting life.

Perhaps it was the cluster of young faces that led the preacher thus to speak, and as he went on, he must have met the earnest

and responsive eyes that are sure to animate a speaker, and the
power and beauty of his words struck every one. To the
Evelyns it was a new and beautiful allegory on a familiar idea.
Janet was divided between discomfort at allusions reminding
her of her secret, and on criticisms of the description of alchemy.
Her mother's heart beat as if she were hearing an echo of her
husband's thoughts about his Magnum Bonum. Little Armine
was thrilled as, in the awe of drawing near to his first Communion, this golden thread of life was put into his hand. But
it was Jock to whom that discourse came like a beam of light
into a dark place. When upon the dreary vista of dull abnega-
tion, on which he had been dwelling for a month past, came this
vision of the beauty, activity, victory, and glory of true manhood, as something attainable, his whole soul swelled and
expanded with joyful enthusiasm. The future that he had
embraced as lead had become changed to gold! Thus the
whole ensuing service was to him a continuation of that blessed
hopeful dedication of himself and all his powers. It was as if
from being a monk he had become a Red Cross Knight of the
Hospital. Yet, after his soiled, spoiled, reckless boyhood, how
could that grand manhood be attained?

Later in the afternoon, when the denizens of the hotel had
gone their several ways, some to look and listen at Benediction
in the Convent church, some to climb through the pine-woods
to the Alp, some to saunter and rest among the nearer trees, the
clergyman, with his Greek Testament in his hand, was sitting
on a seat under one of the trees, enjoying the calm of one of his
few restful Sundays; when he heard a movement, and beheld
the pale thin lad, who still walked so lame, who had been so
silent at the *table d'hôte*, and whose dark eyes had looked up
with such intensity of interest, that he had more than once
spoken to them.

'You are tired,' said the clergyman, kindly making room for him.

'Thanks,' said the boy, mechanically moving forward, but
then pausing as he leant on his stick, and his eyes suddenly
dimmed with tears as he said, 'Oh, sir, if you would only tell
me how to begin——'

'Begin what?' said the old man, holding out his hand.

'To turn it to gold,' said Jock. 'Can I, after being the mad
fool I've been?'

They talked for more than an hour; even till Dr. Medlicott,
coming down from the Alp, laid his hand on Jock's shoulder,
and told him the evening chill was coming, and he must sit still
no longer. And when the boy looked up, the restless weary
distress of his face was gone.

Jock never saw that old clergyman again, nor heard of him,
unless it were his death that he read of in the paper six months
later. But he never heard the name of Engelberg without an
echo of the parting benediction, and feeling that to him it had
indeed been an Angel mountain.

This had been a happy day to several others. Cecil, after
ten minutes with his mother, which filled her with hope and
thankfulness, had gone to show his sister the charms of the
place, and Armine and Babie, on a sheltered seat, were free to
pour out their hearts to one another, ranging from the heights
of pure childish wisdom to its depths of blissful ignorance and
playful folly, as they talked over the past and the future.

Armine knew there was no chance of an immediate and
entire recovery for him, and this was a severe stroke to Babie,
who was quite unprepared. And as her face began to draw up
with tears near the surface, he hugged her close, and consolingly
whispered that now they would be together always, he should
not have to go away from his own dear Babie Bunting, and there
was a little kissing match, ending by Babie saying disconsolately,
'But you did like Eton so, and you were going to get the New-
castle and the Prince Consort's prize, and to be in the eleven
and all—and you were so sure of a high remove! Oh, dear!'
and she let her head drop on his shoulder, and was almost
crying again.

'Don't, don't, Babie! or you'll make me as bad again,' said
Armine. 'It does come over me now and then, and I wish I had
never known what it was to be strong and jolly, and to expect
to do all sorts of things.'

'I shall always be wishing it,' said Babie.

'No, you are not to cry! You would be more sorry if I was
dead, and not here at all, Babie; and you have got to thank
God for that.'

'I do—I have! I've done it ever since we got Johnnie's
dreadful letter. Oh yes, Armine, I'll try not to mind, for perhaps if we aren't thankful, I mayn't keep you at all,' said poor
Babie, with her arms round her treasure. 'But are you quite
sure, Armine? Couldn't Dr. Lucas get you quite well? You see
this Dr. Medlicott is very young,' added the small maiden
sapiently.

'Young doctors are all the go. Dr. Lucas said so when
mother wrote to ask if she had better bring me home for advice,'
said Armine. 'He knows all about Dr. Medlicott, and said he
was first-rate, and they've been writing to each other about me.
The doctor stethoscoped me all over, and then he did a map of
my lungs, Cecil said, to send in his letter.'

'Oh!' gasped Babie, 'didn't it frighten you?'

'I wanted to know, for I saw mother was in a way. She did
talk and whisk about so fast, and made such a fuss, that I
thought I must be much worse than I knew. So I told Dr.
Medlicott I wished he would tell me right out if I was going to
die, in time to see you, and then I shouldn't mind. So he said
not now, and he thought I should get over it in the end, but
that most likely I should have a long time, years perhaps, of
being very careful. And when I asked if I should be able to go
back to Eton, he said he hardly expected it; and that he believed

it was kinder to let me know at once than let me be straining and hoping on.'

'Was it?' said Babie.

'I thought not,' said Armine, 'when I shut my eyes, and the playing-fields and the trees and the river stood up before me. I thought if I could have hoped ever so little, it would have been nice. And then to think of never being able to run, or row, or stay out late, and always to be bothering about one's stockings and wraps, and making a miserable muff of oneself just to keep in a bit of uncomfortable life, and being a nuisance to everybody.'

Babie fairly shrieked and sobbed her protest that he could never be a nuisance to her or mother.

'You are Babie, and mother is mother, I know that; but it did seem such a long burthen and bore, and when—O Babie—don't you know——'

'How we always thought you would go on and be something great, and do something great, like Bishop Selwyn, or like that Mr. Denison that Miss Ogilvie has a book about,' said Babie. 'But you will get well and do it when you are a man, Armie! Didn't you think about it when you heard all about the golden life in the sermon to-day? I thought, "That's going to be Armie's life," and I looked at you, but you were looking down. Were you thinking how it was all spoilt, Armie, poor dear Armie? For perhaps it isn't.'

'No, I know nobody can spoil it but myself,' said Armine. 'And you know he said that one might make weakliness and sickness just as golden, by that great Love, as being up and doing. I was going to tell you, Babie, I was horridly wretched and dismal one day at Leukerbad when I thought mother and all were out of the way—gone out driving, I believe—and then Fordham came in. He had stayed in, I do believe, on purpose——'

'But, but,' said Babie, not so much impressed as her brother wished; 'isn't he rather a spoon? Johnnie said he ought to have been a girl.'

'I didn't think Johnnie was such a stupid,' said Armine. 'I only know he has been no end of a comfort to me, though he says he only wants to hinder me from getting like him.'

'Don't, then,' said Babie, 'though I don't understand. I thought you were so fond of him.'

'So *must* you be,' said Armine; 'I never got on with anybody so well. He knows just how it is! He says if God gives one such a life, He will help one to find out the way to make the best of it for oneself and other people, and to bear to see other people doing what one can't, and we are to help one another. O Babie! you must like Fordham!'

'I must if you do!' said Babie. 'But he is awfully old for a friend for you, Armie.'

'He is nineteen,' said Armine, 'but people get more and more

R

of the same age as they grow older. And he likes all our books, and more too, Babie. He had such a delicious book of French letters, that he lent me, with things in them that were just what I wanted. If we are to be abroad all the winter, he will get his mother to go wherever we do. Suppose we went to the Holy Land, Babie!'

'Oh! then we could find Jotapata! Oh no,' she added humbly, 'I promised Miss Ogilvie not to talk of Jotapata on a Sunday.'

'And going to the Holy Land only to look for it would be much the same thing,' said Armine. 'Besides, I expect it is up among the Druses, where one can't go.'

'Armie,' in the tone of a great confession, 'I've told Sydney all about it. Have you told Lord Fordham?'

'No,' said Armine, who was less exclusively devoted to the great romance. 'I wonder whether he would read it?'

'I've brought it. Nineteen copybooks and a dozen blank ones, though it was so hard to make Delrio pack them up.'

'Hurrah for the new ones! We did so want some for the *Traveller's Joy*, the paper at Leukerbad was so bad. You *should* hear the verses the doctor made on the mud baths. They are as stunning as *Fly Leaves*. Mr. Editor, I say,' as Lord Fordham's tall figure strode towards them, 'she has brought out a dozen clean copybooks. Isn't that a joy for the *Joy*?'

'Had you no other intentions for them?' said Fordham, detecting something of disappointment in Babie's face. 'You surely were not going to write exercises in them?'

'Oh no!' said Babie, 'only——'

'She can't mention it on Sunday,' said Armine, a little wickedly. 'It's a wonderful long story about the Crusaders.'

'And,' explained Babie, 'our governess said we—that is, I—thought of nothing else, and made the Lessons at church and everything else apply to it, so she made me resolve to say nothing about it on Sunday.'

'And she has brought out nineteen copybooks full of it,' added Armine.

'Yes,' said Babie, 'but the little speckled ones are very small, and have half the leaves torn out, and we used to write larger when we began. I think,' she added, with the humility of an aspirant contributor towards the editor of a popular magazine, 'if Lord Fordham would be so kind as to look at it, Armie thought it might do what people call, I believe, supplying the serial element of fiction, and I should be happy to copy it out for each number, if I write well enough.'

The word 'happy' was so genuine, and the speech so comical, that the editor had much ado to keep his countenance as he gave considerable hopes that the serial element should be thus supplied in the MS. magazine.

Meantime the two mothers were walking about and resting together, keeping their young people in some degree in view,

and discussing at first the subject most on their minds, their
sons' bodily health and the past danger, for which Caroline
found a deeply sympathetic listener, and one who took a hopeful view of Armine.

Mrs. Evelyn was indeed naturally disposed to augur well
whenever the complaint was not hereditary, and she was besides
in excellent spirits at the very visible progress of both her sons,
the one in physical, the other in moral health, and she could
not but attribute both to the companionship that she had been
so anxious to prevent. She had never seen Duke look so
well, nor seem so free from languor and indifference, since he
was a mere child, and all seemed due to his devotion to Armine;
while as to Cecil, he seemed to have a new spring of improvement, which he ascribed altogether to his friend.

'It is strange to me to hear this of my poor Jock,' said Caroline, 'always my pickle and scapegrace, though he is a dear
good-hearted boy. His uncle says it is that he wants a strong
hand, but don't you think an uncle's strong hand is much worse
than any mother's weakness?'

'Not than her weakness,' said Mrs. Evelyn. 'It is her love, I
think, that you mean. There are some boys with whom strong
hands are vain, but who will guide themselves for love, and *that*
we mothers are surely the ones to infuse.'

'My boys are affectionate enough, dear fellows,' said Caroline
proudly, forgetting her sore disappointment that neither Allen
nor Robert had chosen to come to her help.

'I did not only mean love of oneself,' said Mrs. Evelyn gently.
'I was thinking of the fine gold we heard of this morning. When
our boys once have found that secret, the chief of our work is
done.'

'Ah! and I never understood how to give them that,' said
Caroline. 'We have been all astray ever since their father
left us.'

'Do you know,' said Mrs. Evelyn, with a certain sweet shyness, 'I can't help thinking that your dear Lucas found that
gold among the stones of the moraine, and will help my poor
weak Cecil to keep a fast hold of it.'

Mrs. Evelyn's opinion was confirmed when a few days later
came the answer to Jock's letter to his tutor, pleasing and
touching both friends so much that each showed it to his
mother. Another important piece of intelligence came in a
letter from John to his cousin, namely, that the present Captain
of the house, with two or three more 'fellows,' were leaving Eton
at the midsummer holidays, and that his tutor had been talking
to him about becoming Captain.

Jock and Cecil greatly rejoiced, for the departing Captain
had been a youth whose incapacity for government had been
much better known to his subordinates than to his master, and
the other two had been the special tempters and evil geniuses
of the house, those who above all had set themselves to make

obedience and religion seem contemptible, and vice daring and manly.

'I should have hated the notion of being Captain,' wrote John, 'if those impracticable fellows had stayed on, and if I did not feel sure of you and Evelyn. You are such a fellow for getting hold of the others, but with you two at my back, I really think the house may get a different tone into it.'

'And every one told us what an excellent character it had,' said Mrs. Evelyn, when the letter, through a chain of strict confidence, came round to her, the boys little knowing how much it did to decide their continuance together, and at Eton. Sir James had never been willing that Cecil should be taken away, and he had become as sensible as any of the rest to the Brownlow charm.

That was a very happy time in the pine-woods and the Alp. The whole of the nineteen copybooks were actually read by Babie to Sydney and Armine ; and Lord Fordham, over his sketches, submitted to hear a good deal. He told his mother that the story was the most diverting thing he had ever heard, with its queer mixture of childish simplicity and borrowed romance, of natural poetry and of infantine absurdity, of extraordinary knowledge and equally comical ignorance, of originality and imitation, so that his great difficulty had been not to laugh in the wrong place, when Babie had tears in her eyes at the heights of pathos and sublimity, and Sydney was shedding them for company. It was funny to come to places where Armine's slightly superior age and knowledge of the world began to tell, and when he corrected and criticised, or laughed, with appeals to his elder friend. Babie was so perfectly good-humoured about the sacrifice of her pet passages, and even of her dozen copybooks, that the editor of the *Traveller's Joy* could not help encouraging the admission of 'Jotapata' into the magazine, in spite of the remonstrances of the rest of his public, who declared it was merely making the numbers a great deal heavier for postage, and all for nothing.

The magazine was well named, for it was a great resource. There were illustrations of all kinds, from Lord Fordham's careful water-colours, and Mrs. Brownlow's graceful figures or etchings, to the doctor's clever caricatures and grotesque outlines, and the contributions were equally miscellaneous. There were descriptions of scenery, fragmentary notes of history and science, records, more or less veracious or absurd, of personal adventures and conversations, and advertisements, such as—

*Stolen or strayed.*—A parasol, white above, black below, minus a ring, with an ivory loop handle, and one broken whalebone. Whoever will bring the same to the Señora Donna Elvira de Menella will be handsomely rewarded with a smile or a scowl, according to her mood.

*Lost.*—On the walk from the Alp, of inestimable value to the owner, and none to any one else, an Idea, one of the very few originated by the Honble. C. F. Evelyn.

Small wit went a good way and personalities were by no means prohibited, since the editor could be trusted to exercise a safe discretion in the riddles, acrostics, and anagrams deposited in the bag at his door ; and immense was the excitement when the numbers were produced, with a pleasing irregularity as to time, depending on when they became bulky enough to look respectable, and not too thick to be sewn up comfortably by the great Reeves, who did not mind turning his hand to anything when he saw his lordship so merry.

The only person who took no interest in the *Traveller's Joy* was Janet, who could not think how reasonable people could endure such nonsense. Her first affront had been taken at a most absurd description which Jock had illustrated by a fancy caricature of 'The Fox and the Crow,' 'Woman's Progress,' in which 'Mr. Hermann Dowsterswivel' was represented as haranguing by turns with her on the steamer, and, during her discourse, quietly secreting her bag. It was such wild fun that Lord Fordham never dreamt of its being an affront, nor perhaps would it have been, if Dr. Medlicott would have chopped logic, science, and philosophy with her in the way she thought her due from the only man who could be supposed to approach her in intellect. He, however, took to chaff. He *would* defend every popular error that she attacked, and with an acumen and ease that baffled her, even when she knew he was not in earnest, and made her feel like Thor, when the giant affected to take three blows with Miölner for three flaps of a rat's tail.

The magazine contained a series of notes on the nursery rhymes, where the 'Song of Sixpence' was proved to be a solar myth. The pocketful of rye was the yield of the earth, and the twenty-four blackbirds sang at sunrise while the king counted out the golden drops of the rain, and the queen ate the produce, while the maid's performance in the garden was, beyond all doubt, symbolic of the clouds suddenly broken in upon by the lightning !

Moreover the man of Thessaly was beautifully illustrated, blinding himself by jumping into the prickly bush of science, where each gooseberry was labelled with some pseudo study. When he *saw* his eyes were out, he stood wondrously gazing after them with his sockets while they returned a ludicrous stare from the points of thorns, like lobsters. In his final leap deeper into truth, he scratched them in again, and walked off, in a crown of laurels, triumphant.

Janet was none the less disposed to leap into her special gooseberry-bush ; and her importunity prevailed, so that before Dr. Medlicott returned to England he escorted her and her mother to Zurich. Then after full inquiries it was decided that she should have her will, and follow out her medical course of study, provided she could find a satisfactory person to board with.

She proposed, and her mother consented, that the two Miss

Rays should be her chaperons, of course with liberal payment.
Nita could carry on her studies in art, and made the plan
agreeable to Janet, while old Miss Ray's eyes, which had begun
to suffer from the copying, would have a rest, and Mrs. Brownlow had as much confidence in her as in any one Janet would
endure.

## CHAPTER XXV

### THE LAND OF AFTERNOON

'And all at once they sang, "Our island home
Is far beyond the wave, we will no longer roam." '

TENNYSON.

WE must pass over three more years and a half, and take up
the scene in the cloistered court of a Moorish house in Algeria,
adapted to European habits. The slender columns supporting
the horse-shoe arches were trained with crimson passion-
flower and bougainvillia, while orange and gardenia blossom
scented the air, and in the midst of a pavement of mosaic
marbles was a fountain, tinkling coolness to the air, which was
already heated enough to make it impossible to cross the court
without protection from the sunshine even at nine o'clock in
the morning.

Mrs. Brownlow had a black lace veil thrown over her head ;
and both she and the clergyman with her, in muslin-veiled hat,
had large white sunshades.

'Little did we think where we should meet again, and why,
Mr. Ogilvie. Do you feel as if you had got into *Tales of the
Alhambra*, or into the *Tempest* ?'

'I hope not to continue in the *Tempest*, at any rate, after this
Argier wedding.'

'Though no doubt you feel, as I do, that the world goes very
like a game at consequences. Who would ever have put
together *The Vicar of Benneton* and *Mary Ogilvie* in the amphitheatre at Constantina, eating lion-steaks. Consequence was,
an engaged ring. What the world said, "Who would have
thought it ?"'

'The world in my person should say you have been Mary's
kindest friend, Mrs. Brownlow. Little did I think, when I persuaded Charles Morgan to give himself six months' rest from
his parish by reading with Armine, that this was to be the end
of it, though I am sure there is not a man in the world to whom
I am so glad to give my sister.'

'And is it not delightful to see dear old Mary ? She looks
younger now than ever she did in her whole life, and has broken
out of all her primmy governessy crust. Oh ! it has been such
fun to watch it, so entirely unconscious as both of them were.
Mrs. Evelyn and I gloated over it together, all the more that
the children had not a suspicion. I don't think Babie and

Sydney realise any one being in love nearer our own times than *Waverley* at the very latest. They received the intelligence quite as a shock. Allen said, as if they had heard that the Greek lexicon was engaged to the French grammar! It will be their first bridesmaid experience.'

'Did they miss the wedding at Kenminster?'

'Yes; Jessie's old General chose to marry her in the depth of winter, when we could not think of going home. You know I have not been at Belforest for four years.'

'Four years! I suppose I knew, but I did not realise it.'

'Yes. You know there was the first summer, when, just as we got back to London after our Italian winter, poor Armie had such a dreadful attack on the lungs that Dr. Medlicott said he was in more danger than when he was at Schwarenbach; and, as soon as he could move, we had to take him to Bournemouth, to get strength for going to the Riviera. I can say now that I never did expect to bring him back again! But I am thankful to say he has been getting stronger ever since, and has scarcely had a real drawback.'

'Yes, I was astonished to see him looking so well. He would scarcely give a stranger the impression of being delicate.'

'They told me last summer in London that the damage to the lungs had been quite outgrown, and that he would only need moderate care for the future. Indeed, we should have stayed at home this year, but last summer twelvemonth there was a fever, and that set on foot a perquisition into our drains at Belforest, and it was satisfactorily proved that we ought by good rights to have been all dead of typhoid long ago. So we turned the workmen in, and they *could* not of course be got out again. And then Allen fell in love with parquet and tiles, and I was weak enough to think it a good opportunity when all the floors were up. But when a man of taste takes to originality, there's no end of it. Everything has had to be made on purpose, and certain little tiles five times over; for when they did come out the right shape, they were of a colour that Allen pronounced utter demoralisation. However, we are quite determined to get home this summer, and you and Mary must meet there, and show old Kenminster to Mr. Morgan. Ah! here she comes, and I shall leave you to enjoy this lucid interval of her while Mr. Morgan is doing his last lessons with the children.'

'How exactly like herself!' exclaimed Mr. Ogilvie, as Mrs. Brownlow vanished under one of the arches.

'Like! yes; but much more, much better,' said Mary eagerly.

'Ah, do you remember when you told me coming to her was an experiment, and you thought it might be better for the old friendship if you did not accept the situation?'

'You triumph at last, David; but I can confess now that for the first four years I held to that opinion, and felt that my poor Carey and I could have loved each other better if our relative situations had been different, and we had not seen so much of one another. My life used to seem to me half-unspoken remonstrance, half-truckling compliance, and nothing but our mutual loyalty to old times, and dear little Babie's affection, could have borne us through.'

'And her extraordinary sweetness and humility, Mary.'

'Yes, I allow that. Very few employers would have treated me as she did, knowing how I regretted much that went on in her household. However, when I met her at Pontresina, after the boys' terrible adventure in Switzerland, there was an indefinable change. I cannot tell whether it is owing to the constant being with such a boy as Armine while he was for more than a year between life and death, or whether it was from the influence of living with Mrs. Evelyn, but she has certainly ever since had the one thing that was wanting to all her sweetness and charm.'

'I never thought so!'

'No; but you were never a fair judge. I think she has owed unspeakably much to Mrs. Evelyn, who, so far as I can see, is the first person who, at any rate since the break-up of the original home, made conscientiousness, or indeed religion, appear winning to her, neither stiff, nor censorious, nor goody.'

'Is not this close combination of the two families rather odd?'

'I don't think it is. Poor Lord Fordham is very fond of Armine, and he hates the being driven abroad every winter so much, that the meeting Armine is the only pleasant ingredient. And it has been convenient for Sydney to join our schoolroom party. I was very glad also, that these last two summers there have been visits at Fordham. Staying there has given Mrs. Brownlow and the younger ones some insight into what the life at Belforest might be, but never has been; and they will not be kept out of it any longer.'

'Then they are going home!'

'After the London season.'

'Why, little Barbara is surely not coming out yet?'

'No; but Elvira is.'

'Ah! by the by, was I not told that I was to have two weddings?'

'Allen wished it, but the Elf won't hear of it. She says she has no notion of turning into a stupid old married woman before she has had any fun.'

'Does she care for him?'

'I don't think she is capable of caring for any one much. I don't know whether she may ever soften with age; but——'

'Say it, Mary—out with it.'

'I never saw such a heartless little butterfly! She did not care a rush when her good old grandfather died, and I don't believe she has one fraction more love for Mrs. Brownlow, or Allen, or anybody else. The best thing I can see is that she is too young to perceive the prudence of securing Allen , but perhaps that is only frivolity, and he, poor fellow, is so devoted to her that it is quite provoking to see how she trifles with and torments him.'

'Isn't it rather good for the great Mr. Brownlow? Not much besides has contradicted him, I should imagine.'

'His mother thinks that it is the perpetual restlessness in which Elvira keeps him that renders him so unsettled, and that if they were once married he would have some peace of mind, and be able to begin life in earnest. But to hurry on the marriage is such a fearful risk, with such a creature as that sprite, that she has persuaded him to wait, and let the child be satisfied by this season in London, that she may not think they are cheating her of her young lady life.'

'It is on the cards, I suppose, that she might see some one whom she preferred to him?'

'Which might, in some aspects of the matter, be the best thing possible ; but Mrs. Brownlow would have many conscientious scruples about the property, and Allen would be in utter despair.'

'Though, of course, all this would be far better than exposing that tropical-natured Spanish butterfly to meeting the subject of a grand passion too late,' said Mr. Ogilvie.

'Yes ; of course that must be in his mother's mind, though I don't suppose she expresses it even to herself. Miss Evelyn is coming out too, and is to be presented, which reconciles the younger ones to putting off all their schemes for working at Belforest, after the true Fordham and story-book fashion. Besides, Mrs. Brownlow always feels that she has a duty towards Elvira, even apart from Allen.'

'And what do you think of Allen? He seems very pleasant and gentlemanly.'

'That's just what he is! He has always been as agreeable and nice as possible all these eight years that I have been with them, and has treated me entirely as his mother's old friend. I can't help liking Allen very much, and wondering what he would have been if—if he had had to work for his living—or if Elvira had not been such a little tormenting goose—or if, all manner of ifs—indeed ; but they all resolve themselves into one question if there be much stuff in him !'

'If not, he is the only one of the family without, except, perhaps, Jock.'

'Oh ! if you saw Jock now, you would not doubt that there's plenty of substance in him ! He has been a very different person ever since his illness in Switzerland, as full of life and fun as ever, but thoroughly in earnest about doing right. He had an immense number of marks for the army examination, and seems by all accounts to be keeping up to regular work, now that it is more voluntary.'

'Is he not rather wasted on the Guards ?'

'Well, that was Sir James Evelyn's doing. They are glad
enough to have him there to look after his friend, Mr. Evelyn,
and it was one of the cases where the decision for life has to be
made before the youth is old enough to understand his full
capabilities. I expect Lucas, to give him his right name, will
do something distinguished yet, perhaps be a great General;
and I hope Sir James has interest enough to get him employment before he has eaten his heart out on drill and parade.
Now that Armine's health is coming round, I do leave Caroline
very happy about the younger half of her family.'

'And the elder half?'

'Well! I sometimes think that there must have been something defective in the management of that excellent doctor and
his mother, as if they had never taught the children proper
loyal respect for her! The three younger ones have it all right,
and the two elder sons are as fond of her as possible; but she
never had any authority over those three from the first. Only
Allen is too gentle and has too much good taste to show it;
while as to the other two, Bobus's contempt is of a kindly, filial,
petting description; Janet's, a nasty, defiant, overt disregard.'

'Impossible! They could not dare to despise her.'

'They do, for the very things that are best in her; and so
far I think the Evelyn intercourse has been unlucky, since they
ascribe her greater religiousness to what it suits their democratic
notions to scorn. Not that there is much to complain of in
Bobus's manner when we do see him. He only uses little stings
of satire, chiefly about Lord Fordham. I don't think he would
knowingly pain his mother if he could help it; and for that
reason there is a reserve between them.'

'He is eating his terms in the Temple, is he not? And
Janet? Is she studying medicine still? Does she mean to
practise?'

'I can't make out. She has only been with us twice in these
four years, once at Sorrento and once in London; but she has a
very active dislike to Mrs. Evelyn, and vexes her mother by
making no secret of it. I believe she is to take her degree at
Zurich this spring, but I don't think she means to practise.
She is too well off for the drudgery, but she is bent on making
researches of some kind, and I think I heard of some plan of her
going to attend lectures, to which her degree may admit her,
but I am not sure where. The two Miss Rays seem to be happy
to escort her anywhere, and that is a sort of comfort to Mrs.
Brownlow. Miss Ray keeps us informed of their comings and
goings, for Janet seldom deigns to write.'

'It is very strange that there should be such alienation, and
from such a mother.'

'The two characters are as unlike as can be, but I have
always thought there must be some cause that no one but Janet
herself could perhaps explain. I cannot help thinking that she
has some definite purpose in this study of medicine; for I do

not think it is for the sake either of the emancipation of women
or of general philanthropy. They must be an odd party. Miss
Ray attends to the household matters, mends the clothes, and
pays the bills. Nita sketches, reads at the libraries, and talks
at the *table d'hôte*, like a strong-minded woman, as she is ; and
Janet goes her own way. Bobus looked in on them once and
described them to us with great gusto.'

There Mary's face became illuminated as a step approached,
and a gentleman with grizzled hair and a thoughtful, gentle
face came out, and sat down on her other side.

He had been college tutor to her brother, though not much
older, and had stayed on at Oxford, till two years back he had
taken a much-neglected living. His health had broken down
under the severe work of organising, and he had accepted the
easy task of reading with Armine Brownlow for the winter in a
perfect climate, as a welcome mode of recruiting his strength.
He had truly recruited it in an unexpected manner, and was
about to take home with him one who would prove such a
helpmeet as would lighten all the troubles and difficulties that
had weighed so heavily on him, and remove some of them
entirely.

So he came out and testified to the remarkable ability and
zeal he had found in his pupil, and likewise to the spirit of
industry which had prevented the desultory life of travelling
and ill-health from having made him nearly so much behindhand as might have been expected. If he only had health to
work steadily for the next two years, he would be quite as well
prepared to matriculate at the university as all but the very
foremost scholars from the public schools. Mr. Morgan thought
his intellect equal to that of his brother Robert, who had taken
a double first-class, but of a finer order, being open to those
poetical instincts which went for nothing with the materialistic
Bobus.

Wherewith the friends fell into conversation more immediately interesting to themselves, while at the other end of the
court, sheltered by a great orange-tree, a committee of the
*Traveller's Joy* was held.

For that serial still survived, though it could never be called
a periodical, since it was an intermittent, and sometimes came
out very rapidly, sometimes with intervals of many months ;
but it was always sent to, and greatly relished by, the absent
members of the original party, at first at Eton, and later, two
in their barracks, and one at his college at Oxford, whither, to
his great satisfaction, he had gone by means of a well-won
scholarship, not at his aunt's expense.

Jotapata's lengthy romance had died a natural death in the
winter that had been spent between Egypt and Palestine. So
far from picking up ideas from it there, Babie, in the actual
sight of Mount Hermon's white crown, had begged not to be
put in mind of such nonsense, and had never recurred to it ; but

the wells of fancy had never been dried, and the young people
were happily putting together their bits of journal, their bits of
history, the description of the great amphitheatre, a poem of
Babie's on St. Louis's death, a spirited translation in Scott-like
metre of Armine's of the opening of the *Æneid*, also one from
the French, by Sydney, on Arab customs, and all Lord Fordham
had been able to collect about Hippo, also 'The Single Eye,' by
Allen, and 'Marco's Felucca,' by Armine and Babie in partner-
ship, and a fair proportion of drollery.

'There was a space left for the wedding, the greatest event
the *Traveller's Joy* had ever had on record,' said Sydney, as
she touched up the etching at the top of her paper, sitting on a
low stool by a low mother-of-pearl inlaid Eastern table.

'The greatest and the last,' chimed in Babie, as she worked
away at the lace she was finishing for the bride.

'I don't see why it should be the last of the poor old *Joy*,'
said Lord Fordham, sorting the MSS. which were scattered
round him on the ground.

'Well, somehow I feel as if we had come to the end of a
division of our lives,' returned Babie.

'Having done with swaddling bands, eh, Infanta?' said Lord
Fordham, while Armine hastily sketched in pen and ink, Babie,
with her hair flying and swaddling bands off, executing a war-
dance. She did not like it.

'For shame, Armine! Don't you know how dreadful it is to
lose dear Miss Ogilvie?'

'Of course, Babie,' said her brother, 'I didn't think you were
such a Babie as not to know that things go by contraries.'

'It is too tender a spot for irony, Armie,' said Lord Fordham.

'Well,' said Armine, 'I shall be obliged to do something out-
rageous presently, so look out!'

'Not really!' said Sydney.

'Yes, really,' said Babie, recovering; 'I see what he means.
He would like to do anything rather than sit and think that
this is the last time we shall all be together again in this
way.'

'I'm sure I don't see why we should not,' said Sydney. 'To
say nothing of meetings in England; Duke and Armine have
only to cough three times in October, and we should all go off
together again, and be as jolly as ever.'

'I don't mean to cough,' said Armine gravely, 'I've wasted
enough of my life already.'

'In our company, eh?' said Sydney, 'or are you to be taken
by contraries?'

'No,' said Armine. 'One has duties, and lotus-eating is
uncommonly nice, but it won't do to go on for ever. I wouldn't
have given in to it this winter if Allen hadn't *floored* us.'

'And then when you thought I had got a tutor and should
do some good with him,' chimed in Babie, 'he must needs go and
fall in love and spoil our Miss Ogilvie.'

The disgust with which she uttered the words was so comic that all the others burst out laughing.

And Fordham said—

'The Land of Afternoon was too strong for him. Shall you really pine much for Miss Ogilvie, Infanta?'

'I shall miss her dreadfully,' said Babie, 'and I think it is very stupid of her to leave mother, whom she has known all her life, and all of us, for a strange man she never saw till four months ago.'

'O Babie, you to be the author of a chivalrous romance!' said Fordham.

'I was young and silly then,' said the young lady, who was within a month of sixteen.

'And all your romances are to be henceforth without love,' said Armine.

'I think they would be much more sensible,' said Babie. 'Why do you all laugh so? Don't you see how stupid poor Allen always is? And it can even spoil Miss Ogilvie, and make her inattentive.'

'Poor Allen,' echoed one or two voices, in the same low tone, for as they peeped out beyond the orange-tree, Allen might be seen, extended on a many-coloured rug, in an exceedingly deplorable attitude.

'Oh yes,' said Sydney; 'but if one has such a—such a—such an object as *that*, one must expect to be stupid and miserable sometimes!'

'She must have been worrying him again,' said Babie.

'Oh yes, didn't you see?' said Armine. 'No, I remember you didn't go out riding early to-day.'

'No, I was finishing Miss Ogilvie's wedding lace.'

'Well, that French captain, that Elfie went on with at the commandant's ball, came riding up in full splendour, and trotted alongside of her, chattering away, she bowing and smiling, and playing off all her airs, and at last letting him give her a great white flower. Didn't you see it in her breast at breakfast? Poor Allen was looking as if he had eaten wormwood all the time when he was forced to fall back upon me, and I suppose he has been having it out with her and has got the worst of it.'

'Oh, it is that, is it?' said Lord Fordham; 'I thought she wanted to pique Allen, she was so *empressée* with me.'

'If people will be so foolish as to care for a pretty face,' sagely said Sydney.

'You know it is not only that,' said Babie; 'Allen is bound in honour to marry Elvira, to repair the great injustice. It is a great pity she will not marry him now at once, but I think she is afraid, because then, you know, she would get to have a soul, like Undine, and she doesn't want one yet.'

'That's a new view of the case,' said Lord Fordham in his peculiar lazy manner, 'and taken allegorically it may be the true one.'

'But one would like to have a soul,' said Sydney.

'I'm not sure,' said Babie, with a great look of awe. 'One would know it was best, but it would be very tremendous to feel all sorts of thoughts and perceptions swelling up in one.'

'If that is the soul,' said Armine.

'Which is the soul?' said Babie, 'our understanding, or our feelings, or both?'

'Both,' said Sydney undoubtingly.

'I don't know,' said Babie. 'Poor little Chico has double the heart of his mistress.'

'It is quite true,' said Fordham. 'We may share intellect with demons, but we do share what is called heart with animals.'

'I think good animals have a sort of soul,' observed Armine.

'And, of course, Elvira has a soul,' said Sydney, who was getting bewildered.

'Theologically speaking—yes,' said Armine, making them all laugh, 'and I suppose Undine hadn't. But it was sense and heart that was wanting.'

'The heart would bring the sense,' said Lord Fordham, 'and so we have come round to the Infanta's first assertion that the young lady shrinks from the awakening.'

'I'll tell you what she really does care for,' said Babie, 'and what I believe would waken up her soul much better than marrying poor Allen.'

The announcement was so extraordinary that they all turned their heads to listen.

'Her old black nurse at San Ildefonso,' said Babie. 'I believe going back there would do her all the good in the world.'

'There's something in that notion,' said Armine. 'She is always better-tempered in a hot country.'

'Yes,' added Babie, 'and you didn't see her when somebody advised our trying the West Indies for the winter. Her eyes gleamed, and she panted, and I didn't know what she was going to do. I told mother at night, but she said she was afraid of going there, because of the yellow fever, and that San Ildefonso had been made a coaling station by the Americans, so it would only disappoint her. But Elfie looked—I never saw any one look as she did—fit to kill some one when she found it was given up, and she did not get over it for ever so long.'

'Take care; here's an apparition,' said Armine, as a brilliant figure darted out in a Moorish dress, rich jacket, short full white tunic, full trousers tied at the ankles, coins pendulous on the brow, bracelets, anklets, and rows of pearls. It was a dress on which Elvira had set her heart in readiness for fancy balls, it had been procured with great difficulty and expense, and had just come home from the French *modiste*, who had adapted it to European wear.

Allen started up in admiration and delight. Even Mr. Morgan was roused to make an admiring inspection of the curious ornaments and devices; and Elvira, with her perfect features, rich complexion, dark blue eyes, Titian-coloured hair, fine figure, and Oriental air, formed a splendid study.

Lord Fordham begged her to stand while he sketched her; and Babie, with Sydney, was summoned to try on the bridesmaids' apparel.

The three girls—Elvira, Sydney, and Barbara—acted as bridesmaids the next day, when, in the English chapel, Mr. Ogilvie gave his sister to his old friend, to begin her new life as a clergyman's wife.

What could be called Elvira de Menella's character? Those who knew her best, such as Barbara Brownlow, would almost as soon have thought of ascribing a personal character to a cloud as to her. She smiled into glorious loveliness when the sun shone; she was gloomy and thunderous when displeased, and though she had a passionate temper, and could be violent, she had no fixed purpose, but drifted with the external impulse of the moment. She had not much mind or power of learning, and was entirely inattentive to anything intellectual, so that education had not been able at the utmost to do more than fit her to pass in the crowd, and could get no deeper; and what principles she had it was not easy to tell. Not that she did or said objectionable things, since she had outgrown her childish outbreaks; but she seemed to have no substance, and to be kept right by force of circumstances. She had the selfishness of any little child, and though she had never been known to be untruthful, this might be because there was not the slightest temptation to deceive. She was just as much the spoilt child, to all intents and purposes, as if she had been the heiress; perhaps more so, for Mrs. Brownlow had always been so remorseful for the usurpation as to be extra indulgent—lenient to her foibles, and lavish in gifts and pleasures, even inconveniencing herself for her fancies; whilst Allen had, from the first, treated her with the devotion of a lover. No stranger had ever supposed that she was not the equal in all respects of the rest of the family, nor had she realised it herself.

# CHAPTER XXVI

## MOONSHINE

'But still the lady shook her head,
And swore by yea and nay,
My whole was all that he had said,
And all that he could say.'

W. M. PRAED.

MRS. BROWNLOW had intended to go at once to London on her return to England, but the joint entreaties of Armine and Bar-

bara prevailed on her to give them one week at Belforest, now
in that early spring beauty in which they had first seen it.

How delightful the arrival was! Easter had been very late,
so it was the last week of the vacation, and dear old Friar John's
handsome face was the first thing they saw at the station, and
then his father's portly form, with a tall pretty creature on each
side of him, causing Babie to fall back with a cry of glad
amazement, 'Oh! Essie and Ellie! Such women!'

Then the train stopped, and there was a tumult of embracings
and welcomes, in the midst of which Jock appeared, having just
come by the down train.

'You'll all come to dinner this evening?' entreated Caroline.
'My love to Ellen. Tell her you must all of you come.'

It was a most delightsome barouche full that drove from the
station. Jock took the reins, and turned over coachman and
footman to the break, and, in defiance of dignity, his mother
herself sprang up beside him. The sky was blue, the hedges
were budding with pure light-green above, and resplendent with
rosy campion and white spangles of stitchwort below. Stars of
anemone, smiling bunches of primrose, and azure clouds of blue-
bell made the young hearts leap as at that first memorable sight.
Armine said he was ready to hurrah and throw up his hat, and
though Elvira declared that she saw nothing to be so delighted
about, they only laughed at her.

Gorgeous rhododendrons and gay azaleas rose in brilliant
masses nearer the house, beds of hyacinths and jonquils per-
fumed the air, judiciously-arranged parterres of gay little Van
Thol tulips and white daisies flashed on the eyes of the arriving
party, while the exquisite fresh green provoked comparisons
with parched Africa.

Bobus was standing on the steps to receive them, and when
they had crossed the hall, with due respect to its Roman mosaic
pavement, they found the Popinjay bowing, dancing, and
chattering for joy, and tea and coffee for parched throats in the
favourite Dresden set in the morning-room, the prettiest and
cosiest in the house.

'How nice it is! We are all together except Janet,' exclaimed
Babie.

'And Janet is coming to us in London,' said her mother.
'Did you see her on her way to Edinburgh, boys?'

'No,' said Jock. 'She never let us know she was there.'

'But I'll tell you an odd thing I have just found out,' said
Bobus. 'It seems she came down here on her way, unknown to
any one, got out at the Woodside station, and walked across
here. She told Brock that she wanted something out of the
drawers of her library-table, of which the key had been lost,
and desired him to send for Higg to break it open; but Brock
wouldn't hear of it. He said his Missus had left him in charge,
and he could not be answerable to her for having locks picked
without her authority—or leastways the Colonel's. He said

Miss Brownlow was in a way about it, and said as how it was
her own private drawer that no one had a right to keep her out
of, but he stood to his colours ; he said the house was Mrs.
Brownlow's, and under his care, and he would have no tamper-
ing with locks, except by her authority or the Colonel's.  He
even offered to send to Kenminster if she would write a note to
my uncle, but she said she had not time, and walked off again,
forbidding him to mention that she had been here.'

'Janet always was a queer fish !' said Jock.

'Poor Janet, I suppose she wanted some of her notes of
lectures,' said her mother.  'Brock's sound old house-dog instinct
must have been very inconvenient to her.  I must write and ask
what she wanted.'

'But she forbade him to mention it,' said Bobus.

'Of course that was only to avoid the fuss there would have
been if it had been known that she had been here without
coming to Kencroft.  By the by, I didn't tell Brock those good
people were coming to dinner.  How well the dear old Monk
looks, and how charming Essie and Ellie !  But I shall never
know them apart, now they are both the same size.'

'You won't feel that difficulty long,' said Bobus.  'There
really is no comparison between them.'

'Just the insipid English Mees,' said Elvira.  'You should
hear what the French think of the ordinary English girl !'

'So much the better,' said Bobus.  'No respectable English
girl would wish for a foreigner's insulting admiration.'

'Well done, Bobus !  I never heard such an old-fashioned
insular sentiment from you.  One would think it was your
namesake.  By the by, where is the great Rob ?'

'At Aldershot,' said Jock.  'I assure you he improves as
he grows older.  I had him to dine the other day at our mess,
and he cut a capital figure by judiciously holding his tongue
and looking such a fine fellow, that people were struck with
him.'

'There,' said Armine slyly, 'he has the seal of the Guards'
approval.'

Jock could afford to laugh at himself, for he was entirely
devoid of conceit, but he added good humouredly—

'Well, youngster, I can tell you it goes for something.  I
wasn't at all sure whether the ass mightn't get his head out of
the lion-skin.'

'Oh yes ! they are all lions and no asses in the Guards,' said
Babie ; whereupon Jock fell on her, and they had a playful
skirmish.

Nobody came to dinner but John and his two sisters.  It had
turned out that the horse had been too much worked to be
used again, and there was a fine moon, so that the three had
walked over together.  Esther and Eleanor Brownlow had
always been like twins, and were more than ever so now, when
both were at the same height of five feet eight ; both had the

same thick glossy dark-brown hair, done in the very same rich
coils, the same clearly-cut regular profiles, oval faces, and soft
carnation cheeks, with liquid brown eyes, under pencilled
arches. Caroline was in confusion how to distinguish them, and
trusted at first solely to the little coral charms which formed
Esther's ear-rings, but gradually she perceived that Esther was
less plump and more mobile than her sister—her colour was
more variable, and she seemed as timid as ever, while Eleanor
was developing the sturdy Friar texture. Their aunt had been
the means of sending them to a good school, and they had a
much more trained and less homely appearance than Jessie at
the same age, and seemed able to take their part in conversation
with their cousins, though Essie was manifestly afraid of her
aunt. They had always been fond of Barbara, and took eager
possession of her, while John's Oxford talk was welcome to all,
—and it was a joyous evening of interchange of travellers'
anecdotes and local and family news, but without any remarkable feature till the time came for the cousins to return. They
had absolutely implored not to be sent home in the carriage,
but to walk across the park in the moonlight ; and it was such
a lovely night that when Bobus and Jock took up their hats to
come with them, Babie begged to go too, and the same desire
strongly possessed her mother, above all when John said, 'Do
come, Mother Carey,' and 'rowed her in a plaidie.'

That youthful inclination to frolic had come on her, and she
only waited to assure herself that Armine did not partake of
her madness, but was wisely going to bed. Allen was holding out a scarf to Elvira, but she protested that she hated
moonlight, and that it was a sharp frost, and she went back to
the fire.

As they went down the steps in the dark shadow of the house,
John gave his aunt his arm, and she felt that he liked to have
her leaning on him, as they walked in the strong contrasts of
white light and dark shade in the moonshine, and pausing to
look at the wonderful snowy appearance of the white azaleas,
the sparkling of the fountain, and the stars struggling out in
the pearly sky ; but John soon grew silent, and after they had
passed the garden, said—

'Aunt Caroline, if you don't mind coming on a little way, I
want to ask you something.'

The name 'Aunt Caroline' alarmed her, but she professed her
readiness to hear.

'You have always been so kind to me' (still more alarming,
thought she) ; 'indeed,' he added, 'I may say I owe everything
to you, and I should like to know that you would not object to
my making medicine my profession.'

'My dear Johnnie !' in an odd, muffled voice.

'Had you rather not ?' he began.

'Oh no ! Oh no, no ! It is the very thing. Only when you
began I was so afraid you wanted to marry some dreadful person !'

You needn't be afraid of that. *Ars Medica* will be bride enough for me till I meet another Mother Carey, and that I shan't do in a hurry.'

'You silly fellow, you aren't practising the smoothness of tongue of the popular physician.'

'Don't you think I mean it?' said John, rather hurt.

'My dear boy, you must excuse me. It is not often one gets so many compliments in a breath, besides having one of the first wishes of one's heart granted.'

'Do you mean that you really wished this?'

'So much that I am saying, "Thank God!" in my heart all the time.'

'Well, my father and mother thought you might be wishing me to be a barrister, or something swell.'

'As if I could—as if I ever could be so glad of anything,' said she with rejoicing that surprised him. 'It is the only thing that could make up for none of my own boys taking that line. I can't tell you now how much depends on it, John; you will know some day. Tell me what put it into your head——'

He told her, as he had told his father nearly four years before, how the dim memory of his uncle had affected him, and how the bent had been decidedly given by his attendance on Jock, and his intercourse with Dr. Medlicott. At Oxford, he had availed himself of all opportunities, and had come out honourably in all examinations, including physical science, and he was now reading for his degree, meaning to go up for honours. His father, finding him steady to his purpose, had consented, and his mother endured, but still hoped his aunt would persuade him out of it. She was so far from any such intention, that a hint of the Magnum Bonum had very nearly been surprised out of her. For the first time since Belforest had come to her, did she feel in the course of carrying out her husband's injunctions; and she felt strengthened against that attack from Janet to which she looked forward with dread. She talked with John of his plans till they actually reached the lodge gate, and there found Jock, Babie, and Eleanor chattering merrily about fire-flies and glow-worms a little way behind, and Bobus and Esther paired together much farther back. When all had met at the gate and the parting good-nights had been spoken, Bobus became his mother's companion, and talked all the way home of his great satisfaction at her wandering time being apparently over, of his delight in her coming to settle at home at last, his warm attachment to the place, and his desire to cultivate the neighbouring borough with a view to representing it in Parliament, since Allen seemed to be devoid of ambition, and so much to hate the mud and dust of public life that he was not likely to plunge into it unless Elvira should wish for distinction. Then Bobus expatiated on the awkward connection the Goulds would be for Allen, stigmatising the amiable Lisette, who of course by this time had married poor George Gould, as

an obnoxious, presuming woman, whom it would be very difficult to keep in her right position. It was not a bad thing that
Elvira should have a taste of London society, to make her less
likely to fall under her influence.'

'That is not a danger I should have apprehended,' said
Caroline.

'The woman can fawn, and that is exactly what a haughty
being like Elvira likes. She is always pining for a homage she
does not get in the family.'

'Except from poor Allen.'

'Except from Allen, but that is a matter of course. He is a
slave to be flouted! Did you ever see a greater contrast than
that between her and our evening guests?'

'Esther and Eleanor? They have grown up into very sweet-
looking girls.'

'Not that there can be any comparison between them.
Essie has none of the ponderous Highness in her—only the
Serenity.'

'Yes, there is a very pleasant air of innocent candour about
their faces——'

'Just what it does a man good to look at. It is like going
out into the country on a spring morning. And there is very
real beauty too——'

'Yes, Kencroft monopolises all the good looks of the family.
What a fine fellow the dear old Friar has grown!'

'If you bring out those two girls this year, you will take the
shine out of all the other chaperons.'

'I wonder whether your aunt would like it.'

'She never made any objection to Jessie's going out with you.'

'No. I should like it very much; I wonder I had not thought
of it before, but I had hardly realised that Essie and Ellie were
older than Babie, but I remember now, they are eighteen and
seventeen.'

'It would be so good for you to have something human and
capable of a little consideration to go out with,' added Bobus,
'not to be tied to the tail of a will-of-the-wisp like that Elf—I
should not like that for you.'

'I am not much afraid,' said Caroline. 'You know I don't
stand in such awe of the little donna, and I shall have my
Guardsman to take care of me when we are too frivolous for
you. But it would be very nice to have those two girls, and
make it pleasanter for my Infanta, who will miss Sydney a good
deal.'

'I thought the Evelyns were to be in town.'

'Yes, but their house is at the other end of the park. What
are Jock and the Infanta looking at?'

Jock and Babie, who were on a good way in advance in very
happy and eager conversation, had come to a sudden stop, and
now turned round, exclaiming, 'Look, mother! Here's the
original Robin Goodfellow.'

And on the walk there was a most ludicrous shadow in the moonlight, a grotesque, dancing figure, with one long ear, and a hand held up in warning. It was of course the shadow of the Midas statue, which the boys had never permitted to be restored to its pristine state. One ear had, however, crumbled away, but in the shadow this gave the figure the air of cocking the other, in the most indescribably comical manner, and the whole four stood gazing and laughing at it. There was a certain threatening attitude about its hand, which, Jock said, looked as if the ghost of old Barnes had come to threaten them for the wasteful expenditure of his hoards. Or, as Babie said, it was more like the ghastly notion of Bertram Risingham in *Rokeby*, of some phantom of a murdered slave protecting those hoards.

'I don't wonder he threatens,' said Caroline. 'I always thought he meant that audacious trick to have forfeited the hoards.'

'Very lucky he was balked,' said Bobus, 'not only for us, but for human nature in general. Fancy how insufferable that Elf would have been if she had been dancing on gold and silver.'

'Take care!' muttered Jock, under his breath. 'There's her swain coming; I see his cigar.'

'And we really shall have it Sunday morning presently,' said his mother, 'and I shall get into as great a scrape as I did in the old days of the Folly.'

It was a happy Sunday morning. The Vicar of Woodside had much improved the church and services with as much assistance in the way of money as he chose to ask for from the lady of Belforest, though hitherto he had had nothing more; but he and his sister augured better things when the lady herself with her daughter and her two youngest sons came across the park in the freshness of the morning to the early Celebration. The sister came out with them and asked them to breakfast. Mrs. Brownlow would not desert Allen and Bobus, but she wished Armine to spare himself more walking. Moreover, Babie discovered that some desertion of teachers would render their aid at the Sunday school desirable on that morning.

This was at present her ideal of Sunday occupation, and she had gained a little fragmentary experience under Sydney's guidance at Fordham. So she was in a most engaging glow of shy delight, and the tidy little well-trained girls who were allotted to her did not diminish her satisfaction. To say that Armine's positive enjoyment was equal to hers would not be true, but he had intended all his life to be a clergyman, and he was resolved not to shrink from his first experience of the kind. The boys were too much impressed by the apparition of one of the young gentlemen from Belforest, to comport themselves ill, but they would probably not have answered his questions even had they been in their own language, and they stared at him in a stolid way, while he disadvantageously contrasted them with the little ready-tongued peasant boys of Italy. However, he had just found the touch of nature which made the world kin, and had made their eyes light up by telling them of a scene he had beheld in Palestine, illustrating the parable they had been repeating, when the change in the church bells was a signal for leaving off.

Very happy and full of plans were the two young things, much pleased with the clergyman and his sister, who were no less charmed with the little, bright, brown-faced, lustrous-eyed girl, with her eager yet diffident manner and winning vivacity, and with the slender, delicate, thoughtful lad, whose grave courtesy of demeanour sat so prettily upon him.

Though not to compare in numbers, size, or beauty with the Kencroft flock, the Belforest party ranged well in their seat at church, for Robert never failed to accompany his mother once a day, as a concession due from son to mother. It was far from satisfying her. Indeed there was a dull, heavy ache at her heart whenever she looked at him, for however he might endeavour to conform, like Marcus Aurelius sacrificing to the gods, there was always a certain half-patronising, half-criticising superciliousness about his countenance. Yet, if he came for love of her, still something might yet strike him and win his heart? Had her years of levity and indifference been fatal to him? was ever her question to herself as she knelt and prayed for him.

She felt encouraged when, at luncheon, she asked Jock to walk with her to Kenminster for the evening service, after looking in at Kencroft, Robert volunteered to be one of the party.

Caroline, however, did not think that he was made quite so welcome at Kencroft as his exertion deserved. Colonel and Mrs. Brownlow were sitting in the drawing-room with the blinds down, presumably indulging in a Sunday nap in the heat of the afternoon, for the Colonel shook himself in haste, and his wife's cap was a little less straight than suited her serene dignity, and though they kissed and welcomed the mother, they were rather short and dry towards Bobus. They said the children had gone out walking, whereupon the two lads said they would try to meet them, and strolled out again.

This left the field free for Caroline to propose the taking the two girls to London with her.

'I am sure,' said Ellen, 'you have always been very kind to the children. But indeed, Caroline, I did not think you would have encouraged it.'

'It?—I don't quite understand,' said Caroline, wondering whether Ellen had suddenly taken an evangelically serious turn.

'There!' said the Colonel, 'I told you she was not aware of it,' and on her imploring cry of inquiry, Ellen answered, 'Of this folly of Robert.'

'Bobus, do you mean?' she cried. 'Oh!' as conviction flashed on her, 'I never thought of *that*.'

'I am sure you did not,' said the Colonel kindly.

'But—but,' she said, bewildered, 'if—if you mean Esther—why did you send her over last night, and let him go out to find her now?'

'She is safe, reading to Mrs. Coffinkey,' said Ellen. 'I did not know Robert was at home, or I should not have let her come without me.'

'Esther is a very dear, sweet-looking girl,' said Caroline. 'If only she were any one else's daughter! Though that does not sound civil! But I know my dear husband had the strongest feeling about first cousins marrying.'

'Yes, I trusted to your knowing that,' said the Colonel. 'And I rely on you not to be weak nor to make the task harder to us. Remembering, too,' he added in a voice of sorrow and pity that made the words sound not unkind, 'that even without the relationship, we should feel that there were strong objections.'

'I know! My poor Bobus!' said Caroline sadly. 'That makes it such a pity she is his cousin. Otherwise she might do him so much good.'

'I have not much faith in good done in that manner,' said the Colonel.

Caroline thought him mistaken, but could not argue an abstract question, and came to the personal one. 'But how far has it gone? How do you know about it? I see now that I might have detected it in his tone, but one never knows, when one's children grow up.'

'The Colonel was obliged to tell him in the autumn that we did not approve of flirtations between cousins,' said Mrs. Brownlow.

'And he answered——?'

'That flirtation was the last thing he intended,' said the Colonel. 'On which I told him that I would have no nonsense.'

'Was that all?'

'Except that at Christmas he sent her, by way of card, a drawing that must have cost a large sum,' said the Colonel. 'We thought it better to let the child keep it without remark, for fear of putting things into her head; though I wrote and told him such expensive trumpery was folly that I was much tempted to forbid. So what does he do on Valentine's Day but send her a complete set of ornaments like little birds, in Genoa silver—exquisite things. Well, she was very good, dear child. We told her it was not nice or maidenly to take such valuable presents; and she was quite contented and happy when her mother gave her a ring of her own, and we have written to Jessie to send her some pretty things from India.'

'She said she did not care for anything that Ellie did not have too,' added her mother.

'Then you returned them?'

'Yes, and my young gentleman patronisingly replies that he

"appreciates my reluctance, and reserves them for a future time."'

'Just like Bobus!' said Caroline. 'He never gives up his purpose! But how about dear little Esther? Is she really untouched?'

'I hope so,' replied her mother. 'So far it has all been put upon propriety, and so on. I told her, now she was grown up and come home from school she must not run after her cousins as she used to do, and I have called her away sometimes when he has tried to get her alone. Last evening she told me, in a very simple way—like the child she is—that Robert would walk home with her in the moonlight, and hindered her when she tried to join the others, telling me she hoped I should not be angry with her. He seems to have talked to her about this London plan; but I told her on the spot it was impossible.'

'I am afraid it is!' sighed Caroline. 'Dear Essie! I will do my best to keep her peace from being ruffled, for I know you are quite right; but I can't help being sorry for my boy, and he is so determined that I don't think he will give up easily.'

'You may let him understand that nothing will ever make me consent,' returned the Colonel.

'I will, if he enters on it with me,' said Caroline; 'but I think it is advisable as long as possible to prevent it from taking a definite shape.'

Caroline was much better able now to hold her own with her brother and sister-in-law. Not only did her position and the obligations they were under give her weight, but her character had consolidated itself in these years, and she had much more force, and appearance of good sense. Besides, John was a weight in the family now, and his feeling for his aunt was not without effect. They talked of his prospects and of Jessie's marriage, over their early tea. The elders of the walking party came in with hands full of flowers, namely, the two Johns and Eleanor, but, ominously enough, Bobus was not there. He had been lost sight of soon after they had met.

Yes, and at that moment he was loitering at a safe distance from the door of the now invalid and half-blind Mrs. Coffinkey, to whom the Brownlow girls read by turns. She lived conveniently up a lane not much frequented. This was the colloquy which ensued when the tall, well-proportioned maiden, with her fresh, modest, happy face, tripped down the steps—

'So the Coffinkey is unlocked at last! Stern Proserpine relented!'

'Robert! You here?'

'You never used to call me Robert.'

'Mamma says it is time to leave off the other.'

'Perhaps she would like you to call me Mr. Robert Otway Brownlow.'

'Don't talk of mamma in that way.'

'I would do anything my queen tells me except command my tones when there is an attempt to stiffen her. She is not to be made into buckram.'

'Please, Robert,' as some one met and looked at them, 'let me walk on by myself.'

'What? Shall I be the means of getting you into trouble?'

'No, but I ought not——'

'The road is clear now, never mind. In town there are no gossips, that's one comfort. Mother Carey is propounding the plan now.'

'Oh, but we shall not go. Mamma told me so last night.'

'That was before Mother Carey had talked her over.'

'Do you think she will?'

'I am certain of it! You are a sort of child of Mother Carey's own, you know, and we can't do without you.'

'Mother would miss us so, just as we are getting useful.'

'Yes, but Ellie might stay.'

'Oh! we have never been parted. We *couldn't* be.'

'Indeed! Is there no one that could make up to you for Ellie?'

'No, indeed!' indignantly.

'Ah, Essie, you are too much of a child yet to understand the force of the love that——'

'Don't,' broke in Esther, 'that is just like people in novels; and mamma would not like it.'

'But if I feel ten times far more for you than "the people in novels" attempt to express?'

'Don't,' again cried Esther. 'It is Sunday.'

'And what of that, my most scriptural little queen?'

'It isn't a time to talk out of novels,' said Esther, quickening her pace, to reach the frequented road and throng of church-goers.

'I am not talking out of any novel that ever was written,' said Bobus seriously; but she was speeding on too fast to heed him, and started as he laid a hand on her arm.

'Stay, Essie; you must not rush on like a frightened fawn, or people will stare,' he said; and she slackened her pace, though she shook him off and went on through the numerous passengers on the footpath, with her pretty head held aloft with the stately grace of the startled pheasant, not choosing to seem to hear his attempts at addressing her, and taking refuge at last in the innermost recesses of the family seat at church, though it was full a quarter to five.

There the rest of the party found her, and as they did not find Bobus, they concluded that all was safe. However, when the two Johns were walking home with Mother Carey, Bobus joined them, and soon made his mother fall behind with him, asking her, 'I hope your eloquence prevailed.'

'Far from it, Bobus,' she said. 'In fact you have alarmed them.'

'H.S.H. doesn't improve with age,' he replied carelessly 'She never troubled herself about Jessie.'

'Perhaps no one gave her cause. My dear boy, I am very sorry for you,' and she laid her hand within his arm.

'Have they been baiting you? Poor little Mother Carey!' he said. 'Force of habit, you know, that's all. Never mind them.'

'Bobus, my dear, I must speak, and in earnest. I am afraid you may be going on so as to make yourself and—some one else unhappy, and you ought to know that your father was quite as determined as your uncle against marriages between first cousins.'

'My dear mother, it will be quite time to argue that point when the matter becomes imminent. I am not asking to marry any one before I am called to the bar, and it is very hard if we cannot, in the meantime, live as cousins.'

'Yes, but there must be no attempt to be "a little more than kin."'

'Less than kind comes in on the other side!' said Bobus, in his throat. 'I tell you the child *is* a child who has no soul apart from her sister, and there's no use in disturbing her till she has grown up to have a heart and a will of her own.'

'Then you promise to let her alone?'

'I pledge myself to nothing,' said Bobus in an impracticable voice. 'I only give warning that a commotion will do nobody any good.'

She knew he had not abandoned his intention, and she also knew she had no power to make him abandon it, so that all she could say was, 'As long as you make no move there will be no commotion, but I only repeat my assurance that neither your uncle nor I, acting in the person of your dear father, will ever consent.'

'To which I might reply, that most people end by doing that against which they have most protested. However, I am not going to stir in the matter for some time to come, and I advise no one else to do so.'


## CHAPTER XXVII

### BLUEBEARD'S CLOSET

'A moment then the volume spread,
And one short spell therein he read.'

SCOTT.

THE reality of John's intention to devote himself to medicine made Caroline anxious to look again at the terms of the trust on which she held the Magnum Bonum secret.

Moreover, she wanted some papers and accounts, and therefore on Monday morning, while getting up, she glanced towards the place where her davenport usually stood, and to her great surprise missed it. She asked Emma, who was dressing her, whether it had been moved, and found that her maid had been as much surprised as herself at its absence, and that the house-keeper had denied all knowledge of it.

'Other things is missing, ma'am,' said Emma; 'there's the key of the closet where your dresses hangs. I've hunted high and low for it, and nobody hasn't seen it.'

'Keys are easily lost,' said Caroline, 'but my davenport is very important. Perhaps in some cleaning it has been moved into one of the other rooms and forgotten there. I wish you would look. You know I had it before I came here.'

Not only did Emma look, but as soon as her mistress was ready to leave the room she went herself on a voyage of dis-covery, peeping first into the little dressing-room, where, seeing Babie at her morning prayers, she said nothing to disturb her, and then going on to look into some spare rooms beyond, where she thought it might have been disposed of, as being not smart enough for my lady's chamber. Coming back to her room she found, to her extreme amazement, the closet open, and Babie pushing the davenport out of it, with her cheeks crimson and a look of consternation at being detected.

'My dear child! The davenport there! Did you know it? How did it get there?'

'I put it,' said Barbara, evidently only forced to reply by sheer sincerity.

'You! And why?'

'I thought it safer,' mumbled Babie.

'And you knew where the key of the closet was?'

'Yes.'

'Where?'

'In my doll's bed, locked up in the baby-house.'

'This is most extraordinary. When did you do this?'

'Just before we came out to you at Leukerbad,' said Babie, each reply pumped out with great difficulty.

'Four years ago! It is a very odd thing. I suppose you had a panic, for you were too old then for playing monkey tricks.'

To which Babie made no answer, and the next minute her mother, who had become intent on the davenport, exclaimed, 'I suppose you haven't got the key of this in your doll's bed?'

'Don't you remember, mother,' said Barbara, 'you sent it home to Janet, and it was lost in her bag on the crossing?'

'Oh yes, I remember! And it is a Bramah lock, more's the pity. We must have the locksmith over from Kenminster to open it.'

The man was sent for, the davenport was opened, desk, drawers, and all. Caroline was once more in possession of her papers. She turned them over in haste, and saw no book of Magnum Bonum. Again, more carefully she looked. The white slate, where those precious last words had been written, was there, proving to her that her memory had not deceived her, but that she had really kept her treasure in that davenport.

Then, in her distress, she thought of Barbara's strange behaviour, went in quest of her, and calling her aside, asked her to tell her the real reason why she had thought fit to secure the davenport in the closet.

'Why,' asked Babie, her eyes growing large and shining, 'is anything missing?'

'Tell me first,' said Caroline, trembling.

Then Babie told how she had wakened and seen Janet with the desk part raised up, reading something, and how, when she lay watching and wondering, Janet had shut it up and gone away. 'And I did not feel comfortable about it, mother,' said Babie, 'so I thought I would lock up the davenport, so that nobody could get at it.'

'You did not see her take anything away?'

'No, I can't at all tell,' said Babie. 'Is anything gone?'

'A book I valued very much. Some memoranda of your father were in that desk, and I cannot find them now. You cannot tell, I suppose, whether she was reading letters or a book?'

'It was not letters,' said Babie, 'but I could not see whether it was print or manuscript. Mother, I think she must have taken it to read and could not put it back again, because I had hidden the davenport. Oh! I wish I hadn't, but I couldn't ask any one, it seemed such a wicked, dreadful fancy that she could meddle with your papers.'

'You acted to the best of your judgment, my dear,' said Caroline. 'I ought never to have let it out of my own keeping.'

'Do you think it was lost in the bag, mother?'

'I hope not. That would be worst of all!' said Caroline. 'I must ask Janet. Don't say anything about it, my dear. Let me think it over.'

When Caroline recollected Janet's attempt, as related by Robert, to break open her bureau, she had very little doubt that the book was there. It could not have been lost in the bag, for, as she remembered, reference had been made to it when Janet had extorted permission to go to Zurich, and she had warned her that even these studies would not be a qualification for the possession of the secret. Janet had then smiled triumphantly, and said she would make her change her mind yet; had looked, in fact, very much as Bobus did when he put aside her remonstrances. It was not the air of a person who had lost the records of the secret and was afraid to confess, though it was possible she might have them in her own keeping. Caroline longed to search the bureau, but however dishonourably Janet might have acted towards herself, she could not break into her private receptacles without warning So, after some consideration, she made Barbara drive her to the station, and send the following telegraphic message to Janet's address at Edinburgh :—

Come home at once. Father's memorandum book missing. Must be searched for.

All that day and the next the sons wondered what was amiss with their mother, she was so pensive, with starts of flightiness. Allen thought she was going to have an illness, and Bobus that it was a very strange and foolish way of taking his resistance, but all the time Armine was going about quite unperceiving, in a blissful state. The vicar's sister, a spirited, active, and very winning woman of thirty-five, had captivated him, as she did all the lads of the parish. He had been walking about with her, being introduced to all the needs of the parish, and his enthusiastic nature throwing itself into the cause of religion and beneficence, which was in truth his congenial element ; he was ready to undertake for himself and his mother whatever was wanted, without a word of solicitation, nay rather, the vicar, who thought it all far too good to be true, held him back.

And when he came in and poured out his narrative, he was, for the first time in his life, even petulant that his mother was too much preoccupied to confirm his promises, and angry when Allen laughed at his vehemence, and said he should beware of model parishes.

By dinner-time the next day Janet had actually arrived. She looked thin and sharp, her keen black eyes roamed about uneasily, and some indescribable change had passed over her. Her brothers told her study had not agreed with her, and she did not, as of old, answer tartly, but gave a stiff, mechanical smile, and all the evening talked in a woman-of-the-world manner, cleverly, agreeably, not putting out her prickles, but like a stranger, and as if on her guard.

Of course there was no speaking to her till bed-time, and Caroline at first felt as if she ought to let one night pass in peace under the home roof ; but she soon felt that to sleep would be impossible to herself, and she thought it would be equally so to her daughter without coming to an understanding. She yearned for some interchange of tenderness from that first-born child from whom she had been so long separated, and watched and listened for a step approaching her door ; till at last, when the maid was gone and no one came, she yielded to her impulse ; and in her white dressing-gown, with softly-slippered feet, she glided along the passage with a strange mixed feeling of maternal gladness that Janet was at home again, and of painful impatience to have the interview over.

She knocked at the door. There was no answer. She opened it. There was no one there, but the light on the terrace below, thrown from the windows of the lower room, was proof to her that Janet was in her sitting-room, and she began to descend the private stairs that led down to it. She was as light in figure and in step as ever, and her soft slippers made no noise as she went down. The door in the wainscot was open, and from the foot of the stairs she had a strange view. Janet's candle was on the chair behind her, in front of it lay half a dozen different keys, and she herself was kneeling before the bureau, trying one of the keys into the lock. It would not fit, and in turning to try another she first saw the white figure, and started violently at the first moment, then, as the trembling, pleading voice said, 'Janet,' she started to her feet, and cried out angrily—

'Am I to be always spied and dogged?'

'Hush, Janet,' said her mother in a voice of grave reproof. 'I simply came to speak to you about the distressing loss of what your father put in my charge.'

'And why should I know anything about it?' demanded Janet.

'You were the last person who had access to the davenport,' said her mother.

'This is that child Barbara's foolish nonsense,' muttered Janet to herself.

'Barbara has nothing to do with the fact that I sent you the key of the davenport where the book was. It is now missing. Janet, it is bitterly painful to me to say so, but your endeavours to open that bureau privately have brought suspicion upon you, and I must have it opened in my presence.'

'I have a full right to my own bureau.'

'Of course you have; but I had these notes left in my trust. It is my duty towards your father to use every means for their recovery.'

'You call it a duty to my father to shut up his discovery and keep it useless for the sake of a lot of boys who will never turn it to profit.'

'Of that I am judge. My present duty is to recover it. Your conduct is such as to excite suspicion, and I therefore cannot allow you to take anything out of that bureau except in my presence, till I have satisfied myself that his memoranda are not there. I would not search your drawers in your absence, and therefore telegraphed for you.'

'Thank you. Since you like to treat your daughter like a maidservant, you may go on and search my boxes,' said Janet sulkily.

'I beg your pardon, my poor child, if I am unjustly causing you this humiliation,' said Caroline humbly, as Janet sullenly flumped down into a chair without answering. She took up the keys that Janet had brought with her, and tried them one by one, where Janet had been using them. The fourth turned in the lock, and the drawer was open! 

'I will disarrange nothing unnecessarily,' said Caroline. 'Look for yourself.'

Janet would not, however, move hand, foot, or eye, while her mother put in her hand and took out what lay on the top. It was the Magnum Bonum. She held it to the light and was sure of it; but she had taken up an envelope at the same time, and her eye fell on the address as she was laying it down. It was to—'James Barnes, Esq.' And as her eye caught the pencilled word 'My Will,' a strange electric thrill went through her, as she exclaimed, 'What is this, Janet? How came it here?'

'Oh! take it if you like,' said Janet. 'I put it there to spare you worry; but if you *will* pursue your researches, you must take the consequences.'

Caroline, thus defied, still instinctively holding Magnum Bonum close to her, drew out the contents of the envelope, and caught in the broken handwriting of the old man, the words— 'Will and Testament—George Gould—Wakefield—Elvira de Menella—whole estate.' Then she saw signature, seal, witnesses —date, '24th April 1862.'

'What is this? Where did it come from?' she asked.

'I found it—in his table drawer; I saw it was not valid, so I kept it out of the way from consideration for you,' said Janet.

'How do you know it was not valid?'

'Oh—why—I didn't look much, or know much about it either,' said Janet in an alarmed voice. 'I was a mere child then, you know. I saw it was only scrawled on letter-paper, and I thought it was only a rough draft, which would just make you uncomfortable.'

'I hope you did, Janet. I hope you did not know what you were doing!'

'You don't mean that it has been executed?'

'Here are witnesses,' said Caroline—her eyes swam too much to see their names. 'It must be for better heads than ours to decide whether this is of force; but oh, Janet! if we have been robbing the orphan all these years!'

'The orphan has been quite as well off as if it had been all hers,' said Janet. 'Mother, just listen! Give me the keeping of my father's secret, and—even if we lose this place—it shall make up for all——'

'You do not know what you are talking of, Janet,' said Caroline, pushing back those ripples of white hair that crowned her brow, 'nor indeed I either! I only know you have spoken more kindly to me, and that you are under my own roof again. Kiss me, my child, and forgive me if I have pained you. You did not know what you did about the will, and as to this book, I *know* you meant to put it back again.'

'I did—I did, mother—if Barbara had not hidden the desk,' cried Janet. And as her mother kissed her, she laid her head on her shoulder, and wept and sobbed in an hysterical manner, such as Caroline had never seen in her before. Of course she was tired out by the long journey and the subsequent agitation; and Caroline soothed and caressed her, with the sole effect of

making her cry more piteously ; but she would not hear of her
mother staying to undress and put her to bed, gathered herself
up again as soon as she could, and when another kiss had been
exchanged at her bedroom door, Caroline heard it locked after
her.

Very little did Caroline sleep that night. If she lost consciousness at all, it was only to know that something strange
and 'wonderful was hanging over her. Sometimes she had a
sense that her trust and mission as a rich woman had been ill-
fulfilled, and therefore the opportunity was to be taken away ;
but more often there was a strange sense of relief from what she
was unfit for. She remembered that strange dream of her
children turning into statues of gold, and the Magnum Bonum
disenchanting them, and a fancy came over her that this might
yet be realised, a fancy to whose lulling effect she was indebted
for the sleep she enjoyed in the morning, which made her unusually late, but prevented her from looking as haggard as
Janet did, with eyelids swollen, as if she had cried a good deal
longer last night.

. The postbag was lying on the table, and directly after family
prayers (which she had for some years begun when at home),
Mrs. Brownlow beguiled her nervousness by opening it, and
distributing the letters.

The first she opened was such a startling one, that her head
seemed to reel, and she doubted whether the shock of last night
was confusing her senses.

MY DEAR MRS. BROWNLOW—What will you think of us now that
the full truth has burst on you ? Of me especially, to whom you en-
trusted your dear daughter. I never could have thought that Nita would
have lent herself to the transaction, and alas ! I let the two girls take
care of themselves more than was right. However, I can at least give you
the comfort of knowing that it was a perfectly legal marriage, for Nita
was one of the witnesses, and looked to all that——

Here Caroline could read no more. Sick and stunned, she
began to dispense her teacups, and even helped herself to some
of the food that was handed round, but her hand trembled so,
and she looked so white and bewildered, that Allen exclaimed—

'Mother, you are really ill. You should not have come
down.'

She could not bear the crowd and buzz of voices and all the
anxious eyes any longer. She pushed back her chair, and as
sons came hurrying round with offered arms, she took the
nearest, which was Jock's, let him take her to the morning-
room, and there assured him she was not ill, only she had had
a letter. She wanted nothing, only that he should go back, and
send her Janet. She tried once more to master the contents of
Miss Ray's letter, but she was too dizzy ; and when Janet came
in, she could only hold it out to her.

'Oh !' said Janet, 'poor old Maria has forestalled me. Yes, mother, it is what I meant to tell you, only I thought you could not bear a fresh shock last night.'

'Married ! O Janet ; why thus ?'

'Because we wished to avoid the gossip and conventionality. My uncle and aunt were to be avoided.'

'Let me hear at once who it is,' said Caroline, with the sharpness of misery.

'It is Professor Demetrius Hermann, a most able lecturer, whose course we have been following. I met him a year ago, at the *table d'hôte*, at Zurich, where he delivered a series of lectures on physiology on a new and original system. He is now going on with them in Scotland, where his wonderful acuteness and originality have produced an immense sensation, and I have no doubt that in his hands this discovery of my father's will receive its full development.'

There was no apology in her tone ; it was rather that of one who was defying censure ; and her mother could only gasp out—

'How long ?'

'Three weeks. When we heard you were returning, we thought it would save much trouble and difficulty to secure ourselves against contingencies, and profit by Scottish facilities.' Wherewith Janet handed her mother a certificate of her marriage, at Glasgow, before Jane Ray and another witness, and taking her wedding-ring from her purse, put it on, adding, 'When you see him, mother, you will be more than satisfied.'

'Where is he ?' interrupted Caroline.

'At the Railway Hotel, waiting till you are prepared to see him. He brought me down, but he is to give a lecture at Glasgow the day after to-morrow, so we can only remain one night.'

'O Janet—Janet, this is very fearful !'

At that moment, Johnnie strolled up to the window from the outside, and, as he greeted Janet with some surprise, he observed—

'There's a most extraordinary-looking foreign fellow loitering about out here. I warned him he was on private ground, and he made me a bow, as if I, not he, were the trespasser.'

On this Janet darted out at the window without another word, and John exclaiming in dismay—

'Mother Carey ! what is the matter ?'

She gasped out, 'O Johnnie ! she's married to him ! And the children don't know it. Send them in—Allen and Bobus, I mean—make haste ; I must prepare them. Take that letter, and let the others know.'

John saw the truest kindness was implicit obedience ; and Allen and Bobus instantly joined her, the latter asking what new tomfoolery Janet had brought home, Allen following with a cup of coffee.

T

Caroline's lips felt too dry to speak, and she held out the certificate.

It was received by Allen with the exclamation—

'By Jove!'

And by Bobus, with an odd, harsh laugh—

'I thought she would do something monstrous one of these days.'

'Did you ever hear of him, Bobus?' she found voice to say, after swallowing a mouthful of coffee.

'I fancy I have. Yes, I remember now; he was lecturing and vapouring about at Zurich; he is half Greek, I believe, and all charlatan. Well, Janet *has* been and gone and done for herself now, and no mistake.'

'But he is a professor,' pleaded Caroline. 'He must be of some university.'

'Don't make too sure,' said Allen. 'A professor may mean a writing master. Good heavens! what a connection.'

'It can't be so bad as that,' said Caroline. 'Remember, your sister is not foolish.'

'Flatter an ugly woman,' said Bobus, 'and it's a regular case of fox and crow.'

'Mercy! here they come!' cried Allen.

'Mother, do you go away! This is not work for you. Leave us to settle the rascal,' said Bobus.

'No, Bobus,' she said; 'this ought to be settled by me. Remember that, whatever the man may be, he is Janet's husband, and she is your sister.'

'Worse luck!' sighed Allen.

'And,' she added, 'he has to go away to-morrow, at latest,' a sentence which she knew would serve to pacify Allen.

They had crossed the parterre by this time, and were almost at the window.

It was Bobus who took the initiative, bowing formally as he spoke in German—

'Good morning, Herr Professor. You seem to have a turn for entering houses by irregular methods.'

The newcomer bowed with suavity saying, in excellent English—

'It is to your sister that in both senses I owe my entrance, and to the lady, your mother, that I owe my apology.'

And before Caroline well knew what was going on, he had one knee to the ground, and was kissing her hand.

'The tableau is incomplete, Janet,' said Bobus, whom Caroline heartily wished away. 'You ought to be on your knees beside him.'

'I have settled it with my mother already,' said Janet.

Both Caroline and her eldest son were relieved by the first glance at the man. He was small, and had much more of the Greek than of the German in his aspect, with neat little features, keen dark eyes, and no vulgarity in tone or appearance. His hands were delicate ; there was nothing of the 'greasy foreigner' about him, but rather an air of *finesse*, especially in his exquisitely-trimmed little moustache and pointed beard, and his voice and language were persuasive and fluent. It might have been worse, was the prominent feeling, as she hastily said—

'Stand up, Mr. Hermann ; I am not used to be spoken to in that manner.'

'Nor is it an ordinary occasion on which I address madame,' said her new son-in-law, rising. 'I am aware that I have transgressed many codes, but my anxiety to secure my treasure must plead for me ; and she assured me that she might trust to the goodness of the best of mothers.'

'There is such a thing as abusing such goodness,' said Bobus.

'Sir,' said Hermann, 'I understand that you have rights as eldest son, but I await my sentence from the lips of madame herself.'

'No, he is not the eldest,' interrupted Janet. 'This is Allen —Allen, you were always good-natured. Cannot you say one friendly word ?'

Something in the more childish, eager tone of Janet's address softened Allen, and he answered—

'It is for mother to decide on what terms we are to stand, Janet, and strange as all this has been, I have no desire to be at enmity.'

Caroline had by this time been able to recover herself, and spoke—

'Mr. Hermann can hardly expect a welcome in the family into which he has entered so unexpectedly, and—and without any knowledge of his antecedents. But what is done cannot be undone ; I don't want to be harsh and unforgiving. I should like to understand all about everything, and of course to be friends ; as to the rest, it must depend on how they go on, and a great deal besides.'

It was a lame and impotent conclusion, but it seemed to satisfy the gentleman, who clasped her hand and kissed it with fervour, wrung that of Allen, which was readily yielded, and would have done the same by that of Bobus if that youth had done more than accord very stiff cold tips.

Immediately after, John said at the door—

'Aunt Caroline, my father is here. Will you see him ?'

That was something to be got over at once, and she went to the Colonel, who was very kind and pitiful to her, and spared her the 'I told you so.' He did not even reproach her with being too lenient, in not having turned the pair at once out of her house ; indeed, he was wise enough to think the extremity of a quarrel ought to be avoided, but he undertook to make every inquiry into Mr. Demetrius Hermann's history, and observed that she should be very cautious in pledging herself as to what she would do for him, since she had, as he expressed it, the whip-hand of him, since Janet was totally dependent upon her.

'Oh! but, Robert, I forgot ; I don't know if there is anything for anybody,' she said, putting her hand to her forehead ; 'there's that other will ! Ah ! I see you think I don't know what I am saying, and my head is getting past understanding much, but I really did find the other will last night.'

'What other will ?'

'The one we always knew there must be, in favour of Elvira. This dreadful business put it out of my head ; the children don't know it yet, and I don't seem able to think or care.'

It was true ; severe nervous headache had brought her to the state in which she could do nothing but lie passively on her bed. The Colonel saw this, and bade her think of nothing for the present, and sent Barbara to take care of her.

She spent the rest of the day in the sort of *anéantissement* which that sort of headache often produces, and in the meantime everybody held *têtes-à-têtes*. The Colonel held his peace about the will not half crediting such a catastrophe, and thinking one matter at a time quite enough for his brain ; but he talked to the Professor, to Janet, to Allen, and to Bobus, and tried to come to a knowledge of the bridegroom's history, and to decide what course ought to be pursued, feeling as the good man always did and always would do, that he was, or ought to be, the supreme authority for his brother's widow and children.

Allen was quite placable, and ready to condone everything. He thought the Athenian Professor a very superior man, with excellent classical taste, by which it was plain that his mosaic pavement, his old china, and his pictures had met with rare appreciation. Moreover, the Professor knew how to converse, and could be brilliantly entertaining ; there was nothing to find fault with in his appearance ; and if Janet was satisfied, Allen was. He knew his uncle hated foreigners, but for his own part, he thought nothing so dull as English respectability.

For once the Colonel declared that Bobus had more sense ! Bobus had come to a tolerably clear comprehension of the matter, and his first impressions were confirmed by subsequent inquiries. Demetrius Hermann was the son of some lawyer of King Otho's court who had married a Greek lady. He had studied partly at Athens, partly at so many other universities, that Bobus thought it rather suspicious ; while his uncle, who held that a respectable degree *must* be either of Oxford or Cambridge, thought this fatal to his reputation. He had studied medicine at one time, but had broached some theory which the German faculty were too narrow to appreciate ; 'Which means,' quoth Bobus, 'either that he could not get a licence to practise, or else had it revoked.'

Then he had taken to lecturing. The professorship was obscure ; he said it was Athenian, and Bobus had no immediate means of finding out whether it were so or not, nor of analysing

the alphabet of letters that followed his name upon the advertisement of his lectures.

Apparently he was a clever lecturer, fluent and full of illustration, with an air of original theory that caught people's
attention. He knew his ground, and, where critically scientific
men were near to bring him to book, was cautious to keep
within the required bounds, but in the freer and less regulated
places he discoursed on new theories and strange systems connected with the mysteries of magnetism, and producing extraordinary and unexplained effects.

Robert and Jock were inclined to ascribe to some of these
arts the captivation of so clever a person as their sister, by
one whom they both viewed with repulsion as a mere ad-
venturer.

They had not the clue which their mother had to the history
of the matter, when the next day, though still far from well,
she had an interview with her daughter and the Athenian Professor before their return to Scotland.

He knew of the Magnum Bonum matter. It seemed that
Janet, as her knowledge increased, had become more sensible of
the difficulties in the pursuit, and being much attracted by his
graces and ability, had so put questions for her own enlighten-
ment as to reveal to him that she possessed a secret. To
cajole it from her, so far as she knew it, had been no greater
difficulty than it was to the fox to get the cheese from the
crow : and while to him she was the errant unprotected young
lady of large and tempting fortune, he could easily make himself appear to her the missing link in the pursuit. He could do
what as a woman she could not accomplish, and what her
brothers were not attempting.

In that conviction, nay, even expecting her mother to be
satisfied with his charms and his qualifications, she claimed
that he might at least read the MS. of the book, assuring her
mother that all she had intended the night before was to copy
out the essentials for him.

'To take the spirit and leave me the letter?' said Caroline.
'O Janet, would not that have been worse than carrying off
the book?'

'Well, mother, I maintain that I have a right to it,' said
Janet, 'and that there is no justice in withholding it.'

'Do you or your husband fulfil these conditions, Janet?' and
Caroline read from the white slate those words about the one
to whom the pursuit was intrusted being a sound religious
man, who would not seek it for his own advancement but for
the good of others.

Janet exultantly said that was just what Demetrius would
do. As to the being a sound religious man, her mother might
seek in vain for a man of real ability who held those old-
fashioned notions. They were very well in her father's time,
but what would Bobus say to them?

She evidently thought Demetrius would triumph in his private interview with her mother, but if Caroline had had any doubt before, that would have removed it. Janet honestly had a certain enthusiasm for science, beneficence, and the honour of the family, but the Professor besieged Mrs. Brownlow with his entreaties and promises just as if—she said to herself—she had been the widow of some quack doctor for whose secret he was bidding.

If she would only grant it to him and continue her allowance to Janet while he was pursuing it, then there would be no limit to the share he would give her when the returns came in. It was exceedingly hard to answer without absolutely insulting him, but she entrenched herself in the declaration that her husband's conditions required a full diploma and degree, and that till all her sons were grown up she had been forbidden to dispose of it otherwise. Very thankful she was that Armine was not seventeen, when a whole portfolio of testimonials in all sorts of languages were unfolded before her! Whatever she had ever said of Ellen's insular prejudices, she felt that she herself might deserve, for she viewed them all as utterly worthless compared with an honest English or Scottish degree. At any rate, she could not judge of their value, and they did not fulfil her conditions. She made him understand at last that she was absolutely impracticable, and that the only distant hope she would allow to be wrung from her by his coaxing, wheedling tones, soft as the honey of Hybla, was, that if none of her sons or nephews were in the way of fulfilling the conditions, and he could bring her satisfactory English certificates, she might consider the matter, but she made no promises.

Then he most politely represented the need of a maintenance while he was thus qualifying himself. Janet had evidently not told him about the will, and Caroline only said that from a recent discovery she thought her own tenure of the property very insecure, and she could undertake nothing for the future. She would let him know. However, she gave him a cheque for £100 for the present, knowing that she could make it up from the money of her own which she had been accumulating for Elvira's portion.

Then Janet came in to take leave. Mr. Hermann described what the excellent and gracious lady had granted to him, and he made it sound so well, and his wife seemed so confident and triumphant, that her mother feared she had allowed more to be inferred than she intended, and tried to explain that all depended on the fulfilment of the conditions of which Janet at least was perfectly aware. She was overwhelmed, however, with his gratitude and Janet's assurances, and they went away, leaving her with a hand much kissed by him, and the fondest, most lingering embrace she had ever had from Janet. Then she was free to lie still, abandoned to fears for her daughter's future and repentance for her own careless past, and, above all, crushed by the ache that would let her really feel little but pain and oppression.

## CHAPTER XXVIII

### THE TURN OF THE WHEEL

'Is there, for honest poverty,
    That hangs his head and a' that,
The coward slave, we pass him by,
    A man's a man for a' that.'

BURNS.

THINKING and acting were alike impossible to Caroline for the remainder of the day when her daughter left her, but night brought power of reflection, as she began to look forward to the new day, and its burthen.

Her headache was better, but she let Barbara again go down to breakfast without her, feeling that she could not face her sons at once, and that she needed another study of the document before she could trust herself with the communication. She felt herself too in need of time to pray for right judgment and steadfast purpose, and that the change might so work with her sons that it might be a blessing, not a curse. Could it be for nothing that the finding of Magnum Bonum had wrought the undoing of this wrong? That thought, and the impulse of self-bracing, made her breakfast well on the dainty little meal sent up to her by the Infanta, and look so much refreshed that the damsel exclaimed—

'You are much better, mother! You will be able to see Jock before he goes——'

'Fetch them all, Babie; I have something to tell you——'

'Writs issued for a domestic parliament,' said Allen, presently entering. 'To vote for the grant to the Princess Royal on her marriage? Do it handsomely, I say, the Athenian is better than might be expected, and will become prosperity better than adversity.'

'Being capable of taking others in besides Janet,' said the opposition in the person of Bobus. 'He seemed so well satisfied with the Gracious Lady house-mother that I am afraid she has been making him too many promises.'

'That was impossible. It was not about Janet that I sent for you, boys. It was to think what we are to do ourselves. You know I always thought there must be another will. Look there!'

She laid it on the table, and the young men stood gazing as if it were a venomous reptile which each hesitated to touch.

'Is it legal, Bobus?' she presently asked.

'It looks—rather so——' he said in an odd, stunned voice.

'Elvira, by all that's lucky!' exclaimed Jock. 'Well done, Allen, you are still the Lady Clare!'

'Not till she is of age,' said Allen, rather gloomily.

'Pity you didn't marry her at Algiers,' said Jock.

'Where did this come from?' said Bobus, who had been examining it intently.

'Out of the old bureau.'

'Mother!' cried out Barbara, in a tone of horror, which perhaps was a revelation to Bobus, for he exclaimed—

'You don't mean that Janet had had it, and brought it out to threaten you?'

'Oh no, no! it was not so dreadful. She found it long ago, but did not think it valid, and only kept it out of sight because she thought it would make me unhappy.'

'It is a pity she did not go a step farther,' observed Bobus. 'Why did she produce it now?'

'I found it. Boys, you must know the whole truth, and consider how best to screen your sister. Remember she was very young, and fancied a thing on a common sheet of paper, and shut up in an unfastened table drawer, could not be of force, and that she was doing no harm.' Then she told of her loss and recovery of what she called some medical memoranda of their father, which she knew Janet wanted, concluding—'It will surely be enough to say I found it in his old bureau.'

'That will hardly go down with Wakefield,' said Bobus; 'but as I see he stands here as trustee for that wretched child, as well as being yours, there is no fear but that he will be conformable. Shall I take it up and show it to him at once, so that if by any happy chance this should turn out waste paper, no one may get on the scent?'

'Your uncle! I was so mazed and stupefied yesterday that I don't know whether I told him, and if I did, I don't think he believed me.'

'Here he comes,' said Barbara, as the wheels of his dog-cart were heard below the window.

'Ask him to come up. It will be a terrible blow to him. This place has been as much to him as to any of us, if not more.'

'Mother, how brave you are!' cried Jock.

'I have known it longer than you have, my dear. Besides, the mere loss is nothing compared with that which led to it. The worst of it is the overthrow of all your prospects, my dear fellow.'

'Oh,' said Jock brightly, 'it only means that we have something and somebody to work for now;' and he threw his arms round her waist and kissed her.

'Oh! my dear, dear boy, don't! Don't upset me, or your uncle will think it is about this.'

'And don't, for Heaven's sake, talk as if it were all up with us,' cried Bobus.

By this time the Colonel's ponderous tread was near, and Caroline met him with an apology for giving him the trouble of the ascent, but said that she had wanted to see him in private.

'Is this in private?' asked the Colonel, looking at the five young people.

'Yes.  They have a right to know all.  Here it is, Robert.'

He sat down, deliberately put on his spectacles, took the will, read it once, and groaned, read it twice, and groaned more deeply, and then said—

'My poor dear sister!  This is a bad business!  a severe reverse!  a very severe reverse!'

'He has hit on his catch-word,' thought Caroline, and Jock's arm still round her gave a little pressure, as if the thought had occurred to him.  The moment of amusement gave a cheerfulness to her voice as she said—

'We have been doing sad injustice all this time; that is the worst of it.  For the rest, we shall be no worse off than we were before.'

'It will be in Allen's power to make up to you a good deal.  That is a fortunate arrangement, but I am afraid it cannot take place till the girl is of age.'

'You are all in such haste,' said Bobus.  'It would take a good deal to make me accept such an informal scrap as this.  No doubt one could drive a coach and horses through it.'

'That would not lessen the injustice,' said his mother.

'Could there not be a compromise?' said Allen.

'That is nonsense,' said his uncle..  'Either *this* will stand, or *that*, and I am afraid this is the later.  18th April.  Was that the time of that absurd practical joke of yours?'

'Too true,' said Allen.  'You recollect the old brute said I should remember it.'

'Witnesses——? There's Gomez, the servant who was drowned on his way out after his dismissal—Elizabeth Brook—is it— servant.—Who is to find her out?'

'Richards may know.'

'It is not our business to hunt up the witnesses.  That's the look-out of the other party,' said Bobus impatiently.

'You don't suppose I mean to contest it?' said his mother. 'It is bad enough to go on as we have been doing these eight years.  I only want to know what is right and truth, and if this be a real will.'

'Where did it come from?' asked the Colonel, coming to the critical question.  'Did you say you found it yourself, Caroline?'

'Yes.'

'Where?'

'In the old bureau.'

'What! the one that stood in his study?  You don't say so! I saw Wakefield turn the whole thing out, and look for any secret drawer before I would take any steps; I could have sworn that not the thickness of that sheet of paper escaped us. I should like, if only out of curiosity, to see where it was.'

'Just as I said, mother,' said Bobus ; 'there's no use in trying to blink it to any one who knows the circumstances.'

'You do not insinuate that there was any foul play !' said his uncle hotly.

'I don't know what else it can be called,' said Caroline faintly , 'but please, Robert, and all the rest, don't expose her. Poor Janet found the thing in the back of the bedside table-drawer, fancied it a mere rough draft, and, child-like, put it out of sight in the bureau, where I lighted on it in looking for something else. Surely there is no need to mention her ?'

'Not if you do not contest the will,' replied the Colonel, who looked thunderstruck ; 'but if you did, it must all come out to exonerate us, the executors, from shameful carelessness. Well, we shall see what Wakefield says ! A severe reverse ! a very severe reverse !'

When he found that Bobus meant to go in search of the lawyer that afternoon, he decided on accompanying him. And with a truly amazing burst of intuition, he even suggested carrying off Elvira to spend the day with Essie and Ellie, and even that an invitation might arise to stay all night, or as long as the first suspense lasted. Then muttering to himself, 'A severe reverse—a most severe reverse !' he took his leave. Caroline went downstairs with him, as thinking she could the most naturally administer the invitation to Elvira, and the two eldest sons proceeded to make arrangements for the time of meeting and the journey.

'A severe reverse !' said Jock, finding himself alone with the younger ones. 'When one has a bitter draught, it is at least a consolation to have labelled it right.'

'Shall we be very poor, Jock ?' asked Barbara.

'I don't know what we were called before,' he said ; 'but from what I remember, I fancy we had about what I have been using for my private delectation. Just enough for my mother and you to be jolly upon.'

'That's all you think of !' said Armine.

'All that a man need think of,' said Jock ; 'as long as mother and Babie are comfortable, we can do for ourselves very well.'

'Ourselves !' said Armine bitterly. 'And how about this wretched place that we have neglected shamefully all these years ?'

'Armine !' cried Jock indignantly. 'Why, you are talking of mother !'

'Mother says so herself.'

'You went on raging about it ; and, just like her, she did not defend herself. I am sure she has given away loads of money.'

'But see what is wanting ! The curate, and the school chapel, and the cottages ; and if the school is not enlarged, they will have a school board. And what am I to say to Miss Parsons? I promised to bring mother's answer about the curate this afternoon at latest.'

'If she has the sense of a wren, she must know that a cataclysm like Janet's may account for a few trifling omissions.'

'That's true,' said Babie. 'She can't expect it. Do you know, I am rather sorry we are not poorer? I hoped we should have to live in a very small way, and that I should have to work like you—for mother.'

'Not like us, for pity's sake, Infanta!' cried Jock. 'We have had enough of that. The great use of you is to look after mother; and keep her from galloping the life out of herself, and this chap from worrying it out of her.'

'Jock!' cried Armine indignantly.

'Yes, you will, if you go on moaning about these fads, and making her blame herself for them. I don't say we have all done the right thing with this money, I'm sure I have not, and most likely it serves us right to lose it, but to have mother teased about what, after all, was chiefly owing to her absence, is more than I will stand. The one duty in hand is to make the best of it for her. I shall run down again as soon as I hear how this is likely to turn out—for Sunday, perhaps. Keep up a good heart, Babie Bunting, and whatever you do, don't let him worry mother. Good-bye, Armie! What's the use of being good, if you can't hold up against a thing like this?'

'Jock doesn't know,' said Armine, as the door closed. 'Fads indeed!'

'Jock didn't mean that,' pleaded Babie. 'You know he did not; dear, good Jock, he could not!'

'Jock is a good fellow, but he lives a frivolous, self-indulgent life, and has got infected with the spirit and the language,' said Armine, 'or he would understand that myself or my own loss is the very last thing I am troubled about. No, indeed, I should never think of that! It is the ruin of these poor people and all I meant to have done for them. It is very strange that we should only be allowed to waken to a sense of our opportunities to have them taken away from us!'

No one would have expected Armine, always regarded as the most religious of the family, to be the most dismayed, and neither he nor Barbara could detect how much of the spoilt child lay at the bottom of his regrets; but his little sister's sympathy enabled him to keep from troubling his mother with his lamentations.

Indeed Allen was usually in presence, and nobody ever ventured on what might bore Allen. He was in good spirits, believing that the discovery would put an end to all trifling on Elvira's part, and that he and she would thus together be able to act the beneficent genii of the whole family. Even their mother had a sense of relief. She was very quiet, and moved about softly, like one severely shaken and bruised; but there was a calm in knowing the worst, instead of living in continual vague suspicion.

The Colonel returned with tidings that Mr. Wakefield had no doubt of the validity of the will, though it might be possible to contest it if Elizabeth Brook, the witness, could not be found ; but that would involve an investigation as to the manner of the loss and the discovery. It was, in truth, only a matter of time ; and on Monday Mr. Wakefield would come down and begin to take steps. That was the day on which the family were to have gone to London, but Caroline's heart failed her, and she was much relieved when a kind letter arrived from Mrs. Evelyn, who was sure she could not wish to go into society immediately after Janet's affair, and offered to receive Elvira for as long as might be convenient, and herself—as indeed had been already arranged—to present her at court with Sydney. It was a great comfort to place her in such hands during the present crisis, all the more that Ellen was not at all delighted with her company for Essie and Ellie. She rushed home on Saturday evening to secure Delrio, and superintend her packing up, with her head a great deal too full of court dresses and ball dresses, fancy costumes, and Parisian hats, to detect any of the tokens of a coming revolution, even in her own favour.

Jock too came home that same evening, as gay and merry apparently as ever, and after dinner claimed his mother for a turn in the garden.

'Has Drake written to you, mother?' he asked. 'I met him the other day at Mrs. Lucas's, and it seems his soul is expanding. He wants to give up the old house—you know the lease is nearly out—and to hang out in a more fashionable quarter.'

'Dear old house!'

'Now, mother, here's my notion. Why should not we hide our diminished heads there? You could keep house while the Monk and I go through the lectures and hospitals, and King's College might not be too far off for Armine.'

'You, Jock, my dear.'

'You see, it is a raving impossibility for me to stay where I am.'

'I am afraid so ; but you might exchange into the line.'

'There would be no great good in that. I should have stuck to the Guards because there I am, and I have no opinion of fellows changing about for nothing—and because of Evelyn and some capital fellows besides. But I found out long ago that it had been a stupid thing to go in for. When one has mastered the routine, it is awfully monotonous ; and one has nothing to do with one's time or one's brains. I have felt many a time that I could keep straight better if I had something tougher to do.'

'Tell me, just to satisfy my mind, my dear, you have no debts.'

'I don't owe forty pounds in the world, mother ; and I shall

not owe that, when I can get my tailor to send in his bill. You
have given me as jolly an allowance as any man in the corps,
and I've always paid my way. I've got no end of things about
my rooms, and my horses and cab, but they will turn into
money. You see, having done the thing first figure, I should
hate to begin in the cheap and nasty style, and I had much
rather come home to you, Mother Carey. I'm not too old, you
know—not one-and-twenty till August. I shall not come
primed like the Monk, but I'll try to grind up to him, if you'll
let me, mother.'

'O Jock, dear Jock!' she cried, 'you little know the
strength and life it gives me to have you taking it so like a
young hero.'

'I tell you I'm sick of drill and parade,' said Jock, 'and
heartily glad of an excuse to turn to something where one can
stretch one's wits without being thought a disgrace to
humanity. Now, don't you think we might be very jolly
together?'

'Oh, to think of being there again! And we can have the
dear old furniture and make it like home. It is the first definite
notion any one has had. My dear, you have given me something to look forward to. You can't guess what good you have
done me! It is just as if you had shown me light at the end of
the thicket; ay, and made yourself the good stout staff to lead
me through!'

'Mother, that's the best thing that ever was said to me yet;
worth ever so much more than all old Barnes's money-bags.'

'If the others will approve! But any way it is a nest egg
for my own selfish pleasure to carry me through. Why, Jock,
to have your name on the old door would be bringing back the
golden age!'

Nobody but Jock knew what made this such a cheerful
Sunday with his mother. She was even heard making fun, and
declaring that no one knew what a relief it would be not to
have to take drives when all the roads were beset with traction
engines. She had so far helped Armine out of the difficulties
his lavish assurances had brought him into, that she had written
a note to the vicar, Mr. Parsons, telling him that she should be
better able to reply in a little while; but Armine, knowing that
he must not speak, and afraid of betraying the cause of his
unhappiness and of the delay, was afraid to stir out of reach of
the others lest Miss Parsons should begin an inquiry.

The Vicar of Woodside was, in fact, as some people
mischievously called her, the Reverend Petronella Parsons.
Whether she wrote her brother's sermons was a disputed question. She certainly did other things in his name which she had
better have let alone. He was three or four years her junior,
and had always so entirely followed her lead, that he seemed to
have no personal identity, but to be only her male complement.
That Armine should have set up a lady of this calibre for the

first goddess of his fancy was one of the comical chances of life,
but she was a fine, handsome, fresh-looking woman of five-and-
thirty, with a strong vein of sentiment—ecclesiastical and
poetic—just ignorant enough to gush freely, and too genuine
to be *always* offensive. She had been infinitely struck with
Armine, had hung a perfect romance of renovation on him,
sympathised with his every word, and lavished on him what
perhaps was not quite flattery, because she was entirely in
earnest, but which was therefore all the worse for him.

Barbara had a natural repulsion from her, and could not
understand Armine's being attracted, and for the first time in
their lives this was creating a little difference between the
brother and sister. Babie had said, in rather an uncalled-for
way, that Miss Parsons would draw back when she knew the
truth, and Armine had been deeply offended at such an un-
generous hint, and had reduced her to a tearful declaration that
she was very sorry she had said anything so uncalled for.

Petronella herself had been much vexed at Armine's three
days' defection, which was ascribed to the worldly and anti-
ecclesiastical influences of the rest of the family. She wanted
her brother to preach a sermon about Lot's wife ; but Jemmie,
as she called him, had on certain occasions a passive force of his
own, and she could not prevail. She regretted it the less when
Armine and Babie duly did the work they had undertaken in
the Sunday-school, though they would not come in for any
intermediate meals.

'What did Mrs. Brownlow tell you in her note ?' she asked of
her brother while giving him his tea before the last service.

'That in a few days she shall be able to answer me.'

'Ah, well ! Do you know there is a belief in the parish that
something has happened—that a claim is to be set up to the
whole property, and that the whole family will be reduced to
beggary ?'

'I never heard of an estate to which there was not some
claimant in obscurity.'

'But this comes from undoubted authority.' Mr. Parsons
smiled a little. 'One can't help it if servants *will* hear things.
Well ! any way it will be overruled for good to that dear boy—
though it would be a cruel stroke on the parish.'

It was the twilight of a late spring evening when the congregation streamed out of church, and Elvira, who had managed
hitherto to avoid all intercourse with the River Hollow party,
found herself grappled by Lisette without hope of rescue. 'My
dear, this is a pleasure at last ; I have so much to say to you.
Can't you give us a day ?'

'I am going to town to-morrow,' said Elvira, never gracious
to any Gould.

'To-morrow ! I heard the family had put off their migra-
tion.'

'I go with Lucas. I am to stay with Mrs. Evelyn, Lord

Fordham's mother, you know, who is to present me at the Drawing-room,' said Elvira magnificently.

'Oh! if I could only see you in your court dress it would be memorable,' cried Mrs. Gould. 'A little longer, my dear, our paths lie together.'

'I must get home. My packing——'

'And may I ask what you wear, my dear? Is your dress ordered?'

'Oh yes, I had it made at Paris. It is white satin, with lilies —a kind of lily one gets in Algiers.' And she expatiated on the fashion till Mrs. Gould said—

'Well, my love, I hope you will enjoy yourself at the Honourable Mrs. Evelyn's. What is the address, in case I should have occasion to write?'

'I shall have no time for doing commissions.'

'That was not my meaning,' was the gentle answer; 'only if there be anything you ought to be informed of——'

'They would write to me from home. Why, what do you mean?' asked the girl, her attention gained at last.

'Did it never strike you why you are sent up alone?'

'Only that Mrs. Brownlow is so cut up about Janet.'

'Ah! youth is so sweetly unconscious. It is well that there are those who are bound to watch for your interests, my dear.'

'I can't think what you mean.'

'I will not disturb your happy innocence, my love. It is enough for your uncle and me to be awake, to counteract any machinations. Ah! I see your astonishment! You are so simple, my dear child, and you have been studiously kept in the dark.'

'I can't think what you are driving at,' said Elvira impatiently. 'Mrs. Brownlow would never let any harm happen to me, nor Allen either. Do let me go.'

'One moment, my darling. I must love you through all, and you will know your true friends one day. Are you—let me ask the question out of my deep, almost maternal, solicitude—are you engaged to Mr. Brownlow?'

'Of course I am!'

'Of course, as you say. Most ingenuous! Ah, well, may it not be too late!'

'Don't be so horrid, Lisette! Allen is not half a bad fellow, and frightfully in love with me.'

'Exactly, my dear unsuspicious dove. There! I see you are impatient. You will know the truth soon enough. One kiss, for your mother's sake.'

But Elvira broke from her, and rejoined Allen.

'I have sounded the child,' said Lisette to her husband that evening, 'and she is quite in the dark, though the very servants in the house are better informed.'

'Better informed than the fact, may be,' said Mr. Gould (for a man always scouts a woman's gossip).

'No, indeed. Poor dear child, she is blinded purposely. She never guessed why she was sent to Kencroft while the old Colonel was called in, and they all agreed that the will should be kept back till the wedding with Mr. Allen should be over, and he could make up the rest. So now the child is to be sent to town, and surrounded with Mrs. Brownlow's creatures to prey upon her innocence. But you have no care for your own niece—none!'

## CHAPTER XXIX

### FRIENDS AND UNFRIENDS

'Ay, and, I think,
One business doth command us all; for mine
Is money.'

*Timon of Athens.*

BEFORE the door of one of the supremely respectable and aristocratic but somewhat gloomy-looking houses in Cavendish Square, whose mauve plate-glass windows and link-extinguishers are like fossils of a past era of civilisation, three riding-horses were being walked up and down, two with side-saddles and one for a gentleman. They were taken aside as a four-wheel drove up, while a female voice exclaimed—

'Ah! we are just in time!'

Cards and a note were sent in with a request to see Miss Menella.

Word came back that Miss Menella was just going out riding; but on the return of a message that the visitors came from Mrs. Brownlow on important business, they were taken upstairs to an ante-room.

They were three—Mr. Wakefield and Mr. Gould, and, to the great discontentment of the former, Mrs. Gould likewise. Fain would he have shaken her off; but as she truly said, who could deprive her of her rights as kinswoman, and wife to the young lady's guardian?

After they had waited a few moments in the somewhat dingy surroundings of a house seldom used by its proper owners, Elvira entered in plumed hat and habit, a slender and exquisite little figure, but with a haughty twitch in her slim waist, superb indifference in the air of her little head, and a grasp of her coral-handled whip as if it were a defensive weapon, when Lisette flew up to offer an embrace with—

'Joy, joy, my dear child! Remember, I was the first to give you a hint.'

'Good morning,' said Elvira, with a little bend of her head, presenting to each the shapely tip of a gauntleted hand, but ignoring her uncle and aunt as far as was possible. 'Is there anything that need detain me, Mr. Wakefield? I am just going out with Miss Evelyn and Lord Fordham, and I cannot keep them waiting.'

'Ah! it is you that will have to be waited for now, my sweet one,' began Mrs. Gould.

'Here is a note from Mrs. Brownlow,' said Mr. Wakefield, holding it to Elvira, who looked like anything but a sweet one. 'I imagine it is to prepare you for the important disclosure I have to make.'

A hot colour mounted in the fair cheek. Elvira tore open the letter and read—

MY DEAR CHILD—I can only ask your pardon for the unconscious wrong which I have so long been doing to you, and which shall be repaired as soon as the processes of the law render it possible for us to change places.—Your ever loving                    MOTHER CAREY.

'What does it all mean?' cried the bewildered girl.

'It means,' said the lawyer, 'that Mrs. Brownlow has discovered a will of the late Mr. Barnes more recent than that under which she inherited, naming you, Miss Elvira Menella, as the sole inheritrix.'

'My dear child, let me be the first to congratulate you on your recovery of your rights,' said Mrs. Gould, again proffering an embrace, but again the whip was interposed, while Elvira, with her eyes fixed on Mr. Wakefield, asked 'What?' so that he had to repeat the explanation.

'Then does it all belong to me?' she asked.

'Eventually it will, Miss Menella. You are sole heiress to your great-uncle, though you cannot enter into possession till certain needful forms of law are gone through. Mrs. Brownlow offers no obstruction, but they cannot be rapid.'

'All mine!' repeated Elvira, with childish exultation. 'What fun! I must go and tell Sydney Evelyn.'

'A few minutes more, Miss Menella,' said Mr. Wakefield. 'You ought to hear the terms of the will.'

And he read it to her.

'I thought you told me it was to be mine. This is all you and uncle George.'

'As your trustees.'

'Oh, to manage as the Colonel does. You will give me all the money I ask you for. I want some pearls, and I must have that duck of a little Arab. Uncle George, how soon can I have it?'

'We must go through the Probate Court,' he began, but his wife interrupted—

'Ways and means will be forthcoming, my dear, though for my part I think it would be much better taste in Mrs. Brownlow to put you in possession at once.'

'Mr. Wakefield explained, my dear,' said her husband, 'that, much as Mrs. Brownlow wishes to do so, she cannot; she has no power. It is her trustees.'

U

'Oh yes, I know every excuse will be found for retaining the property as long as possible,' said the lady.

'Then I shall have to wait ever so long,' said the young lady. 'And I do so want the Arab. It is a real love, and Allen would say so.'

'I have another letter for you,' said Mr. Wakefield, on hearing that name. 'We will leave it with you. If you wish for further information, I would call immediately on receiving a line at my office.'

Just then a message was brought from Mrs. Evelyn inviting Miss Menella's friends to stay to luncheon. It incited Elvira, who knew neither awe nor manners, to run across the great drawing-room, leaving the doors open behind her, to the little morning-room, where sat Mrs. Evelyn, with Sydney, in her habit, standing by the mantelpiece.

'Oh, Mrs. Evelyn,' Elvira began, 'it is Mr. Wakefield and my uncle and his wife. They have come to say it is all mine; Uncle Barnes left it all to me.'

'So I hear from Mrs. Brownlow,' said Mrs. Evelyn gravely.

'Oh, Elfie, I am so sorry for you. Don't you hate it?' cried Sydney.

'Oh, but it is such fun! I can do everything I please,' said the heiress.

'Yes, that's the best part,' said Sydney. 'I do envy you the day when you give it all back to Allen.'

That reminded Elvira to open the note, and as she read it her great eyes grew round.

SWEETEST AND DEAREST—How I have always loved, and always shall love you, you know full well. But these altered circumstances bring about what you have so often playfully wished. Say the word and you are free, no longer bound to me by anything that has passed between us, though the very fibres of my heart and life are as much as ever entwined about you. Honour bids my dissolution of our engagement, and I await your answer, though nothing can ever make me other than your wholly devoted          ALLEN.

Mrs. Evelyn had been prepared by a letter from her friend for what was now taking place, Mr. Wakefield had likewise known the main purport of Allen's note, and had allowed that Mr. Brownlow could not as a gentleman do otherwise than release the young lady; though he fully believed that it would be only as a matter of form, and that Elvira would not hear of breaking off. He had in fact spent much eloquence in persuading Mrs. Brownlow to continue to take the charge of the heiress during the three years before her majority. Begun in generous affection by Allen long ago, the engagement seemed to the lawyer, as well as to others, an almost providential means of at least partial restitution.

He had meant Elvira to read her letter alone, but she had opened it before the two ladies, and her first exclamation was a startled, incredulous—

'Ha! What's this? He says our engagement is dissolved.'

'He is of course bound to set you free, my dear,' said Mrs. Evelyn, 'but it only depends on yourself.'

'Oh! and I shall tease him well first,' cried Elvira, her face lighting up with fun and mischief. 'He was so tiresome, and did bother so! Now I shall have my swing! Oh, what fun! I won't let him worry me again just yet, I can tell him!'

'You don't seem to consider,' began Sydney—but Mrs. Gould took this moment for advancing.

From the whole length of the large drawing-room the trio had been spectators, not quite auditors, though perhaps enough to perceive what line the Evelyns were taking.

So Mrs. Gould advanced into the drawing-room ; Mrs. Evelyn came forward to assume the duties of hostess ; and Sydney turned and ran away so precipitately that she shut the door on the trailing skirt of her habit and had to open it again to release herself.

Mr. Wakefield hoped the young ladies would pardon him for having spoilt their ride, and Elvira was going off to change her dress, when, to his dismay, Mrs. Evelyn desired her to take her aunt to her room to prepare for luncheon. He had seen enough of Mrs. Gould to know that this was a most unlucky measure of courtesy on good simple Mrs. Evelyn's part, but of course he could do nothing to prevent it, and had to remain with Mr. Gould, both speaking in the strongest manner of Mrs. Brownlow's uprightness and bravery in meeting this sudden change. Mr. Wakefield said he hoped to prevail on her to retain the charge of the young lady for the present, and Mr. Gould assented that she could not be in better hands. Then Mrs. Evelyn (by way of doing anything for her friend) undertook to make Elvira welcome as long as it might be convenient, and was warmly thanked. She further ascertained that the missing witness had been traced ; and that the most probable course of action would be that there would be an amicable suit in the Probate Court, and then another of ejectment. Until these were over, things would remain in their present state, for how many weeks or months would depend upon the Law Courts, since Mrs. Brownlow's trustees would be legally holders of the property until the decision was given against them, and Miss Menella would be as entirely dependent on her bounty as she had been all these years. Meanwhile, as Mrs. Brownlow had no inclination to come to London and exhibit herself as a disinherited heroine, Mr. Wakefield and the Colonel strongly advised her remaining on at Belforest.

All this Mrs. Evelyn had been anxious to understand, and thus was more glad of the delay of Elvira and her aunt upstairs than she would have been if she could ever have guessed what work a designing, flattering tongue could make with a vain, frivolous, selfish brain, with the same essential strain of vulgarity and worldliness.

Still, Elvira was chiefly shallow and selfish, and all her affection and confidence naturally belonged to her home of the last eight years. She was bewildered, perhaps a little intoxicated, at the sense of riches, but was really quite ready to lean as much as ever upon her natural friends and protectors.

However, Lisette's congratulations and exultation rang pleasantly upon her ear, and she listened and talked freely, asking questions and rejoicing.

Now Mrs. Gould, to do her justice, measured others by herself, and really and truly believed that only accident had disconcerted a plan for concealing the will till Elvira should have been safely married to Allen Brownlow, and that thus it was the fixed purpose of the family to keep her and her fortune in their hands, a purpose which every instinct bade Mrs. Lisette Gould to traverse and overthrow, if only because she hated such artfulness and meanness. Unfortunately, too, as she had been a governess, and her father had been a Union doctor, she could put herself forward as something above a farmer's wife, indeed 'quite as good as Mrs. Brownlow.'

All Mrs. Evelyn's civility had not redeemed her from the imputation of being 'high,' and Elvira was quite ready to call hers a very dull house. In truth, there was only moderate gaiety, and no fastness. The ruling interests were religious and political questions, as befitted Fordham's maiden session, the society was quietly high-bred and intelligent, and there was much attention to health; for, strong as Sydney was, her mother would have dreaded the full whirl of the season as much for her body as for her mind.

At all this the frivolous, idle little soul chafed and fretted, aware that the circle was not a fashionable one, eager for far more diversion and less restraint, and longing to join the party in Hyde Corner, where she could always make Allen do what she pleased.

With the obtuseness of an unobservant, self-occupied mind, she was taken by surprise when Mrs. Gould said that Mrs. Brownlow was not coming to town, adding, 'It would be very unbecoming in her, though of course she will hold on at Belforest as long as there is any quibble of the law.'

'Oh, I don't want to lose the season; she promised me!'

Then Mrs. Gould made a great stroke.

'My dear, you could not return to her. Not when the young man has just broken with you. You would have more proper pride.'

'Poor Allen!' said Elvira. 'If he would only let me alone, to have my fun like other girls.'

'You see he could not afford to let you gratify your youthful spirits. Too much was at stake, and it is most providential that things had gone no further, and that your own good sense has preserved you to adorn a much higher sphere.'

'Allen could be made something,' said Elvira, 'I know, for

he told me he could get himself made a baronet. He always
does as I tell him. Will they be very poor, Lisette?'

'Oh no, my dear, generous child, Mrs. Brownlow was quite
as well provided for as she had any right to expect. You need
have no anxieties on that score.'

To Elvira, the change from River Hollow to the Pagoda had
been from rustic to gentle life, and thus this reply sounded
plausible enough to silence a not much awakened compassion,
but she still said, 'Why can't I go home? I've nowhere else to
go. I could not stay at the Farm,' she added in her usual
uncomplimentary style.

'No, my dear, I should not think of it. An establishment
must be formed, but in the meantime it would be quite beneath
you to return to Mrs. Brownlow, again to become the prey of
underground machinations. Besides, how awkward it would be
while the lawsuits are going on. Impossible! No, my dear,
you must only return to Belforest in a triumphal procession.
Surely there must be a competition for my lovely child among
more congenial friends.'

'Well,' said Elvira, 'there were the Folliotts. We met them
at Nice, and Lady Flora did ask me the other day, but Mrs.
Brownlow does not like them, and Allen says they are not good
form.'

'Ah! I knew you could not want for friends. You are not
bound by those who want to keep you to themselves for reasons
of their own.'

Thus before Elvira brought her aunt downstairs, enough had
been done to make her eager to be with one who would discuss
her future splendour rather than deplore the change to her
benefactor, and thus she readily accepted a proposal she would
naturally have scouted, to go out driving with Mrs. Gould.
She came back in a mood of exulting folly, and being far too
shallow and loquacious to conceal anything, she related in full
all Mrs. Gould's insinuations, which, to do her justice, the poor
child did not really understand. But Sydney did, and was
furious at the ingratitude which could seem almost flattered.
Mrs. Evelyn found the two girls in a state of hot reproach and
recrimination, and cut the matter short by treating them as if
they were little children, and ordering them both off to their
rooms to dress for dinner.

Elvira went away sobbing, and saying that nobody cared for
her ; everybody was wrapped up in the Brownlows, who had
been enjoying what was hers ever so long.

And Sydney presently burst into her mother's room to pour
out her disgust and indignation against the heartless, ungrateful,
intolerable——

'Only foolish, my dear, and left all day in the hands of a
flattering, designing woman.'

'To let such things be said. Mamma, did you hear——?'

'I had rather not hear, Sydney ; and I desire you will not

repeat them to any one. Be careful, if you talk to Jock to-night. To repeat words spoken in her present mood might do exceeding mischief.'

'She speaks as if she meant to cast them all off—Allen and all.'

'Very possibly she may see things differently when she wakes to-morrow. But, Sydney, while she is here, the whole subject must be avoided. It would not be acting fairly to use any influence in favour of our friends.'

'Don't you mean to speak to her, mamma?'

'If she consults me, of course I shall tell her what I think of the matter, but I shall not force my advice on her, or give these Goulds occasion to say that I am playing into Mrs. Brownlow's hands.'

They were going to an evening party, and Lucas and Cecil came to dinner to go with them. Cecil looked grave and gloomy, but Jock rattled away so merrily that Sydney began to wonder whether all this were a dream, or whether he were still unaware of the impending misfortune.

But Jock only waited for the friendly cover of a grand piece of instrumental music to ask Mrs. Evelyn if she had heard from his mother, and she was very glad to go into details with him, while he was infinitely relieved that the silence was over, and he could discuss the matter with his friends.

'Tell me truly, Jock, will she be comfortably off?'

'Very fairly. Yes, indeed. My father's savings were absolutely left to her, and have been accumulating all this time, and they will be a very fair maintenance for her and Babie.'

'There is no danger of her having to pay the mesne profits?'

'No, certainly not, as it stands. Mr. Wakefield says that cannot happen. Then the old house in Bloomsbury, where we were all born, is our own, and she likes the notion of returning thither. Mrs. Evelyn, after all you and Sir James have done for me, what should you think of my giving it up, and taking to the pestle and mortar?'

'My dear Lucas!' Then after a moment's reflection, 'I suppose it would be folly to think of going on as you are?'

'Raving insanity,' said Jock, 'and this notion really does seem to please my mother.'

'Is it not just intolerable to hear him?' said Cecil, who had made his way to them.

'"What is bred in the bone——"' said Jock. 'What's that? Chopin? Sydney, will you condescend to the apothecary's boy?'

As he led her to the dancing-room, she asked, 'You can't really mean this, Jock. Cecil is breaking his heart about it.'

'There are worse trades.'

'But it is such a cruel pity!'

'What? The execution I shall make,' he said lightly

'For shame, Jock!'

But he went on teasing her, because their hearts were so very full. ''Tis just the choice between various means of slaughter.'

'Don't!' she exclaimed. 'Something can be done to prevent your throwing yourself away. Why can't you exchange?'

'It is too late to get into any corps where I should not be an expense to my mother,' said Jock, regretting his decision a good deal more when he found how she regarded it.

'Well, sacrifice is something!' sighed Sydney

Jock defied strange feelings by a laugh and the reply, 'Equal to the finest thing in the *Traveller's Joy*, and that was the knight who let the hyena eat up his hand that his lady might finish her rosary undisturbed.'

'It is as bad—or as good—to let the hyena eat up your sword hand as to cut yourself off from all that is great and noble—all we used to think you would do.'

So spoke Sydney Evelyn in her girlish prejudice, and the prospects that had recently seemed to Lucas so fair and kindly, suddenly clouded over and became dull, gloomy, and despicable. She felt as if she were saving him from becoming a deserter as she went on—

'I am sure Babie must be shocked!'

'I don't know whether Babie has heard. She has serious thoughts of coming out as a lady-help, editing the *Traveller's Joy* as a popular magazine, giving lessons in Greek, or painting the crack picture in the Royal Academy. In fact, she would rather prefer to have the whole family on her hands.'

'It is all the spirit of self-sacrifice,' said Sydney; 'but oh, Lucas, let it be any sacrifice but that of your sword! Think how we should all feel if there was a great glorious war, and you only a poor creature of a civilian, instead of getting—as I know you would—lots of medals and Victoria Crosses, and knighthood—real knighthood! O Jock, think of that! When your mother thinks of that, she can't want you to make any such mistaken sacrifice to her. Live on a crust if you like, but don't—don't give up your sword.'

'This is coming it strong,' muttered Jock. 'I did not think any one cared so much.'

'Of course I care.'

The words were swept off as they whirled together into the dance, where the clasping hands and flying feet had in them a strange impulse, half tenderness, half exultation, as each felt an importance to the other unknown before. Childishness was not exactly left behind in it, but a different stage was reached. Sydney felt herself to have done a noble work, and gloried in watching till her hero should have achieved greatness on a crust a day, and Jock was equally touched and elated at the intimation that his doings were so much to her.

Friendship sang the same note. Cecil, honest lad, had never

more than the average amount either of brains or industry, and despised medicines to the full as much as did his sister. Abhorring equally the toil and the degradation, he deemed it a duty to prevent such a fall, and put his hope in his uncle. Nay, if his mother had not assured him that it was too late, he would have gone off at once to seek Sir James at his club.

Lord Fordham had been in bed long before the others returned, but in the morning a twisted note was handed to his mother, briefly saying he was running down to see how it was with them at Belforest.

When a station fly was seen drawing to the door, Allen, who was drearily leaning over the stone wall of the terrace, much disorganised by having received no answer to his letter, instantly jumped to the conclusion that Elvira had come home, sprang to the door, and when he only saw the tall figure emerge, he concluded that something dreadful had happened, grasped Fordham's hand, and demanded what it was.

It fell flat that she had last been seen full-dressed going off to a party.

'Then, if there's nothing, what brought you here? I mean,' said poor Allen, catching up his courtesy, 'I'm afraid there's nothing you or any one else can do.'

'Can I see your mother?'

Allen turned him into the library and went off to find his mother, and instruct her to discover from 'that stupid fellow' how Elvira was feeling it. When, after putting away the papers she was trying to arrange, Caroline went downstairs, she had no sooner opened the door than Barbara flew up to her, crying out—

'O mother, tell him not!'

'Tell him what, my dear?' as the girl hung on her, and dragged her into the ante-room. 'What is the matter?'

'If it is nonsense, he ought not to have made it so like earnest,' said Babie, all crimson, but quite gravely.

'You don't mean——'

'Yes, mother.'

'How could he?' cried Caroline, in her first annoyance at such things beginning with her Babie.

'You'll tell him, mother. You'll not let him do it again?'

'Let me go, my child. I must speak to him and find out what it all means.'

Within the library she was met by Fordham.

'Have I done very wrong, Mrs. Brownlow? I could not help it.'

'I wish you had not.'

'I always meant to wait till she was older, and I grew stronger, but when all this came, I thought if we all belonged to one another it might be a help——'

'Very, very kind, but——'

'I know I was sudden and frightened her,' he continued; 'but if she could——'

'You forget how young she is.'

'No, I don't. I would not take her from you. We could all go on together.'

'All one family? Oh, you unpractised boy!'

'Have we not done so many winters? But I would wait, I meant to have waited, only I am afraid of dying without being able to provide for her. If she would have me, she would be left better off than my mother, and then it would be all right for you and Armine. What are you smiling at?'

'At your notions of rightness, my dear, kind Duke. I see how you mean it, but it will not do. Even if she had grown to care for you, it would not be right for me to give her to you for years to come.'

'May not I hope till then?'

She could not tell how sorry she should be to see in her little daughter any dawnings of an affection which would be a virtual condemnation to such a life as his mother's had been.

'You don't guess how I love her! She has been the bright light of my life ever since the Engelberg—the one hope I have lived for!'

'My poor Duke!'

'Then do you quite mean to deny me all hope?'

'Hope must be according to your own impressions, my dear Fordham. Of course, if you are well, and still wishing it four or five years hence, it would be free to you to try again. More I cannot say. No, don't thank me, for I trust to your honour to make no demonstrations in the meantime, and not to consider yourself as bound.'

It was a relief that Armine here came in, attracted by a report of his friend's arrival, and Mrs. Brownlow went in search of her daughter, to whom she was guided by a sonata played with very unnecessary violence.

'You need not murder Haydn any more, you little barbarian,' she said, with a hand on the child's shoulder, and looking anxiously into the gloomy face. 'I have settled him.'

Babie drew a long breath, and said—

'I'm glad! It was so horrid! You'll not let him do it any more?'

'Then you decidedly would not like it?' returned her mother.

'Like it? Poor Duke! Mother! As if I could ever! A man that can't sit in a draught, or get wet in his feet!' cried Babie, with the utmost scorn; and reading reproof as well as amused pity in her mother's eyes, she added, 'Of course, I am very sorry for him; but fancy being very sorry for one's love!'

'I thought you liked wounded knights?'

'Wounded! Yes, but they've done something, and had glorious wounds. Now Duke—he is very good, and it is not his fault but his misfortune ; but he is such a — such a muff !'

'That's enough, my dear ; I am quite content that my Infanta should wait for her hero. Though,' she added, almost to herself, 'she is too childish to know the true worth of what she condemns.'

She felt this the more when Babie, who had coaxed the housekeeper into letting her begin a private school of cookery, started up, crying—

'I must go and see my orange biscuits taken out of the oven ! I should like to send a taste to Sydney !'

Yes, Barbara was childish for nearly sixteen, and, as it struck her mother at the moment, rather wonderfully so considering her cleverness and romance. It was better for her that the softening should not come yet, but, mother as she was, Caroline's sympathies could not but be at the moment with the warm-hearted, impulsive, generous young man, moved out of all his habitual valetudinarian habits by his affection, rather than with the light-hearted child, who spurned the love she did not comprehend, and despised his ill-health. Had the young generation no hearts? Oh no—no—it could not be so with her loving Barbara, and she ought to be thankful for the saving of pain and perplexity.

Poor Armine was not getting much comfort out of his friend, who was too much preoccupied to attend to what he was saying, and only mechanically assented at intervals to the proposition that it was an inscrutable dispensation that the will and the power should so seldom go together. He heard all Armine's fallen castles about chapels, schools, curates, and sisters, as in a dream, really not knowing whether they were or were not to be. And with all his desire to be useful, he never perceived the one offer that would have been really valuable, namely, to carry off the boy out of sight of the scene of his disappointment.

Fordham was compelled to stay for an uncomfortable luncheon, when there were spasmodic jerks of talk about subjects of the day to keep up appearances before the servants, who flitted about in such an exasperating way that their mistress secretly rejoiced to think how soon she should be rid of the fine courier butler.

Just as the pony-carriage came round for Armine to drive his friend back to the station, the Colonel came in, and was an astonished spectator of the farewells.

'So that's your young lord,' he said. 'Poor lad ! if our nobility is made of no tougher stuff, I would not give much for it. What brought him here ?'

'Kindness — sympathy — ' said Caroline, a little awkwardly.

'Much of that he showed,' said Allen, 'just knowing nothing at all about anybody ! No ! If it were not so utterly ridiculous, I should think he had come to make an offer to Babie ;' and as his sister flew out of the room, 'You don't mean that he has, mother?'

'Pray, don't speak of it to any one!' said Caroline. 'I would not have it known for the world. It was a generous impulse, poor dear fellow ; and Babie has no feeling for him at all.'

'Very lucky,' said the uncle. 'He looks as if his life was not worth a year's purchase. So you refused him? Quite right too. You are a sensible woman, Caroline, in the midst of this severe reverse!'

## CHAPTER XXX

### AS WEEL OFF AS AYE WAGGING

'Lesbia hath a beaming eye,
      But no one knows for whom it beameth ;
Right and left its arrows fly,
      But what they aim at, no one dreameth.'

By the advice, or rather by the express desire, of her trustees, Mrs. Brownlow remained at Belforest, while they accepted an offer of renting the London house for the season. Mr. Wake-field declared that there was no reason that she should contract her expenditure ; but she felt as if everything she spent beyond her original income, except of course the needful outlay on keeping up the house and gardens, were robbery of Elvira, and she therefore did not fill up the establishment of servants, nor of horses, using only for herself the little pair of ponies which had been turned out in the park.

No one had perhaps realised the amount of worry that this arrangement entailed. As Barbara said, if they could have gone away at once and worked for their living like sensible people in a book, it would have been all very well—but this half-and-half state was dreadful. Personally it did not affect Babie much, but she was growing up to the part of general sympathiser, and for the first time in their lives there was a pull in contrary directions by her mother and Armine.

Every expenditure was weighed before it was granted. Did it belong rightly to Belforest estate or to Caroline Brownlow? And the claims of the church and parish at Woodside were doubtful. Armine, under the influence of Miss Parsons, took a wide view of the dues of the parish, thought there was a long arrear to be paid off, and that whatever could be given was so much out of the wolf's mouth.

His mother, with 'Be just before you are generous' ringing in her ears, referred all to the Colonel, and he had long had a fixed scale of the duties of the property as a property, and was only rendered the more resolute in it by that vehemence of Armine's which enhanced his dislike and distrust of the family at the vicarage.

'Bent on getting all they could while they could,' he said,

quite unjustly as to the vicar, and hardly fairly by the sister, whose demands were far exceeded by those of her champion.

The claims of the cottages for repair, and of the school for sufficient enlargement and maintenance to obviate a School Board, were acknowledged; but for the rest, the Colonel said, 'his sister was perfectly at liberty. No one could blame her if she threw her balance at the bank into the sea. She would never be called to account; but since she asked him whether the estate was bound to assist in pulling the church to pieces, and setting up a fresh curate to bring in more absurdities, he could only say what he thought,' etc.

These thoughts of his were of course most offensive to Armine, who set all down to sordid Puritan prejudice, could not think how his mother could listen, and, when Babie stood up for her mother, went off to blend his lamentations with those of Miss Parsons, whose resignation struck him as heroic. 'Never mind, Armine, it will all come in time. Perhaps we are not fit for it yet. We cannot expect the world's justice to understand the outpouring of the saints' liberality.'

Armine repeated this interesting aphorism to Barbara, and was much disappointed that the shrewd little woman did not understand it, or only so far as to say, 'But I did not know that it was saintly to be liberal with other people's money.'

He said Babie had a prejudice against Miss Parsons; and he was so far right that the Infanta did not like her, thought her a humbug, and sorely felt that for the first time something had come between herself and Armine.

Allen was another trouble. He did not agree to the retrenchments, in which he saw no sense, and retained his horse and groom. Luckily he had retained only one when going abroad, and at this early season he needed no more. But his grievous anxiety and restlessness about Elvira did not make him by any means insensible to the effects of a reduced establishment in a large house, and especially to the handiwork of the good woman who had been left in charge, when compared with that of the £80 cooks who had been the plague of his mother's life.

No one, however, could wonder at his wretchedness, as day after day passed without hearing from Elvira, and all that was known was that she had left Mrs. Evelyn and gone to stay with Lady Flora Folliott, a flighty young matron, who had been enraptured with her beauty at a *table d'hôte* a year ago, and had made advances not much relished by the rest of the party.

No more was to be learnt till Lucas found a Saturday to come down. Before he could say three words, he was cross-examined. Had he seen Elvira?

'Several times.'

'Spoken to her?'

'Yes.'

'What had she said?'

'Asked him to look at a horse.'

'Did she know he was coming home?'

'Yes.'

'Had she sent any message?'

'Well—yes. To desire that her Algerine costume should be sent up. Whew!' as Allen flung himself out of the room. 'How have I put my foot in it, mother?'

'You don't mean that that was all?'

'Every jot! What, has she not written? The abominable little elf! I'm coming.' And he shrugged his shoulders as Allen, who had come round to the open window, beckoned to him.

He was absolutely grappled by a trembling hand, and a husky voice demanded, 'What message did she really send? I can't stand foolery.'

'Just that, Allen—to. Emma. Really just that. You can't shake more out of me. You might as well expect anything from that Chinese lantern. Hold hard. 'Tis not I——'

'Don't speak! You don't know her! I was a fool to think she would confide to a mere buffoon,' cried poor Allen, in his misery. 'Yet if they were intercepting her letters——'

Wherewith he buried himself in the depths of the shrubbery, while Jock, with a long whistle, came back through the library window to his mother, observing—

'Intercepted! Poor fellow! Hardly necessary, if possible, though Lady Flora might wish to catch her for Clanmacnalty. Has the miserable imp really vouchsafed no notice of any of you?'

'Not the slightest ; and it is breaking Allen's heart.'

'As if a painted little marmoset were worth a man's heart! But Allen has always been infatuated about her, and there's a good deal at stake, though, if he could only see it in the right light, he is well quit of such a bubble of a creature. I wouldn't be saddled with it for all Belforest.'

'Don't call her any more names, my dear! I only wish any one would represent to her the predicament she keeps Allen in. He can't press for an answer, of course ; but it is cruel to keep him in this suspense. I wonder Mrs. Evelyn did not make her write.'

'I don't suppose it entered her mind that the little wretch (I beg your pardon) had not done it of her own accord, and with those Folliotts there's no chance. They live in a perpetual whirl, enough to distract an Archbishop. Twenty-four parties a week at a moderate computation.'

'Unlucky child !'

'Wakefield is heartily vexed at her having run into such hands,' said Jock ; 'but there is no hindering it ; no one has any power, and even if he had, George Gould is a mere tool in his wife's hands.'

'Still, Mr. Wakefield might insist on her answering Allen one way or the other. Poor fellow ! I don't think it would cost her

much, for she was too childish ever to be touched by that
devotion of his. I always thought it a most dangerous experiment, and all I wish for now is that she would send him a
proper dismissal, so that his mind might be settled. It would
be bad enough, but better than going on in this way.'

'I'll see him,' said Jock, 'or may be I can do the business myself, for, strange to say, the creature doesn't avoid me, but rather
runs after me.'

'You meet her in society ?'

'Yes, I've not come to the end of my white kids yet, you see.
And mother, I came to tell you of something that has turned up.
You know the Evelyns are all dead against my selling out. I
dined with Sir James on Tuesday, and found next day it was
for the sake of walking me out before Sir Philip Cameron, the
Cutteejung man, you know. He is sure to be sent out again in
the autumn, and he has promised Sir James that if I can get
exchanged into some corps out there, he will put me on his staff
at once. Mother !'

He stopped short, astounded at the change of countenance,
that for a moment she could neither control nor conceal, as she
exclaimed 'India !' but rallying at once she went on. 'Sir
Philip Cameron ! My dear boy, that's a great compliment.
How delighted your uncle will be !'

'But you, mother !'

'Oh yes, my dear, I shall, I will, like it. Of course I am glad
and proud for my Jock ! How very kind of Sir James !'

'Isn't it ? He talked it over with me as if I had been Cecil,
and said I was quite right not to stay in the Guards ; and that
in India, if a man has any brains at all and reasonable luck, he
can't help getting on. So I shall be quite and clean off your
hands, and in the way of working forward, and perhaps of doing
something worth hearing of. Mother, you will be pleased
then ?'

'Shall I not, my dear, dear Jockey ! I don't think you could
have a better chief. I have always heard that Sir Philip was
such a good man.'

'So Mrs. Evelyn said. She was sure you would be satisfied.
You can't think how kind they were, making the affair quite
their own,' said Jock, with a little colour in his face. 'They
absolutely think it would be wrong to give up the service.'

'Yes ; Mrs. Evelyn wrote to me that you ought not to be
thrown away. It was very kind and dear, but with a little of
the aristocratic notion that the army is the only profession in
the world. I can't help it ; I can't think your father's profession unworthy of his son.'

'She didn't say so !'

'No, but I understood it. Perhaps I am touchy ; I don't
think I am ungrateful. They have always made you like one
of themselves.'

'Yes, so much that I don't like to run counter to their wishes

when they have taken such pains. Besides, there are things
that can be thought of, even by a poor man, as a soldier, which
can't in the other line.'

This speech, made with bent head, rising colour, and hand
playing with his mother's fan, gave her, all unwittingly on his
part, a keen sense that her Jock was indeed passing from her ;
but she said nothing to damp his spirits, and threw herself
heartily into his plans, announcing them to his uncle with
genuine exultation. To this the Colonel fully responded, telling
Jock that he would have given the world thirty years ago for
such a chance, and commending him for thus getting off his
mother's hands.

'I only wish the rest of you were doing the same,' he said ;
'but each one seems to think himself the first person to be
thought of, and her the last.'

The Colonel's wish seemed in course of fulfilment, for when
Lucas went a few days later to his brother Robert's rooms, he
found him collecting testimonials for his fitness to act as Vice-
principal to a European college at Yokohama for the higher
education of the Japanese.

' Mother has not heard of it,' said Jock.

'She need not till it is settled,' answered Bobus. 'It will
save her trouble with her clerical friends if she only knows too
late for a protest.'

Jock understood when he saw the stipulations against
religious teaching, and recognised in the Principal's name an
essayist whose negations of faith had made some stir. However, he only said, ' It will be rather a blow.'

'There are limits to all things,' replied Bobus. 'The truest
kindness to her is to get afloat away from the family raft as
speedily as possible. She has quite enough to drag her down.'

' I should hope to act the other way,' said Jock.

'Get your own head above water first,' said Bobus. ' Here's
some good advice gratis, though I've no expectation of your
taking it. Don't go in for study in the old quarters ! Go to
Edinburgh or Paris or anywhere you please, but cut the connection, or you'll never be rid of loafers for life. Wherever mother
is, all the rest will gravitate. Mark me, Allen is spoilt for anything but a walking gentleman, Armine will never be good for
work, and how many years do you give Janet's Athenian to
come to grief in ? Then will they return to the domestic hearth
with a band of small Grecians, while Dr. Lucas Brownlow is
reduced to a *rotifer* or wheel animal, circulating in a trap collecting supplies, with "*sic vos non vobis*" for his motto.'

Jock looked startled. 'How if there be no such *rotifer* ?' he
said. ' You don't really think there will be nothing to depend
on when we are both gone ?'

' When ?'

' Yes, I've a chance of getting on Cameron's staff in
India.'

'Oh, that's all right, old fellow! Why, you'll be my next neighbour.'

'But about mother? You don't seriously think Ali and Armie will be nothing but dead weights on her?'

'Only as long as there's anybody to hold them up,' said Bobus, perceiving that his picture had taken an effect the reverse of what he intended. 'They have no lack of brains, and are quite able to shift for themselves and mother too, if only they have to do it, even if she were a pauper, which she isn't.'

But it was with a less lightsome heart that Jock went to his quarters to prepare for a fancy ball, where he expected to meet Elvira, though whether he should approach her or not would depend on her own caprice.

It was a very splendid affair. A whole back garden had been transformed into a vast pavilion, containing an Armida's garden, whose masses of ferns and piles of gorgeous flowers made delightful nooks for strangers who left the glare of the dancing-room, and the quaint dresses harmonised with the magic of the gaslight and the strange forms of the exotics.

The simple scarlet of the young Guardsman was undistinguished among the brilliant character-groups which represented old fairy tales and nursery rhymes. There were 'The White Cat and her Prince,' 'Puss-in-Boots and the Princess,' 'Little Snowflake and her Bear,' and, behold, here was the loveliest Fatima ever seen, in the well-known Algerine dress, mated with a richly robed and turbaned hero, whose beard was blue, though in ordinary life red, inasmuch as he was Lady Flora's impecunious and not very reputable Scottish peer of a brother. That lady herself, in a pronounced bloomer, represented the little old woman of doubtful identity, and her husband the pedlar, whose 'name it was Stout'; while not far off the Spanish lady, in garments gay, as rich as may be, wooed her big Englishman in a dress that rivalled Sir Nicolas Blount's.

There was a pretty character quadrille, and then a general *mêlée*, in which Jock danced successively with Cinderella and the fair equestrian of Banbury Cross, and lost sight of Fatima, till, just as he was considering of offering himself to little Bo-peep, he saw her looking a good deal bored by the Spanish lady's Englishman.

Tossing her head till the coins danced on her forehead, she exclaimed, 'Oh, there's my cousin; I must speak to him!' and sprang to her old companion as if for protection. 'Take me to a cool corner, Jock,' she said, 'I am suffocating.'

'No wonder, after waltzing with a mountain.'

'He can no more waltz than fly! And he thinks himself irresistible! He says his dress is from a portrait of his ancestor, Sir Somebody; and Flora declares his only ancestor must have been the Fat Boy! And he thought I was a Turkish Sultana! Wasn't it ridiculous? You know he never says anything but "Exactly."'

'Did he intone it so as to convey all this?'

'He is a little inspired by his ruff and diamonds. Flora says he wants to dazzle me, and will have them changed into paste before he makes them over to his young woman. He has just tin enough to want more, and she says I must be on my guard.'

'You want no guard, I should think, but your engagement.'

'What are you bringing that up for? I suppose you know how Allen wrote to me?' she pouted.

'I know that he thought it due to you to release you from your promise, and that he is waiting anxiously for your reply. Have you written?'

'Don't bore so, Jock,' said Elvira pettishly. 'It was no doing of mine, and I don't see why I should be teased.'

'Then you wish me to tell him that he is to take your silence as a release from you.'

'I authorise nothing,' she said. 'I hate it all.'

'Look here, Elvira,' said Jock, 'do you know your own mind? Nobody wants you to take Allen. In fact, I think he is much better quit of you; but it is due to him, and still more to yourself, to cancel the old affair before beginning a new one.'

'Who told you I was beginning a new one?' asked she pertly.

'No one can blame you, provided you let him loose first. It is considered respectable, you know, to be off with the old love before you are on with the new. Nay, it may be only a superstition.'

'Superstition!' she repeated in an awed voice that gave him his cue, and he went on—'Oh yes, a lady has been even known to come and shake hands with the other party after he had been hanged to give back her troth, lest he should haunt her.'

'Allen isn't hanged,' said Elvira, half frightened, half cross. 'Why doesn't he come himself?'

'Shall he?' said Jock.

'My dear child, I've been running madly up and down for you!' cried Lady Flora, suddenly descending on them, and carrying off her charge with a cursory nod to the Guardsman, marking the difference between a detrimental and even the third son of a millionaire.

He saw Elvira no more that night, and the next post carried a note to Belforest.

*31st May.*

DEAR ALLEN—I don't know whether you will thank me, but I tried to get a something definite out of your tricksy Elf, and the chief result, so far as I can understand the elfish tongue, is, that she sought no change, and the final sentence was, 'Why doesn't he come himself?' I believe it is her honest wish to go on, when she is left to her proper senses; but that is seldom. You must take this for what it is worth from the buffoon,

J. L. B.

Allen came full of hope, and called the next morning. Miss Menella was out riding. He got a card for a party where she was sure to be present, and watched the door, only to see her going away on the arm of Lord Clanmacnalty to some other entertainment. He went to Mr. Folliott's door, armed with a note, and heard that Lady Flora and Miss Menella were gone out of town for a few days. So it went on, and he turned upon Jock with indignation at having been summoned to be thus deluded. The undignified position added venom to the smart of the disregarded affection and the suspense as to the future, and Jock had much to endure after every disappointment, though Allen clung to him rather than to any one else because of his impression that Elvira's real preference was unchanged (such as it was), and that these failures were rather due to her friends than to herself.

This became more clear through Mrs. Evelyn. Her family had connections in common with the Dowager Lady Clanmacnalty, and the two ladies met at the house of their relation. Listening in the way of duty to the old Scottish Countess's profuse communications, she heard what explained a good deal.

Did she know the Spanish girl who was with Flora—a handsome creature and a great heiress? Oh yes; she had presented her. Strange affair! Flora understood that there was a deep plot for appropriating the young lady and her fortune.

'She had been engaged to Mr. Brownlow long before her claims were known,' began Mrs. Evelyn.

'Oh yes! It was very ingeniously arranged, only the discovery was made too soon. I have it on the best authority When the girl came to stay with Flora, her aunt asked for an interview—such a nice sensible woman—so completely understanding her position. She said it was such a distress to her not to be qualified to take her niece into society, yet she could not take her home, living so near, to be harassed by this young man's pursuit.'

'I saw Mrs. Gould myself,' said Mrs. Evelyn. 'I cannot say I was favourably impressed.'

'Oh, we all know she is not a lady; never professes it, poor thing. She is quite aware that her niece must move in a different sphere, and all she wants is to have her guarded from that young Brownlow. He follows them everywhere. It is quite the business of Flora's life to avoid him.'

'Perhaps you don't know that Mrs. Brownlow took that girl out of a farmhouse, and treated her like a daughter, merely because they were second or third cousins. The engagement to Allen Brownlow was made when the fortune was entirely on his side.'

'Precaution or conscience, eh?' said the old lady, laughing. 'By the by, you were intimate with Mrs. Brownlow abroad. How fortunate for you that nothing took place while they had such expectations! Of no family, I hear; of quite low extraction. A parish doctor he was, wasn't he?'

'A distinguished surgeon.'

'And *she* came out of some asylum or foundling hospital?'

'Only the home for officers' daughters,' said Mrs. Evelyn, not able to help laughing. 'Her father, Captain Allen, was in the same regiment with Colonel Brownlow, her husband's brother. I assure you the Menellas and Goulds have no reason to boast.'

'A noble Spanish family,' said the dowager. 'One can see it in every gesture of the child.'

It was plain that the old lady intended Mr. Barnes's hoards to repair the ravages of dissipation on the never very productive estates of Clanmacnalty, and that while Elvira continued in Lady Flora's custody, there was little chance of a meeting between her and Allen. The girl seemed to be submitting passively, and no doubt her new friends could employ tact and flattery enough to avoid exciting her perverseness. No doubt she had been harassed by Allen's exaction of response to his ardent affection, and wearied of his monopoly of her. Maiden coyness and love of liberty might make her as willing to elude his approach as her friends could wish.

Once only, at a garden party, did he touch the tips of her fingers, but no more. She never met his eye, but threw herself into eager flirtation with the men he most disliked, while the lovely carnation was mounting in her cheek, and betraying unusual excitement. It became known that she was going early in July into the country with some gay people who were going to give a series of *fêtes* on some public occasion, and then that she was to go with Lady Clanmacnalty and her unmarried daughter to Scotland, to help them entertain the grouse-shooting party.

Allen's stay in London was clearly of no further use, as Jock perceived with a sensation of relief, for all his pity could not hinder him from being bored with Allen's continual dejection, and his sighs over each unsuccessful pursuit. He was heartily tired of the part of confidant, which was the more severe, because, whenever Allen had a fit of shame at his own undignified position, he vented it in reproaches to Jock for having called him up to London; and yet as long as there was a chance of seeing Elvira, he could not tear himself away, was wild to get invitations to meet her, and lived at his club in the old style of expense.

Bobus was brief with Allen, and ironical on Jock's folly in having given the summons. For his own part he was much engrossed with his appointment, going backwards and forwards between Oxford and London, with little time for the concerns of any one else; but the evening after this unfortunate garden party, when Jock had accompanied his eldest brother back to his rooms, and was endeavouring, by the help of a pipe, to endure the reiteration of mournful vituperations of destiny in the shape of Lady Flora and Mrs. Gould, the door suddenly opened, and Bobus stood before them with his peculiarly brisk, self-satisfied air, in itself an aggravation to any one out of spirits.

'All right,' he said, 'I didn't expect to find you in, but I thought I would leave a note for the chance. I've heard of the very identical thing to suit you, Ali, my boy.'

'Indeed,' said Allen, not prepared with gratitude for his younger brother's patronage.

'I met Bulstrode at Balliol last night, and he asked if I knew of any one (a perfect gentleman he must be, that matters more than scholarship) who would take a tutorship in a Hungarian Count's family. Two little boys, who live like princes, tutor the same, salary anything you like to ask. It is somewhere in the mountains, a feudal castle, with capital sport.'

'Wolves and bears,' cried Jock, starting up with his old boyish animation. 'If I wasn't going pig-sticking in India, what wouldn't I give for such a chance. The tutor will teach the young ideas how to shoot, of course.'

'Of course,' said Bobus. 'The Count is a diplomate, and there's not a bad chance of making oneself useful, and getting on in that line. I should have jumped at it, if I hadn't got the Japs on my hands.'

'Yes, you,' said Allen languidly.

'Well, you can do quite as well for a thing like this,' said Bobus, 'or better, as far as looking the gentleman goes. In fact, I suspect as much classics as Mother Carey taught us at home would serve their countships' turn. Here's the address. You had better write by the first post to-morrow, for one or two others are rising at it; but Bulstrode said he would wait to hear from you. Here's the letter with all the details.'

'Thank you. You seem to take a good deal for granted,' said Allen, not moving a finger towards the letter.

'You won't have it?'

'I have neither spirits nor inclination for turning bear-leader, and it is not a position I wish to undertake.'

'What position would you like?' cried Jock. 'You could take that rifle you got for Algeria, and make the Magyars open their eyes. Seriously, Allen, it is the right thing at the right time. You know Miss Ogilvie always said the position was quite different for an English person among these foreigners.'

'Who, like natives, are all the same nation,' quietly observed Allen.

'For that matter,' said Jock, 'wasn't it in Hongarie that the beggar of low degree married the king's daughter? There's precedent for you, Ali!'

Allen had taken up the letter, and after glancing it slightly over, said—

'Thanks, Vice-principal, but I won't stand in the light of your other aspirants.'

'What can you want better than this?' cried Jock. 'By the time the law business is over, one may look in vain for such a chance. It is a new country too, and you always said you wanted to know how those fellows with long-tailed names lived in private life.'

Both brothers talked for an hour, till they hoped they had persuaded him that even for the most miserable and disappointed being on earth the Hungarian castle might prove an interesting variety, and they left him at last with the letter before him, undertaking to write and make further inquiries.

The next day, however, just as Jock was about to set forth, intending, as far as might be, to keep him up to the point, Bobus made his appearance, and scornfully held out an envelope. There was the letter, and therewith these words :—

On consideration, I recur to my first conclusion, that this situation is out of the question. To say nothing of the injury to my health and nerves from agitation and suspense, rendering me totally unfit for drudgery and annoyance, I cannot feel it right to place myself in a situation equivalent to the abandonment of all hope. It is absurd to act as if we were reduced to abject poverty, and I will never place myself in the condition of a dependent. This season has so entirely knocked me up that I must at once have sea air, and by the time you receive this I shall be on my way to Ryde for a cruise in the *Petrel.*

'*His* health!' cried Bobus, his tone implying three notes, scarcely of admiration.

'Well, poor old Turk, he is rather seedy,' said Jock. 'Can't sleep, and has headaches! But 'tis a regular case of having put him to flight!'

'Well, I've done with him,' said Bobus, 'since there's a popular prejudice against flogging, especially one's elder brother. This is a delicate form of intimation that he intends doing the *dolce* at mother's expense.'

'The poor old chap has been an ornamental appendage so long that he can't make up his mind to anything else,' said Jock.

'He is no worse off than the rest of us,' said Bobus.

'In age, if in nothing else.'

'The more reason against throwing away a chance. The yacht, too! I thought there was a Quixotic notion of not dipping into that Elf's money. I'm sure poor mother is pinching herself enough.'

'I don't think Ali knows when he spends money more than when he spends air,' returned Jock. 'The *Petrel* can hardly cost as much in a month as I have seen him get through in a week, protesting all the while that he was living on absolutely nothing.'

'I know. You may be proud to get him down Oxford Street under thirty shillings, and he never goes out in the evening much under half that.'

'Yes, he told me selling my horses was shocking bad economy.'

'Well, it was your own doing, having him up here,' said Bobus.

'I wonder how he will go on when the money is really not there.'

'Precisely the same,' said Bobus; 'there's no cure for that sort of complaint. The only satisfaction is that we shall be out of sight of it.'

'And a very poor one,' sighed Jock, 'when mother is left to bear the brunt.'

'Mother can manage him much better than we can,' said Bobus; 'besides, she is still a youngish woman, neither helpless nor destitute; and as I always tell you, the greatest kindness we can do her is to look out for ourselves.'

Bobus himself had done so effectually, for he was secure of a handsome salary, and his travelling expenses were to be paid, when, early in the next year, he was to go out with his Principal to confer on the Japanese the highest possible culture in science and literature without any bias in favour of Christianity, Buddhism, or any other sublime religion.

Meantime he was going home to make his preparations, and pack such portions of his museum as he thought would be unexampled in Japan. He had fulfilled his intention of only informing his mother after his application had been accepted; and as it had been done by letter, he had avoided the sight of the pain it gave her and the hearing of her remonstrances, all of which he had referred to her maternal dislike of his absence, rather than to his association with the Principal, a writer whose articles she kept out of reach of Armine and Barbara.

The matter had become irrevocable and beyond discussion, as he intended, before his return to Belforest, which he only notified by the post of the morning before he walked into luncheon. By that time it was a *fait accompli*, and there was nothing to be done but to enter on a lively discussion on the polite manners and customs of the two-sworded nation, and the wonderful volcanoes he hoped to explore.

Perhaps one reason that his notice was so short was that there might be the less time for Kencroft to be put on its guard. Thus, when, by accident of course, he strolled towards the lodge, he found his cousin Esther in the wood, with no guardians but the three youngest children, who had coaxed her, in spite of the heat, to bring them to the slopes of wood strawberries on their weekly half-holiday.

He had seen nothing, but had only been guided by the sound of voices to the top of the sloping wooded bank, where, under the shade of the oak-trees, looking over the tall spreading brackens, he beheld Essie in her pretty gipsy hat and holland dress, with all her bird-like daintiness, kneeling on the moss far below him, threading the scarlet beads on bents of grass, with the little ones round her.

'I heard a chattering,' he said, as, descending through the fern, he met her dark eyes looking up like those of a startled fawn; 'so I came to see whether the rabbits had found tongues.

How many more are there? No, thank you,' as Edmund and Lina answered his greeting with an offer of very moist-looking fruit, and an ungrammatical

'Only us.'

'Then us run away. They grow thick up that bank, and I've got a prize here for whoever keeps away longest. No, you shan't see what it is. Any one who comes asking questions will lose it. Run away, Lina, you'll miss your chance. No, no, Essie, you are not a competitor.'

'I must, Robert; indeed I must.'

'Can't you spare me a moment when I am come down for my last farewell visit?'

'But you are not going for a good while yet.'

'So you call it, but it will seem short enough. Did you ever hear of minutes seeming like diamond drops meted out, Essie?'

'But, you know, it is your own doing,' said Essie.

'Yes, and why, Essie? Because misfortune has made such an exile as this the readiest mode of ceasing to be a burden to my mother.'

'Papa said he was glad of it,' said Esther, 'and that you were quite right. But it is a terrible way off!'

'True; but there is one consideration that will make up to me for everything.'

'That it is for Aunt Caroline?'

'Partly, but do you not know the hope which makes all work sweet to me?' And the look of his eyes, and his hand seeking hers, made her say—

'Oh, don't, Robert, I mustn't.'

'Nay, my queen, you were too duteous to hearken to me when I was rich and prosperous. I would not torment you then, I meant to be patient; but now I am poor and going into banishment, you will be generous and compassionate, and let me hear the one word that will make my exile sweet.'

'I don't think I ought,' said the poor child under her breath. 'O Robert, don't you know I ought not?'

'Would you if that ugly cypher of an ought did not stand in the way?'

'Oh, don't ask me, Robert; I don't know.'

'But I do know, my queen,' said he. 'I know my little Essie better than she knows herself. I know her true heart is mine, only she dares not avow it to herself; and when hearts have so met, Esther, they owe one another a higher duty than the filial tie can impose.'

'I never heard that before,' she said, puzzled, but not angered.

'No, it is not a doctrine taught in schoolrooms, but it is true and universal for all that, and our fathers and mothers acted on it in their day, and will give way to it now.'

Esther had never been told all her father's objections to her

cousin. Simple prohibition had seemed to her parents sufficient
for the gentle, dutiful child. Bobus had always been very kind
to her, and her heart went out enough to him in his trouble to
make coldness impossible to her. Tears welled into her eyes
with perplexity at the new theory, and she could only falter
out—

'That doesn't seem right for me.'

'Say one word and trust to me, and it shall be right. Yes,
Esther, say the word, and in it I shall be strong to overcome
everything, and win the consent you desire. Say only that,
with it, you would love me.'

'If?' said Esther.

It was an interrogative *if*, and she did not mean it for 'the
one word,' but Bobus caught at it as all he wanted. He meant
it for the fulcrum on which to rest the strong lever of his will,
and before Esther could add any qualification he was overwhelming her with thanks and assurances so fervent that she
could interpose no more doubts, and yielded to the sweetness of
being able to make any one so happy, above all the cousin whom
most people thought so formidably clever.

Edmund interrupted them by rushing up, thus losing the
prize, which was won by the last comer, and proved to be a
splendid *bonbon;* but there was consolation for the others, since
Bobus had laid in a supply as a means of securing peace.

He would fain have waited to rivet his chains before mani-
festing them, but he knew Essie too well to expect her to keep
the interview a secret ; and he had no time to lose if, as he intended, though he had not told her so, he was to take her to
Japan with him.

So he stormed the castle without delay, walked to Kencroft
with the strawberry-gatherers, found the Colonel superintending the watering of his garden, and, with effrontery of which
Essie was unconscious, led her up, and announced their mutual
love, as though secure of an ardent welcome.

He did, mayhap, expect to surprise something of the kind
out of his slowly-moving uncle, but the only answer was a
strongly accentuated 'Indeed ! I thought I had told you both
that I would have none of this foolery. Esther, I am ashamed
of you. Go in directly.'

The girl repaired to her own room to weep floods of tears
over her father's anger and the disobedience that made itself
apparent as soon as she was beyond the spell of that specious
tongue. There were a few tears too for his disappointment ;
but when her mother came up in great displeasure, the first
words were—

'O mamma, I could not help it !'

'You could not prevent his accosting you, but you might
have prevented his giving all this trouble to papa. You know
we should never allow it.'

'Indeed I only said if !'

'You had no right to say anything. When a young lady knows a man is not to be encouraged, she should say nothing to give him an advantage. You could never expect us to let you go to a barbarous place at the other end of the world with a man of as good as no religion at all.'

'He goes to church,' said Essie, too simple to look beyond.

'Only here, to please his mother. My dear, you must put this out of your head. Even if he were very different, we should never let you marry a first cousin, and he knows it. It was very wrong in him to have spoken to you.'

'Please don't let him do it again,' said Esther faintly.

'That's right, my dear,' with a kiss of forgiveness. 'I am sure you are too good a girl really to care for him.'

'I wish he would not care for me,' sighed poor Essie wearily. 'He always was so kind, and now they are in trouble I couldn't vex him.'

'Oh, my dear, young men get over things of this sort half a dozen times in their lives.'

Essie was not delighted with this mode of consolation, and when her mother tenderly smoothed back her hair, and bade her bathe her face and dress for dinner, she clung to her and said—

'Don't let me see him again.'

It was a wholesome dread, which Mrs. Brownlow encouraged, for both she and her husband were annoyed and perplexed by Robert's cool reception of their refusal. He quietly declared that he could allow for their prejudices, and that it was merely a matter of time, and he was provokingly calm and secure, showing neither anger nor disappointment. He did not argue, but having once shown that his salary warranted his offer, that the climate was excellent, and that European civilisation prevailed, he treated his uncle and aunt as unreasonably prejudiced mortals, who would in time yield to his patient determination.

His mother was as much annoyed as they were, all the more because her sister-in-law could hardly credit her perfect innocence of Robert's intentions, and was vexed at her wish to ascertain Esther's feelings. This was not easy! the poor child was so unhappy and shamefaced, so shocked at her involuntary disobedience, and so grieved at the pain she had given. If Robert had been set before her with full consent of friends, she would have let her whole heart go out to him, loved him, and trusted him for ever, treating whatever opinions were unlike hers as manly idiosyncrasies beyond her power to fathom. But she was no Lydia Languish to need opposition as a stimulus. It rather gave her tender and dutiful spirit a sense of shame, terror, and disobedience ; and she thankfully accepted the mandate that sent her on a visit to her married sister for as long as Bobus should remain at Belforest.

He did not show himself downcast, but was quietly assured that he should win her at last, only smiling at the useless precaution, and declaring himself willing to wait, and make a home for her.

But this matter had not tended to make his mother more at ease in her enforced stay at Belforest, which was becoming a kind of gilded prison.

## CHAPTER XXXI

### SLACK TIDE

'If . . . .
　Thou hide thine eyes and make thy peevish moan
　Over some broken reed of earth beneath,
　Some darling of blind fancy dead and gone.
　　　　　　　　　　　　　　　　KEBLE.

THERE is such a thing as slack tide in the affairs of men, when a crisis seems as if it would never come, and all things stagnate. The Law Courts had as yet not concerned themselves about the will, vacation time had come, and all was at a standstill, nor could any steps be taken for Lucas's exchange till it was certain into what part of India Sir Philip Cameron was going. In the meantime his regiment had gone into camp, and he could not get away until the middle of September, and then only for a few days. Arriving very late on a Friday night, he saw nobody but his mother over his supper, and thought her looking very tired. When he met her in the morning, there was the same weary, harassed countenance, there were worn marks round the dark wistful eyes, and the hair, whitened at Schwarenbach, did not look as incongruous with the face as hitherto.

No one else except Barbara had come down to prayers, so Jock's first inquiry was for Armine.

'He is pretty well,' said his mother; 'but he is apt to be late. He gets overtired between his beloved parish work and his reading with Bobus.'

'He is lucky to get such a coach,' said Jock. 'Bob taught me more mathematics in a week than I had learnt in seven years before.'

'He is terribly accurate,' said Babie.

'Which Armie does not appreciate,' said Jock.

'I'm afraid not,' said his mother. 'They do worry each other a good deal, and this Infanta most of all, I'm afraid.'

'Oh no, mother,' said Babie. 'Only it is hard for poor Armie to have two taskmasters.'

'What! the Reverend Petronella continues in the ascendant?'

Bobus here entered, with a face that lightened, as did every one's, at sight of Lucas.

'Good morning. Ah! Jock! I didn't sit up, for I had had a long day out on the moors; we kept the birds nearer home for you. There are plenty, but Grimes says he has heard shots towards River Hollow, and thinks some one must have been trespassing there.'

'Have you heard anything of Elvira? à propos to River Hollow,' said his mother.

'Yes,' said Jock. 'One of our fellows has been on a moor not far from where she was astonishing the natives, conjointly with Lady Anne Macnalty. There were bets which of three men she may be engaged to.'

'Pending which,' said his mother, 'I suppose poor Allen will continue to hover on the wings of the *Petrel* ?'

'And send home mournful madrigals by the ream,' said Bobus. 'Never was petrel so tuneful a bird !'

'For shame, Bobus ; I never meant you to see them !'

''Twas quite involuntary ! I have trouble enough with my own pupil's effusions. I leave him a bit of Latin composition, and what do I find but an endless doggerel ballad on What's his name ?—who hid under his father's staircase as a beggar, eating the dogs' meat, while his afflicted family were searching for him in vain ;—his favourite example.'

'St. Alexis,' said Babie ; 'he was asked to versify it.'

'As a wholesome incentive to filial duty and industry,' said Bobus. 'Does the Parsoness mean to have it sung in the school ?'

'It might be less dangerous than "the fox went out one moonshiny night,"' said their mother, anxious to turn the conversation. 'Mr. Parsons brought Mr. Todd of Wrexham in to see the school just as the children were singing the final catastrophe when the old farmer "shot the old fox right through the head." He was so horrified that he declared the schools should never have a penny of his while they taught such murder and heresy.'

'Served them right,' said Jock, 'for spoiling that picture of domestic felicity when "the little ones picked the bones, oh !" How many guns shall we be, Bobus?'

'Only three. My uncle has a touch of gout, the Monk has got a tutorship, Joe has gone back to his ship, but the mighty Bob has a week's leave, and does not mean a bird to survive the change of owners.'

'Doesn't Armine come?'

'Not he !' said Bobus. 'Says he doesn't want to acquire the taste, and he would knock up with half a day.'

'But you'll all come and bring us luncheon ?' entreated Jock. 'You will, mother ! Now, won't you? We'll eat it on a bank like old times when we lived at the Folly, and all were jolly. I beg your pardon, Bob ; I didn't mean to turn into another poetical brother on your hands, but enthusiasm was too strong for me ! Come, Mother Carey, *do* !'

'Where is it to be ?' she asked, smiling.

'Out by the Long Hanger would be a good place,' said Bobus, 'where we found the *Epipactis grandiflora*.'

'Or the heathery knoll where poor little mother got into a scrape for singing profane songs by moonlight,' laughed Jock.

'Ah! that was when hearts were light,' she said; 'but at any rate we'll make a holiday of it, for Jock's sake.'

'Ha! what do I see?' exclaimed Jock, who was opposite the open window. 'Is that Armine, or a Jack-in-the-Green?'

'Oh!' half sighed Barbara. 'It's that harvest decoration!' And Armine, casting down armfuls of great ferns and beautiful trailing plants, made his entrance through the open window, exchanging greetings, and making a semi-apology for his late appearance as he said—

'Mother, please desire Macrae to cut me the great white orchids. He won't do it unless you tell him, and I promised them for the altar vases.'

'You know, Armie,' he said cutting them would be the ruin of the plant, and I don't feel justified in destroying it.'

'Macrae's fancy,' muttered Armine. 'It is only that he hates the whole thing.'

'Unhappy Macrae! I go and condole with him sometimes,' said Bobus. 'I don't know which are most outraged—his Free-kirk or his horticultural feelings!'

'Babie,' ordered Armine, who was devouring his breakfast at double speed, 'if you'll put on your things, I've the garden donkey-cart ready to take down the flowers. You won't expect us to luncheon, mother?'

Barbara, though obedient, looked blank, and her mother said—

'My dear, if I went down and helped at the church till half-past twelve, could not we all be set free? Your brothers want us to bring their luncheon to them at the Hanger.'

'That's right, mother,' cried Jock; 'I've half a mind to come and expedite matters.'

'No, no, Skipjack!' cried Bobus; 'I had that twenty stone of solid flesh whom I see walking up to the house to myself all yesterday, and I can't stand another day of it unmitigated!'

Entered the tall heavy figure of Rob. He reported his father as much the same and not yet up, delivered a note to his aunt, and made no objection to devouring several slices of tongue and a cup of cocoa to recruit nature after his walk; while Bobus reclaimed the reluctant Armine from cutting scarlet geraniums in the ribbon beds to show him the scene in the Greek play which he was to prepare, and Babie tried to store up all the directions, perceiving from the pupil's roving eye that she should have to be his memory.

Jock saw that the note had brought an additional line of care to his mother's brow, and therefore still more gaily and eagerly adjured her not to fail in the Long Hanger, and as the shooting party started, he turned back to wave his cap, and shout, 'Sharp two!'

Two o'clock found three hungry youths and numerous dead

birds on the pleasant, thymy bank beneath the edge of the beech wood ; but gaze as they might through the clear September air, neither mother, brother, nor sister was visible. Presently, however, the pony-carriage appeared, and in it a hamper, but driven only by the stable-boy. He said a gentleman was at the house, and Mrs. Brownlow was very sorry that she could not come, but had sent him with the luncheon.

'I shall go and see after her,' said Jock ; and in spite of all remonstrance, and assurance that it was only a form of Parsonic tyranny, he took a draught of ale and a handful of sandwiches, sprang into the carriage, and drove off, hardly knowing why, but with a yearning towards his mother, and a sense that all that was unexpected boded evil. Leaving the pony at the stables, and walking up to the house, he heard sounds that caused him to look in at the open library window.

On one side of the table stood his mother, on the other Dr. Demetrius Hermann, with insinuating face, but arm upraised as if in threatening.

'Scoundrel !' burst forth Jock. Both turned, and his mother's look of relief and joy met him as he sprang to her side, exclaiming, 'What does this mean ? How dare you ? '

'No, no !' she cried breathlessly, clinging to his arm. 'He did not mean—it was only a gesture !'

'I'll have no such gestures to my mother.'

'Sir, the honoured lady only does me justice. I meant nothing violent. Zat is for you English military, whose veapon is zie horse-vhip.'

'As you will soon feel,' said Jock, 'if you attempt to bully my mother. What does it mean, mother dear ? '

'He made a mistake,' she said, in a quick tremulous tone, showing how much she was shaken. 'He thinks me a quack doctor's widow, whose secret is matter of bargain and sale.'

'Madame ! I offered most honourable terms.'

'Terms, indeed ! I told you the affair is no empirical secret to be bought.'

'Yet madame knows that I am in possession of a portion of zie discovery, and that it is in my power to pursue it further, though, for family considerations, I offer her to take me into confidence, so that all may profit in unison,' said the Greek, in his blandest manner.

'The very word *profit* shows your utter want of appreciation,' said Mrs. Brownlow, with dignity. 'Such discoveries are the property of the entire faculty, to be used for the general benefit, not for private selfish profit. I do not know how much information may have been obtained, but if any attempt be made to use it in the charlatan fashion you propose, I shall at once expose the whole transaction, and send my husband's papers to the *Lancet*.'

Hermann shrugged his shoulders and looked at Lucas, as if considering whether more or less reason could be expected from a soldier than from a woman. It was to him that he spoke.

'Madame cannot see zie matter in zie light of business. I have offered freely to share all that I shall gain, if I may only obtain the data needful to perfect zie discovery of zie learned and venerated father. I am met wit anger I cannot comprehend.'

'Nor ever will,' said Caroline.

'And,' pursued Dr. Hermann, 'when, on zie oder hand, I explain that my wife has imparted to me sufficient to enable me to perfectionate the discovery, and if the reserve be continued, it is just to demand compensation, I am met with indignation even greater. I appeal to zie captain. Is this treatment such as my proposals merit?'

'Not quite,' said Jock. '*That* is to be kicked out of the house, as you shortly will be, if you do not take yourself off.'

'Sir, your amiable affection for madame leads you to forget, as she does, zie claim of your sister.'

'No one has any claim on my mother,' said Jock.

'Zie moral claim—zie claim of affection,' began the Greek; but Caroline interrupted him—

'Dr. Hermann is not the person fitly to remind me of these. They have not been much thought of in Janet's case. I mean to act as justly as I can by my daughter, but I have absolutely nothing to give her at present. Till I know what my own means may prove to be, I can do nothing.'

'But madame holds out zie hope of some endowment. I shall be in a condition to be independent of it, but it would be sweet to my wife as a token of pardon. I could bear away a promise.'

'I promise nothing,' was the reply. 'If I have anything to give—even then, all would depend on your conduct and the line you may take. And above all, remember, it is in my power to frustrate and expose any attempt to misuse any hints that may have been stolen from my husband's memoranda. In my power, and my duty.'

'Madame might have spared me this,' sighed the Athenian. 'My poor Janette! She will not believe how her husband has been received.'

He was gone. Caroline dropped into a chair, but the next moment she almost screamed—

'Oh, we must not let him go thus! He may revenge it on her! Go after him, get his address, tell him she shall have her share if he will behave well to her.'

Jock fulfilled his mission according to his own judgment, and as he returned his mother started up.

'You have not brought him back!'

'I should rather think not!'

'Janet's husband! O Jock, it is very dreadful! My poor child!'

She had been a little lioness in face of the enemy, but she

was trembling so hopelessly that Jock put her on a couch and
knelt with his arm round her while she laid her head on his
strong young shoulder.

'Let me fetch you some wine, mother darling,' he said.

'No, no—to feel you is better than anything,' putting his arm
closer—

'What was it all about, mother?'

'Ah! you don't know, yet you went straight to the point, my
dear champion.'

'He was bullying you, that was enough. I thought for a
moment the brute was going to strike you.'

'That was only gesticulation. I'm glad you didn't knock him
down when you made in to the rescue.'

She could laugh a little now.

'I should like to have done it. What did he want? Money,
of course?'

'Not solely. I can't tell you all about it; but Janet saw
some memoranda of your father's, and he wants to get hold of
them.'

'To pervert them to some quackery?'

'If not, I do him great injustice.'

'Give them up to a rogue like that! I should guess not! It
will be some little time before he tries again. Well done, little
mother!'

'If he will not turn upon her.'

'What a speculation he must have thought her.'

'Don't talk of it, Jock; I can't bear to think of her in such
hands.'

'Janet has a spirit of her own. I should think she could get
her way with her subtle Athenian. Where did he drop from?'

'He overtook me on my way back from the church, for
indeed I did not mean to break my appointment. I don't think
the servants knew who was here. And Jock, if you mention it
to the others, don't speak of this matter of the papers. Call it,
as you may with truth, an attempt to extort money.'

'Very well,' he gravely said.

'It is true,' she continued, 'that I have valuable memoranda
of your father's in my charge; but you must trust me when I
say that I am not at liberty to tell you more.'

'Of course I do. So the mother was really coming, like a
good little Red-riding-hood, to bring her son's dinner into the
forest, when she met with the wolf! Pray, has he eaten up the
two kids at a mouthful?'

'No, Miss Parsons had done that already. They are making
the church so beautiful, and it did not seem possible to spare
them, though I hope Armine may get home in time to get his
work done for Bobus.'

'Is not he worked rather hard between the two? He does
not seem to thrive on it.'

'Jock, I can say it to you. I don't know what to do. The

poor boy's heart is in these Church matters, and he is so bitterly grieved at the failure of all his plans that I cannot bear to check him in doing all he can. It is just what I ought to have been doing all these years ; I only saw my duties as they were being taken away from me, and so I deserve the way Miss Parsons treats me.'

'What way ?'

'You need not bristle up. She is very civil; but when I hint that Armine has study and health to consider, I see that in her eyes I am the worldly obstructive mother who serves as a trial to the hero.'

'If she makes Armine think so——'

'Armie is too loyal for that. Yet it may be only too true, and only my worldliness that wishes for a little discretion. Still, I don't think a sensible woman, if she were ever so good and devoted, would encourage his fretting over the disappointment, or lead him to waste his time when so much depends on his diligence. I am sure the focus of her mind must be distorted, and she is twisting his the same way.'

'And her brother follows suit ?'

'I think they go in parallel grooves, and he lets her alone. It is very unlucky, for they are a constant irritation to Bobus, and he fancies them average specimens of good people. He sneers, and I can't say but that much of what he says is true, but there is the envenomed drop in it which makes his good sense shocking to Armine, and I fear Babie relishes it more than is good for her. So they make one another worse, and so they will as long as we are here. It was a great mistake to stay on, and your uncle must feel it so.'

'Could you not go to Dieppe, or some cheap place ?'

'I don't feel justified in any more expense. Here the house costs nothing, and our personal expenditure does not go beyond our proper means ; but to pay for lodging elsewhere would soon bring me in excess of it, at least as long as Allen keeps up the yacht. Then poor Janet must have something, and I don't know what bills may be in store for me, and there's your outfit, and Bobus's.'

'Never mind mine.'

'My dear, that's fine talking, but you can't go like Sir Charles Napier, with one shirt and a bit of soap.'

'No, but I shall get something for the exchange. Besides, my kit was costly even for the Guards, and will amply cover all that.'

'And you have sold your horses ?'

'And have been living on them ever since ! Come, won't that encourage you to make a little jaunt, just to break the spell ?'

'I wish it could, my dear, but it does not seem possible while those bills are such a dreadful uncertainty. I never know what Allen may have been ordering.'

'Surely the Evelyns would be glad to have you.'

'No, Jock, that can't be. Promise me that you will do nothing to lead to an invitation. You are to meet some of them, are you not?'

'Yes, on Thursday week, at Roland Hampton's wedding. Cecil and I and a whole lot of us go down in the morning to it, and Sydney is to be a bridesmaid. What are you going to do now, mother?'

'I don't quite know. I feel regularly foolish. I shall have a headache if I don't keep quiet, but I can't persuade myself to stay in the house lest that man should come back.'

'What! not with me for garrison?'

'Oh, nonsense, my dear. You must go and catch up the sportsmen.'

'Not when I can get my Mother Carey all to myself. You go and lie down in the dressing-room, and I'll come as soon as I have taken off my boots and ordered some coffee for you.'

He returned with the step of one treading on eggs, expecting to find her half asleep; but her eyes were glittering, and there were red spots on her cheeks, for her nerves were excited, and when he came in she began to talk. She told him, not of present troubles, but of the letters between his father and grandmother, which, in her busy, restless life, she had never before looked at, but which had come before her in her preparations for vacating Belforest. Perhaps it was only now that she had grown into appreciation of the relations between that mother and son, as she read the letters, preserved on each side, and revealing the full beauty and greatness of her husband's nature, his perfect confidence in his mother, and a guiding influence from her, which she herself had never thought of exerting. Does not many an old correspondence thus put the present generation to shame?

Jock was the first person with whom she had shared these letters, and it was good to watch his face as he read the words of the father whom he remembered chiefly as the best of play-fellows. He was of an age and in a mood to enter into them with all his heart, though he uttered little more than an occasional question, or some murmured remark when anything struck him. Both he and his mother were so occupied that they never observed that the sky clouded over and rain began to fall, nor did they think of any outer object till Bobus opened the door in search of them.

'Halloo, you deserter!'

'Hush! Mother has a headache.'

'Not now, you have cured it.'

'Well, you've missed an encounter with the most impudent rascal I ever came across.'

'You didn't meet Hermann?'

'Well, perhaps I have found his match; but you shall hear.

Y

Grimes said he heard guns, and we came upon the scoundrel in Lewis Acre, two brace on his shoulder.'

'The vultures are gathering to the prey,' said his mother.

'I'm not arrived at lying still to be devoured!' said Bobus. 'I gave him the benefit of a doubt, and sent Grimes to warn him off; but the fellow sent his card—*his* card forsooth, "Mr. Gilbert Gould, R.N.,"—and information that he had Miss Menella's permission.'

'Not credible,' said Jock.

'Mrs. Lisette's more likely,' said his mother. 'I think he is her brother.'

'I sent Grimes back to tell him that Miss Menella had as much power to give leave as my old pointer, and if he did not retire at once, we should gently remove his gun and send out a summons.'

'Why did you not do so at once?' cried Jock.

'Because I have brains enough not to complicate matters by a personal row with the Goulds,' said Bobus, 'though I could wish not to have been there, when the keepers would infallibly have done so. Shall I write to George Gould, or will you, mother?'

'Oh dear,' sighed Caroline, 'I think Mr. Wakefield is the fittest person, if it signifies enough to have it done at all.'

'Signifies!' cried Jock. 'To have that rascal loafing about! I wouldn't be trampled upon while the life is in me!'

'I don't like worrying Mr. Gould. It is not his fault, except for having married such a wife, poor man.'

'Having been married by her, you mean,' said Bobus. 'Mark me, she means to get that fellow married to that poor child, as sure as fate.'

'Impossible, Bobus! His age!'

'He is a good deal younger than his sister, and a prodigious swell.'

'Besides, he is her uncle,' said Jock.

'No, no, only her uncle's wife's brother.'

'That's just the same.'

'I wish it were!' But Jock would not be satisfied without getting a Prayer-book, to look at the table of degrees.

'He is really her third cousin, I believe,' said his mother, 'and I'm afraid that is not prohibited.'

'Is he a ship's steward?' said Jock, looking at the card with infinite disgust.

'A paymaster's assistant, I believe.'

'That would be too much. Besides, there's the Scot!'

'I don't think much of that,' said Jock. 'The mother and sister are keen for it, but Clanmacnalty is in no haste to marry, and by all accounts the Elf carries on promiscuously with three or four at once.'

'And she has no fine instinct for a gentleman,' added Bobus. 'It is who will spread the butter thickest!'

'A bad look-out for Belforest,' said Jock.

'It can't be much worse than it has been with me,' said his mother.

'That's what that little ass, Armine, has been presuming to din into your ears,' said Bobus; 'as if the old women didn't prefer beef and blankets to you coming poking piety at the poor old parties.'

'By the by,' cried Caroline, starting, 'those children have never come home, and see how it rains!'

Jock volunteered to take the pony carriage and fetch them, but he had not long emerged from the park in the gathering twilight before he overtook two figures under one umbrella, and would have passed them had he not been hailed.

'You demented children! Jump in this instant.'

'Don't turn!' called Armine. 'We must take this,' showing a parcel which he had been sheltering more carefully than himself or his sister.

'It is cord and tassels for the banner. They sent wrong ones,' said Barbara, 'and we had to go and match it. They would not let me go alone.'

'Get in, I say,' cried Jock, who was making demonstrations with the 'national weapon' much as if he would have liked to lay it about their shoulders.

'Then we must drive on to the Parsonage,' stipulated Armine.

'Not a bit of it, you drenched and foolish morsel of humanity. You are going straight home to bed. Hand us the parcel. What will you give me not to tie this cord round the Reverend Petronella's neck?'

'Thank you, Jock, I'm so glad,' said Babie, referring probably to the earlier part of his speech. 'We would have come home for the pony carriage, but we thought it would be out.'

'Take care of the drip,' was Armine's parting cry, as Babie turned the pony's head, and Jock strode down the lane. He meant merely to have given in the parcel at the door, but Miss Parsons darted out, and not distinguishing him in the dark began, 'Thank you, dear Armine; I'm so sorry, but it is in the good cause and you won't regret it. Where's your sister? Gone home? But you'll come and have a cup of tea and stay to evensong?'

'My brother and sister are gone home, thank you,' said Jock, with impressive formality, and a manly voice that made her start.

'Oh, indeed. Thank you, Mr. Brownlow. I was so sorry to let them go; but it had not begun to rain, and it is such a joy to dear Armine to be employed in the service.'

'Yes, he is mad enough to run any risk,' said Jock.

'Oh, Mr. Brownlow, if I could only persuade you to enter into the joy of self-devotion, you would see that I could not forbid him! Won't you come in and have a cup of tea?'

'Thank you, no. Good-night.' And Miss Parsons was left

rejoicing at having said a few words of reproof to that cynical
Mr. Robert Brownlow, while Jock tramped away, grinning a
sardonic smile at the lady's notions of the joys of self-sacrifice.

He came home only just in time for dinner, and found Armine
enduring, with a touching resignation learnt in Miss Parsons'
school, the sarcasm of Bobus for having omitted to prepare his
studies. The boy could neither eat nor entirely conceal the
chills that were running over him; and though he tried to
silence his brother's objurgations by bringing out his books
afterwards, his cheeks burnt, he emitted little grunting coughs,
and at last his head went down on the lexicon, and his breath
came quick and short.

The Harvest Festival day was perforce kept by him in bed,
blistered and watched from hour to hour to arrest the autumn
cold, which was the one thing dreaded as imperilling him in the
English winter, which he must face for the first time for four
years.

And Miss Parsons, when impressively told, evidently thought
it was the family fashion to make a great fuss about him.

Alas! why are people so one-sided and absorbed in their own
concerns as never to guess what stumbling-blocks they raise in
other people's paths, nor how they make their good be evil
spoken of?

Babie confided her feelings to Jock when he escorted her to
church in the evening, and had detected a melancholy sound in
her voice which made him ask if she thought Armine's attack of
the worst sort.

'Not particularly, except that he talks so beautifully.'

Jock gave a small sympathetic whistle at this dreadful
symptom, and wondered to hear that he had been able to talk.

'I didn't mean only to-day, but this is only what he had made
up his mind to. He never expects to leave Belforest, and he
thinks—O Jock!—he thinks it is meant to do Bobus good.'

'He doesn't go the way to edify Bobus.'

'No, but don't you see? That is what is so dreadful. He
only just reads with Bobus because mother ordered him; and
he hates it because he thinks it is of no use, for he will never be
well enough to go to college. Why, he had this cold coming
yesterday, and I believe he is glad, for it would be like a book
for him to be very bad indeed, bad enough to be able to speak
out to Bobus without being laughed at.'

'Does he always go on in this way?'

'Not to mother; but to hear him and Miss Parsons is enough
to drive one wild. They went on such a dreadful way yesterday
that I was furious, and so glad to get away to Kenminster;
only after I had set off, he came running after me, and I knew
what that would be.'

'What does she do? Does she blarney him?'

'Yes, I suppose so. She means it, I believe; but she does
flatter him so that it would make me sick, if it didn't make me

so wretched! You see he likes it, because he fancies her goodness itself; and so I suppose she is, only there is such a lot of
clerical shop'—then, as Jock made a sound as if he did not like
the slang in her mouth—'Ay, it sounds like Bobus; but if this
goes on much longer, I shall turn to Bobus's way. He has all
the sense on his side!'

'No, Babie,' said Jock very gravely. 'That's a much worse
sort of folly!'

'And he will be gone before long,' said Barbara, much struck
by a tone entirely unwonted from her brother. 'O Jock, I
thought reverses would be rather nice and help one to be heroic,
and perhaps they would, if they would only come faster, and
Armine could be out of Miss Parsons' way; but I don't believe
he will ever be better while he is here. I think!—I think!'
and she began to sob, 'that Miss Parsons will really be the
death of him if she is not hindered!'

'Can't he go on board the *Petrel* with Allen?'

'Mother did think of that,' said Babie, 'but Allen said he
wasn't in spirits for the charge, and that cabin No. 2 wasn't
comfortable enough.'

Jock was not the least surprised at this selfishness, but he
said—

'We *will* get him away somehow, Infanta, never fear! And
when you have left this place, you'll be all right. You'll have
the Friar, and he is a host in himself.'

'Yes,' said Babie ruefully, 'but he is not a brother after all.
O Jock! mother says it is very wrong in me, but I can't
help it.'

'What is wrong, little one?'

'To feel it so dreadful that you and Bobus are going! I
know it is honour and glory, and promotion, and chivalry, and
Victoria Crosses, and all that Sydney and I used to care for;
but, oh! we never thought of those that stayed at home.'

'You were a famous Spartan till the time came,' said Jock
in an odd husky voice.

'I wouldn't mind so much but for mother,' said poor Barbara
in an apologetic tone; 'nor if there were any stuff in Allen;
nor if dear Armie were well and like himself; but, oh dear! I
feel as if all the manhood and comfort of the family would be
gone to the other end of the world.'

'What did you say about mother?'

'I beg your pardon, Jock, I didn't mean to worry you. I
know it is a grand thing for you. But mother was so merry
and happy when we thought we should all be snug with
you in the old house, and she made such nice plans. But
now she is so fagged and worn, and she can't sleep. She began
to read as soon as it was light all those long summer mornings
to keep from thinking; and she is teasing herself over her
accounts. There were shoals of great horrid bills of things
Allen ordered coming in at midsummer, just as she thought she

saw her way! Do you know, she thinks she may have to let
our own house and go into lodgings.'

'Is that you, Barbara?' said a voice at the Parsonage wicket.
'How is our dear patient?'

'Rather better to-night, we think.'

'Tell him I hope to come and see him to-morrow. And say
the vases are come. I thought your mother would wish us to
have the large ones, so I put them in the church. They
are £3.'

Babie thought Jock's face was dazed when he came among
the lights in church, and that he moved and responded like
an automaton, and she could hardly get a word out of him all
the way home. There they were sent for to Armine, who was
sufficiently better to want to hear all about the services, the
procession, the wheat-sheaf, the hymns, and the sermons. Jock
stood the examination well till it came to evensong, when, as his
sister had conjectured, he knew nothing, except one sentence,
which he said had come over and over again in the sermon, and
he wanted to know whence it came. It was, 'Seekest thou
great things for thyself?'

Even Armine only knew that it was in a note in the
*Christian Year*, and Babie looked out the reference, and found
that it was Jeremiah's rebuke to Baruch for self-seeking amid
the general ruin.

'I liked Baruch,' she said. 'I am sorry he was selfish.'

'Noble selfishness, perhaps,' said Armine. 'He may have
aimed at saving his country and coming out a glorious hero,
like Gideon or Jephthah.'

'And would that have been self-seeking too, as well as the
commoner thing?' said Babie.

'It is like a bit of New Testament in the midst of the Old,'
said Armine. 'They that are great are called Benefactors—a
good *sort* of greatness, but still not the true Christian greatness.'

'And that?' said Babie.

'To be content to be faithful *servant* as well as faithful
soldier,' said Armine thoughtfully. 'But what had it to do with
the harvest?'

He got no satisfaction, Babie could remember nothing but
Jock's face, and Jock had taken the Bible, and was looking at
the passages referred to. He sat for a long time resting his head
on his hand, and when at last he was roused to bid Armine
good-night, he bent over him, kissed him, and said, 'In spite of
all, you're the wise one of us, Armie boy. Thank you.'

# CHAPTER XXXII

## THE COST

'O well for him who breaks his dream
With the blow that ends the strife,
And waking knows the peace that flows
Around the noise of life.'

G. MACDONALD.

'Jock ! say this is not true !'

The wedding had been celebrated with all the splendour befitting a marriage in high life. Bridesmaids and bridesmen were wandering about the gardens waiting for the summons to the breakfast, when one of the former thus addressed one of the latter, who was standing gazing, without much speculation in his eyes, at the gold-fish disporting themselves round a fountain.

'Sydney !' he exclaimed, 'are not your mother and Fordham here ? I can't find them.'

'Did you not hear, Duke has one of his bad colds, and mamma could not leave him ? But, Jock, while we have time, set my mind at rest.'

'What is affecting your mind ?' said Jock, knowing only too well.

'What Cecil says, that you mean to disappoint all our best hopes.'

'There's no help for it, Sydney,' said Jock, too heavy-hearted for fencing.

'No help. I don't understand. Why, there's going to be war, real war, out there.'

'Frontier tribes !'

'What of that ? It would lead to something. Besides, no one leaves a corps on active service.'

'Is mine ?'

'It is all the same. You were going to get into one that is.'

'Curious reasoning, Sydney. I am afraid my duty lies the other way.'

'Duty to one's country comes first. I can't believe Mrs. Brownlow wants to hold you back ; she—a soldier's daughter !'

'It is no doing of hers,' said Jock ; 'but I see that I must not put myself out of reach of her.'

'When she has all the others ! That is a mere excuse. If you were an only son, it would be bad enough.'

'Come this way, and I'll tell you what convinced me.'

'I can't see how any argument can prevail on you to swerve from the path of honour, the only career any one can care about,' cried Sydney, the romance of her nature on fire.

'Hush, Sydney,' he said, partly from the exquisite pain she

inflicted, partly because her vehemence was attracting attention.

'No wonder you say "Hush,"' said the maiden, with what she meant for noble severity. 'No wonder you don't want to be reminded of all we talked of and planned. Does not it break Babie's heart?'

'She does not know.'

'Then it is not too late.'

But at that moment the bride's aunt, who felt herself in charge of Miss Evelyn, swooped down on them, and paired her off with an equally honourable best man, so that she found herself seated between two comparative strangers; while it seemed to her that Lucas Brownlow was keeping up an insane whirl of merriment with his neighbours.

Poor child, her hero was fallen, her influence had failed, and nothing was left her but the miserable shame of having trusted in the power of an attraction which she now felt to have been a delusion. Meanwhile the aunt, by way of being on the safe side, effectually prevented Jock from speaking to her again before the party broke up; and he could only see that she was hotly angered, and not that she was keenly hurt.

She arrived at home the next day with white cheeks and red eyes, and most indistinct accounts of the wedding. A few monosyllables were extracted with difficulty, among them a 'Yes' when Fordham asked whether she had seen Lucas Brownlow.

'Did he talk of his plans?'

'Not much.'

'One cannot but be sorry,' said her mother; 'but, as your uncle says, his motives are to be much respected.'

'Mamma,' cried Sydney, horrified, 'you wouldn't encourage him in turning back from the defence of his country in time of war?'

'His country!' ejaculated Fordham. 'Up among the hill tribes!'

'You palliating it too, Duke! Is there no sense of honour or glory left? What are you laughing at? I don't think it a laughing matter, nor Cecil either, that he should have been led to turn his back upon all that is great and glorious!'

'That's very fine,' said Fordham, who was in a teasing mood. 'Had you not better put it into the *Traveller's Joy?*'

'I shall never touch the *Traveller's Joy* again!' and Sydney's high horse suddenly breaking down, she flew away in a flood of tears.

Her mother and brother looked at one another rather aghast, and Fordham said—

'Had you any suspicion of *this?*'

'Not definitely. Pray don't say a word that can develop it now.'

'He is all the worthier.'

'Most true ; but we do not know that there is any feeling on his side, and if there were, Sydney is much too young for it to be safe to interfere with conventionalities. An expressed attachment would be very bad for both of them at present.'

'Should you have objected if he had still been going to India ?'

'I would have prevented an engagement, and should have regretted her knowing anything about it. The wear of such waiting might be too great a strain on her.'

'Possibly,' said Fordham. 'And should you consider this other profession an insuperable objection ?'

'Certainly not, if he goes on as I think he will ; but such success cannot come to him for many years, and a good deal may happen in that time.'

Poor Lucas ! He would have been much cheered could he have heard the above conversation instead of Cecil's wrath, which, like his sister's, worked a good deal like madness on the brain.

Mr. Evelyn chose to resent the slight to his family, and the ingratitude to his uncle, in thus running counter to their wishes, and plunging into what the young aristocrat termed low life. He did not spare the warning that it would be impossible to keep up an intimacy with one who chose to 'grub his nose in hospitals and dissecting-rooms.'

Naturally, Lucas took these as the sentiments of the whole family, and found that he was sacrificing both love and friendship. Sir James Evelyn indeed allowed that he was acting rightly according to his lights. Sir Philip Cameron told him that his duty to a widowed mother ought to come first, and his own colonel, a good and wise man, commended his decision, and said he hoped not to lose sight of him. The opinions of these veterans, though intrinsically worth more than those of the two young Evelyns, were by no means an equivalent to poor Lucas. The 'great things' he had resolved not to seek, involved what was far dearer. It was more than he had reckoned on when he made his resolution, but he had committed himself, and there was no drawing back. He was just of age, and had acted for himself, knowing that his mother would withhold her consent if she were asked for it ; but he was considering how to convey the tidings to her, when he found that a card had been left for him by the Reverend David Ogilvie, with a pencilled invitation to dine with him that evening at an hotel.

Mr. Ogilvie, after several years of good service as curate at a district church at a fashionable south coast watering-place, sometimes known as the English Sorrento, had been presented to the parent church. He had been taking his summer holiday, and on his way back had undertaken to relieve a London friend of his Sunday services. His sister's letters had made him very anxious for tidings of Mrs. Brownlow, and he had accordingly gone in quest of her son.

He ordered dinner with a half-humorous respect for the supposed epicurism of a young Guardsman, backed by the desire to
be doubly correct because of the fallen fortunes of the family,
and he awaited with some curiosity the pupil, best known to
him as a pickle.

'Mr. Brownlow.'

There stood a young man, a soldier from head to foot, slight,
active, neatly limbed, and of middle height, with a clear brown
cheek, dark hair and moustache, and the well-remembered frank
hazel eyes, though their frolic and mischief were dimmed, and
they had grown grave and steadfast, and together with the firm-
set lip gave the impression of a mind resolutely bent on going
through some great ordeal without flinching or murmuring.
With a warm grasp of the hand Mr. Ogilvie said—

'Why, Brownlow, I should not have known you.'

'I should have known you, sir, anywhere,' said Jock, amazed
to find the Ogre of old times no venerable *seignior*, but a man
scarce yet middle-aged.

They talked of Mr. Ogilvie's late tour, in scenes well known
to Jock, and thence they came to the whereabouts of all the
family, Armine's health and Robert's appointment, till they felt
intimate ; and the unobtrusive sympathy of the old friend
opened the youth's heart, and he made much plain that had
been only half understood from Mrs. Morgan's letters. Of his
eldest brother and sister, Jock said little ; but there was no
need to explain why his mother was straitening herself, and
remaining at Belforest when it had become so irksome to her.

'And you are going out to India ?' said Mr. Ogilvie.

'That's not coming off, sir.'

'Indeed, I thought you were to have a staff appointment.'

'It would not pay, sir ; and that is a consideration.'

'Then have you anything else in view ?'

'The hospitals,' said Jock, with a poor effort to seem diverted ;
'the other form of slaughter.' Then as his friend looked at him
with concerned and startled eyes, he added, 'Unless there were
some extraordinary chance of loot. You see the Pagoda tree is
shaken bare, and I could do no more than keep myself and have
nothing for my mother, and I am afraid she will need it. It is
a chance whether Allen, at his age, or Armine, with his health,
can do much, and some one must stay and get remunerative
work.'

'Is not the training costly ?'

'Her Majesty owes me something. Luckily I got my commission by purchase just in time, and I shall receive compensation enough to carry me through my studies. We shall be
all together with Friar Brownlow, who takes the same line, in the
old house in Bloomsbury, where we were all born. That she
really does look forward to.'

'I should think so, with you to look after her,' said Mr.
Ogilvie heartily.

'Only she can't get into it till Lady Day. And I wanted to ask you, Mr. Ogilvie, do you know anything about expenses down at your place? What would tolerable lodgings be likely to come to, rent of rooms, I mean, for my mother and the two young ones? Armie has not wintered in England since that Swiss adventure of ours, and I suppose St. Cradocke's would be as good a place for him as any.'

'I had a proposition to make, Brownlow. My sister and I invested in a house at St. Cradocke's when I was curate there, and she meant to retire to me when she had finished Barbara. My married curate is leaving it next week, when I go home. The single ones live in the rectory with me, and I think of making it a convalescent home; but this can't be begun for some months, as the lady who is to be at the head will not be at liberty. Do you think your mother would do me the favour to occupy it? It is furnished, and my housekeeper would see it made comfortable for her. Do you think you could make the notion acceptable to her?' he said, colouring like a lad, and stuttering in his eagerness.

'It would be a huge relief,' exclaimed Jock. 'Thank you, Mr. Ogilvie. Belforest has come to be like a prison to her, and it will be everything to have Armine in a warm place among reasonable people.'

'Is Kenminster more unreasonable than formerly?'

'Not Kenminster, but Woodside. I say, Mr. Ogilvie, you haven't any one at St. Cradocke's who will send Armine and Babie to walk three miles and back in the rain for a bit of crimson cord and tassels?'

'I trust not,' said Mr. Ogilvie, smiling. 'That is the way in which good people manage to do so much harm.'

'I'm glad you say so,' cried Jock. 'That woman is worse for him than six months of east wind. I declare I had a hard matter to get myself to go to church there the next day.'

'Who is *she*?'

'The sister of the Vicar of Woodside, who is making him the edifying martyr of a goody book. Ah, you know her, I see,' as Mr. Ogilvie looked amused.

'A gushing lady of a certain age? Oh yes, she has been at St. Cradocke's.'

'She is not coming again, I hope!' in horror.

'Not likely. They were there for a few months before her brother had the living, and I could quite fancy her influence bringing on a morbid state of mind. There is something exaggerated about her.'

'You've hit her off exactly!' cried Jock, 'and you'll unbewitch our poor boy before she has quite done for him! Can't you come down with me on Saturday, and propose the plan?'

'Thank you, I am pledged to Sunday.'

'I forgot. But come on Monday then.'

'I had better go and prepare. I had rather you spoke for

me. Somehow,' and a strange dew came in David Ogilvie's
eyes, 'I could not bear to see *her* there, where we saw her installed in triumph, now that all is so changed.'

'You would see her the brightest and bravest of all. Neither
she nor Babie would mind the loss of fortune a bit if it were not,
as Babie says, for "other things." But those other things are
wearing her to a mere shadow. No, not a shadow—that is dark
—but a mere sparkle! But to escape from Belforest will cure
a great deal.'

So Jock went away with the load on his heart somewhat
lightened. He could not get home on Saturday till very late,
when dinner had long been over. Coming softly in, through
the dimly-lighted drawing-rooms, over the deeply-piled carpets,
he heard Babie's voice reading aloud in the innermost library,
and paused for a moment, looking through the heavy velvet
curtains over the doorway before withdrawing one and entering.
His mother's face was in full light, as she sat helping Armine to
illuminate texts. She did indeed look worn and thin, and there
were absolute lines on it, but they were curves such as follow
smiles, rather than furrows of care; feet rather of larks than
of crows, and her whole air was far more cheerful and animated
than that of her youngest son. He was thin and wan, his white
cheeks contrasting with his dark hair and brown eyes, which
looked enormous in their weary pensiveness, as he leant back
languidly, holding a brush across his lips in a long pause, while
she was doing his work. Barbara's bright keen little features
were something quite different as, wholly wrapped up in her
book, she read—

> 'Oh! then Ladurlad started,
> As one who, in his grave,
> Has heard an angel's call,
> Yea, Mariately, thou must deign to save,
> Yea, goddess, it is she,
> Kailyal——'

'Are you learning Japanese?' asked Jock, advancing, so that
Armine started like Ladurlad himself.

'Dear old Skipjack! Skipped here again!' and they were
all about him. 'Have you had any dinner?'

'A mouthful at the station. If there is any coffee and a bit
of something cold, I'd rather eat it promiscuously here. No
dining-room spread, pray. It is too jolly here,' said Jock, dropping into an arm-chair. 'Where's Bob?'

'Dining at the schoolhouse.'

'And what's that Mariolatry?'

'Mariately,' said Babie. 'An Indian goddess. It is the
*Curse of Kehama*, and wonderfully noble.'

'Moore or Browning?'

'For shame, Jock!' cried the girl. 'I thought you did know
more than examination cram.'

'It is the advantage of having no Mudie boxes,' said his mother. 'We are taking up our Southey.'

'And, Armie, how are you?'

'My cough is better, thank you,' was the languid answer. 'Only they won't let me go beyond the terrace.'

'For don't I know,' said his mother, 'that if once I let you out, I should find you croaking at a choir practice at Woodside?'

Then, after ordering a refection for the traveller, came the question what he had been doing.

'Dining with Mr. Ogilvie. It is quite a new sensation to find oneself on a level with the Ogre of one's youth, and prove him a human mortal after all.'

'That's a sentiment worthy of Joe,' said Babie. 'You used to know him in private life.'

'Always with a smack of the dominie. Moreover, he is so young. I thought him as ancient as Dr. Lucas, and behold, he is a brisk youth, without a gray hair.'

'He always was young looking,' said his mother. 'I am glad you saw him. I wish he were not so far off.'

'Well then, mother, here's an invitation from Mahomet to the mountain, which Mahomet is too shy to make in person. That house which he and his sister bought at his English Sorrento has just been vacated by his married curate, and he wants you to come and keep it warm till he begins a convalescent home there next spring.'

'How very kind!'

'O mother, you couldn't,' burst out Armine in consternation.

'Would it be an expense or loss to him, Jock?' said his mother, considering.

'I should say not, unless he be an extremely accomplished dissembler. If it eased your mind, no doubt he would consent to your paying the rates and taxes.'

'But, mother,' again implored Armine, 'you said you would not force me to go to Madeira with the Evelyns!'

'Are they going to Madeira?' exclaimed Jock, thunderstruck.

'Did you not hear it from Cecil?'

'He has been away on leave for the last week. This is a sudden resolution.'

'Yes, Fordham goes on coughing, and Sydney has a bad cold, caught at the wedding. Did you see her?'

'Oh yes, I saw her,' he mechanically answered, while his mother continued—

'Mrs. Evelyn has been pressing me most kindly to let Armine go with them; but as Dr. Leslie assures me it is not essential, and he seems so much averse to it himself——'

'You know, mother, how I wish to hold my poor neglected Woodside to the last,' cried Armine. 'Why is my health always to be made the excuse for deserting it?'

'You are not the only reason,' said his mother. 'It is hard to keep Esther in banishment all this time, and I am in constant fear of a row about the shooting with that Gilbert Gould.'

'Has he been at it again!' exclaimed Jock fiercely.

'You are as bad as Rob,' she said. 'I fully expect a disturbance between them, and I had rather be no party to it. Oh, I shall be very thankful to get away. I feel like a prisoner on parole.'

'And I feel,' said Armine, 'as if all we could do here was too little to expiate past carelessness.'

'Mind, you are talking of mother!' said Jock, firing up.

'I thought she felt with me,' said Armine meekly.

'So I do, my dear; I ought to have done much better for the place, but our staying on now does no good, and only leads to perplexity and distress.'

'And when can you come, mother?' said Jock. 'The house is at your service *instanter*.'

'I should like to go to-night, without telling any one or wishing any one good-bye. No, you need not be afraid, Armie. The time must depend on your brother's plans. St. Cradocke's is too far off for much running backwards and forwards. Have you any notion when you may have to leave us, Jock? You don't go with Sir Philip?'

'No, certainly not,' said Jock. Then, with a little hesitation, 'In fact, that's all up.'

'He has not thrown you over?' said his mother; 'or is there any difficulty about your exchange?'

Here Babie broke in, 'Oh, that's it! That's what Sydney meant! O Jock! you don't mean that you let it prey upon you—the nonsense I talked? Oh, I will never, never say anything again!'

'What did she say?' demanded Jock.

'Sydney? Oh, that it would break her heart and Cecil's if you persisted, and that she could not prevent you, and it was my duty. Mother, that was the letter I didn't show you. I could not understand it, and I thought you had enough to worry you.'

'But what does it all mean?' asked their mother. 'What have you been doing to the Evelyns?'

'Mother, I have gone back to our old programme,' said Jock. 'I have sent in my papers; I said nothing to you, for I thought you would only vex yourself.'

'O Jock!' she said, overpowered; 'I should never have let you!'

'No, mother, dear, I knew that, so I didn't ask you.'

'You undutiful person!' but she held out her arm, and as he came to her, she leant her head against him, sobbing a little sob of infinite relief, as though fortitude found it much pleasanter to have a living column.

'You've done it?' said Armine.

'You will see it gazetted in a day or two.'

'Then it is all over,' cried Babie, again in tears; 'all our dreams of honour, and knighthood, and wounds, and glorious things!'

'You can always have the satisfaction of believing I should have got them,' said Jock, but there was a quiver in his voice, and a thrill through his whole frame that showed his mother that it was very sore with him, and she hastened to let him subside into a chair while she asked if it was far to the end of the canto, and as Babie was past reading, she took the book and finished it herself. Nobody had much notion of the sense, but the cadence was soothing, and all were composed by the time the prayer-bell rang.

'Come to my dressing-room presently,' she said to Lucas, as he lighted her candle for her.

Just as she had gone upstairs, the front door opened to admit Bobus.

'Oh, you are here!' was his salutation. 'So you have done for yourself?'

'How do you know?'

'Your colonel wrote to my uncle. He was at the dinner, and made me come back with him to ask if I knew about it.'

'How does he take it?'

'He will probably fall on you, as he did on me to-night, calling it all my fault.'

'As how?'

'For looking out for myself. For my part, I had thought it praiseworthy, but he says none of the rest of us care a rush for my mother, and so the only one of us good for anything has to be the victim. But don't plume yourself. You'll be the scum of the earth when he has you before him. Poor old boy, it is a sore business to him, and it doesn't improve his temper. I believe this place is a greater loss to him than to my mother. What are your plans?'

'*Rotifer*, as before.'

'*Chacun à son goût*,' said Bobus, shrugging his shoulders.

'I should have thought you would respect curing more than killing.'

'If there were not a whole bag of stones about your neck.'

'Magnets,' said Jock.

'That's just it. All the heavier.'

The brothers went upstairs together, and Jock was kept waiting a little while in the dressing-room, till his mother came out, shutting the door on Barbara.

'The poor Infanta!' she said. 'She is breaking her foolish little heart over something she said to you. "As bad as the woman in the *Black Brunswicker*," she says, only she didn't mean it. Was it so, Jock?'

'I had pretty well made up my mind before. Mother, are you vexed that I did not tell you?'

'You spared me much. Your uncle would never have consented. But oh, Jock! I'm not a Spartan mother. My heart
*will* bound.'

'My colonel said it was right,' said Jock; 'so did Cameron,
and even Sir James, though he did not like it.'

'With such an array of old soldiers on our side we may let
the young ladies rage,' said his mother, but she checked her
mirth on seeing how far from a joke their indignation was to
her son.

He turned and looked into the fire as he said—

'When did Sydney write that letter, mother?'

'Before meeting you at the wedding. She has not written
since.'

'I thought not,' muttered Jock, his brow against the mantelpiece.

'No, but Mrs. Evelyn has written such a nice letter, just like
herself, though I did not understand it then. I think she was
doubtful how much I knew, for she only said how thankworthy
it must be to have such a self-sacrificing spirit among my sons,
moral courage, in fact, of the highest kind, and how those who
were lavish of strong words in their first disappointment would
be wiser by and by. I was puzzled then. But oh, my dear, this
must have been very grievous to you!'

'I couldn't go back, but I did not know how it would be,'
said Jock in a choked voice, collapsing at last, and hiding his
face on his mother's lap.

'My Jock, I am so sorry! I wish it were not too late. I
could not have let you give up so much,' and she fondled his
head. 'I did not think I had been so weak as to let you see.'

'No, mother. It was not that you were so weak, but that
you were so brave. Besides, I ought to take the brunt of it. I
ruined you all by being the prime mover with that assification,
and I was the cause of Armie's illness too. I ought to take my
share. If ever I can be any good to any one again,' he added
in a dejected tone.

'Good!—unspeakably good! This is my first bright spot of
light through the wood. If it were but bright to you! I am
afraid *they* have been very unkind.'

'Not unkind. *She* couldn't be that, but I've shocked and
disappointed her,' and his head dropped again.

'What, in not being a hero? My dear, you are a true hero
in the eyes of us old mothers; but I am afraid that is poor comfort. My Jock, does it go so deep as that? Giving up *all* that
for me! O my boy!'

'It is nonsense to talk of giving up,' said Jock, rousing himself to a common-sense view. 'What chance had I of her if I
had gone to India ten times over?' but the wave of grief broke
over him again. 'She would have believed in me, and, may be,
have waited.'

'She will believe in you again.'

'No, I'm below her.

'My poor boy, I didn't know it had come to this. Do you mean that anything had ever passed between you?'

'No, but it was all the same. Even Evelyn implied it, when he said they must give me up, if we took such different lines.'

'Cecil too! Foolish fellow! Jock, don't care about such absurdity. They are not worth it.'

'They've been the best of my life,' said poor Jock, but he stood up, shook himself, and said, 'A nice way this of helping you! I didn't think I was such a fool. But it is over now. I'll buckle to, and do my best.'

'My brave boy!' and as the thought of the Magnum Bonum darted into her mind, she said, 'You may have greater achievements than are marked by Victoria Crosses, and Sydney herself may own it.'

And Jock went to bed, cheered in spite of himself by his mother's pleasure, and by Mrs. Evelyn's letter, which she allowed him to take away with him.

Colonel Brownlow was not so much distressed by Lucas's retirement as had been apprehended. He knew the life of a soldier with small means too well to recommend it. The staff appointment, he said, might mean anything or nothing, and could only last a short time unless Lucas had extraordinary opportunities. It might be as well, he was very like his grandfather, poor John Allen, and might have had his history over again.

The likeness was a new idea to Caroline and a great pleasure to her. Indeed, she seemed to Armine unfeelingly joyous, as she accepted Mr. Ogilvie's invitation, and hurried her preparations. There was a bare possibility of a return in the spring, which prevented final farewells, and softened partings a little. The person who showed most grief of all was Mrs. Robert Brownlow, who, glad as she must have been to be free of Bobus and able to recall her daughter, wept over her sister-in-law as if she had been going into the workhouse, with tears partly penitent for the involuntary ingratitude with which past kindness had been received. She was, as Babie said, much more sorry for Mother Carey than Mother Carey for herself.

Yet the relief was all the greater that it was plain that Esther was not happy in her banishment; and that General Hood thought her visit had lasted long enough, while the matter was complicated at home by her sister Eleanor's undisguised sympathy with her cousin Bobus, for whom she would have sent messages if her mother had not, with some difficulty, exacted a promise never to allude to him in her letters.

## CHAPTER XXXIII

### BITTER FAREWELLS

' But he who lets his feelings run
  In soft luxurious flow
Shrinks when hard service must be done
And faints at every woe.'

J. H. NEWMAN.

WELCOME shone in Mr. Ogilvie's face in the gaslight on the platform as the train drew up, and the Popinjay in her cage was handed out, uttering, '*Hic, hæc, hoc.* We're all Mother Carey's chicks.'

Therewith the mother and the two youngest of her chicks were handed to their fly, and driven, through raindrops and splashes flashing in the gas, to a door where the faithful Emma awaited them, and conveyed them to a room so bright and comfortable that Babie piteously exclaimed—

'O Emma, you have left me nothing to do !'

Presently came Mr. Ogilvie to make sure that the party needed nothing. He was like a child hovering near, and constantly looking to assure himself of the reality of some precious acquisition.

Later in the evening, on his way from the night-school, he was at the door again to leave a parish magazine with a list of services that ought to have rejoiced Armine's heart, if he had felt capable of enjoying anything at St. Cradocke's, and at which Babie looked with some dismay, as if fearing that they would all be inflicted on her. He was in a placid, martyr-like state. He had made up his mind that the air was of the relaxing sort that disagreed with him, and no doubt would be fatal, though as he coughed rather less than more, he could hardly hope to edify Bobus by his death-bed, unless he could expedite matters by breaking a blood-vessel in saving some one's life. On the whole, however, it was pleasanter to pity himself for vague possibilities than to apprehend the crisis as immediate. It was true that he was very forlorn. He missed the admiring petting by which Miss Parsons had fostered his morbid state ; he missed the occupations she had given him, and he missed the luxurious habits of wealth far more than he knew. After his winters under genial skies, close to blue Mediterranean waves, English weather was trying ; and, in contrast with southern scenery, people, and art, everything seemed ugly, homely, and vulgar in his eyes. Gorgeous cathedrals with their High Masses and sweet Benedictions, their bannered processions and kneeling peasantry, rose in his memory as he beheld the half-restored church, the stiff open seats, and the Philistine precision of the St. Cradocke's Old

Church congregation; and Anglicanism shared his distaste in spite of the fascinations of the district church.

He was languid and inert, partly from being confined to the house on days of doubtful character. He would not prepare any work for Bobus, who, with Jock, was to follow in ten days; he would not second Babie's wish to get up a St. Cradocke's number of the *Traveller's Joy*, to challenge a Madeira one; he did little but turn over a few books, say there was nothing to read, and exchange long letters with Miss Parsons.

'Armine,' said Mr. Ogilvie, 'I never let my friends come into my parish without getting work out of them. I have a request to make you.'

'I'm afraid I am not equal to much,' said Armine, not graciously.

'This is not much. We have a lame boy here for the winter, son to a cabinet-maker in London. His mind is set on being a pupil-teacher, and he is a clever, bright fellow, but his chance depends on his keeping up his work. I have been looking over his Latin and French, but I have not time to do so properly, and it would be a great kindness if you would undertake it.'

'Can't he go to school?' said Armine, not graciously.

'It is much too far off. Now he is only round the corner here.'

'My going out is so irregular,' said Armine, not by any means as he would have accepted a behest of Petronella's.

'He could often come here. Or perhaps the Infanta would fetch and carry. He is with an uncle, a fisherman, and the wife keeps a little shop. Stagg is the name. They are very respectable people, but of a lower stamp than this lad, and he is rather lost for want of companionship. The London doctors say his recovery depends on sea air for the winter, so here he is, and whatever you can do for him will be a real good work.'

'What is the name?' asked Mrs. Brownlow.

'Stagg. It is over a little grocery shop. You must ask for Percy Stagg.'

Perhaps Armine suspected the motive to be his own good, for he took a dislike to the idea at once.

'Percy Stagg!' he began, as soon as Mr. Ogilvie was gone. 'What a detestable conjunction, just showing what the fellow must be. And to have him on my hands.'

'I thought you liked teaching?' said his mother.

'As if this would be like a Woodside boy!'

'Yes,' said Babie; 'I don't suppose he will carry onions and lollipops in his pockets, nor put cockchafers down on one's book.'

'Babie, that was only Ted Stokes!'

'And I should *think* he might have rather cleaner hands, and not leave their traces on every book.'

'He'll do worse!' said Armine. 'He will be vulgarly stuck

up, and excruciate me with every French word he attempts to pronounce.'

'But you'll do it, Armine?' said his mother.

'Oh yes, I will try if it be possible to make anything of him, when I am up to it.'

Armine was not 'up to it' the next day nor the next. The third was very fine, and with great resignation he sauntered down to Mrs. Stagg's.

Percy turned out to be a quiet, gentle, pale lad of fourteen, without cockney vivacity, and so shy that Armine grew shyer, did little but mark the errors in his French exercise, hear a bit of reading, and retreat, bemoaning the hopeless stupidity of his pupil.

A few days later Mr. Ogilvie asked the lame boy how he was getting on.

'Oh, sir,' brightening, 'the lady is so kind. She does make it so plain in me.'

'The lady? Not the young gentleman?'

'The young gentleman has been here once, sir.'

'And his sister comes when he is not well?'

'No, sir, it is his mother, I think. A lady with white hair—the nicest lady I ever saw.'

'And she teaches you?'

'Oh yes, sir! I am preparing a fable in the Latin Delectus for her, and she gave me this French book. She does tell me such interesting facts about words, and about what she has seen abroad, sir! And she brought me this cushion for my knee.'

'Percy thinks there never was such a lady,' chimed in his aunt. 'She is very good to him, and he is ever so much better in his spirits and his appetite since she has been coming to him. The young gentleman was haughty like, and couldn't make nothing of him; but the lady—she's so affable! She is one of a thousand!'

'I did not mean to impose a task on you,' said Mr. Ogilvie, next time he could speak to Mrs. Brownlow.

'Oh! I am only acting stop-gap till Armine rallies and takes to it,' she said. 'The boy is delightful. It is very amusing to teach French to a mind of that age so thoroughly drilled in grammar.'

'A capital thing for Percy, but I thought at least you would have deputed the Infanta.'

'The Infanta was a little overdone with the style of thing at Woodside. She and Sydney Evelyn had a romance about good works, of which Miss Parsons completely disenchanted her—rather too much so, I fear.'

'Let her alone; she will recover,' said Mr. Ogilvie, 'if only by seeing you do what I never intended.'

'I like it, teacher as I am by trade.'

So each day Armine imagined himself bound to the infliction

of Percy Stagg, and compelled by headache, cough, or weather
to let his mother be his substitute.

'She is keeping him going on days when I am not equal to
it,' he said to Mr. Ogilvie.

'Having thus given you one of my tasks,' said that gentleman, 'let me ask whether I can help you in any of your
studies?'

'I have been reading with Bobus, thank you.'

'And now?'

'I have not begun again, though, if my mother desires it, I
shall.'

'So I should suppose; but I am sorry you do not take more
interest in the matter.'

'Even if I live,' said Armine, 'the hopes with which I once
studied are over.'

'What hopes?'

The boy was drawn on by his sympathy to explain his plans
for the perfection of church and charities at Woodside, where
he would have worked as curate, and lavished all that wealth
could supply in all institutions for its good and that of Kenminster. It was the vanished castle over which he and Miss
Parsons had spent so many moans, and yet at the end of it all
Armine saw a sort of incredulous smile on his friend's face.

'I don't think it was impossible or unreasonable,' he said. 'I
could have been ordained as curate there, and my mother would
have gladly given land, and means, and all.'

'I was not thinking of that, my boy. What struck me was
how people put their trust in riches without knowing it.'

'Indeed I should have given up all wealth and luxury. I am
not regretting that!' exclaimed Armine, in unconscious blindness.

'I did not say you were.'

'I beg your pardon,' said Armine, thinking he had not caught
the words.

'I said people did not know how they put their trust in
riches.'

'I never thought I did.'

'Only that you think nothing can be done without them.'

'I don't see how it can.'

'Don't you? Well, the longer I live the more cause I see to
dread and distrust what is done easily by force of wealth. Of
course when the money is there, and is given along with oneself (as I know you intended), it is providential, but I verily
believe it intensifies difficulties and temptations. Poverty is
almost as beneficial a sieve of motives and stimulus to energy
as persecution itself.'

'There are so many things one can't do.'

'Perhaps the fit time is not come for their being done. Or
you want more training for doing them. Remember that to
bring one's good desires to good effect, there is a *how* to be taken
into account. I know of a place where the mere knowledge

that there are unlimited means to bestow seems to produce in-gratitude and captiousness for whatever is done.  On the other hand, I have seen a far smaller gift, that has cost an effort, most warmly and touchingly received.  Again, the power of at once acting leads to over-haste, want of consideration, domineering, expectation of adulation, impatience of counsel or criticism.'

'I suppose one does not know till one has tried,' said Armine, 'but I should mind nothing from Mr. or Miss Parsons.'

'I did not allude to any special case, I only wanted to show you that riches do not by any means make doing good a simpler affair, but rather render it more difficult not to do an equal amount of harm.'

'Of course,' said Armine, 'as this misfortune has happened, it is plain that we must submit, and I hope I am bowing to the disappointment.'

'By endeavouring to do your best for God with what is left you?'

'I hope so, but with my health there seems nothing left for me but unmurmuring resignation.'

Mr. Ogilvie was amused at Armine's notion of unmurmuring resignation, but he added only, 'Which would be much assisted by a little exertion.'

'I did exert myself at home, but it is all aimless now.'

'I should have thought you still equally bound to learn and labour to do your duty in Him and for Him.  Will you think about what I have said?'

'Yes, Mr. Ogilvie, thank you.  I know you mean it kindly, and no one can be expected to enter into my feeling of the use-lessness of wasting my time over classical studies when I know I shall never be able to be ordained.'

'Are you sure you are not wasting it now?'

It was not possible to continue the subject.  Mr. Ogilvie had failed in both his attempts to rouse Armine, and had to tell his mother, who had hoped much from this new influence.  'I think,' he said, 'that Armine is partly feeling the change from invalidism to ordinary health.  He does not know it, poor fellow; but it is rather hard to give up being interesting.'

Caroline saw the truth of this when Armine showed himself absolutely nettled at his brothers on their arrival pronouncing that he looked much better—in fact quite jolly, an insult which he treated with Christian forgiveness.

Bobus had visited Belforest.  His mother had never intended this, and still less that he should walk direct from the station to Kencroft, surprising the whole family at luncheon, and taking his seat among them quite naturally.  Thereby he obtained all he had expected or hoped, for when the meal was over, he was able, though in the presence of all the family, to take Esther by both hands, and say in his resolute earnest voice, 'Good-bye, my sweet and only love.  You will wait for me, and by and by, when I have made you a home, and people see things differently, I shall come for you,' and therewith he pressed on her burning, blushing, drooping brow four kisses that felt like fire.

Her mother might fret and her father might fume, but they were as powerless as the parents of young Lochinvar's bride, and the words of their protest were scarcely begun when he loosed the girl's hands, and, turning to her mother, said, 'Good-bye, Aunt Ellen. When we meet again, you will see things otherwise. I ask nothing till that time comes.'

This was not the part of his visit of which he told his mother, he only dwelt on a circumstance so opportune that he had almost been forgiven even by the Colonel. He had encountered Dr. Hermann, who had come down to make another attempt on the Gracious Lady, and had thus found himself in the presence of a very different person. An opening had offered itself in America, and he had come to try to obtain his wife's fortune to take them out. The opportunity of making stringent terms had seemed to Bobus so excellent that he civilly invited Demetrius to dine and sleep, and sent off a note to beg his uncle to come and assist in a family compact. Colonel Brownlow, having happily resisted his impulse to burn the letter unread as an impertinent proposal for his daughter, found that it contained so sensible a scheme that he immediately conceived a higher opinion of his namesake than he had ever had before.

Thus Dr. Hermann found himself face to face with the very last members of the family he desired to meet, and had to make the best of the situation. Of secrets of the late Joseph Brown-low he said nothing, but based his application on the offer of a practice and lectureship he said he had received from New Orleans. He had evidently never credited that Mrs. Brownlow meant to resign the whole property without giving away among her children the accumulation of ready money in hand, and as he knew himself to be worth buying off, he reckoned upon Janet's full share. He had taken Mrs. Brownlow's own state-ments as polite refusals and a lady's romance until he found the uncle and nephew viewing the resignation of the whole as common honesty, and that she was actually gone. They would not give him her address, and prevented his coming in contact with the housekeeper, so that no more molestation might be possible, and meantime they offered him terms such as they thought she would ratify.

All that Joseph Brownlow had left was entirely in her power, and the amount was such that if she had died intestate, each of her six children would have been entitled to about £1600, exclu-sive of the house in London. Janet had no right to claim any-thing now or at her mother's death, but the uncle and nephew knew that Mrs. Brownlow would not endure to leave her desti-tute, and they thought the deportation to America worth a con-siderable sacrifice. Therefore they proposed that on the actual bonâ fide departure, £500 should be paid down, the interest of the £1100 should be secured to her, and paid half-yearly through

Mr. Wakefield, who was to draw up the agreement; but the final disposal of the sum was not to be promised, but to depend on Mrs. Brownlow's will.

Such a present boon as £500 had made Hermann willing to agree to anything. Bobus had seen the lawyer in London, and with him concocted the agreement for signature, making the payments pass through the Wakefield office, the receipts being signed by Janet Hermann herself.

'Why must all payments go through the office?' asked Caroline.

'Because there's no trusting that slippery Greek,' said Bobus.

'I should have liked my poor Janet to have been forced to communicate with me every half-year,' she sighed.

'What, when she has never chosen to write all this time?'

'Yes. It is very weak, but I can't help it. It would be something only to see her name. I have never known where to write to her, or I would have done so.'

'Oh, very well,' said Bobus, 'you had better invite them both to share the *ménage* in Collingwood Street.'

'For shame, Bobus,' said Jock. 'You have no right to say such things.'

'Only that all this might as well have been left undone if my mother is to rush on them to ask their pardon and beg them to receive her with open arms. I mean, mother,' he added with a different manner, 'if you give one inch to that Greek, he will make it a mile, and as to Janet, if she can't bring down her pride to write to you like a daughter, I wouldn't give a rap for her receipt, and it might lead to intolerable pestering. Now you know she can't starve on £50 a year besides her medical education. Wakefield will always know where she is, and you may be quite easy about her.'

Caroline gave way to her son's reasoning, as he thought, but no sooner was she alone with Jock than she told him that he must take her to London to see Janet in her lodgings before the departure for the States.

He was at her service, and as they did not mean to sleep in town, they started at a preposterously early hour, with a certain mirth and gaiety at thus eloping together, as the mother's spirits rose at the bare idea of seeing the first-born child for whom she had famished so long. Jock was such a perfect squire of dames, and so chivalrously charmed to be her escort, that her journey was delightful, nor did she grow sad till it was over. Then, she could not eat the food he would have had her take at the station, and he saw tears standing in her eyes as he sat beside her in the omnibus. When they were set down they walked swiftly and without a word to the lodgings.

Dr. and Mrs. Hermann had 'left two days ago,' said the untidy girl, whose aspect, like that of the street and house, betokened that Janet was drinking of her bitter brewst.

'What shall we do, mother?' asked Jock. 'You ought to

rest. Will you go to Mrs. Acton or Mrs. Lucas, while I run down to Wakefield's office and find out about them?'

'To Miss Ray's, I think,' she said faintly. 'Nita may know their plans. Here's the address,' taking a little book from her pocket, and ruffling over the leaves, 'you must find it. I can't see. Oh, but I can walk!' as he hailed a cab and helped her into it, finding the address and jumping after her, while she sank back into the corner.

Very small and shrunken did she look when he took her out at the door leading to rooms over a stationer's shop. The sisters were somewhat better off than formerly, though good old Miss Ray was half ashamed of it, since it was chiefly owing to the liberal allowance from Mrs. Brownlow for the chaperonage in which she felt herself to have so sadly failed.

Jock saw his mother safe in the hands of the kind old lady, heard that the pair were really gone, and departed for his interview with Mr. Wakefield. No sooner had the papers been signed, and the £500 made over to them, than the Hermanns had hurried away a fortnight earlier than they had spoken of going. It was much like an escape from creditors, but the reason assigned was an invitation to lecture in New York.

So there was nothing for it but to put up with Miss Ray's account of Janet, and even that was second-hand, for the gentle spirit of the good old lady had been so roused at the treachery of the stolen marriage that she had refused to see the couple, and when Nita had once brought them in, she had retired to her bedroom.

Nita was gone on a professional engagement into the country for a week. According to what she had told her sister, Demetrius and Janet were passionately attached, and his manner was only too endearing; but Miss Ray had disliked the subject so much that she had avoided it in a way she now regretted.

'Everything I have done has turned out wrong,' she said, with tears running down her cheeks. 'Even this! I would give anything to be able to tell you of poor Janet, and yet I thought my silence was for the best, for Nita and I could not mention her without quarrelling, as we had never done before. O Mrs. Brownlow, I can't think how you have ever forgiven me.'

'I can forgive every one but myself,' said Caroline sadly. 'If I had understood how to be a better mother, this would never have been.'

'You! the most affectionate and devoted.'

'Ah! but I see now it was only human love without the true moving spring, and so my poor child grew up without it, and these are the fruits.'

'But, my dear, my dear, one can't *give* these things. Poor Janet always was a headstrong girl, like my poor Nita. I know what you mean, and how one feels that if one had been better oneself,' said poor Miss Ray, ending in utter entanglement, but tender sympathy.

'She might have been a child of many prayers,' said the poor mother.

'Ah! but that she can still be,' said the old lady. 'She will turn back again, my dear. Never fear. I don't think I could die easy if I did not believe she would!'

Jock brought back word that the lawyer had been entirely unaware of the Hermanns' departure, and thought it looked bad. He had seen them both, and his report was less brilliant than Nita's. Indeed Jock kept back the details, for Mr. Wakefield had described Mrs. Hermann as much altered, thin, haggard, shabby, and anxious, and though her husband fawned upon her demonstratively before spectators, something in her eyes betokened a certain fear of him. He had also heard that Elvira was still making visits. There was a romance about her, which, in addition to her beauty and future wealth, made people think her a desirable guest. She was always more agreeable with strangers than in her own family; and as to the needful funds, she had her ample allowance; and no doubt her expectations secured her unlimited credit. Her conduct was another pang, but it was lost in the keener pain Janet had given.

As his mother could not bear to face any one else, Jock thought the sooner he could get her home the better, and all they did was to buy some of Armine's favourite biscuits, and likewise to stop at Rivingtons', where she chose the two smallest and neatest Greek Testaments she could find.

They reached home three hours before they were expected, and she went up at once to her room and her bed, leaving Jock to make the explanations, and receive all Bobus's indignation at having allowed her to knock herself up by such a foolish expedition.

Chill, fatigue, and, far more, grief after her long course of worry really did bring on a feverish attack, so unprecedented in her that it upset the whole family, and if Mr. Ogilvie had not been almost equally wretched himself, he would have been amused to see these three great sons wandering forlorn about the house like stray chicks who had lost their parent hen, and imagining her ten times worse than she really was.

Babie was really useful as a nurse, and had very little time to comfort them. And indeed they treated her as childish and trifling for assuring them that neither patient, maid, nor doctor thought the ailment at all serious. Bobus found some relief in laying the blame on Jock, but when Armine heard the illness ascribed to a long course of anxiety and harass, he was conscience-stricken, as he thought how often his perverse form of resignation had baffled her pleadings and added to her vexations. Words, impatiently heard at the moment, returned upon him, and compunction took its outward effect in crossness. It was all that Jock could do by his good-humoured banter and repartee to keep the peace between the other two, who, when unchecked by regard to their mother and Babie, seemed

bent on discussing everything on which they most disagreed.

Babie was a welcome messenger to Jock at least, when she
brought word that mother hoped Armine would attend to Percy
Stagg, and would take him the book she sent down for him.
Her will was law in the present state of things, and Armine set
forth in dutiful disgust ; but he found the lad so really anxious
about the lady, and so much brightened and improved, that he
began to take an interest in him and, promised a fresh lesson
with alacrity.

His next step in obedience was to take out his books ; but
Bobus had no mind for them, and said it was too late. If
Armine had really worked diligently all the autumn, he might
have easily entered King's College, London ; but now he had
thrown away his chance.

Mr. Ogilvie found him with his books on the table, plunged
in utter despondency. 'Your mother is not worse?' he asked in
alarm.

'Oh no ; she is very comfortable, and the doctor says she may
get up to-morrow.'

'Then is it the Greek?' said Mr. Ogilvie, much relieved.

'Yes. Bobus says my rendering is perfectly ridiculous.'

'Are you preparing for him?'

'No. He is sick of me, and has no time to attend to me
now.'

'Let me see——'

'Oh ! Mr. Ogilvie,' said Armine, looking up with his ingenuous eyes. 'I don't deserve it. Besides, Bobus says it is of no
use now. I've wasted too much time ever to get into King's.'

'I should like to judge of that. Suppose I examined you—
not now, but to-morrow morning. Meantime, how do you construe this chorus? It is a tough one.'

Armine winked out of his eyes the tears that had risen at the
belief that he had really in his wilfulness lost the hope of fulfilling the higher aims of his life, and with a trembling voice
translated the passage he had been hammering over. A word
from Mr. Ogilvie gave him the clue, and when that stumbling-
block was past, he acquitted himself well enough to warrant a
little encouragement.

'Well done, Armine. We shall make a fair scholar of you,
after all.'

'I don't deserve you should be so kind. I see now what a
fool I have been,' said Armine, his eyes filling again with tears.

'I have no time to talk of that now,' said Mr. Ogilvie. 'I
only looked in to hear how your mother was. Bring down
whatever books you have been getting up at twelve to-morrow ;
or if it is a wet day, I will come to you.'

Armine worked for this examination as eagerly as he had
decorated for Miss Parsons, and in the face of the like sneers ;
for Bobus really believed it was all waste of time, and did not

scruple to tell him so, and to laugh when he consulted Jock, whose acquirements lay more in the way of military mathematics and modern languages than of university requirements.

Perhaps the report that Armine was reading Livy with all his might was one of his mother's best restoratives,—and still more that when he came to wish her good-night, he said, 'Mother, I've been a wretched, self-sufficient brute all this time; I'm very sorry, and I'll try to go on better.'

And when she came downstairs to be petted and made much of by all the four, she found that the true and original Armine had come back, instead of Petronella's changeling. Indeed, the danger now was that he would overwork himself in his fervour, for Bobus's continued ill-auguries only acted as a stimulus; nor were they silenced till she begged as a personal favour that he would not torment the boy.

Indeed her presence made life smooth and cheerful again to the young people; there were no more rubs of temper, and Bobus, whose departure was very near, showed himself softened. He was very fond of his mother, and greatly felt the leaving her. He assured her that it was all for her sake, and that he trusted to be able to lighten some of her burdens when his first expenses were over.

'And mother,' he said, on his last evening, 'you will let me sometimes hear of my Esther?'

'O Bobus, if you could only forget her!'

'Would you rob me of my great incentive—my sweet image of purity, who rouses and guards all that is best in me? My "loyalty to my future wife" is your best hope for me, mother.'

'Oh, if she were but any one else! How can I encourage you in disobedience to your father and to hers?'

'You know what I think about that. When my Esther ventures to judge for herself, these prejudices will give way. She shall not be disobedient, but you will all perceive the uselessness of withholding my darling. Meanwhile, I only ask you to let me see her name from time to time. You won't deny me that?'

'No, my dear, I cannot refuse you that, but you must not assume more than that I am sorry for you that your heart is set so hopelessly. Indeed, I see no sign of her caring for you. Do you?'

'Her heart is not opened yet, but it will.'

'Suppose it should do so to any one else?'

'She is a mere child; she has few opportunities; and if she had—well, I think it would recall to her what she only half understood. I am content to be patient—and, mother, you little know the good it does me to think of her and think of you. It is well for us men that all women are not like Janet.'

'Yet if you took away our faith, what would there be to hinder us from being like my poor Janet?'

'Heaven forbid that I should take away any one's honest faith ; above all, yours or Essie's.'

'Except by showing that you think it just good enough for us.'

'How can I help it, any more than I can help that Belforest was left to Elvira? Wishes and belief are two different things.'

'Would you help it if you could?' she earnestly asked.

He hesitated. 'I might wish to satisfy you, mother, and other good folks, but not to put myself in bondage to what has led blindfold to half the dastardly and cruel acts on this earth, beautiful dream though it be.'

'Ah, my boy, it is my shame and grief that it is not a beautiful reality to you.'

'You were too wise to bore us. You have only fancied that since you fell in with the Evelyns.'

'Ah, if I had only bred you up in the same spirit as the Evelyns!'

'It would not have answered. We are of different stuff. And after all, Janet and I are your only black sheep. Jock has his convictions in a strong, practical working order, as real to him as ever his drill and order-book were. Good old fellow, he strikes me a good deal more than all Ogilvie's discussions.'

'Mr. Ogilvie has talked to you?'

'He has done his part both as cleric and your devoted servant, mother, and, I confess, made the best of his case, as an able man heartily convinced can do. Good-night, mother.'

'One moment, Bobus, my dear ; I want one promise from you, to your old Mother Carey. Call it a superstition and a charm if you will, but promise. Take this Greek Testament, keep it with you, and read a few verses every night. Promise me.'

'Dear mother, I am ready to promise. I have read those poems and letters several times in the original.'

'But you will do this for me, beginning again when you have finished? Promise.'

'I will, mother, since it comforts you,' said Bobus, in a tone that she knew might be trusted.

The other little book, with the like request, in urgent and tender entreaty, was made up into a parcel to be forwarded as soon as Mr. Wakefield should learn Janet Hermann's address. It was all that the mother could do, except to pray that this living Sword of the Spirit might yet pierce its way to those closed hearts.

Nor was she quite happy about Barbara. Hitherto the girl had seemed, as it were, one with Armine, and had been led by his precocious piety into similar habits and aspirations, which had been fostered by her intercourse with Sydney and the sharing with her of many a blissful and romantic dream.

All this, however, was altered. Petronella had drawn Armine

aside one way, and now that he was come back again, he did
not find the same perfectly sympathetic sister as before. Bobus
had not been without effect upon her, as the impersonation of
common sense and antagonism to Miss Parsons. It had not
shown at the time, for his domineering tone and his sneers
always impelled her to stand up for her darling ; but when he
was 'poor Bobus' gone into exile and bereft of his love, certain
poisonous germs attached to his words began to grow. There
was no absolute doubt—far from it—but there was an impatience of the weariness and solemnity of religion.

To enjoy Church privileges to the full, and do good works
under Church direction, had in their wandering life been a dream
of modern chivalry which she had shared with Sydney, much as
they had talked of going on a crusade. And now she found
these privileges very tedious, the good works onerous, and she
viewed them somewhat as she might have regarded Cœur de
Lion's camp had she been set down in it. Armine would have
gone on, hearing nothing but 'Remember the Holy Sepulchre,'
but Barbara would soon have seen every folly and failure that
spoiled the glory of the army—even though she might not
question its destination—and would have been unfeignedly
weary of its discipline.

So she hung back from the frequent Church ordinances of
St. Cradocke's, being allowed to do as she pleased about everything extra ; she made fun of the peculiarities of the varieties
of the genus Petronella who naturally hung about it, and adopted
the popular tone about the curates, till Jock told her 'not to
be so commonplace.' Indeed, both he and Armine had made
friends with them, as he did with every one ; and Armine's
enjoyment of the society of a new, young, bright deacon, who
came at Christmas, perhaps accounted for a little of her soreness,
and made Armine himself less observant that the two were
growing apart.

Her mother saw it, though, and being seconded by Jock,
found it easier than of old to keep the tables free from sceptical
and semi-sceptical literature ; but this involved the loss of
much that was clever, and there was no avoiding those envenomed shafts that people love to strew about, and which, for
their seeming wit and sense, Babie always relished. She did
not think—that was the chief charge ; and she was still a joyous
creature, even though chafing at the dulness of St. Cradocke's.

'Gould and another versus Brownlow and another, to be heard
on the 18th,' Mr. Wakefield writes. 'So we must leave our
peaceful harbour to face the world again !'

'Oh, I'm so glad,' cried Barbara. I am fairly tingling to be
in the thick of it again !'

'You ungrateful Infant,' said Armine, 'when this place has
done every one so much good !'

'So does bed ; but I feel as if it were six in the morning and
I couldn't get the shutters open !'

'I wonder if Mr. Ogilvie will think me fit to go in for matriculation for the next term?' said Armine.

'And I ought to go up for lectures,' said Jock, who had been reading hard all this time under directions from Dr. Medlicott. 'I might go on before, and see that the house is put in order before you come home, mother.'

'Home! It sounds more like going home than ever going back to Belforest did!'

'And we'll make it the very moral of the old times. We've got all the old things!'

'What do you know about the old times—baby that you are and were?' said Jock.

'The Drakes move to-morrow,' said his mother. 'I must write to your aunt and Richards about sending the things from Belforest. We must have it at its best before Ali comes home.'

'All right!' said Babie. 'You know our own things have only to go back into their places, and the Drake carpets go on. It will be such fun; as nice as the getting into the Folly!'

'Nice you call that?' said her mother. 'All I remember is the disgrace we got into and the fright I was in! I wonder what the old home will bring us?'

'Life and spirit and action,' cried Babie. 'Oh, I'm wearying for the sound of the wheels and the flow of people!'

'Oh, you little Cockney!'

'Of course. I was born one, and I am thankful for it! There's nothing to do here.'

'Babie!' cried Armine indignantly.

'Well, you and Jock have read a great deal, and he has plunged into night-schools.'

'And become a popular lecturer,' added Armine.

'And you and mother have cultivated Percy Stagg, and gone to church a great deal—pour passer le temps.'

'Ah, you discontented mortal!' said her mother, rising to write her letters. 'You have yet to learn that what is stagnation to some is rest to others.'

'Oh yes, mother, I know it was very good for you, but I'm heartily glad it is over. Sea and Ogre are all very well for once in a way, but they pall, especially in an east wind English fog!'

'My Babie, I hope you are not spoilt by all the excitements of our last few years,' said the mother. 'You won't find life in Collingwood Street much like life in Hyde Corner.'

'No, but it will be life, and that's what I care for!'

No, Barbara, used to constant change, and eager for her schemes of helpfulness, could not be expected to enjoy the peacefulness of St. Cradocke's as the others had done. To Armine, indeed, it had been the beginning of a new life of hope and vigour, and a casting off of the slough of morbid self-contemplation, induced by his invalid life, and fostered at Woodside. He had left off the romance of being early doomed, since his health had stood the trial of the English winter, and under Mr. Ogilvie's bracing management, seconded by Jock's energetic companionship, he had learnt to look to active service and be ready to strive for it.

To Jock, the time had been a rest from the victory which had cost him so dear, and though the wounds still smarted, there had been nothing to call them into action ; and he had fortified himself against the inevitable reminders he should meet with in London. He had been studying with all his might for the pre-liminary examination, and eagerness in so congenial a pursuit was rapidly growing on him, while conversations with Mr. Ogilvie had been equally pleasant to both, for the ex-school-master thoroughly enjoyed hearing of the scientific world, and the young man was heartily glad of the higher light he was able to shed on his studies, and for being shown how to prevent the spiritual world from being obscured by the physical, and to deal with the difficulties that his brother's materialism had raised for him. He had never lost, and trusted never to lose, hold of his anchor in the Rock ; but he had not always known how to answer when called on to prove its existence and trace the cable. Thus the winter at St. Cradocke's had been very valuable to him personally, and he had been willing to make return for the kindness for which he felt so grateful, by letting the vicar employ him in the night-schools, lectures, and parish diversions —all, in short, for which a genial and sensible young layman is invaluable, when he can be caught.

And for their mother herself, she had been sheltered from agitation, and had gathered strength and calmness, though with her habitual want of self-consciousness she hardly knew it, and what she thanked her old friend for was what he had done for her sons, especially Armine. 'He and I shall be grateful to you all the rest of our lives,' she said, with her bright eyes glistening.

David Ogilvie, in his deep, silent, life-long romance, felt that precious guerdons sometimes are won at an age which the young suppose to be past all feeling—guerdons the more precious and pure because unconnected with personal hopes or schemes. He still knew Caroline to be as entirely Joseph Brownlow's own as when he had first perceived it, ten years ago, but all that was regretful jealousy was gone. His idealisation of her had raised and moulded his life, and now that she had grown into the reality of that ideal, he was content with the sunshine she had brought, and the joy of having done her a real service, little as she guessed at the devoted homage that prompted it.

## CHAPTER XXXIV

### BLIGHTED BEINGS

'Allen-a-Dale has no faggot for burning,
Allen-a-Dale has no furrow for turning,
Allen-a-Dale has no fleece for the spinning,
Yet Allen-a-Dale has red gold for the winning.'

SCOTT.

THE little family raft put forth from the haven of shelter into the stormy waves. The first experience was, as Jock said, that large rooms and country clearness had been demoralising, or, as Babie averred, the bad taste and griminess of the Drake remains were invincible, for when the old furniture and pictures were all restored to the old places, the *tout ensemble* was so terribly dingy and confined that the mother could hardly believe that it was the same place that had risen in her schoolgirl eyes as a vision of home brightness. Armine was magnanimously silent, but what would be the effect on Allen, who had been heard of at Gibraltar, and was sure to return before the case was heard in court?

'We must give up old associations, and try what a revolution will do,' Mother Carey said.

'Hurrah!' cried Babie; 'I was feeling totally overpowered by that awful round table, but I thought it was the very core of mother's heart.'

'So did I,' said the mother herself, 'when I remember how we used to sit round with the lamp in the middle, and spin the whole table when we wanted a drawer on the farther side. But it won't bring back those who sat there! and now the light falls anywhere but where it is wanted, and our goods get into each other's way! Yes, Babie, you may dispose of it in the back drawing-room, and bring in your whole generation of little tables.'

There was opportunity for choice, for the house was somewhat over-full of furniture, since besides the original plenishing of the Pagoda, all that was individual property had been sent from Belforest, and this included a great many choice and curious articles, small and great, all indeed that any one cared much about, except the more intrinsically valuable gems of art. It had been all done between Messrs. Wakefield, Gould, and Richards, who had sent up far more than Mrs. Brownlow had marked, assuring her that she need not scruple to keep it.

So by the time twilight came on the second evening, when the whole family were feeling exceedingly bruised, weary, and dusty, such a transformation had been effected that each of the four, on returning from the much-needed toilet, stood at the

2 A

door exclaiming—'This is something like'; and when John arrived a little later, he looked round with—

'This is almost as nice as the Folly. How does Mother Carey manage to make things like herself and nobody else?'

Allen's comment a few days later was—

'What's the use of taking so much trouble about a dingy hole which you can't make tolerable even if you were to stay here.'

'I mean it to be my home till my M.D. son takes a wife and turns me out.'

'Why, mother, you don't suppose that ridiculous will can hold water?'

'You know I don't contest it.'

'I know, but they will not look at it for a moment in the Probate Court.'

Some chance friend whom he had met abroad had suggested this to Allen, and he had gradually let his wish become hope, and his hope expectation, till he had come home almost secure of a triumph, which would reinstate his mother and bring Elvira back to him, having learnt the difference between true friends and false.

It was a proportionate blow when no difficulty was made about proving the will. As the trustees acted, Mrs. Brownlow had not to appear, but Allen haunted the Law Courts with his uncle and saw the will accepted as legal. Nothing remained but another amicable action to put Elvira de Menella in possession.

He was in a state of nervous excitement at every postman's knock, making sure, poor fellow, that Elvira's first use of her victory would be to return to him. But all that was heard of was a grand reception at Belforest, bands, banners, horsemen, triumphal arches, banquet, speeches, toasts, and ball—all, no doubt, in 'Gould taste.' The penny-a-liner of the Kenminster paper outdid himself in the polysyllables of his description, while Colonel Brownlow briefly wrote that 'all was as insolent as might be expected, and he was happy to say that most of the county people and some of the tenants showed their good feeling by their absence.'

Over this Mrs. Brownlow would not rejoice. She did not like the poor girl to be left to such society as her aunt would pick up, and she wrote on her behalf to various county neighbours; but the heiress had already come to the house in Hyde Corner, chaperoned by her aunt, who, fortified by the trust that she was 'as good as Mrs. Joseph Brownlow,' had come to fight the battle of fashion, with Lady Flora Folliott for an ally.

The name of George Gould, Esq., was used on occasion, but he was usually left in peace at his farm with his daughter Mary, with whom her stepmother had decided that nothing could be done. Kate was made presentable by dress and lessons in deportment, and promoted to be white slave, at least so Armine and Barbara inferred, from her constrained and frightened manner when they met her in a shop, though she was evidently trying to believe herself very happy.

Allen was convinced at last that he was designedly given up, and so far from trying to meet his faithless lady, dejectedly refused all society where he could fall in with her, and only wandered about the parks to feed his melancholy with distant glimpses of her on horseback, while Armine and Barbara, who held Elvira very cheap, were wicked enough to laugh at him between themselves and term him the forsaken merman.

Jock had likewise given up his old connections with fashionable life. Several times, if anything were going on, or if he met a former brother officer in the street, he would be warmly invited to come and take his share, or to dine with the mess ; he might have played in cricket matches and would have been welcome as a frequent guest ; but he had made up his mind that this would only lead to waste of time and money, and steadily declined, till the invitations ceased. It would have cost him more had any come from Cecil Evelyn, but all that had been seen of him was a couple of visiting-cards. The rest of the family had not come to town for the season, and though the two mothers corresponded as warmly as ever, and Fordham and Armine exchanged letters, there was a sort of check and chill upon the friendship between the two young girls, of which each understood only her own half.

Jock said nothing, but he seemed to have grown mother-sick, spent all his leisure moments in haunting his mother's steps, helping her in whatever she was about, and telling her everything about his studies and companions, as if she were the great solace of the life that had become so much less bright to him.

In general he showed himself as droll as ever, but there were days when, as John said, 'all the skip was gone out of the Jack.' The good Monk was puzzled by the change, which he did not think quite worthy of his cousin, having—though the son of a military man—a contempt for the pomp and circumstance of war. He marvelled to see Jock affectionately hook up his sword over the photograph of Engelberg above his mantelshelf ; and he hesitated to join the volunteers, as his aunt wished, by way of compelling variety and exercise. Jock, however, decided on so doing, that Sydney might own at least that he was ready for a call to arms for his country. He did not like to think that she was reading a report of Sir Philip Cameron's campaign, in which the aide-de-camp happened to receive honourable mention for a dashing and hazardous ride.

'Why, old fellow, what makes you so down in the mouth?' said John, on that very day as the two cousins were walking home from a lecture. They had had to get into a doorway to avoid the rush of rabble escorting a regiment of household troops on their way to the station, and Lucas had afterwards walked the length of two streets without a word. 'You don't mean that you are hankering after all this style of thing—row and all the rest of it ?'

'There's a good deal more going to it than row,' said Jock, rather heavily.

'What, that donkey, Evelyn, having cut you ? I should not trouble myself much on that score, though I did think better of him at Eton.'

'He hasn't cut me,' Jock made sharp return.

'One pasteboard among all the family,' grunted the Friar. 'I reserve to myself the satisfaction of cutting him dead the next opportunity,' he added magniloquently.

Jock laughed, as he was of course intended to do, but there was such a painful ring in the laugh that John paused and said—

'That's not all, old fellow ! Come, make a clean breast of it, my fair son. Thou dost weary of thy vocation.'

'No such thing,' exclaimed Jock, with an inaudible growl between his teeth. 'Trust Kencroft for boring on !' and aloud, with some impatience, 'It is just what I would have chosen for its own sake.'

'Then,' said John, still keeping up the grand philosophical air and demeanour, though with real kindness and desire to show sympathy, 'thou art either entangled by worldly scruples, leading thee to disdain the wholesome art of healing, or thou art, like thy brother, the victim of the fickle sex.'

'Shut up !' said Jock, pushed beyond endurance ; 'can't you understand that some things can't be talked of ?'

'Whew !' John whistled, and surveyed him rather curiously from head to foot. 'It is another case of deluded souls not knowing what an escape they've had. What ! she thought you a catch in the old days.'

'That's all you know about it !' said Jock. 'She is not that sort. The poverty is nothing, but there's a fitness in things. Women, the best of them, think much of what I suppose you call the row. It fits in with all their chivalry and romance.'

'Then she's a fool,' said John shortly.

'I can't stand any more of this, Monk, I tell you. You know just nothing at all about it, and I've no right to complain, nor any one to bait me with questions.'

The Monk took the hint, and when they reached their own street Jock said—

'You meant it all kindly, Reverend Friar, but there are things that won't stand probing, as you'll know some day.'

'Poor old chap,' said John, with his hand on his shoulder, 'I'll not bother you any more. The veil shall be sacred. If this has been going on all the time, I wonder you have carried it off so well !'

'Ali is a caution,' said Jock, who had shaken himself into his ordinary manner. 'What would become of Babie with two blighted beings on her hands? Besides, he has some excuse, and I have not.'

After this, at every carriage to which Lucas bowed, John frowned, and scanned the inmates in search of the fair deceiver, never making a guess in the right direction.

John had enough of the Kencroft character not to be original. Set him to work, and he had plenty of intelligence and energy, perhaps more absolute force and power than his cousin Lucas; but he would never devise things for himself, and was not discursive, pausing at novelties, because his nature was so thorough that he could not take up anything without spending his very utmost force upon it.

His university training made him an excellent aid to Armine, who went up for his examination at King's College, and acquitted himself so well as to be admitted to begin his terms after the long vacation.

Indeed he and Barbara had drawn together again more. She had her home tasks and her classes at King's College and did not fret as at St. Cradocke's for want of work; she enjoyed the full tide of life, and had plenty of sympathy for whatever did not come before her in a 'goody' aspect, and, though there might be little depth of serious reflection in her, she was a very charming member of the household. Then her enjoyment of society was gratified, for society of her own kind had by no means forgotten one so agreeable as Mrs. Brownlow, and whereas, in her prosperity, she had never dropped old friends, they welcomed her back as one of themselves, resuming the homely inexpensive gatherings where the brains were more consulted than the palate, æsthetics more than fashion. She was glad of it for the young people's sake as well as her own, and returned to her old habit of keeping open house one evening in the week between eight and ten, with cups of coffee and varieties of cheap foreign drinks, and slight but dainty cates made by herself and Babie according to lessons taken together at the school of cookery.

As Allen declared these evenings a grievance, and often thought himself unable to bear family chatter, she had made the old consulting room as like his luxurious apartment at home as furniture and fittings could do, and he was always free to retire thither. Indeed the toleration and tenderness with which his mother treated him were a continual wonder and annoyance to Barbara, the active little busy bee, who not unjustly considered him the drone of the family, and longed to sting him, not to death but to exertion.

It was provoking that when all the other youths had long finished breakfast and gone forth, Mother Carey should wait lingering in the dining-room to cherish some delicate hot *morceau* and cup of coffee, till the tardy, soft-falling feet came down the stairs, and then sit patiently as long as he chose to dally with his meal, telling how little he had slept. Babie had tried her tongue on both, but Allen, when she shouted at his door that breakfast was ready, came forth no sooner, and when he did so, told his mother that he could not have children screaming at his door at all hours of the morning. Mother Carey replied to her impatient champion that while waiting for Allen was her time for writing letters and reading amusing books, and that the day was only too long for him already, poor fellow, without urging him to make it longer.

'More shame for him,' muttered pitiless sixteen.

After breakfast Allen generally strolled out to see the papers or to bestow his time somewhere—in the picture galleries, or in the British Museum, where he had a reading order; but it was always uncertain whether he would disappear for the whole day, shut himself up in his own room, or hang about the drawing-room, very much injured if his mother could not devote herself to him. Indeed she always did so, except when she was bound to take Barbara to some of her classes (including cookery), or when she had promised herself to Dr. and Mrs. Lucas, who were now both very infirm, and knew not how to be thankful enough for the return of one who became like a daughter to them; while Jock, their godson, at once made himself like the best of grandsons, and never failed to give them a brightening, cheering hour every Sunday.

The science of cookery was by no means a needless task, for the cook was very plain, and Allen's appetite was dainty, and comfort at dinner could only be hoped for by much thought and contrivance. Allen was never discourteous to his mother herself, but he would look at her in piteous reproach, and affect to charge all failures on the cook, or on 'children being allowed to meddle,' the most cutting thing to Babie he could say. Then the two Johns always took up the cudgels, and praised the food with all their might. Indeed the Friar was often sensible of a strong desire to flog the dawdling melancholy out of his cousin, and force him no longer to hang a dead weight on his mother; and even Jock began to be annoyed at her unfailing patience and pity, though he understood her compassion better than did those who had never felt a wound.

She did in truth blame herself for having given him no profession, and having acquiesced in the indolent *dilettante* habits which made all harder to him now; and she was not certain how far it was only his fancy that his health and nerves were perilously affected, though Dr. Medlicott, whom she secretly consulted, assured her that the only remedies needed were good sense and something to do.

At last, at midsummer, the crisis came in a heavy discharge of bills, the consequence of Allen's incredulity as to their poverty and incapability of economising. He said 'the rascals could wait,' and 'his mother need not trouble herself.' She said they must be paid, and she found it could be done at the cost of giving up spending August at St. Cradocke's, as well as of breaking into her small reserve for emergencies.

But she told Allen that she insisted on his making some exertion for his own maintenance.

'Yes,' said Allen in languid assent.

'I know it is harder at your age to find occupation.'

'That is not the point. I can easily find something to do. There's literature. Or I could take up art. And last year there was a Hungarian Count who would have given anything to get me for a tutor.'

'Then why didn't you go?'

'Mother, you ask me why!'

'I know you had not made up your mind to the worst, but it is a pity you missed the opportunity.'

'There will be more,' said Allen loftily. 'I never meant to be a burden, but ladies are so impatient. I suppose you do not wish to turn me out instantly to seek my fortune. No, mother, I do not mean to blame you. You have been sadly harassed, and no woman can ever enter into what I have suffered. Put aside those bills. Long before Christmas I shall be able to discharge them myself.'

So Allen wrote to Bobus's friend at Oxford, but he of course did not keep a pocketful of Hungarian Counts. He answered one or two advertisements for a travelling tutor, and had one personal interview, the result of which was that he could have nothing to do with such insufferable snobs. He also concocted an advertisement beginning with 'M.A., Oxford, accustomed to the best society and familiar with European languages,' but though the newspapers charged highly for it, he only received one answer, except those from agents, and that, he said with illimitable disgust, was from a Yankee.

Meantime he turned over his poems, and made Barbara copy out a ballad he had written for the *Traveller's Joy* on some local tradition in the Tyrol. He offered this to a magazine, whose editor, a lady, was an occasional frequenter of Mrs. Brownlow's evenings. The next time she came, she showed herself so much interested in the legend that Allen said he should like to show her another story, which he had written for the same domestic periodical.

'Would it serve for our Christmas number?'

'I will have it copied out and send it for you to look at,' said Allen.

'If it is at hand, I had better cast my eye over it, to judge whether it be worth while to copy it. I shall set forth on my holiday journey the day after to-morrow, and I should like to have my mind at rest about my Christmas number.'

So she carried off with her the Algerine number of the *Joy*, and in a couple of days returned it with a hasty note—

A capital little story, just young and sentimental enough to make it taking, and not overdone. Please let me have it, with a few verbal corrections, ready for the press when I come home at the end of September. It will bring you in about £15.

Allen was modestly elated, and only wished he had gone to one of the periodicals more widely circulated. It was plain that literature was his vocation, and he was going to write a novel to be published in a serial, the instalments paying his expenses for the trial. The only doubt was what it should be about, whether a sporting tale of modern life, or a historical story in which his familiarity with Italian art and scenery would be available. Jock advised the former, Armine inclined to the latter, for each had tried his hand in his own particular line in the *Traveller's Joy*, and wanted to see his germ developed.

To write in the heat and glare of London was, however, manifestly impossible in Allen's eyes, and he must recruit himself by a yachting expedition to which an old acquaintance had invited him half compassionately. Jock shrugged his shoulders on hearing of it, and observed that a tuft always expected to be paid in service, if in no other way, and he doubted Allen's liking it, but that was his affair. Jock himself, with his usual facility of making friends, had picked up a big north-country student, twice as large as himself, with whom he meant to walk through the scenery of Derbyshire and Yorkshire, as far as the modest sum they allowed themselves would permit, after which he was to make a brief stay in his friend's paternal Cumberland farm. He had succeeded in gaining a scholarship at the Medical School of his father's former hospital, and this, with the remains of the price of his commission, still made him the rich man of the family. John was of course going home, and Mrs. Brownlow and the two younger ones had a warm invitation from their friends at Fordham.

'I should like Armie to go,' said the mother in conference with Babie, her cabinet councillor

'Oh yes, *Armie* must go,' said Babie, 'but——'

'Then it will not disappoint you to stay at home, my dear?'

'I had much rather not go, if Sydney will not mind very much.'

'Well, Babie, I had resolved to stay here this summer, and I thought you would not wish to go without me.'

'Oh no, *no*, no, NO, mother,' and her face and neck burnt with blushes.

'Then my Infant and I will be thoroughly cosy together, and get some surprises ready for the others.'

'Hurrah! We'll do the painting of the doors. What fun it will be to see London empty!'

The male population were horribly scandalised at the decision. Jock and Armine wanted to give up their journey, and John implored his aunt to come to Kencroft; but she only promised to send Babie there if she saw signs of flagging, and the Infanta laughed at the notion, and said she had had an overdose of country enough to last her for years. Allen said ladies overdid everything, and that Mother Carey could not help being one of the sex, and then he asked her for £10, and said Babie would have plenty of time to copy out 'The Single Eye.' She pouted 'I thought you were going to put the finishing touches.'

'I've marked them for you. Why, Barbara, I am surprised,' he added in an elder brotherly tone ; 'you ought to be thankful to be able to be useful.'

'Useful ! I've lots of things to do ! And you ?'

'As if I could lug that great MS. of yours about with me on board Apthorpe's yacht.'

'Never mind, Allen,' said his mother, who had not been intended to hear all this. 'I will do it for you ; but Miss Editor must not laugh at my peaked governessy hand.'

'I did not mean that, mother, only Babie ought not to be disobliging.'

'Babie has a good deal to do. She has an essay to write for her professor, you know, and her hands are pretty full.'

Babie too said, 'Mother, I never meant you to undertake it. Please let me have it now. Only Allen will never do anything for himself that he can get any one else to do.'

'He could not well do it on board the yacht, my dear. And I don't want you to have so much writing on your hands.'

'And so you punish me,' sighed Barbara, more annoyed than penitent.

However, nothing could be more snug and merry than the mother and daughter when left together, for they were like two sisters and suited one another perfectly. Babie was disappointed that London would not look emptier even in the fashionable squares, which she insisted on exploring in search of solitude. They made little gay outings in a joyous spirit of adventure, getting up early and going by train to some little station, with an adjacent expanse of wood or heather, whence they came home with their luncheon basket full of flowers, wherewith to gladden Mrs. Lucas's eyes, and those of Mother Carey's district. They prepared their surprises too. Several hopelessly dingy panels were painted black and adorned with stately lilies and irises, with proud reed-maces, and twining honeysuckle, and bryony, fluttered over by dragon-flies and butterflies, from the brush of mother and daughter. The stores from Belforest further supplied hangings for brackets, and coverings for cushions, under the dainty fingers of the Infanta, who had far more of the household fairy about her than had her mother, perhaps from having grown up in a home instead of a school, and, besides, from being bent on having the old house a delightsome place.

Indeed, her mother was really happier than for many years, for the sense of failing in her husband's charge had left her since she had seen Jock by his own free will on the road to the

quest, and likely also to fulfil the moral, as well as the scientific,
conditions attached to it. She did feel as if her dream was
being realised and the golden statues becoming warmed into
life, and though her heart ached for Janet, she still hoped for her.
So, with a mother's unfailing faith, she believed in Allen's dawn-
ing future even while another sense within her marvelled, as
she copied, at the acceptance of 'The Single Eye.' But then,
was it not well known that loving eyes see the most faults, and
was not an editor the best judge of popularity?

She had her scheme too. She had taken lessons some years
ago at Rome in her old art of modelling, and knew her eye and
taste had improved in the galleries. She had once or twice
amused the household by figures executed by her dexterous
fingers in pastry or in butter; and in the empty house, in her
old studio, amid remnants of Bobus's museum, she set to work on
a design that had long been in her mind asking her to bring it
into being.

Thus the *tête-à-tête* was so successful that people's pity was
highly diverting, and the vacation was almost too brief, though
when the young men began to return, it was a wonder how
existence could have been so agreeable without them.

Jock was first, having come home ten days sooner than his
friends were willing to part with him, determined if he found his
ladies looking pale to drag them out of town, if only to Rams-
gate.

They met him in a glow of animation, and Babie hardly gave
him time to lay down his basket of ferns from the dale, and
flowers from the garden, before she threw open the folding-
doors to the back drawing-room.

'Why, mother, who sent you that group? Why do you laugh?
Did Grinstead lend it to Babie to copy? Young Astyanax,
isn't it? And, I say! Andromache is just like Jessie. I say!
Mother Carey didn't do it. Well! She is an astonishing little
mother and no mistake. The moulding of it! Our anatomical
professor might lecture on Hector's arm.'

'Ah! I haven't been a surgeon's wife for nothing. Your
father put me through a course of arms and legs.'

'And we borrowed a baby,' said Babie. 'Mrs. Jones, our old
groom's wife, who lives in the Mews, was only too happy to bring
it, and when it was shy, it clung beautifully.'

'Then the helmet.'

'That was out of the British Museum.'

'Has Grinstead seen it?'

'No, I kept it for my own public first.'

'What will you do with it? Put it into the Royal
Academy?'

'No, it is not big enough. I thought of offering it to the
Works that used to take my things in the old Folly days. They
might do it in terra-cotta, or Parian.'

'Too good for a toy material like that,' said Jock. 'Get some good opinion before you part with it, mother. I wish we could keep it. I'm proud of my Mother Carey.'

Allen, who came home next, only sighed at the cruel necessity of selling [such a work. He was in deplorable spirits, for Gilbert Gould was superintending the refitting of a beautiful steam yacht, in which Miss Menella meant to sail to the West Indies with her uncle and aunt.

'I knew she would! I knew she would,' softly said Babie.

That did not console Allen, and his silence and cynicism about his hosts gave the impression that he had outstayed his welcome, since he had neither wealth, nor the social brilliance or subservience that might have supplied its place. He had scarcely energy to thank his mother for her faultless transcription of 'The Single Eye,' and only just exerted himself to direct the neat roll of MS. to the editor.

The next day a note came for him.

'Mother, what *have* you done?' he exclaimed. 'What *did* you send to the *Weathercock*?'

'"The Single Eye." What? Not rejected?'

'See there!'

DEAR MR. BROWNLOW—I am afraid there has been some mistake. The story I wished for is not this one, but another in the same MS. Magazine; a charming little history of a boy's capture by, and escape from, the Moorish corsairs. Can you let me have it by Tuesday? I am very sorry to have given so much trouble, but 'The Single Eye' will not suit my purpose at all.'

'What does she mean?' demanded Allen.

'I see! It is a story of the children's! "Marco's Felucca." I looked at it while I was copying, and thought how pretty it was. And now I remember there were some pencil-marks!'

'Well, it will please the children,' graciously said Allen. 'I am not sorry; I did not wish to make my *début* in a second-rate serial like that, and now I am quit of it. She is quite right. It is not her style of thing.'

But Allen did not remember that he had spent the £15 beforehand, so as to make it £25, and this made it fortunate that his mother's group had been purchased by the porcelain works, and another pair ordered.

Thus she could freely leave their gains to Armine and Babie, for the latter declared the sum was alike due to both, since if she had the readiest wit, her brother had the most discrimination, and the best choice of language. The story was only signed A. B., and their mother made a point of the authorship being kept a secret; but little notices of the story in the papers highly gratified the young authors.

Armine, who had returned from a round of visits to St. Cradocke's, Fordham, Kenminster, and Woodside, confirmed the report of Elvira's intended voyage; but till the yacht was ready, the party had gone abroad, leaving the management of

the farm and agency of the estate to a very worthy man named
Whiteside, who had long been a suitor to Mary Gould, and
whom she was at last allowed to marry. He had at once made
the Kencroft party free of the park and gardens, and indeed
John and Armine came laden with gifts in poultry, fruit, and
flowers from the dependants on the estate to Mrs. Brownlow.

Armine really looked quite healthy, nothing remaining of his
former ethereal air but a certain expansiveness of brow and
dreaminess of eye.

He greatly scrupled at having the £15 when it was paid, but
Barbara insisted that he must take his share, and he then
said—

'After all, it does not signify, for we can do things together
with it, as we have always done.'

'What things?'

'Well, I am afraid I do want a few books.'

'So do I, terribly.'

'And there are some Christmas gifts I want to send to Woodside.'

'Woodside! oh!'

'And wouldn't it be pleasant to put the choir at the iron
church into surplices and cassocks for Christmas?'

'Oh, Armie, I do think we might have a little fun out of our
own money.'

'What fun do you mean?' said Armine.

'I want to subscribe to Rolandi's, and to take in the *Contemporary*, and to have one real good Christmas party with *tableaux
vivants*, and charades. Mother says we can't make it a mere
surprise party, for people must have real food, and I think it
would be more pleasure to all of us than presents and knick-
knacks.'

'Of course you can do it,' said Armine, rather disappointed.
'And if we had in Percy Stagg, and the pupil teachers, and the
mission people——'

'It would be awfully edifying and good-booky! Oh yes, to
be sure, nearly as good as hiding your little sooty shoeblacks in
surplices! But, my dear Armie, I am so tired of edifying!
Why should I never have any fun? Come, don't look so dismal.
I'll spare five shillings for a gown for old Betty Grey, and if
there's anything left out after the party, you shall have it for
the surplices, and you'll be Roland Græme in my *tableau*.'

The next day Mother Carey found Armine with an elbow on
each side of his book and his hands in his hair, looking so
dreamily mournful that she apprehended a fresh attack of
Petronella, but made her approaches warily.

'What have you there?' she asked.

'Dean Church's lectures,' he said.

'Ah! I want to make time to read them! But why have
they sent you into doleful dumps?'

'Not they,' said Armine; 'but I wanted to read Babie a

passage just now, and she said she had no notion of making Sundays of week-days, and ran away. It is not only that, mother, but what is the matter with Babie? She is quite different.'

'Have you only just seen it?'

'No, I have felt something indefinable between us, though I never could bear to speak of it, ever since Bobus went. Do you think he did her any harm?'

'A little, but not much. Shall I tell you the truth, Armine; can you bear it?'

'What! did I disgust her when I was so selfish and discontented?'

'Not so much you, my boy, as the overdoing at Woodside! I can venture to speak of it now, for I fancy you have got over the trance.'

'Well, mother,' said Armine, smiling back to her in spite of himself, 'I have not liked to say so, it seemed a shame; but staying at the Vicarage made me wonder at my being such an egregious ass last year! Do you know, I couldn't help it; but that good lady would seem to me quite mawkish in her flattery! And how she does domineer over that poor brother of hers! Then the fuss she makes about details, never seeming to know which are accessories and which are principles. I don't wonder that I was an absurdity in the eyes of all beholders. But it is very sad if it has really alienated my dear Infanta from all deeper and higher things!'

'Not so bad as that, my dear; my Babie is a good little girl.'

'Oh yes, mother, I did not mean——'

'But it did break that unity between you, and prevent your leading her insensibly. I fancy your two characters would have grown apart anyhow, but this was the moving cause. Now I fancy, so far as I can see, that she is more afraid of being wearied and restrained than of anything else. It is just what I felt for many years of my life.'

'No, mother!'

'Yes, my boy; till the time of your illness, serious thought, religion, and all the rest, seemed to me a tedious tax; and though I always, I believe, made it a rule to my conscience in practical matters, it has only very, very lately been anything like the real joy I believe it has always been to you. Believe that, and be patient with your little sister, for indeed she is an unselfish, true, faithful little being, and some day she will go deeper.'

Armine looked up to his mother, and his eyes were full of tears, as she kissed him, and said—

'You will do her much more good if you sympathise with her in her innocent pleasures than if you insist on dragging her into what she feels like privations.'

'Very well, mother,' he said. 'It is due to her.'

And so, though the choir did have at least half Armine's

share of the price of 'Marco's Felucca,' he threw himself most
heartily into the Christmas party, was the poet of the versified
charade, acted the strong-minded woman who was the chief
character in 'Blue Bell;' and he and Jock gained universal
applause.

Allen hardly appeared at the party. He had a fresh attack
of sleepless headache and palpitation, brought on by the departure of Miss Menella for the Continent, and perhaps by the
failure of 'A Single Eye' with some of the magazines. He
dabbled a little with his mother's clay, and produced a nymph,
who, as he persuaded her and himself, was a much nobler performance than Andromache, but unfortunately she did not
prove equally marketable. And he said it was quite plain that
he could not succeed in anything imaginative till his health and
spirits had recovered from the blow; but he was ready to do
anything.

So Dr. Medlicott brought in one day a medical lecture that
he wanted to have translated from the German, and told Allen
that it would be well paid for. He began, but it made his head
ache; it was not a subject that he could well turn over to Babie;
and when Jock brought a message to say the translation must
be ready the next day, only a quarter had been attempted.
Jock sat up till three o'clock in the morning and finished it, but
he could not pain his mother by letting her know that her son
had again failed, so Allen had the money, and really believed,
as he said, that all Jock had done was to put the extreme end
to it, and correct the medical lingo, of which he could not be
expected to know anything. Allen was always so gentle,
courteous, and melancholy, that every one was getting out of
the habit of expecting him to do anything but bring home news,
discover anything worth going to see, sit at the foot of the table,
and give his verdict on the cookery. Babie indeed was sometimes provoked into snapping at him, but he bore it with the
amiable magnanimity of one who could forgive a petulant child,
ignorant of what he suffered.

Jock was borne up by a great pleasure that winter. One day
at dinner, his mother watched his eyes dancing, and heard the
old boyish ring of mirth in his laugh, and as she went upstairs
at night he came after and said—

'Fancy, I met Evelyn on the ice to-day. He wants to know
if he may call.'

'What prevents him?'

'Well, I believe the poor old chap is heartily ashamed of his
airs. Indeed he as good as said so. He has been longing to
make a fresh start, only he didn't know how.'

'I think he used you very ill, Jock; but if you wish to be on
the old terms, I will do as you like.'

'Well,' said Jock, in an odd apologetic voice, 'you see the old
beggar had got into a pig-headed sort of pet last year. He said
he would cut me if I left the service, and so he felt bound to be

as good as his word ; but he seems to have felt lost without us,
and to have been looking out for a chance of meeting. He was
horribly humiliated by the Friar looking over his head last
week.'

'Very well. If he chooses to call, here we are.'

'Yes, and don't put on your cold shell, mother mine. After
all, Evelyn is Evelyn. There are wiser fellows, but I shall never
warm to any one again like him. Why, he was the first fellow
who came into my room at Eton ! I am to meet him to-morrow
after the lecture. May I bring him home ?'

'If he likes. His mother's son must have a welcome.'

She could not feel cordial, and she so much expected that the
young gentleman might be seized with a fresh fit of exclusive
disdain, that she would not mention the possibility, and it was
an amazement to all save herself when Jock appeared with the
familiar figure in his wake. Guardsman as he was, Cecil had
the grace to look bashful, not to say shamefaced, and more so
at Mrs. Brownlow's kindly reception than at Barbara's freezing
dignity. The young lady was hotly resentful on Jock's behalf,
and showed it by a stiff courtesy, elevated eyebrows, and the
merest tips of her fingers.

Allen took it easily. He had been too much occupied with
his own troubles to have entered into all the complications with
the Evelyn family ; and though he had never greatly cared for
them, and had viewed Cecil chiefly as an obnoxious boy, he was,
in his mournful way, gratified by any reminder of his former
surroundings. So without malice prepense he stung poor Cecil
by observing that it was long since they had met ; but no one
could be expected to find the way to the other end of nowhere.
Cecil blushed and stammered something about Hounslow, but
Allen, who prided himself on being the conversational man of
the world, carried off the talk into safe channels.

As Cecil was handing Mrs. Brownlow down to the dining-
room, wicked Barbara whispered to her cousin John—

'We've such a nice vulgar dinner. It couldn't have been
better if I'd known it !'

John, whose wrath had evaporated in his 'cut,' shook his head
at her, but partook of her diversion at her brother's resignation at sight of a large dish of boiled beef, with a suet pudding
opposite to it. Allen was too well bred to apologise, but he
carved in the dainty and delicate style befitting the single slice
of meat interspersed between countless *entrées*. Barbara began
to relent as soon as Cecil, after making four mouthfuls of Allen's
help, sent his plate with a request for something more substantial. And before the meal was over, his evident sense of
*bien-être* and happiness had won back her kindness ; she remembered that he was Sydney's brother, and took no more trouble
to show her indignation.

Thenceforth, Cecil was as much as ever Jock's friend, and a
frequenter of the family, finding that the loss of their wealth

and place in the great world made wonderfully little difference to them, and rather enhanced the pleasant freedom and life of their house.  The rest of the family were seen once or twice, when passing through London, but only in calls, which, as Babie said, were as good as nothing, except, as she forgot to add, that they broke through the constraint on her correspondence with Sydney.


## CHAPTER XXXV

### THE PHANTOM BLACKCOCK OF KILNAUGHT

> ' And we alike must shun regard
> From painter, player, sportsman, bard,
> Wasp, blue-bottle, or butterfly,
> Insects that swim in fashion's sky.'
>
> SCOTT.

' AT home?  Then take these.  There's a lot more.  I'll run up,' said Cecil Evelyn one October evening nearly two years later, as he thrust into the arms of the parlour-maid a whole basket of game, while his servant extracted a hamper from his cab, and he himself dashed upstairs with a great bouquet of hothouse flowers.

But in the drawing-room he stood aghast, glancing round in the firelit dusk to ascertain that he had not mistaken the number, for though the maid at the door had a well-known face, and though tables, chairs, and pictures were familiar, the two occupants of the room were utter strangers, and at least as much startled as himself.

A little pale child was hurriedly put down from the lap of a tall maiden who rose from a low chair by the fire, and stood uncertain.

' I beg your pardon,' he said ; ' I came to see Mrs. Brownlow.'

' My aunt.  She will be here in a moment.  Will you run and call her, Lina ?'

' You may tell her Cecil Evelyn is here,' said he ; ' but there is no hurry,' he added, seeing that the child clung to her protector, too shy even to move.  ' You are John Brownlow's little sister, eh ?' he added, bending towards her ; but as she crept round in terror, still clinging, he addressed the elder one : ' I am so glad ; I thought I had rushed into a strange house, and should have to beat a retreat.'

The young lady gave a little shy laugh which made her sweet oval glowing face and soft brown eyes light up charmingly, and there was a fresh graceful roundness of outline about her tall slender figure, as she stood holding the shy child, which made her a wondrously pleasant sight.  ' Are you staying here?' he asked.

' Yes ; we came for advice for my little sister, who is not strong.'

'I'm so glad. I mean I hope there is only enough amiss to make you stay a long time. Were you ever in town before?'

'Only for a few hours on our way to school.'

Here a voice reached them—

> ' Fee, fa, fum,
> I smell the breath of geranium.'

And through the back drawing-room door came Babie, in walking attire, declaiming—

> 'Tis Cecil, by the jingling steel
> 'Tis Cecil, by the pawing bay,
> 'Tis Cecil, by the tall two-wheel,
> 'Tis Cecil, by the fragrant spray.

'O Cecil, how lovely! Oh, the maiden-hair. You've been making acquaintance with Essie and Lina.'

'I did not know you were out, Babie,' said Essie. 'Was my aunt with you?'

'Yes. We just ran over to see Mrs. Lucas, and as we were coming home, a poor woman besought us to buy two toasting-forks and a mouse-trap, by way of ornament to brandish in the streets. She looked so frightfully wretched, that mother let her follow, and is having it out with her at the door. So you are from Fordham, Cecil; I see and I smell. How are they?'

'Duke is rather brisk. I actually got him out shooting yesterday, but he didn't half like it, and was thankful when I let him go home again. See, Sydney said I was to tell you that passion-flower came from the plant she brought from Algiers.'

'The beauty! It must go into Mrs. Evelyn's Venice glass,' said Babie, bustling about to collect her vases.

Lina, with a cry of delight, clutched at a spray of butterfly-like mauve and white orchids, in spite of her sister's gentle 'No, no, Lina, you must not touch.'

Babie offered some China asters in its stead; Cecil muttered 'Let her have it'; but Esther was firm in making her relinquish it, and when she began to cry, led her away with pretty tender gestures of mingled comfort and reproof.

'Poor little thing,' said Babie, 'she is sadly fretful. Nobody but Essie can manage her.'

'I should think not!' said Cecil, looking after the vision, as if he did not know what he was saying. 'You never told me you had any one like *that* in the family?'

'Oh yes; there are two of them, as much alike as two peas.'

'What! the Monk's sisters?'

'To be sure. They are a comely family; all but poor little Lina.'

'Will they be long here?'

'That depends. That poor little mite is the youngest but one, and the nurse likes boys best. So she peaked and pined, and was bullied by Edmund above and Harry below, and was always in trouble. Nobody but Johnnie and Essie ever had a good word for her. This autumn it came to a crisis. You know we had a great meeting of the two families at Walmer, and there the shock of bathing nearly took out of her all the little life there was. I believe she would have gone into fits if mother had not heard her screams, and dashed on the nurse like a vindictive mermaid, and then *made* Uncle Robert believe her. My aunt trusts the nurse, you must know, and lets her ride rough-shod over every one in the nursery. The poor little thing was always whining and fretting whenever she was not in Essie's arms or the Monk's, till the Monk declared she had a weak spine, and he and mother gave uncle and aunt no peace till they brought her here for advice, and sure enough her poor little spine is all wrong, and will never be good for anything without a regular course of watching and treatment. So we have her here with Essie to look after her for as long as Sir Edward Fane wants to keep her under him, and you can't think what a nice little mortal she turns out to be now she is rescued from nurse and those little ruffians of brothers.'

'That's first-rate,' remarked Cecil.

'The eucharis and maiden-hair, is it not? I must keep some sprays for our hairs to-night.'

'Is any one coming to-night?'

'The promiscuous herd. Oh, didn't you know? Our Johns told mother it would be no end of kindness to let them bring in a sprinkling of their fellow-students—poor lads that live poked up in lodgings, and never see a lady or any civilisation all through the term. So she took to having them on Thursday once a fortnight, and Dr. Medlicott was perfectly delighted, and said she could not do a better work ; and it is such fun ! We don't have them unmitigated, we get other people to enliven them. The Actons are coming, and I hope Mr. Esdale is coming to-night to show us his photographs of the lost cities in Central America. You'll stay, won't you?'

'If Mrs. Brownlow will let me. I hope your toasting-fork woman has not spirited her away.'

'Under the eyes of your horse and man.'

'Are you all at home? And has Allen finished his novel?'

Babie laughed, and said—

'Poor Ali ! You see there comes a fresh blight whenever it begins to bud.'

'What has that wretched girl been doing now?'

'Oh, don't you know? The yacht had to be overhauled, so they went to Florence instead, and have been wandering about in all the resorts of rather shady people, where Lisette can cut a figure. Mr. Wakefield is terribly afraid that even poor Mr. Gould himself is taking to gambling for want of something to do. There are always reports coming of Elfie taking up with some count or baron. It was a Russian prince last time, and then Ali goes down into the very lowest depths, and can't do anything but smoke. You know that's good for blighted beings. I cure my plants by putting them into his room surreptitiously.

'You are a hard-hearted little mortal, Babie. Ah, there's the bell!'

Mrs. Brownlow came in with the two Johns, who had joined her just as she had finished talking to the poor woman ; Jock carried off his friend to dress, and Babie, after finishing her arrangements and making the most of every fragment of flower or leaf, repaired with a selection of delicate sprays to the room where Esther, having put her little sister to bed, was dressing for dinner. She was eager to tell of her alarm at the invasion, and of Captain Evelyn's good-nature when she had expected him to be proud and disagreeable.

'He wanted to be,' said Babie, 'but honest nature was too strong for him.'

'Johnnie was so angry at the way he treated Jock.'

'Oh, we quite forget all that. Poor fellow! it was a mistaken reading of *noblesse oblige*, and he is very much ashamed of it. There, let me put this fern and fuchsia into your hair. I'll try to do it as well as Ellie would.'

She did so, and better, being more dainty-fingered, and having more taste. It really was an artistic pleasure to deal with such beautiful hair and such a lovely lay figure as Esther's. With all her queenly beauty and grace, the girl had that simplicity and sedateness which often goes with regularity of feature, and was hardly conscious of the admiration she excited. Her good looks were those of the family, and Kenminster was used to them. This was her first evening of company, for on the only previous occasion her little sister had been unwell, sleepless and miserable in the strange house, and she had begged off. She was very shy now, and could not go down without Barbara's protection, so, at the last moment before dinner, the little brown fairy led in the tall, stately maiden, all in white, with the bright fuchsias and delicate fern in her dark hair, and a creamy rose, set off by a few more in her bosom.

Babie exulted in her work, and as her mother beheld Cecil's raptured glance and the incarnadine glow it called up, she guessed all that would follow in one rapid prevision, accompanied by a sharp pang for her son in Japan. It was not in her maternal heart not to hope almost against her will that some fibre had been touched by Bobus that would be irresponsive to others, but duty and loyalty alike forbade the slightest attempt to revive the thought of the poor absentee, and she must steel herself to see things take their course, and own it for the best.

Esther was a silent damsel. The clash of keen wits and exchange of family repartee were quite beyond her. She had often wondered whether her cousins were quarrelling, and had been only reassured by seeing them so merry and friendly, and her own brother bearing his part as naturally as the rest. She was more scandalised than ever to-day, for it absolutely seemed to her that they were all treating Captain Evelyn, long moustache and all, like a mere family butt, certainly worse than they would have treated one of her own brothers, for Rob would have sulked, and Joe, or any of the younger ones, might have been dangerous, whereas this distinguished-looking personage bore all as angelically as befitted one called by such a charming appellation as the Honourable Cecil Evelyn.

'How about the shooting, Cecil? Sydney said you had not very good sport.'

'Why—no, not till I joined Rainsforth's party.'

'Where was your moor?'

'In Lanarkshire,' rather unwillingly.

'Eh,' said Allen, in a peculiar soft languid tone, that meant diversion. 'Near L——?'

'Yes.'

Then Jock burst out into laughter inexplicable at first, but Allen made his voice gentler and graver as he said, 'You don't mean Kilnaught?' and then he too joined Jock in laughter, as the latter cried—

'Another victim to M'Nab of Kilnaught! He certainly is the canniest of Scots.'

'He revenges the wrongs of Scotland on innocent young Guardsmen.'

'Well, I'm sure there could not be a more promising advertisement.'

'That's just it!' said Jock. 'Moor and moss. How many acres of heather?'

'How was I to expect a man of family to be a regular swindler?'

'Hush! hush, my dear fellow! Roderick Dhu was a man of family. It is the modern form.'

'But I saw his keeper.'

'Oh!' cried Allen. 'I know! Old Rory! Tells you a long story in broad Scotch, of which you understand one word here and there about his Grace the Deuke, and how many miles— miles Scots—he walked.'

'I can see Evelyn listening, and saying "Yes" at polite intervals.'

'How many birds did you actually see?'

'Well, I killed two brace and a half the first day.'

'Hatched under a hen, and let out for a foretaste.'

'And there was one old blackcock.'

'That blackcock! There are serious doubts whether it is a phantom bird, or whether Rory keeps it tame as a decoy. You didn't kill it?'

'No.'

'If you had, you *might* have boasted of an achievement,' said Allen.

'The spell would have been destroyed,' added Jock. 'But

you did not let him finish. Did you say you *saw* the black-cock?'

'I am not sure; I think I heard it rise once, but the keeper was always seeing it.'

Everybody but Essie was in fits of laughing at Cecil's frank air of good-humoured, self-defensive simplicity, and Armine observed—

'There's a fine subject for a ballad for the *Traveller's Joy*, Babie. "The Phantom Blackcock of Kilnaught!"'

Babie extemporised at once, amid great applause—

> 'The hills are high, the laird's purse dry,
>     Come out in the morning early;
> M'Nabs are keen, the Guards are green,
>     The blackcock's tail is curly.

> 'The Southron's spoil, 'tis worthy toil,
>     Come out in the morning early;
> Come take my house and kill my grouse,
>     The blackcock's tail is curly.

> 'Come out, come out, quoth Rory stout,
>     Come out in the morning early,
> Sir Captain mark, he rises! hark,
>     The blackcock's tail is curly.'

'Repetition, Babie,' said her mother; 'too like the Montjoie St. Denis poem.'

'It saves so much trouble, mother.'

'And a recall to the freshness and innocence of childhood is so pleasing,' added Jock.

'How much did the man of family let his moor for?' asked Allen.

There Cecil saw the pitiful and indignant face opposite to him, would have sulked, and began looking at her for sympathy, exclaiming at last—

'Haven't you a word to say for me, Miss Brownlow?'

'I don't like it at all. I don't think it is fair,' broke from Essie, as she coloured crimson at the laugh.

'He likes it, my dear,' said Babie.

'It is a gentle titillation,' said Allen.

'He can't get on without it,' said the Friar.

'And comes for it like the cattle to the scrubbing-stones,' said the Skipjack.

'Yes,' said Armine; 'but he tries to get pitied, like Chico walking on three legs when some one is looking at him.'

'You deal in most elegant comparisons,' said the mother.

'Only to get him a little more pitied,' said Jock. 'He is as grateful as possible for being made so interesting.'

'Hark, there's a knock!' cried Allen. 'Can't you instruct your cubs not to punish the door so severely, Jock? I believe

they think that the more row they make, the more they pro-
claim their nobility !'

'The obvious derivation of the word "stunning,"' said Mother
Carey, as she rose to meet her guests in the drawing-room, and
Cecil to hold the door for her.

'Stay, Evelyn,' said Allen. 'This is the night when unlicked
cubs do disport themselves in our precincts. A mistaken sense
of philanthropy has led my mother to make this house the
fortnightly *salon bleu* of St. Thomas's. But there's a pipe at
your service in my room.'

'Dr. Medlicott is coming,' said Babie, who had tarried behind
the Johns, 'and perhaps Mr. Grinstead, and we are sure to have
Mr. Esdale's photographs. It is never all students, medical or
otherwise. Much better than Allen's smoke, Cecil.'

'I am coming, of course,' he said. 'I was only waiting for
the Infanta.'

It may be doubted whether the photographs, Dr. Medlicott,
or even Jock were the attraction. He was much more fond of
using his privilege of dropping in when the family were alone,
than of finding himself in the midst of what an American guest
had called Mrs. Brownlow's surprise parties. They were on
regular evenings, but no one knew who was coming, from
scientific peers to daily governesses, from royal academicians
to medical students, from a philanthropic countess to a city
missionary. To listen to an exposition of the microphone, to
share in a Shakespeare reading, or worse still, in a paper game,
was, in the Captain's eyes, such a bore that he generally had
only haunted Collingwood Street on home days and on Sundays,
when, for his mother's sake and his own, an exception was made
in his favour.

He followed Babie with unusual alacrity, and found Mrs.
Brownlow shaking hands with a youth whom Jock upheld as a
genius, but who laboured under the double misfortune of always
coming too soon, and never knowing what to do with his arms
and legs. He at once perceived Captain Evelyn to be an 'awful
swell,' and became trebly wretched—in contrast to Jock's open-
hearted, genial young dalesman, who stood towering over every
one with his broad shoulders and hearty face, perfectly at his
ease (as he would have been in Buckingham Palace), and only
wondering a little that Brownlow could stand an empty-headed
military fop like that ; while Cecil himself, after gazing about
vaguely, muttered to Babie something about her cousin.

'She is gone to see whether Lina is asleep, and will be too shy
to come down again if I don't drag her.'

So away flew Babie, and more eyes than Cecil Evelyn's were
struck when in ten minutes' time she again led in her cousin.

Mr. Acton, who was talking to Mrs. Brownlow, said in an
undertone—

'Your model ? Another niece ?'

'Yes ; you remember Jessie ?'

'This is a more ideal face.'

It was true. Esther had lived much less than her elder sister in the Coffinkey atmosphere, and there was nothing to mar the peculiar dignified innocence and perfect unconsciousness of her sweet maidenly bloom. She never guessed that every man, and every woman too, was admiring her, except the strong-minded one, who saw in her the true inane Raffaelesque Madonna on whom George Eliot is so severe.

Nor did the lady alter her opinion when, at the end of a very curious speculation about primeval American civilisation, Captain Evelyn and Miss Brownlow were discovered studying family photographs in a corner, apparently much more interested whether a hideous half-faded brown shadow had resembled John at fourteen, than to what century and what nation those odd curly-whirleys on stone belonged, and what they were meant to express.

Babie was scandalised.

'You didn't listen! It was most wonderful! Why, Armie went down and fetched up Allen to hear about those wonderful walled towns!'

'I don't go in for improving my mind,' said Cecil.

'Then you should not hinder Essie from improving hers! Think of letting her go home having seen nothing but all the repeated photographs of her brothers and sisters!'

'Well, what should she like to see?' cried Cecil. 'I'm good for anything you want to go to before the others are free.'

'The Ethiopian serenaders, or, may be, Punch,' said Jock. 'Madame Tussaud would be too intellectual.'

'When Lina is strong enough she is to see Madame Tussaud,' said Essie gravely. 'Georgie once went, and she has wished for it ever since.'

'Oh, we'll get up Madame Tussaud for her at home, free gratis, for nothing at all!' cried Armine, whose hard work inspirited him to fun and frolic.

So in the twilight hour two days later there was a grand exhibition of human waxworks, in which Babie explained tableaux represented by the two Johns, Armine, and Cecil, supposed to be adapted to Lina's capacity. With the timid child it was not a success, the disguises frightened her, and gave her an uncanny feeling that her friends were transformed; she sat most of the time on her aunt's lap, with her face hidden, and barely hindered from crying by the false assurance that it was all for her pleasure.

But there was no doubt that Esther was a pleased spectator of the show, and her gratitude far more than sufficient to cover the little one's ingratitude.

Those two drifted together. In every gathering, when strangers had departed, they were found *tête-à-tête*. Cecil's horses knew the way to Collingwood Street better than anywhere else, and he took to appearing there at times when he was fully aware Jock would be at the night-school or Mutual Improvement Society.

Though strongly wishing, on poor Bobus's account, that it should not go much farther under her own auspices, day after day it was more borne in upon Mrs. Brownlow that her house held an irresistible attraction to the young officer, and she wondered over her duty to the parents who had trusted her. Acting on impulse at last, she took counsel with John, securing him as her companion in the gaslit walk from a concert.

'Do you see what is going on there?' she asked, indicating the pair before them.

'What do you mean? Oh, I never thought of *that!*'

'I don't think! I have seen. Ever since the night of the Phantom Blackcock of Kilnaught. He did his work on Essie.'

'Essie rather thinks he is after the Infanta.'

'It looks like it! What could have put it into her head? It did not originate there!'

'Something my mother said about Babie being a viscountess.'

'You know better, Friar!'

'I thought so; but I only told her it was no such thing, and I believe the child thought I meant to rebuke her for mentioning such frivolities, for she turned scarlet and held her peace.'

'Perhaps the delusion has kept her unconscious, and made her the sweeter. But the question is, whether this ought to go on without letting your people know?'

'I suppose they would have no objection?' said John. 'There's no harm in Evelyn, and he shows his sense by running after Jock. He hasn't got the family health either. I'd rather have him than an old stick like Jessie's General.'

'Yes, if all were settled, I believe your mother would be very well pleased. The question is, whether it is using her fairly not to let her know in the meantime?'

'Well, what is the code among you parents and guardians?'

'I don't know that there is any, but I think that though the crisis might be pleasing enough, yet if your mother found out what was going on, she might be vexed at not having been informed.'

John considered a moment, and then proposed that if things looked 'like it' at the end of the week he should go down on Saturday and give a hint of preparation to his father, letting him understand the merits of the case. However, in the existing state of affairs, a week was a long time, and that very Sunday brought the crisis.

The recollection of former London Sundays, of Mary Ogilvie's quiet protests, and of the effect on her two eldest children, had strengthened Mrs. Brownlow's resolution to make it impossible to fill the afternoon with aimless visiting and gossiping; and plenty of other occupations had sprung up.

Thus on this particular afternoon she and Barbara were

with the Girls' Friendly Society Classes, of which Babie took the clever one, and she the stupid. Armine was reading with Percy Stagg, and a party of School Board pupil-teachers whom that youth had brought him, as very anxious for the religious instruction they knew not how to obtain. Jock had taken the Friar's Bible Class of young men, and Allen had, as a great favour, undertaken to sit with Dr. and Mrs. Lucas till he could look in on them. So that Esther and Lina were the sole occupants of the drawing-room when Captain Evelyn rang at the door, knowing very well that he was only permitted upstairs an hour later in time for a cup of tea before evensong. He *did* look into Allen's sitting-room as a matter of form, but finding it empty, and hearing a buzz of voices elsewhere, he took licence to go upstairs, and there he found Esther telling her little sister such histories of Arundel Society engravings as she could comprehend.

Lina sprang to him at once ; Esther coloured, and began to account for the rest of the family. 'I hear,' said Cecil, as low tones came through the closed doors of the back drawing-room, 'they work as hard here as my sister does !'

'I think my aunt has almost done,' said Essie, with a shy doubt whether she ought to stay. 'Come, Lina, I must get you ready for tea.'

'No, no,' said Cecil, 'don't go ! You need not be as much afraid of me as that first time I walked in, and thought I had got into a strange house.'

Essie laughed a little, and said, 'A month ago ! Sometimes it seems a very long time, and sometimes a very short one.'

'I hope it seems a very long time that you have known me.'

'Well, Johnnie and all the rest had known you ever so long,' answered she, with a confusion of manner that expressed a good deal more than the words. 'I really must go——'

'Not till you have told me more than that,' cried Cecil, seizing his opportunity with a sudden rush of audacity. 'If you know me, can you—can you like me ? Can't you ? O Essie, stay ! Could you ever love me, you peerless, sweetest, loveliest——'

By this time Mrs. Brownlow, who had heard Cecil's boots on the stairs, and particularly wished to stave matters off till after the Friar's mission, had made a hasty conclusion of her lesson, and letting her girls depart, opened the door. She saw at once that she was too late ; but there was no retreat, for Esther flew past her in shy terror, and Cecil advanced with the earnest, innocent entreaty, 'O Mrs. Brownlow, make her hear me ! I must have it out, or I can't bear it.'

'Oh,' said she, 'it has come to this, has it ?' speaking half-quaintly, half-sadly, and holding Lina kindly back.

'I could not help it !' he went on. 'She did look so lovely, and she is so dear ! Do get her down, that I may see her again. I shall not have a happy moment till she answers me.'

'Are you sure you will have a happy moment *then*?'

'I don't know. That's the thing! Won't you help a fellow a bit, Mrs. Brownlow? I'm quite done for. There never was any one so nice, or so sweet, or so lovely, or so unlike all the horrid girls in society! Oh, make her say a kind word to me!'

'I'll make her,' said little Lina, looking up from her aunt's side. 'I like you very much, Captain Evelyn, and I'll run and make Essie tell you she does.'

'Not quite so fast, my dear,' said her aunt, as both laughed, and Cecil, solacing himself with a caress, held the little one very close to him on his knee, where her intentions were deferred by his watch and appendages.

'I suppose you don't know what your mother would say?' began Mrs. Brownlow.

'I have not told her, but you know yourself she would be all right. Now, aren't you sure, Mrs. Brownlow? She isn't up to any nonsense?'

'No, Cecil, I don't think she would oppose it. Indeed, my dear boy, I wish you happiness, but Esther is a shy, startled little being, and away from her mother; and perhaps you will have to be patient.'

'But will you fetch her—or at least speak to her?' said he, in a tone not very like patience; and she had to yield, and be the messenger.

She found Esther fluttering up and down her room like a newly-caught bird. 'O Aunt Carey, I must go home! Please let me!' she said.

'Nay, my dear, can't I help you for once?' and Esther sprang into her arms for comfort; but even then it was plain to a motherly eye that this was not the distress that poor Bobus had caused, but rather the agitation of a newly-awakened heart, terrified at its own sensations. 'He wants you to come and hear him out,' she said, when she had kissed and petted the girl into more composure.

'Oh, must I? I don't want. Oh, if I could go home! They were so angry before. And I only said "If," and never meant——'

'That was the very thing, my dear,' said her aunt, with a great throb of pain. 'You were quite right not to encourage my poor Bobus; but this is a very different case, and I am sure they would wish you to act according as you feel.'

Esther drew a great gasp; 'You are sure they would not think me wrong?'

'Quite sure,' was the reply, in full security that her mother would be rapturous at the nearly certain prospect of a coronet. 'Indeed, my dear, no one can find any fault with you. You need not be afraid. He is good and worthy, and they will be glad if you wish it.'

'Wish' was far too strong a word for poor frightened Esther; she could only cling and quiver.

'Shall I tell him to go and see them at Kencroft?'

'Oh, do, do, dear Aunt Carey! Please tell him to go to papa, and not want to see me till——'

'Very well, my dear child; that will be the best way. Now I will send you up some tea, and then you shall put Lina to bed; and you and I will slip off quietly together, and go to St. Andrew's in peace, quite in a different direction from the others, before they set out.'

Meantime Cecil had been found by Babie tumbling about the music and newspapers on the ottoman, and on her observation—

'Too soon, sir! And pray what mischief still have your idle hands found to do?'

'Don't!' he burst out; 'I'm on the verge of distraction already! I can't bear it!'

'Is there anything the matter? You're not in a scrape? You don't want Jock?' she said.

'No, no—only I've done it. Babie, I shall go mad if I don't get an answer soon.'

Babie was much too sharp not to see what he meant. She knew in a kind of intuitive, undeveloped way how things stood with Bobus, and this gave a certain seriousness to her manner of saying—

'Essie?'

'Of course, the darling! If your mother would only come and tell me—but *she* was frightened, and won't say anything. If she won't, I'm the most miserable fellow in the world.'

'How stupid you must have been!' said Babie. 'That comes of you, neither of you, ever reading. You couldn't have done it right, Cecil.'

'Do you really think so?' he asked, in such piteous, earnest tones that he touched her heart.

'Dear Cecil,' she said, 'it will be all right. I know Essie likes you better than any one else.'

She had almost added 'though she is an ungrateful little puss for doing so,' but before the words had time to come out of her mouth, Cecil had flown at her in a transport, thrown his arms round her and kissed her, just as her mother opened the door, and uttered an odd incoherent cry of amazement.

'O Mother Carey,' cried Cecil, colouring all over, 'I didn't know what I was doing! She gave me hope!'

'I give you hope too,' said Caroline, 'though I don't know how it might have been if *she* had come down just now!'

'Don't!' entreated Cecil. 'Babie is as good as my sister. Why, where is she?'

'Fled, and no wonder!'

'And won't she, Esther, come?'

'She is far too much frightened and overcome. She says you may go to her father, and I think that is all you can expect her to say.'

'Is it? Won't she see me? I don't want it to be obedience.'

'I don't think you need have any fears on that score.'

'You don't? Really now? You think she likes me just a little? How soon can I get down? Have you a train-bill?'

Then during the quest into trains came a fit of humility. 'Do you think they will listen to me? You are not the sort who would think me a catch, and I know I am a very poor stick compared with any of you, and should have gone to the dogs long ago but for Jock, ungrateful ass as I was to him last year. But if I had such a creature as that to take care of, why, it would be like having an angel about one. I would—indeed I would—reverence, yes, and worship her all my life long.'

'I am sure you would. I think it would be a very happy and blessed thing for you both, and I have no doubt that her father will think so too. Now here are the others coming home, and you must behave like a rational being, even though you don't see Essie at tea.'

Mother Carey managed to catch Jock, give a hint of the situation, and bid him take care of his friend. He looked grave. 'I thought it was coming,' he said. 'I wish they would have done it out of our way.'

'So do I, but I didn't take measures in time.'

'Well, it is all right as regards them both, but poor Bobus will hardly get over it.'

'We must do our best to soften the shock, and as it can't be helped, we must put our feelings in our pocket.'

'As one has to do most times,' said Jock. 'Well, I suppose it is better for one in the end than having it all one's own way. And Evelyn is a generous fellow, who deserves anything!'

'So, Jock, as we can do Bobus no good, and know besides that nothing could make it right for his hopes to be fulfilled, we must throw ourselves into this present affair as Cecil and Essie deserve.'

'All right, mother,' he said. 'There's not stuff in her to be of much use to Bobus if he had her, besides the other objection. It is the hope that he will sorely miss, poor old fellow!'

'Ah! if he had a better hope lighted as his guiding star! But we must not stand talking now, Jock; I must take her to church quietly with me.'

To Cecil's consternation, his military duties would detain him all the forenoon of the next day; and before he could have started, the train that brought John back also brought his father and mother, the latter far more eager and effusive than her sister-in-law had ever seen her. 'My dear Caroline, I thought you'd excuse my coming, I was so anxious to see about my little girl, and we'll go to an hotel.'

'I'll leave you with her,' said Caroline, rushing off in haste to let Esther utter her own story as best she might, poor child! Allen was fortunately in his room, and his mother sprang down to him to warn him to telegraph to Cecil that Colonel Brownlow was in Collingwood Street; the fates being evidently determined to spare her nothing.

Allen's feelings were far less keen as to Bobus than were Jock's, and he liked the connection; so he let himself be infected with the excitement, and roused himself not only to telegraph, but go himself to Cecil's quarters to make sure of him. It was well that he did so, for just as he got into Oxford Street he beheld the well-known bay fortunately caught in a block of omnibuses and carts round a tumble-down cab-horse and some gasfitting. Such was the impatience of the driver of the hansom, that Allen absolutely had to rush desperately across the noses of half a dozen horses, making wild gestures, before he was seen and taken up by Cecil's side.

'The most wonderful thing of all,' said Cecil afterwards, ' was to see Allen going on like that!'

In consequence of his speed, Colonel and Mrs. Brownlow had hardly arrived at Esther's faltered story, and come to a perception which way her heart lay, when she started and cried, 'Oh, that's his hansom!' for she perfectly well knew the wheels.

So did her aunt and Babie, who had taken refuge in the studio, but came out at Allen's call to hear his adventures, and thenceforth had to remain easily accessible, Babie to take charge of Lina, who was much aggrieved at her banishment, and Mother Carey to be the recipient of all kinds of effusions from the different persons concerned. There was the mother: 'Such a nice young man! So superior! Everything we could have wished! And so much attached! Speaks so nicely! You are sure there will be no trouble with his mother?'

'I see no danger of it. I am sure she must love dear little Esther, and that she would like to see Cecil married.'

'Well, you know her! but you know she might look much higher for him, though the Brownlows are a good old family. Oh, my dear Caroline, I shall never forget what you have done for us all.'

Her Serenity in a flutter was an amusing sight. She was so full of exultation, and yet had too much propriety to utter the main point of her hopes, fears, doubts, and gratitude; and she durst not so much as hazard an inquiry after poor Lord Fordham, lest she should be suspected of the thought that came uppermost.

However, the Colonel, with whom that possibility was a very secondary matter, could speak out: 'I like the lad; he is a good, simple, honest fellow, well-principled, and all one could wish. I don't mind trusting little Essie with him, and he says his brother is sure to give him quite enough to marry upon, so they'll do very well, even if—— How about that affair which was hinted of at Belforest, Caroline? Will it ever come off?'

'Probably not. Poor Lord Fordham's health does not improve, and so I am very thankful that he does not fulfil Babie's ideal.'

'Poor young man!' said Ellen, with sincere compassion but great relief.

'That's the worst of it,' said the father gravely. 'I am afraid it is a consumptive family, though this young fellow looks hearty and strong.'

'He has always been so,' said Caroline. 'He and his sister are quite different in looks and constitution from poor Fordham, and I believe from the elder ones. They are shorter and sturdier, and take after their mother's family.'

'I told you so, papa,' said Ellen. 'I was sure nothing could be amiss with him. You can't expect everybody to look like our boys. Well, Caroline, you have always been a good sister; and to think of your having done this for little Essie! Tell me how it was. Had you suspected it?'

It was all very commonplace and happy. Colonel and Mrs. Brownlow were squeezed into the house to await Mrs. Evelyn's reply, and Cecil and Esther sat hand-in-hand all the evening, looking, as Allen and Babie agreed, like such a couple of idiots that the intimate connection between *selig* and 'silly' was explained.

Mrs. Robert Brownlow whiled away the next day by a grand shopping expedition, followed by the lovers, who seemed to find pillars of floorcloth and tracery of ironwork as blissful as ever could be pleached alley. Nay, one shopman flattered Cecil and shocked Esther by directing his exhibition of wares to them, and the former was thus excited to think how soon they might be actually shopping on their own account, and to fix his affections on an utterly impracticable fender as his domestic hearth. Meanwhile Caroline had only just come in from amusing Mrs. Lucas with the story, when a cab drove up, and Mrs. Evelyn was with her, with an eager 'Where are they?'

'Somewhere in the depths of the city with her mother, shopping. Ought I to have told you?'

'Of course I trust you. She must be nice—your Friar's sister; but I could not stay at home, and Duke wished me to come——' 'How is he?'

'So very happy about this—the connection especially. I don't think he could have borne it if it had been the Infanta. How is that dear Babie?'

'Quite well. I left her walking with Lina in the Square gardens.'

'As simple and untouched as ever?'

'As much as ever a light-hearted baby.'

'Ah! well, so much the better. And let me say, once for all, that you need not fear any closer intercourse with us. My poor Duke has made up his mind that such things are not for him, and wishes all to be arranged for Cecil as his heir. Not that he is any worse. With care he may survive us all, the doctors say; but he has made up his mind, and will never ask Babie again. He says it would be cruel; but he does long for a sight of her bright face!'

'Well, we shall be brought into meeting in a simple natural way.'

'And Babie? How does she look? I am ashamed of it; but I can't help thinking more about seeing her than this new cousin. I can fancy her—handsome, composed, and serene.'

'That may be so ten or twenty years hence! but now she is the tenderest little clinging thing you ever saw.'

'And my ideal would have been that Cecil should have chosen some one superior; but after all, I believe he is really more likely to be raised by being looked up to. He has been our boy too long.'

'Quite true; I have watched him content with the level my impertinent children assign him here, but now trying to be manly for Essie's sake. You have not told me of Sydney.'

'So angry at the folly of passing over Babie, that I was forced to give her a hint to be silent before Duke. She collapsed, much impressed. Forgive me, if it was a betrayal; but she is two years older now, and would not have been a safe companion unless warned. Hark! Is that the door-bell?'

Therewith the private interview period set in, and Babie made such use of her share of it, that when Lina was produced in the drawing-room before dinner she sat on Cecil's knee, and gravely observed that she had a verse to repeat to him—

> 'The phantom blackcock of Kilnaught
> Is a marvellous bird yet uncaught;
>    Go out in all weather,
>    You see not a feather,
> Yet a marvellous work it has wrought,
> That phantom blackcock of Kilnaught.'

'What is that verse you are saying, Lina?' said her mother.

Lina trotted across and repeated it, while Cecil shook his head at wicked Babie.

'I hope you don't learn nursery rhymes about phantoms and ghosts, Lina?' said Mrs. Robert Brownlow.

'This is an original poem, Aunt Ellen,' replied Babie gravely.

'More original than practical,' said John. 'You haven't accounted for the pronoun?'

'Oh, never mind that. Great poets are above rules. I want Essie to promise us bridesmaids blackcock tails in our hats.'

'My dear!' said her aunt, in serious reproof, shocked at the rapidity of the young lady's ideas.

'Or, at least,' added Babie, 'if she won't, you'll give us blackcock lockets, Cecil. They would be lovely—you know—enamelled!'

'That I will!' he cried. 'And, Mother Carey, will you model me a group of the birds? That would be a jolly present!'

'Better than Esther's head, eh? I have done that three times, and you shall choose one, Cecil.'

Nothing would serve Cecil but an immediate expedition to the studio, to choose as well as they could by lamp-light.

And during the examination, Mrs. Evelyn managed to say to Caroline, 'I'm quite satisfied. She is as bright and childish as you told me.'

'Essie?'

'No, the Infanta.'

'If she is not a little too much so.'

'Oh no, don't wish any difference in those high spirits!'

'She makes it a cheerful house, dear child; and even Allen has brightened lately.'

'And Jock? He looks hard-worked, but brisk as ever.'

'He does work very hard in all ways; but he thoroughly enjoys his work, and is as much my sunshine as Babie. There are golden opinions of him in the Medical School; indeed there are of both my Johns.'

'They are quite the foremost of the young men of their year, and carry off most of the distinctions, besides being leaders in influence. So Dr. Medlicott told us,' said Mrs. Evelyn; 'and yet he said it was delightful to see how they avoided direct rivalry, or else were perfectly friendly over it.'

'Yes, they avoid, when it is possible, going in for the same things, and indeed I think Jock has more turn for the scientific side of the study, and the Friar for the practical. There is room for them both!'

'And what a contrast they are! What a very handsome fellow John has grown! So tall, and broad, and strong, with that fine colour, and dark eyes as beautiful as his sister's!'

'More beautiful, I should say,' returned Caroline; 'there is so much more intellect in them—raising them out of the regular Kencroft comeliness. True, the great charm of the stalwart Friar, as we call him, is—what his father has in some degree— that quiet composed way that gives one a sense of protection. I think his patients will feel entire trust in his hands. They say at the hospital the poor people always are happy when they see one of the Mr. Brownlows coming, whether it be the big or the little one.'

'Not so very little, except by comparison; and I am glad Jock keeps his soldierly bearing.'

'He is a Volunteer, you know, and very valuable there.'

'But he has not an ounce of superfluous flesh. He puts me in mind of a perfectly polished, finished instrument!'

'That is just what used to be said of his father. Colonel Brownlow says he is the most like my poor young father of all the children.'

'He is the most like you.'

'But he puts me most of all in mind of my husband, in all his ways and manner; and our old friends tell me that he sets about things exactly like his father, as if it were by imitation. I like to know it is so.'

## CHAPTER XXXVI

### OF NO CONSEQUENCE

> ' Fell not, but dangled in mid air,
> For from a fissure in the stone
> Which lined its sides, a bush had grown,
> To this he clung with all his might.'
>
> ARCHBISHOP TRENCH.

LORD FORDHAM made it his most especial and urgent desire that his brother's wedding, which was to take place before Lent, should be at his home instead of at the lady's. Otherwise he could not be present, for Kenminster had a character for bleakness, and he was never allowed to travel in an English winter. Besides, he had set his heart on giving one grand festal day to his tenantry, who had never had a day of rejoicing since his great-uncle came of age, forty years ago.

Mrs. Robert Brownlow did not like it at all, either as an anomaly or as a disappointment to the Kenminster world, but her husband was won over, and she was obliged to consent. Mother Carey and her brood were of course to be guests, but her difficulty was the leaving Dr. and Mrs. Lucas. The good old physician was failing fast, and they had no kindred near at hand, or capable of being of much comfort to them, and she was considering how to steer between the two calls, when Jock settled it for her by saying that he did not mean to go to Fordham, and, if Mrs. Lucas liked, would sleep in the house. There was much amazement and vexation. He had of course been the first best man thought of, but he fought off, declaring that he could not afford to miss a single lecture or demonstration. Friar John's University studies had given him such a start that he had to work less hard than his cousin, and could afford himself the week for which he was invited ; but Jock declared that he could not even lose the thirty-six hours that Armine was to take for the journey to Fordham and back. Every one declared this nonsense, and even Mrs. Lucas could not bear that he should remain, as she thought, on her account ; but his mother did not join in the public outcry, and therefore was admitted to fuller insight, as he was walking back with her, after listening to the old lady's persuasions.

'I think she would really be better pleased to spare you for that one day,' said Caroline.

'May be, good old soul,' said Jock ; 'but as *you* know, mother, that's not all.'

'I guessed not. It may be wiser.'

'Well! There's no use in stirring it all up again, after having settled down after a fashion,' said Jock. 'I see clearer than ever how hopeless it is to have anything fit to offer a girl in her

position for the next ten years, and I must not get myself betrayed into drawing her in to wait for me. I am such an
impulsive fool, I don't know what I might be saying to her, and
it would not be a right return for all they have been to me.'

'You will have to meet her in town ?'

'Perhaps; but not as if I were in the house and at the
wedding. It would just bring back the time when she bade me
never give up my sword.'

'Perhaps she is wiser now.'

'That would make it even more likely that I should say
what would be better left alone. No, mother! Ten years
hence, if——'

She thought of Magnum Bonum, and said, 'Sooner, perhaps!'

'No,' he said, laughing. 'It is only in the *Traveller's Joy*
that all the bigwigs are out of sight, and the apothecary's boy
saved the Lord Mayor's life.'

With that laugh, rather a sad one, he inserted the latch-key
and ended the discussion.

Whether Barbara were really unwilling to go was not clear,
for she had no such excuse as her brother; but she grumbled
almost as much as her aunt at the solecism of a wedding in the
gentleman's home; and for the only time in her life showed ill-
humour. She was vexed with Esther for her taste in bridesmaid's attire (hers was given by her uncle); sarcastic to Cecil
for his choice of gifts; cross to her mother about every little
arrangement as to dress; satirical on Allen's revival of spirits
in prospect of a visit to a great house; annoyed at whatever
was done or not done; and so much less tolerant of having
little Lina left on her hands, that Aunt Carey became the
child's best reliance.

Some of this temper might be put to the score of that pity
for Bobus which Babie in her caprice had begun to dwell on,
most inconsistently with her former gaiety; but her mother
attributed it to an unconfessed reluctance to meet Lord Fordham again, and a sense that the light thoughtlessness to which
she had clung so long might perforce be at an end.

So sharp-edged was her tongue, even to the moment of
embarkation in the train, that her mother began to fear how
she might behave, and dreaded lest she should wound Fordham;
but she grew more silent all the way down, and when the
carriage came to the station, and they drove past banks starred
by primroses, and with the blue eyes of periwinkles looking out
among the evergreen trailers, she spoke no word. Even Allen
brightened to enjoy that lamb-like March day; and John, with
his little sister on his knee, was most joyously felicitous. Indeed, the tall, athletic, handsome fellow looked as if it were
indeed spring with him, all the more from the contrast with
Allen's languid, sallow looks, savouring of the fumes in which
he lived.

Out on the steps were Fordham, wrapped up to the ears;

Sydney, ready to devour Babie, who passively submitted ; and
Mrs. Evelyn, as usual, giving her friend a sense of rest and
reliance.

The last visit, though only five years previous to this one,
had seemed in past ages, till the familiar polished oak floor was
under foot, and the low tea-table in the wainscoted hall, before
the great wood fire, looked so homelike and natural that the
newcomers felt as if they had only left it yesterday.  Fordham,
having thrown off his wraps, waited on his guests, looking
exceedingly happy in his quiet way, but more fragile than ever.
He had a good deal of fair beard, but it could not conceal the
hollowness of his cheeks, and there were great caves round his
eyes, which were very bright and blue.  Yet he was called well,
waited assiduously on little Lina, and talked with animation.

'We have nailed the weathercock,' he said, 'and telegraphed
to the clerk of the weather-office not to let the wind change for
a week.'

'Meantime we have three delicious days to ourselves,' said
Sydney, 'before any of the nonsense and preparation begins.'

'Indeed !  As if Sydney were not continually drilling her
unfortunate children !'

'If you call the Psalms and hymns nonsense, Duke——'

'No ! no !  But isn't there a course of instruction going on,
how to strew the flowers gracefully before the bride ?'

'Well, I don't want them thrown at her head, as the children
did at the last wedding, when a great cowslip ball hit the bride
in the eye.  So I told the mistress to show them how, and the
other day we found them in two lines, singing—

'"This is the way the flowers we strew !"'

'I suppose Cecil is keeping his residence ?'

'No.  Did you not know that this little church of ours is not
licensed for weddings ?  The parish church is three miles off
and a temple of the winds.  This is only a chapelry, there is a
special license, and Cecil is hunting with the Hamptons, and
comes with them on Monday.'

'Special license !  Happy Mrs. Coffinkey !' ejaculated Babie.

'Everybody comes then,' said Sydney ; 'not that it is a very
large everybody after all, and we have not asked more neighbours than we can help, because it is to be a feast for all the
chief tenants—here in this hall—then the poor people dine in
the great barn, and the children drink tea later in the school.
Come, little Caroline, you've done tea, and I have my old baby-
house to show you.  Come, Babie !  Oh ! isn't it delicious to
have you ?'

When Sydney had carried off Babie, and the two mothers
stood over the fire in the bedroom, Mrs. Evelyn said—

'So Lucas stays with his good old godfather.  I honour him
more than I can show.'

'We did not like to leave the old people alone. They were
my kindest friends in my day of trouble.'

'You will not let me press him to run down for the one day,
if he cannot leave them for more? Would he, do you think?'

'I believe he would, if *you* did it,' said Caroline slowly; 'but
I ought not to let you do so, without knowing his full reason
for staying away.'

They both coloured as if they had been their own daughters,
and Mrs. Evelyn smiled as she said—

'We have outgrown some of our folly about choice of profession.'

'But does that make it safer? My poor boy has talked it
over with me. He says he is afraid of his own impulses, leading
him to say what would not be an honourable requital for all
your kindness to him.'

'He is very good. I think he is right—quite right,' said Mrs.
Evelyn. 'I am afraid I must say so. For anything to begin
afresh between them might lead to suspense that my child's
constitution might not stand, and I am very grateful to him for
sparing her.'

'Afresh? Do you think there ever was anything?'

'Never anything avowed, but a good deal of sympathy. Indeed, so far as I can guess, my foolish girl was first much
offended and disquieted with Jock for not listening to her persuasions, and then equally so with herself for having made
them, and now I confess I think shame and confusion are pre-
dominant with her when she hears of him.'

'So that she is relieved at his absence.'

'Just so, and it is better so to leave it; I should be only too
happy to keep her with me waiting for him, only I had rather
she did not know it.'

'My dear friend!' And again Caroline thought of Magnum
Bonum. All the evening she said to herself that Sydney showed
no objection to medical students when she was looking over the
Engelberg photographs with John, who had been far more her
companion in the mountain rambles they recalled than had
Jock in his half-recovered state.

The mother could not help feeling a little pang of jealousy
as she owned to herself that the Friar was a very fine-looking
youth, with the air of a university man, and of one used to good
society, and that he did look most perilously happy. He was
the next thing to her own son, but not quite the same, and she
half repented of her candour to Mrs. Evelyn, and wished that
the keen, sensitive face and soldierly figure could be there to
reassert their influence.

There ensued a cheerful, pleasant Saturday, which did much
to restore the ordinary tone between the old friends and to take
off the sense of strangeness. It was evident that Lord Fordham
had insensibly become much more the real head and master of
the house than at the time when the Brownlow party had last

been there, and that he had taken on him much more of the duties of his position than he had then seemed capable of fulfilling. It might cost much effort, but he had ceased to be the mere invalid, and had come to take his part thoroughly and effectively, and to win trust and confidence. It was strange to think how Babie could ever have called him a muff merely to be pitied.

The Sundays at Fordham were always delightful. The little church was as near perfection as might be. It was satisfactory to see that Fordham's gentleness and courtesy had dispelled all the clouds, and Barbara had returned to her ordinary manner; perhaps a little more sedate and gentle than usual, and towards him she was curiously submissive, as if she had a certain awe of the tenderness she had rejected.

After the short afternoon service, Sydney waited to exercise her choir once more in their musical duties; but Babie, hearing there was to be no rehearsal of the flower-strewing, declared she had enough of classes at home, and should take Lina for a stroll on the sunny terrace among the crocuses, where Fordham joined them till warned that the sun was getting low.

One there was who would have been glad of an invitation to join in the practice, but who did not receive one. John lingered with Allen about the gardens till the latter disposed of himself on a seat with a cigar beyond the public gaze. Then saying something about seeing whether the stream promised well for fishing, John betook himself to the bank of the river, one of the many Avons, probably with a notion that by the merest accident he might be within distance at the break-up of the choir practice.

He was sauntering with would-be indifference towards the foot-bridge that shortened the walk to the church, but he was still more than one hundred yards from it, when on the opposite side he beheld Sydney herself. She was on the very verge of the stream, below the steep, slippery clay bank, clinging hard with one hand to the bared root of a willow stump, and with the other striving to uphold the head and shoulder of a child, the rest of whose person was in the water.

One cry, one shout passed, then John had torn off coat, boots, and waistcoat, and plunged in to swim across, perceiving to his horror that not only was there imminent danger of the boy's weight overpowering her, but that the bank, undermined by recent floods, was crumbling under her feet, and the willow-stump fast yielding to the strain on its roots. And while each moment was life or death to her, he found the current unexpectedly strong, and he had to use his utmost efforts to avoid being carried down far below where she stood watching with cramped, strained, failing limbs, and eyes of appealing, agonising hope.

One shout of encouragement as he was carried past her, but stemming the current all the time, and at last he paddled back

towards her, and came close enough to lay hold of the
boy.

'Let go,' he said, 'I have him.'

But just as Sydney relaxed her hold on the boy the willow
stump gave way and toppled over with an avalanche of clay
and stones.  Happily Sydney had already unfastened her grasp,
and so fell, or threw herself backwards on the bank, scratched,
battered, bruised, and feeling half buried for an instant, but
struggling up immediately, and shrieking with horror as she
missed John and the boy, who had both been swept in by the tree.
The next moment she heard a call, and scrambling up the
bank, saw John among the reedy pools a little way down,
dragging the boy after him.

She dashed and splashed to the spot and helped to drag the
child to a drier place, where they all three sank on the grass,
the boy, a sturdy fellow of seven years old, lying unconscious,
and the other two sitting not a little exhausted, Sydney
scarcely less drenched than the child.  She was the first to
gasp—

'The boy?'

'He'll soon be all right,' said John, bending over him.  'How
came——'

'I came suddenly on them—him and his brother—birds'-
nesting.  In his fright he slipped in.  I just caught him, but
the other ran away, and I could not pull him up.  Oh! if you
had not come.'

John hid his face in his hands with a murmur of intense
thanksgiving.

'You should get home,' he said.  'Can you?  I'll see to the
boy.'

At this moment the keeper came up full of wrath and consternation, as soon as he understood what had happened.  He
was barely withheld from shaking the truant violently back to
life, and averred that he would teach him to come birds'-nesting
in the park on Sunday.

And when, after he had fetched John's coat and boots,
Sydney bade him take the child, now crying and shivering, back
to his mother, and tell her to put him to bed and give him something hot, he replied—

'Ay, ma'am, I warrant a good warming would do him no
harm.  Come on, then, you young rascal; you won't always find
a young lady to pull you out, nor a gentleman to swim across
that there Avon.  Upon my honour, sir, there ain't many could
have done that when it is in flood.'

He would gladly have escorted them home, but as the boy
could not yet stand, he was forced to carry him.

'You should walk fast,' said John, as he and Sydney
addressed themselves to the ascent of the steep sloping ground
above the river.

She assented, but she was a good deal strained, bruised, and spent, and her heavy winter dress, muddied and soaked, clung to her and held her back, and both laboured breathlessly without making much speed.

'I never guessed that a river was so strong,' she said. 'It was like a live thing fighting to tear him away.'

'How long had you stood there?'

'I can't guess. It felt endless! The boy could not help himself, and I was getting so cramped that I must have let go if your call had not given me just strength enough! And the tree would have come down upon us!'

'I believe it would,' muttered John.

'Mamma must thank you,' whispered Sydney, holding out her hand.

He clasped it, saying almost inwardly—

'God and His Angels were with you.'

'I hope so,' said Sydney softly.

They still held one another's hands, seeming to need the support in the steep, grassy ascent, and there came a catch in John's breath that made Sydney cry—

'You are not hurt?'

'That snag gave me a dig in the side, but it is nothing.'

As they gained the level ground, Sydney said—

'We will go in by the servants' entrance, it will make less fuss.'

'Thank you;' and with a final pressure she loosed his hand, and led the way through the long, flagged, bell-hung passage, and pointed to a stair.

'That leads to the end of the gallery; you will see a red baize door, and then you know your way.'

Sydney knew that at this hour on Sunday, servants were not plentiful, but she looked into the housekeeper's room, where the select grandees were at tea, and was received with an astonished 'Miss Evelyn!' from the housekeeper.

'Yes, Saunders; I should have been drowned, and little Peter Hollis too, if it hadn't been for Mr. Friar Brownlow. He swam across Avon, and has been knocked by a tree; and Reeves, would you be so *very* kind as to go and see about him?'

Reeves, who had approved of Mr. Friar Brownlow ever since his race at Schwarenbach, did not need twice bidding, but snatched up the kettle and one of Mrs. Saunders's flasks, while that good lady administered the like potion to Sydney and carried her off to be undressed. Mrs. Evelyn was met upon the way, and while she was hearing her daughter's story, in the midst of the difficulties of unfastening soaked garments, there was a knock at the door. Mrs. Saunders went to it, and a young housemaid said—

'Oh, if you please, ma'am, Mr. Friar Brownlow says it's of no consequence, but he has broken two of his ribs, and Mr. Reeves thinks Mrs. Evelyn ought to be informed.'

She spoke so exactly as if he had broken a window, that at first the sense hardly reached the two ladies.

'Broken what?'

'His ribs, ma'am.'

'Oh! I was sure he was hurt!' cried Sydney. 'O mamma! go and see.'

Mrs. Evelyn went, but finding that Reeves and Fordham were with John, and that the village doctor, who lived close by the park gates, had been sent for, she went no farther than the door of the patient's room, and there exchanged a few words with her son. Sydney thought her very hard-hearted, and having been deposited in bed, lay there starting, trembling, and listening, till her brother, according to promise, came down.

'Well, Sydney, what a brave little woman you have shown yourself! John has no words to tell how well you behaved.'

'Oh, never mind that! Tell me about him. Is he not dreadfully hurt?'

'He declares these particular ribs are nothing,' said Fordham, indicating their situation on himself, 'and says they laugh at them at the hospital. He wanted Reeves to have sent for Oswald privately, and then meant to have come down to dinner as if nothing had happened.'

'Mr. Oswald does not mean to allow that,' said Miss Evelyn.

'Certainly not; I told him that if he did anything so foolish I should certainly never call him in. Now let me hear about it, Sydney, for he was in rather too much pain to be questioned, and I only heard that you had shown courage and presence of mind.'

The mother and brother might well shudder as they heard how nearly their joy had been turned into mourning. The river was a dangerous one, and to stem the current in full flood had been no slight exploit; still more the recovery of the boy after receiving such a blow from the tree.

'Very nobly done by both,' said Fordham, bending to kiss his sister as she finished.

'Most thankworthy,' said Mrs. Evelyn.

There was a brief space spent silently by both Mrs. Evelyn and her son on their knees, and then the former went up to the little bachelor-room, where in the throng of guests John had been bestowed, and where she found him lying, rather pale, but very content, and her eyes filled with tears as she took his hand, saying—

'You know what I have come for?'

'How is she?' he said, looking eagerly in her face.

'Well, I think, but rather strained and very much tired, so I shall keep her in her room for precaution's sake, as to-morrow will be a bustling day. I trust you will be equally wise.'

'I have submitted, but I did not think it requisite. Pray don't trouble about me.'

'What, when I think how it would have been without you? No, I will not tease you by talking about it, but you know how we shall always feel for you. Are you in much pain now?'

'THEN I THOUGHT OF—

"TIME, WITH ITS EVER-ROLLING STREAM,
IS BEARING THEM AWAY."'

'Nothing to signify, now it has been bandaged, thank you. I shall soon be all right. Did she make you understand her wonderful courage and resolution in holding up that heavy boy all that time?'

Mrs. Evelyn let John expatiate on her daughter's heroism till steps were heard approaching, and his aunt knocked at the door. Perhaps she was the person most tried when she looked into his bright, dark eyes, and understood the thrill in his voice as he told of Sydney's bravery and resolution. She guessed what emotion gave sweetness to his thankfulness, and feared if he did not yet understand it he soon would, and then what pain would be in store for one or other of the cousins. When Mrs. Evelyn asked him if he had really sent the message that his fractured ribs were of no consequence, his aunt's foreboding spirit feared they might prove of only too much consequence; but at least, if he were a supplanter, it would be quite unconsciously.

As Barbara said, when she came up from the diminished dinner-party to spend the evening with her friend—

'Those delightful things always do happen to other people!'

'It wasn't very delightful!' said Sydney.

'Not at the time, but you dear old thing, you have really saved a life! That was always our dream!'

'The boy is not at all like our dream!' said Sydney. 'He is a horrid little fellow.'

'Oh, he will come right now!'

'If you knew the family, you would very much doubt it.'

'Sydney, why will you go on disenchanting me? I thought *the real thing* had happened to you at last as a reward for having been truer to our old woman than I.'

'I don't think you would have thought hanging on that bank much reward,' said Sydney.

'Adventures aren't nice when they are going on. It is only *meminisse juvat*, you know. You must have felt like the man in Rückert's Apologue, with the dragon below, and the mice gnawing the root above.'

'My dear, that story kept running in my head, and whenever I looked at the river it seemed to be carrying me away, bank, and stump, and all. I'm afraid it will do so all night. It did, when some hot wine and water they made me have with my dinner sent me to sleep. Then I thought of—

> '"Time, with its ever-rolling stream,
> Is bearing them away,"

and I didn't know which was Time and which was Avon.'

'In your sleep, or by the river?'

'Both, I think! I seem to have thought of thousands of things, and yet my whole soul was one scream of despairing prayer, though I don't believe I said anything except to bid the boy hold still, till I heard that welcome shout.'

'Ah, the excellent Monk! He is the family hero. I wonder if he enjoys it more than you? Did he really never let you guess how much he was hurt?'

'I asked him once; but he said it was only a dig in the side, and would go off.'

'Ah, well! Allen says it is accident that makes the hero. Now the Monk has been as good as the hyena knight of the Jotapata, who was a mixture of Tyr, with his hand in the wolf's mouth, and of Kunimund, when he persuaded Amala that his blood running into the river was only the sunset.'

'Don't,' said Sydney. 'I won't have it made nonsense of!'

'Indeed,' said Babie, almost piteously, 'I meant it for the most glorious possible praise ; but somehow people always seem to take me for a little hard bit of spar, a barbarian or a baby; I wish I had a more sensible name!'

'Infanta, his princess, is what Duke always calls you,' said Sydney, drawing her fondly to nestle close to her on the bed in her fire-lit room. 'Do you know one of the thoughts I had time for in that dreadful eternity by the river, was how I wished it were you that were going to be a daughter to poor mamma.'

'Esther will make a very kind, gentle, tender one.'

'Oh yes; but she won't be quite what you are. We have all been children together, and you have *fitted* in with us ever since that journey when we talked incessantly about Jotapata.' Then, as Babie made no answer, Sydney gave her a squeeze, and whispered, 'I know!'

'Who told you?' asked Babie, with eyes on the fire.

'Mamma, when I was crazy with Cecil for caring for a pretty face instead of real stuff. She thought it would hurt Duke if I went on.'

'Does he care still?' said Babie in a low voice.

'Oh, Babie, don't you feel how much?'

'Do you know, Sydney, sometimes I can't believe it. I'm sure I have no right to complain of being thought a childish, unfeeling little wretch, when I recollect how hard, and cold, and impertinent I was to him three years ago.'

'It *was* three years ago, and we were very foolish then,' consolingly murmured the wisdom of twenty, not without recollections of her own.

'I hope it was only foolishness,' said Barbara; 'but I have only now begun to understand the rights of it, only I could not bear the thoughts of seeing him again. And now he is so kind!'

'Do you wish you had?'

'Not that. I don't think anything but fuss and worry would have come of it then. I was only fifteen, and my mother could never have let it go on, and even if——; but what I am so grieved and ashamed at is my fancying him not enough of a man for such a self-sufficient ape as I was. And now I have seen more of the world, and know what men are, I see his generosity, and that his patient fight with ill-health, to do his best and his duty, is really very great and good.'

'I wish you could tell him so. No, I know you can't; but you might let him feel it, for you need not be afraid of his ever asking you again. They have had a great examination of his lungs, and there's only part of one in any sort of order. They say he may go on with great care unless he catches cold, or sets the disease off again, and upon that he made up his mind that it was a very good thing he had not disturbed your peace.'

'As if I should not be just as sorry!' said Babie. 'O Sydney, what a sad world it is! And there is he going about as manful, and pleased, and merry about this wedding as if it were his own. And the worst of it is, though I do admire him so, it can't be real, proper, lover's love, for I felt quite glad when you said he would never ask me, so it is all wasted.'

The mothers would hardly have liked the subject of the maidens' talk in their bower, and Barbara bade good-night, feeling as if she should never look at Fordham with the same eyes again; but the light of day restored commonplace thoughts of the busy Monday.

Reeves, having been sent up by his lord with inquiries, found the patient's toilet so far advanced, that under protest he could only assist in the remainder. So the hero and heroine met on the stairs, and clasped hands in haste to the sound of the bell for morning prayers in the household chapel, to which they carried their thankful hearts.

The Fordham household was not on such a scale that the heads of the family could sit still in dignified ease on the eve of such a spectacle. Every one was busy adorning the hall or the tables, and John would not be denied his share, though, as he could neither stoop, lift, nor use his right arm, he was reduced to making up wreaths and bouquets, with Lina to supply him with flowers, since he was the one person with whom she never failed to be happy or good. Fordham was entreated to sit still and share the employment, but his long thin hands proved utterly wanting in the dexterity that the Monk displayed. He was, moreover, the man in authority constantly called to give orders, and in his leisure moments much more inclined to haunt his Infanta's winged steps, and erect his tall person where she could not reach. Artistic taste rendered her, her mother, and Allen most valuable decorators, and it might be doubted whether Allen had ever toiled so hard in his life. In pity to the busy servants, luncheon was served up cold on a side-table, when Barbara, who had rallied her spirits to nonsense pitch, declared that, metaphorically, Fordham and the agent carved the meal with gloves of steel, and that the workers drank the red wine through the helmet barred. In the midst, however, in marched Reeves with a tray and a napkin, and a regular basin of invalid soup, which he set down before John in his easy-chair. There was something so exceedingly ludicrous in the poor Friar's endeavour to be gratified, and his look of dismay and disgust, that the public fairly shrieked with laughter, in which he would fain have joined, but had to beg pardon for only looking solemn ; laughter was a painful matter

However, later in the afternoon, when he was looking white and tired, his host came and said—

'Your object is to be about, and not make a sensation when people arrive. Come and rest then ;' then landed him on his own sofa in his sitting-room, which was kept sacred from all confusion.

About half an hour later Mrs. Evelyn said—

'Sydney, my dear, Willis is come for the tickets. Are they ready ?'

'Oh, mother, I meant to have done them yesterday evening !'

'You had better take them to Duke's room, it is the only quiet place. He is not there ; I wish he were. Willis can wait while you fill them up,' said Mrs. Evelyn, not at all sorry to pin her daughter down for an hour's quiet, and unaware that the room was occupied.

So Sydney, with a list of names and packet of cards, betook herself to her brother's writing-table, never perceiving that there was anybody under the Algerine rug, till there was a movement, suddenly checked, and a voice said—

'Can I help ?'

'Oh ! don't move. I'm so sorry, I hope——'

Oh no ! I beg your pardon,' he said with equal incoherency, and raising himself more deliberately. 'Your brother put me here to rest, and I fell asleep, and did not hear you come in.'

'Oh, don't ! Pray, don't ! I am so sorry I disturbed you. I did not know any one was here——'

'Pray, don't go ! Can't I help you ?'

Sydney recollected that in the general disorganisation pen, ink, and table were not easy to secure, and replied—

'It is the people in the village who are to dine here to-morrow. They must have tickets, or we shall have all manner of strangers. The stupid printer only sent the tickets yesterday, and the keeper is waiting for them. It would save time if you would read out the names while I mark the cards ; but please lie still, or I shall go.' And she came and arranged the cushions, which his movements had displaced, till he pronounced himself quite comfortable.

Hardly a word passed but 'Smith, James, two ; Bennet, Widow, one ; Hacklebury, Nicholas, three ;' with a 'Yes' after each, till they came to 'Hollis, Richard.'

'That's the boy's father,' then said Sydney.

'Have you heard anything of him ?' asked John.

'Oh yes ! his mother dragged him up to beg pardon and return thanks, but mamma thought you would rather be spared the infliction.'

'Besides that, they were not my due,' said John. 'I never thought of the boy.'

'If you did not, you saved him twice!'

'A Newfoundland-dog instinct. But I am glad the little scamp is not the worse. I suppose he is to appear to-morrow?'

'Oh yes! and the vicar begs no notice may be taken of him. He is really a very naughty little fellow, and if he is made a hero for getting himself and us so nearly drowned by birds'-nesting on a Sunday in the park, it will be perfectly demoralising!'

'You are as bad as your keeper!'

'I am only repeating the general voice,' said Sydney, with a gleam upon her face, half-droll, half-tender. 'Poor little man! I got him alone this morning, while his mother was pouring forth to mine, and I think he has a little more notion where thanks are due.'

'I should like to see him,' said John. 'I'll try not to demoralise him; but he has given me some happy moments.'

The voice was low, and Sydney blushed as she laughed and said—

'That's like Babie, saying it was delightful.'

'She is quite right as far as I am concerned.'

The hue on Sydney's cheek deepened excessively, as she said—

'Is George Hollis next?'

They went on steadily after that, and Willis was not kept long waiting. Then came the whirl of arrivals, Cecil with his Hampton cousins, Sir James Evelyn and Armine, Jessie and her General, and the Kenminster party. Caroline found herself in great request as general confidante, adviser, and medium, as being familiar with all parties, and it was evidently a great comfort to her sister-in-law to find some one there to answer questions and give her the *carte-du-pays*. Outwardly, she was all the Serene Highness, a majestic matron, overshadowing everybody, not talkative, but doing her part with dignity, in great part the outcome of shyness, but rather formidable to simple-minded Mrs. Evelyn.

She heard of John's accident with equanimity amazing to her hostess, but befitting the parent of six sons who were always knocking themselves about. Indeed, John was too well launched ever to occupy much of her thoughts. Her pride was in her big Robert, and her joy in her little Harry, and her care for whichever intermediate one needed it most. This one at the moment was of course pretty, frightened, blushing Esther, who was moving about in one maze and dazzle of shyness and strangeness, hardly daring to raise her eyes, but fortunately graceful enough to look her part well in the midst of her terrors. Such continual mistakes between her and Eleanor were made, that Cecil was advised to take care that he had the right bride; but Ellie, though so like her sister outwardly, was of a very different nature, neither shy nor timid, but of the sturdy Friar texture.

She was very unhappy at the loss of her sister, and had an odd little conversation with Babie, who showed her to her room, while the rest of the world made much of the bride.

'Ellie, the finery and flummery is to be done in Aunt Ellen's dressing-room,' explained Babie ; 'but Essie is to sleep here with you to-night.'

Poor Ellie ! her lip quivered at the thought that it was for the last time, and she said bluntly—

'I didn't want to have come ! I hate it all !'

'It can't be helped,' said Barbara.

'I can't think how you and Aunt Carey could give in to it !'

'It was the real article, and no mistake,' said Babie.

'Yes ; she is as silly about him as possible. A mere fine gentleman ! Poor Bobus has more stuff in him than a dozen of him !'

'He is a real, honest, good fellow,' said Babie. 'I'm sorry for Bobus, but I've known Cecil almost all my life, and I can't have him abused. I do really believe that Essie will be happier with a simple-hearted fellow like him than with a clever man like Bobus, who has places in his mind she could never reach up to, and lucky for her too,' half whispered Babie at the end.

'I thought you would have cared more for your own brother.'

'Remember, they all said it would have been wrong. Besides, Cecil has been always like my brother. You will like him when you know him.'

'I can't bear fine folks.'

'They are anything but fine !' cried Babie indignantly.

'They can't help it. That way of Lord Fordham's, high-breeding I suppose you call it, just makes me wild. I hate it !'

'Poor Ellie. You'll have to get over it, for Essie's sake.'

'No, I shan't. It is really losing her, as much as Jessie——'

'Jessie looks worn.'

'No wonder. Jessie was a goose. Mamma told her to marry that old man, and she just did it because she was told, and now he is always ordering her about, and worries and fidgets about everything in the house. I wish one's sisters would have more sense and not marry.'

Which sentiment poor Ellie uttered just as Sydney was entering by an unexpected open door into the next room, and she observed, 'Exactly ! It is the only consolation for not having a sister that she can't go and marry ! O Ellie, I am so sorry for you.'

This somewhat softened Ellie, and she was restored to a pitch of endurance by the time Essie was escorted into the room by both the mothers.

That polished courtesy of Fordham's which Ellie so much disliked had quite won the heart of her mother, who, having viewed him from a distance as an obstacle in Esther's way, now underwent a revulsion of feeling, and when he treated her with marked distinction, and her daughter with brotherly kindness, was filled with mingled gratitude, admiration, and compunction.

When, after dinner, Fordham had succeeded in rousing his uncle and the other two old soldiers out of a discussion on promotion in the army, and getting them into the drawing-room, the Colonel came and sat down by his 'good little sister' to confide to her, under cover of Sydney's music, that he was very glad his pretty Essie had chosen a younger man than her elder sister's husband.

'Very opinionated is Hood!' he said, shaking his head. 'Stuck out against Sir James and me in a perfectly preposterous way.'

Caroline was not prepossessed in favour of General Hood, either by his conversation with herself at dinner, or by the startled way in which Jessie sat upright and put on her gloves as soon as he came in ; but she did not wish to discuss him with the Colonel, and asked whether John had gone to bed.

'Is he not here ? I thought he had come in with the young ones ? No ? then he must have gone to bed. Could Armine or any of them show me the way to his room ?—for I should like to know how the boy really is.'

'I doubt if Armine knows which is his room. I had better show you, for he is not unlikely to be lying down in Fordham's sitting-room. Otherwise you must prepare for many stairs. I suppose you know how gallantly he behaved,' she added, as they left the room.

'Yes, Mrs. Evelyn told me. I am glad he has not lost his athletics in his London life. I always tell his mother that John is the flower of the flock.'

'A dear, good, brave fellow he is.'

'Yes, you have been the making of him, Caroline. If we don't say much about it, we are none the less sensible of all you have been to our children. Most generous and disinterested !'

This was a speech to make Caroline tingle all over, and be glad both that she was a little in advance, and at the door of Fordham's room, where John was not. Indeed, he proved to be lying on his bed, waiting for some one to help him off with his coat, and he was gratified and surprised to the utmost by his father's visit, for in truth John was the one of all the sons who most loved and honoured his father.

If that evening were a whirl, what was the ensuing day, when all who stood in the position of hosts or their assistants were constantly on the stretch, receiving, entertaining, arranging, presiding over toilettes, getting people into their right places, saving one another trouble ? If Mrs. Joseph Brownlow was an invaluable aid to Mrs. Evelyn, Allen was an admirable one to Lord Fordham, for his real talent was for society, and he had shaken himself up enough to exert it. There might have been an element of tuft-hunting in it, but there was no doubt

that he was doing a useful part. For Robert was of no use at
all, Armine was too much of a mere boy to take the same part,
and John was feeling his injury a good deal more, could only
manage to do his part as bridegroom's man, and then had to go
away and lie down, while the wedding-breakfast went on. In
consequence he was spared the many repetitions of hearing how
he had saved Miss Evelyn from a watery grave, and Allen made
a much longer speech than he would have done for himself when
undertaking, on Rob's strenuous refusal, to return thanks for
the bridesmaids.

That which made this unlike other such banquets, was that
no one could help perceiving how much less the bridegroom was
the hero of the day to the tenants than was the hectic young
man who presided over the feast, and how all the speeches, however they began in honour of Captain Evelyn, always turned
into wistful good auguries for the elder brother.

There was no worship of the rising sun there, for when Lord
Fordham, in proposing the health of the bride and bridegroom,
spoke of them as future possessors, in the tone of a father
speaking of his heir-apparent, there was a sub-audible 'No, no,'
and poor Cecil fairly and flagrantly broke down in returning
thanks.

Fordham's own health had been coupled with his mother's,
and committed to a gentleman who knew it was to be treated
briefly; but this did not satisfy the farmers, and the chief
tenant rose, saying he knew it was out of course to second a
toast, but he must take the opportunity on this occasion. And
there followed some of that genuine native heartfelt eloquence
that goes so deep, as the praise of the young landlord was
spoken, the strong attachment to him found expression, and
there were most earnest wishes for his long life, and happiness
like his brother's.

Poor Fordham, it was very trying for him, and he could only
command himself with difficulty and speak briefly. He thanked
his friends with all his heart for their kindness and good
wishes. Whatever might be the will of God concerning himself,
they had given him one of the most precious recollections of his
life, and he trusted that when sooner or later he should leave
them, they would convey the same warm and friendly feelings
to his successor.

There were so many tears by that time, and Mrs. Evelyn felt
so much shaken, that she made the signal for breaking up.
No one was more relieved than Barbara. She must go to her
room to compose herself before she could bear a word from any
one, and as soon as she could gain the back stair, she gathered
up her heavy white silk and dashed up, rushing along the
gallery so blinded by tears under her veil that she would have
had a collision if a hand had not been put out as some one drew
aside to let her fly past if she wished; but as the mechanical
'Beg pardon' was exchanged, she knew Fordham's voice and

paused. 'I was going to look after the wounded Friar,' he said, and then he saw her tearful eyes, and she exclaimed, 'I could not help it! I could not stay! You would say such things. O Duke! Duke!'

It was the first time she had used the familiar old name, but she did not know what she said. He put her into a great carved chair, and knelt on one knee by her, saying, 'Poor Rogers, I wish he had let it alone. It was hard for my mother and Cecil.'

'Then how could you go on and break all our hearts!' sobbed Babie.

'It will make a better beginning for Cecil. I want them to learn to look to him. I thought every one knew that each month I am here is like an extra time granted after notice, and that it was no shock to any one to look forward to that fine young couple.'

'Oh, don't! I can't bear it,' she exclaimed, weeping bitterly.

'Don't grieve, dearest. I have tried hard, but I find I cannot do my work as it ought to be done. People are very kind, but I am content, when the time comes, to leave it to one to whom it will not be such effort and weariness. This is really one of the most gladsome days of my life. Won't you believe it?'

'I know unselfish people are happy.'

'And do you know that you are giving me the sweetest drop of all, to-day?' said Fordham, giving one shy, fervent kiss to the hand that clasped the arm of the chair just as sounds of ascending steps caused them to start asunder and go their separate ways.

## CHAPTER XXXVII

### THE TRAVELLER'S JOY

'   'Tis true bright hours together told,
      And blissful dreams in secret shared,
   Serene or solemn, gay or bold,
      Still last in fancy unimpaired.'

                                        KEBLE.

To his mother's surprise, Lucas did not betray any discomfiture at Sydney's adventure, nor even at John's having, of necessity, been left behind for a week at Fordham after all the other guests were gone. All he said was that the Friar was in luck.

He himself was much annoyed at the despatch he had received from Japan. Of course there had been much anxiety as to the way in which Bobus would receive the tidings of Esther's engagement; and his mother had written it to him with much tenderness and sympathy. But instead of replying to her letter, he had written only to Lucas, so entirely ignoring the whole matter that, except for some casual allusion to some other subject, it would have been supposed that he had not

received it.   He desired his brother to send him out the rest of
his books and other possessions which he had left provisionally
in England ; and he likewise sent a manuscript with orders to
him to get it published and revise the proofs.   It proved to be a
dissertation on Buddhism, containing such a bitter attack upon
Christianity that Jock was strongly tempted to put it in the fire
at once, and had written to Bobus to refuse all assistance in its
publication, and to entreat him to reconsider it.   He would not
telegraph, in order that there might be more time to cool down,
for he felt convinced that this demonstration was a species of
revenge, at least so far that there was a certain satisfaction in
showing what lengths the baffled lover might go to, when no
longer withheld by the hope of Esther or by consideration for
his mother.

Jock would have kept back the knowledge from her, but she
was too uneasy about Bobus for him not to tell her.   She saw it
in the same light, feared that her son would never entirely forgive her, but went on writing affectionate letters to him all the
same, whether he answered them or not.   Oh, what a pang it
was that she had never tried to make the boy religious in his
childhood !

Then she looked at Jock, and wondered whether he would
harbour any such resentment against her when he came to perceive what she had seen beginning at Fordham.

John came back most ominously radiant.   It had been very
bad weather, and he and Sydney seemed to have been doing a
great quantity of fretwork together, and to have had much
music, only chaperoned by old Sir James, for Fordham had been
paying for his exertions at the wedding by being confined to
his room.

He had sent Babie a book, namely, Vaughan's beautiful *Silex
Scintillans*, full of marked passages, which went to her heart.
She asked leave to write and thank him, and in return his
mother wrote to hers—

Duke is much gratified by the dear Infanta's note.   He would like to
write to her unless he knows you would object.

To which Caroline replied—

Let him write whatever he pleases to Barbara.   I am sure it will only
be what is good for her.

Indeed Babie had been by many degrees quieter since her return.

So a correspondence began, and was carried on till after
Easter, when the whole party came to London for the season.
Mrs. Evelyn wished Fordham to be under Dr. Medlicott's eye ;
also to give Sydney another sight of the world, and to superintend Mrs. Cecil Evelyn's very inexperienced *début*.

The young people had made a most exquisitely felicitous tour
in the South of France and North of Spain, and had come back
to a pleasant little house, which had been taken for them near
the Park.   There Cecil was bent on giving a great house-warm-

ing, a full family party. He would have everybody, for he had prevailed to have Fordham sleeping there while his room in his own house received its final arrangements ; and Caroline had added to Ellen's load of obligation by asking her and the Colonel to come for a couple of nights to behold their daughter dressed for the Drawing-room.

That would no doubt be a pretty sight, but to others her young matronly dignity was a prettier sight still, as she stood in her soft dainty white, receiving her guests, the rosy colour a little deepened, though she knew and loved them all, and Cecil by her side, already having made a step out of his boyhood by force of adoration and protection.

But their lot was fixed, and they could not be half so interesting to Caroline as the far less beautiful young sister, who could only lay claim to an honest, pleasant, fresh-coloured, intelligent face, only prevented by an air of high-breeding from being milkmaid-like. It was one of those parties when the ingenuity of piercing a puzzle is required to hinder more brothers and sisters from sitting together than could be helped.

So fate or contrivance placed Sydney between the two Johns at the dinner-table, and Mother Carey, on the other side, felt that some indication must surely follow. Yet Sydney was apparently quite unconscious, and she was like the description in *Rokeby*—

> ' Two lovers by the maiden sate
> Without a glance of jealous hate ;
> The maid her lovers sat between
> With open brow and equal mien ;
> It is a sight but rarely spied,
> Thanks to man's wrath and woman's pride.'

Were these to awaken ? They seemed to be all three talking together in the most eager and amiable manner, quite like old times, and Jock's bright face was full of animation. She had plenty of time for observation, for the Colonel liked a good London dinner, and knew he need not disturb his enjoyment to make talk for ' his good little sister.' Presently, however, he began to tell her that the Goulds and Elvira had really set out for America, and when her attention was free again, she found that Jock had been called in by Fordham to explain to Essie whether she had, or had not, seen Roncesvalles, while Sydney and John were as much engrossed as ever.

So it continued all the rest of the dinner-time. Jock was talked to by Fordham, but John never once turned to his other neighbour. In the evening the party divided, for it was very warm, and rather than inconvenience the lovers of fresh air Fordham retreated into the inner drawing-room, where there was a fire. He had asked Babie to bring the old numbers of the *Traveller's Joy*, as he had a fancy for making a selection of the more memorable portions, and having them privately printed as a memorial of those bright days. Babie and Armine were there looking them over with him, and the former would fain

have referred to Sydney, but on looking for her, saw she was
out among the flowers in the glass-covered balcony, too much
absorbed even to notice her summons. Only Jock came back
with her, and sat turning over the numbers in rather a dreamy
way.

The ladies and the Colonel were sent home in Mrs. Evelyn's
carriage, where Ellen purred about Esther's happiness and good
fortune all the way back. Caroline lingered, somewhat purposely, writing a note that she might see the young men when
they came back.

They wished her good-night in their several fashions.

'Good-night, mother. Well, some people are born with silver
spoons ! '

'Good-night, mother dear. Don't you think Fordham looks
dreadful ? '

'Oh no, Armie ; much better than when I came up to
town.'

'Good-night, Mother Carey. If those young folks make all
their parties so jolly, it will be the pleasantest house in London !
Good-night ! '

'Mother,' said Jock, as the cousin, softly humming a tune,
sprang up the stairs, 'does the wind sit in that quarter ? '

'I am grievously afraid that it does,' she said.

'It is no wonder,' he said, doctoring the wick of his candle
with her knitting-needle. 'Did you know it before ? '

'I began to suspect it after the accident, but I was not sure ;
nor am I now.'

'I am,' said Jock quietly.

'She is a stupid girl ! ' burst out his mother.

'No ! there's no blame to either of them. That's one comfort. She gave me full warning, and he knew nothing about it,
nor ever shall.'

'He is just as much a medical student as you ! That vexes
me.'

'Yes, but he did not give up the service for it, when she
implored him.'

'A silly girl ! O Jock, if you had but come down to Fordham ! '

'It might have made no odds. Friar was so aggressively jolly
after his Christmas visit, that I fancy it was done then. Besides,
just look at us together ! '

'He will never get your air of the Guards.'

'Which is preposterously ridiculous in the hospital,' said Jock,
endeavouring to smile. 'Never mind, mother. It was all up
with me two years ago, as I very well knew. Good-night.
You've only got me the more whole and undivided, for the ex-
tinction of my will-of-the-wisp.'

She saw he had rather say no more, and only returned his
fervent embrace with interest ; but Babie knew she was restless
and unhappy all night, and would not ask why, being afraid to

hear that it was about Fordham, who coughed more, and looked frailer.

He never went out in the evening now, and only twice to the House, when his vote was more than usually important ; but Mrs. Evelyn was taking Sydney into society, and the shrinking Esther needed a chaperon much more, being so little aware of her own beauty that she was wont to think something amiss with her hair or her dress when she saw people looking at her.

Sydney had no love for the gaieties, and especially tried to avoid their own county member, who showed signs of pursuing her. Her real delight and enthusiasm were for the surprise parties, to which she always inveigled her mother when it was possible. Mrs. Evelyn was not by any means unwilling, but Cecil and Esther loved them not, and much preferred seeing the Collingwood Street cousins without the throng of clever people, who were formidable to Esther and wearisome to Cecil.

Jock seldom appeared on these evenings. He was working harder than ever. He was studying a new branch of his profession, which he had meant to delay for another year, and had an appointment at the hospital which occupied him a great deal. He had offered himself for another night-school class, and spent his remaining leisure on Dr. and Mrs. Lucas, who needed his attention greatly, though Mrs. Lucas had her scruples, feared that he was overdoing himself, and begged his mother to prohibit some of his exertions. Dr. Medlicott himself said something of the same kind to Mrs. Brownlow. 'Young men will get into a rush, and suffer for it afterwards,' he said, 'and Jock is looking ill and overstrained. I want him to remember that such an illness as he had in Switzerland does not leave a man's heart quite as sound as before, and he must not overwork himself.'

'And yet I don't know how to interfere,' said his mother. 'There are hearts and hearts, you know,' she added.

'Ah ! Work may sometimes be the least of two evils,' and the doctor said no more.

'So Jock will not come,' said Mrs. Evelyn, opening a note declining a dinner in Cavendish Square.

'His time is very much taken up,' said his mother. 'It is one of his class-nights.'

'So he says. It is a strange question to ask, but I cannot help it. Do you think he fully enters into the situation ?'

'I say in return, Do you remember my telling you that the two cousins always avoided rivalry ?'

'Then he acts deliberately. Forgive me ; I felt that unless I was certain of this virtual resignation of the unspoken hope, I was not acting fairly in allowing—I cannot say encouraging —what I cannot help seeing.'

'Dear Mrs. Evelyn ! you understand that it is no slight to Sydney, but you know why he held back ; and now he sees that his absence has made room for John, he felt that there was no

chance for him, and that the more he can keep out of the way
the better it is for all parties.  Honest John has never had the
least notion that he has come between Jock and his hopes, and
it is our great desire that he should not guess it.'

'Well! what can I say?  You are generous people, you and
your son; but young folks' hearts will go their own way.  I
had made up my mind to a struggle with the prejudices of all
the family, and I had rather it had been for Jock; but it can't
be helped, and there is not a shadow of objection to the other
John.'

'No, indeed!  He is only not Jock——'

'And I do not think my Sydney was knowingly fickle, but
she thought she had utterly disgusted and offended Jock by
her folly about the selling out, and that it was a failure of
influence.  Poor child! it was all a cloud of shame and grief to
her.  I think he would have dispelled it if he had come to the
wedding, but as he did not——'

'The Adriatic was free,' said Caroline, trying to smile.  'I
see it all, dear Mrs. Evelyn.  I neither blame you nor Sydney;
and I trust all will turn out right for my poor boy.'

'He deserves it!' said Mrs. Evelyn, with a sigh.

There was a good deal more intercourse between Cavendish
Square and Collingwood Street than Mother Carey had expected.  Mrs. Evelyn and her son and daughter fell into the
habit of coming, when they went out for a drive, to see whether
Mrs. Brownlow or Barbara would come with them; and as it
was almost avowed that Babie was the object, she almost
always went, and kept Fordham company in the carriage,
whilst his mother and sister were shopping or making calls.
He had certainly lost much ground in these few weeks; he had
ceased to ride, and never went out in the evening; but the
doctors still said he might live for months or years if he avoided
another English winter.  His mother was taking Sydney into
society, and Esther was always happier when under their wing,
being rather frightened by the admiration of which Cecil was
so proud.  When they went out much before Fordham's bed-
time, he was thankful for the companionship of Allen or
Armine, generally the former, for Armine was reading hard,
and working after lectures for a tutor; while Allen, unfortunately, had nothing to prevent him from looking in whenever
Mrs. Evelyn was out, to play chess, read aloud, or assist in that
re-editing of the cream of the *Traveller's Joy,* which seemed
the invalid's great amusement.  Fordham had a few scruples
at first, and when Allen had undertaken to come to him for the
whole afternoon of a garden-party, he consulted Barbara
whether it was not permitting too great a sacrifice of valuable
time.

'You don't mean that for irony?' said Babie.  'It is only so
much time subtracted from tobacco.'

'Will you let me say something to you, Infanta?' returned

Fordham, with all his gentleness. 'It seems to me that you are not always quite kind in your way of speaking of Allen.'

'If you knew how provoking he is!'

'I have a great fellow-feeling for him, having grown up the same sort of helpless being as he has been. I should be much worse in his place.'

'Never!' cried Babie. 'You would never hang about the house, worrying mother about eating and fiddle-faddles, instead of doing any one useful thing!'

'But if one can't?'

'I don't believe in can't.'

'Happy person!'

'Oh, Duke, you know I never meant health; you know I did not,' and then a pang shot across her as she remembered her past contempt of him whom she now reverenced.

'There are other incapacities,' he said.

'But,' said Babie, half-pleading, half-meditating, 'Allen is not stupid. He used to be considered just as clever as Bobus; and he is so now to talk to. Can there be any reason but laziness, and want of application, that makes him never succeed in anything, except in answering riddles and acrostics in the papers? He generally just begins things, and makes mother or Armie finish them for him. He really did set to work and finish up an article on Count Ugolino since we came home from Fordham, and he has tried all the periodicals round, and they won't have it, not even the editors that know mother!'

'Poor fellow! And you have no pity!'

'Don't you think it is his own fault?'

'It is quite possible that he would have done much better if he had always had to work for his livelihood. I grant you that even as a rich man he ought to have avoided the desultory ways, which, as you say, are more likely to have caused his failures than want of native ability. But I don't like to see you hard upon him. You hardly realise how cruelly he has been treated in return for a very deep and generous attachment, or how such a grief must make it more difficult for him to exert his powers.'

'I don't like you to think me hard and unkind,' said Babie sadly.

'Only a little over just,' said Fordham. 'I am sure you could do a great deal to help and brighten Allen; and,' he added, smiling, 'in the name of spoilt and shiftless heirs, I hope you will try.'

'Indeed I will,' said Babie earnestly, as the footman at the shop door signalled to the coachman that his ladies were ready.

She found it the less difficult to remember what he had said, because Allen himself was much less provoking to her. Something was due to the influence and example of the strenuous endeavour that Fordham made to keep up to such duties as he had undertaken, not indeed onerous in themselves, but a severe labour to a man in his state. It had been intimated to him also that his saturation with tobacco was distressing to his friend, and he was fond enough of him to abstain from his solace, except when walking home at night.

Perhaps this had cleared his senses to perceive habits of consideration for the family, which he had never thought incumbent on himself, whatever they might be in his brothers ; and his eyes were open, as they had never yet been, to his mother's straits. It was chiefly, indeed, through his fastidiousness. His mother and Babie had existed most of this time upon their Belforest wardrobe ; indeed, the former, always wearing black, was still fairly provided ; but Babie, who had not in those days been out, was less extensively or permanently provided ; and Allen objected to the style in which she appeared in the enamelled carriage, 'like a nursery governess out for an airing.'

'Or not so smart,' said Babie, merrily putting on her little black hat with the heron's plume, and running downstairs.

'She does not care,' said Allen ; ' but, mother, how can you let her ?'

'I can't help it, Allen. We turned out all the old feathers and flowers to see if I could find anything more respectable ; but things don't last in Bloomsbury, and they only looked fit to point a moral, and not at all to adorn a tail or a head.'

'I should think not. But can't the poor child have something fresh, and like other people ?'

No ; her uncle had given her bridesmaid's dress, but there had been expenses enough connected with the journey to Fordham to drain the dress purse, and the sealskin cap that had been then available could not be worn in the sun of June. There had been sundry incidental calls for money. Mother Carey had been disappointed in the sale of a somewhat ambitious set of groups from Fouqué's *Seasons*, which were declared abstruse and uninteresting to the public. She had accepted an order for some very humble work, not much better than chimney ornaments, for which she rose early, and toiled while Babie was out driving with her friends. When she had the money for this she would be more at ease, and if it came to a little more than she durst reckon upon, she could venture on some extras.

'Babie might earn it for herself ; she is full of inventions.'

'There is nothing more strongly impressed on me than that those children are not to begin being made literary hacks before they are come to maturity. One Christmas tale a year is the utmost I ought to allow.'

'I wish I could be a literary hack, or anything else,' sighed poor Allen.

It was the first time he really let himself understand what a burden he was, and as Fordham was one of those people who involuntarily almost draw out confidence, he talked it over with him. Allen himself was convinced, by having really tried, that he was not as available clever as others of his family. Whether nature or dawdling was to blame, he had neither originality nor fire. He could not get his plots or his characters to work, even when his mother or Babie jogged them on by remarks: his essays were heavy and unreadable, his jokes hung fire, and he had so exhausted every one's patience, that the translations and small reviewing work which he could have done were now unattainable. He was now ready to do anything, and he actually meant it, but there seemed nothing for him to do. Mrs. Evelyn succeeded in getting him two pupils, little pickles whom their sister's governess could not manage, and whom he was to teach for two hours every morning in preparation for their going to school.

He attended faithfully, but he was not the man to deal with pickles. The mutual aversion with which the connection began, increased upon further acquaintance. The boys found out his weak points, and played tricks, learnt nothing, and made his life a burden to him ; and though the lady mother liked him extremely, and could not think why her sons were so naughty with him, it would not be easy to say which of the parties concerned looked with the strongest sense of relief to the close of the engagement.

The time spent with Fordham was, however, the compensation. There was sincere liking on both sides, and such helpfulness that Fordham more than once wished he had some excuse for making Allen his secretary ; and perhaps would have done so if he had really believed such a post would be permanent.

Armine's term likewise ended, and his examination being over with much credit, he wished for nothing better than to resume the pursuits he had long shared with Fordham. He had not Jock's facility in forming intimacies with youths of his own age. His development was too exclusively on the spiritual and intellectual side to attract ordinary lads, and his home gave him sufficient interests outside his studies ; and thus Fordham was still his sole, as well as his earliest, friend outside the family. Their intercourse had never received the check that circumstances had interposed between others of the two families, Armine had spent part of almost all his vacations with the Evelyns, the correspondence had been a great solace to the invalid, and the friendship grew yearly more equal.

Armine was to join the Evelyn party when they went to the seaside, as they intended to do on leaving London. It was the fashion to say he looked pale and overworked, but he had really attained to very fair health, and was venturing at last to look forward in earnest to a clerical life ; a thought that began to colour and deepen all his more intimate conversations with his friend, who could share with him many of the reflections

matured in the seclusion of ill-health. For they were truly
congenial spirits, and poor Fordham was more experienced in
the lore of suffering and resignation than his twenty-seven years
seemed to imply.

Meantime the work of editing the *Traveller's Joy* was carried
on. Some five-and-twenty copies were printed, containing all
the favourite papers—a specimen from each contributor, from a
shocking bad riddle of Cecil's to Dr. Medlicott's commentary
upon the myths of the nursery; from Armine's original acrostic
on the 'Rhine and Rhone,' down to the 'Phantom Blackcock of
Kilnaught;' the best illustrations from Mrs. Brownlow's
sketches and Dr. Medlicott's clever pen-and-ink outlines were
reproduced; and, with much pains and expense, Fordham had
procured photographs of all the marked spots, from Schwarenbach even to Fordham Church, so that Cecil and Esther considered it a graceful memorial of their courtship.

'So very kind of Duke,' they said.

Esther had quite forgotten all her dread of him, and never
was happier than when he was listening to all that had amused
her in the gaieties which she liked much better in the past than
in the present.

The whole was finished at last, after many a pleasant discussion and reunion scene, and the books were sent to the
binder. Fordham was eager for them to come home, and rather
annoyed at some delays which made it doubtful whether they
would be received before he, with his mother and sister, left
town. It was late, and June had come in, and the weight of
London air was oppressing him and making him weaker, and
his mother, anxious to get him into sea air, had made no fresh
engagements. It was a surprise to meet him at All Saints' on
St. Peter's Day.

'Come with us, Infanta,' he said, pausing at the door of the
carriage. 'I am to have my drive early to-day, as the ladies are
going to this great garden-party.'

Sydney said she would walk home with Mrs. Brownlow, and
be taken up when Babie was set down.

Fordham gave the word to go to the binder's.

'I should have thought you had better have gone into some
clearer air,' said his mother, for he looked very languid.

'There will be time for a turn in the Park afterwards,' he
said; 'and the books were to be ready yesterday, if there is any
faith in binders.'

The books were ready, and Fordham insisted on having them
deposited on the seat beside him, in spite of all offers of sending
them; and a smiling—

'Oh, Duke, your name should have been Babie,' from his
mother.

They then drove to Cecil's house, where Mrs. Evelyn went in
to let Esther know her hour of starting; but where Cecil came
running down, and putting his head into the carriage, said—

'Come in, mamma; here's the housemaid been bullying Essie, and she wants you to help her. These two can go round the Park by themselves, can't they?'

'Those are the most comical pair of children,' said Fordham, laughing, as the carriage moved on. 'Will Esther ever make a Serene Highness?'

'It is not in her,' said Babie. 'It might have been in Jessie, if her General was not such a horrid old martinet as to hinder the development; but Essie is much nicer as she is.'

Meantime, Fordham's fingers were on the knot of the string of his parcel

'Oh, you are going to peep in? I am so glad.'

'Since mamma is not here to laugh at me.'

'You'll tell her you did it to please the Babie!'

'There, it is you that are doing it now,' as her vigorous little fingers plucked far more effectively at the cord than his thin weak ones.

Out came at last one of the choice dark green books, with a clematis wreath stamped on the cover, and it was put into Barbara's lap.

'How pretty! This is mother's own design for the title-page! And oh—how capital! Dr. Medlicott's sketch of the mud baths, with Jock shrinking into a corner out of the way of the fat Gräfin! You have everything. Here is Armine's Easter hymn!'

'I wished to commemorate the whole range of feeling,' said Fordham.

'I see; you have even picked out the least ridiculous chapter of Jotapata. I wish some one had sketched you patiently listening to the nineteen copybooks. It would have been a monument of good nature. And here is actually Sydney's poem about wishing to have been born in the twelfth century—

'Would that I lived in time of faith,
   When parable was life,
When the red cross in Holy Land
   Led on the glorious strife.
Oh! for the days of golden spurs,
   Of tournament and tilt,
Of pilgrim vow, and prowess high,
   When minsters fair were built;
When holy priest the tonsure wore,
   The friar had his cord,
And honour, truth, and loyalty
   Edged each bold warrior's sword.'

'The solitary poetical composition of our family,' said Fordham, 'chiefly memorable, I fear, for the continuation it elicited.'

'Would that I lived in days of yore,
   When outlaws bold were rife,

> The days of dagger and of bowl,
>     Of dungeon and of strife.
> Oh ! for the days when forks were not,
>     On skewers came the meat ;
> When from one trencher ate three foes :
>     Oh ! but those times were sweet !
> When hooded hawks sat overhead,
>     And underfoot was straw,
> Where hounds and beggars fought for bones
>     Alternately to gnaw.'

'That was Jock's, I believe. How furious it did make us ! Good old Sydney, she has lived in her romance ever since.'

'Wisely or unwisely.'

'Can it be unwisely, when it is so pure and bright as hers, and gives such a zest to common things ?'

'Glamour sometimes is perplexing.'

'Do you know, Duke, I would sometimes give worlds to think of things as I used in those old times.'

'You a world-wearied veteran !'

'Don't laugh at me. It was when Bobus was at home. His common sense made all we used to care for seem so silly that I have never been able to get back my old way of looking at things !'

'I am afraid glamour once dispelled does not return. Yet, after all, truth is the greater. And I am sure that poor Bobus never loosened my Infanta's hold on the real truth.'

'I don't know,' she said, looking down ; 'he or his books made me afraid to think about it, and like to laugh at some things—no, I never did before you. You hushed me on the very borders of that kind of flippancy, and so you don't guess how horrid I am, or have been, for you have made things true and real to me again.'

' "Fancy may die, but Faith is there," ' said Fordham. 'I think you will never shut your eyes to those realities again,' he added gently. 'It is there that we shall still meet. And my Infanta will make me one promise.'

'I would promise you *any* thing.'

'Never knowingly to read those sneering books,' he said, laying his hand on hers. 'Current literature is so full of poisoned shafts that it may not be possible entirely to avoid them, and there may sometimes be need to face out a serious argument ; but you will promise me never to take up that scoffing style of literature for mere amusement ?'

'Never, Duke, I promise,' she said. 'I shall always see your face, and feel your hand forbidding me.'

Then as he leant back, half in thankfulness, half in weariness, she went on looking over the book, and read a preface, new to her : —

I have put these selections together, thinking that to the original 'Travellers' it may be a joy to have a memorial of happy days full of much innocent pleasure and wholesome intercourse. Let me here express my warm gratitude for all the refreshments afforded by the friendships it commemorates, and which makes the name most truly appropriate. As a stranger and pilgrim whose journey may be near its close, let me be allowed thus to weave a parting garland of some of the brightest flowers that have bloomed on the wayside, and in dedicating the collection to my dear companions and fellow-wanderers in the scenes it records, let me wish that on the highway of life that stretches before them, they may meet with many a 'Traveller's Joy,' as true as they have been to the Editor.

F——.

Babie, with eyes full of tears, was looking up to speak, when the carriage, having completed the round, again stopped, and Mrs. Evelyn came down, escorted by Cecil, with hearty thanks.

'Essie's nice clean, fresh, country notions were scouted by the London housemaid,' she said. 'I am happy to say the child held her own, though the woman presumed outrageously on her gentleness, and neither of the two had any notion how to get rid of her.'

'Arcadia had no housemaids,' said Fordham, rallying.

'If not, it must have been nearly as bad as Jock's twelfth century,' said Babie, in the same tone.

'Ah! I see!' said Mrs. Evelyn, laughing.

And there was a little playful banter as to which had been the impatient one to open the parcel, each pretending to persuade her that it had been a mere yielding to the other. Thus they came to Collingwood Street, where Babie would have taken out her book

'No, no, wait,' said Fordham. 'I want to write your name in it first. I'll send it this evening. Ali and Armie are coming to me while these good people are at their Duchess's.'

'Our last gaiety, I am thankful to say,' returned his mother, as Barbara felt a fervent squeeze of the hand, which she knew was meant to remind her of the deeper tone of their conversation.

It was a very hot day, and in the cool of the evening the two Johns beguiled Mrs. Brownlow and Babie into a walk. They had only just come home when there was a hurried peal at the bell, and Armine, quite pale, dashed upstairs after them.

'Mother, come directly! I've got a hansom.'

'Fordham?' asked John.

Armine sighed an affirmative.

'Allen sent me for mother. He said one of you had better come. It's a blood-vessel. We have sent for Medlicott, and telegraphed for the others. But oh! they are so far off!'

Mrs. Brownlow gave Barbara one kiss, and put her into Jock's arms, then sprang into the cab, followed by John, and was driven off. The other three walked in the same direction, almost unconsciously, as Armine explained more fully.

Fordham had seemed tired at first, but as it became cooler, had roused himself, seated himself at his writing-table, and made one by one the inscriptions in the volumes, including all their party of travellers, even Janet and Bobus; Reeves, who had been their binder, Mrs. Evelyn's maid, and one or two intimate friends—such as Mr. Ogilvie and his sister—and almost all had some kind little motto or special allusion written below the name, and the date. It had thus taken a long time, and Fordham leant back so weary that Allen wanted him to leave the addressing of the books, when wrapped up, to him and Armine; but he said there were some he wished to direct himself, and he was in the act of asking Bobus's right address when a cough seized him, and Allen instantly saw cause to ring for Reeves. The last thing that Armine had seen was a wave of the hand to hasten his own departure, as Allen despatched him for his mother, and gave orders for the summoning of others more needed, but who might not be fetched so promptly.

Then Jock had time to question whether Barbara ought to go on with him and Armine to the door, but there was a sound in her 'Let me! I must!' that they could not withstand; and they walked on in absolute silence, except that Jock said Reeves knew exactly what to do.

Dr. Medlicott's carriage was at the door, and on their ringing they were silently beckoned into the dining-room, where their mother came to them. She could not speak at first, but the way in which she kissed Barbara told them how it was. All had been over before she reached the house. Dr. Medlicott had come, but could do nothing more than direct Allen how to support the sufferer as he sank, with but little struggle, while a sudden beam of joy and gladness lit up his face at the last. There had been no word from the first. By the time the flow of blood ceased, the power of speech was gone, and there was thus less reason to regret the absence of the nearest and dearest.

Mrs. Brownlow said she must await their return with Allen, who was terribly shocked and overcome by this his first and sudden contact with death. John, too, had better remain for his sister's sake, but the others had better go home.

'Yes, my child, you must go,' she said, laying her hand on the cold ones of Barbara, who stood white, silent, and stunned by the shock.

'Oh, don't make me,' said a dull, dreamy, piteous voice.

'Indeed you must, my dear. It would only add to the pain and confusion to have you here now. They may like to have you to-morrow. Remember, he is not here. Take her, Jock. Take care of her.'

The coming of Sir James Evelyn at that moment gave Babie the impulse of movement, and Dr. Medlicott hurrying out to offer the use of his carriage, made her cling to Jock, and then to sign rather than speak her desire to walk with her brothers.

Swiftly and silently they went along the streets on that June night in the throng of carriages carrying people to places of amusement, the wheels surging in their ears with the tramp and scuffle of feet on the pavement like echoes from some far-off world. Now and then there was a muffled sound from Armine, but no word was spoken till they were within their own door.

Then Jock saw for one moment Armine's face perfectly writhen with suppressed grief ; but the boy gave no time for a word, hurrying up the stairs as rapidly as possible to his own room.

'Will not you go to bed ? Mother will come to you there,' said Jock to his sister, who was still quite white and tearless.

'Please not,' was her entreaty. 'Suppose they sent for me !'

He did not think they would, but he let her sit in the dark by the open window, listening ; and he put his arm round her, and said gently—

'You are much honoured, Babie. It is a great thing to have held so pure and true a heart, not for time, but eternity.'

'Don't, Jock. Not yet. I can't bear it,' she moaned ; but she laid her head on his shoulder, and so rested till he said—

'If you can spare me, Babie, I think I must see to Armie. He seemed to me terribly overcome.'

'Armine has lost his very best and dearest friend,' she said, pressing her hands together. 'Oh yes, go to him ! Armie can feel, and I can't ! I can only choke !'

Jock apprehended a hysterical struggle, but there only came one long sob like strangulation, and he thought the pent-up feeling might better find its course if she were left alone, and he was really anxious about Armine, remembering what the loss was to him, that it was his first real grief, and that he had had a considerable share of the first shock of the alarm.

His soft knock was unheard, and as he gently pushed open the door, he saw Armine kneeling in the dark with his head bowed over his prayer-desk, and would have retreated, but he had been heard, and Armine rose and came forward.

The light on the stairs showed a pale, tear-stained face, but calm and composed ; and it was in a steady, though hushed, voice that he said—

'Can I be of any use ?'

'I am sorry to have disturbed you. I only came to see after you. This is a sore stroke on you, Armie.'

'I can stand it better now. I have given him up to God as he bade me,' said Armine. 'It had been a weary, disappointed, struggling life, and he never wished it to last.' The tears were choking him, but they were gentle ones. 'He thought it might be like this—and soon—only he hoped to get home first. And I can give thanks for him, what he has been to me, and what he will be to me all my life.'

'That is right, Armie. John did great things for us all when he caught the carriage.'

'And how is Babie ?'

'Poor child, she seems as if she could neither speak nor cry.

It is half hysterical, and I was going to get something for her to take. Perhaps seeing you may be good for her.'

'Poor little thing, she is almost his widow, though she scarcely knows it,' said Armine, coming down with his brother.

They found Babie still in the same intent, transfixed, watching state; but she let Armine draw her close to him, and listened as he told her, in a low tender voice, of the talks he had had with Fordham, who had expressed to his young friend, as to no one else, his own feelings as to his state, and said much that he had spared others, who could not listen with that un-realising calmness that comes when sorrow, never yet experi-enced, is almost like a mere vision. And as Babie listened, the large soft tears began to fall, drop by drop, and the elder brother's anxiety was lessened. He made them eat and drink for one another's sake, and watched over them with a care that was almost parental, till at nearly half-past twelve o'clock the other three came home.

They said Mrs. Evelyn had come fully prepared by the tele-gram, and under an inexplicable certitude which made it need-less to speak the word to her. She was thankful that Marmaduke had been spared the protracted weeks of struggle in which his elder brothers' lives had closed, and she said—

'We knew each other too well to need last words.'

Indeed she was in the exalted state that often makes the earlier hours and days of bereavement the least distressing, and Sydney was absorbed in the care of her. Neither had been nearly so much overcome as Cecil and Esther, who had been hunted up with difficulty. He seemed to be as much shocked and horrified as if his brother had been in the strongest possible health, and poor Esther felt it wicked and unfeeling to have been dancing, and cried so bitterly that the united efforts of her aunt and brother could not persuade her that what was done in simple duty and obedience need give no pang, and that Mrs. Evelyn never thought of the incongruity.

It was only her husband's prostration with grief and desola-tion that drew her off, to do her best with her pretty childish caresses and soothings; and when the two had been sent to their own home, Mrs. Evelyn was so calm that her friend felt she might be left with her daughter for the night, and returned, bringing her tender love to 'Our Babie,' as she called the girl.

She clung very much to Barbara in the ensuing days. The presence of every one seemed to oppress her except that of her own children and the two youngest Brownlows, for had not Armine been the depositary of all Fordham's last messages? What she really seemed to return to as a refreshment after each needful consultation with Sir James on the dreary tasks of the mourners, was to finish the packing of those *Traveller's Joys* which lay strewn about Fordham's sitting-room, open at the fly-leaves, that the ink might dry.

Esther was very gentle and sweet, taking it quite naturally that Babie should be a greater comfort to her mother-in-law than herself ; and content to be a very valuable assistant herself, for the stimulus made her far more capable than she had been thought to be. She managed almost all the feminine details, while Sir James attended to the rest. She answered all the notes, and wrote all the letters that did not necessarily fall on her husband and his mother ; and her unobtrusive helpfulness made her a daughter indeed.

All the young men went to the funeral ; but Mrs. Brownlow felt that it was a time for friends to hold back till they were needed, when relations had retreated ; so she only sent Babie, whom Mrs. Evelyn and Sydney could not spare, and she followed after three weeks, when Allen was released from his unwelcome work.

She found Mrs. Evelyn feeling it much more difficult to keep up than it had been at first, now that she sorely missed the occupation of her life. For full twenty years she had had an invalid on her mind, and Cecil's marriage had made further changes in her life. It was not the fault of the young couple. They did not love their new honours at all. Apart from their affection, Cecil hated trouble and responsibility, and could not bear to shake himself out of his groove, and Esther was frightened at the charge of a large household. Their little home was still a small paradise to them, and they implored their mother to allow things to go on as they were, and Cecil continue in the Guards, while she reigned as before at Fordham ; letting the Cavendish Square house, which Essie viewed with a certain nervous horror.

Mrs. Evelyn had so far consented that the change need not be made for at least a year. Her dower house was let, and she would remain as mistress of Fordham till the term was over, by which time the young Lady Fordham might have risen to her position, and her Lord be less unwilling to face his new cares.

'And they will be always wanting me to take the chair,' said he, in a deplorable voice that made the others laugh in spite of themselves ; and he was so grateful to his mother for staying in his house, and letting him remain in his regiment, that he seemed to have quite forgotten that the power was in his own hands.

2 E

# CHAPTER XXXVIII

### THE TRUST FULFILLED

'You know my father left me some prescriptions
Of rare and prov'd effects, such as his reading,
And manifest experience, had collected
For general sovereignty ; and that he will'd me
In heedfullest reservation to bestow them,
As notes, whose faculties inclusive were,
More than they were in note.'

*All's Well that Ends Well.*

ANOTHER year had come and gone, with its various changes, and
the mother of the Collingwood Street household felt each day
that the short life of Marmaduke Viscount Fordham had not
been an unimportant one to her children.

It had of course told the most on Barbara. Her first great
grief seemed to have smoothed out the harsher lines of her
character, and made her gentle and tolerant as she had never
been ; or more truly, she had learnt charity at a deeper source.
That last summer had lifted her into a different atmosphere.
What she had shared with Fordham she loved. She had felt the
reality of the invisible world to him, and knew he trusted to her
meeting his spirit there even in this life, and the strong faith of
his mother had strengthened the impression.

'Heavenly things had seemed more true,
And came down closer to her view,'

now that his presence was among them. She had by no means
lost her vivacity. There would always be a certain crispness,
drollery, and keenness about her, and she had too much of her
mother's elasticity to be long depressed ; but instead of looking
on with impatient criticism at good works, she had learnt to be
ardent in the cause, and she was a most effective helper. To
Armine, it was as if Fordham had given him back the sister of
his childhood to be as thoroughly one in aims and sympathies as
ever, but with a certain clearness of eye, brisk alacrity of execution, and quickness of judgment that made her a valuable
assistant, the complement, as it were, of his more contemplative
nature.

He had just finished his course at King's College, and taken
a fair degree, and he was examining advertisements, with a
view to obtaining some employment in teaching that would put
a sufficient sum in his hands to enable him to spend a year at
one of the theological colleges, in preparation for Ordination.
His mother was not happy about it, she never would be quite
easy as to Armine's roughing it at any chance school, and she
had much rather he had spent the intervening year in working

as a lay assistant to Mr. Ogilvie, who had promised to give him a title for Orders, and would direct his reading.

Armine, however, said he could neither make himself Mr. Ogilvie's guest for a year, nor let his mother pay his expenses; also that he wished to do something for himself, and that he felt the need of definite training. All he would do was to promise that if he should find himself likely to break down in his intended employment of tuition, he would give up in time and submit to her plan of boarding him at St. Cradocke's.

'But,' as he said to Babie, 'I don't think it is self-will to feel bound to try to exert myself for the one great purpose of my life. I am too old to live upon mother any longer.'

'How I do wish I could do anything to help you to the year at C——. Mother has always said that she will let me try to publish *Hart's-tongue Well* when I am twenty-one!'

'Living on you instead of mother?'

'Oh no, Armie, you know we are one. Though perhaps a mere story like that is not worthy to do such work. Yet I think there must be something in it, as Duke cared for it.'

'That would be proof positive but for the author,' said Armine, smiling; 'but poor Allen's attempts have rather daunted my literary hopes.'

'I really believe Allen would write better sense now, if he tried,' said Babie. 'I believe Lady Grose is making something of him!'

'Without intending it,' said Armine, laughing.

'No; but you see snubbing is wholesome diet, if it is taken with a few grains of resolution, and he has come to that now!'

For Allen had continued not only to profess to be, but to be willing to do anything to relieve his mother, and Dr. Medlicott had, with much hesitation and doubt, recommended him for what was called a secretaryship to a paralytic old gentleman, who had been, in his own estimation, eminent both in the scientific and charitable worlds, and still carried on his old habits, though quite incapable. It really was, as the Doctor honestly told Allen, very little better than being a male humble companion, for though old Sir Samuel Grose was fussy and exacting from infirmity, he was a gentleman; but he had married late in life a vulgar, overbearing woman, who was sure to show insolent want of consideration to any one she considered her inferior. To his surprise, Allen accepted the situation, and to his still greater surprise, endured it, walking to Kensington every day by eleven o'clock, and coming home whenever he was released, at an hour varying from three to eleven, according to my Lady's will. He became attached to the old man, pitied him, and did his best to satisfy his many caprices and to deal with his infirmities of brain and memory; but my Lady certainly was his *bête noire*, though she behaved a good deal better to him after she had seen him picked up in the Park by Lady Fordham's carriage. However, he made light of all he underwent from her, and did not break down even when it was known that though poor George Gould had died at New York, his widow showed no intention of coming home, and wrote confidently to her step-daughters of Elvira marrying her brother Gilbert. She was of age now, there was nothing to prevent her, and they seemed to be only waiting for a decent interval after her uncle's death. Allen, a couple of years ago, would have made his mother and all the family as wretched as he could, and would have dropped all semblance of occupation but smoking. Now Lady Grose would not let him smoke, and Sir Samuel required him to be entertaining; but the continual worry he was bearing was making him look so ill that his mother was very anxious about him. She had other troubles. It was eighteen months since Janet Hermann had drawn her allowance. Her husband once had written in her name, saying that she was ill, but Mr. Wakefield had sent an order payable only on her signature, and it had never been acknowledged or presented! Could Janet be living? Or could she be in some such fitful state of prosperity as to be able to disregard £25?

Her mother spent many anxious thoughts and prayers on her, though the younger ones seemed to have almost forgotten her, so long it was since she had been a part of their family life. Nor did Bobus answer his mother's letters, though he continued to write fully and warmly to Jock. As to the MS., he said he had improved upon it, and had sent a fresh one to a friend who would have none of the scruples of which physical science ought to have cured Jock. It came out in a review, but without his name, and though it was painful enough to all who cared for him, it had been shorn of several of the worst and most virulent passages; so that Jock's remonstrance had done some good.

Jock himself had come into possession of £200, and the like sum had been left to his mother by their good old friends the Lucases, who had died, as it is given to some happy old couples to leave this world, within three days of one another.

The other John, in the last autumn, had taken both his degrees at Oxford and in London with high credit, and had immediately after obtained one of those annual appointments in his hospital which are bestowed upon the most distinguished of the students, to enable them to gain more experience; but as it did not involve residence, he continued to be one of the family in Collingwood Street. However, in the early spring, a slight hurt to his hand festered so as to make the doctors uneasy, and his sister set her heart on taking him to Fordham for Easter, for a more thorough rest than could be had at Kencroft, while the younger ones were having measles.

John, however, had by this time learnt enough of his own feelings to delay consent till he had written to ask Mrs. Evelyn whether she absolutely objected to his entertaining any future hopes of Sydney, when he should have worked his way upward, as his recent success gave him hopes of doing in time.

Sydney's fortune was not overpowering. £10,000 was settled on each of the younger children, and it had only been Fordham's liberality in treating Cecil as his eldest son that had brought about his early marriage. Thus she was no such heiress that her husband would be obliged to feel as if he were living on her means, or that exertion could be dispensed with, and thus, though he must make his way before he could marry, there was no utter inequality for one who brought a high amount of trained ability and industry.

Mrs. Evelyn could only answer as she would once have answered Jock, and on these terms he went. In the meantime Sydney had rejected the honourable young rector of the next parish, and was in the course of administering rebuffs to the county member, who was so persuaded that he and Miss Evelyn were the only fit match for one another, that no implied negative was accepted by him. Her brother, whom he was coaching in his county duties, was far too much inclined to bring him home to luncheon ; and in the clash and crisis, without any one's quite knowing how it happened, it turned out that Mrs. Evelyn had been so imprudent as to sanction an attachment between her daughter and that great lout of a young doctor, Lady Fordham's brother ! Not only the M.P., but all the family shook the head and bemoaned the connection, for though it was to be a long engagement and a great secret, everybody found it out. Lucas had long made up his mind that so it would end, and told his mother that it was a relief the crisis had come. He put a good face on it, wrung his cousin's hand with the grasp of a Hercules, observed 'Well done, old Monk,' and then made the work for his final examination a plea for being so incessantly occupied as to avoid all private outpourings. And if he had very little flesh on his bones, it was hard work and anxiety about his examination.

That final ordeal was gone through at last ; John Lucas Brownlow was, like his cousin, possessor of a certificate of honour and a medal, and had won both his degrees most brilliantly. He had worked the hardest and had the most talent, and his achievement was perhaps the most esteemed because of his lack of the previous training that Friar had brought from Oxford. Professors and physicians wrote his mother notes to express their satisfaction at the career of their old friend's son, and Dr. Medlicott came to bring her a whole bouquet of gratifying praise and admiration from all concerned with him, ranging from the ability of his prize essay to the firm delicacy of his hand ; and backed up by the doctor's own opinion of the blameless conduct and excellent influence of both the cousins. And now Dr. Medlicott declared he must have a good rest and holiday, after the long strain of hard toil and study.

It came like a dream to Caroline that the conditions imposed by her husband fifteen years before, when Lucas was a mischievous imp of a Skipjack, had been thus completely worked out, not only the intellectual, but the moral and religious terms being thus fulfilled.

The two cousins had come home to dinner in high spirits at the various kind things that had been said to, and of, Jock, and discussing the various suggestions for the future that had been made to them. They thought Mother Carey strangely silent, but when they rose she called her son into the consulting room, as she still termed it.

'My dear,' she said, 'this slate will tell you why this is the moment I have looked forward to from the time your dear father was taken from us with his work half done. He had been working out a discovery. He was sure of it himself, but none of the faculty would believe in it or take it up. Even Dr. Lucas thought it was a craze, and I believe it can only be tested by risky experiments. All that he had made out is in this book. You know he could not speak for that dreadful throat. This is what he wrote. I copied it again, putting in my answers lest it should fade, but these are his very words, and that is my pledge. Magnum Bonum was our playful pet name for it between ourselves.

'"I promise to keep the Magnum Bonum a secret, till the boys are grown up, and then only to confide it to the one that seems fittest, when he has taken his degree, and is a good, religious, wise, able man, with brains and balance, fit to be trusted to work out and apply such an invention, and not make it serve his own advancement, but be a real good and blessing to all." And oh, Jock,' she added, 'am I not thankful that after all it should have come about that you should fulfil those conditions!'

'Did you not once mean it for John?' said Jock, hastily looking up.

'Yes, when I thought that hateful money had turned you all aside.'

'Then I think he ought to share this knowledge.'

'I thought you would say so, but it is your first right.'

'Perhaps,' said Jock. 'But he is superior in his own line to me. He gave himself up to this line of his own free will, not like me, as a resource. And moreover, if it should bring any personal benefit, as an accident, it would be more important to him than to me. And these other conditions he fulfils to the letter. Mother, let me fetch him.'

She kissed his brow by way of answer, and a call brought John into the room. The explanation was made, and John said, 'If you think it right, Aunt Caroline. No one can quite fulfil the conditions, but two may be better than one.'

'Then I will leave you to read it together,' she said, after pointing them to the solemn words in the first page. 'Oh, you cannot think how glad I am to give up my trust.'

She went upstairs to the drawing-room, and about half an hour had passed in this way, when Jock came to the door, and said, 'Mother, would you please to come down?'

It was a strange, grave voice in which he spoke, and when she reached the room, they set Allen's most luxurious chair for her, but she stood trembling, reading in their faces that there was something they hesitated to tell her. They looked at one another as if to ask which should do it, and a certain indignation and alarm seized on her. 'You believe in it!' she cried, as if she suspected them of disloyalty.

'Most entirely!' they both exclaimed.

'It is a great discovery,' added Jock, 'but——'

'But,' said John, as he hesitated, 'it has been worked out within the last two years.'

'Not Dr. Hermann!' she cried.

'No indeed!' said Jock. 'Why?'

'Because poor Janet overheard our conversation, and obtained a sight of the book. It was her ambition. I believe it was fatal to her. She may have caught up enough of the outline to betray it. Jock, you remember that scene at Belforest?'

'I do,' said Jock; 'but this is not that scoundrel. It is Ruthven, who has worked it out in a full and regular way. It is making a considerable sensation, though it has scarcely yet come into use as a mode of treatment. Mother, do not be disappointed. It will be the blessing that my father intended, all the sooner for not being in the hands of two lads like us, whom all the bigwigs would scout!'

'And what I never thought of before,' said John. 'You know we are so often asked whether we belong to Joseph Brownlow, that one forgets to mention it every time; but that day, when Dr. Medlicott took me to the Westminster hospital, we fell in with Dr. Ruthven, and after the usual disappointment on finding I was only the nephew and not the son, he said, "Joseph Brownlow would have been a great man if he had lived. I owe a great deal to a hint he once gave me:"'

'He ought to see these notes,' said Jock. 'It strikes me that there is a clue here to that difficulty he mentions in that published paper of his.'

'You ought to show it to him,' said John.

'You ought,' said Jock.

'Do you know much about him?' asked Mother Carey. 'I don't think I ever saw him, though I know his name. A fashionable physician, is he not?'

'A very good man,' said John. 'A great West-end swell just come to be the acknowledged head in his own line. I suppose it is just what my uncle would have been ten years ago, if he had been spared.'

'May we show it to him, mother?' said Jock. 'I should

think he was quite to be trusted with it. I see! I was reading
an account of this method of his to Dr. Lucas one day, and he
was much interested and tried to tell me something about my
father; but it was after his speech grew so imperfect, and he
was so much excited and distressed that I had to lead him away
from the subject.'

'Yes, Dr. Lucas's incredulity made all the difference. How
old is Dr. Ruthven, John?'

'A little over forty, I should say. He may have been a pupil
of my uncle's.'

After a little more consultation, it was decided that John
should write to Dr. Ruthven that his cousin had some papers of
his father's which he thought the doctor might like to see, and
that they would bring them if he would make an appointment.

And so the Magnum Bonum was no longer a secret, a burden,
and a charge!

It was not easy to tell whether she who had so long been its
depositary felt the more lightened or disappointed. She had
reckoned more than she knew upon the honour of the discovery
being connected with the name of Brownlow, and she could not
quite surmount the feeling that Dr. Ruthven had somehow
robbed her husband, though her better sense accepted and
admired the young men's argument that such discoveries were
common property, and that the benefit to the world was the
same.

Allen was a good deal struck when he understood the matter.
He said it explained a good deal to him which the others had
been too young to observe or remember both in the old home and
afterwards.

'One wonderful part of it is how you kept the secret, and
Janet too!' he said. 'And you must often have been sorely
tempted. I remember being amused at your disappointment
and her indignation when I said I didn't see why a man was
bound to be a doctor because his father was before him; and I
suppose if Bobus or I had taken to it, this Ruthven need not
have been beforehand with us!'

'It would have been transgressing the conditions to hold it
out to you.'

'I don't imagine I could have done it any way,' said Allen,
sighing. 'I never can enter into the taste the others have for
that style of thing; but Bobus might have succeeded. You
must have expected it of him, at the time when he and I used
to laugh at what we thought was a monomania on your part for
our taking up medical science as a tribute to our father, when
we did not need it as a provision.'

'You see, if any of you had taken up the study from pure
philanthropy, as some people do—well, at any rate in George
Macdonald's novels—it would have been the very qualification.
But I had little hope from the time that the fortune came. I
dreamt the first night that Midas had turned the whole of you

to gold statues, and that I was wandering about like the Princess Paribanou to find the *Magnum Bonum* to disenchant you.'

'It has come pretty true,' said Allen thoughtfully; 'that inheritance did us all a great deal of mischief.'

'And it took a greater *magnum bonum*, a *maximum bonum*, to disenchant us,' said Armine.

'Which I fear did not come from me,' said his mother, 'and I am most grateful to the dear people who applied it to you. I wish I saw my way to the disenchantment of the other two !'

'I suppose you quite despaired till John took his turn in that direction,' said Allen. 'Bobus could really have done better than any of us, I fancy, but he would not have fulfilled the religious condition, as *sine quâ non*.'

'Bobus is not really cleverer than Jock,' said Armine.

'Yet the Skipjack seemed the most improbable one of all,' said his mother. 'I wish he were not deprived of it, after all !'

'Perhaps he is not,' said Armine. 'He told me he had been comparing the MS. notes with Dr. Ruthven's published paper, and he thought my father saw farther into the capabilities.'

'Well, he will do right with it. I am thankful to leave it in such hands as his and the Monk's.'

'Then it was this,' continued Allen, 'that was the key to poor Janet's history. I suppose she hoped to qualify herself when she was madly set on going to Zurich.'

'Though I told her I could never commit it to her ; but she knew just enough to make that wretched man fancy it a sort of quack secret, and he managed to persuade her that he had real ability to pursue the discovery for her. Poor Janet ! it has been no *magnum bonum* to her, I fear. If I could only know where she is.'

A civil, but not a very eager note came in reply to John from Dr. Ruthven, making the appointment, but so dispassionately that he might fairly be supposed to expect little from the interview.

However, they came home more than satisfied. Perhaps in the interim Dr. Ruthven had learnt what manner of young men they were, and the honours they had won, for he had received them very kindly, and had told them how a conversation with Joseph Brownlow had put him on the scent of what he had since gradually and experimentally worked out, and so fully proved to himself, that he had begun treatment on that basis, and with success, though he had only as yet brought a portion of his fellow-physicians to accept his system.

Lucas had then explained as much as was needful, and shown him the notes. He read with increasing eagerness, and presently they saw his face light up, and with his finger on the passage they had expected, he said, 'This is just what I wanted. Why did I not think of it before?' and asked permission to copy the passage.

Then he urged the publication of the notes in some medical journal, showing true and generous anxiety that honour should be given where honour was due, and that his system should have the support of a name not yet forgotten. Further, he told his visitors that they would hear from him soon, and altogether they came home so much gratified that the mother began to lose her sense of being forestalled. She was hard at work in her own way on a set of models for dinner-table ornaments which had been ordered. 'Pot-boilers' had unfortunately much more success than the imaginary groups she enjoyed.

Therefore she stayed at home and only sent her young people on a commission to bring her as many varieties of foliage and seed-vessels as they could, when Jock and Armine spent this first holiday of waiting in setting forth with Babie to get a regular good country walk, grumbling horribly that she would not accompany them.

She was deep in the moulding of a branch of chestnut, which carried her back to the first time she saw those prickly clusters, on that day of opening Paradise at Richmond, with Joe by her side, then still Mr. Brownlow to her, Joe, who had seemed so much closer to her side in these last few days. The Colonel might call Armine the most like Joe, and say that Jock almost absurdly recalled her own soldier-father, Captain Allen ; but to her, Jock always the most brought back her husband's words and ways, in a hundred little gestures and predilections, and she had still to struggle with her sense of injury that he should not be the foremost.

The maid came up with two cards : Dr. and Mrs. Ruthven. This was speedy, and Caroline had to take off her brown holland apron, and wash her hands, while Emma composed her cap, in haste and not very good will, for she could not but think them her natural enemies, though she was ready to beat herself for being so small and nasty 'when they could not help it, poor things.'

However, Mrs. Ruthven turned out to be a pleasant lively *table d'hôte* acquaintance of six or seven years ago in her maiden days, and her doctor an agreeable Scotsman, who told Mrs. Brownlow that he had been here on several evenings in former days, and did not seem at all hurt that she did not remember him. He seemed disappointed that neither of the young men was at home, and inquired whether they had anything in view. 'Not definitely,' she said, and she spoke of some of the various counsels Dr. Medlicott and others had given them.

In the midst she heard that peculiar dash with which the Fordham carriage always announced itself. Little Esther might be ever so much a Viscountess, but could she ever cease to be shy ? In spite of her increasing beauty and grace, she was not a success in society, for the ladies said she was slow ; she had no conversation, and no dash or rattle to make up for

it, and nothing would ever teach her to like strangers. They were
only so many disturbances in the way of her enjoyment of her
husband and her baby ; and when she could not have the former
to go out driving with her, she always came and besought for
the company of Aunt Caroline and Babie ; above all, when she
had any shopping to do. She knew it was very foolish, but she
could never be happy in encountering shop people, and she
wanted strong support and protection to prevent herself from
being made a lay figure by urgent dressmakers. Her home
only gave her help and company on great occasions, for Eleanor
persisted in objecting to fine people, was determined against
attracting another Guardsman, and privately desired her sister
to abstain from inviting her. Essie was aware that this was all
for the sake of a certain curate at St. Kenelm's, and left Ellie
to carry out her plan of passive resistance, becoming thus the
more dependent on her aunt's family.

In she came, too graceful and courteous for strangers to
detect the shock their presence gave her, but much relieved to
see them depart. Her husband was on guard, and she had a
whole list of commissions for mamma, which would be much
better executed without him. Moreover, baby must have a new
pelisse and hat for the country, and might not she have little
stockings and shoes, in case she should want to walk before the
return to London ?

As little Alice was but four months old, and her father's
leave was only for three months, this did not seem a very probable contingency, but Mother Carey was always ready for
shopping. She had never quite outgrown the delight of the
change from being a penniless schoolgirl, casting wistful fleet-
ing glances at the windows where happier maidens might enter
and purchase.

Then there was to be a great review in two days' time ; Cecil
would be with his regiment, and Esther wanted the whole
family to go with her, lunch with the officers, and have a
thorough holiday. Cecil had sent a message that Jock must
come to have the cobwebs swept out of his brain, and see his
old friends before he got into harness again. It was a well-
earned holiday, as Mother Carey felt, accepting it with eager
pleasure for all who could come, though John's power of so
doing must be doubtful, and there was little chance of a day
being granted to Allen.

In going out with her niece, Caroline's eye had fallen on an
envelope among the cards on the hall table, ambiguously
addressed to 'J. Brownlow, Esq., M.B.' and on her return home
she was met at the door by Jock with a letter in his hand.

'So Dr. Ruthven has been here,' he said, drawing her into
the consulting-room.

'Yes. I like him rather. He seems to wish to make any
amends in his power.'

'Amends ! you dear old ridiculous mother ! Do you call this

amends?' holding up the letter. 'He says, now this discovery
is getting known and he has a name for the sort of case, his
practice is outgrowing him, and he wants some one to work
with him who may be up to this particular matter, and all he
has heard of us convinces him that he cannot do better than
propose it to whichever of us has no other designs.'

'Very right and proper of him. It is the only thing he can
do. I suppose it would be the making of one of you. Ah!' as
she glanced over the letter. 'He gives the preference to you.'

'He was bound to do that, but I think he would prefer the
Monk. I wonder whether you care very much about my
accepting the offer.'

'Would this house be too far off?'

'I don't know his plans enough to tell. That was not what
I was thinking of, but of what it would save *her*. Essie said she
was not looking well; and no doubt waiting is telling on her,
just as her mother always feared it would.'

'John has just not had the forbearance you have shown!'

'That is all circumstance. There was the saving her life, and
afterwards the being on the spot when she was tormented about
the other affair. He has no notion of having cut me out, and I
trust he never will.'

'No, I do him that justice.'

'Then he has the advantage of me every way, out and out in
looks and University training; and it was to him that Ruthven
first took a fancy.'

'You surpassed him in your essay, and in——'

'Oh yes, yes,' interrupted Jock hastily, 'but you see work
was my refuge. I had nothing to call me off. Besides, I have
my share of your brains, instead of her Serenity's; but that's all
the more reason if you would listen to me. Depend upon it,
Ruthven, if he knew all, would much prefer the connection
John would have, and *she* would bring means to set up
directly.'

'I suppose you will have it so,' replied she, looking up to him
affectionately.

'I should like it,' he said. 'It is the one thing for them, and
waiting might do her infinite harm; the dear old Monk
deserves it every way. Remember how it all turned on his
desperate race. If your comfort depended on my taking it,
that would come first.'

'Oh no.'

'But there is sure to turn up plenty of other work without
leaving you,' he continued. 'I don't fancy getting involved in
West-end practice among swells, and not being independent.
I had rather see whether I can't work out this principle further,
devoting myself to reading up for it, and getting more hospital
experience to go upon.'

'I dare say that is quite right. I know it is like your
father, and indeed I shall be quite content however you decide.

Only might it not be well to see how it strikes John, before you absolutely make it over to him ?'

'You are trying to be prudent against the grain, Mother Carey.'

'Trying to see it like your uncle. Yes, exactly as if I were trying to forestall his calling me his good little sister.'

'I don't know what he would call me,' said Jock, 'for at the bottom is a feeling that, after reading my father's words, I had rather not, if I can help it, begin immediately to make all that material advantage out of "Magnum Bonum," as you call it.'

'Well, my dear, do as you think right ; I trust it all to you. It is sure to turn out the right sort of " Magnum Bonum " to you——'

The Monk's characteristic ring at the bell was heard, and the letter was, without loss of time, committed to him, while both mother and son watched him as he gathered up the sense.

'Well, this is jolly !' was his first observation. 'Downright handsome of Ruthven !' and then as the colour rose a little in his face, 'Just the thing for you, Jock, home work, which is exactly what you want.'

'I'm not sure about that,' said Jock ; 'I don't want to get into that kind of practice just yet. It is fitter for a family man.'

'And who is a family man if you are not ?' said John. 'Wasn't it the very cause of your taking this line ?'

'There's a popular prejudice in favour of wives, rather than mothers,' said Jock. 'I should have said you were more likely to fulfil the conditions.'

'Oh !' and there was a sound in that exclamation that belied the sequel, 'that's just nonsense ! The offer is to you primarily, and it is your duty to take it.'

'I had much rather you did, and so had Dr. Ruthven. I want more time for study and experience, and have set my heart on some scientific appointment——'

'Come now, my good fellow—why, what are you laughing at ?'

'Because you are such a good imitation of your father, my dear Johnnie,' said his aunt.

'It is just what my father would say,' returned John, taking this as a high compliment ; 'it would be very foolish of Lucas to give up a certainty for this just because of his Skipjack element, which doesn't want to get into routine harness. Now, don't you think so, Mother Carey ?'

'If I thought it was the Skipjack element,' she said, smiling.

'If it is not,' he said, the colour now spreading all over his face, 'I am all the more bound not to let him give up all his prospects in life.'

'All my prospects ! My dear Monk, do you think they don't go beyond a brougham and unlimited staircases ?'

'I only know,' cried John, nettled into being a little off his guard, 'that what you despise would be all the world to me!'

The admission was hailed triumphantl , but the Kencroft nature was too resolute, and the individual conscience too generous, to be brought round to accept the sacrifice, which John estimated at the value of the importance it was to himself, viewing what was real in Lucas's distaste as mere erratic folly, which ought to be argued down. Finally, when the argument had gone round into at least its fiftieth circle, Mother Carey declared that she would have no more of it. Lucas should write a note to Dr. Ruthven, accepting his proposal for one or other of them, and promising that he should know which, in the course of a few days; so that John, if he chose, could write to his father or *any one* else. Meantime there was to be no allusion to 'the raid of Ruthven' till the day of the review was over. It was to be put entirely off the tongue, if not out of the head!'

And the two young doctors were weary enough of the subject to rejoice in obedience to her.

The day was perfect, except that poor Allen was pinned fast by his tyrant; all the others gave themselves up to the enjoyment of the moment. They understood the sham fight, and recognised all the corps, with Jock as their cicerone; they had a good place at the marching past, and Esther had the crowning delight of an excellent view of Captain Viscount Fordham with his company, and at the luncheon. Jock received an absolutely affectionate welcome from his old friends, who made as much of his mother and sister for his sake, as they did of the lovely Lady Fordham for her husband's, finding them, moreover much more easy to get on with.

## CHAPTER XXXIX

### THE TRUANT

'The bird was sitting in his cage,
　And heard what he did say;
He jumped upon the window-sill,
　"'Tis time I was away."'

*Ballad.*

'THERE is a young lady in the drawing-room, ma'am,' said the maid, looking rather puzzled and uncertain, on the return of the party from the review.

'A stranger? How could you let her in?' said John.

At that moment a face appeared at the top of the stairs, a face set in the rich golden auburn that all knew so well, and half-way up, Mrs. Brownlow was clasped by a pair of arms, and there was a cry, 'Mother Carey, Mother Carey, I'm come home!'

'Elvira! my dear child! When—how did you come?'

'From the station, in a cab. I made her let me in, but I thought you were never coming back. Where's Allen?'

'Allen will come in by and by,' said the astonished Mother Carey, who had been dragged into the drawing-room, where Elvira embraced Babie, and grasped the hands of the others.

'Oh, it is so nice,' she cried, then nestling back to Mother Carey.

'But where did you come from? Are you alone?'

'Yes, quite alone. Janet would not come with me after all.'

'Janet, my dear! Where is she?'

'Oh, not here—at Saratoga, or at New York. I thought she was coming with me, but when the steamer sailed she was not there, only there was a note pinned to my berth. I meant to have brought it, but it got lost somehow.'

'Where did you see her?'

'At the photographer's at Saratoga. I should never have come if she had not helped me, but she said she knew you would take me home, and she wrote and took my passage and all. She said if I did not find you, Mr. Wakefield would know where you were, but I did so want to get home to you! Please, may I take off my things? I don't want to be such a fright when Allen comes in.'

It was all very mysterious, but Elvira must be much altered indeed if her narrative did not come out in an utterly complicated and detached manner. She was altered certainly, for she clung most affectionately to Mother Carey and Barbara when they took her upstairs. She had a little travelling-bag with her; the rest of her luggage would be sent from the station, she supposed, for she had taken no heed to it. She did so want to get home.

'I did feel so hungry for you, Mother Carey. Mother, Janet said you would forgive me, and I thought, if you were ever so angry, it would be *true*, and that would be nicer than Lisette; and, indeed, it was not so much my doing as Lisette's.'

Whatever 'it' was, Mother Carey had no hesitation in replying that she had no doubt it was Lisette's fault.

'You see,' continued Elvira, 'I never meant anything but to plague Allen a little at first. You know he had always been so tiresome and jealous, and always teased me when I wanted any fun—at least I thought so, and I did want to have my swing before he called me engaged to him again. I told Jock so, but then Lisette and Lady Flora and old Lady Clanmacnalty went on telling me that you knew the money was mine all the time, and that it was only an accident that it came out before I was married.'

'Oh, Elvira, you could not have thought anything so wicked,' cried Babie.

'They all went on so, and made so sure,' said Elvira, hanging her head, 'and I never did know the real way the will was

found till Janet told me.  Babie, if you had heard Lady Clanmacnalty clear her throat when people talked about the will
being found, you would have believed she knew better than any
one.'

So it was.  The girl, weak in character, and far from sensible,
full of self-importance, and puffed up with her inheritance, had
been easily blinded and involved in the web that the artful
Lisette had managed to draw round her.  She had been totally
alienated from her old friends, and by force of reiteration had
been brought to think them guilty of defrauding her.  In truth,
she was kept in a whirl of gaiety and amusement, with little
power of realising her situation, till the breach had grown too
wide for the feeble will of a helpless being like her to cross it.
Though she had flirted extensively, she had never felt capable
of accepting any one of her suitors, and in these refusals she
had been assisted by Lisette, who wanted to secure her for her
brother, but thanks to warnings from Mr. Wakefield, and her
husband's sense of duty, durst not do so before she was of age.

Elvira's one wish had been to visit San Ildefonso again.  She
had a strong yearning towards the lovely island home which she
gilded in recollection with all the trails of glory that shine round
the objects of our childish affections.  Lisette always promised
to take her, but found excuses for delay in the refitting of
the yacht, while she kept the party wandering over Europe in
the resorts of second-rate English residents.  No doubt she
wished to make the most of the enjoyments she could obtain,
as Elvira's chaperon and guardian, before resigning her even to
her brother.  At last the gambling habits into which her husband fell, for lack, poor man, of any other employment, had
alarmed her, and she permitted her party to embark in the
yacht, where Gilbert Gould acted as captain.

They reached the island.  It had become a coaling station.
The bay where she remembered exquisite groves coming down
to the white beach, was a wharf, ringing with the discordant
shouts of negroes and cries of sailors.  The old nurse was dead,
and fictitious foster brothers and sisters were constantly turning up with extravagant claims.

'Oh, I longed never to have come,' said Elvira; 'and then I
began to get homesick, but they would not let me come!'

No doubt Lisette had feared the revival of the Brownlow influence if her charge were once in England, for she had raised
every obstacle to a return.  Poor Gould and his niece had both
looked forward to Elvira's coming of age as necessarily bringing
them to England, but her uncle's health had suffered from the
dissipation he had found his only resource.  Liquor had become
his consolation in the life to which he was condemned, and in
the hotel life of America was only too easily attainable.

His death deprived Elvira of the last barrier to the attempts
of an unscrupulous woman, who was determined not to let her
escape.  Elvira's longing to return home made her spread her

toils closer. She kept her moving from one fashionable resort to another, still attended by Gilbert, who was beginning to grow impatient to secure his prize.

'How I hated it!' said Elvira. 'I knew she was false and cruel by that time, but it was just like being in a trap between them. I loathed them more and more, but I couldn't get away.'

Nurtured as she had been, she was helpless and ignorant about the commonest affairs of life, and the sight of American independence never inspired her with the idea of breaking the bondage in which she was spellbound. Still, she shrank back with instinctive horror from every advance of Gilbert's, and at last, to pique her, Lisette brought forward the intelligence that Allen Brownlow was married.

The effect must have surprised them, for Elvira turned on her aunt in one of those fits of passion which sometimes seized her, accused her vehemently of having poisoned the happiness of her life, and taken her from the only man she could ever love. She said and threatened all sorts of desperate things; and then the poor child, exhausted by her own violence, collapsed, and let herself be cowed and terrified in her turn by her aunt's vulgar sneers and cold determination.

Yet still she held out against the marriage. 'I told them it would be wicked,' she said. 'And when I went to church, all the Psalms and everything said it would be wicked. Then Lisette said it was wicked to love a married man, and I said I didn't know, I couldn't help it, but it would be more wicked to vow I would love a man whom I hated, and should hate more every day of my life. Then they said I might have a civil marriage, and not vow anything at all, and I told them that would seem to me no better than not being married at all. Oh! I was very, very miserable!'

'Had you no one to consult or help you, my poor child?'

'They watched me so, and whenever I was making friends with any nice American girl, they always rattled me off somewhere else. I never did understand before what people meant when they talked about God being their only Friend, but I knew it then, for I had none at all, none else. And I did not think He would help me, for now I knew I had been hard, and horrid, and nasty, and cruel to you and Allen, the only people who ever cared for me for myself, and not for my horrid, horrid money, though I was the nastiest little wretch. Oh, Mother Carey, I did know it then, and I got quite sick with longing for one honest kiss—or even one honest scolding of yours. I used to cry all church-time, and they used to try not to let me go—and I felt just like the children of Israel in Egypt, as if I had got into heavy bondage, and the land of captivity. Oh, do speak, and let me hear your voice once more! Your arm is so comfortable.'

Still it seemed that Elvira had resisted till another attempt

2 F

was made. While she was at a boarding-house on the Hudson a large picnic party was arranged, in which, after American fashion, gentlemen took ladies 'to ride' in their traps to and from the place of rendezvous. In returning, of course, it had been as easy as possible for her chaperon to contrive that she should be left alone with no cavalier but Gilbert Gould, and he of course pretended to lose his way, drove on till night-fall, and then judgmatically met with an accident, which hurt nobody, but which he declared made the carriage incapable of proceeding.

After walking what Elvira fancied half the night, shelter was found in a hospitable farmhouse, where the people were wakened with difficulty. They took care of the benighted wanderers, and the farmer drove them back to the hotel the next morning in his own waggon. They were received by Mrs. Gould with great demonstrations both of affection, pity, and dismay, and she declared that the affair had been so shocking and compromising that it was impossible to stay where they were. She made Elvira take her meals in her room rather than face the boarding-house company, paid the bills (all, of course, with Elvira's money), and carried her off to the Saratoga Springs, having taken good care not to allow her a minute's conversation with any one who would have told her that the freedom of American manners would make an adventure like hers be thought of no consequence at all.

The poor girl herself was assured by Mrs. Gould that this 'unhappy escapade' left her no alternative but a marriage with Gilbert. She would otherwise never be able to show her face again, for even if the affair were hushed up, reports would fly, and Mrs. Lisette took care they should fly, by ominous shakes of the head, and whispered confidences such as made the steadier portion of the Saratoga community avoid her, and brought her insolent attention from fast young men. It was this, and a cold 'What can you expect?' from Lisette that finally broke down her defences, and made her permit the Goulds to make known that she was engaged to Gilbert.

Had they seized their prey at that moment of shame and despair, they would have secured it, but their vanity or their self-esteem made them wish to wash off the mire they had cast, or to conceal it by such magnificence at the wedding as should outdo Fifth Avenue. The English heiress must have a wedding-dress that would figure in the papers, and, even in the States, be fabulously splendid. It must come from Paris, and it must be waited for. All the bridesmaids were to have splendid pearl lockets containing coloured miniature photograph portraits of the beautiful bride, who for her part was utterly broken-hearted. 'I thought God had forgotten me, because I deserved it ; and I only hoped I might die, for I knew what the sailors said of Gilbert.'

Listless and indifferent, she let her tyrants do what they

would with her, and it was in Gilbert's company that she first
saw Janet at the photographer's. Fortunately he had never
seen Miss Brownlow, and Elvira had grown much too cautious
to betray recognition ; but the vigilance had been relaxed since
the avowal of the engagement, and the colouring of the photographs from the life was a process so wearisome that no one
cared to attend the sitter, and Elvira could go and come, alone
and unquestioned.

So it was that she threw herself upon Janet. Whatever had
been their relations in their girlhood, each was to the other the
remnant of the old home and of better days, and in their stolen
interviews they met like sisters. Janet knew as little as Elvira
did of her own family, rather less indeed, but she declared Mrs.
Gould's horror about the expedition with Gilbert to have been
pure dissimulation, and soon enabled Elvira to prove to herself
that it had been a concerted trick. In America it would go for
nothing. Even in England, so mere an accident (even if it had
really been an accident) would not tell against her. But then,
Elvira hopelessly said, Allen was married !

Again Janet was incredulous, and when she found that Elvira
had never seen the letter in which Kate Gould was supposed to
have sent the information, and knew it only upon Lisette's
assertion, she declared it to be probably a fabrication. Why
not telegraph ? So in Elvira's name and at her expense, but
with the address given to Janet's abode, the telegram was sent
to Mr. Wakefield's office, and in a few hours the reply had come
back : 'Allen Brownlow not married, nor likely to be.'

There was no doubt now of the web of falsehood that had
entangled the poor girl ; but she would probably have been too
inert and helpless to break through it, save for her energetic
cousin, who nerved her to escape from the life of utter misery
that lay before her. What was to hinder her from setting off
by the train, and going at once home to England by the steamer ?
There was no doubt that Mrs. Brownlow would forgive and
welcome her, or even if that hope failed her, Mr. Wakefield was
bound to take care of her. She had a house of her own standing empty for her, and the owner of £40,000 a year need never
be at a loss.

Had she enough money accessible to pay for a first-class
passage ? Yes, amply even for two. She had always been so
passive and incapable of all matters of arrangement, that Mrs.
Gould had never thought it worth while to keep watch over her
possession of 'the nerves and sinews of war,' being indeed
unwilling to rouse her attention to the fact that she was paying
the by no means moderate expenses of both her tyrants.

Janet found out all about the hours, secured — as Elvira
thought — two first-class berths, met her when she crept like a
guilty thing out of the hotel at New York, took her to the
station, went with her to an outfitter to be supplied with necessaries for the voyage, for she had been obliged to abandon

everything but a few valuables in her hand-bag, and saw her safely on board, introduced her to some kind friendly English people, then, on some excuse of seeing the steward, left her, as Elvira found, to make the voyage alone !

It turned out that Janet had spoken to the gentleman of this party, and explained that her young cousin was going home alone, asking him to protect her on landing ; and that she had come to London with them and been there put into a cab, giving the old address to Collingwood Street, where with much difficulty she had prevailed on the maid to let her in to await the return of the family.

Nothing so connected as this history came to the ears of Mrs. Brownlow or her children.  That evening they only heard fragments, much more that was utterly irrelevant, and much that was inexplicable, all interspersed with inquiries and caresses and intent listening for Allen.   Elvira might not have acquired brains, but she had gained in sweetness and affection.   The face had lost its soulless, painted-doll expression, and she was evidently happy beyond all measure to be among those she could love and trust, sitting on a footstool by Mrs. Brownlow's knee, leaning against her, and now and then murmuring: 'O Mother Carey, how I have longed for you !'

She was not free from the fear that Lisette and Gilbert could still 'do something to her,' but the Johns made large assurances of defence, and Mr. Wakefield was to be called in the next day. It must be confessed that everybody rather enjoyed the notion of the pair left at Saratoga with all their hotel bills to pay, and the wedding-dress on their hands, but Elvira knew they had enough to clear them for the week, and only hoped it was not enough to enable them to follow her.

Fragments of all this came out in the course of the evening. Allen did not come home to dinner, and the other young men left the coast clear for confidences, which were uttered in the intervals of listening, till after all her excitement, her landing and her journey, Elvira was so tired out that she had actually dropped asleep, with her head on Mother Carey's knee, when his soft weary step came up the stairs, and perceiving, as he entered, that there was a hush over the room, he did not speak. Babie looked up from her work with an amused smile of infinite congratulation.  There was a glance from his mother.  Then, as Babie put it, the Prince saw the Sleeping Beauty, and, with a strange long half-strangled gasp and clasped hands, went down on one knee.   At that very moment Elvira stirred, opened her eyes, put her hand over them, bewildered, as if thinking herself dreaming, then with a sort of shriek of joy, flung herself towards him, as he held out his arms with 'My darling !'

'Oh, Allen, can you forgive me ?  And oh ! do marry me before they can come after me !'

So much Mother Carey and Babie heard before they could remove themselves from the scene, which they felt ought to be a *tête-à-tête.* They shut the lovers in. Babie said, 'Undine has found a heart, at least,' and then they began to piece out the story by conjecture, and they then discovered how little they had really learnt about Janet. They supposed that the Hermanns must be living and practising at Saratoga, and in that case it was no wonder she could not come home, the only strange thing was Elvira's expecting it. Besides, why had not Mrs. Gould taken alarm at the name, and why was her husband never mentioned ? Was there no message from her ? Most likely there was, in the note that was lost, and moreover, Elvira might be improved, but she was Elvira still, and had room for very little besides herself in her mind's eye.

They must wait to examine her till these first raptures had subsided, and in the meantime Caroline wrote a telegram to go as early as possible to Mr. Wakefield. It showed a guilty conscience that Mrs. Gould should not have telegraphed to him Elvira's flight.

When at last Mrs. Brownlow held that the interview must come to an end, and with preliminary warning opened the door, there they were, with clasped hands, such as Elvira had never endured since she was a mere child ! Allen looking almost too blissful for this world, and Elvira with eyes glistening with tears as she cried, 'O Mother Carey, you never told me how altered he was, I never knew how horrible I had been till I saw how ill he looks ! What can we do for him ?'

'You are doing everything, my darling,' said Allen.

'He of course thinks her as irresponsible as if she had been hanging up by the hair all this time in a giant's larder,' whispered Babie to Armine.

But Elvira was really unhappy about the worn, faded air that made Allen look much older than his twenty-nine years warranted. The poor girl's nerves proved to have been much disturbed ; she besought Barbara to sleep with her, and was haunted by fears of pursuit and capture, and Gilbert claiming her after all. She kept on starting, clutching at Babie, and requiring to be soothed till far on into the night, and then she slept so soundly that no one had the heart to wake her. Indeed it was her first real peaceful repose since her flight had been planned, nor did she come down till half-past ten, just when Mr. Wakefield drove up to the door, and Jock had taken pity on Allen, and set forth to undertake Sir Samuel for the day. Mr. Wakefield was the less surprised at the sight of the young lady, having been somewhat prepared by her telegraphic inquiry about Allen, which he had not communicated to the Brownlows, for fear of raising false expectations.

There was a great consultation. Elvira was not in the least shy, and only wanted to be safely Mrs. Allen Brownlow before the Goulds should arrive, as she expected, in the next steamer to pursue her *vi et armis.* If it had depended on her, she would have sent Allen for a special licence, and been married in her travelling-dress that very day. Mr. Wakefield, solicitor as he was, was quite ready for speed. He had always viewed the marriage with Allen Brownlow as a simple act of restitution, and the trust made settlements needless. Still he did not apprehend any danger from the Goulds, when he found that Elvira had never written a note to Gilbert in her life. Nay, he thought that if they even threatened any annoyance, they had given cause enough to have a prosecution for conspiracy held over them in wholesome terror.

And considering all the circumstances, Mrs. Brownlow and Allen were alike determined against undignified haste. Miss Menella ought to be married from among her own kindred, and from her own house ; but this was not easy to manage ; for poor Mary Whiteside and her husband, though very worthy, were not exactly the people to enact parents in such a house as Belforest ; and Mrs. Brownlow could see why she herself should not, though Elvira could not think why she objected. At last the idea was started that the fittest persons were Mr. and Mrs. Wakefield. The latter was a thorough lady, pleasant and sensible. The only doubt was whether so very quiet a person could be asked to undertake such an affair, and her husband took leave, that he might consult her and see whether she could bring herself to be mother for the nonce to the wild heiress, of whom his family were wont to talk with horrified compassion.

When he was gone, it was possible to come to the examination upon Janet for which Mother Carey had been so anxious. How was she looking ?

'Oh ! so old, and worn and thin. I never should have guessed it was Janet, if I had not caught her eye, and then I knew her eyebrows and nose, because they are just like Allen's,—and her voice sounded so like home that I was ready to cry, only I did not dare, as Gilbert was there.'

'I wonder they did not alarm at her name.'

'I don't imagine they ever heard it ?'

'Not when she was living there ! Was not her husband practising ?'

'Her husband ! Oh no, I never heard anything about him. I thought you knew I found her at the photographer's ?'

'Met her as a sitter ?'

'Oh dear, no ! I thought you understood. It was she that was doing my picture. She finishes up all his miniature photographs.'

'My dear Elvira, do you really mean that my poor Janet is supporting herself in that way ?'

'Yes, indeed I do ; that was why I made sure she would have come home with me. I was so dreadfully disappointed when I found only her note.'

'And are you sure you have quite lost it ?'

'Yes, I turned out every corner of my bag this morning to

look for it. I am so sorry, but I was so ill and so wretched that I could not take care of anything. I just wonder how I lived through the voyage, all alone.'

'Was there no message? Nothing for me?'

'Yes, I have recollected it now, or some of it. She said she durst not go home, or ask anything of you, after the way she had offended. Oh! I wonder how she could send me, for I know I was worse.'

'But what did she say?' said Caroline, too anxious to listen to Elvira's own confessions. 'Was there nothing for me?'

'Yes. She said, "Tell her that I have learnt by the bitterest of all experience the pain I have given her, and the wrong I have done!" Then there was something about being so utterly past forgiveness that she could not come to ask it. Oh, don't cry so, Mother Carey, we can write and get her back, and I will send her the passage money.'

'Ah! yes, write!' cried out the mother, starting up. "When he was yet a great way off." Ah! why could she not remember that?' But as she sat down to her table, 'You know her address?'

'Yes, certainly, I went to her lodgings once or twice; such a little bit of a room, up so many stairs.'

'And you did not hear how that man, her husband, died?'

'I don't know whether he is dead,' said this most unsatisfactory informant. 'She does not wear black, nor a cap, and I am almost sure that he has run away from her, and that is the reason she cannot use her own name.'

'Elfie!'

'Oh, I thought you knew! She calls herself Mrs. Harte. She took my passage in that name, and that must be why my things have never come. Yes, I asked her why she did not set up for a lady doctor, and she said it was impossible that she could venture on showing her certificates or using her name—either his or hers.'

That was in the main all that could be extracted from Elvira, though it was brought out again and again in all sorts of forms. It was plain that Janet had been very reticent in all that regarded herself, and Elvira had only had stolen interviews, very full of her own affairs, and, besides, had supposed Janet to intend to return with her. Both wrote; Elfie, to announce her safety, and Caroline, an incoherent, imploring, forgiving letter, such as only a mother could write, before they went out to supply Elvira's lack of garments, and to procure the order for the sum needed for her passage. Caroline was glad they had gone independently, for, on their return, Babie reported to her that her little Ladyship was so wroth with Elfie as to wonder at them for receiving her so affectionately. It was very forgiving of them, but she should never forget the way in which poor Allen had been treated.

'I told her,' said Babie, 'that was the way she talked about

Cecil, and you should have seen her face! She wonders that Allen has not more spirit, and indeed, mother, I do rather wish Elfie could have come back with nothing but her little bag, so that he could have shown it would have been all the same.'

'A comfortable life they would have had, poor things, in that case,' laughed her mother, 'though I agree that it would have been prettier. But I don't trouble myself about that, my dear. You know, in all equity, Allen ought to have a share in that property. It was only the old man's caprice that made it all or none ; and Elvira is only doing what is right and just.'

'And Allen's love was a real thing, when he was the rich one. So I told Essie : and besides, Allen would never make any hand of poverty, poor fellow.'

'I think and hope he will make a much better hand of riches than he would have done without all he has gone through,' said her mother.

Allen showed the same feeling when he could talk his prospects over quietly with his mother. These four years had altered him at least as much for the better as Elfie. He would not now begin in thoughtless self-indulgence, refined indeed and never vicious, but selfish, extravagant, and heedless of all but ease, pleasure, and culture. Some of the enervation of his youth had really worn off, though it had so long made him morbid, and he had learnt humility by his failures. Above all, however, his intercourse with Fordham had opened his eyes to a sense of the duties of wealth and position, such as he had never before acquired, and the religious habits that had insensibly grown upon him were tincturing his views of life and responsibility.

It was painful to him to realise that he was returning to wealth and luxury, indeed, monopolising it,—he the helpless, undeserving, indolent son, while all the others, and especially his mother, were left to poverty.

Elfie wanted Mother Carey and all to make their home at Belforest, and still be one family as of old. Indeed, she hung on Mother Carey even more than upon Allen, after her long famine from the motherly tenderness that she had once so little appreciated.

Of such an amalgamation, however, Mrs. Brownlow would not hear, nor would she listen to a proposal of settling on her a yearly income, such as would dispense with economy, and with the manufacture of 'pot-boilers.'

No, she said, she was a perverse woman, and she had never been so happy as when living on her husband's earnings. The period of education being over, she had a full sufficiency, and should only meddle with clay again for her own pleasure. She was beginning already a set of dining-table ornaments for a wedding present, representing the early part of the story of Undine. Babie knew why, if nobody else did. Perhaps she should one of these days mould a similar set for Sydney of the crusaders of Jotapata! Then Allen bethought him of putting into Elvira's head to beg, at least, to undertake Armine's expenses at the theological college for a year, and to this she consented thankfully. Armine had been thinking of offering himself as Allen's successor for a year with Sir Samuel; but two days' experience as substitute convinced him that Allen was right in declaring that my Lady would be the death of him. Lucas could manage her, and kept her well-behaved and even polite, but Armine was so young and so deferential that she treated him even worse than she did her first victim! She had begun by insisting on a quarter's notice or the forfeiture of the salary, as long as she thought £25 was of vital importance to Allen, but as soon as she discovered that the young lady was a great heiress, she became most unedifyingly civil, called in great state in Collingwood Street, and went about boasting of having patronised a sort of prince in disguise.

Meantime Dr. Ruthven's offer seemed left in abeyance. Colonel Brownlow had all his son's scruples, and more than his indignation at Lucas's folly in hesitating; and John was so sure that he ought not to accept the proposal, that he would not stir in the matter, nor mention it to Sydney. At last Lucas acted on his own responsibility, and had an interview with Dr. Ruthven, in which he declined the offer for himself, but made it known that his cousin was not only brother to the beautiful Lady Fordham who had been met in Collingwood Street, but was engaged to Lord Fordham's sister. At which connection the fashionable physician rubbed his hands with so much glee, that Jock was the more glad not to have to hunt in couples with him.

The magnificent wedding-dress had been stopped by telegram, just as it was packed for New York, and was despatched to Belforest. Mrs. Wakefield undertook the task imposed upon her, and the wedding was to be grand enough to challenge attention, and not be liable to the accusation of being done in a corner. It might be called hasty, for only a month would have passed since Elvira's arrival, before her wedding-day; but this was by her own earnest wish. She made it no secret that she should never cease to be nervous till she was Allen Brownlow's wife, even though a letter to her cousins at River Hollow had removed all fear of pursuit by Mrs. Gould; she seemed bent on remaining at New York, and complained loudly of 'the ungrateful girl,' whose personal belongings she retained by way of compensation.

It would have been too much to expect that Elvira should be a wise and clever woman, but she had really learnt to be an affectionate one, and in the school of adversity had parted with much of her selfish petulance and arrogance. Allen, whose love had always been blindly tender, more like a woman's or a parent's love than that of an ordinary lover, was rapturous at the response he at last received. At the same time, he knew her too well to expect from her intellectual companionship, and would be quite content with what she could give.

They were both of them chastened and elevated in tone by their five years' discipline.

The night before the party went down to Belforest, where they were to meet the Evelyns, Allen lingered with his mother after all the rest had gone upstairs.

'Mother,' he said, 'I have thought a great deal of that dream of yours. I hope that the touch of Midas may not be baneful this time.'

'I trust not, my dear; you have had a taste of the stern, rugged nurse.'

'And, mother, I know I failed egregiously where the others rose.'

'But you were rising.'

'Then you will let me do nothing for you, and I feel myself sneaking into your inheritance, to the exclusion of all the rest, in a back-door sort of way.'

'My dear Allen, it can't be helped, you have honestly loved your Elf from her infancy, when she had nothing, and she really loved you at the very worst. Love is so much more than gold, that it really signifies very little which of you has the money. You and she have both gone through a good deal, and it depends upon you now whether the possession becomes a blessing to yourselves and others. Don't vex about our not having a share, you know yourself how much happier we all are without the load, and there will never be any anxiety now. I shall always fall back on you, if I want anything.'

'That is right,' said Allen, clearing up a good deal as she looked up brightly in his face. 'You promise me.'

'Of course I do,' she said, smiling. 'I'm not proud.'

'And you did make Armine consent to our paying those expenses of his. That was good of you, but the boy only does it out of obedience.'

'Yes, he would like a little bit of self-willed penance, but it is much better for him to submit, bodily and mentally.'

'Elvira has asked me whether we can't, after all, build the church and all the rest which he wanted so much, and give it to him.'

Caroline smiled, she would not vex Allen by saying how this was merely in the spirit of the story book, endowing everybody with what they wanted, but she said, 'Build by all means, and endow when you have had time to see what is needed, and what is good for the people, but not for Armine's sake, you know He had much better serve his apprenticeship and learn his work somewhere else. He would tell you so himself.'

'I daresay. He would talk of the touch of Midas again. Elvira will be sadly disappointed. She had some fancy of presenting him to it as soon as he was ordained!'

'Getting the fairies meantime to build the whole concern in secret? Dear Elfie, her plans are generous and kind. Tell her, with my love, that her church must not be a shrine for Armine, but that perhaps he and it will be fit for each other in some five years' time. Meantime, if she wants to make somebody happy, there's that excellent hard-working curate of Eleanor's, who has done more good in Kenminster than I ever saw done there before.'

'I don't see why Kencroft should get *all* the advantages!'

'Ah! You ungrateful boy! Now if Rob had carried off Elfie, you might complain!'

At which Allen could not but laugh.

'And now, good-night, Mr. Bridegroom; you want your beauty sleep, though I must say you look considerably younger than you did two months ago.'

The wedding was a bright one, involving no partings, only joy and gladness, and the sole drawback to the general rejoicings seemed to be that it was not Mrs. Brownlow herself who was returning to take possession.

But on that very afternoon came a chill on her heart. Her own letter and Elvira's to Janet were returned from America! It was quite probable that the right address might have been in Elvira's lost note, and that Janet might be easily found through the photographer. 'But,' said her mother, 'I do not believe she will ever come home unless I go to fetch her.'

'The very thing I was thinking of doing,' said Jock. 'Letters will hardly find her now, and I have not settled to anything. The dear old Doctor's legacy will find the means.'

'And I am sure you want the rest of the voyage. I don't like the looks of you, my Jockey.'

'I shall be all right when *this* is over,' said Jock, with an endeavour at laughing; 'but I find I am a greater fool than I thought I was, and I had much better be out of the way of it all till it is a *fait accompli*.'

'It' was of course John's marriage. This was the first time Jock had seen the lovers together. In spite of vehement talking and laughing, warm greetings to every one, and playing at every interval with the little cousins, Jock could not hide from either of the mothers that the sight cost him a good deal, all the more because the showing the Belforest haunts to Sydney had always been a favourite scheme, hitherto unfulfilled; nor was there any avoiding family consultations, which resulted in the fixing of the wedding for the middle of September, so that there might be time for a short tour before they settled down to John's work in London.

Mrs. Evelyn begged that Barbara would come to her whilst her mother and brother were away; Armine would be at his theological college, and there was nothing to detain Mrs. Brownlow and her son from the journey, to which both looked forward with absolute pleasure, not only in the hope of the meeting, but in the being together, and throwing off for a time the cares of home and gratifying the spirit of enterprise.

Jock had one secret. He had reason to think that Bobus

would have a kind of vacation at the time, and he telegraphed to Japan what their intended voyage was to be, with a hope he durst not tell, that his favourite brother would not throw away the opportunity of meeting them in America.

## CHAPTER XL

### EVIL OUT OF GOOD

'And all too little to atone
For knowing what should ne'er be known.'

SCOTT.

THE season at Saratoga was not yet over, the travellers were told at New York, though people were fast thronging back into 'the city.' Should they go on thither at once, or try to find the photographer nearer at hand? It was on a Friday that they . landed, and they resolved to wait till Monday, Jock thinking that a rest would be better for his mother.

The early autumn sun glowed on the broad streets as they walked slowly through them, halting to examine narrowly every display of portraits at a photographer's door.

It was a right course; they came upon some exquisitely-finished ones, among which they detected unmistakably the coloured likeness of Elvira de Menella. They went into the studio and asked to look at it. 'Ah, many ask that,' they were told, 'though the sensation was a little gone by.'

'What sensation?' Jock asked, while his mother trembled so much that she had to sit down on one of the velvet chairs.

'I guess you are a stranger, sir, from England? Then no doubt you have not heard of the great event of the season at Saratoga, the sudden elopement of this young lady, a beautiful English heiress, on the eve of marriage, these very portraits ordered for the bridesmaids' lockets.'

'Whom did she elope with?' asked Jock.

'That's the remarkable part of it, sir. Some say that she was claimed in secret by a lover to whom she had been long much attached; but we are better informed. I can state to a certainty that she only fled to escape the tyranny of an aunt. She need only have appealed to the institutions of the country.'

'Very true,' said Jock. 'Let me ask if your informant was not the lady who coloured this photograph, Mrs. Harte?' 'Yes.' 'And is she here?'

'No, sir,' with some hesitation.

'Can you give me her address? I am her brother. This lady is her mother, and we are very anxious to find her.'

The photographer was gained by the frank address and manner. 'I am sorry,' he said, 'but the truth is that there was a monster excitement about the disappearance of the girl, and as Mrs. Harte was said to have been concerned, there was constant resort to the studio to interview her ; and I cannot but think she treated me ill, sir, for she quitted me at an hour's notice.'

'And left no address?' exclaimed her mother, grievously disappointed.

'Not with me, madam ; but she was intimate with a young lady employed in our establishment, and she may know where to find her.'

And, through a tube, the photographer issued a summons, which resulted in the appearance of a pleasant-looking girl, who, on hearing that Mrs. Harte's mother and brother were in search of her, readily responded that Mrs. Harte had written to her a month ago from Philadelphia, asking her to forward to her any letters that might come to the room she usually occupied at New York. She had found employment, and there could be no doubt that she would be heard of there.

It was very near now. There was something very soothing in the services of that Sunday of waiting, when the church seemed a home on the other side the sea, and on the Monday they were on their way, hearing, but scarcely heeding, the talk in the cars of the terrible yellow-fever visitation then beginning at New Orleans.

They arrived too late to do anything, but in early morning they were on foot, breakfasting with the first relay of guests at the hotel, and inquiring their way along the broad tree-planted streets of the old Quaker city.

It was again at a photograph shop that they paused, but as they were looking for the number, the private door opened, and there issued from it a gray figure, with a black hat, and a bag in her hand. She stood on the step, they on the side-walk. She had a thin, worn, haggard face, a strange, gray look about it, but when the eyes met on either side there was not a moment's doubt.

There was not much demonstration. Caroline held out her hand, and Janet let hers be locked tight into it. Jock took her bag from her, and they went two or three paces together as in a dream, till Jock spoke first.

'Where are we going? Can we come back with you, Janet, or will you come to the hotel with us?'

'I was just leaving my rooms,' she said. 'I was on my way to the station.'

'You will come with me,' said Caroline under her breath ; and Janet passively let herself be led along, her mother unconsciously holding her painfully fast.

So they reached the hotel, and then Jock said, 'I shall go and read the papers ; send a message for me if you want me. You had rather be left to yourselves.'

The mother knew not how she reached her bedroom, but once there, and with the door locked, she turned with open arms. 'O Janet, one kiss!' and Janet slid down on the floor before her, hiding her face in her dress and sobbing, 'O mother, mother, I am not worthy of this!'

Then Caroline flung herself down by her, and gathered her into her arms, and Janet rested her head on her shoulder for some seconds, each sensible of little save absolute content.

'And you have come all this way for me?' whispered Janet, at last raising her head to gaze at the face.

'I did so long after you! My poor, poor child, how you have suffered!' said Caroline, drawing through her fingers the thin, worn, bony, hard-worked hand.

'I deserved a thousand times more,' said Janet. 'But it seems all gone since I see you, mother. And if you forgive, I can hope God forgives too.'

'My child! my child!' and as the strong embrace, and the kiss was on her brow, Janet lay still once more in the strange rest and relief. 'It is very strange,' she said. 'I thought the sight of you would wither me with shame, but somehow there's no room for anything but happiness.'

Renewed caresses, for her mother was past speaking.

'And Lucas is with you? Not Babie?'

'No, Babie is left with Mrs. Evelyn.'

'So poor little Elvira came safe home?'

'Yes, and is Mrs. Allen Brownlow. Poor child, you rescued her from a sad fate. She believed to the last you were coming with her, and she lost your note, or you would have heard from us sooner.'

Janet went on asking questions about the others. Her mother dreaded to put any, and only replied. Janet asked where they had been living, and she answered—

'In the old house, while the two Johns have been studying medicine.'

'Not Lucas!' cried Janet, sitting upright in her surprise.

'Yes, Lucas. The dear fellow gave up all his prospects in the army, because he thought it would be more helpful to me for him to take this line, and he has passed so well, Janet. He has got the silver medal, and his essay was the prize one.'

'And——' Janet stood up and walked to the window, as she said 'and you have told him——'

'Yes. But, Janet, it was too late. Some hints of your father's had been followed up, and the main discovery worked out, though not perfected.'

Janet's eyes glistened for a moment as they used to do in angry excitement, and she asked, 'Could he bear it?'

'He was chiefly concerned lest I should be disappointed. Then he reminded me that the benefit to mankind had come all the sooner.'

'Ah!' said Janet with a gasp, 'there's the difference!' She did not explain further, but said, 'It has not poisoned his life!'

Then seeking in her bag, she took out a packet. 'I wish you to know all about it, mother,' she said. 'I wrote this to send home by Elvira, but then my heart failed me. It was well, since she lost my note. I kept it, and when I did not hear from you, I thought I would leave it to be posted when all was over with me. I should like you to read it, and I will tell you anything else you like to know.'

There came the interruption of the hotel luncheon, after which a room was engaged for Janet, and the use of a private parlour secured for the afternoon and evening. Jock came and went. He was very much excited about the frightful reports he heard of the ravages of yellow fever in the south, and went in search of medical papers and reports. Janet directed him where to seek them. 'I was just starting to offer myself as an attendant,' she said. 'I shall still go, to-morrow.'

'You? O Janet, not now!' was her mother's first exclamation.

'You will understand when you have read,' quietly said Janet.

All that afternoon, according to her manifest wish, her mother was reading that confession of hers, while she sat by replying to each question or comment, in the repose of a confidence such as had not existed for fifteen years.

Magnum Bonum (wrote Janet). So my father named it. Alas! it has been Magnum Malum to me. I have thought over how the evil began. I think it must have been when I brooded over the words I caught at my father's death-bed, instead of confessing to my mother that I had over-heard them. It might be reserve and dread of her grief, but it was not wholly so. I did not respect her as I ought in my childish conceit. I was an old-fashioned girl. Grandmamma treated her like a petted eldest child, and I had not learnt to look up to her with any loyalty. My uncle and aunt too, even while seeming to uphold her authority, betrayed how cheaply they held her.

'No wonder,' said Caroline. 'I was a very foolish creature then.'

'I saw you differently too late,' said Janet.

Thus unchecked by any sober word, my imagination went on dwelling on those words, which represented to me an arcanum as wonderful as any elixir of life that alchemists dream of, and I was always figuring to myself the honour and glory of the discovery, and fretting that it was destined to one of my brothers rather than myself. Even then, I had some notion of excelling them, and fretted at our residence at Kenminster because I was cut off from classes and lectures. Then came the fortune, and I saw at the first glance that wealth would hinder all the others, even Robert, from attempting to fulfil the conditions, and I imagined myself persevering and winning the day. As to the concealment of the will, I can honestly say that, to my inexperienced fancy, it appeared utterly unlike my father's and grandmother's, and at the moment I hid it, I only thought of the disturbance and discomfort which scruples of my mother's would create, and the unpleasantness it would make with Elvira, with whom I had just been quarrelling. When as I grew older, and found the validity of wills did not depend on the paper they were written upon, I had qualms which I lulled by thinking that when my education was safe, and Elvira safely married to Allen, I would look again, and then bring it to light, if needful. My mother's refusal to commit the secret to me on any terms entirely alienated me, I am grieved to say. I have learnt since that she was quite right, and that she could not help it. It was only my ignorance that rebelled; but I was enraged enough to have produced the will, and perhaps should have done so, if I had not been afraid both of losing my own medical training, and of causing Robert to take up that line, in which I knew he could succeed better than any one.

'Janet, this must be fancy!'

'No, mother. There's no poison like a blessing turned into a curse. This is the secret history of what made me such a disagreeable, morose girl.'

Then came the opportunity that enabled me to glance at the book of my father's notes. Barbara's eyes made me lock the desk in haste and confusion. It was really and truly accident that I locked the book out instead of in. As you know, Barbara hid away the davenport, and I could not restore the book, when I had pored over it half the night, and found myself quite incompetent to understand the details, though I perceived the main drift. I durst not take the book out of the house, and the loss of my keys cut me off from access to it. Meantime I studied, and came to the perception that a woman alone could never carry out the needful experiments, I must have a man to help me, but I was too much warped by this time to see how my mother was thus justified. I still looked on her as insanely depriving me of my glory, the world of the benefit for a mere narrow scruple. Then I fell in with Demetrius Hermann. How can I tell the story? How he seemed to me the wisest and acutest of human beings, the very man to assist in the discovery, and how I betrayed to him enough by my questions to make him think me a prize, both for my secret and my fortune. He says I deceived him. Perhaps I did. Any way, we are quits. No, not quite, for I loved him as I should not have thought it in me to love any one, and the very joy and gladness of the sensation made me see with his eyes, or else be preposterously blind. I think his southern imagination made his expectations of the secret unreasonable, and I followed his bidding blindly and implicitly in my two attempts to bring off Magnum Bonum, which I had come to believe my right, unjustly withheld from me. The second attempt, as you know, ended in the general crash.

Afterwards, all the overtures were made by my husband. I would not share in them. I was too proud and would not come as a beggar, or see him threaten and cringe as unhappily I knew he could do, nor would I be seen by my mother or brothers. I knew they would begin to pity me, and I could not brook that. My mother's assurance of exposure, if he made any use of the stolen secret, made Demetrius choose to go to America.

'He said it all came out before my military brother. Did that change Lucas's destination?' said Janet, looking up.

'Ask him.'

'No, indeed,' said Jock, when he understood. 'I turned doctor as the readiest way of looking after mother.'

'Did you understand nothing?'

'Only that she had some memoranda of my father's, that the sc— that Hermann wanted. I never thought of them again till she told me.'

Mrs. Brownlow started at the next few words.

My child was born only two days after we landed at New York.

But a quick interrogative glance kept her silent.

She was very small and delicate, and her father was impatient both of her weakness and mine. I think that was when I began to long for my mother. He made me call her Glykera, after his mother. I had taught him to be bitter against mine.

'O mother, if you could have seen her,' suddenly exclaimed Janet, 'she was the dearest little thing,' and she drew from her bosom a locket with a baby face on one side, and some soft hair on the other, put it into her mother's hand and hid her face on her shoulder.

'Oh! my poor Janet, you have suffered indeed! How long did you keep the little darling?'

'Two years. You will hear! I was not quite wretched while I had her. Go on, mother. There's no talking of it.'

We tried both practising and lecturing, feeling our way meantime towards the Magnum Bonum. We found, however, in the larger cities that people were quite as careful about qualifications as at home, and that we wanted recommendations. I could have got some practice among women if Demetrius would have rested long enough anywhere, but he liked lecturing best. I had been obliged to perceive that he had very little real science, and indeed I had to give him the facts and he put them in his flowery language. While as to Magnum Bonum, he had gained enough to use it in a kind of haphazard way, for everything. I trembled at what he began doing with it, when in the course of our wanderings we got out of the more established regions into the south-west. In Texas we found a new township, called Burkeville, without a resident medical man, and the fame of his lectures had gone far enough for him to be accepted. There we set up our staff, and Demetrius—it makes me sick to say so—tried to establish himself as the possessor of a new and certain cure. I was persuaded that he did not know how to manage it, I tried to make him understand that under certain conditions it might be fatal, but he thought I was jealous. He had had one or two remarkable successes, his fame was spreading, he was getting reckless, and I could not watch as carefully as I sometimes did, for my child was ill, and needed all my care. The favourite of all the parish was the minister's daughter, a beautiful, lively, delicate girl, loved and followed like a sort of queen by the young men, of whom there were many, while there were hardly any other young women, none to compare with her. Demetrius had lost some patients, it was a sickly season, and I fancy there was some mistrust and exasperation against him already, for he was incompetent, and grew more averse to consulting me when his knowledge was at fault. I need not blame him.

Every one at home knows that I do not always make myself agreeable,
and I had enough to exacerbate me, with my child pining in the unhealthy
climate, and my father's precious secret used with the rough ignorance of
an empiric.  I knew enough of the case of this Annie Field to be sure that
there were features in it which would make that form of treatment
dangerous.  I tried to make him understand.  He thought me jealous of
his being called in rather than myself.  Well—she died, and such a storm
of vengeance arose as is possible in those lawless parts.  I knew and
heeded nothing of it, for my little Glykera was worse every day, and I
thought of nothing else, but it seems that reports unfavourable to us had
come from some one of the cities where we had tried to settle, and thus
grief and rage had almost maddened one of Annie's lovers, a young man
of Irish blood, a leader among the rest.  On the day of her funeral all the
ruffianism in the place was up in arms against us.  My husband had warning, I suppose, for I never saw or heard of him since he went out that
morning, leaving me with my little one moaning on my lap.  She was
growing worse every hour, and I knew nothing else, till my door was burst
open by a little boy of eight or ten years old, crying out, 'Mrs. Hermann,
Mrs. Hermann, quick, they are coming to lynch you ! come away, bring
the baby.  If father can't stop them, there's no place safe but our house.'

And indeed upon the air came the sound of a great, horrible, yelling
roar unspeakably dreadful.  It seems never to have been out of my ears
since.  I do not know whether an American mob would have proceeded
to extremities with a lonely woman and dying child, but there was an
Irish and Spanish element of ferocity at Burkeville, and the cold, hard
Englishwoman was unpopular ; besides that, I was supposed to share in
the irregular practice that had had such fatal effects.  But with that
horrible sound, one did not stop to weigh probabilities.  I gathered up
my child in her bed-clothes, and followed the boy out at the back door,
blindly.  And where do you think I found myself ? where but in the
minister's house ?  His wife, whose daughter had just been carried out to
her grave, rose up from weeping and praying, to take me into the innermost chamber, where none could see me, and when she saw my darling's
state, to give me all the help and sympathy a good woman could.  Oh !
that was my first true knowledge of Christian charity.

Mr. Field himself was striving at the very grave itself to turn away the
rage of these men against those whom they held his daughter's murderers,
but he was as nothing against some fifty or sixty gathered, I suppose, some
by real or fancied wrongs, some from mere love of violence.  Any way,
when he found himself powerless against the infuriated speeches of the
young Irish lover, he put his little boy over the graveyard wall, and sent
him off to take me to the last place where the mob would look for me, the
very room where Annie died.  Those howls and yells round the empty
house, perhaps, too, the shaking of my rapid run, hastened the end with
my precious child.  I do not believe she could have lived many hours,
but the fright brought on shudderings and convulsions, and she was gone
from me by nine that evening.  They might have torn me to pieces then,
and I would have thanked them !  I cannot tell you the goodness of the
Fields.  It could not comfort me then, but I have wondered over it often
since.  [There were blistered, blotted tear-marks here.]  They knew it
was not safe for me to remain, for there had been wild talk of a warrant
out against us for manslaughter.  They would have had me leave my
little darling's form to their care, but they saw I dreaded (unreasonably I
now think) some insult from those ruffians for her father's sake.  Mr.

Field said I should lay my little one to her rest myself. They found a long basket like a cradle. We laid her there in her own night-dress, looking so sweet and lovely. Mr. Field himself went out and dug the little grave, close to Annie's, and there by mooonlight we laid her, and the good man put one of the many wreaths from Annie's grave upon hers, and there we knelt and he prayed. I don't know what denomination his may be, but a Christian I know he is. Cruel as the very sight of me must have been, they kept me in bed all the next day ; and the minister went to see what he could save for me. Finding no one, the mob had wreaked their vengeance on our medicine bottles and glasses, smashed everything, and made terrible havoc of all our books, clothes, and furniture. Almost the only thing Mr. Field had found unhurt was mother's little Greek Testament, which I had carried about, but utterly neglected till then. Mr. Field saw my name in it, brought it to me, and kindly said he was glad to restore it ; none could be utterly desolate whose study lay there. I was obliged to tell him how you had sent it after me with that entreaty, which I had utterly neglected, and you can guess how he urged it on me.

'You have gone on now?' said her mother, looking up at her.

Janet's reply was to produce the little book from her hand-bag, showing marks of service, and then to open it at the fly-leaf. There Caroline herself had written 'Janet Hermann,' with the reference to St. Luke xv. 20. She had not dared to write more fully, but the good minister of Burkeville had, at Janet's desire, put his own initials, and likewise written in full :

'Refrain thy voice from weeping, and thine eyes from tears, for thy work shall be rewarded, saith the Lord, and they shall come again from the land of the enemy. And there is hope in thine end, saith the Lord, that thy children shall come again to their own border.'

'He might have written it for me,' said Caroline. 'My child —one at least is come to me.'

'Or you have gone into her far country to seek her,' said Janet.

'Can I write to this good man?' asked Caroline. 'I do long to thank him.'

'Oh yes. I wrote to him only the day before yesterday.'

There was but little more of the narrative.

At night he borrowed a waggon, and drove me to a station in time to take the early train for the north-east, supplying me with means for the journey, and giving me a letter to a family relation of his, in New York State. I was most kindly sheltered there for a few days while I looked out for advertisements. I found, however, that I must change my name, for the history of the Burkeville affair was copied into all the papers, and there were warnings against the two impostors, giving my maiden name likewise, as that in which my Zurich diploma had been made out. This cut me off from all medical employment, and I had to think what else I could do, not that I cared much what became of me. Seeing a notice that an assistant was wanted to colour and finish photographs, I thought my drawing, though only schoolroom work, might serve. I applied, showed specimens, and was thought satisfactory. I sent my address to Mr. Field, who had promised to let me know in case my husband made any attempt to trace me, or if I could find my way back to him, but up to this time I have heard absolutely nothing. The few white days in my life are, however, when I get a cheering, comforting letter from him. How I should once have laughed their phraseology to scorn, but then I did not know what reality meant, and they are the only balm of my life now, except mother's little book, and what they have led me to.

But you see why I cannot come with Elvira. Not only do I not dare to meet my mother, but it might bring down upon her one whom she could not welcome. Besides, it is clearly fit that I should strive to meet him again ; I would try to be less provoking to him now.

'I see, my dear,' said Caroline. 'But why did you never draw on Mr. Wakefield all this time?'

'I never thought we ought to take that money,' said Janet. 'I could maintain myself, and that was all I wanted. Besides, I was ashamed to bid him use a false name, and I durst not receive a letter under my own, nor did I know whether Demetrius might go on applying.'

'He did once, saying that you were unwell, but Mr. Wakefield declined to let him be supplied without your signature.'

Janet eagerly asked the when and the where.

'I am glad,' said her mother, 'to find that your change of name was not in order to elude him, as I feared at first.'

'No,' said Janet, 'he never knew he was cruel, but he had made a mistake altogether in me. I was a disappointment to begin with, owing to my own bad management, you see, for if I had brought off the book, and destroyed the will, his speculation would have succeeded. And then, for his comfort, he should have married a passive, ignorant, senseless, obedient Oriental, and he did not know what to do with a cold, proud thing, who looked most hard when most wretched, who had understanding enough to see his blunders, and remains of conscience enough to make her sour. Poor Demetrius ! He had the worst of the bargain ! And now——' She turned the leaf of the manuscript, and showed, with a date three days back—

Mr. Field has written to me, sending a cutting of an advertisement of a month back of a spiritualist from Abville, which he thinks may be my husband's. I am sure it is, I know the Greek idiom put into English. It decides me on what I had thought of before. I shall offer my services as nurse or physician, or whatever they will let me be in that stress of need. I may find him, or if he have fled, I may, if I live, trace him. At any rate, by God's grace, I may thus endeavour to make a better use of what has never yet been used for His service.

And in case I should add no further words to this, let me conclude by telling my dear, dear mother that my whole soul and spirit are asking her forgiveness, and by sending my love to my brothers and sister, whom I love far better now than ever I did when I was with them. And to Elvira too—perhaps she is my sister by this time.

Let them try henceforth to think not unkindly of

JANET HERMANN.

This had been enclosed in an envelope addressed to Mrs. Joseph Brownlow, to the care of Wakefield and Co., solicitors.

'You see I cannot go back with you, mother dear,' she said, 'though you have come to seek me.'

'Not yet,' said Caroline, handing the last page to Jock, who had come back again from one of his excursions.

'Look here, Janet,' said Jock, 'mother will not forbid it, I know. If you will wait another day for me to arrange for her, I will go with you. This is a place specially mentioned as in frightful need of medical attendance, and I already doubted whether I ought not to volunteer, but if you have an absolute call of duty there, that settles it. Mother, do you remember that American clergyman who dined with us? I met him just now. He begged me with all his heart to persuade you to come and stay with his family. I believe he is going to bring his wife to call. I am sure they would take care of you.'

'I don't want care. Jock, Jock, why should I not go and help? Do you think I can send my children into the furnace without me?'

Jock came and sat down by her with his specially consoling caress. 'Mother dear, I don't think you ought. We are trained to it, you see, and it is part of our vocation; besides, Janet has a call. But your nursing would not make much difference, and besides, you don't belong only to us—Armine and Babie need their home. And suppose poor Bobus came back. No, I am accountable to them all. They didn't send me out in charge of my Mother Carey that I should run her into the jaws of Yellow Jack. I can't do it, mother. I should mind my own business far less if I were thinking about you. It would be just like your coming after me into a general engagement.'

'Lucas is quite right,' said Janet. 'You know, mother, this is a special kind of nursing, that one does not understand by the light of nature, and you are not strong enough or tough enough for it.'

'I flattered myself I was pretty tough,' said her mother, with trembling lip. 'What sort of a place is it? Could not I—even if you won't let me nurse—be near enough to rest you, and feed you, and disinfect you? That is my trade, Jock will allow, as a doctor's wife and mother. And I could collect things and send them to the sick. Would that not be possible, my dears?'

Jock said he would find out. And then he told them he had found a church with a daily service, to which they went.

And then those three had a wonderfully happy evening together.

## CHAPTER XLI

### GOOD OUT OF EVIL

'How the field of combat lay
By the tomb's self ; how he sprang from ambuscade—
Captured Death, caught him in that pair of hands.'
BROWNING.

'JOHN,' said Sydney, as they were taking their last walk together as engaged people on the banks of their Avon, 'there's something I think I ought to tell you.'

'Well, my dearest.'

'Don't they say that there ought not to be any shadow of concealment of the least little liking for any one else, when one is going to be married ?' quoth Sydney, not over lucidly.

'I'm sure I can safely acquit myself of any such shadow,' said John, laughing. 'I never had the least little liking for anybody but Mother Carey, and that wasn't a least little one at all !'

'Well, John, I'm very much ashamed of it, because he didn't care for me, as it turned out ; but if he had, as I once thought, I should have liked him,' said Sydney, looking down, and speaking with great confusion out of the depths of her conscience, stirred up by much 'Advice to Brides' and Sunday novels, all turning on the lady's error in hiding her first love ; and then perhaps because the effect on John was less startling than she had expected, she added with another effort, 'It was Lucas Brownlow.'

'Jock !' cried John. 'The dear fellow !'

'Yes—I did think it, when he was in the Guards, and always about with Cecil. It was very silly of me, for he did not care one fraction.'

'Why do you think so ?' said John hoarsely.

'Well, I know better now, but when he made up his mind to leave the army, I fancied it was no better than being a recreant knight, and I begged and prayed him to go out with Sir Philip Cameron, and as near as I dared told him it was for my sake. But he went on all the same, and then I was quite sure he did not care, and saw what a goose I had made of myself. Oh, Johnnie, it has been very hard to tell you, but I thought I ought, and I hope you'll never think of it more, for Lucas just despised my foolish forwardness, and you know you have every bit of my heart and soul. What is the matter, John ? Oh ! have I done harm when I meant to do right ?'

'No, no, my darling, don't be startled. But do you mean that you really thought Jock's disregard of your entreaties came from indifference ?'

'It was all one mixture of pain and anger,' said Sydney. 'I can't define it. I thought it was one's duty to lead a man to be courageous and defend his country, and of course he thought me *such* a fool. Why, he has never really talked to me since!'

'And you thought it was indifference,' again repeated John, with an iteration worthy of his father.

'Oh, John, you frighten me. Wasn't it? Did you know this before?'

'No, most certainly not. I did know thus much, that in giving up the army Jock had given up his dearest hopes; but I thought it was some fine fashionable lady, whom he was well rid of, though he didn't know it. And he never said a word to betray it, even when I came home brimful and overflowing with happiness. And you know it was his doing that my way has been smoothed. O Sydney, I don't know how to look at it!'

'But indeed, John dear, I couldn't help loving you best. You saved me, you know, and I feel to fit in, and understand you best. I can't be sorry as it has turned out.'

'That's very well,' said John, trying to laugh, 'for you couldn't be transferred back to him, like a bale of goods. And I could not have helped loving you; but that I should have been a robber, Jock's worst enemy!'

'I can't be sorry you did not guess it,' said Sydney. 'Then I never should have had you, and somehow——'

'And you thought him wanting in courage,' recurred John.

'Only when I was wild and silly, talking out of the *Traveller's Joy*. It was hearing about his going into that dreadful place that stirred it all up in my mind, because I saw what a hero he is.'

'God grant he may come safe out of it!' said John. 'I'll tell you what, Sydney, though, it is a shame, when I am the gainer: I think your romance went astray; more faith and patience would have waited to see the real hero come out, and so you have missed him and got the ordinary jog-trot, commonplace fellow instead.'

'Ah! but love must be at the bottom of faith and patience,' said Sydney, 'and that was scared away by shame at my own forwardness and foolishness. And now it is all gone to the jog-trot! I want no better hero!'

'What a confession for the maiden of the twelfth century!'

'I'm very glad you don't feel moved to start off to the yellow fever.'

'Do you know, Sydney, I do not know what I don't feel moved to sometimes, I cannot understand this silence!'

'But you said the telegram that he was mending was almost better than if he had never been ill at all.'

'So I thought then; but why do we not hear, if all is well with them?'

Three weeks since, a telegram had been received by Allen, containing the words, 'Janet died at 2.30 A.M. Lucas mending.'

It had been resolved not to put off the wedding, as much in-

convenience would have been caused, and poor Janet was only
cousin to John, and had been removed from all family interests
so long, even Mrs. Robert Brownlow saw no impropriety, since
Barbara went to Belforest for a fortnight, returning to Mrs.
Evelyn on the afternoon of the wedding-day itself to assist in
her move to the Dower House. Esther, who had never professed
to wish for a hero, had been so much disturbed by the recent
alarms of war, that she was only anxious that her Guardsman
should safely sell out in the interval of peace ; and he had
begun to care enough about the occupations at Fordham to wish
to be free to make it his chief dwelling-place.

The wedding was as quiet as possible. Sydney was disappointed of the only bridesmaid she cared much about, and
Barbara felt a kind of relief in not having a second time to
assist at the destruction of a brother's hopes. She was very
glad to get back to Fordham, reporting that Allen and Elvira
were so devotedly in love that a third person was very much *de
trop;* though they had been very kind, and Elvira had mourned
poor Janet with real gratitude and affection. Still they did not
take half so much alarm at the silence as she did, and she was
relieved to be with the Evelyns, who were becoming very
anxious. The bridegroom and bride could not bear to go out
of reach of intelligence, and had limited their tour to the nearest
place on the coast, where they could hear by half a day's
post.

No news had come except that seven American papers had
been forwarded to Barbara, giving brief accounts of the pesti-
lence in the southern cities. The numbers of deaths in Abville
were sensibly decreased, one of these papers said. The arrival
of an English physician, Dr. Lucas Brownlow, and his sister
had been noticed, and also that the sister had succumbed to the
disease, but that he was recovering. These were all, however,
only up to the date of the telegram, and the sole shadow of encouragement was in the assurances that any really fatal news
would have been telegraphed. Mrs. Evelyn and Barbara were
very loving companions during this time. Together they looked
over those personal properties of Duke's which rather belonged
to his mother than his heir Mrs. Evelyn gave Barbara several
which had special associations for her, and together they read
over his papers and letters, laughing tenderly over those that
awoke droll remembrances, and perfectly entering into one
another's sympathies.

'Yet, my dear,' said Mrs. Evelyn, 'I do not know whether I
ought to let you dwell on this : you are too young to be looking
back on a grave when all life is before you.'

'Nay,' said Babie, 'it was he that showed me how to look
right on through life ! You cannot tell how delightful it is to
me to be brought near to him again, now I can understand him
so much better than ever I did when he was here.'

'Yet it was always his fear that he might sadden your life.'

'Sadden? Oh no! It was he who put life into my hands, as something worth using,' said Babie. 'Don't you know it is the great glory and quiet secret treasure of my heart that, as Jock said that first night, I have that love not for time but eternity?'

And their thoughts could not but go back to the travellers in America, and all the possibilities, for were not whole families swept off by the disease, without power of communication?

However, at last, four days after the wedding, Barbara received a letter.

ASHTON VINEYARD, VIRGINIA, 30th September.

MY DEAREST BABIE—I have left you too long without tidings, but I have had little time, and no heart to write, and I could not bear to send such news without details. Of the ten terrible days at Abville I may, if I can, tell you when we meet. I was in a sort of country-house a little above the valley of the shadow of death, preparing supplies, and keeping beds ready for any of the exhausted workers who could snatch a rest in the air of the hill. I scarcely saw my poor Janet. She had made out that her husband had been one of the first victims, before she even guessed at his being there. She only came once to tell me this, and they would not even allow me to come down to the church, where all the clergy, doctors, and sisters who could, used to meet every morning and evening.

On the tenth day she brought home Jock, smitten down after incessant exertion. Every one allows that he saved more cases than any one, though he says it was the abatement of the disease. Janet declares that his was a slight attack. If *that* was slight! She attended to him for two days, then told me the crisis was past and that he would live, and almost at the same time her strength failed her. The last thing she said consciously to me was, 'Don't waste time on me. I know these symptoms. Attend to Jock. That is of use. Only forgive and pray for me.' Very soon she was insensible, and was gone before twenty-four hours were over. The sister whom they spared to help me said she was too much worn out to struggle and suffer like most, indeed as Jock had done.

That Sister Dorothea, a true divine gift, a sweet and fair vision of peace, is a Miss Ashton, a Virginian. She broke down, not with the disease, only fatigue, and I gave her such care as I could spare from my dear boy. When her father, General Ashton, came to take her home, he kindly insisted on likewise carrying us off to his beautiful home, on a lovely hillside, where we trusted Jock's strength would be restored quickly. But perhaps we were too impatient, for the journey was far too much for him. He fainted several times, and the last miles were passed in an unconscious state. There has come back on him the intermittent fever which often succeeds the disease; and what is more alarming is the faintness, oppression, and difficulty of breathing, which he believes to be connected with the slight affection of heart remaining from his rheumatic fever at Schwarenbach. Then it is very difficult to give him nourishment except disguised with ice, and he is altogether fearfully ill. I send such an account of the case as I can get for John or Dr. Medlicott to see. How I long for our kind home friends! This place is, unhappily, very far from everywhere, a lone village in the hills; the nearest doctor twelve miles off. The Ashtons think highly of him; but he is old, and I can't say that I have any confidence in his treatment. Jock allows that he should do otherwise, but he says he

has no vigour or connection of ideas to be fit to treat himself consistently,
and that he should only do harm by interfering with Dr. Vanbro; indeed
I fear he thinks that it does not make much difference. If patience and
calmness can bring him through, he would live, but, my dear Babie, I
greatly dread that I shall not bring him back to the home he made so
bright. He seldom rouses into talking much, but lies passive and half
dozing when the feverish restlessness is not on him. He told me just now
to send his love to you all, especially to the Monk and Sydney, with all
dear good wishes to them both. No one can be kinder than the Ashtons;
they are always trying to help in the nursing, and sending for everything
that can be thought of for Jock. Sister Dorothea and Primrose are as
good and loving as Sydney herself could be, and there is an excellent
clergyman who comes in every day, and prays for my boy in church.
Ask them to do the same at Fordham, and at our own churches. As long
as I do not telegraph, remember that while there is life there is hope.—
Your loving                                             MOTHER C.

This letter was sent on to John. Two days later a fly drove
up to the Dower House, and Sydney walked into the drawing-
room alone.

Where did she come from?

From Liverpool. John was gone to America.

'I wanted to go too,' she said, tears coming into her eyes;
'but he said he could go faster without me, and he could not
take me to these Ashtons, or leave me alone in New York.'

'It was very noble and good in you to let him go, Sydney,'
cried Babie.

'It would have broken his heart for ever,' said Sydney, 'if he
had not tried to do his utmost for Jock. He says Jock has been
more than a brother to him, and that he owes all that he is, and
all that he has, to him and Mother Carey, and that even—if—if
he were too late, he should save her from coming home alone.
You think he was right, mamma?'

'Right indeed, and I am thankful that my Sydney was unselfish, and did not try to keep him back.'

'Oh, mamma, I could never have looked him in the face again
if I had hindered him! And so we went up to London, and
luckily Dr. Medlicott was at home, and he was very eager that
John should go. He says he does not think it will be too late,
and they talked it over, and got some medicines, and then John
let me come down to Liverpool with him and see him on board,
and we telegraphed the last thing to Mrs. Brownlow, so that it
might be too late for her to stop him.' While that message was
rushing on its way beneath the Atlantic, it was the early morning of the ebb tide of the fever, and the patient was resting
almost doubled over with his head on pillows before him, either
slumber or exhaustion, so still that his mother had yielded to
urgent persuasion and lain down in the next room to sleep in
the dreamless repose of the overworn watcher.

For over him leant a sturdy, dark-browed, dark-bearded
figure, to whom she had ventured to entrust him. Some four-

teen hours before, Robert had with some difficulty found them
out at Ashton Vineyard, having been irresistibly drawn by
Jock's telegram to spend in the States an interval of leisure in
his work, caused by his appointment as principal to another
Japanese college. He had gone to the bank where Jock had
given an address, and his consternation had been great on
hearing the state of things. All this, however, he had left
unexplained, and his mother had hardly even thought of asking
where he had dropped from. For Jock was in the midst of one
of his cruellest attacks of the fever, and all she had been
conscious of was a knock and summons to the door, where Primrose Ashton gently whispered, ' Here is some one you will be
glad to see !' and Robert's low deep voice, almost inaudible with
emotion, asked, ' May I see him ?'

'He will not know you,' she said, with the sad composure of
one who has no time to grieve. But even in the midst of the
babbling moan of fevered weakness, there was half a smile as
of pleased surprise, and an evident craving for the strong support of his brother's arm, and by and by Jock looked up with
meaning and recognition in his eyes, though quite unable to
speak, in that faint and exhausted state indeed that verged
nearer to death after every attack.

This had passed enough for her to know there would be a
respite for perhaps a good many hours, and she had yielded to
the entreaty or command of Bobus that she would lie down and
sleep, trusting to him to call her at any moment.

Presently, as morning light stole in, Jock's eyes were open,
gazing at him fondly, and he whispered, ' Dear old Bob,' then
presently, 'Open the window.'

The sun was rising, and the wooded hillside opposite was all
one gorgeous mass of autumn colouring, of every shade from
purple to golden yellow, so glorious that it arrested Bobus's
attention even at that instant.

'Beautiful, isn't it ?' asked the feeble voice.

'Wonderful, as we always heard.'

'Lift me a little. I like to see it. Not fast—or high—so.'

Bobus raised the white wasted form, and rested the head
against his square firm shoulder. 'Dear old Bob! This is
jolly! I'm not cramping you ?'

'Oh no, but should not you have something ?'

'What time is it ?'

'6.30.'

'Too soon yet for that misery ;' then, after some silence, 'I'm
so glad you are come. Can you take mother home ?'

'I would ; but you will.'

'I don't think so.'

'Now, Jock, you are not getting into Armine's state of mind,
giving yourself up and wishing to die ?'

'Not at all. There are hosts of things I want to do first.
There's that discovery of father's. With what poor Janet told

me of Hermann's doings, and what I saw at Abville, if I could only get an hour of my proper wits, I could put the others up to a wrinkle that would make the whole thing comparatively plain.'

'Should not you be better if you dictated it, and got it off your mind?'

'So I thought and tried, but presently I saw mother looking queer, and she said I was tired, and had gone on enough. I made her read it to me afterwards, and I had gone off into a muddle, and said something that would have been sheer murder. So I had better leave it alone. Old Vanbro mistrusts every word I say because of the Hermann connection, and indeed I may not always have talked sense to him. Those things work out in God's own time, and the Monk is on the track. I'd like to have seen him, but I've got you.'

This had been said in faint slow utterances, so low that Bobus could hardly have heard a couple of feet farther off, and with intervals between, and there was a gesture of tender perfect content in the contact with him that went to his heart, and, before he was aware, a great hot tear came dropping down on Jock's forehead and caused an exclamation.

'I beg your pardon,' said Bobus. 'O Jock, you don't know what it is to find you like this. I came with so much to ask and talk of to you.'

Jock looked up inquiringly.

'You were right to suppress that paper of mine,' continued Bobus, 'I wouldn't have written it now. I have seen better what a people are without Christianity, be the code what it may, and the civilisation, it can't produce such women as my mother, no, nor such men as you, Jockey, my boy,' he muttered much lower.

'Are you coming back, dear old man?' said Jock, with eyes fixed on him.

'I don't know. Tell me one thing, old man : I always thought, when you took to using your brains and getting up physical science, that you must get beyond what satisfied you as a soldier. Now, have the two, science and religion, never clashed, or have you kept them apart?'

'They've worked in together,' said Jock.

'You don't say so because you ought, and think it good for me?'

'As if I could, lying here. "All Thy works praise Thee, O God, and Thy saints do magnify Thee."'

Bobus was not sure whether this were a conscious reply, or only wandering, and his mother here came in, wakened by the murmur of voices.

The brothers could not bear to lose sight of one another, though Jock was too much exhausted by this conversation, and by the sickness that followed any endeavour to take food, to speak much again. Thus, when the rector came, Bobus asked whether he must be sent out of the room ; Jock made an earnest sign to the contrary, and he stayed.

There was of course nothing to concern him, especially in the brief reading and prayer ; but his mother, looking up, saw that he was finding out the passage in the little Greek Testament.

Janet's lay on a little table close by the bedside. The two copies had met again. The work of one was done. Was the work of the other doing at last?

However that might be, nothing could be gentler, tenderer, or more considerate towards his mother than was Bobus, and her kind friends felt much relieved of their fears for her, since she had such a son to take care of her.

Towards the evening, the negro servant knocked at the door, and Bobus took from him a telegram envelope. His mother opened it and read—

Friar Brownlow to Mrs. Brownlow. I embark to-day.

A smile shone out on Jock's white weary face, and he said, 'Good old Monk ! If I can but hold out till he comes, I shall get home again yet. I should like to do him credit.'

ASHTON VINEYARD, 12th October.

MY DEAREST CHILD—You know the main fact by telegram, and now I can write, I must tell you all in more order. We thought our darkest hour was over when the dear John's telegram came, and the hope helped us up a little while. To Jock himself it was like a drowning man clinging to a rope with the more exertion because he knew that a boat was putting off. At least so it was at first, but as his strength faded, his brain could not grasp the notion any longer, and he generally seemed to be fancying himself on the snow with Armine, still, however, looking for John to come and save them, and sometimes, too, talking about Cecil, and being a true brother in arms, a faithful servant and soldier. The long severe strain of study, work, and all the rest which he has gone through, body and mind, coming on a heart already not quite sound, throughout the past year, was, John thinks, the real reason of his being unable to rally when the fever had brought him down, after the dreadful exertion at Abville. Dear fellow, he never let us guess how much his patience cost him. I think we had looked to John's arrival as if it would act like magic, and it was very sore disappointment when his treatment was producing no change for the better, but the prostration went on day after day. Poor Bobus was in utter despair, and went raging about, declaring that he had been a fool ever to expect anything from Kencroft, and at last he had to be turned out of the sick-room. For I should tell you that the one thing that kept me up was the entire calm, grave composure that John preserved throughout, and which gave him the entire command. He never showed any consternation or dismay, nor uttered an augury, but he went quietly and vigilantly on, in a manner that all along gave me a strange sense of confidence and trust, that all that could be done was being done, and the issue was in higher hands. He would not let any one really help him but Sister Dorothea, with her trained skill as a nurse. I don't think even I should have been suffered in the room, if he had not thought Jock might be more conscious than was apparent, for he had not himself received one token of recognition all those three days. Poor Bobus ! the little gleam of light that Jock had let in on him seemed all gone. I do not know what would have become of him but for the good Ashtons. He had been persuaded for a time that what was so real to Jock must be true; but when Jock was no longer conscious, he had nothing to help him, and I am afraid he spoke terrible words when Primrose talked of prayer and faith. I believe he declared that to see one like his brother snatched away when just come to the perfection of his early manhood, with all his capacity and all his knowledge in vain, convinced him either that this universe was one grim, pitiless machine, grinding down humanity by mere law of necessity, or if they would have it that there was supernatural power, it could only be malevolent; and then Primrose, so strong in faith as to venture what I should have shrunk from as dangerous presumption, dared him to go on in his disbelief, if his brother were given back to prayer.

She pitied him so much, the sweet bright girl, she had so pitied him all along, that I believe she prayed as much for him as for Jock.

Of course I did not know all this till afterwards, for all was stillness in that room, except when at times the clergyman came in and prayed.

The next thing I am sure of, was John's leaning over me, and his low steady voice saying, 'The pulse is better, the symptoms are mitigating.' Sister Dorothea says they had both seen it for some hours, but he made her a sign not to agitate me till he was secure that the improvement was real. Indeed there was something in that equable firm gentleness of John's that sustained me, and prevented my breaking down. Even then it was another whole day before my darling smiled at me again, and said 'Thanks' to John, but oh! with such a look.

When Bobus heard his brother was better, he gave a sob, such as I shall never forget, and rushed away into the pine-wood on the hillside, all alone. The next time I saw him he was walking in the garden with Primrose, and with such a quieted, subdued, gentle look upon his face, it put me in mind of the fields when a great storm has swept over them, and they are lying still in the sunshine afterwards.

Since that day, when John said we might send off that thankworthy telegram, there has been daily progress. I have had one of my headaches. That monarch John found it out, and turned me out. I could bear to go, for I knew my boy was safe with him. He made me over to Primrose, who nursed me as tenderly as my Babie could have done, and, indeed, I begin to think she will soon be as near and dear to me as my Sydney or Elvira. She has a power over Bobus that no one else ever had, and she is very lovely in expression as well as features, but how will so ardent a Christian as she is receive one still so far off as my poor Robert, though *indeed* I think he has at least come so far as the cry, 'Help Thou mine unbelief.'

So now they have let me come back to my Jock, and I see visibly his improvement. He holds out his hand, and he smiles, and he speaks now and then, the dreadful oppression is gone, and all the dangerous symptoms are abating, and I cannot tell how happy and thankful we are. 'Send my love, and tell **Sydney** she has a blessed **Monk**,' he says, as he wakes, and sees me writing.

That dear **Monk** says he will not go home till he can carry home his patient. When that will be I cannot tell, for he cannot sit up in bed yet. Dear Sydney, how I thank her! John says it was not his treatment, but, under Divine Providence, youthful nature that had had her rest, and begun to rally her strength. But under that blessing, it was John's steady, faithful strength and care that enabled the restoration to take place.—My dear child's loving                              MOTHER CAREY.

# CHAPTER XLII

## DISENCHANTED

' Whatever page we turn,
However much we learn,
Let there be something left to dream of still.'

LONGFELLOW.

IT was on a very cold day of the cold spring of 1879 that three ladies descended at the Liverpool station, escorted by a military-looking gentleman. He left them standing while he made inquiries, but his servant had anticipated him. 'The steamer has been signalled, my Lord. It will be in about four o'clock.'

'There will be time to go to the hotel and secure rooms,' said one lady.

'Oh, Reeves can do that. Pray, let us come down to the docks and see them come in.'

No answer till all four were seated in a fly, rattling through the street, but on the repetition of 'Are we going to the docks?' his Lordship, with a resolute twirl of his long, light moustache, replied, 'No, Sydney. If you think I am going to have you making a scene on deck, falling on your husband's breast, and all that sort of thing, you are much mistaken! I shall lodge you all quietly in the hotel, and you may wait there, while I go down with Reeves, and receive them like a rational being.'

'Really, Cecil, that's too bad. He let me come on board!'

'Do you think I should have brought you here if I had thought you meant to make yourself ridiculous?'

'It is of no use, Sydney,' said Babie; 'there's no dealing with the stern and staid *père de famille*. I wonder what he would have liked Essie to do, if he had had to go and leave her for nearly two months when he had only been married a week?'

'Essie is quite a different thing—I mean she has sense and self-possession.'

'Mamma, won't you speak for us?' implored Sydney. 'I did behave so well when he went! Nobody would have guessed we hadn't been married fifty years.'

'Still I think Cecil is quite right, and that it may be better for them all to manage the landing quietly.'

'Without a pack of women,' said Cecil. 'Here we are! I hope you will find a tolerable room for him and no stairs.'

As if poor Mrs. Evelyn were not well enough used to choosing rooms for invalids!

Twilight had come, the gas had been turned on, and the

three anxious ladies stood in the window gazing vainly at end-less vehicles, when the door opened and they beheld sundry figures entering.

Sydney and Barbara flew, the one to her husband, the other to her mother, and presently all stood round the fire looking at one another. Mrs. Evelyn made a gesture to a very slender and somewhat pale figure to sit down in a large easy chair.

'Thank you, I'm not tired,' he briskly said, standing with a caressing hand on his friend's shoulder. 'Here's Cecil can't quite believe yet that I have the use of my limbs.'

'Yes,' said John, 'no sooner did he come on board, than he made a rush at the poor sailor who had broken his leg, and was going to be carried ashore on a hammock. He was on the point of embracing him, red beard and all, when he was forcibly dragged off by Jock himself, whom he nearly knocked down.'

'Well,' said Cecil, as Sydney fairly danced round him in revengeful glee, 'there was the Monk solicitously lifting him on one side, and Mother Carey assisting with a smelling-bottle on the other, so what could I suppose?'

'All for want of us,' said Sydney.

'And think of the cunning of him,' added Babie; 'shutting us up here that he might give way to his feelings undis-turbed!'

'I promised to go and speak about that poor fellow at the hospital,' cried John, with sudden recollection.

'You had better let me,' said Jock.

'You will stay where you are.'

'I consider him my patient.'

'If that's the way you two fought over your solitary case all the way home,' said Babie, 'I wonder there's a fragment left of him.'

'It was only three days ago,' said John, 'and Jock has been a new man ever since he picked the poor fellow up on deck, but I'm not going to let him stir to-night.'

'Let me come with you, Johnnie,' entreated Sydney; 'it will be so nice! Oh no, I don't mind the cold!'

'Here,' added her brother, 'take the poor fellow a sovereign.'

'In compensation for the sudden cooling of your affection,' said Jock. 'Well, if it is an excuse for an excursion with Sydney I'll not interfere, but ask him for his sister's address in London, for I promised to tell her about him.'

'Oh,' cried Babie, at the word 'London,' 'then you have heard from Dr. Medlicott?'

'I did once,' said John, 'with some very useful suggestions, but that was a month ago or more.'

'I meant,' said Babie, 'a letter he wrote for the chance of Jock's getting it before he sailed. There's the assistant lecture-ship vacant, and the Professor would not like any one so much. It is his own appointment, not an election matter, and he meant to keep it open till he could get an answer from Jock.'

'When was this?' asked Jock, flushing with eagerness.

'The 20th. Dr. Medlicott came down to Fordham for Sunday, to ask if it was worth while to telegraph, or if I thought you would be well enough. It is not much of a salary, but it is a step, and Dr. Medlicott knows they would put you on the staff of the hospital, and then you are open to anything.'

Jock drew a long breath and looked at his mother. 'The very thing I've wished,' he said.

'Exactly. Must he answer at once?'

'The Professor would like a telegram, Yes or No, at once.'

'Then, you wedded Monk, will you add to your favours by telegraphing for me?'

'Yes. Of course it is "Yes"? How soon should you have to begin, I wonder?'

'Oh, I'm quite cheeky enough for that sort of work. If you'll telegraph, I'll write by to-night's post.'

'I'll go and do the telegraphing,' said Cecil; 'I don't trust those two.'

'As if John ever made mistakes,' cried Sydney.

'In fact, I want to send a telegram home.'

'To frighten Essie. She will get a yellow envelope saying you accept a lectureship, and the Professor urgent inquiries after his baby.'

'Sydney is getting too obstreperous, Monk,' said Cecil. 'You had better carry her off. I shall come back by the time you have written your letters, Jock.'

'Those two are too happy to do anything but tease one another,' said Mrs. Evelyn, as the door shut on the three. 'My rival grandmother, as Babie calls her, was really quite glad to get rid of Cecil; she declared he would excite Esther into a fever.'

'He did alarm her Serenity herself,' said Babie, laughing. 'When she would go on about grand sponsors and ancestral names, he told her that he should carry the baby off to church and have him christened Jock out of hand, and what a dreadful thing that would be for the peerage. I believe she thought he meant it.'

'The name is to be John,' said Mrs. Evelyn—'John Marmaduke. He has secured his godmother'—laying a hand affectionately on Babie—'but I must not forestall his request to his two earliest and best friends.'

'Dear old fellow!' murmured Jock.

'Everybody is somewhat frantic,' said Barbara. 'Jock's varieties of classes were almost distracted and besieged the door, till Susan was fain to stick the last bulletins in the window to save answering the bell; then no sooner did they hear he was better than they began getting up a testimonial. Percy Stagg wrote to me, to ask for his crest for some piece of plate, and I wrote back that I was sure Dr. Lucas Brownlow would like it best to go in something for the Mission Church ; and if they wanted to give him something for his very own, suppose they got him a brass plate for the door ?'

'Bravo, Infanta ; that *was* an inspiration !'

'So they are to give an alms-dish, and Ali and Elfie give the rest of the plate. Dr. Medlicott says he never saw anything like the feeling at the hospital, or does not know what the nurses don't mean to get up by way of welcome.'

'My dear Babie, you must let Jock write his letters,' interposed her mother, who had tears in her eyes and saw him struggling with emotion. 'In spite of your magnificent demonstrations, Jock, you must repair your charms by lying down.'

She followed him into his room, which opened from the sitting-room, and he turned to her, speaking from a full heart. 'O mother ! It seems all given to me, the old home, the very post I wished for, and all this kindness, just when I thought I had taken leave of it all.' He sobbed once or twice for very joy.

'You are sure it suits you ?'

'If I only can suit it equally well ! Oh, I see what you mean. That is over now. I suppose the fever burnt it out of me, for it does not hurt me now to see the dear old Monk beaming on her. I am glad she came, for I can feel sure of myself now. So there's nothing at present to come between me and my Mother Carey. Thanks, mother, I'll just fire off my two notes , and establish myself luxuriously before Cecil comes back ! I say, this is the best inn's best room. Poor Mrs. Evelyn must have thought herself providing for Fordham. Oh yes, I shall gladly lie down when these notes are done, but this is not a chance to be neglected. Now, *Deo gratias*, it will be my own fault if Magnum Bonum is not worked out to the utmost ; yes, much better than if we had never gone to America. Even Bobus owns that all things *have* worked together for good !'

His mother, with another look at the face, so joyous though still so wasted and white, went back to the other room, with an equally happy though scarcely less worn countenance.

'I hope he is resting,' said Mrs. Evelyn. 'Are you quite satisfied about him ?'

'Fully. He may not be strong for a year or two, and must be careful not to overtask himself, but John made him see one of the greatest physicians in New York, to whom Dr. Medlicott had sent letters of introduction—as if they were needed, he said, after Jock's work at Abville. He said, as John did, there was no lasting damage to the heart, and that the attack was the consequence of having been brought so low ; but he will be as strong and healthy as ever, if he will only be careful as to exertion for a year or so. This appointment is the very thing to save him. I know his friends will look after him and keep him from doing too much. Dr. —— was quite grieved that he had no notion how ill Jock had been, or he would have come to Ashton. Any of the faculty would, he said, for one of the "true chivalry of 1878." And he was so excited about the Magnum Bonum.'

'Do you think you and he can bear to crown our great thanksgiving feast?'

'My dear, my heart is all one thanksgiving!'

'Cecil's rejoicing is quite as much for Jock's sake as over his boy. He told me how they had been pledged as brothers in arms, and traces all that is best in himself to those days at Engelberg.'

'Yes, that night on the mountain was the great starting-point, thanks to dear little Armine.'

'I am writing to him and to Allen,' said Barbara from a corner.

'My love a thousand times, and we will meet at home!'

'Then our joy will not feel incongruous to you?' said Mrs. Evelyn.

'No, I am too thankful for what I know of my poor Janet. She is mine now as she never was since she was a baby in my arms. I scarcely grieve, for happiness was over for her, and hers was a noble death. They have placed her name in the memorial tablet in Abville church, to those who laid down their lives for their brethren there. I begged it might be, "Janet Hermann, daughter of Joseph Brownlow"—for I thank God she died worthy of her father. In all ways I can say of this journey, my children were dead and are alive again, were lost and are found.'

'Ah! I was sure it must be so, if such a girl as Miss Ashton could accept Robert.'

'I am happier about him than I ever thought to be. I do not say that his faith is like John's or Armine's, but he is striving back through the mists, and wishing to believe, rather than being proud of disbelieving, and Primrose knows what she is doing, and is aiding him with all her power.'

'As our Esther never could have done,' said Mrs. Evelyn, 'except by her gentle innocence.'

'No. She could only have been to him a pretty white idol of his own setting up,' said Babie.

'Now,' added her mother, 'Primrose is fairly on equal grounds as to force and intellect. She has been all over Europe, read and thought much, and can discuss deep matters, while the depth of her religious principle impresses him. They fought themselves into love, and then she was sorry for him, and so touched by his wretchedness and longing to take hold of the comfort his reason could not accept. I wish you could have seen her. This photograph shows you her fine head; but not the beautiful clear complexion, and the sweetness of those dark gray eyes!'

'I liked her letter,' said Babie, 'and I am glad she was such a daughter to you, mother. Allen says he is thankful she is not a Japanese with black teeth.'

'He wrote very nicely to her, and so did Elfie,' said her mother. 'And Armine wrote a charming little note, which pleased Primrose best of all.'

'Poor Armine has felt all most deeply,' said Babie. 'Do you remember when he thought it his mission to die and do good to Bobus? Well, he was sure that, though, as he said, his own life then was too shallow and unreal for his death to have done any good, Jock was meant to produce the effect.'

'And he has——'

'Yes, but by life, not death! Armie could hardly believe it. You know he was with us at Christmas; and when he found that Bobus was to be led, not by sorrow, but by this Primrose path, it was quite funny to see how surprised he was.'

'Yes,' said Mrs. Evelyn, 'he went about moralising on the various remedies that are applied to the needs of human nature.'

'It made into a poem at last, such a pretty one,' said Babie. 'And he says he will be wiser all his life for finding things turn out so unlike all his expectations.'

'I have a strange feeling of peace about all my children,' said Caroline. 'I do feel as if my dream had come true, and life, true life, had wakened them all.'

'Yes,' said Mrs. Evelyn, 'I think they all, in their degree, may be said to have learnt or be learning the way to true Magnum Bonum.'

'And oh, how precious it has been to me!' said the mother. 'How the guarding of that secret aided me through the worst of times!'

THE END

*Printed by* R. & R. CLARK, LIMITED, *Edinburgh*.

# MESSRS. MACMILLAN AND CO.'S PUBLICATIONS.

*UNIFORM EDITION OF THE NOVELS AND TALES OF*

# CHARLOTTE M. YONGE.

In Crown 8vo, Cloth extra. Illustrated. 3s. 6d. each.

MACMILLAN AND CO., Ltd., LONDON.

# BY RUDYARD KIPLING.

**THE DAY'S WORK.** Forty-sixth Thousand. Crown 8vo. 6s.

*MORNING POST.*—"The book is so varied, so full of colour and life from end to end, that few who read the first two or three stories will lay it down till they have read the last."

**PLAIN TALES FROM THE HILLS.** Thirty - ninth Thousand. Crown 8vo. 6s.

*SATURDAY REVIEW.*—"Mr. Kipling knows and appreciates the English in India, and is a born story-teller and a man of humour into the bargain. . . . It would be hard to find better reading."

**LIFE'S HANDICAP.** Being Stories of Mine Own People. Twenty-eighth Thousand. Crown 8vo. 6s.

*BLACK AND WHITE.*—"*Life's Handicap* contains much of the best work hitherto accomplished by the author, and, taken as a whole, is a complete advance upon its predecessors."

**MANY INVENTIONS.** Twenty-fifth Thousand. Crown 8vo. 6s.

*PALL MALL GAZETTE.*—"The completest book that Mr. Kipling has yet given us in workmanship, the weightiest and most humane in breadth of view. . . . It can only be regarded as a fresh landmark in the progression of his genius."

**THE LIGHT THAT FAILED.** Rewritten and considerably enlarged. Twenty-eighth Thousand. Crown 8vo. 6s.

*ACADEMY.*—"Whatever else be true of Mr. Kipling, it is the first truth about him that he has power, real intrinsic power. . . . Mr. Kipling's work has innumerable good qualities."

**SOLDIER TALES.** With Illustrations by A. S. HARTRICK. Ninth Thousand. Crown 8vo. 6s.

*ATHENÆUM.*—"By issuing a reprint of some of the best of Mr. Kipling's *Soldier Tales*, Messrs. Macmillan have laid us all under an obligation."

**WEE WILLIE WINKIE, and other Stories.** Crown 8vo. 6s.

**SOLDIERS THREE, and other Stories.** Crown 8vo. 6s.

*GLOBE.*—"Containing some of the best of his highly vivid work."

**THE JUNGLE BOOK.** With Illustrations by J. L. KIPLING, W. H. DRAKE, and P. FRENZENY. Forty-third Thousand. Crown 8vo, Cloth gilt. 6s.

*PUNCH.*—"'Æsop's Fables and dear old Brer Fox and Co.,' observes the Baron sagely, 'may have suggested to the fanciful genius of Rudyard Kipling the delightful idea, carried out in the most fascinating style of *The Jungle Book.*'"

**THE SECOND JUNGLE BOOK.** With Illustrations by J. Lockwood Kipling. Thirtieth Thousand. Crown 8vo, Cloth gilt. 6s.

*DAILY TELEGRAPH.*—"The appearance of *The Second Jungle Book* is a literary event of which no one will mistake the importance. Unlike most sequels, the various stories comprised in the new volume are at least equal to their predecessors."

**"CAPTAINS COURAGEOUS."** A STORY OF THE GRAND BANKS. Illustrated by I. W. TABER. Twenty-second Thousand. Crown 8vo, Cloth gilt. 6s.

*ATHENÆUM.*—"Never in English prose has the sea in all its myriad aspects, with all its sounds and sights and odours, been reproduced with such subtle skill as in these pages."

**A FLEET IN BEING.** NOTES OF TWO TRIPS WITH THE CHANNEL SQUADRON. Forty-first Thousand. Crown 8vo. Sewed, 1s. net; Cloth, 1s. 6d. net.

*ARMY AND NAVY GAZETTE.*—"A very admirable picture of the life of officers and men who go down to the sea in the ships of Her Majesty's fleet."

**THE KIPLING BIRTHDAY BOOK.** Compiled by JOSEPH FINN. Authorised by the Author, with Illustrations by J. LOCKWOOD KIPLING. 16mo. 2s. 6d.

*STANDARD.*—"Will make a welcome present to girls. Mr. Finn has done his work exceedingly well."

MACMILLAN AND CO., Ltd., LONDON.